FIRSTBORN

The Finest in Fantasy from
MICHELLE WEST

The House War:
THE HIDDEN CITY (Book One)
CITY OF NIGHT (Book Two)
HOUSE NAME (Book Three)
SKIRMISH (Book Four)
BATTLE (Book Five)
ORACLE (Book Six)
FIRSTBORN (Book Seven)
WAR (Book Eight)*

The Sun Sword:
THE BROKEN CROWN (Book One)
THE UNCROWNED KING (Book Two)
THE SHINING COURT (Book Three)
SEA OF SORROWS (Book Four)
THE RIVEN SHIELD (Book Five)
THE SUN SWORD (Book Six)

The Sacred Hunt:
HUNTER'S OATH (Book One)
HUNTER'S DEATH (Book Two)

* Coming soon from DAW

FIRSTBORN

A House War Novel

MICHELLE WEST

DAW BOOKS, INC.

DONALD A. WOLLHEIM, FOUNDER

1745 Broadway, New York, NY 10019

ELIZABETH R. WOLLHEIM

SHEILA E. GILBERT

PUBLISHERS

www.dawbooks.com

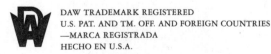

For Uncle Sho & Uncle Eiji.

Thank you for being father and older brother to my mother for so long.

We're going to miss you.

Acknowledgments

Terry Pearson read this book when it was being written, a chapter at a time. He read it when it was the first half of a book that was way too long. He read it when it had fifty thousand different words, and didn't complain *too* much about the twenty or so that disappeared.

He provided a place to hide from the world when I revised *Firstborn* so that it would—hopefully—stand as a book in the series, rather than half a book.

He was not the only person who had to endure my anxiety and the whining it produced.

My sons did their best not to mock me, although older son said it filled him with a certain nostalgia. Thomas attempted to divert me from anxiety about the finished book. And, failing that—and the writer's brain, sadly, is a well of neurosis and fear that is endless, unlike oil wells—kept my house sane and running. And fed.

With help, of course, from my mother, who lost her oldest brother this year.

Also: the godfather, John, his wife Kristen, who keep our home interesting at least two nights a week, and added some sense of normalcy—for my household—throughout.

But it was Sheila Gilbert, as usual, to the rescue. When I turned in a last book that was too long, she worked with me to let me preserve the story I'd written. If it weren't for her, in the end, I would have had to lose about 150,000 words in order to patch what was left together in a way that somehow structurally worked. This would mean, for my process, starting over, pretty much.

Jody Lee had to produce a cover for this book on short notice—because of course she had done the work for the novel called *War.* Which is coming out in four months. Not the book you now hold.

Joshua Starr was on the receiving end of the messiest page proofs I have ever turned in. But the errors and difficulties contained in the book are, sadly, mine.

Prologue

H E WAS OLD.
   He had never denied his age, and if at times he resented the slow accretion of inefficiencies that were age's legacy, he did not decry them; they were what they were. Nor did he dread death as some did; it held no fear for him. Death, like age, was an inevitability, a proof in some fashion of life's progression.

He was aware that experience might, were its oft humiliating lessons absorbed, grant wisdom; wisdom was the minor victory that could be abstracted from disaster, if one survived.

He was not certain he would survive this.

The winter winds were bitterly cold; the sky, a ceaseless, perfect blue, seemed to mock the desire for warmth. The man who required that warmth huddled against whatever shelter he could find, shorn of the dignity or majesty of those who might once have lived among these ruins.

He could see the uneven edges of what had once been external walls; some of those walls retained height. One was at his back now. All else appeared to be covered in snow and ice, but the irregularities that implied buildings also implied that these had been grand, majestic, large. White snow and ice obliterated color, texture. Time had done the rest.

And time was not his friend. He had never felt so cold, so exhausted, so *old*, at any other point in his life, and he had not been considered young for decades.

*   *   *

Service meant many things to many people. Each man, each woman, who chose a life of service did so for their own reasons. For some, it was employment, pure and simple. Of the hundreds of men and women who comprised the Household Staff of the Terafin manse, employment was the primary concern. He did not fault them for it. They worked long hours, under the oversight of a woman who could, with a side-glance, reduce them to tears.

Had he made different choices, he might have been content to be one such servant; he had not, and even in this nightmare winter landscape, he did not regret it.

Ah, idle thoughts, idle, all. The cold was bitter here. Surrounded by forest, he nonetheless lacked wood for fire, and only the ruins of a half-wall protected him from the biting, stinging wind. He did not expect to survive the storm but did not—yet—have surrender in him.

Possibly the most defining lesson he had learned before youth had deserted him was to recognize power. To recognize the potential *for* power. It was not a simple task, this last big lesson. To the young, power was often mistaken for appearance, wealth, brutality. Many who sought power wore masks; many claimed power they did not, in the end, possess. Many claimed weakness and turned it on its edge, playing a binding, crippling game. In their weakness, they exerted influence on people who claimed none.

"I have told you before: we choose our service. What we choose defines us, Ellerson." Akalia had not been, then, the guildmaster, inasmuch as the domicis had one—but she would rise to that responsibility in time. He remembered her clearly as she was on that day: forbidding, attractive, aloof. And disapproving. "What you have not, clearly, understood is that what we choose defines those we serve as well.

"You think of service as a young man thinks. But you will not *be* of service if you do not lose that notion. You are not meant to be obedient and pliant; you are not meant to be mindless. There are many who choose service as a way of avoiding responsibility."

"I am not—"

"No. Not entirely, or I would not have allowed you to cross our threshold." She rose from the chair behind a desk that was both worn and impressive and began to pace, the desk between them covered in inkstands and parchment. "Ryan chose to serve Varile of House Demonde. You did not. It is the only thing that gives me hope." This last was said in her dry, dry tone, the hint of a smile curving her lips. It was not a kind smile.

"Yet Ryan is one of your prized students, is he not?"

"Indeed."

He found Akalia frustrating on the best of days. This was not one of them. On the worst of days she was an obstacle the like of which he had very seldom encountered.

"What is it you want from me?" he demanded. He had been a very tired man, on the other precipice of youth.

"You fail to understand—again—what you must understand. It is not what *I* want that will be definitional. It is what *you* want." She stopped her pacing for a moment, meeting and holding his gaze. "I am not the master you have chosen to serve. Even were I, you would not be the domicis I would choose."

"And who would you choose?" Yes, he'd been young. Young, angry, restless. He had hoped to find answers in this guildhall. He had hoped that those with the greater breadth of experience could provide them. Akalia had that experience, but none of it had made her genial, none had made her kind. If she was wiser than he—and he had bitterly begrudged acknowledgment of that difference—her wisdom was sharp, cutting, even dismissive. It made him feel callow.

She had been silent for long enough he thought she would not answer. And perhaps because it would have been kind if she had chosen to maintain her silence, she spoke.

"Service is not a contest, Ellerson. It is not merely a matter of worth, of being 'worthy.' You are not a child, to wait upon the approval of the nearest adult. If that is the total of your aspiration, you will not find the answers you seek here. What do you want, Ellerson?

"Before you attempt to answer, consider your audience with care."

As if he had ever done anything else while standing in the shadow of this particular desk. The answer came to his lips but did not leave them. It was Akalia's wont to poke holes in every sentence; to reveal the construction of each as faulty, the logic behind it untenable.

The wind was harsh; were his hands not tucked into his armpits, he was almost certain he would lose the use of his fingers. The trees—the shadows of trees—rose above him, cast into velvet and midnight by the light of a single moon. That moon was more disturbing than even the winter itself although, in the end, it was the winter that would kill him. He could not see the second moon.

He did not believe it was in the sky.

*   *   *

What did he want?

The question maddened him, the answer was so obvious. He wanted purpose. He wanted a place. He wanted to be of use, of aid, of help. Thus did every applicant to the guildhall respond. It had been said well, said emphatically, said with fervent belief, and it had been enough to grant him small rooms within the student body. It had been enough to qualify him to take the lessons, many and varied, that were offered.

Choosing which had been difficult, of course. The choice itself was vetted, watched, commented on; it was questioned. Within a hall that was to give answers that might guide an entire life—or the remainder of one—questions were paramount.

The answers he offered to any other master were considered satisfactory.

And perhaps that was why, in this night in which his breath was so visible it was almost solid, he remembered none of them. He remembered Akalia—and at that, Akalia in a youth that he suspected she, too, had failed to appreciate for what it was at the time: strength, vitality.

She would have recognized his smile.

What had he wanted?

I want to serve a great man, a great woman.

Akalia had, predictably, been disappointed with the answer. She dismissed it out of hand. She did not, however, dismiss him. His only companions as he stood in the lee of her desk were frustration, anger, and exhaustion—but this was common; she seemed to invoke them by presence alone. She had allowed him to accept only two contracts, each of a length less than a year, and she was the choke point through which more permanent vocational work would come. Or not.

He had not disgraced the domicis; that much had been made clear at the outset of this interview—but it was made clear in a cool, casual way; there was no praise in it. Nor, he thought, should there be. If the lack stung, it was his to deal with. He wished merely that he could deal with it without also having to deal with Akalia.

"What does that mean?" she had asked, after several minutes of awkward, shuttered silence.

"You did not ask this of Ryan."

"No. You are not Ryan. You feel, perhaps, that I favor him?"

He was not fool enough to say *yes*, although it was a close-run thing.

"You were offered House Demonde. Why did you not accept?"

He was underslept and hungry. This was not the state in which to confront—or be confronted with, rather, as he wasn't a fool—Akalia. "Varile," he replied, "is repulsive."

One dark brow rose as the syllables echoed into stillness. "Varile is considered, by many, a man destined for greatness."

Having stuck out his neck, he could not now withdraw. From another speaker, perhaps, but not Akalia.

"By whom?"

Her lips twitched. "By many."

"Then this mythical many may have the privilege of serving him."

"Indeed. Do you feel that Ryan is a fool?"

Ellerson stilled. After a much more careful pause, he said, "No."

"No, indeed. And yet he was willing to serve. He was willing to bind his life to a man you consider contemptible."

He did not argue with the choice of word. It was not the one he had chosen, but in a pinch, it would do.

"If Ryan is not a fool, is he a mendicant? Do you think he seeks to somehow enrich himself?"

Ellerson turned toward the door. He did not answer her question; he was angry enough that he intended never to answer another.

"Ellerson."

He froze, his hand on the handle. "I have not always agreed with Ryan." This was a gross understatement. "But I have never said he does not have his principles. He is a domicis. He understands service."

"And he has chosen to serve a man you believe unworthy of that service."

Ellerson turned; he kept the door at his back. "Yes. And that is, as we have been taught, his choice; it is not mine to judge."

"And yet you do."

"No, Akalia, I do not." He spoke with force, with heat—and with truth, although he had not once said this out loud. Had not perhaps said this even in the quiet of his thoughts. "Were I to serve Demonde, I would judge myself, and judge myself harshly."

He expected anger. Or contempt. She was very adept at both. But she offered silence instead, watching him, her hands by her sides, her eyes only slightly narrowed.

"And what can Ryan offer that you cannot?"

"Respect." He bowed his head. Lifted it again. "Respect for Varile's authority. Respect for his position. Respect for the responsibilities he has chosen to undertake—and in my opinion, to undermine. Varile does things by halves, and *only* by halves."

"He is, surely, young."

"Then he is too young to have the power he's been granted. He does not know how to use it wisely."

"And you would." It was not a question.

Ellerson had never been humble; he had merely been silent. "Yes."

"If that is the case—and I will not argue the point—why are you here?"

I do not know.

He had been young. He thought it perhaps the last month of his life in which he could truly say that. The single moon shed enough light that he could see the outline of ruined buildings. He was not, of course, dressed for the cold. Lighting a fire was not beyond his ability, but lighting a fire from nothing was. This landscape was, in all ways, magical. Wild.

The sound of hooves cut the wind; the sound of horns joined it, an odd blend of harmony and disharmony, as if wind and horn struggled for dominance of the aerial landscape, neither with any certainty of supremacy. He had managed to avoid those hooves; the snow here was thick and hard, not brittle. It carried his weight and left little evidence of his passing.

He was not certain he would survive.

Akalia was not angered by his answer. If not for the very slight dip of her chin, he might have believed she had not heard it at all; it was quietly spoken. Quietly, exhaustedly spoken. She dismissed him. He left.

He returned to the rooms students—of various ages and various competencies—occupied. He returned quickly, and he did not seek his own room. He sought, instead, Ryan's. Ryan, who would not be a student in these halls for much longer. Ryan's door, a narrow wooden door very much like Ellerson's own, was ajar; light in the shape of a doorframe's corners cut the darker floor of the hall.

He hesitated, wavering in his resolve.

"Ellerson?"

He was not surprised to be recognized; he himself could identify the footfalls of most of the people who graced his classes and the student halls. He hesitated, thinking the better of the long, swift strides that had brought him here.

The door opened.

Ryan, his raven hair drawn back in a long braid, stood in the frame, his face shadowed by the interior light of rooms that would soon no longer bear his name.

They could not be said to be friends; they could not be said to be enemies. There was, in their anger and hostility, a type of wary respect. They were not—exactly—rivals, but it occurred to Ellerson, as he met Ryan's gaze, that were they, Ryan would have been a worthy opponent. He wondered if Ryan saw him in the same light.

"Have you come to see me off? You are hours and a day too early."

Ellerson shook his head, and Ryan stepped back into a room made chaotic by his intent to vacate. Shirts were strewn across each flat surface, as were robes, pants, and two tailored jackets.

Ellerson grimaced and looked at Ryan; Ryan shrugged. "I've never had much in the domicis hall," he said—and there was something in his voice that Ellerson could not immediately name—"but . . ." he held out an arm to indicate the mess.

Ellerson entered the room. He was silent; they both were. And then, because Ellerson had no words, having arrived in anger and frazzled desperation, he fell back on very early training. He liberated a hanger from beneath the piles of cloth of one sort or another and lifted the nearest shirt.

Ryan hesitated again before he joined Ellerson, and they worked side by side, taking comfort from the simple, domestic actions that had been their earliest lessons.

"Why?" Ellerson was surprised to find that he had chosen to break the almost companionable silence.

Nor did Ryan pretend to misunderstand. "I am not—I have never been—like you. What I want is simple."

"What I want is simple as well."

"Is it?"

Ellerson glanced at Ryan; Ryan continued his fastidious handling of shoes.

"I have never been as certain as you, as quick to assess. I have never been as practical. No, don't say it. We're unlikely to meet again in the near future. We're unlikely to argue, to clash, to turn lessons into debates—or worse." He said the last with a wry smile. "I understand my weaknesses. I may not yet understand my strengths—but it's the weaknesses I've spent so long assessing, I know them better than I know how to fold a sheet.

"You frustrate me, it's true. You see the world so narrowly. You admit to far fewer possibilities than almost any other student who has chosen to remain in these halls. But there's a consistency to your views—and your choices—that make the rest of us almost envious."

Ellerson said nothing—because he had, of a sudden, nothing to say.

"I've surprised you. At least I've managed that before I leave." He set the shoes down carefully and lifted boots. These boots were less well-tended; they were older.

"Leave them," Ellerson said. "They won't suit the service you've chosen."

Ryan set the boots aside very slowly. "Do you recognize them?"

Ellerson frowned. Stopped. Lifted them. He felt something like pain as he looked at the inside of the worn leather and saw his own initials. "Yes." But he hadn't until Ryan had asked.

"You do not approve of Patris Varile. I understand this. Half the student body understands it," he added, with a grimace.

"Why?" Ellerson asked again. "Why him?"

"Because if he is all of the things you have claimed that he is—and I will not lie, you are not wrong—he is still more, besides."

"He is—"

"He is fragile in a way you are not. He is, perhaps, fragile in a way I once was. You see him as lazy and irresponsible."

Ellerson nodded. He did not speak.

"And, in part, he is. Don't make that face. This is the last time I will be able to discuss him with you or anyone else except the guildmaster." Ryan glanced at Ellerson, at the boots in Ellerson's suddenly nerveless fingers. He took them back, folded their heights carefully, and set them beside the shoes and short boots that *were* suitable. "In part, his irresponsibility comes from fear and uncertainty. Have you met his mother?"

"No."

"His father?"

"No."

"Neither were inclined to part with either their power or their influence—nor are they now. They do not live under the same roof; did they, there would only be one. Varile has long had to balance between the animosities of his parents. He fears to make the wrong decision—and so he often makes none.

"And yes, Ellerson, it *is* a weakness. It is, further, a weakness to which he will not admit. Do not think that I have agreed to serve him because I intend to change him—that, at least, would be too much of a disgrace to both of our teachers. I see him as he is. And I see his fear. I believe that were the shadows of that fear less dark and less cold, he would make different choices and different decisions—and I have bet my life on it."

"And you would be willing to serve, regardless?"

"I am. He is not the master for you. You were wise enough to realize it instantly. But you and I are not the same man, Ellerson. We do not have the same desires. We do not have the same talents. Given the past two years, it is odd to say this to you—but I *will* say it. It is your disappointment that has made this choice so difficult. Not Akalia's, not the guildmaster's, but yours."

Ellerson closed his eyes. Opened them to see Ryan's, clear and unblinking. "I did not mean—"

"No, of course not. My only regret in leaving the guildhall is that I might never see the master you would be willing to devote your life—and not months of your life—to. You've always said you have interest in serving men of power—but you don't trust them. You can't. You've come close, in your time, to being one.

"And I hope, one day, to see the lord that you're willing to serve." He bowed then.

So you can judge him as harshly? he thought but did not say.

Ryan shook his head; the air was charged, and the thought was not silent enough.

He did not often think of Ryan. Nor did he think, often, of the guildhall.

He thought, instead, of Finch, Teller, Jester; of Arann and Angel and Carver. He could not, in good conscience, have remained by Jewel's side as domicis, and was surprised, still, by the pain that had caused him. But he had known that she was seer-born. He had known that if she was not born to power—and she had not been—she would have no choice but to rise to it. Given her gift, given her almost singular talent, she would not long survive it without some intervention; she required someone with power beyond his own. And he had not, in his own estimation, been wrong. If anything, he had underestimated the dangers she would face.

The danger, he thought, shivering, that she would *become*.

But her den?

They had come to him.

He had gone to speak with Akalia, that interview so very, very different from the early ones. She had, as guildmaster, handled their request. She had, as guildmaster, no advice to offer him—he was retired, or should have been; he had become a permanent fixture, a teacher in the domicis halls.

He had waited, as he could not easily wait in his youth, while she had explained what was desired, what had been requested, and what his responsibilities, should he choose to accept, would be.

It was—they both knew it—pro forma. She had known what his answer would be before he had even opened her door. But he surprised her on that day, perhaps for the last time. He had bowed—a gesture of respect, yes, but also a gesture of leave-taking, and he had said, in his quiet, unadorned voice—so different from the voice of his younger self—"I am grateful for every hard-fought lesson you have chosen to teach me. I am grateful for the opportunities you provided, and for the patience you managed, however nearly, to show."

She said nothing as he rose.

"Everything you have taught me, deliberately or incidentally, leads to this. This is why I came to the guildhall. This is why I stayed."

She understood then. "I do not believe they have asked that you serve permanently."

"No," he said, smiling. "They have not. But I will serve them until I am incapable of service. There will be no other master."

It was her turn to bow, then. "Will you tell them that the terms of the contract have changed?"

He shook his head. "It is not necessary. Nothing need be said."

He was far from Terafin. Far from home. Far from the responsibilities that he had chosen to undertake. And he could not undertake them in this winterscape of bitter cold and ancient ruins. His breath hung about him like a pall; the horns passed by. He rose then.

He did not know by what magic he had found this place; he knew only that some magic might reverse his course. He was Ellerson, domicis; he knew his duty, and he had not yet surrendered it.

How long did it take a man to freeze to death? Less time, Ellerson felt certain, than had passed since he had found himself in the heart of Winter. He was not, and had not been, attired for the bitter cold; his breath hung about him in thin, almost tangible clouds. His hands and his feet ached; his legs were stiff enough that walking caused pain. He walked, regardless.

He could.

This meant either that his sense of the passage of time was flawed, or that time did not pass in this place with its single moon the same way it did in Averalaan. He was hungry, but the hunger was a secondary concern. If he did not find shelter of some kind soon, it was not starvation that would kill him.

Thrice more that eve, the horns sounded. The third time, he could see the hunters passing yards ahead of where he cowered. They rode the wind, or so it seemed to Ellerson; perhaps the wind merely followed in their wake. He knew that he was not the target of this hunt, because he knew that were he, he would have died the first time the horns had clashed with the wind's howl for dominance.

But he knew, as well, that the hunters were not human. Silvered by moonlight, they carried spears whose heads absorbed light, rather than reflecting it, and their hair, cloaks of platinum that parted as they moved. They were of a height, apparently of a gender, and they did not ride horses.

They were Lord Celleriant's people.

He had always recognized Lord Celleriant as a power—and at that, a dangerous one. But Lord Celleriant served Jewel. He served in a way that the winged cats did not, and probably could not, given their nature. Ellerson had never seen that man in his element—and his element was Winter. Jewel had, and she had not only survived, but triumphed.

It was daunting, to realize just how far above them she had risen.

She did not see it herself, of course; it was her nature to cling, to hold, to bind herself. She looked to her den, the heart of the home she had built. It was a struggle for her to look in any other direction. Ellerson had watched it, seen it, recognized it. He had offered her the only help he could: he had taken her den and its affairs in Terafin in hand.

He wished her to know that they were safe. And he understood that she could not know this because she was seer-born, and it wasn't true. He had walked into a wardrobe. He had stepped into Winter. He had had no way to return to the Terafin manse.

Perhaps this odd translocation was due to the nature of The Terafin's personal chambers; they existed in a space that was joined to the rest of the manse only through the doors that granted entry. Those doors were guarded by Chosen, as was their right and duty—but that duty had become decorative.

No one that passed through those doors without invitation or permission would find The Terafin. But Ellerson had had both invitation and permission. He had been in the act of performing the duties that had been requested, although technically they were not his.

He was here.

He wondered how many of the Household Staff would join him—if they joined him at all. The sky above what the Terafin library had become was an unchanging amethyst; the sky here had passed from perfect azure to midnight, a blue black that was startling in its clarity.

Were it not for the driving wind and the fear of the Hunt itself, Ellerson would have avoided the ruins; he did not know why the hunters chose, always, a path that bypassed them. He could not imagine they were men subject to fear—but that was irrelevant. They did not seem to feel cold, either; they were certainly untouched by something as trivial as age.

Anything that roused caution or fear in the Wild Hunt would destroy him. But many, many things that did not would kill him first. Cold. Hunger.

* * *

The edges of walls and foundation stones peered above the endless snow, redefining the shape of the drifts. Some were no taller than his ankles—most, in fact. They would not be useful. But farther in, he could see broken walls that stretched to his thigh, to his chest. It was to these that he headed. He was cautious in his footing, and kept his eyes open, but he moved quickly. No trees provided visual cover for him; until he reached that part of the ruins, nothing could provide shelter.

If he was not the target of the Hunt, he had no doubt that he would draw their interest if they sighted him. Nor had he any doubt what would follow.

He was surprised to find walls that were taller than he was. Time had had its effect, of course; if the walls remained, what had once been roof had long since decayed. But there were window casements in the longest, whole section of wall he could find; they contained no glass. He could not immediately determine which side of the wall was the interior side—not until he found a corner, and another preserved wall that was sheared at an angle.

He walked around that second wall and came to an immediate halt.

There was a woman standing against the stone between those empty windows. She was not tall enough to be a hunter, and she did not gleam the way they did. No, she wore robes. For a moment Ellerson thought she might be Evayne a'Nolan—but that was a delusion of hope. Her robes were not midnight blue, and they did not move and rustle with an apparent will of their own.

"You should not be here," the stranger said.

He executed a shallow but entirely proper bow—as if this woman, in her robes beneath the open sky, were the owner of what remained of this building. "My apologies," he replied, rising. "I did not realize that any of the buildings in these ruins could serve as a home to anyone."

The woman lifted her hands slowly, as if to make clear they were empty, before she pulled back the hood of her robe. Ellerson had never seen her before. Had he, he was not certain he would have remembered her; everything about her was nondescript. She was neither too tall nor too short, too heavy or too slender, too old or too young. Her hair was not dark, but it was not light; it fell in that range that was considered mousy.

But her smile, if brief, was genuine. He was certain nothing else about her—except perhaps the robe—was. "You did not realize it because of course it is not true. No one calls this city home now. Well met, Ellerson of the domicis. Ellerson of Terafin."

"I am not ATerafin," he replied.

"No, of course you are not. But Terafin has defined your life for years, or rather, it has defined the shape of your life. Were it not for Terafin, you would not be here now. Come. If you approach these empty windows, the air is much less chill."

He accepted the instruction as if it were an invitation.

"You should not be here," the stranger repeated.

"I would not be here had I the choice," Ellerson replied. "Nor will I remain if I can find a passage back. I have responsibilities and duties that are being neglected in my absence."

She smiled again. "You do." The smile faltered. "Understand that I cannot interfere directly. I cannot guide you to a passage that will take you back to your Terafin and the lords you serve."

Ellerson was silent for a beat. "Cannot, or will not?"

"Cannot and would not."

"Why are you here?"

"If I cannot grant you passage back to your world and your time, I can ameliorate some of the difficulties you now face. I have already done so, of course." Studying his carefully neutral expression, she added, "Or perhaps I have merely arranged that it be done. These walls stand because of enchantments laid upon them at their building. So, too, the floors."

Ellerson found, to his surprise, that the air was distinctly less chill by the windows, as the woman had said. He took care to keep a respectful distance between them. He was not Haval Arwood. His appearance was not a mask or a feint. "You expected to find me today."

"Yes, as you've surmised." She gestured to the floor, and he saw that she spoke truth; although it was dusted with snow, the snow was thin. There was no ice beneath it. "There is a door, of sorts. It will open on command."

"And it has never been discovered?"

"It hears only the voice of mortals. No, it has not yet been discovered. You will find clothing, supplies, and food; you will find shelter, of a kind."

"The food—"

"As the walls were, it is enchanted; unlike those walls, the enchantment has never been under siege. There are no treasures contained therein that would justify the use of the magics required to break it. Any who know how to look can see what is contained," she added. "Or such magics would have been brought to bear.

"There is history here. Your Empire did not exist when this city fell. Your kind did not exist."

He did not ask her how enchantments could be keyed to mortality if mortals did not exist. It was irrelevant, and he felt that the questions he would be allowed were few, the time for them passing as the night darkened.

"You will not find your way to Terafin on your own. That is not the nature of this most ancient of places. Not all the beings that dwell here are inimical to you and your kind; some will be curious. Some will be fanciful. Some will destroy you not because they desire destruction, but because you are so fragile."

She opened her mouth, and horns robbed the air of the sound of her words. Her brow creased as she lifted her chin and turned, briefly, to glance out of the open casement to which she was closest. "Do not fear the Hunt here," she told him. "What you see of the Hunt is memory, not reality. Those horns have not been sounded in this landscape since—" She fell silent. "Soon, Ellerson. Soon. It will be over, one way or the other."

She was not old but sounded, momentarily, ancient, the weight of the burden she carried apparent in her voice, her expression, her endless weariness. "This is all I can offer you; it is meager. But you are not mine; you are not my distant kin. Could you take and survive my test, I could offer more—but even were you born to see, you could not now undertake it. You have made choices for the whole of your life that have defined the choices you might make now. And your choices are binding."

"And yours, lady?" he asked softly.

"Do not pity me."

"I could not." It was truth. "You are the Oracle."

"I am, yes."

"Have you seen The Terafin? Have you seen Angel ATerafin?"

Understanding that he must ask the questions, no matter what his current situation, she nodded. "Yes."

"Did she pass your test?"

"It was not my test," the Oracle replied softly. "But her own. Inasmuch as she could, she did—but . . ."

"It is not yet over."

"No. That is the nature of the seer-born."

"Does she know?"

"I do not know. She will, if she does not yet." The Oracle lifted the folds of the hood from her shoulders and pulled them over her head again. "I cannot stay. Your presence here is faint enough that it might continue undetected— but even hidden as I am, mine is not." She surprised him; she bowed.

It was a complicated gesture, too formal for all but the ceremonial investitures of the highest echelons of the patriciate. He could not return it in kind, but he offered her the bow that was appropriate for his own station in the life he had chosen. "You wish to resume your responsibilities," she told him as she rose. "As you must. But you are mistaken if you believe that you must return to Terafin to do so."

He stiffened.

"You walked into this landscape from a wardrobe."

Breath held, he nodded.

"When you did not return, Jewel went in search of you—but she had waited too long. She entered a different dream, a different geography. Before she did, however, Carver entered the wardrobe."

"Carver's here?"

"Yes. But I must warn you, he is not as you are. The dreams of this place are more real to him; he does not know how to avoid them. Find him—and find him soon."

Ellerson nodded and bowed again. He was not surprised to find her gone when he rose—and had she not been, it would not have mattered. He began to search the floor upon which she'd been standing. As it was solid stone, he could not find the trapdoor he'd expected, and after a few more minutes, he gave up on that notion.

He spoke. He spoke in his authoritative, quiet voice. The word *open* did nothing. He tried it in all the languages he knew—it was a rudimentary word, and he could speak it efficiently in almost a dozen ways. He tried *shelter* next, and as *open*, it did nothing. He then tried *help, succor, sanctuary.*

He was not the den; he didn't give way to cursing until he had run down the list of obvious words, and when he did, he did it deliberately, each word tested in the languages he knew.

When he had exhausted even those, he tried different words, each with a decreasing amount of hope, an increasing amount of urgency. After this, he slumped against the wall and closed his eyes, listening to the howl of wind and the horns.

The Oracle had come to him. She had come to where she knew he would be. Jewel didn't speak with any frequency about the Oracle or the firstborn, but he understood what the Oracle could do.

She could have found Carver instead. She could have delivered the same message; she could have led him to the same shelter. She had done none of those things. She had come to Ellerson.

Ellerson seldom thought of the guildhall of the domicis. But he had stumbled through the ruins, thinking of his past, the sharper images and interactions, the odd illuminations. His friendship—his rivalry—with Ryan had not defined him. His clashes with Akalia had shaped what was already there.

But those memories folded into a single word, which remained unchanged no matter which language he might choose to speak it in.

Terafin.

The ground beneath his feet began to glow with a faint, pale light that was reminiscent of moon, not sun. There was no other change, but he could see that the glow was confined to—and defined by—a specific area. He cleared the light snow with his feet, and as he worked, he thought of Ryan. He had not seen Ryan in years, had had no reason to speak with him.

If he returned, if he survived, he would seek him out. He could not, of course, introduce Ryan to his lord—it would be difficult to gather the den in one place, given their disparate responsibilities. But he could tell Ryan at least this much of them: their names.

Finch.

Teller.

Angel.

Arann.

Jester.

He watched the glow brighten, and he heard something crack or snap beneath his feet. He spoke the last name because, at the moment, it was the most important.

Carver.

A staircase opened up before his feet. It opened not into the darkness of disused cellar, the mustiness of crypt; it was brightly lit, a stretch of hall visible from the height of the stairs. He descended quickly but carefully; he could not afford to fall, and his limbs were thick and stiff with cold.

Chapter One

"**Y**OU *STEPPED* ON MY *tail*!" The outraged yowl of a great black cat echoed off the uneven walls and the rounded ceiling of the tunnel.

"It's dark," Adam said. He might have lifted his hands in a gesture of placation, but they were full. The thick wire of a lantern hung from the crook of his right elbow, swaying as he attempted to avoid compounding his sin. "It's dark and the tunnel is narrow. I told you you should let me walk ahead."

"What if something tries to *eat* you?"

He prevented himself from grimacing, a skill he had learned in his years overseeing the very tired younglings in his care. "This is the stronghold of the Oracle. There is nothing in these tunnels that will eat me unless she commands it."

And nothing—not even the cats—that would save him from death if she so desired it.

"What if *I* try to *eat* you?" Night stopped walking. His tail twitched as it lay, extended, on the floor at his back. If Adam's hands had not been full, he might have smacked the cat's head in frustration.

He avoided the tail a second time; he strongly suspected he had avoided it the first time as well. There was no point arguing with Night. Although his brothers, Snow and Shadow, did, they were also cats. Mortals didn't emerge from scuffles like this uninjured.

The cats were bored. They were so so *bored*. When bored, they shared. Adam was heartily sick of bored cats. His sense of self-preservation had dwindled with the passage of days; not even the most cautious of men could consider these whiny, tired *children* a serious threat. Not even when he had almost died at their hands. Or claws.

Jewel was the Matriarch of Terafin.

The Oracle was the Matriarch of Matriarchs.

In these halls—some constructed of worked stone that was smooth as glass, with ceilings higher than any the Terafin manse could boast, and some rough tunnels that were narrow and twisting—it was the Oracle's word that was law. She did not speak often; Shianne disliked her intensely. Shadow concurred. Avandar would answer questions on the rare occasions she chose to appear and interact. For the most part, she kept her distance.

But she had asked Adam to run small errands for her, as if he were the most junior of children, and he had agreed because she was Matriarch here, and it was always wisest to stay on the good side of a Matriarch. He had, at her command, filled the lanterns that he found in empty rooms. She did not tell him which rooms, of course, but he understood her command; if the doors were open, the lanterns within were to be filled.

Many of the doors did not open and would not. Nor did Adam attempt to force them. No, Night did that, shredding wood in his sulky boredom. The great cats could not, however, destroy the locked doors.

Adam had also been sent to the lake that existed in just one branch of this place, and he had drawn water in buckets—a familiar activity. These, he returned to the room in which Jewel slept. He did not accompany Jewel when she rose in the morning; Shadow did. But he was there when she returned, with water, with light. Water, however, could not wash away the dark circles under her eyes, and her hair had become tangled in the way it did when she worried. He did not ask her what lessons the Oracle imparted; he truly did not want to know.

Today, however, he had been asked to carry clothing.

"You will find a chest in a room across the hall from Jewel's room," the Oracle told him. "And in it, you will find a set of robes. They are dark, but the cloth is thick; it is perfect for this endless Winter."

"You wish me to bring these robes to Jewel?"

"No, child. I wish you to bring them to someone else. I would carry them myself, but she will not accept anything from my hands, not even food."

He knew what the next task would be.

He had hooked a food basket—an awkward size and shape, but the Oracle had not seen fit to supply him with another—over his left arm; the handle nestled into the crook of his elbow. The rest of his attention was upon the robes. She had not told him to be careful, but he understood that caution was absolutely required, because he had seen the chest that contained them. And when he had—hesitantly—attempted to pull the robes out of that chest the first time, he had paused, his hands an inch above the cloth. He had then washed those hands as thoroughly as possible.

He told himself that the robes were valuable, but that had been a lie. Ah, no, he believed they were of incalculable value, but that did not account for his hesitance. Something about the cloth and the color was a warning; these were not meant to be touched. Not by Adam. Even Night had sniffed in disdain, but he had kept his distance.

That distance had evaporated; the cats were very single-minded, and Night's mind was on boredom and the injustice of being forced to endure it. When Adam failed to step on his tail a third time, the great black cat took a forceful step back, and a paw landed on the trailing length of the robe.

The cat shrieked, a yowling sound that devolved almost instantly into a guttural snarl; his fur rose as he gained size through outrage and resultant fury. There was an enemy here, carried in Adam's arms, and he intended to do battle.

"That is quite enough."

Night hissed but froze in place. The Oracle appeared in the hall, casting a shadow that encompassed only the cat. Even in the dull lamplight, the cat seemed to dissolve into the darkness.

"My apologies, Adam. I forget the wild ones and their constant, querulous mischief."

Night had disappeared.

Alarmed, Adam opened his mouth, but the Oracle shook her head. "He will find himself back in The Terafin's rooms where he will argue with Snow."

"I'm not sure that's better."

"It is better," the Oracle observed, "for the cat. You have done well. I will be in your debt."

He froze.

"I am not a Matriarch, Adam of Arkosa. Nor am I one of the Winter people. I do not feel lessened by debt or obligation; they arise naturally from my sense of gratitude for services rendered. The gratitude of the firstborn is not the resentment of those who came after; nor is such gratitude onerous to us. If you proceed down the hall, you may set the robes down." She glanced at them, the shape of her eyes changing.

"I have waited for you," she said. "I cannot carry them myself. Even if I could, as I said before, she would not accept them from me. But you will survive the carrying, and no one else would."

*　　*　　*

The door at the end of the hall appeared as Adam approached it. In any other dwelling, he would assume this appearance the artifact of light. Here, he did not. The Oracle had given him directions, and the tunnels conformed to her desire. She wished this door to be open, and it was now open. Light shone through the crack between hard door and frame. Something about the way it fell against the uneven floor felt strangely lonely.

On the open road, one learned to hoard one's privacy; to make a space inside oneself where one could retreat while surrounded by the noise of the children. One learned—slowly—to recognize the signs of that retreat in the adults, and as one approached adulthood, to make allowances for it. Sometimes people needed to be alone.

But loneliness was different. It was an isolation that was not desired, although it could exist side by side with those who desired privacy. Sometimes it could exist no matter how immersed one became in the noise and the chatter of family, of kin. Adam had learned early to tell the difference between these two states.

He therefore approached the door, pausing there. His hands were full. On the open road, there were sounds and signs that one used to ask permission to encroach; in the Terafin manse, one hit the harder doors and waited. If one were expected, the doors would open at the hands of a page or servant. If not, one left.

Today, Adam waited. He heard nothing; no movement, no voice.

After a pause, he said, "Hello?" And when no answer came, he tried again, this time in Weston. He waited, his arms full of cloth, the basket on one and the lamp on the other growing weightier in the stillness.

At length, he pushed the door open with his foot and entered a room that should not have been at the end of a poorly carved tunnel. It was a bright room, the floors gleaming where they could be seen beneath the knotted fringes of a large, oval rug. There was a table pushed up against one wall, the wood of its legs light against the darker grain of floor. There were windows; curtains had been drawn and roped to either side of each. Sunlight touched floor, changing the color of the carpet; it stretched to touch everything, even the bed.

The bed, like Weston beds, was above the ground, and it was occupied.

Its occupant was covered by heavy blankets, but they had bunched beneath the crook of her left arm; she slept on her side, her back toward the wall. She did not wake as Adam entered the room; given her appearance, he wondered if she would wake at all. He set the basket and the lantern down and carefully placed the mass of robes on the single chair tucked beneath the table. Long after he'd finished, the cloth rustled, the noise louder than breathing. He turned his back on it and headed toward the room's occupant, but he stopped before he reached the bedside.

Her hair was a tangled, black mess; her skin was not ruddy, but dark with what appeared to be soot. Soot that still bore the marks of tears. Her hand—or the hand that could be seen—was not much cleaner, and there was a trace of dried blood on the tips of the exposed fingers. She was wearing clothing that was about as clean as she herself.

He wondered where she'd come from. He thought her fifteen or sixteen years old, although sleep often deprived a face of the weight and characteristics of age. He hesitated for one long moment, and then went in search of water.

By the time he returned, the girl was no longer sleeping. She was seated across the bed, her back against the wall, her body still tangled and covered in blankets. Her hair was not less of a mess—but even this, the Oracle had foreseen; the water had already been warmed and a brush and comb lay on a tray beside an enormously heavy bucket. He had tucked them into his satchel and carried the water back to the room. There was no bath, and no lake or river, but there was easily enough water to clean one girl.

The girl, however, did not appear to want to be clean. Or to want to clean up while Adam was anywhere near her. Her eyes were so narrow it was hard to see their color, but when he did, he froze. They appeared to be violet.

Voice almost a whisper, he spoke a name. *Evayne.* Her eyes widened, and yes, they were violet, a particular shade that he associated with only one person.

Her eyes narrowed again, her body stiffening. "Are you one of the Oracle's people?"

"Ah, no. No. I serve Terafin."

Her brows rose again, in concert. "Terafin? You mean one of The Ten? You're a long way from home."

He reddened. "I serve The Terafin while I remain in her Northern city. I am of Arkosa. My Matriarch is Margret. My home is the Voyanne."

"We're not in Averalaan, are we?"

"No. We are in the Oracle's domain. We have taken shelter here while the demons hunt us."

She was pale then, as if she had never seen sunlight. He could see the whites of her eyes. "They came to you? They came to you, too?"

"They have been hunting the Matriarch," Adam replied. "But, yes, demons also hunted my kin in the Sea of Sorrows." He would have died there, so much mortal detritus, in the wake of a battle that had broken earth and unleashed storms in the hard, baked clay of the desert. He would have died had his talent not manifested itself then. And he would have been broken permanently had it not been for . . . her. Evayne.

But this girl and that woman were not the same; he could see the shape of the older face in the younger one—but none of her experience, none of the measured and weary control she exerted over her expression.

"Have you—have you taken the Oracle's test?" he finally asked.

She lowered her chin toward the knees she had folded into her chest. ". . . No." She shuddered at the question. Adam could understand this. The Oracle was a power the like of which existed only in stories told to children. But so much of the world he had experienced since his mother's death was. If she had not yet taken that test, she would. He was certain of it; he'd seen proof of it, held in the hands of the older Evayne—and any age was older, compared to this girl.

Ah, he'd been mistaken. She wasn't shuddering. She was weeping.

Adam understood the difference between being alone and being lonely. He understood, as well, the different shades of pain; the pain that was a wall, and the pain that could be a bridge. He was Adam of Arkosa; this was a bridge, and he crossed it before he could stop to think because he had done it so often in his life.

He slid an arm around her shoulder, dropped beside her on the bed, curving his knees beneath his free arm to lessen his height, to make his size as insignificant as he could. She stiffened but didn't push him away. Had she, he would have released her, moved back, and waited. It was always easier with small children; they were still young enough to seek comfort, to accept it.

As they grew, what brought them comfort changed, and sometimes there was no comfort that could be offered or, rather, none that could be taken. He accepted that, too. Trying was necessary; accepting rejection was simply a part of that. He had learned, with time, to understand the instant rejection that was part of a child's rage—that they might push him away and then scream when he actually attempted to leave.

But he understood, as well, when walls had been erected that could not be climbed or breeched. She did not speak, but she did not push him away. She was lonely; pain had dulled the edge of suspicion—or overwhelmed it.

He did not speak. He did not ask questions. He did not offer her platitudes or promises that things would be all right. How could he? His mother could have. Adam, however, was neither a good liar nor an authority. What comfort could she take from his words? And he knew that there was no safety for Evayne. And no home. The Voyanne at least allowed families to be together. The road she walked did not.

He sat with her for an hour, perhaps longer, before she stopped shaking. She had fallen asleep.

When Adam disentangled himself—taking care not to wake her—he carefully folded the robes she was to wear. He would have cleaned the room, but there were no brooms, no cloths, no odd Western dusters. Night did not return. The door did not open into the same crude tunnel that had led to it; it opened into sunlight and greenery. The room, which had not seemed dark in comparison to the tunnel from which he'd first emerged, was no match for the light that now streamed in through the open door. The light cast shadows, and his shadow fell upon the bed and the girl who lay in it.

As if that shadow had substance, she stirred, turning away from the light—and then, in turn, toward it. Her eyes opened to Adam framed by the door and what might appear like escape. She shed blankets and sheets and swung her legs toward the floor.

"I'm sorry," he said in quiet Weston. "This is not escape or freedom."

"There is no freedom," was her equally quiet reply. "But—there's been so little light. So little air." She reached up to her neck with both hands, her eyes widening in alarm.

"No," Adam said quickly. "It is on the small table."

She all but leaped toward that table, her arms shaking and outstretched. Her hands closed instantly around the only item of value she seemed to carry: a metallic lily, a flower in worked silver, caught and held by a slender, silver chain. She put it on—or tried; her hands were shaking, and the clasp was un-done. Adam left the doorway to come to her aid.

She lifted her chin as he held both ends of the chain and lowered it again as he worked the odd clasp. "It's my birthday present," she told him, although he had not asked. "My sixteenth birthday present. It's the only one I could carry—it's the only one I had in my hands when—" She stiffened. Adam continued to ask no questions.

After a pause, he said, "It is lovely. The craftsman who made it was skilled."

"He is!" She turned then, the lily on the outside of her clothing, her hair a sleepy mess. "He doesn't make much like this—there's so little call for it in the village. Mostly, he works with my father. The blacksmith. But he made this for me. I don't know when he did the work—he—" The smile fled instantly. "He'll never see me wear it."

"Are you so certain?" Adam was not. Of a sudden, he thought the opposite.

"He won't survive." Her hands became fists, but she did not remove the lily. Would never, he thought, remove it.

"He lived when you last saw him?"

"He was trying to *fight*," she said. "He'd gone back for his sword."

"Against demons?"

"Against demons. Because he used to be a soldier before he lost part of his leg. He has a leg—my father helped to craft it—so he can walk." But not well enough to fight, in her opinion. Adam slid an arm around her shoulder, holding her up, bracing some part of her weight against his chest. She wasn't a child, but the pain and the fear were familiar to him. Had he not felt it himself?

When she fell silent, he began to speak. It was harder to converse in Weston than Torra, but this young woman spoke the Weston of the Free Towns. He told her of the Arkosan Voyani. Of their Matriarch, his mother; of her death. Of their Matriarch, his sister. He spoke of the Serra Diora, her beauty a story, a legend in and of itself; he spoke of her isolation and her bitter loss; he spoke of the lute he had borrowed from one of the bards who now traveled with the caravan.

The rains had carried it away.

He had promised to return it—and he understood that he *must* keep that promise; the lute itself was special to the bard in a way other instruments were not.

And then he spoke of drowning, of dying.

She was silent, now, caught in his voice and his story—because Adam could tell stories. It was one of the ways in which he entertained the young. He did not have a bard's voice; he understood that. But in Weston it was harder, and the words were simpler because they had to be.

"I did not die," he added, smiling. "As you can see. I am here." The smile dimmed. "I would have died. All help—and there was help—was too late. But I am healer-born. It was on that day that my powers woke. I . . . came back. I was not conscious when I did. I was not breathing, and then I was." He looked at his free hand. Lifted it. It was a normal hand in all ways.

He told her of the healer-born, although she knew the stories. He told her of Levec, both grimacing and smiling as he did. He told her of the terror of being alone—made harder by far by the absence of every adult and child he had ever known. He had not understood, waking alone, a grim terror of a giant at his bedside, that had he remained, he might have destroyed both himself and those who loved him because his power was wild and uncontrolled and his desperate need to destroy the isolation itself was far too strong to be denied.

"I might have died anyway," he continued. "But I was saved. And my kin.

And I learned about the powers I have. I learned how to heal, and when to heal, and . . . when not to heal."

"How did you reach the Houses of Healing?"

She was shorter than he was; he realized this as he tucked the top of her head under his chin. His Onas would be so surprised when he finally made his way back home: he would be taller than them.

"A woman," he said quietly. "A stranger. Not kin, not family."

"Who?"

"Her name was Evayne."

She was silent for long enough, Adam was afraid that he had offended her. But she did not draw back or pull away, not immediately. Breeze ruffled her hair—and his—and he said, "Let's go outside. There's sun. It's warm."

She did not answer, but did not resist as he drew her gently outside. The skies above were an azure broken by tufts of clouds too slight to block sun for long. There were trees, however; branches cast shadows to lessen the heat of the sun. There were no insects, no birds; the sound of moving water implied that there was a stream, a brook, nearby.

The door of Evayne's room, however, did not appear to be attached to something as mundane, as ordinary, as a wall. He could see the open door, and he could see the room they had exited, but the door was not attached to a frame. If he closed it, he wondered if it would vanish into the scenery.

He almost wanted to close it.

Jewel was here because she had been determined to take the Oracle's test. She had felt it necessary, and Adam understood why. But Jewel was a woman, full-grown; she was a power. She had the full might of a clan, or its equivalent in the Northern Empire, at her disposal. She wanted for nothing; not food, not money, not companions. She had fought her way through demons, had survived assassins, had trod ancient and abandoned halls; her allies were ancient, immortal, and wild.

Evayne had none of those things. She was older than Adam, but felt, in this moment, much younger.

He found a large, mossy rock, near the brook that passed through these lands, and there, he and Evayne stopped. They were silent as they sat, adjusting their positions, lost in their own thoughts. This time, it was Evayne who broke the silence.

"My parents live in Callenton. It's one of the Free Towns."

Adam knew very little of Imperial geography, but it was irrelevant. He nodded.

"My father was the blacksmith. I——" She hesitated, as if searching for words and abandoning them unsaid. "I wasn't their natural child."

Adam said nothing, but he did not look away. He slid an arm loosely around Evayne's shoulder, prepared to remove it instantly if she tensed or in any way rejected the comfort he might have offered a young child.

She did not. She didn't react at all. Her focus, her intent, was on the story she was, even now, attempting to convey.

"I was left on the doorstep of the Mother's church. In swaddling cloth that the mother-born found strange. The priests there didn't believe I was a child abandoned by one of the villagers. It's not like the city you live in; there aren't as many people, and everyone knows everyone else. It would be hard—not impossible, but very difficult—to hide a pregnancy and a childbirth.

"At the time, one of the Mother's Daughters was passing through. It happens often, in the Free Towns. She saw the child—saw me—and saw the swaddling cloth, and she decided to bespeak the Mother personally.

"The Mother understood why, I think. My own mother told me this today." She tensed. "Today," she repeated, her voice softer. "This morning. My sixteenth birthday," she added, a tinge of bitterness in the depths of the words. "I was the unwanted orphan, given to the blacksmith and his wife, who had no children of their own to raise. Everyone knew it. Every child in the village. Every child who attended the Mother's service."

Adam could not conceive of an abandoned child among his own kin. Even the children who were the product of violence were taken in by their mother, by the tribe. But the Voyani were not so numerous as the citizens of Averalaan, and perhaps the rules of the Northern Houses were different. They did not appear to value blood-kin, blood ties—and they were proud of that.

But absent blood ties, they still built families; he thought of the den. They did not share parents, but that didn't seem to matter. They were kin, and bound by ties of kinship, in the way the Voyani were bound by ties of blood.

Evayne shook herself. "My parents loved me," she continued. "And I loved them. Neither my mother nor my father acknowledged the truth that the rest of the village knew: I wasn't theirs. My mother didn't birth me. My father was strict, and often silent, but . . . there was a warmth to his silence, and sometimes, when he worked, a kind of excitement. I wanted to be a blacksmith," she added.

"My mother was chattier—but that wasn't hard. She was the smith's wife, and she was held in some regard. But she tried to be friendly and helpful when help was needed, and she was of the village. She was still treated as the black-smith's wife after my father's death."

"You were of the village, as well."

"No, not really. I was a child from nowhere. I had no history in the village."

"You had your entire life!"

"It doesn't count. I was a stranger."

Adam's arm tightened; he forced it to relax.

"When my mother got quiet, it was bad. And she got a lot quieter in the past year. She'd look at me as if—" Evayne didn't finish the sentence.

Adam didn't require it, though. Her mother must have been told something by the Mother's Daughter at the time she had been found.

"I had friends," she said softly, after another long pause. "Not many. But— friends. Most of the villagers didn't care for me. They tolerated me for the sake of my parents, and after my father died, my mother. I tried *so hard* to be a good daughter. To be what the village wanted. But I couldn't be. I was a foreigner, an outsider."

Adam did not understand the village.

"Wylen was a year younger than me. He was also the child of people who had come to settle in the village. We started spending time together because we had that in common—but Wylen at least knew who his parents were. And Darguar. He did some of the smithing work my father had once done—but he was an outsider as well. He was respected because he could do some of the necessary work.

"He was missing a foot. He'd fought in the wars in the South—I don't know which ones. He wouldn't say. He told us that he'd been a soldier, that he'd lost a foot—but we stopped asking questions because he'd stop, sometimes, and just stare off into the distance, as if—as if he couldn't see us anymore.

"He'd come to the village. I think he wanted to farm." She shook her head. "He wasn't raised to a farm, and he didn't know what he was doing. But he knew how to work in a forge. He wasn't as good as my father, but his early training was in silver and gold—very different things. He was a big bear of a man, and when he was angry, he was terrifying. He never hit us," she added quickly. She had loved this man, whoever he was. "But you just—you wanted to stay away until it passed.

"He was an outsider, too, but he was more accepted because of what he did." She glanced up at Adam, her smile wan. "We were all outsiders, and we made our own inside."

She fell silent again. Adam thought she might stop and accepted that; his curiosity was not her problem. Or it shouldn't be; he was no longer four years old, asking questions in an innocence that would never be accepted from adults.

She had not finished.

"Last night—late last night—I had a visitor." Her hands became fists. She drew her knees tightly into her chest, dropping her chin; hair obscured her face. "It was my sixteenth birthday." She buried her face briefly. "Three visitors," she added. "For my birthday."

"The first was a man I had never seen before. Never seen but knew. He told me—he told me he was grateful to see that I had survived to be sixteen. He said he was my father. My real father.

"But my *real* father was the man who found me and raised me. My *real* father was the man who loved me. Who died. I didn't want to listen to him—I was angry. I—it was late, I'd been sleeping."

There was no need to make excuses now, no need to explain—but she did. To Adam, her words made sense, but the Voyani were never completely safe on the open road. One didn't always know, in times of violence, who one's father was. One knew one's mother. And one's tribe.

"He asked me to go with him. He seemed to expect that I would; that he'd tell me he was my real father and I'd follow him, deserting my mother. I said . . . no. I said . . . a lot more, but it all meant no. He just bowed and told me he would come again."

"I thought—" She shook her head. "I woke. I was awake. I've always had trouble with sleep. It's the dreams," she added quietly. "Or nightmares. I went to check on my mother, who's never had trouble with sleep. She was there. She was sleeping. But she stirred because I'd checked, and she woke. And I don't know what she knew—but she knew something was wrong. Even in the lamplight, she was so pale.

"She was afraid. She was afraid I would leave her." Silence, the sound of swallowing, of unsaid words. "I asked her what was happening.

"She asked me why I was awake. I answered—but . . . she knew something. It was something she'd never told me." She swallowed again. "I—" she fell silent, curling further in on herself.

Adam understood. "We say things," Adam said softly, "in anger. But anger is not our only truth. She is your mother. She understands."

"She knew," Evayne said, to her knees. "She knew that someone would come for me on my sixteenth birthday." Evayne exhaled. "She wouldn't have taken me. Wouldn't have raised me. He—he wanted to come back when I was twelve, and my mother said—my mother said that twelve was too young. If he meant to take me back at twelve, he could find some other woman to parent. She said my dad never intended to give me up at all.

"But—sixteen seemed old enough to my mother, when I was a babe in arms. Until I turned fifteen. And then it seemed too young. She wanted a child. They both did. And he told her—"

"He?"

"The man who claimed to be my real father. He told her that I was—" She laughed, bitterly, derisively, "the hope of the world. The hope upon which all others depended. My mother asked him why someone so important was to be left to a blacksmith and his wife in the Free Towns. She didn't believe him.

"But if she'd told me, I wouldn't have believed him, either."

"He answered," Adam said, certain, although it was a guess.

Evayne was crying now; the sound was in all the syllables, changing their weight and breaking them in different places. "He said—" She stopped, started again. "She said he said it was because they would love me. What I needed—" But the words were lost again. When they resumed, they were low. "He'd been told that they would love me and protect me better than anyone else, anywhere. All he needed for me was that.

"And he told them that the choice—to stay or to leave—would be mine, in the end. That he would come to me at the start of my sixteenth year."

"I think my parents believed that if it was my choice, I would never leave them." And then, she wept anew.

"Your second visitor was the Oracle?" He asked the question only when she had stilled and her tears had stopped. He had no doubt they would start again. *They would love you*, he thought. That was what her parent had desired. And they had. Love begets love.

It seemed cruel to Adam. He understood that Evayne would have to surrender all of that love. All of the life she had built. He had seen her before and was certain he would see her again—but she would never be this girl again. She would be a young woman, and an old woman, and the ages in between, who had faced and passed the Oracle's test. She would learn the arts of the Sword's Edge; she would walk in dark and fell places. She would face demons, and worse.

She would be what her father had intended her to be—but she would know, always, what she had lost. What she had chosen to give up.

"The Oracle came next," Evayne said, confirming what seemed obvious to Adam. "She came when my mother had left the room—and time seemed to stop around her. I dropped a cup. It didn't land.

"She expected me to go with her. She had come to take me someplace. To test me. To—" She shook her head. "She thought I had made my decision."

This seemed impossible to Adam. The Oracle saw everything that had happened, and everything that might. Or so he had been told, and he believed it. But the Oracle was ancient, inhuman; lies told to mortals would be trivialities, things of little note, as all things that lacked consequences became.

"But she—she pulled out her *heart*, and she—she offered to let me look at it."

"Did you?"

Evayne shook her head. Swallowed. There were more tears. "She told me that she had tried, and she bowed, and she walked through a wall. And then the cup landed, and my mother heard it and came running. And I told her—I told her I didn't *want* to leave. I didn't want—it would have been different. Maybe it would have been different if my father was still alive. They had no other children. They—" She shook herself. "But he's dead. I'm all she has.

"I think she was happy. Sometimes, with my mother, it's hard to tell. We went back to sleep."

Her back was shaking. Her shoulders. Her head was bowed; she was speaking to her knees. Or not speaking, for three long breaths. "And then they came."

Adam stiffened.

"I woke—there was so much noise. I could hear things breaking—wood, glass—I could hear people screaming. I—I told my mother to stay in the house. She told me to stay with her, but—I knew. I *knew*. I made her promise. That was the only smart thing I did. I made her promise, and I promised her that I would survive, I would be careful—

"Have you ever seen a demon?"

"Yes," Adam said softly.

She looked up; her face was a tear-streaked red mess.

"It is why we are here, in the Oracle's home. I told you—the Matriarch of Terafin seeks to take—has taken—the Oracle's test."

"Did she survive it?"

"Yes, although she sleeps."

"Is she sane?"

"She is Matriarch," Adam replied, as if that were an answer. To Adam, it was. Matriarchs saw more than the rest of their clan. They saw farther. They made decisions based on things that none of their kin could see. And it broke them, in small ways. He was certain that Jewel would break, too. His role—if he discounted the healing which no other clan member possessed—was to stop

the small cracks from becoming huge fissures. That had been his role in Arkosa, as well.

But Evayne, he thought, would carry a burden far heavier than Jewel's in the
end. Heavier, lonelier. Shadow believed that Jewel would fall if she did not
have her den— and Adam understood this. No one survived long without kin,
without family. If her den was not bound by ties of blood, it merely proved that
blood was irrelevant.

Evayne would have no kin.

He could not tell her this, but he did not need to. If she was here, she was
beginning to understand it. What had his mother said? *You cannot prevent pain.
You should not cause it, but you cannot prevent it. Pain is our forge, Adam. It breaks
us, or it makes us stronger—and we have need of strength.*

Adam did not believe this to be true, except in one regard. He could not
prevent pain because life had pain. But life had joy as well. And joy was
strength, too.

"Demons came. To Callenton. They brought fire and death with them. If
they hadn't—" She almost raised her hands to her ears, as if the echoes of
screams were still too loud, too visceral. "I ran to Wylen's. He was alive. He
was terrified because he's not stupid—but he was alive. He asked about Darguar, but his father dragged him off, toward the Mother's church. He tried to
take me with him—Wylen did—but I had to find Darguar." She swallowed.

"I met him on the road to my house. He had a sword in hand, a shield over
his back; he was wearing a dented helm. We'd always wanted to see him in
armor—but not like this. Not like this." Her voice dropped. "He was angry
that I was alone, but relieved to see me. And he intended to gather up the
people who could fight. He meant to go to the Town Hall. I told him not to.
Not there.

"He didn't argue. I don't know if that meant that he understood—but I
knew it would be bad. They'd die. They'd be too close together, and the demons would go to where the people were.

"There were no god-born priests in our village. No mage-born researchers.
There were no soldiers, and the armed men were caravan guards. That's it.
That's all we had. I don't know why—" she swallowed. "I don't know why the
demons came to Callenton." She looked to Adam as if he could provide answers. He couldn't.

"When was this?" he asked softly.

"Today."

He hesitated and then said, "What was the date? Does Callenton use the
Weston calendar?"

"It was the eighth of Wittan."

"The year?"

"431."

Three years from now, Adam thought. In three short years, the demons would be so bold they could sweep through a single mortal village without fear. He wondered, then, what Averalaan would look like. Would there be demons there as well? Ah, no. The demons already hunted the streets of that enormous city. But not openly. Not like this.

He apologized for interrupting her, and she once again found the threads of a story that was far too new to be comfortable, if it would ever be comfortable. "They were killing people. They were killing people slowly. They weren't afraid of us, of any of us. Darguar told me to go home—or to go somewhere safe. As if anywhere was safe. But he—he gave me something before he left. I don't know why—he had a birthday present for me."

"It was your birthday."

"Yes—but why would he even think of carrying it then?"

"I don't know. Maybe he intended to give it to you when the demons attacked. It wasn't large." He thought of the box she had carried in her hands, set aside on the table in the room she would occupy for the next small while. Thought, again, of the Oracle.

"There was nothing we could do," she continued. "Except die. Some people tried to flee the village; I think they were caught well before they'd managed to find the road. It was dark."

She swallowed. "I knew. I knew this was why he'd come. I knew this is what the Oracle wanted me to see. I called my—the person who said he was my father.

"He came. I asked him to help. I begged him to help. Because he *could*. He could hear me, he could appear *out of nowhere* when I called him. He—I knew he could."

"He wouldn't."

"No. He said I had to do it. *Me.* I could do what he asked, or I could die. And everyone I knew and loved—or hated, it made no difference—would die with me. And if I waited—if I wasted more time—those people *would* die, because . . . because what I'd seen once, I couldn't change. What happened remained fixed.

"It made no sense. No, it *should* have made no sense. But I understood it. Wylen was alive. Darguar was alive. But if they died, they'd be dead no matter what I did. The Oracle came out of nowhere to stand beside him, and this time—this time, I went with her."

"You didn't look at her heart?"

"She didn't offer. And I didn't want to see it. I didn't want to see anything else." She leaned into him, her arms still wrapped around her knees, her head bowed.

Adam held her, carefully, until she slept.

"She is *noisy*," Snow said. Of course it was Snow. He appeared only after Adam had carried Evayne back to the bed in her room. She woke briefly, eyes wide; her lids grew heavy once she'd caught sight of him. For this reason, he did not wish to leave her side.

"She is not nearly as noisy as you or your brothers," Adam replied. "Have you come to fetch me?"

"*Fetch?*"

"Has the Matriarch sent you to bring me back to her side?"

"*Fetch!*"

"If you cannot behave, go elsewhere. Now."

Snow's fur joined his ears as he turned a baleful glare on the Oracle. "Make *me*."

"They are not the wisest of creatures," the Oracle said to Adam, as Snow vanished. "But you may as well take advantage of the peace and quiet. Beyond this place, Adam, there will be very, very little of it in your future."

"You want me to stay with Evayne."

"I cannot compel you to do so. She does not seem strong, to you."

"No one is strong when stripped of kin and home. No one. She is . . . young."

"Yes. She is young. And precious," she added softly. "Stay with her until she confronts what she must confront."

"I will have to accompany the Matriarch."

"Yes. But in this place, there will be no conflict. I am not Neamis. I am not your Matriarch. I cannot compel. Or perhaps I will not. What she needs now, I cannot give her. And so, in some fashion, I have brought her here, to you."

"I cannot—"

"You cannot give her all that she needs, no. But no single person can give another everything that they need. What you can give will make a difference—perhaps a small difference, but a difference nonetheless. Give her what you can. I will not negotiate," she continued when Adam said nothing. "I will not bribe. What you offer has value to Evayne because it *is* offered." She looked at Evayne, sleeping in the bed, and stretched out one arm—but she did not cross the threshold. "She feels she was given no choice. That is not true. She was given choice. None were good choices. None were happy choices.

"But they were choices, and she was free to make either. Understand that, Adam of Arkosa, for it is something your Terafin must come to understand as well. She has made a very unfortunate decision, an impulsive one.

"It is Evayne, in the end, who must see that the consequence of that single, simple decision does not destroy everything The Terafin has ever chosen to do."

Chapter Two

20th day of Morel, 428 A.A.
Order of Knowledge, Averalaan Aramarelas

SIGURNE MELLIFAS WOKE BEFORE the break of dawn. In the sky beyond her tower windows, night had not yet surrendered to brightness and color. She glanced at the complicated web of orange and gold that overlaid her doors, her walls, and one significant window and saw, immediately, the cause for her broken sleep.

The remnants of sleep fled as she rose, flinging wardrobe doors open with a flick of fingers before her feet touched the harsh chill of stone floor; she reached for her robes in the same way. Sigurne disdained the use of magic to accomplish mundane tasks—but anything that saved time was now essential.

She had not summoned Matteos. She had summoned no one. But she paused at her dresser for one long moment. Her hands shook as she fumbled with the top drawer, cursing age and cold. She was no longer a child, no longer a prisoner, and yet she felt something akin to the same fear that she had known as both in the Northern Wastes.

She did not name it.

Instead, her hands closed around a small box; shaking, they opened it. A ring was nestled within folds of what felt, to the touch, like velvet. She had examined the ring; she was magi, First Circle, and if she was not the scholar that many of her confederates were, she was not without curiosity or caution.

In the dim light, she could see a simple band which contained one embedded stone. A careless person might consider it a diamond, or even one of the lesser stones that mimicked them. It was not, or perhaps it was not simply diamond.

The ring was not enchanted. The essence of it, the whole of it, was a creation of magic. More than that, she had been unable to determine. She could see the shimmering of color just beneath its surface—and in the growing light of encroaching dawn, the surface was platinum, not gold; it lacked something as essential as gold's visual warmth.

Not yet, Meralonne had said. *Not yet, but soon.*

But she knew, as the ring gained weight and lost warmth in the cup of her palm, that *soon* might arrive without warning.

She had been surprised to receive a gift of this nature from Meralonne APhaniel, a First Circle mage who had shown very, very little regard for material possessions, even as a statement of the power of the individual who owned them. His clothing was donned as an afterthought, and he had frequently appeared in lecture halls—when he could be forced to enter them at all—without shoes.

Only when he fought, only when he joined a battle that would kill lesser mages, did he don the most forbidding of his regalia. And it *was* regalia, in Sigurne's observation. The armor. The sword. He had drawn no shield in over a decade, and that troubled her, although she never put the reason into words; she had shied away from even that much truth.

And it was not her way to do so.

When he had placed the small box in her hands, his eyes had been silver, narrow, his expression remote. *I leave this in your care.*

She had not opened the small box. Instead, she had looked up—had had to look up, more aware of the difference in their heights than she had been in decades. *There is already too much in my care. If this is your responsibility, I beg you to continue to carry it.*

It is not, little Sigurne. It is . . . a sign. It is a symbol. I have never worn it, and I never will. It was meant to be worn by those I chose worthy.

She had shaken her head; her hands had remained steady. She could almost see her reflection in his eyes: an aged and austere woman whom time had slowly but irrevocably bent.

I did not say that you must agree with my choice. And this time, his lips folded into a more familiar smile. *We have seldom agreed, in that regard. You have, after all, accepted Matteos. And no, I do not need to hear his many sterling qualities enumerated yet again; I have only just finished breakfast and would like to retain some of it.* And he had summoned his pipe. *It is simply a reminder. A guarantee that I will know you as Sigurne Mellifas. You have been the most rewarding, and the most difficult, of my many, many students. And Sigurne?*

Silence, then and now.

You will be my last.

And she had understood.

This ring was an ending, the close of a long story whose beginning she would never know. Had he been any other man, she would have pressed him for explanations about the ring: who had made it, of what, how long ago. But she knew without asking that there would be no answers.

And that was dishonest. It was truth, but it was not the whole of the truth, and it was not the reason she had retreated from anything except a shaky acceptance. She understood that the gift was not meant to be questioned or examined; that in the eyes of Meralonne APhaniel, he had bestowed upon her a singular honor—an honor that was to be gratefully, gravely accepted.

She had always understood—in her youth, in this foreign, crowded city, and as she learned the lessons that he was willing to teach her—that Meralonne was a power. The magi did not discuss him. They did not discuss his age, or any part of his tenure within the Order; they *did* complain and resent, but given his attitude that was almost inevitable, and their resentment only amused him.

But she had never forgotten the sight of him, sword and shield in hand, a small demonic army arrayed against him. She had heard his battle cry over the howling of the winds in the Northern Wastes. He had reminded her then of the most powerful of the demons the Ice Mage had summoned—and she had known that that demon, ancient, wise, and deadly, possessed merely an echo of this man's power and grandeur.

She had known that Meralonne APhaniel was not, could not be, mortal.

And she had hungered for the sight of him, for each glimpse that time could afford her. She had known that he would be her death; that everyone and everything who served the demonologist in the Northern Wastes would perish that day. She had welcomed that death, had even anticipated it with something akin to desire—it was the only freedom she thought she could have.

But only, and ever, at his hands.

So many memories of the life between that day and this one had dimmed; she could not, without effort, remember what she had eaten a handful of days ago; could not remember the passing triviality of social conversations.

But she remembered clearly every time she had seen Meralonne draw his sword; it was the only time he truly seemed to be alive, shaking off existence in the Order as if waking from slumber. Decades had passed before she understood how very, very much she wished him not to wake. She could no more put an earthquake or tidal wave to sleep. But she had never considered them to be beautiful or compelling because they lacked intellect, will.

She closed her eyes, understanding that even that was not the whole of the truth. The ring was cool in her palm; her hands were cold. She did not ask Meralonne if it was time. She had no need.

She slid his gift onto a finger of her left hand; should it prove dangerous in ways she could not determine, she did not wish to lose use of the dominant hand.

She then lifted brush to hair, taking time for no other vanities before she departed her chambers.

The stairs were dark and long. She wished, as she began her descent, that she could dispense with the pretense of these drafty rooms; that she could reside much closer to the ground and the rest of the Order's many halls. But Kings did not discard either throne or crown, and if she was not monarch, she was ruler, here: guildmaster of the Order of Knowledge. She would be guildmaster for as long as she lived—and, at the moment, she was uncertain that her reign would last another month.

Too much was changing, too quickly.

Magic had, as Meralonne predicted, become elemental and infinitely more dangerous; it was difficult to control the intensity of summoned power; fires to light simple candles became raging bonfires in an instant—without notably draining the caster. Small accidents had become the norm within the Order's practice halls.

Had they occurred only there, Sigurne might have considered the change a boon—but, of course, they had not. She had three missives that had arrived in the hands of royal couriers who were polite enough to "invite" a response. And she had no response to give. The magi who were adept at detection of magic had been put to work, like the least senior of students, to study the change in the flow of, the availability of, magic. Had they not been as concerned as Sigurne, they would have resented the task—but she had made it clear that she could not trust the youngsters—men of a mere four decades—to understand the whole of what they observed.

Ah, flattery.

And yet there was truth in it. Which was why it had worked and continued to do so.

When she reached the most secure chambers in her Tower—in the whole of the Order—she was not surprised to find Matteos Corvel. She had not summoned him, of course; she had done nothing to disturb his sleep. She had, in fact, done the opposite.

He was as hastily dressed as she herself, as grim. His gaze accused her. Had he been alone in the room, he would have accompanied the look with words, and the discussion, while familiar, would burn with the acquired heat and worry of the past few weeks.

He was not, however, alone.

A man, dressed in the very fine uniform of personal servant to a rich patris, stood by the long, tall windows through which one could look down into the isle's streets—or across, to *Avantari*, the palace which the Kings called home. His gloved hands were loosely clasped behind his back.

He turned as Sigurne entered the room and executed a bow that implied the difference in their social status. She waited until he rose and offered him the same bow, absent his fluid grace and certainty. She doubted that she could have matched his gesture in her distant youth; she had not been taught the trivial formalities of the complicated hierarchy of Imperial interactions until she had been too old to take to them naturally. Her master, her second master, had disdained them.

"Andrei."

"Guildmaster." He started to speak and stopped as his gaze fell to her ring. His dark brows rose as obvious surprise transformed his expression for one long breath; he mastered that expression, but the words were slower to follow. "Forgive me for the hour of my arrival."

"No apology is necessary," Sigurne replied. "Will you take refreshments?"

A glimmer of something—distaste, perhaps—turned the corners of his mouth down. He declined politely.

"I see," she said, because she did, "that you have dined in the Order's halls before."

"I have."

"Will you partake of a drink?"

"No. We have the luxury of very, very little time. I am here to deliver a warning, as promised."

Matteos had come to stand behind Sigurne and to the left.

"Is Hectore well?"

"As well as one would expect. He dislikes the disruption, and he has been in company with Jarven ATerafin far too often of late. Normally, I discourage the connection."

"We are grateful that you have not done so. I have watched Jarven play many, many games over the course of decades, and often felt there was not a game he could not, in the end, win. But he is not what he once was. Were he young again—" she shook her head.

"I would like to know more of your history with Jarven."

"There is little of it. I was trained by a demonologist; I learned to note danger, and the dangerous, as my first lesson, and I did not forget." Her gaze as she met Andrei's changed. "I did not see you in the same light."

"You did not apprehend my nature." The answer was smooth as glass.

"I do not believe I understand it now," she replied. "Oh, I've heard the words. But I cannot make sense of them." He had not even blinked at the mention of the forbidden arts. So. Hectore knew that much.

"Where is Meralonne APhaniel?" Andrei asked.

It was not the question she had been expecting, but these days, it was the question she herself feared to ask. She did not answer. She was not young enough to find silence uncomfortable—not when it was of her choosing.

Andrei's slight nod acknowledged this. When conversation resumed, he carried it. "I am Hectore of Araven's personal servant. I am his bodyguard. I am his errand boy. There is very little that one can ignore when one is all of those positions at once—Hectore is not, and has never been, a cautious man by either inclination or nature. He desires the safety of this city, this Empire; he desires the safety of his family.

"He has elected to forgo their summer retreat, and they remain in the city, under bristling guard. You might know of at least two of those guards," Andrei added.

"Ah, yes. He poached among the Second Circle, and I allowed it."

Andrei's brow rose. "Allowed? Given his commentary after your discussion, he considered it a very near-run negotiation. And an expensive one."

"Very expensive," Sigurne agreed. "I would, of course, have let him have them in return for your dedicated services. He was not inclined to agree."

"I would not have agreed, had he been so inclined."

"I know. It is why I accepted a hefty sum of gold in your place." In a more serious tone, she added, "I cannot afford to have the magi hired away at this time, as you well know. The price he did pay would be considered staggering for the length of hire and the duties desired. It is not a price that could be matched by many."

"And the mages who are under permanent contract to their various Houses?"

Sigurne chuckled. "And so we come back to Meralonne."

He inclined his head. His eyes were a steady shade of brown as he waited, unblinking.

"I do not know where he is. I know only that he lives in the Terafin manse and makes The Terafin's personal chambers his home. It is *highly* unusual; I have quashed the rumors within easy reach, but rumor travels like fire."

"Faster."

"There is truth to these rumors, of course. I expect you understand that."

"I do. I have spent some time in The Terafin's quarters of late. The wilderness is waking, Sigurne. It is my fear—" He stopped. "We have had no word from The Terafin since the sixteenth of Morel. But it is not of The Terafin that I have come to speak."

"You have found the heralds."

"It would be difficult to find them before Illaraphaniel does. Of his own herald, there has been no sightings, but it is only a matter of time. Illaraphaniel does not sleep as the Sleepers do. He does not live in their slumber. His herald, if he arrives, is like to arrive through the city gates, just another traveler in Averalaan."

She swallowed. "Why have you come?"

"One of the eldest found me." He winced. "He is not . . . pleased . . . at my presence in The Terafin's wilderness, but he acknowledges as truth that she has accepted me and has granted all permissions required for my safe passage. And he understands, as well, that the permissions granted to Illaraphaniel are contingent upon . . . the absence of his herald."

"They are *helping* us?"

"Are you so surprised?"

"I am. Things ancient—and sentient—very seldom have the interests of the merely mortal at heart."

"They seldom have hearts, yes," was Andrei's grave reply. "Two among the denizens of the ancient wilderness led the heralds astray; he is hunting them now, having been distracted from his duties. Such enchantments as they have the power to cast, they have cast; they have led many, many in pointless, forgetful hunts in their time. I have come to tell you that you do not have much time until he recalls what his duties are and completes them."

"How much time?"

"According to the elders, a week, Sigurne. Perhaps two."

20th day of Morel, 428 A.A.
Terafin Manse, Averalaan Aramarelas

Teller ATerafin lifted his head at the sound of a knock on his door. He did not close the book he was examining; he flipped, instead, to a different page, one of many that were bookmarked. The pages fell flat to either side, and words rearranged themselves—literally—as he watched.

The door opened; Barston stood in its frame. "Patris Araven," he said.

"Please see him in." Barston nodded but did not leave. "The Chosen?" His tone was pointed, but not yet barbed.

"Of course. Are the captains available?"

"By some great coincidence, right-kin, both captains are not only available but present." This was said with more sarcasm than Barston usually employed where men of note—outsiders—might possibly hear him.

Teller nodded, his expression grave. "My word, Barston, that I will attempt to conform to a more regular schedule soon."

"I would settle for a discussion of the schedule you *do* keep," was the secretary's rather barbed reply. Teller did not blame him.

He remembered the former right-kin, Gabriel ATerafin, and the right-kin's interactions with Barston; it was clear as drinking water that Gabriel trusted Barston more than he trusted any other individual within the manse. Teller wanted to do the same.

And Barston knew that he did not. His dignity was offended; his pride, somewhat injured. But Teller thought it was more than that—and it was the more that troubled him. He had trusted Barston every day of his apprenticeship. He had trusted Barston every day of his tenure as right-kin.

But in the absence of The Terafin, demons had come to the manse; they had infested members of the *House Council.* They had hunted and almost murdered one of the younger under-servants. None of these things could be discussed openly with any safety—and all discussions were open.

He might have escaped the censure in Barston's gaze if it had only been the captains of the Chosen and Hectore of Araven who had arrived at his door. But Jarven ATerafin had, of course, *also* arrived.

Teller had all but begged Finch to keep Jarven in his own office in the Merchant Authority—and he had done so entirely for the sake of his relationship with Barston. Finch had promised only that she would try.

"No, don't bother announcing me," Jarven now told Barston. He lifted his hand to display the prominent and somewhat ostentatious House Council ring. "I'm certain the right-kin knows who I am."

Teller considered telling Barston to eject him. He was surprised at the effort it took not to give in to the impulse. Teller was not Jay; he generally *liked* Jarven. He just liked him at a greater distance.

Jarven took a chair as Hectore was more correctly ushered into the right-kin's presence. Andrei accompanied his master and looked about as happy to see Jarven as Teller felt. The captains took their posts by the wall that also contained the door as Jester and Birgide entered the room.

Only when they were all present did the door close. Teller opened the book beneath his hands to a different page.

Jester said nothing to antagonize Jarven, which was a good sign, since Jarven consistently failed to be antagonized. He never failed to be amused.

Today, however, he was alert, his eyes slightly narrowed, his expression sharp. To Teller's eye, he looked younger, leaner, than he had in years, possibly a decade. Finch considered this a good sign, but Teller wasn't as certain.

As it was his office, he opened their theoretically informal meeting. "We have had word from the Order of Knowledge."

Jarven said, without preamble, "There have been forty-eight instances of magic running wild within the city proper. There have been over three hundred such instances beyond the city's walls, such as they are."

Jester's mouth was a narrow line, but he held his tongue.

Hectore nodded. He was not precisely a friend to Jarven—Jarven did not collect friends—but was, perhaps, as close to a worthy rival as Jarven could have. There was respect between the two men, and the type of wary trust that existed when you knew your opponent so well you knew with certainty where the dangers lay.

"Work has not yet been completed on the Merchant guildhall—but we have acquired the services of an Artisan and several of the maker-born, and we expect to have a fundamentally safe home within the fortnight. But the caravan routes to the west are also reporting difficulties." Hectore didn't ask about the Order of Knowledge's incident report. Clearly, he had no need.

"Difficulties?" Jester said quietly, the first time he had chosen to speak. The word was sharp.

"Some of the merchants have lost guards."

"To what?"

Hectore glanced at Andrei. Technically, Andrei was a servant, and for reasons of his own, preferred to preserve this pretense. He therefore winced and shook his head. Hectore's gaze grew more pointed.

And, as always, Andrei surrendered. "The description is literal. They have disappeared."

"Disappeared?"

"Yes. In one incident, one of the wagons vanished, with everything—and everyone—it contained."

"Vanished." Jester tried for nonchalance. Teller watched as his lips folded into a smile reminiscent of, well, Jarven. He wasn't Jarven; he failed. The trick to Jarven ATerafin's ability to control his reaction, in Teller's opinion, was that Jarven truly didn't care. It wasn't, as so many people assumed it must be, an act. Jester, in spite of all attempts to the contrary, did.

Andrei nodded. "They are not the only losses; there have been deaths."

Teller didn't bother to ask about bandits. Andrei would not consider deaths of that nature relevant to a discussion of this one.

"The merchants carry gossip from the Free Towns as well," Hectore continued, in the wake of Andrei's silence.

"There have been disappearances there?" Jester now allowed Teller to resume the questioning, and given his expression, he was going to leave it in Teller's hands.

"Yes. More. There have been deaths, as well. The Order of Knowledge has dispatched their own investigators, but that is recent, and the situation is unlikely to be resolved by the magi—if indeed the magi come to any resolution at all." Hectore glanced at Andrei again; the servant was silent. "In our opinion—and by our, I mean Andrei's—the only mage likely to come up with relevant conclusions would be Meralonne APhaniel."

Who was under exclusive contract to House Terafin. House Terafin was in no hurry to return his services to the Order of Knowledge and, therefore, the Crowns. Even if Finch were willing to allow it, Meralonne would not go. Everyone in this room knew it.

Jarven glanced at Hectore; the look that passed between them heavily implied some prior discussion to which the rest of the room's occupants—with the exception of Andrei—had not been not privy. "Given the population of Averalaan, the number of unusual disappearances is much lower than we would expect. Our investigators have sifted through reports of people who have gone missing in each of the hundred holdings, and we've made educated guesses as to the nature of those disappearances."

Teller watched the flow of conversation as it moved, without apparent effort, to encompass Birgide. She was a gardener, a member of the Household Staff whose oversight was given to the Master Gardener and not the Master of the Household Staff. She was also The Terafin's Warden. Teller didn't understand how she accomplished the role she had accepted, but he understood her purpose. She was the guardian of the wild and hidden forest that lay in wait behind the Terafin manse. To Birgide was given the task of both guardian and steward.

"The forest doesn't exist in its entirety in the grounds at the back of the manse." This was common knowledge to this small council. "I have attempted to ascertain the physical boundaries of the lands that are claimed by The Terafin."

"And?" It was Jarven. Something in his voice immediately set Jester on edge. This time, Teller felt uncomfortable as well.

She met his gaze, tilting her head as she observed him for a few seconds longer than a man in Jarven's position was accustomed to, given that Birgide was technically a servant. She seemed to be listening to something no one else in the room could hear—and Jarven must have noticed both her concentration and his own ignorance because his eyes narrowed, his lips turning up in a thin, definitive smile.

"I cannot create a geographical map of the boundaries of the wilderness. I understand them, but the understanding is heartbeat or breath. I could no more explain how breath works to your satisfaction."

"But you could explain how to stop it?"

She didn't blink; Jester's skin, the white paleness of natural redheads, flushed. "Yes, if that is the nature of the discussion you wish to have. I do not believe, however, that I know more in that regard than you."

"You flatter me," Jarven replied.

"Do I?"

Hectore cleared his throat. "I would appreciate if the rest of this conversation about hypotheticals be held in my absence. I am a busy man."

Jarven said nothing. Birgide, however, offered Hectore a shallow bow. "There is no map. I cannot tell you how to navigate the terrain. I am not certain I navigate it, either. I believe I am given permission to traverse the forest."

"Have you ever become lost?" Hectore asked.

This evoked a genuine smile; it was rueful. "I have not been allowed to become lost. Many of the denizens of the forest have ways of making their disapproval of me quite clear, but they have stopped at outright harm." She shrugged. "There is one map, however, that appears to be relevant: Averalaan's. I can—with ease—reach both the Terafin manse and the Common from the forest."

"And *Avantari*? Come, come," Jarven added, at her expression. "We are not fools—or at least *I* am not. These are the three places where the *Ellariannatte* currently grow."

She did not reply. She did not, Teller realized with mild surprise, like Jarven. After a pause, she continued. "If I wish to move instantly from the Isle to the hundred holdings, it is trivial. If I wish, however, to reach the borders of the city, it takes a more concentrated effort."

"But you can do so?" It was Andrei who asked.

Birgide very seldom met Andrei's gaze. Teller, watching, realized that she feared Andrei; she simply mistrusted and disliked Jarven. He understood that she considered Andrei a very real danger yet could not understand why. Nothing his investigations had turned up implied that Andrei was a threat.

"Yes," she finally answered. "I can. If the forest desired it, the travel would extend in both directions; I could enter the city, and anyone in the city could enter—and become lost in—the forest. It is *not* what the Terafin wants. Not yet."

Andrei frowned. "Yet?"

"The denizens of the forest speak a language I do not understand," she said. "I cannot pick out the words or make sense of them in any way other than instinctively." This was clearly not to her taste or, perhaps, her standards. "I have tried. My apologies, Andrei."

Andrei's smile was slight, but it was almost the opposite of Jarven's in texture. "You have accepted an almost impossible task. I do not judge. I may marvel, I may honor, but I do not judge. Do you believe that the forest will change in intent?"

"No, not in intent. The forest doesn't understand precisely what circumstances might cause them to absorb the mortal citizens of this land. But they understand that The Terafin would allow it." She paused. "They sense a coming cataclysm. If it occurs, they will absorb every resident of the city who is capable of reaching the forest itself. Apparently, reaching it will not be a given."

"Do they believe their intervention will be required?" It was Hectore who asked.

"Yes. I have asked them when, and they have given me no useful answer. They have attempted to answer," she added, "and I have been unable to translate that answer in any meaningful fashion. But I have spent the past four days doing nothing but walking the boundaries of the forest where it overlaps with Averalaan." Silence again. Longer and more troubled.

At length, she lifted her face and turned to Teller. "You are right-kin," she said. "In the absence of the regent, you serve as Terafin to me, and I serve as your intermediary to the wilderness."

Teller nodded.

"If there is a chance—any chance at all—that you can find The Terafin, aid her, or speed her on her way, it's imperative that you do so, in my opinion."

Jarven said, "Interesting. Why?"

But Teller lifted a hand, palm out, in Jarven's direction; he did not look away from Birgide's eyes. They were—or had been—brown at some point. They could almost achieve brown now, but brown was no longer their natural color. And at the moment, they were almost bloodred. Jester had mentioned this; Teller hadn't seen it in action until now.

"The forest is not mortal. It is not, in any way, human. There are creatures within it who can adopt forms that are almost human—but not many—and most consider it a game, like a child's tea party. Those that don't consider it a game are almost always predators. The forest accepts them, of course; our forests contain both predators and their prey. To the wilderness, it is a simple extension of nature."

Andrei stiffened then.

"I am Warden, but I am not Lord, not master. It is The Terafin's will that keeps the city safe. I contain . . . what I can. I have that ability. But it is difficult, and it is becoming increasingly more so with the passage of days.

"If it becomes necessary to absorb the citizens of Averalaan in an emergency, the people who do escape into the wilderness will become a simple part of that wilderness—not guest, but prey, if they are not powerful enough. To the forest, this is natural. I will be able to contain some of the damage done—but not, and never, all. My will is not absolute in this regard; if I grant permission to enter, I cannot grant those who flee to the forest *status*. It is why I will not open those borders to our people unless they face certain death in the city's streets."

Silence. A long beat.

"You can open the borders?" Jarven was cold, stiff; he was the only person in the room who was willing or, perhaps, who felt it necessary to ask. Teller wasn't certain why he bothered; he did not seem to be in a mood to annoy.

"Say, rather, that I can keep those borders closed."

"Interesting. Is it becoming more difficult, or is it easier?"

Silence. Birgide's gaze slid off the old ATerafin merchant to meet Jester's. It was Jester's nod, so slight it might have been imagined, that caused her to answer. "It is becoming both, at once. It is easier to maintain the security of the borders I have crossed myself, but there are new waypoints that are beginning to open. It is difficult to be certain that I am aware of all of them. I know, however, when something unusual crosses into the Terafin wilderness." She fell silent. It was clear that she did not intend to continue.

Jarven opened his mouth; it was Andrei who interrupted before he could speak.

"Is this necessary?" The pointed question was aimed, in its entirety, at the Terafin merchant.

"Is what necessary?" The question was mild; the expression behind it, however, was the opposite of benign.

"You mean to ask the Warden what unusual means. You also mean to ask her what cataclysm the elders fear. These would—in other men—be worthy, perhaps necessary, questions. But you already know the answers."

"Indeed."

"Then what do we gain but the waste of the Warden's time? She has spent the past four days in the wilderness, and if, as she contends, that wilderness' overlap of our city is becoming more solid, it is in the wilderness that her duty now lies."

Jarven said, "Jester, would you care to answer Andrei's question?"

"No. I agree with Andrei. It is a waste of time. What the forest fears—what the Kings and gods fear—are the Sleepers."

"And what does The Terafin fear?"

"I don't know," he replied. He was lying. Or perhaps he wasn't; it was surprisingly hard to tell. "Maybe you could ask Finch when you see her." He rose and bowed to Teller.

"The reason," Birgide said, before he could leave the room, "that the disappearances within Averalaan have been far, far fewer than expected, given the population, is The Terafin. Even absent, it is her will that protects the city. But there are things stirring beyond Terafin's forests, and I do not think her passive protections will hold. The House Mage stands guard, in a fashion—but I believe most of what he fights is part of the forest, in much the same way that street gangs are part of the city."

"Most?"

"You are well aware that there have been demons; the demons are not part of the wilderness. Indeed, the wilderness, where it is powerful enough, rejects them utterly." She bowed.

"Birgide," Teller said.

"Right-kin?"

"Can the denizens of the wilderness be moved to protect the city from the creatures who will come through different forests?"

Silence.

Jarven's expression was sour.

Jester exhaled; the Warden and the redhead exchanged a long glance. Jester's hands danced in brief, quick den-sign. *Only you.*

But the gardener met his eyes and smiled. "That has been the subject of much discussion with those who are capable of it. Or inclined to it." She turned to the door, and then turned back. "Thank you, Teller."

"He did not dissemble at all? He made no pretense of either age or weakness?"

Jester sighed. Loudly. He had brandy in one hand and was massaging his forehead with the other. "I don't understand why you don't attend these damn meetings yourself. There aren't many, they don't last long, and you'll get far more information that way."

"I am not fond of Jarven," Haval replied.

"With the single exception of Finch—and possibly Hectore on a good day—no one is. He's taken a dislike to Birgide."

Haval threw Jester a withering glance.

"Birgide, however, trained under stoneface."

"I would suggest you refrain from mocking Duvari, even in the forest."

Which was, to Jester's annoyance, where they currently stood. He didn't care for the forest. He wanted to sit—or lie prone—in one of the chairs in the great room. Haval, however, seemed to like to wander among the foliage. Especially near the tree of fire.

Jester liked fire only when it was contained in a hearth—and he didn't have to personally start it. But Haval could find the tree of fire. He could *easily* find it. It took Birgide, the Warden, longer to reach its bowers.

Jester sipped his drink, resenting the lack of the rest of the bottle—also in the great room. "How is it you can find this damn tree so quickly?" he muttered.

Haval's smile was probably genuine. He didn't answer. "Birgide is occupied?"

"Yes. And before you say it, I've told her to give herself a rest. She's not listening. She is terrified of the future—the very near future—and she's using every waking moment to somehow prepare for it. And frankly, there are far more than the average number of waking minutes in Birgide's life at present."

"You understand what Birgide is attempting to accomplish."

Jester did.

"What is Jarven attempting to accomplish?"

And they were back to Jarven again. Jester was tempted to walk away.

"How much do you distrust him?" Haval asked.

"Completely."

Haval merely waited while Jester sipped more of the brandy that was vanishing by the minute.

"I trust him to amuse himself. I trust him to play to win. But I don't know how the game of amusing himself—and winning—plays out against cataclysm, demons, and gods. I don't think he gives a rat's ass about anyone else in the city. Oh, he might stop to offer Hectore a hand if Hectore falls while fleeing—but he'd walk over almost anyone else. I don't know—I've never known—what that bastard wants. But it's not what the rest of us want."

"Do you think he would consort with—although I find that word harsh—demons? Do you think he would ally himself against The Terafin?"

And that was the heart of Jester's fear. He didn't *know.* He could make guesses. He could make educated guesses, based on Jarven's history as ATerafin, and as the master of the Terafin merchant concerns. But he had an uneasy feeling that becoming that authority had *been* one of Jarven's early goals. He was no longer certain that it would be enough.

And where gods walked, the game could change in disastrous ways.

"Jester?"

"You tell me," was Jester's bitter reply. "Not even Finch can say with certainty that he won't. Finch assumes he's coming to life because he's guaranteed not to be bored."

"You don't agree."

"No. I don't think boredom has ever been his problem. He wants to be necessary. He wants to be at the center of events; he's a spider. He's not happy with a web that he can't, in the end, own."

"Yet he has never attempted to take the Terafin title."

"No."

"Why?"

"It has nothing to offer him."

"Rymark appeared to be quite interested in it, for something that you claim is essentially useless."

"Rymark was a pretentious, preening—" Jester spit. "Haval, I'm exhausted. I hate worry. I hate thinking at this time of day. I took your damn job. I agreed to be your errand runner. I agreed to file reports—although I would have refused that part if I'd realized how much like interrogation your 'reports' are, and how long they last. I didn't agree to *think* all the damn time. I didn't agree to answer your hundred questions before being dismissed.

"I *don't know* what Jarven wants. And if I don't, I can't—" He pulled himself up short.

Haval was smiling. "Jarven was directly responsible for the formation, in the end, of the *Astari*. Jarven was responsible for much of the training grounds and equipment that the *Astari* use. It was Jarven who chose to utilize the servants' halls in the palace, to cut through them in subtle ways, to allow the *Astari* to move—and move quickly—through *Avantari*.

"Jarven was responsible for the training of the Kings' personal bodyguards. He was responsible for making adjustments to every small detail."

"How do you know this?"

"Because I was there."

"I need a drink."

"You have one."

"I need a bigger drink. This one's almost gone."

"You are correct, Jester. If you do not know what he wants, you will not be able to accurately assess what he might, or might not, do."

"And you can't tell me."

"I am uncertain myself. Do not look at me like that; while I do not disdain lies, I choose to use them when they serve a useful function. Jarven has always been an annoyance. But he has been a competent, quick, unpredictable one. We have not always been allies. We have never truly been enemies. That may have come in time, but I disappointed him."

"Disappointed him?"

"Cruelly, as I recall; it was the least . . . colorful word he condescended to use at the time." Haval's smile looked genuine, but it was Haval; all his lies sounded like truth. "I was a different man in my distant youth, and he had hopes of me."

"That's the first thing you've ever said that makes you seem . . ."

"Trustworthy?"

"Likeable."

The grin deepened briefly, and then it was gone. "What happens to the wilderness if Jewel does not return?"

It was not a question anyone had asked. Jester was irritated. It was not a question that needed to be asked, the answer seemed so clear. Taking a page from Haval's book, he failed to answer.

"It is a question that occupies the gods and the god-born with increasing intensity." Haval looked up to the bowers of the burning tree. "I believe Birgide will soon be joining us."

Birgide was not alone. By her side, delicate paws disturbing nothing, was a small golden fox. The Warden came to a stop five yards from the burning tree, her expression opaque. Haval stood beneath its bowers, and Jester, between them. The fox glanced up at Birgide as she came to a halt, following the direction of her gaze. He sauntered across Jester's feet—stepping on both of them—and approached Haval Arwood.

Haval inclined his head, the gesture so respectful it put most formal bows to shame. "Eldest. Have you brought word?"

"You don't require it."

Haval smiled. "It is habit, no more. I may enter the forest on sufferance, but you are of it, and mortals are often blinded by hope."

"It is not hope that blinds them, but greed. Are you a greedy mortal?"

"I have been called so, in my time," was Haval's grave reply. The fact that the fox was golden-furred and spoke perfect, crisp Weston, seemed to signify very little to the older man. Not for the first time, Jester wondered who Haval Arwood had once been. He'd done his own investigating, of course, and had hit seventeen hard walls, but enough information had come in for Jester to realize that *Elemental Fashion* was not a front. It was Haval's home, and the business required the dedicated work of two people, not many.

"But not recently?" the fox chuckled.

"Recently I have been called far worse. My wife is not best pleased with me, at the moment."

Foxes didn't laugh. This one did—and the laugh was low, resonant, and very warm. "It is never a good idea to annoy the mate of a wise and powerful man. Mortals often forget that."

"I assure you, Eldest, I have not." He slid both of his hands behind his back in a loose clasp. "But greedy? Perhaps. I believe you know what I desire—and I believe very little of it is in your power to grant, no matter the sacrifice I might offer."

The fox shook his whiskered face. "It will not do, Haval," he said, as if speaking to a child—but a loved child, an indulged child. "If you truly believed that, you would not spend your precious, dwindling time in my company."

"He lies all the time," Jester said, before he could stop himself. There was something about the fox that implied comfort, belonging, safety. The latter was a pipe dream, of course. But it had never stopped anyone from yearning for it.

Birgide was watching the fox. She looked cautious, perhaps even nervous. Whatever Haval or Jester felt, the small creature clearly hadn't turned its charm on the Warden. Or perhaps Birgide saw what neither Haval nor Jester could. She bowed, however, to the former.

"Duvari wishes to speak with you."

"Of course he does," Haval replied, sounding like a long-suffering parent. "We were, however, discussing Jarven, the other problem child."

She was perfectly capable of controlling every aspect of her expression, but she was more at ease in this forest than she was in the manse. "He is so heavily girded by enchantments it is difficult to separate them," Birgide said, "as you expected. He does not, however, bear the taint of the demonic." She frowned. "I am not cognizant with all forms of enchantment, although I have been privy to many, many papers about magical theory.

"I believe that Jarven is more than cognizant, at this point." She hesitated. Jester marked it. "In the four days since The Terafin's visit, the focus of his enchantments have changed. On the day of the dinner, they were protective in nature. They protected privacy—it was a voluntary enchantment, like stones, but closer held—and protected him from magical attacks and controls. I think he has added a few."

"Their nature?"

"I am uncertain. Enhancement, probably."

"Of what?"

"He is too old for this fight," she said bluntly. "I believe—and this is entirely the guess of a rank amateur—he is attempting to compensate for that. I cannot be certain; if I spent a week or two within the halls of the Order of Knowledge, I would have a far better answer."

"Very well."

It was interesting to watch Birgide and Haval interact. Haval treated her as a subordinate, and she responded as if he were correct. There was no resentment between them, only a fragile trust. He accepted her competence without question; she accepted his in the same way. Haval's trust made sense to Jester; Birgide's did not.

But he had promised to give up on expecting anything sensible to come out of this forest.

The golden fox had once again made his way to Jester's feet as Haval and Birgide continued their not-quite-conversation beneath a tree of fire. He nudged Jester's left shin with his head as if he were a cat, and Jester knelt.

"I will travel with you for the day," the fox surprised him by saying.

"I was going to go back to bed."

"No, you were not. You were going to speak with Finch." The fox leaped into the lap Jester's legs made, and Jester grimaced. It wasn't safe to treat ancient, wild forces as if they were house cats, but in this case, the ancient wild force seemed to—politely, unlike other loud, wild creatures—demand it.

"Yes, I was going to speak with Finch."

"I wish to visit her. She will not come to the forest, no matter how loudly we call her. We have sent invitations," he added, "but she ignores them. We are concerned that perhaps she is deaf." He said this with utter sincerity, and for one long moment, Jester felt the cold, ancient and inevitable, beneath the veneer of warmth and charm. The fox was not, he thought, like the cats; they could rage and threaten and scream; they could be insulted at any passing event at any moment in time. But they forgot quickly.

He lifted his gaze—only his gaze—to Haval, who was watching them both. Haval's smile was rueful, but it didn't reach his eyes. He nodded.

Jester did not want to take the fox to Finch. "She's not ignoring you," he told the golden creature. "You have the Warden. We have Finch. To us, the merely mortal, the forest and the city are distinct. Separate. Finch guards The Terafin's interests in the city.

"Without you, Eldest, The Terafin will not have a home to return to." He hoped this was empty flattery, but he meant it regardless. "Without Finch, the home she returns to will be standing—but it won't be hers, or ours, anymore."

The fox rumbled. Jester shook with the depth and force of the sound, contained entirely in his arms. And yes, the fox was ill-pleased. Jester glanced at Haval, at Haval's dark eyes, and wondered if the clothier chose his position nearest the tree for a practical reason. But Haval nodded once again.

Jester acquiesced. "Can you even leave the forest?"

The fox chuckled. "I never leave the forest. No more than the Warden or the Councillor." He nodded to Birgide and Haval in turn. "And you, Jester? You do not leave it either. After we have spoken to Finch, I will go wherever you choose to take me. I have some desire to see the streets of the city our Lord finds so compelling."

"Will people see you? Or will I be talking to an invisible person the entire time?"

"Which would you prefer?" the fox asked with interest.

"It is not my preference that matters; I will change my behavior if it is required. It is your choice entirely, Eldest."

The small body—which had not felt tense in his arms—relaxed. "Yes," he said. "They will see me."

"You won't find the city impressive," Jester warned him, rising, the impossibly soft and beautiful creature in his arms.

"Will I not?"

"Celleriant didn't."

"Ah. He will before the end . . . if he survives."

"I highly doubt that."

"It will be a battlefield unlike any you have ever seen, and the young hunter revels in war."

Chapter Three

20th day of Morel, 428 A.A.
Merchant Authority, Averalaan

THE DAY HAD BEEN hectic, haunted in things great and small by the absence of the merchants, Terafin and otherwise, who had not survived the demon attack upon the Merchants' guildhall. The building itself looked new—perhaps even better than new—a symbol of the resilience of commerce in the aftermath of war. But the people, unlike the great stone facade, would not return. They would be—slowly—replaced.

James Varson had been promoted in the absence of the entire chain of command above him, victims of a different attack who would also never return. He had not become the head of the Merchant Authority's operations—he was too low-born for that and had not had the fortune to be adopted by one of The Ten—but it was clear that it was James who had kept the Merchant Authority running. Inasmuch as the Merchant Authority had a ruler, James Varson was its regent.

As Finch ATerafin was regent to The Terafin in her absence.

Her tenure as head of the Terafin operations in the Merchant Authority had immediately become a source of conflict for the House Council; she was *regent*. Her absence from the House—a necessity for the duties the merchant operations required—was fast becoming untenable.

Had the conflict been practical, she would have accepted the censure with humility. It was not. It was almost entirely political in nature. Haerrad was the point of that formation; he was the driving force that intended to split her from the Merchant Authority. And in any other circumstance, Finch would have acceded as gracefully as Haerrad allowed. He was not, however, a man to allow anyone else a moment of grace.

He had *not* fought Finch's claim on the regency; he had supported the right-kin's council nomination. The disappearance of Rymark—and the rumors that surrounded that disappearance—had severely weakened the Rymark-led faction within the council, but Finch was not foolish enough to believe difficulty from that quarter was over. And she had forbidden Haerrad one thing. He was not to kill those who were involved. If there were to *be* deaths, the decision would be Finch's.

Finch was regent.

Haerrad was not, however, Finch's chief concern at the moment. Not even when she left these offices.

There was a knock at the door; it was Lucille's. Finch spoke, and the doors opened; she could see the moment the older woman's face creased in several frowns' worth of lines. Lucille carried tea. The tray was bulky, and although Lucille was not a small woman, it was not easily maneuvered in one hand. Because she was Lucille, she waited until she had entered the room—and more important, the door had closed behind her—before she opened her mouth.

"You were carrying the tray," Finch offered, in as meek a voice as she dared.

"So was the *last* assassin." Lucille came to the side table, set the tray down, and marched back to the door. "What have I told you? We spent a small fortune on the brass." The literal brass. She jabbed her finger at the handles that adorned the doors. "And small is relative."

Finch poured her own tea as she listened to a lecture she'd heard a dozen times in far fewer days. The act of pouring tea calmed her, but it brought back a brief memory of Ellerson—and that was never helpful. The tea was served— was *always* now served—in the expensive cups. Finch liked them, while hating the necessity. But they had saved her life twice; they were necessary.

"Finch?"

She looked up. Lucille's arms were crossed, her lips thinned. "Are you watching?"

"Yes, Lucille."

Lucille reached out and gripped the door handles. She did not immediately burst into flame; nor did any part of the door, the carpet, or the painting to the left of the doors.

"I see. You are not a demon."

Lucille's lips twitched at the regent's tone. "I don't want to sound like Jarven," she began.

"But I trust too easily?"

"Yes. You trust me. You can. Even Jarven doesn't badger you into suspicion where I'm concerned." Jarven did, and had, but Finch felt no need to correct Lucille. "But Haerrad was *not* himself."

"Himself is quite deadly and treacherous enough."

"Yes, well. You are to make certain *everyone* who enters the room touches—"

"The doors, yes. Or the carpet runner." That was new as well. Finch had suggested the desk; Jarven declined; the desk was too close to Finch or Jarven, had either been seated.

"I could strangle Jarven," Lucille muttered. It had been the most common Lucille phrase spoken in this room since Finch had assumed the regency. To be fair, it had been a fairly frequent comment before then.

"Don't, please."

"It won't make much difference to your workload these days. He's never here."

"He has been overseeing the Merchants' Guild, Lucille. He is even, I'm told, effectively leading it."

"And if you believe that, you are clearly underslept."

"Jarven was not responsible for the regency," Finch continued. "That was, in its entirety, my own decision."

Lucille exhaled. She looked at the painting on the wall—not at Finch. "I have been at my desk in the Merchant Authority's operations for a very long time."

Finch nodded.

"I know merchants. I know sharks. For the most part, the sharks are easier to deal with. But Jarven in the old days—Finch, you didn't see him. He was a force of nature. He was like a summer storm, a perfect sunrise or sunset, a perfect, clear night. If Jarven chose to engage in a conflict, there was no question in my mind that he would be victorious; if we engaged in bets, we bet on the length of time it would take, or how many would fall before he claimed his victory."

Finch had heard variants of this story before; Lucille was not her only source. And for the most part, the comments were made with a fondness, a nostalgia, that implied that the worst or most terrible of the danger was in the past.

Finch rose, set her teacup aside, and moved toward where Lucille stood. "Do you believe he will hurt me?" she asked.

Lucille didn't even look shocked at the question, and Finch saw that the woman upon whom the Merchant Authority depended was afraid. It was unsettling. "I can't understand what his game is, or I would be able to answer the question. But, Finch—I have not seen him like this for *decades*. I am worried."

Finch exhaled. "So am I. But I've never seen him like this. I believe we're not the only people who are worried, either."

"Assassination attempts?"

"Possibly."

Lucille snorted. "I've never worried about Jarven's life. Just his dignity."

"I," Finch replied, "have never worried about either—but dignity where I grew up had a very different meaning."

"Oh?"

"No begging, no prostitution. I believe, even at his absolute worst, Jarven could manage not to do either."

Lucille's lips twitched again; she held on to worry for another half breath, and then grinned. "If he hadn't scooped you up, I would have."

"I could never run this office the way you do."

"Not the way I do, no. But you could run it. There's steel in you that most don't see."

Finch nodded, aware—as Lucille was aware—that Jarven had.

She managed two meetings with James Varson, one official, one less so, and one meeting with Andrei, shorn of Hectore, but stiff with a high-class servant's dignity; she was visited by a member of the Order of Knowledge, a man named Matteos Corvel; she was visited by a golden-eyed daughter of the Mother, who wished to beg audience with her on her parent's behalf.

She had a missive from Haerrad—he seldom set foot in the Authority offices in person—to her right, an investigative report about missing persons to her left, and beneath that, a demand for compensation, and a list of cargo manifests, itemized and in her opinion largely fabricated, when she heard the door.

It wasn't Lucille, or rather Lucille's knock, and she knew who it was before the door fully opened. Jester.

Jester, she thought, carrying something that looked, from this distance, like a golden-furred cat. The cat in question lifted its head as Jester stepped across the threshold, shifting his hold to close the door. The creature wasn't a cat. It was a fox.

She had seen it once before.

There was a tightness in her breath that not even arguments with Lucille could cause as she met the creature's large, unblinking eyes. They appeared to be lustrous gold from this distance. They were also narrowed.

Finch had looked into the eyes of gods—not often, and not for long— before. These eyes reminded her of those. But gods were confined to the heavens and the Between, the place to which they summoned mortals when they wished to converse in person. The fox? It was held almost cradled in Jester's arms.

"Finch," Jester said, in a tone that implied den-sign would have been more appropriate. His hands, however, were occupied.

Finch was not at all certain that den-sign would be wise, and she was certain that even had they chosen to speak with the silent gestures the den had developed in their youth, the fox would understand it all. And would understand that they had attempted to exclude him.

"Finch," the fox said, before she could gather enough of her thoughts to attempt to address the creature in a fashion it would consider appropriate.

Released from the need for words, she bowed. It was not a shallow bow, and it wasn't short; there was nothing perfunctory about it. She allowed herself one deviation from total obeisance; she did not wait to be told to rise. But she felt the weight of that lack of permission across the whole of her back as she unbent.

Jester seemed confused.

Finch met the eyes of the golden fox and held them through the discomfort of doing so. It wasn't a staring contest. Although she—and the rest of the den—had had some training because the noisy, messy, chaotic cats loved them, she understood that the fox was not like those cats, except in one way. He was wild and ancient and inhuman.

He deserved respect.

He deserved fear.

She had no illusion, meeting his eyes, that his size or his shape mattered, and she knew that even if he was not in his element—the hidden forest was *not* the Terafin offices—his was the greatest power present.

"Eldest," she said, inclining her chin gravely.

"I wished to see what keeps you from us," the fox told her. He jumped lightly down from Jester's arms; Finch thought the floor trembled as he landed. Foxes were not humans; their expressions were limited by the shapes of their jaws, their eyes, noses. But she understood as he landed that he was both angry and slightly disgusted. He did not care for the feel of these floors beneath his paws.

She was afraid, for one held breath, that he would change them.

"This box," he said, "is small and airless."

She went immediately to the windows—windows that were enchanted and were not meant to be open—and flung the curtains back. She struggled to open the latches, and almost gave up. It was Jester, stepping in to join her, who managed to force them.

"Yes, Eldest," she said, turning back to the fox. "It is both of those things."

"There are too many mortals here."

"You are now in the heart of the city's commerce. Some say the Empire's commerce. Yes, there are many mortals here. I am one of them. Jester is another."

"And why are these mortals of more significance to you than *we* are?" Before she could answer, he continued, padding across the carpet and crushing the pile beneath paws that shouldn't have had the weight to do so, "We have been calling you. Could you not hear us?"

Finch frowned. "Calling me?"

The fox, tail swishing, lifted a head to stare at her. He seemed to be assessing her words, and he sniffed, as if those words had a scent he could discern.

Finch had been trained by Jarven. Lies did not enrage her. She was far better at lying than Teller—and everyone was better at lying than Jay. But she did not and would not lie to a god, and she did not lie to the fox. She didn't think such lies would ever be successful, and where a lie was guaranteed to fail, silence—or honesty—was better.

But she needed no lie. She said, "I have not been in the hidden forest since the day The Terafin came—and left it."

"We are *aware* of that. It is why we have called."

"How could I hear you if I haven't entered the forest?"

The fox seemed perplexed. He walked quickly to Finch, and sniffed her feet, moving in circles around her and batting the skirts of her confining dress with his tail. "Do you feel no desire to enter the forest? Do you feel no need for its safety and its privacy?"

The fox was not the only person—if person was the right word—in the room who was now confused. "Yes," Finch finally replied, "I do. I want to search it from top to bottom for Jay. I want to walk through it to Carver—wherever he is. I want to stand beneath the burning bowers of the tree of fire, because I am cold, and I am tired." All of these words were weighted with truth, anchored by it.

Jester put a hand on her shoulder—but gently, lightly; he did not grip.

"Then why do you not come?"

"I can't. This box, as you call it, is the heart of *my* power. But it is not like yours. If I leave it, if I desert it now, I will lose it. Someone else will find it empty, and they'll move in."

The fox said, a shrug implied in its tone, "Then let them have it. It cannot be important. There is almost nothing here."

"Almost?"

"A faint scent. An echo of power, so tiny it could not be considered power in its own right." He looked up, and up again, waiting. And Finch, who had served Jarven at his most querulous for over a decade, knelt and lifted the fox in her arms.

He was surprisingly light, almost weightless; house cats weighed more. And smelled worse, in Finch's opinion. She bent her nose into the fur at the top of his head and inhaled deeply. And she smelled, oddly, honey and corn and fire. She felt warmth. She felt peace and the promise of rest. She was so tired of assassins and death and the need to think of both almost constantly.

"You are cruel," she told the fox.

"Yes. But not always, and not often. You have been summoned, Finch. Is Teller as unhearing?"

"More so. This is the seat of my power. Teller sits beside the seat of Jay's power." Her arms tightened involuntarily, as if to hold the creature closer. As if to absorb what he offered.

The fox shook his head, turned, and licked her cheek.

It hurt.

"You do not understand," the fox said, its voice changing although its form did not. "You are mortal, yes. She is Sen. You should not matter, but you do. She has made a path with, and of, the rest of you; you are important to her. As important as your city. As important as my forests."

"What are you doing?" Jester demanded. He reached for the fox, and the fox turned. Finch couldn't see its expression; Jester could. He paled but held out his arms anyway. Her own tightened. To Finch he said, "Your cheek is bleeding."

"Do not *question me*, little mortal. You do not understand. Do you think *your* Terafin can save your mortal city? A *god* walks the plane. The world once again coalesces, and the ancient things left in the shards of their half-divine sleep *are waking*. Do you think she can stand alone?"

"She won't have to stand alone," Jester said.

The fox growled. It was a sound that implied a dragon's throat. "She *will*. Because *she is Sen*. She is not you. She is not Finch. She is not *us*. Not even we could do what she intends, in her abysmal ignorance, to do. She is not even *aware* of it. She is terrified of it.

"And *you*," he said, head curving to meet Finch's steady—and surprisingly angry—gaze, "will doom her. Do you understand?"

Finch shook her head. "I would never, ever betray her."

The fox's laugh was bitter and wild and achingly lovely. "You are *stupid*. You are *foolish*. You are *ignorant*."

This, oddly, was comforting. It made the fox sound very like the cats. Finch missed them. Missed them but was profoundly and uneasily grateful that Jay hadn't left them behind.

"She is not what she was," the fox said, bringing its voice under control. Finch wondered if he was aware of her comparison. "She is what she *is*. But she has chosen to leave the larger part of herself with you. If you cannot accept her, you will lose her. If you lose her, she will not preserve what she intends to preserve—she will not even *see* it.

"And if she cannot, *you* must. But to do that, Finch, you must see *us*. You must understand what you see. You must be as comfortable with it as you are with this box."

"Nothing in this box can kill me," Finch replied. "Not without effort and not without warning."

"Ah, Finch, I see you are armed with nothing but naïveté this morning."

Finch looked up, arms tightening, to see Jarven almost lounging against the closed doors. She hadn't even heard them open, and from Jester's tight expression, neither had he.

Jarven entered the room, raised a brow at Jester, and stopped to rest against the outer edge of his own desk. "The tea," he told Finch, "will be cold."

Jester bristled—if one knew him well. Finch adjusted her grip on the fox and lifted a hand in den-sign.

"I must admit," Jarven added, as he strode toward his chair, "I didn't expect to see you again so soon." He spoke to Jester, offering him the rare nod that passed between equals.

This unnerved Jester immediately, as Jarven had no doubt intended. Jarven's smile did the rest. It reminded Finch of why Lucille was so uneasy, her wordless uncertainty circulating throughout The Terafin's Merchant Authority offices. Jarven's smile was not the smile of a harmless old man. It was a tight, brittle smile, pasted expertly over a vast well of rage.

Rage.

"You will excuse me," he continued, as he made his way to his chair, "if this meeting was meant to be private or exclusive. I have had a very trying day, and I am not of a mind to retreat from my own office."

"Are you ever of a mind to retreat?" Jester asked, his voice mild. It was, sadly, mild in the same way Haval Arwood's achieved mild.

Jarven would notice, of course. Jarven *did* notice. The shape of his smile changed, and Finch felt some of the tension leave her jaw and shoulders.

"Strategically, yes, now that you inquire. I don't suppose you have anything useful to do?"

"I try to avoid that," Jester replied. "But you're Jarven ATerafin, feared throughout the patriciate."

"It is not the patriciate that is my chief concern at the moment," came the curt reply. Jarven was not in a good enough mood to deflect or deny Jester's mild exaggeration. Finch wanted to know where he'd been, what he'd done—or what he'd failed to do. "If, however, you are otherwise unoccupied, tea would be helpful to those of us who aren't."

Jester lifted brows, very briefly, in Finch's direction; she nodded.

The man whose office Finch now shared—while he lived it would never truly be her own—sat heavily, placing his elbows on the surface of his desk and propping his jaw up with his hands. It was not an act; Jarven was exhausted. Exhausted and furious.

"I will not have you staring at me as if you've already become Lucille," he snapped. "I already have one of those—I do not need another."

"She's just worried."

"Yes. She's breathing."

This startled a chuckle out of Finch.

"I will thank you not to take amusement out of my current predicament," he said, his voice almost superbly waspish, some of the Jarven with whom she was familiar returning to the arched line of brow.

"I am certain," she replied, voice lighter, "that if you explained what your current predicament is, it would destroy all my ability to be amused." She walked toward her own desk—or tried.

She could not move her feet.

"I will assume that you did not actually brawl with Jester," Jarven said, his eyes narrowing slightly.

"Of course not!"

"Then what, Finch, happened to your cheek? You might as well tell me; it will either amuse me or give me a target on which to alleviate my . . . frustration."

Her arms felt weighted, heavy, as she realized that Jarven had entered the office, walked to his desk, noticed the wound on her cheek—and had not, apparently, noticed what she now carried in her arms.

He misread her expression—and for once, not deliberately. "You can't honestly think that anyone would miss it? The polite might refrain from remark, but I am not in a mood to be polite."

"Put me down," the fox told Finch. "Put me down in front of the man."

Finch's arms tightened. She didn't even know why; she felt a sudden chill, as if her burden were ice. Fur-covered, golden ice. She didn't speak, didn't voice her denial. And she could not ask why Jarven couldn't see the fox, because of course, that would alert Jarven himself.

"Finch," the fox said, voice rumbling. "If you do not do as I ask, I will be forced to bite your hands. Or eat one." There was no humor at all in the threat.

Jarven, however, had noticed the changing play of her expressions; he was frowning. It was a sharp thing, that frown, something to cut yourself on a few times before it was gone.

She needed her hands. But she needed Jarven, as well—and even if she hadn't, she was not certain she could blithely do as the fox demanded. She couldn't even name her fear, it was so visceral, so instinctive.

"I will not ask again," the fox told her, voice now soft.

Jarven's hands fell to the desk, as if something in that soft voice had made itself audible. It was clear that the fox remained invisible to him, but he had become aware that there was something to be seen—something that he could not.

She knew that Jarven was the greater danger to her, in the end. But she had lived with Jarven for a decade and a half. She could weather his anger, if it became necessary.

"You will not," Finch told the fox, "command me in *my own* home."

The fox looked up at her, taking his eyes from Jarven for the first time since Jarven had entered the room. She met—and held—his gaze, wondering if the dress she wore was proof in any way against magical teeth and jaws. Her hands, however, like her face, were not covered in the cloth, and she had no doubt—at all—that the creature could, if it desired, carry out its threat.

"Finch."

She looked up to Jarven's distinctly engaged expression; boredom, and even rage, had burned from his face, leaving only their echoes in its lines.

"You are clearly not addressing me."

"No, of course not. I couldn't stop you from commanding me anywhere you chose."

"I am awaiting clarification. It is the elderly who are often expected to loosen their grip on sanity and reality, not the young."

"You've been playing at that for decades. It doesn't work on me."

"No, more's the pity. And I will have an answer to the question." He frowned. "I suppose Jester knows the answer."

Finch nodded.

"Then I will let him back in. I am now in the mood to take tea, and I dislike lukewarm tea."

"Jarven . . ." The fox was watching them both, his head bobbing between them, the menace of him once again hidden, sheathed.

"You gamble," the fox told her.

"I don't, actually," Finch replied, while Jarven's lips tightened. "I would not dream of issuing commands to you in the forest. But you are not in the forest."

"I am, Finch. I never leave it."

"You aren't," she replied. "If you insist that I must see you—the wilderness, the forest—and I must accept you as *part of* me, you must do the same."

The fox looked astonished. Its brows, so much a part of its face she had missed them, rose. She was fixed, frozen, her arms tiring at the weight of him, but she met and held his gaze.

And then, the small creature laughed. The weight left her arms, although the fox did not, and she stumbled as her legs once again moved at her own command.

"Perhaps," the fox said, as it curled into those arms, "you are wise to avoid the forest. You do not understand the necessity of respect."

"Oh, I do. I do. But The *Terafin* demands far more of us than simple respect." She said, to Jarven, "Can you see him now?"

"No. And I am beginning to wonder—" He stopped at the knock on the door. "Enter."

Jester came in, bearing both a tea tray and a frown. The tray, he set down. The frown, he deepened. He held his peace until Jarven lifted a brow at him.

"You can pour for yourself," he said. "I'm getting a drink."

"You don't want to touch that cabinet without my permission."

"Finch, can I have a drink?"

"Jarven," Finch said, which was half an answer, the other half being no.

"Fine. Yes, please *do* help yourself."

"Why can't he see you?" Finch asked the fox. This caused Jester to stop, hand on brass knob; Finch met his gaze reflected in beveled glass. It was a narrow cabinet, and was meant for display, although it was of course perfectly functional—and stocked. Lucille had forbidden its use; she wanted all food and drink in the funnel of her oversight.

Jarven, however, didn't care if Jester was poisoned. Finch did, but thought it so highly unlikely she said nothing.

The fox rumbled. "Because this is your home, not mine."

"Explain, please," Jarven said, at his most pleasant, his most patient.

"Jester came to visit me at the behest of a visitor."

"And that visitor?"

"You might have seen him a few days ago, when Birgide brought us all to the forest."

"Ah." After a longer pause, his less patient expression reemerged, and Finch felt instant relief. "The fox?"

"Very good!" the fox exclaimed, in what sounded to Finch like genuine pleasure.

Jarven did not appear to hear this either, which was just as well. Condescension was only acceptable when it came from Jarven; it did not travel to him unless he desired it. "And why did this fox wish to visit us?"

"Me, Jarven. He wished to visit me."

Jarven swatted the correction away as if it were a fly. A fruit fly. "Do not make that face, Finch. You will wind up looking like a much more elegant and demure version of Lucille—and neither of those looks would work for her."

"They'd work for me," Finch replied stiffly.

Jarven rolled his eyes. He was staring at her as if he could make the fox appear by force of will alone. "Why did he wish to visit?"

"He is displeased with my irresponsibility and wished to know why I am failing him."

The fox nodded, well-pleased with her answer.

Jester, however, was not. He was a curious shade of pale—too pink to be white, but very close. Finch had seldom seen him stand so still. Even the surface of the drink he now held didn't ripple with the usual little movements.

"If he thinks you irresponsible, he is not as perceptive as I would generally expect from those who are ancient and immortal."

"The wisdom of the forest is not the wisdom of the streets," Finch replied, her arms involuntarily tightening.

"Ah, yes. I forget myself." And he did no such thing.

"If it amuses you to test," Finch told him, in her most Lucille-like voice, "Please do it when I am not here. I will, of course, grieve for you should you die—but I cannot afford to die with you at present."

Jarven laughed.

And the laugh tugged at Finch's lips, pulling them up as her own amusement caught light from his. He denied nothing, of course. And while he could do so with grace, he acknowledged Finch's perception.

"Lucille would be proud of you," he said, fondly. "What does the eldest want from you?"

"He desires that I do my duty, nothing more."

"I see you *are* wielding naïveté this morning. Given the immediate future, I am almost disappointed in you."

Finch said nothing.

"In particular, I am disappointed that you feel that it is an appropriate weapon to wield against *me*. Be a mouse if it pleases you. Be a steel mouse. But that is a ridiculous assumption."

"How so?" She did not argue or counter. She waited, the warmth of golden fur heating her arms and her torso.

"Things ancient, things wild, do not define duty the way you do, Finch." He had not said "we." "If you believe that you are called upon to do your duty and nothing more, you fail to understand the ancient concept."

Finch opened her mouth, and the fox very gently bit her hand; he did not draw blood. Her hand didn't hurt. It was almost like a very hard kiss. "Hush, little mortal. I want to hear what he has to say."

She kept her gaze fixed on Jarven, without hope that he would not recognize the little signs in her reaction that betrayed the fox's interjection. *This is my home.* "And what is the ancient concept? You are older and more experienced, but you are—to my knowledge—still as mortal as the rest of us."

"I have not, you may have noticed—and if you haven't, Lucille certainly has—been much in the Merchant Authority offices of late. You do such fine work I feel my presence here almost irrelevant. I am cheered immensely to find that this is not the case this afternoon."

"Jarven."

"I have been speaking," he continued, thoroughly enjoying himself, "to gods, Finch. I did attempt to interact with the god-born, but they do not have answers to the questions I ask—they are slow and intractable, and all conversations end with the equivalent of 'I have to ask my father.' Or mother. It is not *satisfying*, and I have therefore petitioned the cathedrals. I have spent some time in conversation. As a member of the House Council."

Out of the corner of her eye, she saw Jester empty his glass; she hadn't been aware of him drinking from it until now.

"You are not empowered to speak on behalf of Terafin."

"Am I not? A pity. I was forced to be direct, and the political error—if it is indeed considered such—cannot be waved away with a nod to the slow faculties that are a product of age."

"Where did you find him?" the fox asked Finch.

"He was in the office when I was sent here by *my* Lord."

"Interesting." The fox lifted his head; breath tickled her chin. Sweet breath. "He took you in?"

"He was commanded to teach me by the same Lord that commanded me to attend him. Yes, in a fashion."

"And he did not kill you. Did he damage you?"

"Finch," Jarven said, steepling his hands. She realized then that it had been a while since she had seen that familiar, sharp gesture.

"No," she told the fox. "He did not damage me. At the beginning, it would have been like trapping a—a mouse. I had neither defense nor weapon against him. He is not a careful man. If he sets his sights on something, he will move toward it in the most direct path he can take."

Jester snorted. The fox turned instantly toward him. "You do not agree?"

"Jarven's concept of direct or straight would shame a corkscrew. If there was a straight path, he would mistrust it instinctively. If he could walk safely through the front door, he would waste an hour sliding in through a window."

Jarven's raised brow was not entirely friendly; Finch was certain Jester knew it.

The fox, however, nodded thoughtfully. "You do not like him."

"No."

"You do not trust him."

"Gods, no."

The fox turned back to Finch. "He did not harm you because you were not worthy of harm?"

"No one," she said gravely, "is innately worthy of harm. And many of the people he has harmed in the past—or attempted to harm—"

"Does he fail often?"

"Almost never."

"But not never."

"No. And those who have defeated him—or at least have not been defeated by him—are probably as close to friends as he has."

"Would you consider yourself a friend? It is a mortal concept," the fox added, appearing to want to be helpful.

"Of Jarven's?" She frowned. "I think of him that way, yes."

Jarven frowned.

"But no, in the end. I am not what they are. I have not proven myself in his eyes."

"And will you?"

Finch closed her eyes briefly. She didn't know how to answer the question, but she was familiar with it; she had asked it of herself for weeks now, months now. A dozen answers came and went, but she was aware that if Jarven hadn't heard the fox's question, he would hear her answer. She straightened her spine, stiffened her shoulders, lifted her chin, and looked across a desk at the man who had been so central to her for half her life. "Yes."

Jarven's lips quirked in a very unusual smile.

"You wish me not to interfere," the fox said.

"Did I say that?"

"Yes."

Finch frowned.

"You said 'yes,' Finch. Jewel is fond of you. You are sister to her, and in the old world, that is no small thing."

Ah. "And if you interfere, my answer must be no?"

"Will it damage you greatly if that is the outcome? Would Jewel be unhappy?"

"Don't you know?"

"She has a very light touch."

"Why are you asking?" she asked gently.

The fox grinned. "I want him."

"But we need him."

"Yes, exactly." The fox turned to study Jarven, who was now studying Finch as if she had just presented a perplexing problem. It was not yet his contract negotiation face, but it was cool, distant, appraising. It had none of either his usual warmth or his usual frustration—and even if she knew that both were pretense and could be pulled on or put off like clothing, she preferred them. They were what she knew.

"I *want him*," the fox repeated.

"Why?"

"Because he is the first one I've seen—the only one—who might serve our purposes. Look at him, Finch. Look at him. He is old, and age enfeebles the lesser races, but he struggles against it. He burns. How long do you think he will last?" The last comment was made in a conversational tone, as if he were discussing the blooms in a garden hothouse.

She had asked that herself, but never of Jarven. Never of Lucille. "How long," she asked, "could you give him?"

Jarven's eyes were bright, sharp; his body tense. He couldn't see or hear the fox. He could, however, see and hear Finch. And he knew her so well; in some ways, he knew her better than she knew herself, observing all of the small gestures, the small reactions that were so innate to her she wasn't aware of them.

He had made her aware of most of them.

"We cannot make him invulnerable," the fox said. "Nor impervious to harm. He is not, by nature, a cautious man."

"I would not, of course, ask that—and neither would he if he could hear you. What would it cost?"

The fox chuckled, voice low, the sound almost more felt than heard. "That is not a matter for you to discuss. It would not be you who would pay the price."

"I don't think you understand what my duties here are."

"No. But it is irrelevant. I understand our Lord. You cannot barter for him, and you cannot pay in his stead. That would imply that you own him, that he is truly yours. And that is not the case with mortals, or not the ones who serve our Lord."

"Nonetheless," she said gravely, "I will know. You cannot speak to him here, not yet. But you could speak to him in the forest."

The fox nodded.

"Jester will not bring him. But if you satisfy me, *I* will."

Jarven opened his mouth. Finch lifted her head, met his gaze, held it. Whatever he saw in her face caused a flicker of smile, no more. He fell silent, observing. Observing her.

"And if we do not, little mortal?"

"I will not deliver him."

"You understand that he wants what we will offer?"

"Yes. But I am regent, Eldest. There is a reason that I can find your forest if I so choose; a reason that I am not lost in the upper remove of the manse. There is a reason Jarven cannot find the hidden wilds on his own. We both know it. What I consider necessary, The Terafin will accept. There is trust between us. If I accept your offer, the finer details will, of course, be yours to negotiate. But the larger ones? If you demanded one human sacrifice, a single living person, to save the entire city, The Terafin would not accept it."

"Not even if the sacrifice were willing?"

Finch smiled. "Not even then."

"Curious. Why?"

"Because that is where it would start. But 'willing' is a word that has too many shades. If a man volunteers in order to save the lives of his children, one could call him willing. We would not."

"One life for thousands."

"We will lose hundreds before the end," she replied. "If not thousands. But it matters, as you well know."

The fox shook his head, eyes darting to Jarven and back to Finch. "What do you . . . ask?"

"Will he be a sacrifice? Will you kill him?"

The fox exhaled. "No."

"Will your aid kill him, in the end?"

"Harder to say. He is not a cautious man."

"He is enormously cautious."

The fox shook his head, impatient. "We speak of different things, Finch. Once he has begun his game, his hunt, he is cautious—but he is reckless in the choice *of* the game. He is willing, once he engages, to spend the whole of his life, and the lives of others, in pursuit of victory. He sets his own conditions for defeat."

All of it was true. "And you believe that he will choose to play a deeper, deadlier game if he serves you." She emphasized the word "serve" but didn't look to Jarven to see its effect.

"I believe he will be *able* to play."

"You would not compel him?"

"If compulsion were necessary, I would not desire him. No. He will be what he is; to change it too much is to lose his value."

"Will he become immortal?"

The fox wheezed with laughter. "Immortality was ever the lure for the mortal."

Finch shook her head. "I know an immortal man. The only thing he desires is death."

"You speak of Viandaran, of course."

She nodded.

"We are not the gods of old—not yet. We could not curse your Jarven in such a fashion. We do not have that power or that permission." He met her eyes, saw that she would wait, and said, "No."

"Will he keep his soul?"

The tail of the fox rose, then. It grew much longer, although its essential nature appeared to be unchanged. "Is that of concern?"

"It is."

"Why?"

"The bridge awaits us, unless you do not believe in it. It was not meant for you, Eldest. It was meant for mortals."

"We are not *Kialli*, to take the soul and husband it."

She bent and set the fox on the floor. "When we die," she told the fox, "we travel across the bridge to the Halls of Mandaros, where our lives are judged. He claims our memories, and we return, we are reborn. It is the only immortality allowed us. If you kill him, he is free to cross the bridge. If he dies in your service, he is free to cross the bridge.

"But if you hold him, hold his soul somehow, he will be lost to the rest of us forever."

"He will be lost to you, regardless," the fox pointed out. The tail extended again, wrapping itself around Finch's wrist. "And if you chance to meet again, you will not recognize each other. You will not be Finch. He will not be Jarven." The way he said this made her realize that only Jarven would be considered a loss.

But Finch was accustomed to being dismissed and undervalued in this office. It felt like the most natural thing in the world. "You must decide how much you want him. I have seen the Winter King. I know when he lived. I know he will not die unless the Winter Queen does. I don't care what Jarven wants. If that is the fate that awaits him, he can rot to death in this office." Before the fox could reply, she added, "Killing me won't solve the roadblock, Jarven. In this, you could threaten—and no one could threaten me more effectively—and it wouldn't matter. You would never reach the forest, no matter how completely I caved in to that threat."

"I am impressed with the foresight of The Terafin." Jarven's voice was thin.

"It's not foresight—you could game that."

"Seven of your centuries," the fox interrupted, reaching the same conclusion that Jarven had.

"Seven *centuries?*"

"Your centuries. I am fair."

"One. One century."

"That would hardly justify *my* efforts." The fox thwacked the floor. "I would take the one century if it were not cramped by your conception of time."

"How would you define it?"

"By his."

Finch folded her arms, pursed her lips. "I have not insulted your intelligence, Eldest. I would appreciate if you did not insult mine."

The fox wheezed. "If she did not own you, I might change my mind. I think I *would* take you. But it is fair, regardless—it is his perception that will cause suffering. That was the case with Viandaran, and it is still the case."

Finch considered this. "You would do nothing to interfere with that perception? You would not contain or imprison him in the span of a single day in order to extend your ownership? You would accept that his perception was not to be interfered with or gamed?"

"Grudgingly."

"And when he has lived out his indenture, will you release his soul?"

"Yes."

She exhaled. "You will not ask him to do things that The Terafin would never allow."

The fox looked outraged. "He does that *now*, without my interference. I want *him*, Finch. Hobble him too completely and he will not be himself. Do you not trust him?" Sly, sly voice.

"Of course not," she replied. "But he's always been confined by the power of the merely mortal. He is not talent-born; he has had to broker magic for his personal use from the Order. He is not an army, and although he might—just might—be able to hire a small one, he has to do it the hard way. He has to live alongside the laws of the Twin Kings, and if he breaks them—"

"When," the fox said.

"Fine. *When* he breaks them, he is still bound by the necessity to appear to have followed them to the letter."

"He will be himself," the fox replied. "Just . . . better. I will not take him if you attempt to bind him in any way. His conscience, such as it is, will be his own."

Finch nodded.

Throughout this negotiation, Jester had been silent. He set his empty glass down—on Jarven's desk—and scooped the fox up. "We will return home," he told Finch. She nodded. To the fox, he added, "Let go of her wrist. Without breaking it or cutting her. Please."

"Warden," the fox said, nodding—to Finch.

"I'm not—"

"You are. I did not realize it until this afternoon. You are her *mortal* Warden. You are the Warden of the spaces which we do not, and cannot yet, command. You are imperfect, of course; your control and your oversight are crippled. But you are Warden, here."

The single word "yet" remained after Jester had closed the door behind them. Finch turned then to face Jarven.

"I would have accepted the seven centuries," he said, his voice so mild he seemed relaxed, at peace.

"A pity, then, that he was not negotiating with you." She considered remaining on the carpet Jarven had installed to provide protection against magical attack, and decided against it, moving instead to her desk.

"What did he offer?"

"You will have to have that discussion, Jarven. I have literally no idea what he wants from you, or what he'll offer you. None. He might turn you into a giant boar. Or a monkey."

"It is to be hoped not. A century?"

"A century in your perceived time, yes."

"Very well. Shall we go?"

"I have two meetings this afternoon."

"You are wearing your worry."

She shrugged.

"You are afraid of me?"

She shook her head. "Not on my own behalf. I have taken precautions of my own, of course, but I am aware that were my death your goal, I would be dead."

"That is hardly sporting."

Finch nodded. "It isn't. Perhaps my best defense against you has always been that *I* am not much sport." She glanced away. "Perhaps I have hope that in granting this, I will be spared the fate of every other protégé you've taken on."

"You don't believe that."

Finch shrugged. "I'm not you. I've never wanted rivals, worthy or otherwise. I don't enjoy engaging them as you do. I don't feel that it proves anything about me. But I've learned from you. I've learned everything I can. I will never feel ready—but I am not what I once was."

"No. You are Terafin's regent." His smile was fond; Finch thought it was genuine. "You understand," he continued, ignoring his tea, "that I want this?"

She nodded. "And before you feel the need to expound, I'm well aware of what happens to people who choose to stand between you and what you want." Her smile was genuine.

"And you might choose to stand there anyway?" His voice, his posture, were casual.

"If it's on the path between me," she replied, "and what *I* want."

And the sun that entered a window bare, for the moment, of curtains was lovely and warm, as warm as Jarven's expression. And as caring about where it fell as Jarven himself.

But that, she thought, was what she loved about both Jarven and sunlight. They were forces of nature; the sun could be too bright or too punishing in its summer heat, and it could be warmth and succor in the winter, a reminder that ice and snow were not eternal. But they answered to no one, and only a fool tried to tell the sun when, and how, to rise—or fall.

In a fashion, it was kindness. Jarven, no matter how old or frail he might in truth become, expected nothing and judged nothing. If she chose to stab him in the figurative back, he might smile just as he was smiling now: as if she, too, had finally become as uncontained a force of nature as he.

Chapter Four

20th day of Morel, 428 A.A.
Terafin Manse, Averalaan Aramarelas

MERALONNE APHANIEL STOOD IN the folds of wild wind as if he had never touched the ground; as if he never again would. Beneath his feet, the Terafin manse sprawled in the quiet of morning activity. Gardeners—for so they called themselves—tended their tame plots of insignificant foliage, unaware that beyond them, almost beside them, the forest teemed with life. Only one of their number understood the difference; only one was drawn by, compelled by, the wilderness.

It was time. Sigurne Mellifas had donned the ring.

He could see her, a faintly luminous presence, across the bay; she had entered the hundred holdings. He did not know her business there and, were she not the one conducting it, would not have cared. But he guessed where she had gone, for Moorelas' Sanctum was across the bay, at the strained boundary between hundred and sea wall.

The wind called his name. The air, like the hush of the wilderness, promised storm: thunder and lightning. But the sky was unaccountably clear. Was he prepared? Was he ready?

No. He had no shield. He had lost it, in the dark labyrinths of what had once been city, to a Duke of the Hells, a battle he had undertaken for reasons that were growing increasingly dim and inconsequential.

The lack of the shield had not troubled him; even had he held it, its polished surface would be blank, the regalia of the only rank he had ever desired to hold stripped from him by the august displeasure of the White Lady.

He frowned at a flicker of movement on the grounds below.

Finch. Finch ATerafin. He could hear the wilderness speak her name; he could see the trees shuffle to the right or the left to grant her entry because she was mortal and could not enter in any other way. He heard the joy, the excitement, the faint threads of worry, in the rustle of leaves and the movement of the denizens of the wilderness.

Worry?

Ah. She was not alone. From the north, he became aware of the Warden. She labored—had been laboring—in a silence so complete he had not seen her until the moment she responded to the forest's concern, but she, like Finch, had company.

Interesting. Birgide Viranyi had not been Meralonne's choice of Warden, but the forest's itself. Given her interest—her famed and previously derided interest—in the *Ellariannatte*, perhaps this should not have come as a surprise. But he understood that she had been tested, and she had not been found wanting; that she had surrendered some part of her essential self to the forest and the trees that she so unaccountably loved.

He had not expected the enigmatic Haval Arwood to become her most frequent companion while she resided there. Meralonne was not a keen observer of humanity and human nature; he understood well those parts of it that involved a desire for power, for dominance, but the rest was—had always been—inconsequential.

He did not, therefore, understand Haval Arwood or Haval's role. He was not mentor, but he was not servant. He was often resented, and his knowledge was exemplary for a human—deeper and sharper than the knowledge of even The Terafin, who had claimed these lands with an irrevocable authority, a primal certainty.

And yet he was here.

And it appeared that he had chosen—or the forest had chosen—to allow him to accompany the Warden as she moved to cut off Finch, and the guest Finch had chosen to bring with her.

And last, he recognized that guest, and his lips folded in a smile, a complicated expression. He had last seen that man standing on the very slender strip of ground just outside of the Merchant Authority building, while literal demons fought just above his head.

There was a story here—but it was a slight thing, a curiosity; it only barely caught his attention. He knew why as he slowly made his way down from his perch of air.

Shianne.

20th day of Morel, 428 A.A.
Terafin Forest, Averalaan Aramarelas

Haval felt his age keenly as he moved out of the protections granted him by Jewel's tree of fire. Birgide's side shadow, cast groundward by the boughs of fire-limned branches, flickered, longer, straighter, wider than his own. Possessed of neither Birgide's mastery over, nor obsession with, the forest, he nonetheless respected both deeply.

It would devour her life. She understood and accepted that.

"What troubles you?" he asked.

"Finch has come to the forest."

That was not generally considered a sign of trouble. Birgide's tone, however, did not imply that she had fled here, seeking protection or safety. After a brief pause, Haval said, "She has not come alone."

Birgide stilled.

Ah. "Is Finch's companion Jarven ATerafin?"

"Yes."

"I do not suppose you have the authority to refuse him entry?"

"It is . . . complicated. Yes, I have that authority—but he has come as Finch's guest, and Finch is kin. The forest hears her. You might hear the voices of the ancient trees; they are raised in joy."

"Joy?"

"She has come home, a place she does not visit often." Birgide's smile contained a brief flash of bitterness; she shook her head, and the bitterness gave way to rue. It removed years from her face, but years were not a concern of Haval's.

Jarven was.

Birgide said, "You expected this?"

"It is difficult to have expectations of Jarven ATerafin. One is frequently disappointed in them. Has Duvari ever discussed Jarven with you?"

"No. But he has also refused to discuss you."

"Perhaps it is because your control over your own expressions—facial, and body—are poor." He spoke calmly and without disapproval. "It is clear that you can maintain that control, but it is not second nature."

"No. In my defense, I am at home here." She did not move. "We will not have long; the forest is willing to extend the length of the path Finch walks with her guest, but Finch will not be denied forever. What did you expect Duvari to say of Jarven?"

"It is what he will say—to you—in the wake of this visit that should be your chief concern. To be honest, inasmuch as I have that inclination, I believe he has merely been waiting for Jarven to die."

His phrasing caused a frown to ripple up her face, where it remained, longest, in the line of her brow. "You feel that this will change."

"You did not see Jarven in his prime," Haval replied.

"You are not afraid of Jarven."

"I am as afraid of Jarven as I am of tidal waves. I might leave the oceanside to avoid them, but I will never have mastery over them."

She lifted a hand, waving the rest of his words away, her expression shuttered. Ah. "Silence is better than lies, here. It is not fear you feel."

And at that, he bowed his head—not to Birgide, but to the trees. "Apologies, Elders," he whispered, rising only when the breeze moved him to do so. "You are Warden of this unusual landscape. You understand what Meralonne APhaniel fights, on an almost daily basis.

"You understand that the partitions that separate this world from the one in which we live are all but crumbled ruins—or will be soon. And you understand that we—I—am mortal. The Terafin is mortal. Her forest is the seat of her power. Her den is the seat of her sanity.

"Do you honestly think that, as we are now, we have a chance of surviving what must be survived?"

"Yes."

"Then Duvari has, in my opinion, failed you utterly."

Voice flat, she said, "You want Jarven here."

"No. I definitely do not want him here. If it were in my hands, I would have him removed from the Terafin manse entirely. It is not, however, in my hands. Even were The Terafin to return to resume her rule, it would remain outside of my hands. Given the nature of the manse now, he would have to be dead to be carried out.

"And yes, Birgide, perhaps the elders sense my anticipation. Perhaps they sense something akin to relief or even desire. You do not know what has occupied Jarven's time in the past four days, and in the weeks that preceded them. I do. I wondered if this was, at last, the game he must lose or concede."

"You think his presence here changes that?"

"I do. And Birgide, I do not know what his game is. I have almost never understood which of the many games he considers worthy and which he considers beneath him. But I know that the demons and their Lord are the opponents he has chosen. Twice now, he has been the detritus of their attempted assassinations."

"And if they offer him a better deal?"

"A fair question. It is not my chief concern."

She waited.

"Jarven will consider a better deal only after he has won a decisive victory in their eyes. It is not enough now to simply win; they must be forced to acknowledge their own loss. Another observer might consider only the stakes involved."

"You don't."

"No. If he is acknowledged the greater power, he might consider a 'better deal,' as you put it. But I have seen enough of demons to know that that will never happen. They will not and cannot acknowledge a mortal as the greater power. Ah, forgive me. That is hyperbole. The demons that can would never be in a position to offer Jarven more than The Terafin can. The demons who are would perish before they acknowledged his victory."

"And if you are wrong?"

He considered this. Considered, carefully, what he knew, what he'd learned, what he'd gathered in the spaces between words. "I may well be." A name, carried by breeze, formed syllables in the air. "I believe the House Mage is almost upon us."

Meralonne landed silently before the Warden; there he tendered her a perfect bow.

She returned that bow. "The eldest bids you to examine the fountain in the Terafin library," she said, voice grave.

"I have examined it; does the eldest expect changes have been made?"

She did not reply, nor would she. She was Warden, but mortal.

"Which of the eldest?" he asked.

"The great tree."

He felt a pang of something like joy; he could not be certain, it was so unusual. "I did not know that he had awoken."

"I don't think he's fond of the fox," Birgide replied. "They argued." She hesitated.

"You are Warden here," he told her, as if she were the newest mage-born student in a long list of less than impressive candidates. It was clearly a tone with which she was familiar, even comfortable. "As Warden, you need have no fear of my reaction or my opinion."

"It is not fear," Haval said, his voice modulated, his expression respectful but fearless. "You are House Mage. The Terafin accepted you. She granted express permission for you to reside in her rooms, and in this forest. But the forest is aware, APhaniel, that the time is coming when all permissions will be withdrawn; you will not be ally—you will be a different version of *Darranatos,* except in one regard: you will have stood beneath these bowers; you will have seen, and spoken with, the beings who gather here, and who will serve The Terafin until their death. The Warden exercises caution."

"Ah. And should I accept the advice of an elder who will not risk giving me that advice in person?"

Haval Arwood did not blink, although he must have felt the tremors beneath his feet. "You are free, of course, to disregard it. Were it a matter of his own safety, and his alone, I am certain he would demand that you attend him. But he has chosen to treat you with the respect due a powerful outsider, which he fears you will become. It is diplomatic, APhaniel." The tremors stilled.

Meralonne was genuinely surprised. He was aware that the tailor was accorded a position of respect by The Terafin, and he had often considered Haval observant, but it was clear that he had spoken those words to calm the eldest, not the mage who stood in front of him; clear, as well, that the words had been necessary. "Respect is due the eldest," he finally managed to say. "You are, of course, correct. He will not demand; he will invite. And I, who have not walked the forests in his company for endless centuries, would accept that invitation with genuine pleasure." It was not a lie. And because he spoke truth, it was accepted.

Nor was it the reason, in the end, that he had come.

"Why have you allowed Jarven ATerafin entry?" He was no longer surprised when the Warden glanced at Haval and held her peace.

Haval spoke. "He comes as Finch's guest. You are aware that there are two people in Terafin that The Terafin would trust with not only her life, but the lives of those she values."

Was he?

"Finch has chosen. She is regent."

"There are no regents in this forest."

"And yet, APhaniel, she is demonstrably here. She will not tell the forest what to do, nor will she command the Warden."

"And you?"

Haval's smile was slight, almost rueful. "No, she will not command me. Given the state of my workroom, she would not trust me to master the organizational skills to become truly competent. Regardless, she has chosen, and the forest has accepted her choice. In general, the denizens of the wilderness seem remarkably unconcerned about the fate of the mortals beyond its borders. In their lack of concern, they allow decisions about the mortal realm to pass into her hands."

"It will not always be so," Meralonne's voice was quiet, but not soft.

"No," Haval agreed.

"Haval, I am delighted to see you taking fresh air," Jarven said, when they at last came into view.

Finch was not delighted. She adored Hannerle, but she found her enigmatic and somewhat condescending husband more of a trial. She was surprised, however, to see Meralonne APhaniel, and her knees bent into the curtsy her skirts easily allowed before she could stop them.

This caused the ripple of a frown to tug at Haval's lips and eyes. Meralonne, however, didn't appear to notice. He was studying Jarven.

"I am less delighted to see you taking fresh air," Haval replied. "Especially here."

Jarven, Finch thought, was highly amused by this.

"I haven't seen you look so hale in decades," the tailor added.

"You so seldom accept the pleasure of my company, you have little with which to compare. Come, come. That expression will frighten Finch."

"If she has worked under you for over half her life, that is impossible."

"Is it? Perhaps we have discussed your previous career. Your previous vocation."

Haval raised a brow. "You are still breathing."

"True. Disappointed?"

"Frequently. But if it will stop this annoying prodding, I am not particularly disappointed to see you here now. As you are Finch's guest, you are Finch's problem."

"I am capable of handling more than one task at a time."

"When it suits you, and when you so choose, yes. You are incapable of setting aside specific tasks, when those tasks suit literally no one else. It was your besetting sin and your single weakness."

Jarven's brows rose, his lined eyes rounding in what Finch was almost certain was genuine surprise. The laughter that followed tinged the surprise; he was delighted by Haval's very sour expression. She had always known that she would never completely understand Jarven.

"You have not changed, Haval. You have aged, but you have not changed. Tell me, have you spoken with the forest elders?"

"Frequently. Or perhaps it would be more accurate to say they have spoken with me."

"And if you have not offended them, it is unlikely that I will."

"Have you suffered under the misapprehension that you and I are similar?"

"We are."

Haval shook his head. "We are similarly competent, Jarven. But we are not similar men."

"No. Had you not married, we might have been."

Haval shook his head again. "It was not the marriage that changed me," he said quietly. "It was the desire to be married. She offered a life I had never experienced, and I wanted that life."

"And so you became a tailor."

Haval nodded.

"You cannot tell me that the current difficulties do not engage you. You cannot tell me that you are not as fascinated, as interested, as I. You cannot tell me that your thoughts and your dreams and your focus have not turned toward the subject of legend, of myth. Oh, you can," Jarven added, waving a hand. "But you will be lying."

"I do not disdain a well-placed lie."

"And?"

"It is irrelevant. I am engaged, but I am involved because I have something I fear to lose. No, it is more than that. I have something I wish to protect. It is the significant difference between us now. There is nothing you fear to lose."

"Fear of loss dooms men to lives of servitude," Jarven replied. He did not appear to be troubled by Haval's words. Not immediately. "Were you always so judgmental?"

"I do not judge," Haval replied. "I assess—as I was once instructed to do."

Jarven's laugh was bright again, but sharp, and Haval reflected its essence with the darker edge of his smile. "And what arrogant fool told you that?"

"The only man I had ever met I was willing to grant my unqualified respect."

"Ah. And now?"

"Now it is qualified."

Jarven shook his head. "We were both young men."

"I believe you said at the time I was young, and you were in your prime."

Jarven turned to Finch. "Haval puts me in mind of something. You said you wished to avoid the fate that befalls all of my protégés."

She could feel the history—hidden, but deeply rooted—between these two men. She nodded.

"Haval was the most significant of their long number. He survived. Perhaps he will have something to teach you if you care to learn."

Finch expected Haval's expression to sour; she was surprised when it did not. He was, as he had said, assessing Jarven, his face a mask that allowed no expression to escape. It was the single thing about him that she found most difficult, this sudden absence of the warmth of human expression.

"Or perhaps, Jarven," Haval surprised her—surprised them both—by saying, "She will have something to teach you. The games we once played we both survived. This is not that game."

"No. It is a greater game—it is *the* game. All others were echoes—and at that, muted echoes—of this one."

"You sound certain."

"I am. I am, however, less certain of where we are heading."

Birgide looked to Haval and then to Finch.

"No," she told the forest's Warden, "I'm not at all certain it is wise."

"And yet you chose to invite him here under your protection?" It was not Birgide who asked, but Haval.

"The eldest asked it," she replied.

"Of Jarven?"

"Of me." Jarven was watching her with the same intense curiosity that had characterized his entry into this forest. "I do not understand everything that has occurred. Nor do I pretend to understand everything that will. I do not pretend to have control of Jarven. At my most certain, my most arrogant, I could not pretend that—it is the act of a fool."

Haval nodded.

"I think it likely that the elders believe they *will* have control—but I confess uncertainty there, as well."

"You are willing to trust Jarven, then."

Finch shook her head. "It would only insult him. And even if I cared little for his temper and his ruffled pride, I would not. I believe that we won't be his targets. We won't be his opponents. He won't kill us or harm us unless we stand in his way—but that's always been his way. It was his way when The Terafin offered him the House Name. It was his way when she offered him the Merchant Authority."

"She did not offer that," Jarven countered.

Finch ignored this. "People have accused Jarven of being monstrous. I even understand why. But I think—" She stopped, gazing at her feet, youth evident in the line of her chin, her bunched shoulders. She was, for a moment, the girl that Jewel had gone to such lengths to rescue in the streets of the hundred holdings.

She exhaled, lifting her chin. Dispelling the ghost of that waif, she said, "I think we need our own monsters."

"I rather think we have monsters enough." Haval's voice was gentle.

"Not one of them," she said, "could stand against Meralonne APhaniel and survive. Not one could stand against the demons APhaniel dispatched with contempt. Against the greater demons, we're kindling."

"You are wrong," Meralonne said quietly, lifting his gaze for the first time from Jarven and Haval. "The Terafin could do what even I could not. Not yet."

Not yet.

Haval spared the magi an obvious glance, no more. When the Warden had appeared, Finch had done two things. She had relaxed, and she had stopped walking. She did not, in Haval's estimation, intend to continue.

Jarven would notice, of course. But Jarven noticed everything when he was of the mind to pay attention. He had become sloppier with age—but Jarven at his most sloppy was, and had been, a match for Duvari at his most focused.

I think we need our own monsters.

"Ironic, is it not?" Jarven said.

Haval's nod was brief. "Neither of us chose to remain to oversee what we built."

"No. And it changed. Of course it did. It changed enough that it would be a roadblock to those who knew its lay."

"If I recall correctly, you considered the management of men—of people— beneath you at the time."

"And you did not?"

"No."

"And Duvari?"

"He is not a man you can easily manipulate. You can insult him, yes. But he has very little ego, very little vanity."

"And only one ambition."

Haval nodded.

"I would have thought you might choose another."

"I have only once considered those you have chosen to groom worth that choice."

"Ah. You refer to Finch, of course."

Haval nodded. "I approve of Lucille."

"Lucille?"

"Yes."

"She could not do what I have done."

"No. You did not groom Lucille; you accepted her. She is the only person, until Finch, to whom you have ceded any part of your territory."

"But only the boring parts."

"Indeed."

"I do not foresee many boring parts, in this. But there is a curious symmetry in it. Your protégé—"

"The Terafin is *not* my protégé."

"—Is more than mortal, in the eyes of the wilderness; she is a force to be reckoned with—if not now, then in future. And you are stubbornly mortal, stubbornly mundane, but you are also, and have always been, a force to be reckoned with. But I? I am fenced in by a stubbornly mortal—and perhaps worse, stubbornly loyal—woman, the age of your protégé, and it is I who reach for the numinous, the wild. And we four will be here."

"I am not of Terafin," Haval said mildly. Ah, Jarven's eyes. His face. He did not need to stand beneath burning bowers; his gaze was alight, unblinking. He had found some way into terrain he had not entered since Haval himself was young.

And Haval felt a twinge of nostalgia, even of, if not joy, enjoyment nonetheless. Only a fool would have missed this man, but all men were capable of folly.

Jarven glanced at Finch. "We are to wait?"

Finch looked to Birgide. Birgide nodded. To Jarven she said, "Do not leave the path without escort. The forest is not entirely safe."

"It is not secure?"

The gardener smiled. "It is secure; it is not safe." She turned fully to Meralonne APhaniel. "The eldest *invites* you to attend him at your earliest convenience. He, too, would take joy from your company."

"I doubt that," Meralonne replied.

Haval winced but said nothing.

"I merely mean I am not yet what I was. And if it is information about my ancient kin that he seeks—and there was affection between them—I do not have it. I do not understand how Shianne came to be here. But she is companion to The Terafin, and The Terafin is neither ancient nor wild. She will protect Shianne."

"Nonetheless," Birgide continued, "he wishes your company."

The mage bowed then. When he rose, he said, "ATerafin." He spoke to

Jarven. "It is very easy to become lost in this place. Be wary, if that is in your nature."

The fox appeared only after Meralonne had taken his leave.

For a moment, if Finch ignored his unnatural coloring, she could believe him to be the animal he appeared to be. She knelt immediately; he padded over to her lap and leaped delicately into her arms. She then rose, as if she were a living throne or pedestal. The fox was not like the cats; he was politer, softer spoken, and less inherently violent. But she thought him the greater danger, in the long run. And, as the cats, he was neither her responsibility nor her concern.

"You fear him," the eldest said, glancing at Jarven.

"Yes," she said, without regret or embarrassment. "I do."

"And yet you consider him kin."

Did she? "He is ATerafin, as am I."

"He is not ATerafin as you are," the fox replied, voice grave, eyes wide, round, unblinking. They felt, for a moment, like Haval Arwood's eyes when he subjected someone to the whole of his ferocious observation; she was certain they missed nothing.

"No. But he is nothing at all like me."

"He is far more like you than I am."

She nodded. "I believe he wishes he weren't."

"He has never been fond of being discussed in the third person," Jarven interjected.

"No?" the fox seemed genuinely interested in this claim, but he shook his head and turned once again to Finch. "Where was I before I was interrupted? Ah. Yes. You believe he wishes he were less like you?"

Finch hesitated. She had trained with, worked with, Jarven for all of her adult life; she could lie easily, and in truth no longer considered flattery a lie so much as a social necessity, an expedient that manners often required, if not outright demanded.

But she was aware, as the fox regarded her, that her words had a weight here that was, that must be, entirely different.

"I believe," she therefore said, "that he does not consider himself at all like me, except in the sense that we are both people, both mortal. I am ATerafin, as is he, but he would not have noticed me, would never have become mentor to me, were it not for the command of The Terafin.

"He could not disobey a direct command, and I believe he was given exactly that. Among Jarven's strengths is his ability to make do; to work with what is in front of him. He may dream of different clay—or wood, or metal—with which to craft, but he will make the most of, the best of, what he is given."

"He does not complain?"

She was surprised into a quiet laugh. "He's *Jarven*. Of course he complains. I am not what he was in his distant youth."

"I should hope not," Jarven said.

"I have none of his ambition, none of his fire, none of his aggression."

"Ah," the fox said, voice soft. "A pity, really. But you have spoken only of the differences. If he wishes he were less like you—"

"Less mortal," Finch said quietly. "Less fragile. He is, as I said, practical. He takes what he has at hand, and he builds with it, plays with it, games with it. But neither Jarven nor I were talent-born. Neither he nor I were scions of wealth, born to power, born of it.

"What you might offer him is a new material to work with or a new, and better, hand with which to play."

The fox nodded genially; he was not done with Finch. "Will you join us?" It was only barely a request.

But Finch shook her head.

"That is foolish," the fox told her.

"Yes, I know. But it is also wise."

"Oh?"

"Jarven does not forgive men—or women—who see him in any state of weakness he does not voluntarily expose. Lucille might be forgiven, but I? I would not."

"Ah. Then I will tell you this, Finch ATerafin, sister to our lord and much beloved, you are both right and wrong. He is, at times, uneasy in your presence; it is true. But it is not the uneasiness that comes from wariness; he does not expect that you will, like his previous students, attempt to unseat him or harm him. He is accustomed to caution from the powerful—and ambition, it is true—and he has waited for you to join their ranks.

"But, of course, he is wise in a fashion. Waiting, he also knows that you will not, not unless commanded to it. And The Terafin would never make that command. No. His difficulty lies with what you have already said. Can you not see why?"

She frowned.

"If I may, Eldest?" Haval now interrupted.

"Councillor," the fox replied, condescending to nod in the tailor's direction, as he had not yet done in Jarven's. The tailor was the only man present who was not ATerafin, and who Finch was certain would never become so.

"He would never have chosen you," Haval said quietly. "You have surmised this, and I concur."

Finch nodded.

"And, Finch, you are, in the end, the pupil who has shown the most potential. If you desired the House, it would—with some effort—be yours. Jarven is certain of it. And he is correct."

Her frown deepened and then cleared. "He's uneasy because he made a mistake."

"Yes. And now he must wonder: how often has he made similar mistakes? How often has he chosen the wrong pupils?"

"It is more than that," the fox said. "Jarven understands that mortals want power. He understands that every living being wants power. He believes that those without the will or the strength or the cunning will never achieve it. You remind him, uncomfortably, that those with the potential might not have the desire; were it not for The Terafin's need, you would never have become what you are.

"And that is uncomfortable. If he is unscrupulous, he has scruples. You have been waiting, yes? For the thing that will test you, in his eyes. For the event that will start the schism, that will pit him against you. But you have failed to understand, Finch: so has he. He did not decide on a whim to destroy what he had built—"

Jarven said, in a tone of voice Finch had never heard him use, "Enough." The word was soft but sharp, it was cold; it contained every threat that a man of power with few scruples could bring to bear. Jarven meant to be obeyed. Here. In The Terafin's wild forest.

Her arms had tensed, tightened; to an outsider she might have looked like a woman whose visceral maternal instincts had reared their collective heads and was consequently protecting her child, making of her arms the only certain safety the child could have. And none of these things would be true. She wanted to apologize for Jarven, to beg the eldest's forgiveness, to placate—as she had learned to do—without surrender.

She could not, because she understood that Jarven had been pushed as far as he could be pushed. He would never accept protection from her, and he would, in the ice of his rage, be . . . humiliated. She wished Lucille were here, because Lucille *could* be a mother hen. But she suspected that Lucille would have withdrawn in tense, worried silence.

She glanced at Haval, trying in a subtle way to restrain the fox, for all the good that would do. Haval's face was devoid of expression; he watched Jarven. His hands were by his sides, and he was utterly still.

"Councillor?" the fox said. Finch would have to ask him why he referred to Haval that way—but later. She was more afraid for Jarven than she had ever been, wishing desperately that she had refused his request. Their request.

"There is fire in him," Haval replied.

The fox lifted his head thoughtfully. "Yes."

"It has been Jewel's way," Haval continued, "to respect and shelter the dangerous—no matter the circumstances of their birth—when they will tolerate or allow it."

"Indeed," the fox replied, lifting his nose. "Woven into our Lord's complicated commands to those of us who obey her is the daughter of the Lord of the Hells. Ah, Finch. You've met her, I see." He continued to speak to Haval. "And if our Lord is willing to succor and grant freedom to one such as that child, she should not object to Jarven."

Finch said nothing for one long minute. Muscle by muscle, she could see Jarven relax.

"I wished to hear the Councillor's advice. Advice," he added, "does not have to be taken. Surely Jarven has taught you that. The Warden does not desire this, and she has made it known. She *could* interfere. She has earned that right. But she, too, listens to the Councillor. And, Finch, she has listened to you. She has listened to your Jester. She has made her decision, although she teeters on its edge even now."

"Very well," Haval said. He slid his hands behind his back and inclined his chin in the fox's direction. "Although you know what my advice will be."

"I thought mortals liked to hear their own voices."

"Ah. I am not among them. If I can hear my own voice, so can others."

The fox chuckled. "Very well. Your intent is very hard to divine. I can hear rustles, whispers, hints of motion, in every other person present—even your Jarven. But you are so self-contained, so absent of the things we read and hear, you are almost a shadow."

Jarven burst out laughing; his laughter broke the peculiar, strained tension, although he was the only one to be so highly amused.

"He is amused at your expense?" the fox asked.

"Frequently. If you wish my opinion, explicitly stated, we want him. But if he does not meet your criteria, we want him anyway. He is old, yes—and his age is not feigned, although he accentuates it when it suits him. Give him back even a portion of his youth, and he may be the decisive factor in any victory we have. I cannot see how," he added. "And perhaps it is sentiment or nostalgia that clouds my vision."

"Sentiment in the wild is a dangerous vice," the fox replied.

"It is frequently dangerous in the mortal world as well. But it is my suspicion, Eldest, that the sentiment that can and does survive is therefore of incalculable value to you and your kind."

Silence then.

The fox grew heavy, suddenly, in Finch's arms. The motion of the tinkling leaves above their heads stilled; the entire forest seemed to be holding the whole of its collective breath.

It was Jarven who broke the silence; he chuckled. "Be wary," he said, lifting his head to glance around the canopy of branches, silent and still. "Of dangerous old men. We are few indeed. You will not harm The Terafin's Councillor."

"Do not," Birgide said, her lips almost white, the left side of her jaw twitching, "be so certain of that."

"I am certain," Jarven replied, shrugging. "I have considered killing Haval three times in our life together. I did not do so, although there was some pressure toward the end. His value to me outweighed his danger. The wilderness, the ancients, prize danger *as* value."

"They prize their dignity, their pride, and the respect they are due a great deal more than Jarven ATerafin ever has." Birgide spoke through clenched jaws.

"And Haval has injured their dignity? I see."

Throughout, Haval said nothing.

The fox did not grow heavier in Finch's arms—but he didn't grow any lighter, either. Finch took this as a hint and put him down. "You will not come?" he asked again, although he did not look back at her, certain of her answer.

"Jarven is like the forest. It is never wise to injure his dignity."

"Very well." The fox shook his head at Jarven. "You will be far more comfortable in the wilderness than our Lord; it is savage in a fashion that you understand instinctively. The rest? Just details."

Finch watched them go. They stepped off the path, and the diamond trees, glittering and beautiful and hard, seemed to absorb even their voices.

20th day of Morel, 428 A.A.
Terafin Manse, Averalaan Aramarelas

Only when they were ensconced in the West Wing again did Finch speak to Haval. He was unwilling to speak in the great room, and instead retreated—with tea—to his workroom. There was, of course, only one chair fit for use; it was Finch who cleared cloth and beads from another. She could not understand how Haval could work in this space, it was so chaotic. Yet he seemed to know exactly where, in this chaos, to find what he wanted.

In general, Finch was content to let Haval open any discussion he had requested. Today, however, she was not. "You did that on purpose."

He was too tired to use his face as a mask; it was blank, his eyes fixed on a point just past Finch's left shoulder. The door, perhaps.

"You speak of my comment about sentiment?"

"Not specifically that comment."

"What would you have had me do? I have not seen Jarven this impatient, this prickly, for decades. Literally decades." He hesitated, and then shrugged. "This is possibly because I have assiduously avoided him for decades."

Finch exhaled. "I have only known him for two. Less than two. And yes, he is . . . restless."

"Tell me, Finch, would you threaten the elders?"

Since the answer was obvious, she waited.

"Jarven did."

She knew.

"I do not threaten the wilderness. I do not trifle with threats."

"Trifle?"

He did not elaborate. "You are certain the Merchant Authority is secure?"

She nodded.

"Good. If it depends on Jarven's time or attention, you will lose it."

There were many questions Finch wanted to ask, but Haval hadn't answered the first one; she strongly suspected that he would treat the others in the same way. He was not unlike Jarven, in that regard. But he was unlike Jarven in substantial ways.

"You are not afraid," Haval observed.

"Not more so than usual, no." After a pause, she added, "I'm worried about Lucille."

"Were you Jarven, I would accuse you of attempted diversion. You are not. You are worried about her."

"She cares about Jarven. She always has. I think she's more afraid for him than of him, even now. I've only seen her angry at him once—truly angry."

"After the first assassination attempt?"

She nodded. She accepted that Haval knew things. How was an issue, but for the moment, it was not relevant. Later, it would have to be.

"She has seen trade wars from the inside," Haval continued. "Given her role in the Merchant Authority, she has no doubt seen to the removal of bodies; it is quite possible she has even been a target. Her own survival is not in question—and in the end, in her mind, neither is Jarven's, no matter how she frets at him. But yours? Yours is uncertain. I have no doubt she has done everything within her power to protect you; I have no doubt that some of that involved her personal funds, things that could be entirely left off the books.

"But you are not Jarven, and Lucille, I am certain, feels that only the good die young. It is not," he added, "true, of course."

"Of course." Finch thought of Duster. "Can you control him at all?"

"No."

"I can't, either."

"No, of course not. You come closer, Finch, than any before you. Closer, in my opinion, than Lucille. In his fashion, he respects you—but he doesn't know what to do with you, beyond what he has done. He was angry when the assassination attempts began. His overweening arrogance aside, he understands that protection requires that he be lucky one hundred per cent of the time; they only need to be lucky—if that is the word for it—once."

"His anger surprised me."

"Truly?"

Another wry smile. "Truly. He has not groomed you to be a pawn; he has no need of them. He has groomed you to be a ruler." Before she could speak, he lifted a hand. She stopped, closing her mouth. "What do you think a ruler is? You, of all people, must not confuse it with the pomp and circumstance of wealth. Wealth accrues to the powerful, should they seek it. Jewel tolerates the pageantry but does so poorly. She would not be a power were it not for her talent-born gifts."

"Neither would I."

He nodded. "But you do not have her gifts; you have—as Jarven and I—learned other ways. Jewel trusts instinct, and her instincts are good. You have learned to question yours. You look at what is in front of you, Finch. You understand your own goals, your own desires—but you work with what is there. You privilege planning over dreaming, and it is impossible to plan with any intelligence if what you view is the daydream, not the reality.

"You are regent. It is my belief that Terafin will prosper under your regency in a way it would not prosper under Jewel's in more mundane circumstances. You look ill-pleased."

"Do I?"

"Yes."

"I'm probably being overprotective. Jay saved us all. If it weren't for her—"

"Yes, but that is irrelevant, as you should know. I will not press you on this; I am fatigued, and I have much to do in the foreseeable future."

Finch turned toward the door, reached it, turned back. She rested her shoulders and the back of her head against the wooden panels as she regarded Haval. "You believe the regency will not be short."

Haval nodded.

"Jay will come back."

"Yes. I did not say that she would not return." There was a hint of something in him, then, something that felt real. "You will have a very, very short regency if she does not."

"But if she's back—" She cut off the rest of the thought, the sentence, unwilling to expose it.

He heard it anyway. "I believe your regency and her return are fast becoming entirely unrelated. I am sorry." He looked at the scattering of tailoring supplies that carpeted the floor around his feet. "Hannerle is quite angry about it. She has demanded—and begged—that I 'do something.' And so, I am here."

"And Jarven?"

"Is here, as well. Understand what we will build, here. It has already begun."

The tree of fire was not the heart of The Terafin's domain; it was, however, her stronghold. The Terafin did not understand why, and Meralonne was content to leave her ignorant. She would learn, if she survived. Her survival was not in his hands.

It was, he thought, in the hands of those who lived at the forest heart. Chief among them was the being Birgide had called a tree. And perhaps that was not inaccurate; the Warden saw much, saw clearly. But it was, to trees, what the Twin Kings were to short-lived, starving street urchins.

"Illaraphaniel."

Meralonne, who knew what to expect, felt a moment of pale wonder at the man who swept him a wild, chaotic bow. It was not a mortal motion, but it mimicked the Weston gesture of respect.

He knew, had known, that the forest whispered—and shouted—The Terafin's name, but nothing, save the tree of fire, had made so clear how deeply rooted she was in these lands, how clearly they heard her. This man was *arborii*. His hair was, at base, the platinum of the *Arianni*, and his form, like theirs: he was taller than Meralonne by perhaps six inches, but slender in a way that evoked saplings, young trees. His eyes were the color of the Weston sky.

As he rose—and if the bow was fluid and graceful, it was not precise—Meralonne offered a shallower bow, in kind.

"You are surprised."

"I am. I have not seen your kin thus for a very long time."

"And if I stand here," the servant replied, with a broad smile, "you will be able to tell me the exact count of days in your reckoning."

"I have spent much time in mortal lands; the days and hours of that reckoning are hopelessly tangled."

"Ah, perhaps, perhaps. You are expected, and I must not let you tarry. But it has been long, as well, since we have spoken with your kin; we are shaking out our branches and growing our finery and waiting."

"They will not pass this way," Meralonne said softly.

"Oh?" For a moment the *arborii* looked confused. The moment passed. "They will have to pass this way," he said gently. "Or so the ancients say. Do you think they will fight?"

"They will most certainly fight if you mean to hinder their passage. But they will not ride without The Terafin's permission; not through these lands."

"Oh, but they *must*. Is that not why The Terafin has left us?"

"Brother, you speak and speak and *speak*," another voice joined them. Another of the *arborii*. Unlike the first, this one was brown-haired and, instead of streaks of green and red, had actual leaves growing from her braided hair.

"I am not offended, if that is your concern," Meralonne told her. "I am . . . grateful."

"Yes, but if you are grateful to listen, he will plant himself here and take root. We have been rooted for so long, he will waste the spring babbling. And your time, no doubt. Have you eaten?"

"I have."

"I am bid to inform you that you will not light your bowl of fire here. It is tolerated, but it is not welcome; the only fire that should burn in this forest is hers."

"It was not originally hers."

"What it *was* does not matter. What it *is* does. And it only burns the rootless."

The young man tilted his head to the side. "Will it burn you, do you think?"

"Yes."

"Have you tried to touch it?"

"No."

"Maybe you should?"

The *arborii* who had chosen to appear female laughed. "Did I not warn you, Illaraphaniel?"

"Yes." He had been reluctant to come here; he could not remember why. "Have many awakened?"

"Many? By whose reckoning?"

"Yours, perhaps."

"No. By our reckoning, few—but perhaps by yours, many. I do not know if you will recognize them all—I think most were barely planted when you went into exile."

The branches above their heads creaked ominously.

Barely, in this context, was ancient, immortal. "This is not where I should be," Meralonne said softly. "The season is Winter, and I am a Winter Lord."

"The world is in Winter, yes," the *arborii* said, speaking in unison, although their inflections and tones were different. "But you feel it, too: this world is Jewel's, and she has come to it new. It is *spring*, Illaraphaniel. It is not yet Summer, but the Winter holds no sway here."

"Not none."

"Almost none. Look!" And speaking thus, they led him into a clearing of sorts. It was almost a small field, irregular in shape; trees girded it, but had been pulled back to allow sunlight in. The heart of ancient forests could be dark places if the trees were not mindful.

This was not dark. He had seen places such as this in his youth, before wars had destroyed them, and he remembered the screams of burning trees, their voices stilled, their bodies gutted. The warring gods knew no pity when bent upon revenge or conquest.

The forests, however, were not helpless. Not all of them.

They were awake, these trees. Not just the two who had come to escort him—as if he were a child, who might not hear the ancients, or a mortal, too easily lost. He was not inclined to feel insult when moments of wonder were so rare.

The *arborii* numbered in the dozens. They plaited each other's hair, or lay aground, turned upward to face the sun, to absorb it across the entirety of their bodies. Some wore vines and leaves as clothing—the two who met him first had—but others did not. They wanted sun and wind and perhaps even rain.

He could not remember a gathering such as this.

Or perhaps he had never been considered an appropriate guest. What response would he have given before his fall?

He did not know. He was lost, a moment, in the return to a living, breathing forest. When The Terafin had granted him permission to both wander and protect her lands, he had not seen *arborii*, but he had heard their whispers in the rustling of leaves, the shift of their branches. He had been aware, as none but the Warden could be, that the wilderness was waking.

Had he considered it spring? Spring was not one of the true seasons; it was a mortal word, a mortal contrivance, a wish for the end of winter. And yet, the *arborii* spoke of spring, and he could see summer in their awakening and in their youthful joy. Years, centuries, they had slumbered and perhaps dreamed.

Now, they spoke.

Hands were raised in greeting; he was surprised until he realized they were not raised for his benefit, but for the benefit of his escorts. There was no formality in their address or their approach, nor could he tell which of these trees were truly ancient and which, like Celleriant, were merely old in mortal terms.

But he knew that they would not speak thus to the White Lady. The Summer Queen. Even at the height of Summer, she was not given to familiarity; she might hear their voices, and they might know it, but their voices would fall into the hush of awe.

And fear.

"You are thinking of Ariane, yes?" the woman said.

Meralonne did not reply.

"These forests are not hers," the man said gently. "Our Lord is not given to the formality that power often demands; nor does he define dignity in such strict terms."

He glanced at the three who lay flat out on wild grass.

The woman laughed. "Or in any terms, really. The sun is lovely, Illaraphaniel. Perhaps you will join us?"

"It is not for me," he replied. But he replied in the tongue of trees and living things, not his own, and certainly not the Weston beloved of The Terafin.

"It is a pity. Once, we are told, it was. But not all of your kin are so stiff and severe—at least, we hope not. It will be such a disappointment."

"If they ride to war—and it is The Terafin's hope that they will—they will be as much a disappointment as I."

The man shook his head. "They will have time, here, if they choose to spend it. Time, we can give."

They spoke truth. He shook his head in wonder at The Terafin, at her Warden, at the ignorance that was their birthright, and quite probably their doom.

He expected to find the eldest in the center of this clearing; he did not. The eldest stood as part of the periphery. But his roots could be seen and felt long before one could touch the girth of his trunk, and his branches cast long and darkening shadows.

"Thus it is," a new voice said.

Meralonne stilled instantly; without thought, his hand fell to his sword, and his sword came.

At his back, silence fell in a widening circle. Only the woman who had walked by his side—and who had stepped back—spoke. "It is not an ax," she chided, as if speaking to young children. "And he is not our enemy. His was one of the First Voices. He means no harm here."

"Yet harm can be done, regardless," the eldest said, as he stepped out of the shadows his great trunk cast.

Chapter Five

H E WAS TALL. TALLER than Meralonne and taller than any of the *arborii* who had chosen to step away from their literal roots to bask in sunlight and freedom of movement. His hair was not a single color, but all of those found in the nature of the wilderness; dusk, dawn, day, midnight, touched by green and gold and orange. Leaves he wore, but leaves of silver, of gold, of diamond, as if each were individual scales, the whole of which became armor.

And he wore a crown.

Meralonne did not set his sword aside. He lowered it, but it would not leave his hand.

"Illaraphaniel." The eldest nodded, the movement light; he did not bow.

"Eldest."

"Do you not recognize me?"

"I recognize your voice," was the soft reply. It was true.

"You did not think to hear it again, ere the end?"

"No, Eldest."

"You did not visit."

"No."

"You will not tell me that you were much occupied?"

"I would not tell you anything you already know."

"Your heart is a Winter heart."

"Yes, Eldest. And it will be a Winter heart until the coming of Summer. I know no other way."

At some unspoken signal, speech in the clearing resumed; speech, laughter, something that sounded like mortal friendship in both its heat and warmth.

"We used to envy you," the eldest said softly. Given the rising volume, it was a wonder he could be heard at all. "You could travel. We could not. Oh, we could leave our trees—but never for long, and never safely. And yet, we are here, and you, who can travel, cannot ever leave yourself."

"Had I known that you were awake, I would have left the mortal realm."

"Ah. I was not, as you must suspect, awake. You might have spoken; I would not have heard your words, except perhaps in dream. Perhaps your sword would have caused enough pain to break my slumber—but perhaps not. We have been preserved from the malice of man and the malice of other predators, but we lay in Winter as you still do."

"You wished to speak with me?"

"I did. I have desired it since I first became aware of your presence. I forgive the sword; it has long been the first element of greeting between our kin, even if it was not always so. You ride to war."

"I do not ride," Meralonne replied. "But I wait, yes. I will be summoned. I can almost hear the horns."

"It was boon to you, then, that your ancient enemy once again strides these lands?"

"No."

"No? How odd. It is only in his presence that you might redeem yourself."

"It is not redemption," Meralonne replied, his grip on the sword tightening. "We were given a task and we will complete it."

"And when it is complete?"

But he could not speak the words that were the whole of his hope, the whole of his desire. He could not expose them, could not see them shattered. He had waited. He had waited, beyond hope, bereft of the White Lady's voice and favor. He had not died; he could not, not yet. There was only one death that he would pursue, one death that would be *worthy* of her. There was only one thing that he would allow to kill him.

And that being lay in the Northern Wastes, surrounded by *Kialli*, surrounded by the anima of the dead, his sundered kin, those who had betrayed their only true parent in their desperate search for the love of a god.

"You are unkind, Eldest," he finally said.

"Yes, of course. And kind in equal measure. But you serve the will of the White Lady, in your own fashion; I serve The Terafin, in mine."

"She is not the White Lady's equal."

"No. In these lands, she is her superior. The White Lady will not visit these lands without The Terafin's permission. Yet you are here. I find it perplexing. At first, I thought The Terafin did not *know*. Her connection to us was tenuous; we were only barely awake.

"But we heard her, in our slumber, and we lifted our collective branches to better catch the sound of her voice. We heard Ishavriel. We could not move as we now move, but we did what we could. And, Meralonne, she did what she could. Had she consulted us, we would have been horrified, terrified, for she took the fire of the dead, the pyre upon which they lay, but which cannot consume them, and she made it her own.

"And it is here: fire as warmth. Fire as succor. It is a thing that mortals speak of, but until The Terafin, we could not understand why or how. It is her fire that is our spring. And were she stronger or more certain, it is that fire that would become our sun, our summer. It would consume nothing. It is miraculous.

"It is as miraculous, to me, as the first time I heard my own voice. It was a gift I could not even think to ask for, who lived rooted and mute."

"That was not a gift I gave," he whispered.

"No. But you were present when your sister woke me." He looked over Meralonne's head, which required no effort on his part at all, as if aware that this truth was the one that would wound.

Shianne.

"Yes," the eldest said, as if the single word in all its complexity had escaped him. "We thought her dead," he continued softly, "and, in truth, she will be soon. She will live less than a full mortal span of years; she is mortal now, and mortality is part of her essential nature. I do not understand how this came to pass; I see the hand of a god in it, and I will not hazard a guess as to which.

"We have long avoided gods, where it was possible to do so. But, Illaraphaniel, we can still hear her voice when she speaks. She walked in these woods. She spoke. We hear no other voice so clearly as hers, excepting only our lord's. And perhaps not even that. Shianne was once of us in a way that The Terafin cannot be."

He said nothing in reply, listening instead to the distant, playful voices of the *arborii*; feeling, as he did, the absence of warmth and youth. Failure—even if it had not been, in the end, his own—had marked and changed him.

"What do you intend, Illaraphaniel?"

"Was it not you, Eldest, who extended an invitation to me? Should it not be me who therefore asks that question?"

"Perhaps." The eldest lifted his head and gazed to the west. "You have heard the distant horns."

"Yes, Eldest."

"You do not search for them."

"I have been content to wait."

"Why? Beneath the streets of your mortal city, your kin lie sleeping—but they will not sleep much longer. I hear the horns winded that will wake them, although those horns are not yet sounded from my lands."

Meralonne bowed head. "Even from here."

"Yes. I ask again, what will you do? Their heralds cannot reach them, not yet. It is my Lord's desire that the Sleepers not wake. She understands what you are. She understands where your loyalty and duty lie. She understands that your service to Terafin, and to the magi, has been a way to while away your long exile. But you are not yet what you were; you were lessened in every way.

"She knows you will leave—must leave—when you are finally summoned. When you are, Illaraphaniel, these borders will no longer open in welcome to you. There will be no safe place in The Terafin's lands for you or your kin without her permission. But she does not fully understand what that means. She knows only that if the three awaken, she will lose the city.

"And she knows this because you told her."

Meralonne was silent.

"You do not seek your herald."

"No."

"We will not attempt to harm him."

"No."

"I ask a third time, what do you intend? In the heart of the city across the water, I see a token that I have not seen since I was young, and it is worn, not by one of the White Lady's people, but by a mortal."

Meralonne gazed at the eldest in silent wonder. "How powerful has your Lord become?" The words were a whisper; there was no fear in them.

"I do not understand the question," the eldest replied, evincing no confusion whatsoever. Very well. "Why?"

"It is no concern of yours," Meralonne replied, his voice soft, his sword's light brighter, harsher. "I intend her no harm. I intend none of the mortals harm—"

The eldest frowned then, reaching out with one arm to touch the trunk of his body. "What is he doing?" He spoke names that had no analogue in language, and one of the *arborii* rose at once. She did not approach her Lord, but left, her feet quick and light as she gained the wooded circumference of the clearing and disappeared.

"My apologies, Illaraphaniel. I am unaccustomed to the speed at which the living move, it has been so long since I last truly walked. Why does a mortal bear that token? You cannot think it will protect her?"

"Eldest," he replied, "you ask a question for which I have no answer; do you not think I have not asked it of myself? Why ask me what I intend when you know what the answer must be? I am not mortal. My context does not define me as it defines those who are. The life I build does not replace the life from which I was exiled, and no desire that grows from *this* shadow of life can equal or overcome the truth of what I was born to be. I am among the firstborn of the White Lady's Princes. I am the White Lady's. I am her hunter, her prince. There is nothing, no one, I have loved so much as she.

"I have listened to my brothers, buried in sleep decreed by gods who intended to abandon these lands permanently. I have yearned for the youth in which we faced gods in the wars that shaped and broke continents. I can see them—I have always been able to see them—if I but close my eyes. It is at their side that I belong.

"I have fought demons, at the behest of Sigurne Mellifas, the mortal who wears that token. It is only in combat with them that I remember my truest self. Do not mistake fondness for something it is not."

The eldest nodded. "Just so. Do you wish us to release the heralds?"

The sword rose. "What have you done?" The words were visceral, the rage at the presumption of this being, instant.

"Our Lord does not wish the heralds to find their Lords," he replied. He gestured. To his hand, ancient of the woodlands, came a thing that shocked the mage.

It was a sword.

A red, burning blade.

All voices died in the clearing, and with them, all movement. The *arborii* had fled, withdrawing into their bodies as if they were mortal children fleeing for their lives while their father bought them time.

The swords did not clash. Meralonne stared at the blade itself. It was not, as it had appeared, a *Kialli* weapon; it was a thing of fire. Fire, he thought, and a metal that was nothing so mundane as mortal steel.

"The burning tree."

"Even so. It is not the way of my kin to fight armed with such weapons, but some of us have been . . . learning. It is enlightening."

"Learning."

The eldest nodded.

"How?"

"I have been asked, as a condition of such lessons, to hold and keep my peace."

"An oath given to a mortal."

The eldest did not respond.

And Meralonne, who served as guardian, had not seen. He lowered his sword. "You have not harmed my herald."

"No. But he, alone of the four, has not come through the wilderness to reach you, which is unexpected, although perhaps it should not have been. He has lived in long exile, as have you. And as you, he has used his particular gifts to grant mortals knowledge." The red sword vanished.

The blue sword likewise disappeared. Meralonne did not answer.

"I ask an unprecedented fourth time, what do you intend?"

"I? What I have always intended: to return to the White Lady."

"We do not hear her voice," the eldest said.

"I know. But she lives, still." He exhaled. "Your Lord seeks her in the wilderness, even now."

"Yes. She has found Shianne. She will find the White Lady. You cannot aid her in any way on the path she has chosen to walk; even were you not so diminished, you could not. The path, to you, is closed, and will remain so while the Lord of the Hells lives."

He did not reply; he knew. Of course he knew.

"You have no shield, Illaraphaniel."

"No."

"How, then, will you stand against the Lord of the Hells?"

Meralonne did not answer. He longed for two things, and one—ah, one was his pipe.

"Your fire is not her fire," the *arborii* said, as if he could perceive the odd, out-of-place desire. "And her fire is not their fire." He turned, once again, to the trunk of the tree he had shed, touching its bark with the flat of both palms, his back momentarily exposed.

The branches that sheltered them from sunlight descended slowly from a great height. They moved as limbs of trees should not be able to move without breaking. "We cannot remake what was lost and sundered," the eldest said. "That is not our skill."

"Did your lord know that the heralds would come?"

"She did not speak of it to us. But she is as she is. If you asked her, she would tell you that it was coincidence." His smile was slight, almost affectionate. "It is a mortal word: coincidence."

The branches had finally reached Meralonne's eye level; there, they stopped. He frowned, regarding the leaves. They reflected sunlight as they moved, causing light to dance. They were not, however, leaves of silver or gold, and certainly not diamond. He had not seen these leaves in this forest, or any other he could recall.

"What is this?" he asked softly, although his gaze did not stray from the finely veined leaves.

"There is metal here, in the very trees; there is fire in their veins; there is life in both things. You have traversed the Stone Deepings; you thought to do so again, ere the end. I cannot and, therefore, cannot tell you what you might find there, although I hear the voice of stone from this remove."

"There is stone on the Isle," Meralonne replied. "Both in the mortal world and in the hidden. Perhaps it sings."

"Regardless, what I offer is not what the Stone Deepings might offer, and in the Green Deepings, you will not find what you seek."

"Do not bring the Deepings here," Meralonne whispered. "She is Sen, yes, but she is only Sen, and the price the Deepings exact, she will not pay."

The *arborii* lord seemed almost offended. He did not deign to reply, and the moment passed. "Once," he said, "I would have said I understood your kin. I would have said I understood you. But you are grown strange, Illaraphaniel. Perhaps the cause is exile." The branches shook slightly. "But I forget myself.

"Take the leaves, if you will. They will not magically become what you require. We do not work metal here, except perhaps gold, for it is soft and malleable. Even if we did, the arts you require are not arts that we practice; not yet, and perhaps not ever."

Meralonne reached up to touch a leaf with the tips of his fingers. He could not speak for one long moment, and when he did gather his voice, it was rough with things unsaid. "Why?" he asked.

"It is a gift, Illaraphaniel, for you have fought the dead in our stead while we slept. Ours have never been the warrior's arts, and the dead no longer care for the arts that are ours."

"It is not the way of my kin—or yours—to give gifts."

"No, perhaps not. But it is the way of our Lord, and we would do her honor."

"And will this metal be free of your influence?" He lowered his hand.

"It will be of the forest, of the wilderness—but Illaraphaniel, so are you. What you forge of it will decide how that connection is expressed. I would not forge a weapon of it," the eldest added. "I have come to understand something of your weapons. It would not serve you well, in that regard, should we come face-to-face upon a future field of battle; it will not harm us.

"But it is not sword you lack; it is shield. When the branch is sundered from the tree, it dies."

"You are not a tree."

"I am the essence of trees," the eldest replied.

Meralonne bowed. He bowed low. He did not speak and did not rise until bidden. When he did, he raised not one hand, but two, understanding the eldest's intent.

The whole of the branch fell into his upturned hands.

"The rest, I fear, is in your hands."

Meralonne nodded, listening. The branch itself was voiceless, silent save for the tinkling of metal leaves as they made contact with each other. "No one, Eldest, has borne such a shield."

"No one," the eldest replied, "has borne your burden. What obligation we owe you for your service to our Lord, we have paid. And now, Illaraphaniel, I would walk. You must find your smith."

21st day of Morel, 428 A.A.
Avantari, Averalaan Aramarelas

Birgide Viranyi could travel to the palace without fear of mortal interference. The roads and paths between the Terafin manse extended, now, to the Courtyard Garden; Duvari had requested the removal of the *Ellariannatte* but had been dissuaded from commanding it outright. He viewed the trees with great and obvious suspicion, but none of the Master Gardeners would be budged until he had absolute proof of their perfidy. They were called "the Kings' trees," but they had never survived in any soil other than the Common—until now. Natural fear of Duvari—caution being too mild a word—had been set aside by genuine outrage.

Birgide could not restrain a smile at the hilarity and absurdity of the situation—but she gave in to it only here, beneath the boughs of those trees. She would, of course, be seen long before she met with Duvari.

No one moved to intercept her as she entered the palace and walked its halls; she noted the magical protections that were new and paused only a moment to examine them. Duvari would be waiting if she tarried.

"He did *what?*"

"Jarven did not enter the forest on his own recognizance. He entered it with the aid and permission of the regent."

"The regent. Finch."

Birgide nodded.

Duvari was not alone, which was unusual. Devon ATerafin, second in the hierarchy of the Royal Trade Commission, stood beside him. One glance at the room told her they were otherwise unobserved, although magic had been used to capture words. This, she expected; it was an enchantment paid for, requested by, and approved by Patris Larkasir. It was to Devon Duvari now looked.

"Jarven exerts no undue influence on the regent."

"She has never escorted him into the wilderness before."

"She has. The dinner with Patris Araven was held in The Terafin's personal chambers."

"What game is he playing?"

He, Birgide thought, not Finch. As if he could hear the thought, Duvari, in full icy, scowl, turned his glare on Birgide. "Devon spoke of undue influence. It is true. Jarven does not magically control the girl; there is no sign of obvious extortion. If you feel that those are the only relevant forms of control, I have taught you so poorly you have almost no place here."

She considered the information she had relayed from several different angles and finally said, "It was not Finch's suggestion; it was not her idea. Nor was it Jarven's, initially."

"Haval."

"No. I would have assumed Haval Arwood under any other circumstance, but I witnessed Jarven's entry. One of the forest denizens desired Jarven's presence, and Finch did not think it wise to refuse him."

"Would she be capable of it?"

"I cannot say. I would," Birgide added, "but it would be costly. The regent— as any competent regent—chooses battles she is likely to win. It is my belief that she did not feel she could, when confronted with both Jarven and the eldest."

"What did he want?" Duvari was never in what could be called a good mood. Tonight, it was actively foul.

She exhaled. "I believe he wants to be more powerful."

Devon coughed, and Birgide reddened. "Apologies," she said to her master. "I mean, rather, that he believes that the liaison with the eldest will help him achieve that goal."

"And so it is about power at last."

Birgide, however, shook her head. "I seldom interact with Jarven. I have done some research since we encountered The Terafin four days ago. There is no shortage of information on Jarven—but the older that information is, the less reliable; he is lionized."

"Demonized," Devon said.

"I confess I find Jarven difficult to understand. Haerrad makes sense to me. Rymark made sense."

"Has Rymark been found?"

"No. He is not in the wilderness, and he is not—that I have been able to ascertain—in Averalaan. I have not expended resources in such a search; I have not been given funds to cover it." Before Duvari could respond, she added, "Haerrad has all but torn the city apart looking for Rymark, with the regent's tacit approval."

"Tacit?"

It was Devon who said, "Explicit approval. She would very much like to see the problem with Rymark resolved by his death. If he were brought before her, I think it very likely that she would draw the House Sword and relieve him of his head. She would require several layers of permission to do so."

"I believe she would receive most of them," Duvari replied, his tone indicating that this was a tertiary matter at best, left in the hands of others. "You do not trust Jarven."

"No one does," Birgide replied. "He supports the regent in his new role as council member, but the right-kin doesn't trust him either."

"Finch has been under his thumb for long enough that she does?"

Birgide hesitated again, which added expression to Duvari's face, none of it pleasant. "I would say she is fond of him," she finally said. "Where Jarven ATerafin is concerned, she seems to feel that trust is irrelevant. As regent, she has little choice; she will be surrounded by men and women she cannot entirely trust. So was The Terafin. It is a fact of life."

"You attempt to justify a woman who holds political power to me?"

"No. Merely to explain. It is not Jarven that concerns me—"

"Then it must be true that you've had no experience with him."

She had said "little" but offered no correction.

"And not the Terafin regent, either."

"No." Committed, she said, "it is Haval Arwood."

Devon's posture didn't change; he recognized the name though he did not consider the tailor a threat. It was Duvari whose silence shifted; it became a glacial structure, a barrier. Duvari could kill a man without once altering his expression, but there were subtle signs if one observed only the Lord of the Compact, and not his intended victim.

She saw them now.

"He has asked you to deliver another message."

"Yes, in a fashion."

"In a fashion?"

"I believe he intended that I speak with you. He has a way of revealing information without ever stooping to words; he allows more—or less—to be seen."

"And he concerns you how?"

Devon had not uttered a word. He had not only fallen silent, but actually stepped back; she spared him a glance, no more.

"I do not think Haval cares for, or approves of, Jarven ATerafin. I have seldom seen them in the same space together, and the mention of Jarven's name instantly sours the tailor. Jester dislikes Jarven intensely, but that may be because Jarven treats him obviously and visibly as a child. I don't think Jester's information about Jarven is any different than the regent's. The Terafin herself does not care for him.

"I believe that Haval approved of Jarven's decision."

"Pardon?"

"I believe he *wants* Jarven to be the beneficiary of the ancient. I believe he believes it is necessary." She hesitated. Duvari marked it, of course. "The Terafin trusts Haval. Jester trusts him. Finch is neutral, but he adores his wife—and that sentiment has meaning for Finch. Her first avenue of attack, should she wish to interfere with Haval, will be that wife."

"She would not be foolish enough to harm her."

Birgide frowned and then shook her head as if to clear it. Ruefully, she said, "Forgive me. I have clearly spent too long with The Terafin's kin. She would never harm Hannerle. She would never allow her to *be* harmed. She would not attack or threaten—even if it were not clear that that would doom her instantly. No, she would show up at *Elemental Fashion*, she would ask to have a quiet word with Hannerle, and she would pour out her fears and her concerns to the older woman."

Devon coughed, and Birgide looked at him; his eyes were crinkled in the corners with what looked like genuine amusement.

"And she would expect this to have some salutary effect?"

"Yes. And in my opinion, she would not be wrong."

"It is not a tool available to the *Astari*," Duvari finally said.

"No. I do not know how dangerous the tailor is. When I first met him, I would have said that he was not dangerous at all. I know that he worked with—or for—you, but I have inferred that; he does not speak of it. But you do know Haval in a way that I don't. You would threaten his wife only if you were utterly and completely certain that you could kill him almost immediately."

At this, Duvari smiled. It was grim, but genuine; he approved. Approval had once meant safety. Birgide no longer required that safety, but she felt an almost embarrassing warmth, regardless.

"Very well. You are, of course, correct. And Haval's wife would never welcome me into her home in the way she would welcome Finch. Do you believe that it is the wife's concern that motivates Haval now?"

"Yes. I do not think that the regent—or any of the den—have attempted to influence her in that regard. I believe she met them when they were much younger, and where allowed, she worries. Hannerle had no children, and not by choice."

"You asked him this?"

"Jester." She replied. "And regardless, yes. I think that Haval's wife is a large factor in his motivation where Terafin is concerned."

"You are now wasting time," Duvari told her. "Speak the rest of your mind and speak it quickly. I will visit Haval myself."

"You are aware that the forest is alive in a way that most forests are not."

"Time, Birgide," was his impatient response.

"Very well. There are beings that are not human within the confines of the forest. Some can speak explicitly, and some speak in ways that are not simply audible. Haval first found the heart of The Terafin's forest defenses on his own. He entered the back gardens and did not become lost; it was as if the forest itself guided him.

"They refused Jarven entry outright. It wasn't a formal rejection; they simply shut the paths of entry. He spent time in the gardens—but only the formal gardens. He could not find the forest itself."

Duvari nodded.

"Yet Haval was not only allowed to enter, but he was allowed to enter the forest's heart. He did not search for it; he merely . . . walked. He likes the forest," she added. "And no, before you ask, this is observation, no more. His like or dislike, on the face of it, isn't of concern to the wilderness or to us."

"What is?"

"The forest elders, for want of a better word."

"You believe they exert influence over him?"

She shook her head again. "They call him Councillor."

"Councillor? Of who, or what?"

"I assume they refer to The Terafin. But no, it's more than that. I understand my own role in the wilderness, and in the forest. I understand the alterations that have been made in me, that I might better fulfill my duties. But those alterations do not exist solely in the forest. If Jarven is similarly altered—and I assume he will be, and possibly more heavily—"

"Why Jarven?"

"Because his death will not hurt Jewel. If they try, if they fail, it is merely failure to them. Before you ask, my death would not have hurt her either. The cost of failure in either of our cases was deemed acceptable."

"Continue. Haval?"

"Councillor is what they now call him. They call the regent by her name; they call me Warden. They do not seem to care for mortal ranks or titles; they don't disdain them, but they don't feel they serve a useful function. I believe Councillor *is* like Warden, in that regard.

"I assume that The Terafin values his opinions when he chooses to offer them; from Jester, I infer that he does not offer often. Even when she asks for his opinion, he frequently forces her to answer the questions she's asked on her own."

"That was always his way."

"It's his way now. Jester doesn't enjoy it," she added.

"Councillor."

"Yes. The forest is aware of him in a way I was not." She hesitated again. "He is allowed, in all ways, to keep his own counsel."

"Pardon?"

"I believe he is the only person—outside of The Terafin herself—who could enter the wilderness, of whom I would not immediately be aware. I believe he can traverse it in the same fashion. He has been speaking with the elders, and Duvari—they have come, on occasion, to speak with him. He cannot hear them as I hear them, or as The Terafin does; they are sometimes forced to walk.

"But they walk. I saw him talking to one tree-spirit for what felt like hours, once. Or, rather, the spirit spoke; Haval asked a few questions, but seemed content to absorb information rather than share it."

"Would you say that Haval has been altered in any way?"

"No. I am certain he has not."

"You believe *Haval* recommended Jarven ATerafin?"

After a long pause, she shook her head. "No. But I believe he was not ill-pleased that it was Jarven chosen."

"Do you understand Haval Arwood's previous life?"

"No. You have not spoken of it; you will not allow it to be spoken of."

"Very well. Do you understand why Haval Arwood is not dead?"

"No," she said again.

"It would have been too costly to kill him, at the time," Duvari replied. "And I had reason to believe him when he said he was done with that life. I will speak with Haval, and decide; if he has broken his word in any fashion, things will change."

21st day of Morel, 428 A.A.
Terafin Manse, Averalaan Aramarelas

There was a very specific knock at the door of Haval's workroom, a room he occupied less and less often. He had taken a second room in the West Wing, one which was significantly tidier; it was not, however, the room in which he held his meetings. As he expected this one and had scheduled it, in a manner of speaking, he was only surprised at the hour. It was late.

Late enough that he should not have been seated, beading a pale gold silk. Beading was finicky work and required light; the light in the room was therefore bright, being supplied at this point entirely by magestones. But the work itself was soothing, the intricacy demanding some part of his attention.

"Enter."

The door opened slowly. The frame was empty for scant seconds, and then Duvari filled it. Ah, Haval thought.

"You will forgive me for not rising immediately," the tailor said. "Please, take a seat."

Duvari was meticulously tidy. Haval allowed a smile to grace his otherwise focused expression as he met the *Astari's* gaze. He could not abandon his work immediately without losing beads, and took some care to finish, to knot.

"Is there a seat?" Duvari asked.

"Ah, yes. Apologies. I try to leave one free, but I am working on a commission at the moment, from one of my exacting, and impatient, clientele."

"And wealthy?"

"Yes, very. I have been forced to accept fewer commissions of late, and as I am largely unpaid while I remain within Terafin, those I have accepted must be completed. You are late."

Duvari raised a brow. He stepped into the room just far enough that he could close the door; he then stood with his back against it. Jester would be leaning; Duvari did not. "I was unaware that I had committed myself to a specific hour."

"I speak in generalities, of course," Haval replied. "And it is late." Haval carefully set a bead into the jar from which it had come, twisting the lid. Duvari said, "You have your bead jars enchanted." His voice was flat.

"Only for expensive beads," Haval replied.

"And your needles are likewise enchanted."

"Ah, well, yes."

"Because sharp needles are required?" Duvari was clearly tired; his sarcasm was both pointed and edged in mild, undisguised, disgust.

Haval smiled. "Because they are far too easily lost. I have only to speak, and they reveal themselves. It is a variant on the functional enchantment laid upon magestones for illumination."

"They function as magestones."

"They function as needles, but yes."

"I am surprised the cloth is not enchanted."

"Unlike needles or jars, cloth leaves my hands." He folded said cloth very, very carefully, walked it over to the bed, and set it down atop of a pile of other bolts. The needle he added to its brothers on the sash that crossed his apron while Duvari continued his increasingly frustrated examination.

"You did not think I would give up my work?"

"I had expected that you could *contain* your work to your store. I chose to visit that building first."

"Ah. I do hope you did not wake my wife. She will worry."

"I did not wake your wife, to my knowledge."

"If she did not attempt to stave in your skull, she did not wake. She would not, I think, be happy to see you."

"No one is happy to see me," the Lord of the Compact replied. He then shut his mouth for five full beats. "So you are working as a tailor to The Terafin."

"And the right-kin and the regent, yes."

"What other work are you doing here, Haval?"

"I was wondering when you would find it in yourself to ask. If you will not join me here, perhaps you would be interested in a walk?"

"I would join you here if it were possible."

"Finch generally moves things if she wishes to sit."

"Clearly, Finch is treated with far more indulgence than I ever was."

Haval smiled. "And perhaps that is true. My wife is fond of her; in any clash between the two of us, my wife would be certain to take her side."

"Not true."

"Oh, it is. You have failed to understand the essential nature of Jewel and her den-kin if you believe otherwise."

"I have never failed to understand the powerful."

"Yes, Duvari, you have. Your definition of power is merely danger along a single axis." Haval held up a staying hand. "You cannot afford to make a mistake, of course. As a designer and clothier, my mistakes can be rectified; they will not lead to failure and death. I have spent some time crafting for the wealthy and the powerful. In many cases, they are not more cunning, but less; their survival is more certain."

He set his heavy apron upon a peg on the wall nearest the door, a modification he had requested. He had no desire to fuss with closets or unnecessary doors at this particular time. "Shall we?"

"Am I to walk with you alone?"

"Yes, unless you came with escort."

"And if I did?"

Haval sighed. "You did not. But Birgide is still yours, and she is omnipresent. If you require protection from an elderly tailor, she will be more effective than the rest of the *Astari* combined while you are on Terafin grounds."

Haval was uncertain that Duvari would enter the forest; he was uncertain that he *could*. Jewel detested the Lord of the Compact. She did not despise him, precisely, but chaffed under his apparent lack of manners and social grace. Not, of course, that social grace was her particular strength; he suspected that was the reason for her annoyance. Duvari was not held to the same standards; he dismissed all such standards with contempt and ease.

Duvari, Haval had explained, did not rule.

This was not, strictly speaking, truth. Duvari was Lord of the Compact; he had both the ear and the trust of the Kings and their sons. He ruled the *Astari*, and where matters of security were concerned, could override the Kings themselves in a very narrow, specific set of circumstances. He terrified servants and petty nobles alike.

He did not terrify Haval. As Haval had said, it was late. He was not young, and the prospect of walking without reaching a destination had little appeal. If the forest chose to do so, they might walk for hours or days without reaching that destination.

"What are you doing here?" Duvari asked softly. Not good; an outright demand or command would have been a better sign.

"By here, do you mean the forest or House Terafin?"

"Both."

"I am a tailor," he replied, "to Finch and the right-kin. I offered Jewel advice when she was of a mind to ask for it, but she is not currently in residence."

"Pretend for a moment that I have graduated from your infernal lessons."

"Ah. You wish me to assume that you know what I know?"

"Except for the parts I don't, yes. And if you ask me to delineate my ignorance, I may actually lose my temper."

"Very well. In the case of the regent, I intended to do what I could—and it is minimal—to curb Jarven's influence. That has proved largely unnecessary. The right-kin plays chess with me on occasion and discusses the forest. We talk about my commissions—the dress I am making now—and my wife. Occasionally, he asks for advice."

"On?"

"How to deal with the Master of the Household Staff, for the most part. She is a truly intimidating woman. I myself deal with her by vanishing."

"And Jester?"

"Jester runs errands for the regent."

"And the regent's tailor?"

"I do not find him particularly helpful, but on rare occasions he is the most reliable source of gossip I have. When I was in the store more often, I had access to better.

"Vereena, before you ask, is adjusting."

"I had no intention of asking, as you well know."

"Yes. I am relieved to see that you are able to accompany me."

"That was not a given?"

"I rather suspected you would not be. The forest responds to The Terafin's visceral trust—or distrust—of individuals."

"And the forest allows *you* entry."

"Everyone must trust someone, Duvari. Even the Kings. I have told her, repeatedly, that it is almost insulting—to me—to be trusted in this fashion. But where she is concerned, I am trustworthy. At best, my lectures are mixed messages; they are a waste of her time."

Duvari exhaled. "I came to ask you what you want."

"I know," Haval replied. "You are Duvari. You have not appreciably changed in all the years I've known you. You are predictable in intent; you are frequently unpredictable in action. It is an unusual combination." He continued to walk, gazing straight ahead. Duvari did likewise as if assuming that the only danger in this forest was Haval himself.

It was an oddly humbling thought.

"You have spoken to the god-born," Haval continued, when Duvari failed to speak.

Duvari nodded, expression stiff.

"You have spoken to the magi; to Sigurne Mellifas."

"I have. She was singularly unhelpful."

"If I know you, you have spoken with the maker-born." Although Duvari's expression betrayed nothing, Haval could sense his surprise, could feel him struggle to make a decision. He might have told him it was a waste of time; no decision could be made that could not be unmade in the instant that followed it.

"Yes. I assume you have done these things as well."

"Not personally, no. I *am* a tailor, Duvari. I am not the Lord of the Compact."

"You might have been."

"No. What I wanted would not allow that."

"I will never understand you."

Haval smiled; it was genuine. "I am a far more selfish man, in the end, than you are. I am more capricious, as well—but then again, so is stone. I wanted happiness, in my youth. I wanted peace. I did not expect that I would have either, and when the opportunity arose, I took it instantly."

"And without regret?"

"Ah, that is different. Do I miss the life I lived? Perhaps, at times. But I would have missed the life I did not choose more. Ah, we are here." Ahead, in the darkness of night forest, he could see light. It was gold, orange, red; it was white. It was the tree of fire.

Duvari paused as it came into view; he observed it critically, as if it displeased him. "It does not burn."

"No. Not in the sense that wood naturally does. I find it remarkable. And warm." He approached the tree; Duvari, sensibly, lagged behind. "You ask me what I want." When he reached the tree itself, he turned, placing it firmly at his back and above his head. "My answer has not changed."

"Has it not?"

"I want happiness. I want peace. To me, there is only one avenue to both. Do you understand what will happen to this city?"

Duvari's hands slid behind his back. Haval did not tense. He was not concerned. Even had he chosen to remain in the West Wing of the Terafin manse, he would not have been.

Duvari did not answer.

"Very well. Shall I tell you what I believe will happen?"

"Please." Uninflected voice. Hooded expression.

"Beneath the streets of our city, sleeping, lie three of the four Princes who rode to face the god we do not name. They failed in their charge, and in their duty, and when the battle was over, the god was not dead. The wrath of their Lord was great, and the gods agreed; she exiled the four."

"There are only three."

"Yes. One of the four held to his vows."

"Why did she not merely execute them?"

"Why, indeed?" was Haval's soft reply. "Perhaps because she knew that this day would come. The Lord of the Hells has returned to us. In the past, he had his legions, his followers; in the present, he has his demons. And there they lie, the Sleepers, waiting for the moment of his return."

"He has returned."

"Yes. And they are waking. The enchantments of gods are large and not easily diminished." He paused, glancing up, toward heat and light. Toward, in fact, the fire that had been brought to this forest by one of those demons. This was, in Haval's opinion, Jewel's chief strength. She could take the enemy in and make it her own—without demanding that it change its essential nature.

And so she had.

"The gods feared these Princes," Haval continued. "They fear them now. If the Princes wake in this city, they will have a power that we—you and I—have never seen. Did you know that gods warred, when they last walked these lands?"

"I had heard."

"They destroyed mountains. They destroyed oceans. They destroyed each other. What lay between these conflicts—our lives, and the lives of the lesser creatures, as they are called—did not, of course, survive. And so, when the three wake, we will have the equivalent of these gods beneath our very feet."

"Your sources are good."

"If a trifle self-involved, yes. I have grown fond of them. It is a weakness."

"You are fond of The Terafin," Duvari pointed out.

"Yes. And of her den. I admire Finch."

"Teller?"

"He would not have survived either of us; I believe Finch would have. But yes, since you mention him, I am. Do you believe it is fondness that motivates me?"

"Not for them, no. If it became necessary, you would sacrifice any of them."

Haval nodded. "It is the definition of necessity, however, that divides us now. If Jewel does not return, the city will perish. Some small handful of its citizens can be rescued—but even so, it will be a near thing."

"You think The Terafin can stand against three gods?"

"Yes. If she is in *this* city, yes."

"You cannot influence her return."

"No. I cannot. But I can influence what that return will mean. She requires this city," Haval continued. "She requires her den, and her House. She requires the safety of one farmer and one old, irascible tailor, both in the Common. She requires the safety of one tavern. She requires your Kings."

Duvari watched the fire at Haval's back. Reflected in his eyes, it made him look demonic. "You will never return to us."

"No. But you knew that, even then. Had there been any possibility that I would, you would have had me killed."

"I would have killed you myself."

"That is the only way that I would have—possibly—died, yes. I will not interfere in the protection of the Kings; it is not my responsibility, and it is not my job. I will offer you aid in what meaningful way I can, should I have the opportunity. But the Kings are not in my hands. They are in yours."

"If she can stand against the Sleepers that even the gods—when they walked—fear, why does she require the Kings?"

For the first time, Haval glanced down. A branch of fire trembled above his head; it then lowered to touch his shoulder. He felt warmth, not heat, and thought, *affection is always a danger. Love is a weakness.* But no man or woman could be strong for every waking minute of their life. "Mortals were not meant to contain what she might contain. They were not meant to have that power."

Duvari had always been perceptive. "You believe she will not be sane?"

"I believe she will not be fit to rule mortals," he replied. "And the city is mortal. The people who live in its many streets, rich and poor, are likewise mortal." He stared at Duvari as he continued. "Are gods sane, Duvari? If a god desires it, they might make a living, growing tree—of fire. Is that sane? They might, in a night, remake the entirety of their personal quarters, might open doors into worlds that do not or did not exist before the door opened. Is that sane?

"It is not *mortal*. It is not *human*. But insane?"

"If she is so powerful, how is it that she is not what you fear?"

"Because she's human, and she wishes to remain human. On some level, she understands exactly what will happen if she dons the mantle of the power she requires. She has not faced it, not fully. The cats have always understood."

"The den?"

"I believe Teller understands. The rest cannot truly conceive of it; they might pay lip service to the shadow of that fear. Jewel has traveled in order to find another way to stop the Sleepers from destroying her life. She believes she has traveled to find the only way. And I will not lie, Duvari, tempting as it is. I have prayed—"

"You?"

"Even so. I have prayed that she will find that way. If she does not, there is only one stark choice to be made. Her life or the Empire's. In every functional sense, she will be dead to us. But if she finds what she seeks, the battle will be harder and the losses more severe. We will be at war with the wilderness and the demons; we will be at war with gods.

"Her rule of these lands is absolute, even at a distance. I do not understand it, but I accept it. Her people cannot yet walk the lands we normally live in. But as the days pass, I believe it will be possible. Some can leave the forest now, and return; they cannot be seen by most. Soon, they will be visible. Soon, the power they hold in this forest will affect the world beyond its borders.

"I am training those who desire the knowledge," he continued. "I am teaching them, inasmuch as I can, and within the frustrating limits of my own experience and knowledge. No matter what Jewel faces, if she dies, we will *all* perish: King, city, Empire."

"You are creating *Astari* of your own."

"In a fashion, yes. Chief among them will be Jarven ATerafin."

Chapter Six

O N THE SECOND DAY, Adam could not find the door to Evayne's room.

Jewel lay abed, and he did not feel up to the task of joining the conversation among those who waited for her to wake. Two days, she had slept, and looked to sleep for a third. Or longer. But it was Matriarch business, and the decisions reached were not his to make. That they were not anyone's to make did not occur to the others, and he was content to let them discuss and argue in his absence.

The Oracle, however, had other plans. She left the company to its own devices, interfering only when the cats got out of hand. Given that boredom had become the entirety of their litany—eclipsing even *stupid*—interference was frequently required. The cats were not fond of the Oracle, but the Oracle required neither obedience nor respect. If she wished to move them, they moved, without much volition. It didn't improve their mood, on the other hand.

As Evayne was elsewhere in the bowels of this maze of halls and tunnels, Adam was not surprised to find the Oracle, or rather, to be found by her. She appeared by his side in one of the physical, stone halls, rather than the tunnels that seemed older and wilder. Robed, as Evayne the elder was robed, her hood drawn back from her face, she seemed not quite real; a spirit that haunted the caverns.

"Do you understand how time works?" she asked.

Time was not a concept that troubled Adam overmuch.

"You are young," she said. "I am not. Time is the web through which all of my observations must travel, and the web is complex; to shift one strand is not the matter of a moment but often of centuries of foresight."

He nodded. "It is the business of Matriarchs," he said when it became clear she expected a verbal response.

"When you return to Averalaan—if indeed that occurs—and Evayne returns to the world, you will not meet her immediately. Even were you to arrive in the same place, you would not arrive at the same time. You are bound to the time and the stream that birthed you."

"And Evayne is not."

"And Evayne is not. You are aware that her sixteenth birthday occurs three years hence. You are aware that the coming of age that was so necessary has not yet fully occurred. Nor will it, while she remains in my halls. You can meet her before she is of age only here, because my halls were created by me, and they reflect some of my abilities, my duties. Do not attempt to find her in the mortal world; do not attempt to contact her. If you speak, she will come to you—or not at all. Do not speak of what will come," she continued. "Do not speak of it to any save Evayne herself, and only if she raises the subject. You will see her—you have seen her once.

"You think us unkind."

Adam nodded more forcefully.

"And so we are. Although we can see individual lives and individual pain, we can also see the aggregate. Were it a choice between one life and many, what would you expect your Matriarch to choose? What would Yollana of Havalla choose?"

"The many," he said, without hesitation.

"And you would not?"

He looked at her for one long moment. "Were the one life in question mine, I would choose the many," he finally said. "But if neither are mine—the one or the many—how can you expect or ask me to choose? I am not Matriarch. The choice will never be mine.

"Matriarchs can see the future," he continued, when the Oracle failed to either move or speak. "You *know* this. You are Matriarch of Matriarchs. It is why Matriarchs are trusted. If a Matriarch tells us that we must abandon an infant, even those who *hate it* will abide by the decision. But if a stranger tells us that this must be done, that there is purpose to the evil, we cannot trust it. We *should not* trust it.

"It is said that we were given the Matriarchs so that the harshness of the Voyanne would not make monsters of us all. And so it falls on the shoulders of those who *can* see, *to* see."

She looked at him as he stopped, her eyes unlike any eyes he had ever met in his life. "Are you afraid of becoming monstrous?"

"Why do you ask me when you already know?"

"I know the many possible paths you might take," the Oracle replied. "But your fears, where they are not expressed, are opaque. And, Adam, I ask because there are many, many possibilities. You think I have seen everything—and I can. But you do not understand that that everything means, in some fashion, that I have seen nothing."

"But you have planned—"

"I have hoped, child. I have hoped. I have done what I can, when I can, from the moment I first understood that most lives were not lived as mine was—and is."

"I am not afraid of becoming a monster," he told her. "I am only afraid that my sister might be forced to become one."

"Because she is Matriarch."

He nodded. And then, disloyally, added, "Because she is not hard enough and cold enough and certain enough."

"Neither is Jewel."

He nodded again, uneasy now.

"What you have given Evayne, I could not give her, but your role in her life is done, for now. If she had time, I would send you to her. But she does not; nor do you." She closed her eyes. "At the moment, it is Jewel who requires your aid." The Oracle paused. "I will give something into your keeping. It is not yours; it is not of you. But you must hold it now, until it is required."

Adam hesitated. The Oracle's right hand was a fist.

"Adam."

She was not asking permission. She was not asking a favor. She meant him to carry this thing. He nodded. Her fingers unfolded slowly as if it took effort, will, concentration. In her hand she held a ring.

It was the ring of House Terafin's ruler. It was the Matriarch's ring.

"It was left with me, as surety. I will return it to you now. The path I made, she has walked, and the ring is not, therefore, forfeit."

Adam's hands were frozen by his sides. "Can you not give it to her?"

"No. She has not yet finished, but the path made from here is her own path—to follow or to forsake. You will understand when it must be returned, and if you doubt, hold it fast. Do not," she added, "lose it."

Before the Oracle led Adam back to the room in which Jewel slept, Shadow reached her. Adam had never seen the murderous rage with which he now regarded the Oracle—and he had tried, almost successfully, to kill Adam on at least one occasion. He had tried to kill *Jewel* then.

The Oracle stopped instantly. "Eldest," she said, her voice neutral.

Shadow growled. His voice was so bestial it seemed as if the ability to form words had deserted him. His claws, Adam could see, had created grooves and runnels in the floor—which was stone.

Adam was not surprised when Shadow leaped toward the Oracle.

The Oracle gestured, and Shadow froze in mid-leap. "Come, Adam," she said. "You do not want to be standing there when he works himself free."

"What did you do?"

"Some creatures—like your great cats—are only peripherally aware of time and its passage. They have agreed to abide by time's rule, but they are cats; they abide in their own fashion, and their obedience is often hazy. They do not age as you age, of course, but they are more primal than even I. What they were yesterday, they are today; what they will be tomorrow, they were millennia past." She stepped around the silent, snarling, clawed statue. Adam, mindful of dignity, followed.

"Why did they agree to—to obey time, then?" he asked.

"Why do they agree to serve Jewel?"

"I don't know."

"Knowledge accrues over time. Experience begets knowledge. To live free of time in its entirety is to live unchanged. The sum of their knowledge could be confined to the moment of their creation—but it could not grow or expand. And the cats, you might have noticed, are vain; they do not like to be ignorant. In their minds, ignorance is stupidity.

"But even so, when they are not driven by rampant ego, they are comforted by it; at times they feel they have learned everything, and they wander. It is the ability *to* wander that makes them vulnerable to such minor tricks."

Adam hesitated.

"You are wondering if I have answered this question for a reason. You are wondering what purpose I intend the answer to serve."

Adam exhaled. "I was."

"Do you understand that the power you possess is in some fashion a power that affects time in a limited way?"

Did he? He frowned. "It is not," he answered carefully, "just a matter of time."

"No?"

"If the body is injured—if, for instance, the intestinal walls have been pierced or slashed open—time is not guaranteed to save the man or woman so injured. If someone is poisoned, time is not guaranteed to save them, either."

"Then you would argue that time is not involved?"

He shook his head. "Sometimes it's time. The body remembers its healthy state. It has its own imperative. There are injuries that would heal naturally. If an arm is broken, a leg, we can set the bone—and yes, Oracle, in that case, time shifts around that injury."

"You are afraid that Levec will be angry with you for speaking to me."

Adam winced, but he smiled at the mention of Healer Levec. "Levec," he said fondly, "is a very angry man. But his anger is not terrifying." Mostly. "And no, I do not think he would be angry at this discussion. He might be confused by it. He does not think of healing as I think of it."

"Ah. But he is powerful, in his own right."

Adam nodded. "For Levec, time is what heals injuries that don't *require* us. The injuries that do require our intervention are not a simple matter of time. We work against time. It is our responsibility to keep the body and the spirit entwined while we force the body into its proper shape. We cannot force a body to become something different, something other than what it naturally is, and we let the body's knowledge of itself guide us.

"I think it is at least two parts: the first, to force the body to remember what it was, not what it currently is, and the second, to hold that shape, to knit it in place—yes, Oracle. Time."

She smiled again, as if he had answered an especially tricky question. "You are wrong on one count, however."

"Oh?" He did not doubt her; he was not Levec. There was no bluster in him.

"You can force a body to become other than what it is, or what it was born to be. Should you desire it, you could shape living flesh. Should you desire it, you could do what I have done to the cats. I would not recommend it, however—they are not terribly forgiving creatures when their vanity has been deeply wounded."

Shadow was waiting for the Oracle and Adam when they finally reached the room in which Jewel slept. Adam froze, as if he were the one whose time had been stopped. Shadow, however, ignored him. He had eyes for the Oracle. Words for the Oracle, as well—and such words: a torrent of curses for which Adam would have been caned or without the next meal had he been at home among kin.

The words, however, were far less threatening. When the cats were talking— even in outrage—they were as safe as fanged, clawed, winged hunters could be.

The Oracle nodded to the cat. "Eldest," she said politely, as if they had not already crossed paths minutes ago.

Shadow hissed.

"Has she woken?"

"No." Shadow's wings were high. His fur, however, was flat and sleek; his tail swished back and forth.

"She is speaking," Snow added, from farther in the room. "And crying. Even *he* can't make her *wake up*."

"Eldest," the Oracle said quietly, "will you grant me entry?"

Shadow hissed again.

Adam stepped in front of the Oracle. "You can't wake her. The Oracle might—if you allow her entry." He spoke softly, as one did with the cats, but there was no plea, no wheedling, in the words he had chosen.

Snow hissed. "She doesn't *need* our permission, stupid boy."

"Unless she can walk through you, she needs you to move."

"She *can*."

Adam whispered a prayer to the Lady for patience.

The room in which Jewel now slept was not the one in which she had fallen asleep, but close: it was larger. It accommodated the whole of their gathered companions: the three cats, Angel and Terrick, Kallandras and Celleriant, Adam and Shianne, Jewel and her domicis Avandar.

Terrick leaned against one wall, as he had when Adam had departed to find Evayne. The others were seated a little way off, by a long table that was currently empty. Jewel lay abed.

As the cats made way—loudly, and sulking the entire time, as if moving a few feet away from a door was an act of colossal inconvenience—he entered the room, and the Oracle followed in his wake.

There was food here. Warmth. Shelter. There were no demons; the giant, winged serpent could not hunt them. But he was aware that in a peaceful life, the worst enemy one faced was often oneself. One's kin. In the face of greater danger, those things could be put aside—but they had seeds, grew roots, even then.

He did not know the precise details of what the Matriarch of Terafin feared, but he had lived his life in the lee of Matriarchs—his mother, his sister—and he knew the precise details didn't matter. What mattered was survival: the survival of the children, the future of the clan. What mattered was the safety of kin. The Voyanne was—had been—the only home the Voyani knew; they did not therefore have to defend a fixed, immovable space.

Adam had not wanted his sister, Margret, to become Matriarch. And he had known that she must. But she was, he thought, more like Jewel than like

Evallen, their mother. She had failed to kill Nicu when he had betrayed them the first time, choosing love and history and sentiment over the rough and necessary justice of the Voyanne.

And they had paid.

She had paid.

Adam did not see the power the Matriarch wielded; he saw the costs of that power. The burden. The loss. They were never so high as when the Matriarchs dreamed.

Not all dreams, he chided himself. *Not all sleep.*

It was true, but he could not make himself believe it of this sleep. He understood that the Terafin Matriarch had come to this place to find the Oracle; that she had come to take the Oracle's test. To pass it was to gain a type of power that no Matriarch before her had wielded in the history of the Voyanne. But Shadow had made clear—with cold corrections from Avandar—that those who undertook the Oracle's test very seldom passed it. They were broken by it, instead.

Avandar said Jewel had passed.

Shadow, however, had said, "Not yet. She has survived so far. But she has not yet reached the place of choice."

It was Shadow Adam believed correct, and he wished it were not. He made his way to the bedside, knelt on the stone floor; the pallet was barely held above the ground. He took her hand in his; no one stopped him. Angel was here, and Angel was den; he considered Adam kin.

Or he considered Adam harmless. Perhaps both.

The Oracle came to stand beside him. The Matriarch was pale, her eyes ringed with dark half circles that implied too much drink or too little sleep, or both.

But sleep, she had had.

"When she spoke, what did she say?" the Oracle asked.

Silence.

It was Shianne who answered. Of the people in this room, she feared the Oracle least. "We do not know, Eldest."

The Oracle's brows rose, the shape of her eyes widening and narrowing in succession as she absorbed this information and its implications, very few of which were clear to Adam.

"Shadow," Adam said.

"I wasn't *listening*," the cat replied, adding a sniff at the end of the sentence.

"I wasn't *either*," Snow added. "It was too *boring*."

Avandar spoke a single word. Celleriant spoke a different one. A brief flash of light filled the room and the cats mewled in outrage.

"You are very like her, you know," the Oracle said, as she studied Jewel's sleeping face.

Adam blinked, and this time he did look up. The light in the Oracle's cupped hand was . . . her heart. He could see the gaping void in her chest where the heart naturally resided—if natural was a word for such a thing.

"I am nothing like her," he replied. "I do not have her strength. I do not have her burdens. I could not carry them."

"My child," she said, in a voice that was so familiar, "you will have to carry very similar burdens in the end. I am sorry."

"I cannot," he said, with complete conviction. "I cannot be Matriarch. I am male."

"I know," the Oracle replied. "Do you understand why the clans are matrilineal?"

He nodded gravely. "The mother is always known. The father may not be."

"Indeed. And upon the open road it was necessary. But Arkosa has left the Voyanne, and you are of Arkosa. Your sister now rules the ancient, empty city in the Sea of Sorrows. It is there," she added, "that Jewel Markess now walks." She gestured, and Adam rose, hovering, anxious.

"Do you wish to see what she sees in her long dream? Do you wish to know what she does there?"

"He does not."

To Adam's surprise, it was Shianne who spoke. She had come to stand on the other side of the Oracle, and in the light of the Oracle's heart, Shianne's eyes were glinting silver: hard, cold.

The Oracle said, without turning to face her, "It is not of you that the question was asked. It is not for you to answer it."

Adam exhaled. He understood that Shianne did not wish him to look, and he did not wish to see what Jewel saw; it was not truth, but possibility. Yet possibility had created a burden of fear that had destroyed greater men than Adam. He did not decline, not yet; there was one question he had to ask.

"Will it help to wake her?"

The Oracle did not reply.

Shianne stepped forward, and the illumination in the Oracle's hand was eclipsed, for a moment, by the light that surrounded her. She was mortal, yes. Pregnant. But she was filled with a strange brightness and power that implied—to Adam, from the Dominion—that she was Sword's Edge. Magi.

"You will answer his question, Eldest."

He was afraid for her then. "Lady—"

"Nothing the Oracle does is an act of kindness. Nothing. Even stray comments have an edge and a weight—and a cost—that is only apparent when it has become far too late to avoid the debt." She spoke with certainty, and with anger.

Adam did not understand it. Almost gently, he stepped between this pale, Winter woman and the bent and wizened Oracle. "I know that," he told Shianne, his voice as gentle as it ever was when he spoke with adults, not those reckoned children.

"He *does*," Shadow said, growling. Shadow had never liked Adam. "He knows her. He *sees* her. And she sees *him*."

"He is naive," Shianne told Shadow, the edge off the chill of her voice. "He is young. In my youth, a being such as he would not yet be complete; his creator would not allow him the freedom of choices such as these."

"You are *wrong*," the gray cat replied. "But even if he *were* old, he would still be *stupid*. You are mortal, Shianne. You *chose* mortality. How could you choose it when you do not *understand* it at all?"

Throughout their discussion, the Oracle waited with outward calm. Adam turned to her and bowed. "I am sorry," he said, in Weston.

"Sorry?"

"We often can't see the burdens we haven't yet carried ourselves," was his grave reply. He studied her expression.

"You are wondering if perhaps there is any point in speaking to me at all," the Oracle said. It was not a question.

"I am wondering, rather, if there is anything I might say or do that you have not already seen."

"No. No, Adam of Arkosa, there is not." The Oracle's smile was an odd, broken thing. "But it is, perhaps, like mortal love before it has been uttered, offered."

Adam was confused.

"That I know does not change the comfort—and even the occasional joy—I derive from hearing the words. Mortals are fixed in time."

Adam glanced at Avandar.

"Even he. There is only forward, for mortals, no matter when they are. I knew that Jewel would not wake. But I knew also," she added, at Shadow's growl, "that she would. Or that she would not dream. Or that she would not survive. All of these variants are true, in a fashion; they all have the potential to be real."

"You chose the now to be the one in which she does not wake."

"No, Adam. *Jewel* chose that now. She has the ability to control the gift she has cursed so often since her childhood—but it is not perfect. The seer-born cannot see too much. What they take from me is the ability to see—for a time—almost as I do. It is akin to a second, an eyeblink, no more, but mortals were not created to contain and sustain such an endless, eternal second."

"And me?"

The Oracle waited, the light in her hands pulsing faintly.

"What do you want of me, then? How can I wake her if she can't wake herself? I have tried to heal—to use my power as I have used it in the past."

"Have you?"

"When she was dreaming, yes." He stopped, his brows raised as he considered the Oracle. Finally, he said, "Oh."

"Even so. This is not the first time The Terafin has lain abed in sleep."

"But you're the Oracle. The Wardens aren't *here*."

"No. But, perhaps, Adam, neither is Jewel."

"What does she speak of?" Shianne now demanded. Shadow sniffed and stalked to the farthest edge of the room, in a definitive bad mood. A very declarative one.

"You're *always* in a *bad* mood," Snow told him. But Snow was likewise disgruntled.

"Why are they annoyed?" Shianne asked again.

"The Oracle reminds me—or allows me to remind myself—that I've met the Matriarch in her own dreams before."

"You have already tried to wake her."

Adam nodded. "I was not the only one to walk in her dreams that night."

Shadow growled. Shianne's perfect brow rippled once in understanding. She fell silent, and when the silence broke, she said "I have need of you, Adam of Arkosa. If I understand what you are, and what must come to pass, the life for which I have sacrificed eternity may well require your aid. Having surrendered so much to the Oracle, I wish to lose nothing else."

He bowed, his cheeks warm, as if her declaration of his usefulness was akin to a declaration of love. He was momentarily giddy because she had said she had a use for him.

"The Oracle doesn't want me dead," he told Shianne. "Whatever role she sees for me, it can't end here."

"You do not understand the nature of time," the Oracle told him quietly. "It *can* end here. But it could have ended in the forest, as well. It could end on the

Winter road—and that is the most likely outcome of your journey, by far. I think the likelihood that you will die here is small.

"It is not nearly so small as the possibility that your Jewel will succeed in the task she has undertaken. She is not what the Sen once were. She is too much like you." A ripple of expression passed; it left her face serene and untouched. "Decide, Adam of Arkosa."

He had already decided. He lifted his head and looked into the heart in her hands.

"No," she told him.

He looked up from the clouds that roiled, trapped between her palms and walls of what seemed to be glowing crystal. He saw the heart of the storm there—the Southern Winds in which all history, all death, were trapped. He could almost hear their howl.

She waited until he looked up to meet her eyes before she spoke again. "It is not enough for you to look."

"I don't understand."

"Place your hands upon the crystal," were the words her mouth formed. But what he heard, what he felt, were different words. *You must touch my heart.*

And how, he thought, did one touch the heart of a god? He knew, of course. On one level there was only one answer. And perhaps on all levels, for Adam, there was only one answer. She was Matriarch of Matriarchs; she carried the burdens his mother, and her mother, and her mother's mother, stretching back to the first step Arkosa had taken upon the Voyanne, had carried. But she carried them all simultaneously.

It was death to know too much about the business of Matriarchs.

But they had always been people. They had never been gods. Adam thought that he could never know too much of the Oracle's business. His life—his entire life—would not be enough time to even attempt to learn that much. He exhaled. Nodded.

He heard two voices shrieking in unison as he set his hands to either side of the crystal before slowly forcing his palms to touch the crystal's sides.

Stupid, stupid boy!

The wind howled, its voice piercing. It was not a winter wind; it was not cold. There was no snow beneath his feet, and he saw that his feet were neatly gloved in familiar shoes.

There was sand here. It stretched for as far as most eyes could see. Adam had always had exceptional vision. He started to walk toward the small shape that broke the line of a horizon of azure and gold when a second howling joined the first.

"Why are you *so stupid?*" To his right stalked the great, gray cat.

"How are you here?" Adam whispered.

The cat's expression made clear that Adam had descended to even lower depths of stupidity, which should have been impossible while he still breathed. Adam, however, had discovered that there was no lower limit beyond which the cat's respect could not plummet.

"Why do *I* have to save *you?*"

"Shadow, I'm not actually here."

Shadow's roar broke the wind's voice. His expression teetered between complete disgust and astonishment and, because it was Shadow, fell into disgust. This disgust was not, of course, silent.

The Terafin Matriarch was not Voyani. She did not, therefore, have Adam's experience of the desert; she had crossed it only once in her life, and there had been no ceremony in it, no glimpse of the wastes beneath which lay her ancient home.

Adam did not, therefore, understand why Jewel dreamed of desert. This was the Sea of Sorrows; he was certain of it. Shadow padded in voluble disgust by his side, and the cat could, without effort, remain disgusted for a very long time. The only cure for it was distraction.

"What are you *looking* at, stupid boy?"

Adam had been wondering that himself. The shape on the horizon had not fully resolved itself, but it was not human. Nor was it large. He understood that the logic of dreaming was not reality; it could warp and twist between one step and the next. Things gifted by dreams—flight, strength—could be lost in an instant, and dreams also deprived him of simple things: the ability to run, for instance. Or to speak.

He was not afraid of the dream itself. The Warden of Dreams was imprisoned in the heart of the Matriarch's hidden lands. Such imprisonment could not last forever, but it would be some time yet before the Warden visited those who slept again. He thought they might never visit Jewel and stopped to examine that thought.

He wasn't certain where the thought had come from. He glanced at the great, gray cat. "Can you fly?"

Shadow hissed, flexing his wings.

"I mean here and now," Adam added hastily.

Shadow was sulking. He sent dry, arid sand into the air in a fine mist. "It's not safe," he muttered. "It's *your* fault."

"I am preventing you from flying?"

The great, gray cat rolled eyes that were predominantly gold—the color, oddly, of the sand itself. "*She* should have come *instead.*"

"She?"

He hissed.

"You refer to Shianne?"

"Stupid, *stupid, stupid.*"

Adam sighed. "Why would Shianne be a better choice?"

"She would *know.*"

Adam had no desire to force a pregnant woman into the Sea of Sorrows. But he kept this thought to himself. He knew that Shianne, her body so visibly sheltering an infant, was, and would remain, far more dangerous than he.

When he was halfway to the shape he had first spotted, he stopped in surprise. He had spent so much time in Averalaan, he thought with guilt, that he could not even recognize a *wagon*. In his own defense, it was not quite like the wagons that had been home to his family's supplies for his entire living memory—but it was not so very different. Not as different, certainly, as the vast, forbidding interiors of the Terafin manse; not as different as the more modest and yet equally forbidding Houses of Healing.

It was not moving. His first thought, seeing it, was that it had been abandoned. He saw no horses, no mules, no oxen, nothing that might pull the wagon; nor did he see the carved symbols with which the Matriarchs gifted their wagons with flight in the seas.

But perhaps, he thought, he was not yet close enough. He quickened his pace and noted only as he drew close to the wagon that Shadow had fallen silent. When he glanced at the cat, he noted the difference in his wings, his fur, his narrowed eyes.

Twenty yards became ten; ten became five. The wagon was much larger than the wagons from which Arkosa's Matriarch ruled. The whole of the clan did not travel together; they dispersed throughout the Terreans. Adam had distant cousins he had met no more than a handful of times. None, however, traveled in wagons like this.

"Is it safe?" Adam asked the cat.

"Nothing is safe," the cat replied. There had been no mention of stupidity. Adam kept five yards distance between himself and the exterior of the wagon. He had initially approached the wagon's back and moved now to view its front.

There, he stopped. Across the front of the wagon, there *were* marks, written in red. They were symbols he recognized immediately, although he'd never seen them on a Voyani wagon before.

"It's—it's Weston." Ellerson had insisted that Adam be educated.

Ellerson. Adam winced. He had not spent his life in the care of the old man, but it was impossible not to admire someone who was so quietly, so completely, dedicated to service. Worse, it had been impossible not to come to depend on him. His absence made the whole of the West Wing seem funereal.

"What is Weston?" Shadow asked, a growl at the back of his throat, his eyes facing forward.

"The language of The Terafin's people," Adam replied. "This is Weston. You can't read it?"

Shadow didn't respond in outrage at what would normally have been perceived as a terrible insult. "I *can*."

Adam said, "What does it say?"

This did get an annoyed hiss from the cat. "*You* can't read it?"

"I've been trying to learn to read it. I'm not very good at it yet. Only the trade words." Which these were definitely not.

"It is her name," Shadow told Adam. "Her name and her many vows."

"Vows?"

"The things she has promised," the cat continued, once again taking no time to insult Adam's ignorance.

"To who?"

This, on the other hand, caused the cat's brows to rise, changing the shape of his eyes. "To the *only* person that *matters,* you foolish, foolish *child*. To *herself*."

Adam did not explain vows or oaths to Shadow. Nor did he quibble with the cat's astonished, disgusted statement, although he could have. He had known the Terafin Matriarch for long enough to know that it was the vows she had sworn to every other person that would matter.

Shadow hissed anyway. "Are you *listening*?" he demanded, pawing sand. "If you do not, I will fly away and leave you here *forever*." As if he were, in truth, a very annoyed Ono or Ona.

"I always listen to you," Adam said, completely truthfully.

"You think of vows as *words*. You even call them that. You give your *word*."

Adam nodded.

"But words are just moving air, *dead* air. They are *sound*. They mean as much as the breeze. There are no Oathbinders *left*," he continued. "When they walked, words could be sealed and bound. They could be wed to life—and the breaking, to death. But now? Nothing."

"My word is not worth nothing," Adam said. Shadow seldom offended him, but this was important.

"Can you fly?" the cat asked.

Adam blinked. ". . . No."

"Tell me you can."

"Why? It would be—"

"A lie, perhaps. Yes. But you *could* tell me that lie. There are *other* lies. There are truths that become *lies*. There are lies that become *truth*. It is all just words." He hissed, sent sand up in a spray, and padded toward the wagon.

"Shadow, wait—"

"For *what?*" the cat countered, flicking his wings as if to literally swat Adam's concerns away. "You will tell me that *your word* has meaning, yes?"

Adam nodded. And then spoke, because the cat didn't bother to look back. "Yes."

"You will tell me that *her* word has meaning."

"Yes, of course."

"This is *why*, stupid boy. She has carved words of dead air and daydream here, at the heart of herself. These are her vows. She has made them all but unbreakable."

Adam frowned. "Do I have words like this?"

"How should *I* know?"

"Can you tell me what they say? Can you read them out loud to me?"

Shadow snorted. "You should have studied *harder*," he said, with a kind of bored condescension. He was not afraid of Jewel's vows.

"Shadow . . ."

"What *now?*" The gray cat leaped lightly over the small railings that had been lifted; this was truly a Matriarch's wagon.

"The forest—the forest beings—seem to understand what the Matriarch wants. They understood it before she'd ever spoken to them. She's never given them orders—that I know of—and yet they obey what has never been spoken. I don't think they care much for us," he added, "but they care for the things *she* cares for."

"Yesssssss?"

"Is this why?"

"Yes. You are being less stupid today."

"Have you always seen them?"

". . . But not *much* less stupid."

Adam, however, continued. The cat used the word *stupid* the way most people drew breath. "If these are her vows, and these are her words, why has she abandoned this wagon?"

The cat turned fully to face him and sat heavily in sun-hot sand. He was staring at Adam, something almost predatory in his face. Something beyond the prominent fangs.

"Why," he asked, tail swishing, "do you think it is abandoned?"

"It does not fly," Adam replied. "It does not hover. It does not move."

"Perhaps she is *inside*." But he looked to the sand that surrounded them, not to the wagon. "Perhaps she has gone to *her* city."

Adam couldn't leap the guardrail; he climbed over it instead while the cat snickered. The Weston words were written across the narrow door. Not all the wagons in the south were built this way; some created interior space with stretched, oiled cloth, and some were even more open. But this was very old in both style and substance.

"Are you *sure* you should touch that?" Shadow asked.

"I'm certain of nothing," Adam replied, "except that you should stop scratching the floor."

Shadow sniffed.

Adam opened the door. He half expected that it would be locked—or worse, guarded—but it wasn't; the door slid easily into the small enclosure. Adam froze in the frame, while Shadow butted him in the small of the back with what was probably his head.

"What? What? *What?*"

Adam had spent his life in wagons and tents. He had been allowed free rein of his mother's wagon—the Matriarch's wagon—one of the few who was. Margret was allowed the same theoretical freedom, but his mother's expectations, and frequently bitter disappointments, had made the wagon cage to his sister.

Cage, not home.

"Yes," his mother had said, her voice so bitter there was almost nothing else in it. "It's a cage. It's her cage. If she can't learn to *live in it*, you will all perish when I'm gone." Adam's hands had massaged her stiff neck as she spoke. "You think I'm harsh. You think I'm hard on her. No, don't speak—you know how I feel about lying." He had intended to say nothing, understanding that this— this listening to whatever she felt she could safely share—was the only gift he could offer his mother.

"I'm not nearly as hard on her as life will be. I'm not nearly as demanding. I get angry at her. But, Adam, if she cannot become stronger, life will break her. She carries the weight of Arkosa. You don't understand what that means."

"But I do," he said, the words not protest, but quiet confirmation. "I've watched you all my life."

"Aye, you have, little peacemaker," his mother said fondly, some of the bitterness seeping out of her voice. She never, ever spoke this way to Margret. He wished, not for the first time, and certainly not the last, that she would. "But you're a boy. You're a son. You will never be called upon to bear the burden I bear. You will never be forced to be mother to Arkosa."

"I would be father, if I could."

"Yes, love, you would. But fathers cannot carry life. And if you were a daughter, you would not love me nearly so much, and you would not trust me."

He remembered his outrage. "Margret trusts you—you are Arkosa!"

"Margret is a fool," his mother replied. "She needs and wants too much. But she is not so much of a fool as that. You don't understand. Affection is a luxury. It is an indulgence. To give it, to receive it—that is not the purpose of the Matriarch. She does not trust me, Adam, because she cannot trust me. I will hurt her more than any enemy she will ever face."

Her neck was stiff again. Adam's hands were trembling.

"It is what my mother did to me. I am stronger than your sister. Go. Talk to her. Comfort her if you can."

He hesitated, torn between the two women to whom he was most closely related, each of them in pain.

He shook himself. This wagon was not that wagon, and his mother was dead. Even the memories she had left for his sister were like scars: faded with time, a reminder of the pain that had caused them. Jewel Markess ATerafin, The Terafin, had not grown up in this wagon. It had never been her cage.

It was empty. Of course it was empty. Light streamed in through the open, narrow windows, the shutters absent; it hit a threadbare rug, an empty chair. On the slender windowsill was a worn pipe, empty of leaf and ash. He did not recognize the pipe, nor did he recognize the rug or the chair. His gaze moved past them until he saw a door; it was not the one he had entered. Weston in style, it was not the more common Southern hangings found in the interiors of a building.

Shadow's low growl—always more threatening than his complaints— brought Adam fully back to himself. "It's a . . . door. Jewel's not here."

The cat's hiss was a physical sensation; his mouth might have been near Adam's ear. "Why are you *standing there*?"

Hand trembling, although he could not later say why, he reached for the door's handle. It was worn, brass, but it was comfortingly solid, neither too warm nor too cold. Drawing breath, he opened the door and stood staring at the busy streets of Averalaan.

"I don't understand." Adam pivoted in the doorway to see the wagon abandoned in the golden sand of the Sea of Sorrows.

"No," Shadow agreed, grooming his paw. "You don't."

"Is the Matriarch—was she—Voyani? Some make their way to your smelly, crowded city."

"It is not *my* smelly, crowded city—it is *hers*."

"What are we doing here, Shadow?" Adam asked, almost bewildered.

"I am protecting *you*. You are being *stupid*."

"Ah, apologies. I meant, what are we supposed to be doing here?"

"Oh, that."

Adam had assumed that this was Jewel's dream—or nightmare. Now, he wasn't certain. He knew that he couldn't wake her. He'd tried. He was here *to* wake her. He was here.

You are only a son.

"Yes, Matriarch." He stepped through the door into familiar streets.

Although he seldom ventured into the hundred holdings, the Common wasn't unfamiliar. He recognized it because merchants parked their wagon stalls beneath the bowers of Birgide's trees. Had he not reached these streets through that open door, he would have assumed it was real.

He listened to passing conversations, some of them arguments, some gossip; he had learned early to weed out the constant barking of merchants. Everything about this place was as he remembered it. At no point did the dream shift to include him; at no point did it create improbability—if one did not consider a city of this size to be improbable—to terrify or lull him.

But as he knelt beside one of the great trees, Shadow hissed. Adam picked up a leaf, and then two.

"You are *wasting* time."

Adam nodded, almost absently. "I am. But this is a dream, and time has different rules in dreams."

Shadow shrieked. This caused ripples of panic to spread throughout the dense crowd. Adam placed the leaves against his chest, beneath the cloth of his shirt. He then frowned and, frowning, headed toward the Merchant Authority.

The guards were not polite—or they wouldn't have been, had Adam been without Shadow. One of the two appeared to recognize the cat, or at least associate him with The Terafin. They didn't like the look of Adam, but as Voyani he was accustomed to that. They really didn't like the look of the gray cat, and a conference of whispers produced a third guard. He was obviously in charge, but he didn't have the authority to allow Adam to enter with a dangerous animal.

Shadow was outraged.

Adam said, "Please—there are Terafin Chosen outside of the Terafin offices. One of them will vouch for me and my—my cat."

One of the younger guards was sent up the stairs, and he returned with one of the Chosen. To Adam's surprise, it was Captain Arrendas. He shook himself. Why would that be surprising? It was Jewel's dream.

"*Stupid* boy."

Arrendas was surprised, not at the insult—none of the Chosen could be surprised at what fell out of the mouths of these cats—but by Adam himself. He turned to the Merchant Authority guard and said, "Yes, he is one of the Terafin's personal servants. He is not ATerafin, but he is much trusted."

The guards, with some relief that the decision—and its resultant consequences—was not theirs, moved aside to let Adam and Shadow pass.

Arrendas marched in silence to the Terafin offices. He opened the door with a word, not a hand, and walked Adam—and Shadow, who was now looking dangerously interested—to the front desk.

The woman behind it stared at the gray cat. She then rose instantly and headed toward a door behind her and to the side; it opened, she spoke—he couldn't catch the words—and returned to his side. "Captain," she said, to Arrendas, "Finch bids you enter as well, if you wish."

He wasn't surprised that Finch was happy to see him—Finch had always been happy to see him. She was, Adam understood, like an Ona, a sister to The Terafin, and trusted as if she were kin.

She was already almost all the way across the room before the door had closed, and she enveloped him in a hug. He leaned into it, inhaling; everything about Finch was as he remembered it. Everything.

"Is Jay back, too?" she asked, when she was willing to let him go.

"She is not," Shadow informed her, pouting.

Finch immediately dropped her hand to his head and began to scratch behind his ears. "You're not to destroy anything here," Finch told him gently. "Unless it's to save a life."

Adam, however, was staring. He held a hand out to Finch, and said, "May I—may I heal you?" It was awkwardly phrased, but it was an awkward question, which was why he had chosen to ask it in Weston.

"I'm not injured," Finch said, obviously confused. "Why?"

"It's like pinching yourself in a dream," Adam told her.

Finch looked down at Shadow again, her expression changing as he watched it.

"It will only take a second."

"Take as long as you think you need," Finch said, offering her hand.

He hadn't lied. He only needed a second. What he felt beneath his fingers was life; Finch's life.

Adam was in Averalaan.

22nd day of Morel, 428 A.A.
Merchant Authority, Averalaan Aramarelas

"I don't understand," Adam whispered.

Finch, who had been overjoyed to see him, gently retrieved her hand. He barely noticed. He looked around the office in a state of utter confusion. For a moment, he reminded her of the lonely, frightened boy she had first met in the Houses of Healing. Without thought, she shifted into Torra.

He must have understood why; he flushed.

"Jay isn't with you," she said.

"She is. I mean—she was. I mean, I was with her."

Shadow began to snicker, and Finch placed a firm hand on his head. "You are all *so stupid.*"

"Where were you? Let me get tea."

Adam shook his head. Wanly, he added, "I have no appetite. At all." He was staring at her, a mixture of longing and dread crowding his expression. "We were—we are—in a room in a cave. I—" He shook his head again. "The Matriarch met the Oracle. The Oracle's with us. We've been with her for a few days; she's been learning what the Oracle is willing to teach.

"But she didn't wake up yesterday morning. She's alive," he added quickly. "She's dreaming. But she won't wake. Even the cats couldn't wake her."

Finch fixed Shadow with a questioning glance. She hoped it was suitably firm. The cats were almost physically incapable of admitting to limitations, and failure would be high on their list.

Shadow, however, flicked his tail rather than avoiding her gaze. In a voice shorn of his customary good temper—which is to say, whining—he said, "I could not *find* her."

"What do you mean?"

"*You* know."

And the odd thing was, she did. The cats were the definition of frivolity—murderous frivolity—most of the time. They squabbled like young siblings. They complained about boredom, which was apparently the besetting sin of the entirety of humanity. But they had come from the forest. "You guard her dreams."

"Yesssss."

"You tried to keep her safe from the Warden."

"Yesssss."

"You could do this because you can enter her dreams."

He sniffed. "I *know* this *already*."

"My apologies," she told him, shifting her hand to scratch behind his ears. "I needed to make certain I knew it. You couldn't enter this dream. Have the Wardens somehow escaped?"

The great cat snorted; warm air brushed past Finch's face. "No."

"Shadow, *please*—that carpet is worth more than my life!"

"It is *ugly*. It *offends* me."

Finch sighed. To Adam she said, "Clearly, he's bored. Have things stopped trying to kill you?"

"For four days, nothing has been able to find us—or so I've been told."

"Is that why Shadow can't reach Jay's dreams?"

Adam frowned. "I don't know. Shadow?"

Shadow flicked his wings dismissively.

"Never mind. Sit down, Adam. I need to cancel my next appointment." Finch left him quickly, without pausing to see if he obeyed.

"You touched the Oracle's crystal."

Adam nodded.

"You can't feel it now."

"How could I? My hands are here. With me. In your city." He hesitated, and then said, "I started out in the desert. In the Sea of Sorrows. That means nothing to you—it was, and is, a place of sun and sand and wind. But when I opened the wagon door, it opened here. I thought it was like the Sea of Sorrows. I thought it was part of her dream.

"But you're not a dream."

"Possibly a nightmare, given current events. Ah, no—we're fine. We're all fine. When Jay wakes, if you're with her, tell her that. Shadow, do you know what's happening?"

"Yesssss. *Nothing* is happening."

It was so easy to forget just how deadly the great cats were. Finch exhaled. "We're not wise. We're not ancient. We're not—at least I'm not—magical. I'm sorry I don't know these things. I probably should, but I've always relied on you and your brothers to tell me what I need to know, because you know everything."

She felt Adam's gaze drill the side of her face. He was earnest and honest both, and he found obvious lies uncomfortable. But these weren't entirely falsehoods. The cats were everything she was not. The cats—especially Shadow—stood guard over and around Jay, and they did what they could to both infuriate her and keep her alive. They could do things Finch couldn't do.

Shadow growled but was obviously pleased. The cats loved flattery.

"She is *Sen*," Shadow told Finch, looking down his august nose although his head was at a lower level than hers. "This is the heart of her power." That nose wrinkled. "It is smelly and ugly and crowded and *stupid*, but so is everything she loves. We are here because she is here."

Adam shook his head. "She's not. She can't be."

Shadow yowled in outrage.

Finch, however, closed her desk drawer. "I declare it a state of emergency," she said, smiling. "Let's go back to the manse."

"But she can't be here."

"Neither can you."

Chapter Seven

FINCH ENTERED THE WEST Wing in a rush of skirts, Adam to the left, Shadow to the front and right. Arrendas preceded her into the manse, his presence signaling her early return from the Merchant Authority. As regent, she was entitled to the protection of the Chosen. She had tried to argue against it, pointing out that Teller was the right-kin, and in greater need.

Teller accepted the Chosen without complaint, which meant Finch had very little choice in the matter. She hated to divert resources, but she was comfortable with the Chosen, especially their captains.

The cat muttered and cursed and sulked from the foyer at which the carriage had let them off to the residential rooms. It would have been useful if the cats were capable of making themselves invisible, but at least in these halls the servants had become accustomed to them.

And the servants would gossip; gossip would spread like fire across dry kindling. Rumors would circulate: The Terafin had returned. Adam was here. Shadow was here. She could almost see relief and hope, yet she hated to raise either without cause.

Especially when she herself found that hope its own special agony.

They found Jester in his room; they found Ariel in hers, and she let out a shriek of almost unintelligible Torra when Shadow and Adam stepped through her door—of the denizens of the Wing, she was closest to, most trusting of, them.

"I'm sorry," she told the girl, in her own gentle Torra, "they can't stay. Jay is waiting for them." But she hated to tear them away immediately, and after a brief pause, said, "I'll try to find food."

"I'm not—"

"I want to see if you can take something back with you."

"I have no idea how to *get* back."

"We'll work on that. But—visit with Ariel. I think Shadow should stay with you, but I don't have to. I'll be back soon."

Arrendas had clearly sent Arann to the West Wing; he was there when Finch left Jester's empty room. It was early for Jester to be so awake; he'd been out the previous evening, in company not noted for its sobriety.

"Adam and Shadow are back," she told Arann, before he could ask. She saw the subtle shift in the line of his shoulders, and signed, *she's safe.*

"Arrendas said you're to accept escort in the manse, unless Shadow is with you."

"Given his mood this morning, the person who'll need protection *is* Shadow. I can't believe I actually miss the cats when they're not here." Haval's room was empty as well. Finch said, "Is Teller in his office?"

Arann nodded.

"I don't suppose you could run to his office and tell him to meet me at The Terafin's chambers?"

"Not if I don't want to commit ritual suicide, no." No other member of the Chosen would say this. In general, when presented with a request that directly interfered with their duties, they said a lot of nothing. But Arann was allowed a certain amount of leeway in his formalities: he lived in the West Wing when he wasn't on duty. He was The Terafin's brother in all but blood.

"Fine. We're taking a detour to the right-kin's office, where I will no doubt annoy poor Barston."

"Why?"

"I need the House Mage. I want Jester and Birgide. I'll accept Haval."

"We're going outside, then."

"Yes. After we find the House Mage, who's usually in Jay's rooms. Or above them fighting winged monsters."

Finch didn't answer Teller's questions. Hope had become a fear, and she wanted to hoard that fear; to keep it to herself where it wouldn't cause injury to people she loved when they could do nothing about it, either.

But that was unfair. She knew it. She wondered if all protective impulses were as unfair, as diminishing, as this one. "Adam was with Jay," she told Teller. "He arrived here—somehow, I'm not sure even he understands how—while trying to wake her up. He's afraid he can't go back."

"And you're not?"

"No. I don't think he'll be able to stay. I've left him and Shadow with Ariel while I find Meralonne."

Teller rose. He tidied his desk and then headed out to inform Barston that he would be missing meetings for the next two hours. Barston was annoyed but glanced at the regent; whatever he saw in Finch's face calmed him somewhat. He didn't ask her if everything was well. But he never asked that. She inclined her head.

In theory, it was Barston's responsibility to arrange Finch's schedule. In practice, as Finch had not forsaken the Merchant Authority, it was Lucille's. Barston accepted this with the good grace one would assume of a territorial traditionalist, but he *did* accept it. He was not of a mind to trust Jarven and felt that Finch's exodus from that office would require exactly that trust.

Teller and Finch were met at The Terafin's chambers by the two captains of the Chosen. They joined Arann and Marave, releasing the two Chosen who had accompanied Teller back to their duties.

Torvan generally did the talking for the captains when they had something to say, but as he was on guard duty, he was silent. Arrendas had, apparently, filled him in on the basics, because he did ask after Adam and Shadow.

No one attempted to keep Finch from The Terafin's chambers; nor did they question Teller's presence. The doors were opened swiftly. Finch wondered if the library that could be seen from this side of the open doors existed anymore. It had been one of Jay's favorite rooms until the changes had occurred.

She stepped into it, and arrived in the room that had replaced it, if it could be called a room at all, as it lacked a ceiling or obvious walls. Teller followed. None of the den were precisely comfortable in The Terafin's personal chambers, too aware that it was here that Ellerson and Carver had been lost.

But the sky was a steady amethyst; there were no visible clouds overhead, and there was no flash of lightning in the distance—the surest sign that Meralonne had located an enemy. "Where is the House Mage?" Finch asked Torvan.

"Here, somewhere."

"How do you summon him when his presence is required?"

"There is no place his presence is required more," was Torvan's grave reply.

"So . . . you don't summon him."

"No, Regent."

"I should have inquired before we came here," she told him. "I think we are working to deadline, and I'm not certain we have the time required to locate the mage, if there is no formal procedure in place."

"That deadline?"

"I don't know." She lifted her face into the passing breeze; it was gentle and cool. "I want news," she told Torvan, her voice dropping in volume. "I want it so badly I'm afraid to hope. And I don't want to frighten Adam."

"Adam is not easily shaken."

"You didn't see him in the Merchant Authority offices," she said, with a slender grin, "when he realized that I was not a figment of dream or daydream."

The breeze grew stronger, tugging at the hair she kept pinned and oiled and confined. She closed her eyes, inhaled, and opened them again. Meralonne was aware of their presence.

She found him unsettling, but she always had. He was mage-born and, more-over, barely leashed; she was convinced that he was malleable only because of his great respect for Sigurne Mellifas, and not because Sigurne wielded any significant power over him should he step out of line. But he had become, in the passage of weeks, stranger and more wild.

He was always beautiful now. She had seen glimpses of a cold and harsh perfection in him when they had first met—but only, and always, when he fought the demons. Now, it was there almost all the time. The querulous man who smoked his pipe as an act of lazy aggression had all but vanished.

She found herself missing that man. But that man, she thought, could not do what this man had undertaken: defend The Terafin's lands from the incursion of demons and monsters.

And what will defend these lands against him? She shook the thought away as unprofitable and stopped herself from bowing. Here, now, the bow was unnecessary, and she felt instinctively that granting him visible signs of respect that rank did not demand was no longer completely safe. It had been . . . once.

He seemed to read her thoughts from his perch of air; he came toward the floor without ever once condescending to touch it with his feet. His eyes were silver, bright, his hair a platinum cloak. He sheathed his sword—which meant, in his case, that the sword vanished.

He did bow.

Finch inclined her head, but it took effort to limit herself to that. She wished that Jarven were here, caught herself mid-wish, and almost shook her head. Jarven was not regent. Meralonne was one of the things that she would have to be capable of confronting on her own, even if she never became comfortable doing so.

Teller, however, did bow. "APhaniel," he said gravely. "We continue grateful."

"You did not come to offer me gratitude, surely?"

"No," he said. "Nor pipe weed, either."

"Ah. You've been speaking with the Master of the Household Staff."

Teller's wince was visible, obvious.

"I have, however, tobacco of my own," the mage replied. And speaking thus, he retrieved his pipe from the folds of his robe and sank, at last, to the ground.

Jester, Haval, and Birgide were waiting for them at the edge of the forest. To Finch's mild surprise, so were Adam and Shadow. Jester signed to Adam, who hesitated before signing back; Finch thought it was because he was still uncertain of how to use den-sign quickly. Haval frowned.

Birgide, however, was staring at Shadow, her brows creased.

Meralonne nodded to the gray cat. "Eldest," he said, and then, after a pause, "Shadow."

"Yessssssss?"

"You have left The Terafin's side."

Shadow hissed. "It's not *my* fault." He glared at Adam, who actually flushed.

"Adam?" Jester said.

But Finch said, "I wish to go to the tree of fire before we have this conversation." To her surprise, Haval concurred.

And there, they gathered, as if the tree were a great bonfire. The forest gloom was lifted in that light, but the light implied burning, not dawn or day. It was not comfortable. Adam stayed beside Finch for most of the walk, which would have been silent were it not for Shadow. Shadow was not bored, not exactly, but he was offended by the ignorance of the rest of his companions, and as always, felt compelled to share. It was strangely comforting.

Finch offered Adam a hand, and he took it without thought. But he was aware that this was not a Weston custom, except where children were involved. At the moment, in this unnatural forest, Weston custom did not concern him.

He told them about the Matriarch's predicament. It felt almost wrong to do so, but these were her closest kin; he knew that were she here, it would be the Chosen who would remain by her side at all times; it would be Finch and Teller who would tend her. It would be the den to whom she would come for counsel.

Haval was staring at him. "You accepted the Oracle's help, you touched the Oracle's version of a crystal ball, and you came here." It was not a question so much as a repetition of facts.

Adam nodded. "With Shadow."

"Who did not touch the Oracle's crystal."

Shadow hissed.

Meralonne exhaled. Smoke traveled from his lips in wreaths. "Adam, do you understand that the Oracle is the first child of the gods? She was born when the gods you now worship were a distant possibility, although in name, they could be said to exist. She was born when the wild gods had only barely sunk roots into this world."

"Why did she not leave when the gods left?" It was Finch who asked.

"She could not," Meralonne replied. "She was born to this plane. She is *of* it in a way that the gods were not. Do not ask me," he added, affecting a boredom that only the cats could achieve without effort, "why the gods were not; it is complicated theology and, frankly, it is irrelevant."

"If she is the child of gods, does she have the powers of her parents?"

"Some, certainly. And she has abilities that are unique; those abilities have none of her parents in them."

"But it's said the gods could remake the continents—or destroy them—without much effort."

"Destroy, perhaps. Creation was always more difficult. If you wonder why Adam is here, however, you fail to understand what the Oracle is." His eyes—eyes that had always seemed disconcertingly cold to Adam—narrowed. "You said that The Terafin chose to take the Oracle's test. You implied that she had passed it."

Adam hesitated. Finch's hand tightened briefly around his, as if she intended to transmit some of her strength to him by simple touch alone.

Shadow, however, said, "She did not *die*. She is not *insane*. But she has not *finished*."

"Why does she not wake?" the mage asked—of the cat.

Shadow hissed. He didn't answer, which meant he didn't know.

"How long has she slept?"

"Two days, perhaps? It is hard to gauge time in the wilderness."

"For *you*," Shadow muttered. He began to clean his paws.

"Why did the Oracle feel that you could wake The Terafin?" the mage continued, ignoring the cat. He had never liked them, Adam recalled.

"I think . . ."

"Because you've woken her once when she couldn't wake on her own." It was Jester who spoke.

Adam nodded. "I had tried," he added, voice lower, gaze turned briefly inward. "I had tried, and she did not wake. But the Oracle felt I was not trying the right thing, that I was somehow doing something different. And it was true. The first time I woke her, I attempted to heal her. I did what I did for those with the sleeping sickness under Levec's care."

"Was it different?"

Adam's gaze grazed Shadow, but he understood that nearly dying to the great, gray cat was not, in fact, what the mage meant. Had it been different then?

No, he thought. Not completely. It had felt different at the time because the Matriarch had always been in control of her dreams; he could not shift them as he had shifted the others. Oh, the dreams had shifted—but she had done that. And she had done that because she had seen Adam and had recognized almost instantly that Adam was not a phantasm of dream.

Adam had been there.

It had been easier for Adam. The dreamers did not have multiple incidences of themselves in their dreams; they were at the center of the dream that held them fast. They did not doubt the truth of their dreams, but they did not realize that they could affect their outcomes. The other dreamers accepted that Adam was real because they believed the dreams they were living in were real.

Jewel had known, the minute she had seen Adam, that the two were different.

He frowned.

"I could not reach her dreaming," he finally said. "Until I touched the Oracle's heart, I could not reach it."

Silence. The crackle of flame, of fire. The movement of branches. Adam startled, looked up, saw that those branches did not move as tree branches did: they moved like snakes, although they retained the appearance of burning wood.

It was Haval Arwood who said quietly, "It has begun, then."

Adam was confused for one long moment; it was clear that he had company. Birgide, Jester, and Finch were frowning in a way that implied thought. Teller, however, was not. He did not look to Haval; he did not look to the mage. He looked, instead, to the gray cat. Shadow flicked wings and padded over to Teller's side, where he sat on the right-kin's foot.

"Do you know where she is?" Teller asked Shadow.

Shadow said nothing.

Teller exhaled and tried again. "Is she here?"

Shadow said more nothing.

It was Adam who answered. "I think she must be. But I think she could be anywhere in Averalaan." He hesitated. "She will be her dreaming self."

"What exactly does that mean?" Jester demanded.

"She will be young, like me, or younger, or old like you. She will be powerful, or powerless. She will be rich or poor. She will have a husband and family. She will be a desperate orphan. She will be dreaming."

"And she will be here," Haval said. He looked almost ashen as the words left his mouth.

"Haval, what is going on?" Jester demanded. "No, don't ask me questions. Don't make another lecture or lesson of this—we don't have the time."

"I do not understand it well enough to make a lesson of it," Haval replied, with brittle dignity. "I do not understand what being Sen means." He glanced at Meralonne.

"She is not powerful enough," the mage said quietly, "to do what must be done. I am sorry."

"She is not," Haval replied, "powerful enough yet."

"You assume that she will be."

"Yes. You assume she will not. I have always had a great respect for the depth of your knowledge about things ancient."

"And not things mortal?"

"And not," Haval inclined his head, "mortals." To Jester, he said, "Her power is centered in this city—all of it. Birgide can map its boundaries because Birgide is aware of all of them. She cannot extend her territory. In my opinion, it will never be larger than it currently is. We know that within the boundaries of these lands, she has the power to alter reality as the rest of us perceive it."

Shadow sniffed.

Jester signed. Teller signed. Finch signed. Adam had difficulty catching the whole of the exchange. They were all so quick, and he had practiced very, very little since leaving the manse. He caught perhaps half of what was signed and had to work to piece it together. Ah. They were speaking of The Terafin's personal chambers. They did not agree with Haval precisely, but they could not disagree with any conviction.

Jester swallowed. "How can she be in both places simultaneously?"

Haval replied with care. "I would not say that she is. The part of her that sleeps is here—somewhere. The part of her that does not is where Adam was when he accepted the Oracle's aid. I believe—and now I am speculating wildly—that Adam is to find her here, and to wake her, here."

Adam said, "If she is physically *here*, how can I wake her?"

"That would be my question as well," Haval replied, in the mildest of voices. He turned to Birgide and said, "Tell me, where is Jewel now?"

"Councillor," a new voice said, "that is not a fair question, as you well know." A small, golden fox entered the clearing. By his side was a man Adam recognized: Jarven ATerafin.

He tensed—almost everyone did, even Finch, to whom he was almost an Ono. Jarven, however, was staring at Shadow. And Adam. His lips turned up in the smile that the Matriarch liked least. One glance at Haval made it clear that he agreed with the Matriarch, at least in this.

Haval, however, accepted the interruption—and the correction—in stride. "I am uncertain why, Eldest."

"Because the Warden will not, of course, be able to answer. She will sense what we all sense: our Lord's presence. But we sense it regardless. She is *of* these lands; these lands are *of* her. Ask us instead which part of the forest she *does not* inhabit."

"Which part, then, Eldest?"

"None. There is no part of the forest that she does not inhabit."

"And the city, then?"

"Where it overlaps the forest? She is omnipresent."

"Then she cannot yet—"

"She can. She is of both worlds. She is Sen."

It was Haval who said to the den, without further preamble, "We will start in the twenty-fifth holding."

Neither Finch nor Teller had the time to search through the entire city looking for a figment of Jay made somehow disturbingly real. Jarven, who had not, in theory, been present for most of the discussion, said, "I will go to the Authority offices for the afternoon—or at least until you have abandoned or fulfilled your quest."

That left Teller with a glacially annoyed Barston. "I will only go as far as the twenty-fifth holding," he said quietly.

"You need not be apologetic," Haval told him, almost gently. "It is my belief that Adam will not be able to do what is necessary without your presence."

22nd day of Morel, 428 A.A.
Twenty-fifth Holding, Averalaan

Haval knew where they had once lived.

"Of course," he said, voice fully neutral.

"Why 'of course'?" Jester looked up to see shutters—some open, some closed, most warped. They were not dressed for the twenty-fifth holding in any way. Jester appreciated the irony. He also appreciated the guards. Meralonne had not elected to accompany them. Nor, in the end, had Birgide. Only the absence of the latter made him uneasy.

"I was hired to teach her. I was not certain that it was wise, and I did some very minor research."

"Meaning you sent some poor apprentice—"

"Sadly, no. You are the first assistant I have had since I began to fashion clothing for the patriciate. The research was done by me. That, I believe, was one of two windows into the apartment you once called home."

Jester looked up. The building had not changed much since they had fled, leaving almost everything they owned—not that it had ever been much—behind. Leaving, he thought, Duster as well. He had seldom looked at their home from the vantage of the street; he felt no prickling nostalgia as he nodded. He glanced at Teller and Finch. Teller lifted a hand in quick den-sign.

Yes.

"Why did you want to start here?" Teller asked the tailor.

"A hunch," Haval replied. "I am not possessed of The Terafin's instincts. That aside, I trust mine."

"We've been ATerafin for over half our lives."

"And you lived in this place for three years. Maybe four."

Teller nodded.

"But it was here, Teller, that Jewel made her home and finished building her family. It was here that she dreamed—of safety, of security, of a place where her den might live in peace. It was here that she truly began to build."

Finch glanced at Haval. "Angel came to us here. But the rest of us, she already had."

"True. But Ararath is dead."

The stairs were as narrow and rickety—as noisy—as they had always been. They seemed flimsy now, too small; the ceilings were low and the hall poorly lit. Jester remembered his life in the holdings. He remembered, as he walked here, how much like wealth it had seemed, how much like freedom. Life itself made changes, but he had never been sentimental.

What Jay had built, he had chosen—albeit more slowly—to love as well, inasmuch as he was capable of that emotion. He hadn't tested her. Even if he'd desired to do so, he'd've had to wait in line. It was a short line consisting of one: Duster.

She pushed. She pushed constantly. She trusted nothing. She couldn't trust Jay. And yet she had.

"Why," he asked Finch, "did you trust Jay?"

Finch said, "She saved my life. She saved me from literal demons."

"She saved Duster as well."

"Not the same way." But Finch understood the question Jester hadn't quite asked. "I prayed," she said. "The way even you pray when things have gone south. I was cold, I was barefoot, I was in a night shift designed for—" she shook her head. "I was scrawny. I knew how to scrap a bit, but I didn't know how to fight. Duster? She knew how to fight." The shadow of a smile touched her lips as she mounted familiar stairs.

"I expected to die. I didn't expect Jay. And Carver." She turned to look down a step at Adam, whose hand she still held. "This is where we lived."

He nodded. "Will the stairs hold Shadow?"

"Shadow could walk across stretched gauze without tearing or breaking it—if he wanted."

Adam looked highly dubious. "He's heavy."

"I *can*," Shadow said.

"You're too heavy—"

"Am *not*."

Jester kept a grin off his lips. "Shadow," he told the gray cat, "We're too heavy, and we're probably a third of your weight."

Shadow was incensed. Loudly. But Jester noted that the stairs no longer creaked beneath the cat's feet—only theirs.

When Haval reached the door, there was a small tussle for position; the halls would not easily accommodate them all unless they stood in a line. The twenty-fifth holding was not as dangerous as the thirty-second, but it wasn't precisely safe, either. People knew when to mind their own business and did so with alacrity.

For reasons that were not clear, Haval suggested that Adam open the door. Adam, however, shook his head. He turned to Teller. "If she is somehow here," he said quietly, "she will expect you. Or Finch. Or Jester." He glanced to the back of the hall. "Arann?"

Arann, on duty, hadn't spoken a word. He conferred briefly with the Chosen present, then nodded. Normally, the Chosen would open the door. Arann was both Chosen and den, the only person who was.

"What do you expect to find?" Adam asked Haval.

"I do not expect to find anything," Haval replied. "Ah, no, that is imprecise. I expect to find young Jewel. But if I do not, and we have walked into someone else's life and home, I will accept this as information, and we will continue. There is no ego involved. That is the important thing that many people your age forget. They are afraid of mistakes, of making mistakes; they are afraid of feeling—or being—stupid. Mistakes, however, are our finest teachers."

"If we survive them," Jester said, voice sour.

"Indeed. It is the only time in which the mistakes of others can still prove instructive."

"And you won't feel guilty if you've ordered someone else to make mistakes in your stead." It wasn't a question. Adam didn't understand why Jester disliked Haval. Then again, Jester disliked everyone who wasn't den-kin, he was just usually much better at hiding it.

"No, Jester. You are correct. There is no profit in guilt."

"Without it, there's no responsibility either."

"Is that how you see responsibility?"

Arann had reached the door. Shadow was standing on one of his feet.

"Do you want to open it?" he asked the cat, without heat.

It occurred to Adam that Shadow rarely tormented Arann. Arann was physically large—the largest of the den—but Shadow had fought demons with glee and invective; his decision to more-or-less leave Arann alone had nothing to do with size, prowess, or training on Arann's part.

Adam privately thought it had more to do with Arann's steadiness. He accepted Shadow standing on his foot without irritation or comment. The cats really were like children.

This one hissed. "He's right," he said, glaring at Haval.

This confused Adam. It did not appear to confuse anyone else. Arann rapped on the door. It wasn't knocking, not precisely, and it wasn't a single tap. It was a series of taps.

Finch was smiling, except it didn't quite look like a smile. Teller was still. Jester was grinning. Adam felt very much the outsider here. This was a part of their life he had never seen and had only rarely heard about. They had been young, here. They had been the age Adam was now.

Matriarch business, he told himself. He let the pang fade.

The door opened.

* * *

Arann froze in the doorway. Shadow hissed. The sound seemed to bounce off ceiling and walls, growing in volume.

"Arann?" It was Finch. Of course it was Finch.

He didn't answer. And as he stepped over the threshold, through the doorway, it became clear that he wouldn't. His armor melted away, as if it were a thin sheet of pretty, Northern ice; what remained was the clothing he had worn beneath it.

Except it wasn't that clothing. No one in the Terafin manse dressed like this. If it weren't for his coloring, Arann might have been Voyani. He wore too-large clothing, of mismatched color. The stitching that held the parts together was good, though.

Finch froze. Jester froze. Teller closed his eyes.

"You took your time," someone said, from inside the apartment. "We're almost out of food."

It was Arann who said "Angel."

"What?" And it was Angel's voice.

"Who let *Angel* start eating?"

"Duster," an unfamiliar voice replied.

Silence. A silence that robbed everyone still standing in the hall of breath, of motion. The voice was clearly unfamiliar only to Adam. And possibly to Shadow, but no one was asking the cat. No one cared enough to ask him. Finch reached out to touch Arann, possibly to grab his shoulder, but it had taken her too long to shake herself free of whatever shock held her.

Arann headed into the apartment.

"You three coming?"

"Depends," Jester said—from the hall. "Did you let Carver cook?"

"Does it look like the place is on fire?"

"That only happened once!" Carver said.

Adam felt a peculiar knot in his throat, in his chest.

Jester walked through the door. And Jester, the most fastidious of the den, the most careful with his appearance, changed just as Arann had done. His hands were lifted and flying in den-sign too complicated for Adam to read. But someone in the room laughed. Someone else threatened to remove his hands. Unfamiliar voice, again.

But that voice sent a ripple through Finch, a kind of odd shudder. She looked at Teller. Teller was staring. Staring with something like fear and something like yearning.

"Go in," Finch told him gently. "For us, I think it's safe."

"But it's not—"

"Go."

"You?"

"I'll be—I'll follow."

Teller walked into the apartment.

Adam could now see through the open doorway; the door hadn't slammed in his face. A very short hall opened into a room. There was a small table to one side, and a few chairs—but not enough for the people currently gathered there. They sat on the floor; some sat against the wall between the windows. There were bowls in their laps, and their hands flew as they chatted, some mix of den-sign and Weston.

He recognized Arann, Jester, Teller. He recognized Jewel. Farther in, he saw Carver, and Angel with his very peculiar hair. But there were others, here, that he didn't know, and he understood why everyone else had frozen.

He turned to Finch.

Haval had turned to her as well.

She was signing, although her eyes didn't leave the open door. Adam didn't recognize the words. Not until she signed *Angel, Carver, Arann, Jester, Teller* did he understand that the first gestures, the early ones, had also been names. Names he had not been taught. The last name she signed was *Jay*.

These, then, were her dead.

There was noise in that room. An argument. A girl Adam's age who was cleaning her fingernails with her dagger's tip, glaring out at the world. A boy who was sitting beside Arann as if he were a happy, living shadow.

"What will you do, Regent?" Haval asked.

"What can I do?" she whispered, as young in that moment as the people in that small space. "It wasn't easy, living here," she continued. "I remember. It wasn't easy. But the good parts were *good*, Haval. We had food, and we had a roof that wasn't going to collapse in a strong wind or a heavy rain. We had each other."

Haval nodded. "Yes. All of this is true. You understand that it is not, however, real."

"Do I?"

"Do you not?" He turned to Adam. "I am not certain you will be able to enter that room."

Shadow, however, said, "He can."

"He was not of the den of that time."

"He is of it *now*."

"And you?" Haval asked the cat.

The cat said, "I cannot enter."

Adam blinked, and blinked again. "What do you mean?" he asked in Torra.

"Are you *stupid*? I *said*, 'I cannot enter.' Which word wasn't clear *enough* for you?"

"He meant to ask why," Finch told the cat, dropping a hand, automatically, to the top of his head.

"Because *I* am not *hers*."

"Interesting," Haval said.

"She will not let me enter." He sniffed.

"You are hers, though." It was Adam who spoke, to Finch. His hand was still laced in hers. "You don't want me to wake her."

"I do," Finch whispered. "I do." Her eyes were filmed, her voice thick. "But you know, Adam, I don't remember things. I grieve for the dead, but I don't remember them. I don't remember what they looked like. I don't remember what they sounded like. I remember *being here*. I remember laughing. I remember feeling almost safe. I remember Duster was dangerous. I remember Lefty was shy and awkward—but so sharp. I remember Fisher—he's the silent guy with the perfect jaw over there. I remember Lander. He only spoke in den-sign.

"But I don't remember them like this. I don't remember, most days, what they really looked like. Even when I try. The only place—the *only* place—I see them is in dreams. But in that apartment, in that room—that's what we were like."

"Yes," Adam agreed. More gently, he added, "But you can't live here anymore. They're not real."

Finch nodded. It was the truth. But it was not truth *enough*, Adam realized. Not quite. He said, "What happened to the people who were living here, before Jewel started to dream?"

"Living here?"

"Your city is very crowded. There are people everywhere. The Matriarch is in these apartments now. Do you think there was no one here before?"

Finch closed her eyes.

It was Haval who said, "There were people living here before."

Finch listened, for one long minute, to the sounds of conversation. She knew why the laughter and warmth had ended. She knew what had happened. She knew why this was no longer the den's home. It had been hollowed out slowly by the disappearances: Lefty, Fisher, Lander. Duster had not died here, but had it not been for Duster, they would never have made it to Terafin.

And before that, before they'd run for their lives, there had been money—or rather, lack of money. There had been hard choices to make, hard things to *do*. It wasn't, she had told Haval, easy. But the good parts *had* been good. That was what this was: a dream of the good parts, before Lefty had disappeared.

Before he had died.

No bodies had ever been found, not even Duster's.

"How do you wake her?" Finch asked, without looking away. She had not seen that expression on Arann's face since they'd lost Lefty. Lefty had been his family. Lefty had been his choice. They'd almost lost Arann after they'd lost Lefty.

"I don't know," Adam replied. Haval cleared his throat. Finch grimaced at the sound, signing, *ignore*. "I think she has to see me." He looked at Finch for one long moment. "Will you go in and speak with your dead?"

Her dead. She wanted it. She wanted it almost as much as Arann clearly did and had. It was a dream. It was a good dream. Jay clearly had some control; she had chosen this.

"Finch?"

"I can't," she whispered. "I think if I leave you on the outside, the door will close forever." And that would be a bad thing. She knew it. But she didn't feel it the way she felt the yearning and the pain. And it didn't matter. Jay wasn't actually here. Finch was regent.

She remembered that she had wanted the regency. It was harder, at the moment, to remember why. To preserve the House for Jay? To preserve the den? She was certain that if she entered that apartment, she would be *safe*. She would be safe in a way she had not been safe for years, if ever. It was visceral certainty. Nothing in her could deny it. There would be nothing to worry about preserving. Nothing to fight against. No reason to fight at all, except for the usual: food, sleeping space, shoes.

But Adam's question remained. Did she believe the apartment had been empty yesterday? Not likely. The building was more-or-less warm, more-or-less clean. Someone—someone else—had called this home. Where had they gone? Were they dead?

And if they were already dead, if that price had been paid, did it matter?

She reached for Adam's hand again; she had dropped it to sign. Yes. Yes it mattered. Jay would never have turned a family out of their home. She would never have killed them to take it over. She would never do it now, consciously.

But she was, Adam had said, dreaming. And in dreams, things happened offstage. They happened before the dream itself started, their history accepted, immutable, known.

Adam's hand tightened around hers; it was no longer clear who was offering the comfort and who was receiving it.

"I will wait," Haval told them both. "I will make inquiries in your absence."

"Inquiries?" Finch asked, voice as hollow as she felt.

"Answers to Adam's question."

She didn't want the answer. She was afraid of it. She was afraid she knew what it was. *Jay.* Lifting her voice, she said, "Is there *any* food left?"

"Some," Jester answered, grinning. "Carver's sitting on Angel." It was a literal description. Angel wasn't thrilled about it either. She felt the smile tug at her lips, felt the old exasperation, and walked into her home, her heart's home.

The door, open until that moment, closed at her back. Adam, however, was not on the outside. He'd been wrong, Finch thought; she'd been right. Adam was den, even if he had been adopted in Jay's absence. He knew her. He had saved her life. He had kept her from the bridge, knitting her wounds whole while they both slept.

And Jay, sleeping or waking, knew him. She accepted him. But he didn't belong in this here-and-now, and she knew this, too.

Who? Lander signed, from the far wall. Finch wasn't certain anyone had seen it; they'd spoken the words out loud, except for Duster, who glared. Finch looked down to see that her clothing hadn't changed. She was dressed as the regent of House Terafin. Her hair was uncomfortably bound, her feet restricted by very fine boots.

"Jay," she said, turning.

Jay was standing to one side of a table too small to eat at, a bowl in her hands. The bowl had been meant for Finch, but she set it down, frowning, her brows drawn together in confusion. "Finch?"

"You've been dreaming," Finch said. Here, in this room, she let the tears slide. She was with kin here. The only person who'd hate it was Duster, and Duster was dead. She lifted her hand, and Adam's rose with it. "They can't wake you. They're afraid."

"I've been . . . dreaming." She looked around the room, and many of its occupants froze. Three did not: Arann, Jester, Teller. Their clothing, unlike Finch's, remained Helen's creations: solid and well-made, but of scraps and ends large enough to be useful. It wasn't just their clothing, of course; they were fourteen or fifteen years of age again.

Arann bowed head into hands for a long, long breath.

"Yes, Matriarch." Adam's voice was soft, his expression one of open worry. "You have been learning what the Oracle can teach you. We do not know what the lessons entail—I have been too afraid to ask."

"Afraid?"

"It is the business of Matriarchs—and the Oracle is the first Matriarch. She terrifies me."

"Me, too. Not as much as Yollana did, though."

Adam privately agreed. The Oracle knew *everything*, or she could know it. When everything was your secret, your knowledge, it was less dangerous to know something of your business—you knew something simply by breathing.

"You're here to wake me."

Adam nodded.

"And Finch is here to help you?"

Finch nodded.

Wanly, Jay said, "I don't want to wake up."

"What we had here was good. Better than a House Council plotting your downfall. Better than the demons. Better than a god. Not much quieter than a wing full of cats, though." She wanted to say, *but it's not real*. She couldn't. The dreams that Adam had entered had led him to Averalaan. They'd led him to Finch. They'd led him to reality.

Finch let go of Adam's hand and crossed the room. She wanted to hug Jay but didn't. "I'm regent. I'll hold things together here. Come home."

"I think I may have been trying to do that," Jay answered. And she aged as she spoke. The room emptied, not slowly, but instantly; only the living—or the waking—remained.

Teller blinked and looked around. The room felt empty, almost funereal—but the living did remain: Finch, Jester, Arann. *Angel?* he signed.

Alive. Eating, Jay signed back. "Thanks for letting me take him. It helps."

Jester signed, *Carver?*

Jay signed, *Alive.*

She stopped. Looked at her hands as if they belonged to someone else. Turned them up, regarding the cup of empty palms attached to her own arms. Her eyes widened, her breath sharpened, her mouth opened, corners turned up in what might become a genuine smile—

And then she was gone.

The room was empty. The furniture—such as it was—remained. The bowls, mostly empty. The remnants of food.

Jester swore, and Finch realized that the clothing—such as it was—also remained. "Don't," she told him mildly. "Arann's going to be in actual trouble—his armor wasn't cheap."

Neither was his sword, and the sword was also gone. He had daggers, and they weren't particularly good daggers, although they'd been considered great, back in the day.

"Carver's alive," Teller said.

"Has she found him, then?"

"No," Adam said. "We haven't, not yet."

"But he's alive. You saw her face. You saw her eyes. She answered. She *knew*." Jester turned toward the windows. "Doesn't mean he'll stay that way, but still."

It was Arann who said, "He's alive for now. That's enough."

Finch walked to the table, knelt beside it, and lifted a dagger that remained on the floor. "Recognize this?" she asked, lifting its scabbard.

"Duster's," Teller replied.

"She was so pissed off," Jester added, grinning. "We were lucky no one died. But she kept it. No one was allowed to touch the damn thing without losing fingers."

"It was the best knife in the house," Finch said. "And it was all hers. From us." She was crying and didn't care. "We have to get back." She turned to Adam.

Adam was gone.

The Matriarch woke him. Jewel. The Terafin. Jay.

His throat was dry, his eyes almost sandy with sleep. He sat up in a darkened room, and realized it was the same room in which he'd accepted the Oracle's help. He listed to the left, but Jewel caught his shoulder before he fell out of bed. Since the beds were so close to the floor—much closer than the towering beds in the Terafin manse—falling wouldn't injure him.

Shadow's growl came from the left into which he would have fallen, and he changed his mind.

"You were dreaming," the Matriarch said.

It had felt so real. "So were you." He looked past her to Angel and signed. *What happened?*

"You touched the Oracle's crystal," Angel—hair no longer rising in a spire—said.

"And I collapsed?"

Angel's hesitation was marked. "No. You faded."

"Faded."

"We watched you disappear." He glanced at Shianne and away. "We were worried until Snow pointed out that Shadow had gone with you."

The Oracle was no longer in the room, Adam saw. "What did the Oracle say?"

"She said it was a very good sign."

"That Shadow came with me?"

"That you took so long to . . . vanish."

Jewel, seated on the side of the bed, was staring into her empty hands. "Adam, will you walk with me? When you can actually stand without falling over, I mean."

Standing without falling over took another hour. During that hour he drank a clear, dark tea. It was bitter and faintly spicy. He ate some kind of northern stew. He listened to the cats insult each other. He listened to Shianne talk, although she was speaking to someone across the room.

During this time, the Matriarch was silent. She signed to Angel, but kept to herself, her shoulders slumped, her gaze apprehensive. As if, Adam thought, she was trying to memorize every detail of this room and its occupants.

He knew that Matriarchs dreamed. They dreamed of the future, a future dressed in veils that only experience of the actual events pierced completely. He remembered the discussions his own mother had had with her daughter and her closest sister when she had experienced a prophetic dream and couldn't make sense of it.

He wondered if Jewel's dreams would ever be so merciful again. He had come to understand that there was mercy of a kind in ignorance.

The Oracle's abode was bright with artificial light. It was a warren of halls and rooms. Adam had thought the Terafin manse confusing and confining when he had first come to Averalaan—but the geography of the manse made sense. He could, and did, memorize it until he no longer got lost when he walked its halls.

He would never know enough of these caves that he could do so here. It had taken him two days to understand that the halls and the rooms changed. They weren't illusory—he could, and did, open doors at random, and they opened into perfectly normal rooms, although some were very oddly decorated. But he could not depend on their location.

Only the rooms in which the Matriarch's companions resided were fixed in place, and Adam suspected that they, too, would be unanchored and free to wander when they were at last vacated.

Jewel, however, seemed to be able to navigate here. She was not—according to Carver—very good with geography or maps; she had been the last person to become comfortable with the layout of the Terafin manse. Here, however, she knew where she was going.

"It's easier," she said, when he asked. "In the Oracle's domain, you only have to focus on where you want to go and start walking. Everything here changes constantly, so there's no point in memorizing all the halls or rooms between where you were and where you want to go. It's like it was designed for me." She spoke Torra. "Do you remember my dream?"

He nodded, reached into his pocket, and found—by touch—a small, silvered ball. It hung from a chain.

Jewel stared at it, arrested.

"Finch insisted I take it," he said. "She wanted me to bring food."

"That's not food."

"It's her compromise. It's tea."

Jewel had paled; she resumed her walk, and Adam fell in beside her. His was the longer stride. It wasn't difficult to keep up. He'd considered keeping the sieve hidden, allowing the Matriarch to believe that she'd had an unusual dream, a gift of learning to better understand her own power. But he was not comfortable knowing more about a Matriarch's business than she knew herself.

And that was not the whole of the reason for his hesitation. Haval had said there had definitely been people living in that apartment before the Matriarch had started dreaming. Adam had no way of knowing whether or not those people would—or could—return to the home she had reclaimed. He had no idea what had happened to them.

He knew only that if Haval was correct, they had ceased to exist the minute she had sought a dream of family and home.

One wanted, when one was young, family. Love. The Voyani considered the Voyanne their home—but even they dreamed of a time when they could at last set down their burdens and rest. The Voyanne was a road to be walked until they *could* return home.

But the Voyani could not merely wish something into being.

Even Adam, as a small child, had wished. He had daydreamed. He now understood how dangerous even the most benign of daydreams could be if they could be made real instantly.

"It was real," Jewel said, accepting the filled tea ball.

He said nothing.

"Tell me what happened. Tell me what happened to you."

As they walked, he did. She stopped him once or twice, to ask questions or to clarify for herself what he was describing; she didn't seem best pleased to hear that Jarven had been not only in her forest on his own, but near her burning tree. But she kept turning the tea ball over and over in her hands as she listened.

And when he got to the end, she said, "I don't know what happened to the people who were living in the apartment. You were right," she added, voice dropping. "There's no way those rooms were empty."

She looked at the ball again, and then looked up. "Carver's alive. When Jester asked, I answered—he's still alive."

"They know," Adam replied. "They knew what it meant the minute you signed the word. Where are we going?"

"Oh, outside." She smiled at his expression. "You won't need winter clothing where we're going."

She was right. The final door she touched opened into a forest. It was green and warm and noisy the way forests are noisy. There was a large rock in a small clearing—it wore a skirt of moss and was bathed in sunlight. He thought he recognized it.

She led him to the rock and then sat across its gentle, concave surface; Adam joined her. "You're worried," she said, her knees folded up beneath her chin.

"Not as worried as you are."

"You woke me."

"You woke yourself, I think. I was there, yes—but you saw me, and you remembered. I tried to wake you before that, and nothing happened. Whatever your dreams are now, they're not like the dreams the Wardens manipulated." He spoke Torra as well, for ease and for comfort. He didn't dislike Weston, but to Adam, Weston was always going to be a merchant language, a language of commerce. Torra was the language of kin and family.

She didn't argue.

"I couldn't reach you at all without the Oracle's intervention."

"Did you see her?" Jewel asked. It was a strange question, but Adam understood what she meant.

"I didn't look."

"No?"

"I was trying to find you. I was focused only on that. But she's the Oracle, a child of gods, and we already know that she can appear anywhere. She can animate stone and force it to speak with her voice."

"You think she sent you to Averalaan." It wasn't a question.

But it wasn't accurate, either. Adam frowned. After a pause in which he poked at the niggling doubt, he said, "No. I think she allowed me to enter your dreams."

"But you were *in* Averalaan." She held up the tea ball; it caught sunlight, reflecting it on nearby tree trunks.

He nodded again. "I think your dreams brought me to Averalaan."

"The wagon?"

"Yes. I don't understand it, but yes. I did enter your dreams." Thought now coalesced into something he could capture with words. "I think I faded from here not when I touched the Oracle's crystal, but when I opened the door of the Matriarch's wagon and stepped into the city itself. If I had never found the wagon, I would not have found you—I think the Oracle gave me a vision of the wagon itself, but not—not more."

At the end of the waking day, Jewel came to the small oasis. She had never owned a garden, no matter how small, and while she could be said to own the many gardens—some enclosed in expensive glass—of Terafin, she did not consider them hers. But she owned the forest into which those gardens and grounds now led. This oasis was not her forest; she had not created this small space.

The earth beneath her feet, the trees above her head, the breeze that tugged at her hair, even the insects that buzzed near her ear, seemed to sing. She could not join them; she couldn't pronounce the words she heard. On the third day, she recognized the odd song as a name. A long, complicated name.

"Yes," the Oracle said. "It is mine."

And that made sense to Jewel. She was The Terafin, but she had the name she was born with. No one but den used it now. No one would until she died, and even then, only if some of what she loved and had built survived.

The night that Adam had returned her to the Oracle's caverns had been long and sleepless, by design. Adam had collapsed instantly; Jewel had collapsed slowly.

"Will it always be like this?" she asked.

The Oracle understood the question. "I do not know, daughter. You are not Evayne, and it was she I worked with most closely in all of your long history." The history, Jewel thought, of mortals. "Had I the time, I would work thus with you—but this is your final day. You must leave—and leave soon. Your path is not as difficult to walk as hers has been and will be. But you could not walk it as she has. You are not god-born."

"Do you know what happened to the former occupants of that apartment?"

"Do you not?"

Jewel's hands became fists. "I've spent all day searching." She grimaced. "Nine hours, heart exposed, eyes watering. I can't find anything."

"That is your answer, then."

Silence. Jewel forced herself to break it. "What do you mean?"

"They do not exist, Jewel."

"They're dead?"

"That is not what I said. They do not exist. Not now."

"Did they?"

"That is a question you should be able to answer at this point in your training. But you have spent a day searching. I have allowed it. You learn best when you have immediate incentive. You have now reached the point where the exercise and the search have nothing left to teach you.

"You are not Evayne. You are Jewel Markess. You were born in, and of, Averalaan. Beneath your feet, the firstborn lay imprisoned in their long sleep, their dreams of failure and conquest. Across your bay, the god-born rule; the spires of the three stretch to the heights of sky. In your streets, the *Kialli* walk again. And in your garden, the *Ellariannatte* bloom.

"You are not immortal. You are not a god. You are confined by time while you walk here. There are answers you might search for within your own lands; there are answers you search for in mine. But only in these places can you impede time's flow, and even then, it is a pocket. You will age while you work and learn, even if time outside of you does not pass.

"That is not true anywhere else. I have watched you. You can summon your heart, and it holds. You can search it. You can accept the pain of what you see. And your heart, Jewel, does not shatter."

Jewel stopped, arrested. "Shatter?"

"Yes."

Silence for a long, long beat. "Does that happen often?"

"You must define often. Has it happened? Yes. More than once? Yes."

The sunlight on the rock was warm; Jewel exposed her eyelids to its light. "Did they lose their power?"

"You must also define power," the Oracle replied. "If you mean to ask did they die, the answer is no. Did they lose their gift? Not as such."

"I don't understand."

"No," the Oracle said quietly. "No, you don't." She lifted her chin. "You have met Yollana in your travels. You fear her. She did not come to me, in the end, but we have spoken."

"You didn't test her."

"No."

"Why?"

"There are two reasons, Jewel. First and foremost, it was not necessary. Understand that I cannot travel in time. Understand that Evayne a'Nolan does not travel at her own will—but she is the only one who *can*. I am said to see everything that might possibly occur in the future. I do, on a much larger scale, what you are learning to do. I search, child."

"Even now?"

"Yes, even now. There is one outcome I desire. To reach that outcome, there are many, many things that must happen. Yollana is, and has been, some part of that."

"But you didn't teach her."

"No. There are forks, always, in paths that lead to desired outcomes. There are things I cannot control, events I cannot influence. Could I simply choose to achieve the desired outcome, you would not be here at all. I cannot. In Yollana's case, the possibility of failure was too high. I could not increase those odds. Nor, in the end, could I increase yours. Do you understand? I could see many roads that would lead you to my domain, and I could see many roads that would lead you away.

"But passing—or failing—is not in my hands; it is not I who am being tested."

"And my chance of failure?"

"Not as high as Yollana's. But it is irrelevant. Yollana was not, could not become, *Sen*. You are and can. Some risks, we have no choice but to take. In Yollana's case, what she could do without passing my test was enough. It was risky, but it was enough.

"You understand what the seer's crystal is. You have seen some of the harshest of Yollana's choices, and you have seen the price she has paid. You think of her as strong, cold, proud. She is all those things. Could you hold her heart in your hands? Could you hold yours if you had been forced to make the choices she has made?

"But I wander. You cannot remain here indefinitely. What I can teach you, I have taught. The rest is in your hands. Now you must return to time. You must make the choices that build a future in which your lands and your people survive."

"Tell me," Jewel said. "How do I find Ariane?"

The Oracle raised a brow. "Daughter," she said, reaching out to brush a strand of hair from Jewel's face, "that is not the question you have been asking. When you have not searched for the people who have vanished, you have been searching for your kin. But if you do not, cannot, find your way to the Hidden Court, the rest of your kin will perish.

"You do not have the time I have. You do not have the ability to hold what I hold. The time you've been given *must* be used wisely; there is so little of it left. When you leave this place, time will enfold you differently. You cannot go back; there is only forward. But when you return to your own lands, you live in the time stream you were meant to occupy. And there, daughter, time is among your greatest foes.

"Tomorrow, if you wake, you must leave."

If.

Chapter Eight

The Hidden Wilderness

THERE WERE NO DREAMS.

In the darkness of what seemed perpetual twilight, there was cold and pain, although pain receded. Carver knew this was not a good sign, but good or bad didn't matter here. He was in a wilderness that even the wildest streets of his city had not prepared him for, and he was not dressed for cold. Dressing for cold had been one of Jay's primary concerns when the den had lived in the twenty-fifth holding.

He lifted a hand to his throat, grasping air. The locket was gone. And the leaf she had left in its place, which was of no use to him, remained. Jay had been here, somehow. In a dream.

There were no dreams now. No sleep. No people. In the distance, Carver could hear the baying of horns, as if the horns themselves were alive. They were not close, not yet, but would be soon. He rose. His back, pressed against the half-height of a ruined wall, was once again exposed to wind, but the stones themselves had been cold as ice. He moved, stumbling forward, the effort almost involuntary. He had come to hear horns in his sleep, a certain sign that he was not alone.

Here, he thought not of survival, but death. Of the many deaths in his life. Of pain and triumph, of guilt, of regret. Lefty, Lander, Fisher, Duster. Duster. He wondered if anyone would be waiting for him when he crossed the bridge. He was half-certain he would see Duster, and she'd snap at him because she wasn't *waiting*. She just happened to *be there*, and he could mind his own damn business.

He wondered what the dead talked about. How they died? What killed them? He had a story or two to add. The thought made him smile.

He shook the smile off, forced himself to his feet again.

I'll have your back.

I don't need *anyone at my back.*

I need someone to have your back. Jay. What Duster wouldn't accept from any of them, she'd accept from Jay. Didn't mean she wasn't angry about it, but Duster was always angry. Everything with Duster was about strength or weakness. Needing someone at her back was definitely the latter.

Carver didn't care. Hadn't cared then. Duster didn't have partners. She didn't have family. She didn't have friends. But she stayed with the den while loudly making clear that she didn't need them. She didn't need anyone.

He had her back. In the worst of the scuffles with rival dens, he had had her back since the day she'd joined the den. *I've got your back.*

She stopped telling him she didn't need him. Stopped telling him he was getting in the way. She never thanked him—no, that wasn't true. She had offered, once or twice, when things had gotten really dicey—a grunt, a nod of acknowledgment, unadorned by simple words.

And she had had his back. Wordless, refusing to acknowledge even that much, she'd had his back. She didn't like him. She didn't like any of them. But they weren't outsiders. They weren't enemies. When push came to shove, she was there.

When push came to shove.

Duster had gone to face the demon. Duster had gone alone. It was the biggest fight she—or any of the den—had ever faced. It was the toughest.

Had she been afraid?

He pushed himself up, off the ground, off snow that was hard as ice, and just as warm.

Had she been afraid of the demon, of the death? She'd gone knowing that Carver wouldn't be there. Carver wouldn't have her back. None of them would. They'd escape, maybe. That was the entire point. Duster was the only person who stood half a chance of delaying the demon for long enough all the rest of the den would survive. Only Duster.

But she must have known. She must have.

Carver stood no chance of surviving the Wild Hunt. No chance, if he did, of surviving the winter that enveloped them both, hunter and hunted. But it was different, wasn't it? The rest of the den weren't here. Carver's death would mean nothing.

He wished, then, that he had had Duster's back one more time.

Carver lost consciousness for minutes at a time but struggled back to grim reality. He could no longer feel his face, his feet, his hands, and this was a mercy. The last time he fell, the horns were closer. He could not rise. His arms would not support his weight.

But something did. Someone spoke.

The voice was familiar; it implied warmth and safety, although it could barely be heard over the howl of the wind, the winding of horns.

He had thought there were no dreams here. No more dreams; Jay had taken them with her. But she had left one, just one, and it was perfect.

Ellerson.

The wind was gone. The wind and the cold. He ached, his throat was dry, his eyes teared at artificial light. But to his side—or the side he could see without rising and turning his head—there were walls. Walls, not half-walls, not ruins.

"Master Carver, you are in no condition to rise without aid."

Had he been trying? Yes. He sank back into a bed made of blankets and warm stone. Ellerson, however, now provided the aid that had been lacking. Also: food.

"I do not believe you will lose the fingers, and your injuries do not seem fevered or infected. Inasmuch as one can be said to be lucky in these circumstances, you have been lucky."

If he had thought Ellerson a fever dream, doubts vanished as the domicis continued to speak. This was Ellerson. The domicis was not wearing Terafin clothing or colors; he wasn't wearing anything that would have been suitable for his role in the West Wing. Which meant he had found clothing, people, or both. He had clearly found some way of lighting a fire because the liquid in the mug he now offered to Carver was warm. No, it was *hot*.

"Where are we?" he asked, after he had stopped coughing.

"We are in an underground shelter. The shelter itself is, as you can see, whole. Whatever transpired above ground has not transpired here. There are supplies that we can safely use, and there is both food and water. Neither will last indefinitely."

Carver listed to the side, and Ellerson caught him. "Food?"

"Yes. I do not think you will be up to travel for a few days yet. It was a near thing."

Carver disagreed with Ellerson by the end of the first day. He pulled himself out of bed, left the room, and began to explore the shelter. He had expected to find another room—perhaps another two, at most—but had been mistaken. There were several rooms. The rooms themselves had no obvious magestones, but the light emitted from the ceilings and walls was similar to the familiar illumination the stones provided. None of the doors were locked; none of the doors appeared to *have* locks. Carver didn't manage to make it through most of the rooms, though; although he had recovered too much to lie abed—or aground, more accurately—Ellerson had been right. He was not yet fit to travel for any length of time. Even moving in the safety of these halls and rooms had left him exhausted.

He slept soundly and dreamlessly, waking with no sense of time of day, not that being outside in the winter landscape would have changed that. Time did not work the way he was accustomed to here.

Ellerson shared the room in which Carver was expected to recover. Carver noted that he had backpacks—two—that appeared to be stuffed. There were cloaks as well as boots, both of which would be welcome, and neither of which were proof against the winter.

"No," the domicis said, as Carver raised a silent brow. "These were left for our use, and they will be better than nothing. As will the blankets. There are very few things here, and we will carry them all."

"Where are we going?"

"Away," Ellerson replied, "from the ghosts of the Wild Hunt. Away from this place. It is not safe to remain here for longer than absolutely necessary."

It was enough of an answer. Carver ate food that seemed oddly bland; it was like bread, but with seeds and a strange sweetness that lingered on the tongue long after he'd swallowed. He drank hot water—Ellerson trusted food that had been here for gods knew how long, but not water.

On the third day of an increasingly frustrating convalescence, Carver took the metallic blue leaf from its place between shirt and skin, and held it by the stem, twirling it slowly to see how it caught and reflected—light.

Ellerson entered the room and stopped, arrested. "Where did you find that leaf?"

"Not far from here," Carver replied. "Not far from where you found me." He hesitated and then, with his free hand, signed a single word.

Ellerson knew it. The old man had never used den-sign; the den had never condescended to teach him because they'd known that he'd never agree. But Carver had always suspected that the domicis could read the signs if he could not communicate with them, and Ellerson's expression confirmed it.

"I met her. She said she was dreaming—and she meant it. She thought I was dreaming, as well. I gave her something to take home. She left me with this." His smile was affectionate, rueful, tired. "It's not one of her leaves. I mean, it's not from the trees that grow in her forest."

"What did she intend you to do with it?"

"I don't know. She didn't either. I think she wanted to leave me with *something*, and this is the first thing she could reach. She said she wasn't home. Angel was with her. The cats. That must mean Avandar is here as well."

But Ellerson said quietly, "No. It means they are with her. I do not believe she is here."

"It's here that I saw her."

"Yes—but she was dreaming."

"She couldn't be dreaming. I still have the leaf. I don't have my pendant."

Ellerson nodded, frowning. He stood. "We are not in Averalaan. These lands do not conform to our lives the way our own do. We reached them through a wardrobe. She dreamed. If I recall correctly, she almost died in one such dream. Do you remember what happened?"

And he did. She had never left her bed.

"I believe that Jewel could find you—in her dreams—because that is the nature of the ruins beneath which we shelter. It is part memory, part dream."

"Whose?"

"The Oracle did not say—and even had she, I think it highly unwise to mention the dreamer by name. The Hunt that you saw was not reality, but memory. According to the Oracle." Carver's cheek would heal; Ellerson had said there would be no scar. But his arm? That would scar.

"Eat," the domicis said quietly, "and sleep."

The only thing Ellerson had not found in his inspection of the shelter during Carver's extended and necessary sleep were the rings. He had gathered gaudy blankets, boots that appeared to be of a size although there were two pairs, rope, netting that seemed to be made of fine golden links, more suitable to jewelry than practical use. He had found the cloaks, the food, and skins meant to carry water, and also the packs that were meant to contain them.

But he had not found the rings. Carver found those. There were—as there were with other items that were clearly meant to be worn—two; they were remarkably simple bands of white gold or gold. The light made it hard to discern.

"Where did you find those?" The domicis appeared to be uneasy.

"In the room at the end of the hall. It's the one with the half-height entrance."

"I saw no door there."

Carver grinned. "How well do you know the back halls?"

"Passingly well. Or I did until the change in The Terafin's chambers."

"I'll show you."

Ellerson could not see the door.

He could see Carver. He could see Carver enter it. He could not see the door itself, and when he attempted to follow Carver's lead, he hit solid rock. This was uncomfortably similar to wardrobes that opened into icy hell. Carver was grateful that he had been able to return.

Ellerson was troubled. "Rope," he said.

Carver nodded. He wound a length of rope around his waist. The twine was thicker than string; it wasn't thick enough to bear much weight, but weight wasn't their only concern. He was reminded, as Ellerson tied knots, of his early days with the den in the undercity. Those had been good days, foraging in deserted, shattered streets and broken homes occupied only by the dead.

And those had led to bad days, and then, very bad days. Their survival had depended on the streets of that hidden city, and their losses—until Duster—had come as a result of that dependence, that familiarity.

He shook his head. These rooms were not the undercity. They were lit, dry, warm. They were not endless. Whatever had been left here—according to Ellerson—had been left for them.

The room remained as Carver had found it. He could hear Ellerson's voice through the open door he perceived; Ellerson could not hear his. He wasn't certain why he could see the door, and why Ellerson couldn't, but whoever had once lived here was long gone.

"I am not certain," Ellerson said, "that we were meant to take these."

Carver shrugged. "They're not being used by anyone now."

"No." Ellerson opened the small box that Carver had dragged back into the hall.

"There wasn't any more food," he said. "No rope, no blankets."

Ellerson watched Carver. After a moment, he said, "Give me the leaf."

Carver shrugged and removed the metallic blue leaf from its resting place against his skin. He handed it to the domicis. He felt no hesitation at all.

Ellerson examined the leaf carefully, his frown one of intense concentration. "My eyes," he finally said, "are not what they were." He turned to the end of the hall, as did Carver. Ellerson, as he'd clearly expected, could now see the half-height passage. Carver no longer could.

"These rings," the domicis said, "were not created for our use. I am not certain why they were left here. Perhaps they serve no useful function."

"Most jewelry doesn't."

Ellerson frowned but kept his peace.

"I think we should take them," Carver continued. "We don't know if they're special, by the standards of the wild and ancient. But we also don't know if we'll need to trade or barter with whatever we meet on the open road—if it doesn't try to kill us first." He took the leaf that Ellerson handed him, and carefully returned it to its place between shirt and chest.

"We do not even know where we are going."

"Home," Carver replied. "And now that you're here, I think we have a chance of reaching it."

The first thing Carver discovered was that the ruins had boundaries. They were boundaries that he'd never crossed. Ellerson had explained that the people whose spears had injured him weren't real; the Oracle had called them memories or echoes. Memories could—and often did—cause pain; even Carver acknowledged that. But not like this.

Perhaps because Ellerson was with him, and perhaps because he carried the strange single leaf that Jay had handed him, he did not hear the hunting horns. He didn't hear the clopping of multiple hooves. He saw ruins that spoke of age and destruction, open air reminders of the hidden city.

He was not sorry to leave them.

Ellerson chose a direction. He had a compass, a small, pocket instrument that was clearly brought from home, not the enchanted basement. It was completely useless. Whatever made it point in some true direction in Averalaan had remained in Averalaan when the two of them had been swallowed by a wardrobe and spit out here.

There was sunlight, or what appeared to be sunlight. Ellerson chose to use that light as a rougher, less certain compass. It didn't work. Or perhaps it did—but only if they chose to travel toward that unseen sun. It made no difference to Carver, but Ellerson didn't like it. He set a course away from that light, and the landscape shifted.

The light was the center of this place, and all things must move toward the center, as if it were the bottom of a vast, slow whirlpool.

The cold, however, was not a problem. The cloaks that had seemed such meager winter wear were warm, in a fashion. When donned, the cold did not touch them at all. It might have been high spring or early summer. The boots were likewise warm—but better; they did not slip or slide. Ice beneath the snow was not a hazard, and snow that hid deeper dells or drops did not break. The boots conformed perfectly to the feet that were in them; they did not appear to be made in a specific size.

Ellerson was unwilling to test the rings that Carver had found.

They had found no tents, no tenting, and no bedrolls in the underground rooms. "They would not be required," he told Carver, "by the people who lived in that long-ago city."

"No?"

"I believe they were kin to Lord Celleriant."

Carver's grimace was genuine.

"Tell me, have you ever seen Lord Celleriant sleep?"

". . . No."

"He does not, except when injured—and even then, not for long. I believe he considers the need for sleep a besetting weakness."

"He probably considers the need to breathe a major weakness, as well."

Ellerson nodded. "How often have you see him eat?"

"He never ate with us."

Ellerson nodded again. "I think the food left will keep us for some time, but we will have to make do with the blankets; I do not think they required, or pitched, tents that were not decorative or celebratory in nature."

But, as it happened, the blankets—which Carver had considered far too colorful and bright—served a different function. A better one. They were—like everything else in this godsforsaken place—magical in nature. When laid against the ground, they functioned as the cloaks did. Snow, wind, and cold did not touch them.

No, Carver thought, it was more than that. Where they were set down, something else touched the snow and the cold. He thought, at first, it was a barrier of some kind—something to keep the weather out. This made some sense. Even if you didn't need sleep, you probably didn't enjoy a faceful of rain or icy wind while you were eating.

But Ellerson pointed out that the trees, where their branches crossed the perimeter of the loudly colorful boundaries defined by the edge of blanket, changed. The branches lost snow and the buds that had wintered—possibly for millennia—blossomed. Their blankets were not the only color in this wilderness. Wherever they were set down, leaves and blossoms, grass and wildflowers, bloomed.

The blankets appeared to bring summer to the winter landscape.

Carver's awe was silent; it was tinged with unspoken wonder.

Ellerson's silence was not; it was laden with worry. Carver tried not to resent it, and almost failed. But he wasn't sixteen, and Ellerson was no longer responsible for his manners, his bearing, his education. They were in this together.

He tried to think as Ellerson must be thinking. "These—these blankets—were left for us," he said.

Ellerson nodded. "You thought them ridiculous."

"I did—snow's white. Everything here is white. I thought we'd be seen for miles."

"I think," Ellerson said softly, "we will. These are not made of the same fabric as the cloaks—and that is what I expected. The cloaks are the color of winter tree bark, winter stone. They are not meant to trumpet our presence. The blankets, however, would do that no matter how drab their base fabric is. Look at the leaves."

"You don't want to use them."

"We don't have a choice," Ellerson replied.

"The cloaks are warm," Carver countered. "I've spent a winter or two shivering in alleys so cold I couldn't open my mouth without biting my own tongue. I survived it. I could survive a damn sight better wrapped in this cloak and sitting up against the trunk of that tree."

"That specific tree?"

"It's wide enough. If you're worried about the attention we'll draw, we don't have to use the blankets here." Carver said it with a genuine pang. There was something about those leaves that filled him with belief that there would be a spring, and a future, beyond this winter world.

Ellerson said softly, "It is a false spring, a false summer. When we leave, the leaves will freeze and die. I, too, find peace and contentment beneath these branches."

"But you think about the cost."

"Perhaps. These trees are not our trees."

But the thought of these branches freezing as sudden warmth was just as suddenly withdrawn was oddly painful. "You win. We don't need the blankets to survive—and until we do, we'll keep them packed."

Ellerson was silent for a full beat. "I think," he said at last, "the blankets were meant to serve some function. I do not know what the Oracle said to those long-ago denizens of this winter place."

"You're worried." Flat words.

"Perhaps. We are living on borrowed time. We are alive because the Oracle chose—long before even the Empire was born—to intervene."

Carver was silent.

"I do not believe she chose to intervene without reason. She foresaw a use for us."

"Use?"

Ellerson nodded. "It is not for our sake that she intervened."

Carver shrugged uneasily. He had learned early that nothing in life was free; that a deal that looked too good was, always, too good. He closed his eyes. Opened them again. "Did I ever tell you about the first time I met Jay?"

Ellerson shook his head. "No."

And he smiled, seeing the old man's face. "But you know."

"I have heard, yes."

"She wasn't looking for me. I wasn't one of her visions. She'd come to find Finch—to save Finch. I followed her out of an alley entirely unlike this—" he lifted an arm, swept it out, to encompass the white and the bitter cold. "And into Taverson's. I don't know what I expected. I can't remember what I said. Does memory always do that?" he added.

"Do what?"

"Shift. Change."

"We look at our memories in retrospect," Ellerson replied, in his teaching voice. "Our knowledge colors our understanding of them."

"I don't remember what I was thinking. I don't remember what she said. Not exactly. But I remember her expression. We were kids," he added, gazing at his bent knee. "Kids. And she'd come to rescue someone her own age. She wasn't ever big, you know? And her hair was always a mess." He smiled. "I couldn't see the color of her eyes, in the alley. I knew she was afraid—but that was just smart. She was out, in the streets, past dark; she was alone. She shouldn't have been," he added. "And she wouldn't have been, if not for Finch."

"I had nowhere to go." His shoulders tightened. "By choice, I had nowhere to go. Nowhere was better than where I had been. I hadn't thought much about where I was going. It wasn't cold enough to freeze to death. I thought, if I survived another couple of years, I could join the Kings' army."

"Were you expecting trouble?"

"Some. I thought I could take care of myself. I didn't make much noise. I wasn't trying to stake a claim. I just wanted away."

"May I ask why?"

Carver grimaced. "I'd just broken someone's hand. I mean that. Hand, fingers. It was a test. Of me. I was given orders."

"You think you failed."

"Yeah." His shrug was tighter. "I followed 'em. I followed, and I hated it. I couldn't apologize—wouldn't've changed a damn thing. Words don't paper over broken bones." He looked at his own hands. "I'm fine with killing," he continued. "To survive. I'd knifed men—kids, like me—before. Someone's at you with a blade, you do what you have to do to make sure you're not the one on the ground at the end of it.

"I was good with that. I *am* good with that, even now. But—the hand was different. There was no fight in the guy. I wasn't stupid. I followed orders. But I knew that I'd be walking away, and I knew how to do it more-or-less safely. None of that involved saying no."

"You've never spoken to Jewel about it."

Carver shook his head. "Her rules: past doesn't count. And I didn't want to live in that past. Now? Now I wouldn't be under someone who gave orders like that. I'm not a kid. I've got other options—and I can see them. Then?" He shook his head. "I had no idea who Jay was." He looked up then to meet Ellerson's steady gaze.

"I wasn't looking for a new boss. I would have said I wasn't looking for anything. But I saw her. I asked her why she was there. She said she was going to rescue a friend. And you know? She meant it. I thought she'd just get the crap beaten out of her—if she was that lucky.

"But I had nothing to do. Nowhere I had to be. And I wanted—I think I wanted—to see it, you know? To see her *try*. When I found out that she was trying to rescue a girl she didn't know, had never even *met*—" He shook his head.

"She didn't know how to use what was around her. She didn't know how to fight." He smiled then, seeing her. She never looked young in his memories. She always looked like Jay, as if the heart of her, the essence of her, was ageless or unchanging. "I helped where I could. We found Finch. We ran. We made it.

"And there I was. Finch, she'd come to save. Me? She'd stumbled across me, trying to hide in an alley. She'd fed me at the tavern. She had money. To me, she had money. But it wasn't that. She didn't ask me why. She didn't ask me what I wanted. She just—I came in Finch's wake, and she let me stay.

"And I wanted it," he said. "I wanted it. I'm not that different from Finch or Teller. Their situations were more extreme. If she hadn't intervened, they'd've died. She saved their lives. Teller's, in a winter like this—but in our streets, not this forest.

"She saved mine, as well." He looked up at budding branches across an endless sky. "I couldn't get the hang of the patricians. Duster called me the patrician when she was in a mood. But I didn't fit in. Terafin was uncomfortable. It was everything I'd daydreamed about, when I had the time to waste. Teller went to the right-kin's office. Finch went to the Merchant Authority. Jay went tromping through the streets with Meralonne. Arann joined the House Guard. Angel was as uncomfortable as I was—mostly because Jay wasn't with us. Jay wasn't giving us our orders.

"He'd never take orders from anyone else. Me?" Carver shrugged. "She'd never given much in the way of orders before. But before then, I'd been useful. I was muscle. Terafin didn't need muscle. Jay didn't need muscle. Arann knew instantly. But I think—" He shook his head again. "He adapted to the House because of the healer. Alowan. Alowan had spent decades as a non-Terafin member of the manse.

"Jester. Me. I started talking to the servants. I think I intended to be one, until I caught my first glimpse of the Master of the Household Staff. And I couldn't do it. What she wanted from Household Staff was far above me. You taught us," he added. "How to speak. How to read. How to interact with the servants. You told me—"

"That even if you were qualified, you could not be a servant while living in the West Wing."

Carver nodded. "I landed on my feet. I did what I could." He stood.

Ellerson stood as well.

"Merry is ATerafin." It was the first time he'd spoken her name to the domicis.

Ellerson nodded, as if this was not a surprise. It probably wasn't.

"She's a servant."

He nodded again.

"She's a servant in the West Wing, among her other duties. We're not—we don't care about the hierarchy of the back halls. She knows that. But she knows she has to. She couldn't live with us and *be* a servant. What you said of me was true. But it was true of Merry in a different way. No one daydreams about being a servant."

"That is not true," Ellerson said quietly, closing his pack and shouldering it beneath the length of his cloak.

"She was proud of the House Name. We got it for nothing—all of us but

Jay. Merry worked, and worked hard, to earn it. She worked in service. She endured the Master of the Household Staff. I—she was warm. She laughed, and she was warm. She accepted us. She told us the Household Staff was grateful—*grateful*—because Jay'd saved The Terafin's life when the demon dressed like Rath came to visit.

"We milked that for all it was worth. It gave us the only edge we were ever going to have." He exhaled. "She couldn't live with us and be a servant. And I couldn't live with her because she was one, and I was Jay's. Jay was House Council. I didn't want to break anything. Not the West Wing. Not my life. Not Merry's.

"And right now? It seems stupid. I don't know if I'll ever see her again."

Ellerson's voice was gentle. "Is it Merry you're worried for?"

"Meaning, not Jay?"

Ellerson was quiet, waiting.

"I worry about them both. But Jay is Jay. She'll land on her feet, even if she doesn't like where she's landed. She's got the cats. Avandar. Celleriant. Merry's—" he shook his head. "She can't *be* den, but she could have been. She's not talent-born. She's not valuable to the House the way Jay is." His smile was almost self-conscious. "Neither am I."

After a very long pause, Ellerson said, "When we get back, what will you do?"

"When?" Carver's laugh was brief and bitter. "If?"

"We each have our duties. I will not question how you do yours; I understand, however, what mine entail."

Carver shook his head. "I don't know. I've lived with Jay for over half my life. It's home. It's home to me. But for all the reasons I've stated, Merry can't live with us. Maybe . . . maybe we both give up our rooms on the Isle. Maybe we both find a place that belongs to the two of us, away from Terafin." He looked up, and up again, before he met Ellerson's eyes. "Tell me I'm wrong." His voice was low.

"I would, if I could in good conscience do so." The domicis did not look surprised by anything Carver had said. "You are not wrong. Could you give her the choice?"

Carver said, "What kind of a choice is that? Choose me and walk away from everything you've ever wanted and built for yourself?" He shook his head. "It'd be like telling her to choose *me* over herself. What kind of love is that, in the end? The one where I have to be more important than she is? If it were something trivial, I'd do it. It's not. And I won't lie. I've wanted to. I've wanted to tell her to throw it away, to give it up, to be with me. I've given her every chance to do it. She's never offered. What she does is important to her—if it weren't, she'd never have been given the House Name.

"And she's important to me."

"Yes. Does Jewel know?"

"Jay's never asked." He hesitated. "And no, probably not. We're part of her home, but she's never expected that home will be all of our lives. She doesn't ask Jester where he goes—unless the House Council collectively drops on her head because he's offended someone powerful. She doesn't ask Arann about the Chosen, unless she needs the information to make decisions. She knows there are things Finch won't tell her.

"She's never demanded that our home be our only life. She trusts that if it's important enough, she'll hear." He fell silent. It didn't last. Carver was not one of nature's silent people. "Thanks."

"For?"

"Listening. Pretending to be interested."

"It was not pretense, Master Carver."

"Do you ever talk about yourself?"

"Infrequently, yes. And as you suspect, given your expression, only at need."

"So you'll listen to me talk, but you won't talk yourself?"

"Unless it is relevant and necessary, no."

Carver's smile was sly. "We're going to be perfect traveling companions, then." He stepped off the blanket, glanced at the flowering branches above it, and grimaced. But he rolled it up, shoved it into his own pack, and shouldered it.

Carver did talk. He never raised his voice, and he paused mid-sentence whenever there was a sharp or loud noise, but he resumed talking the minute Ellerson had ascertained—inasmuch as that was possible in this landscape—that there was no danger. No danger, the domicis thought wryly, beyond the cold and the passing dreams of the Hunt. Although the Oracle had said they were not real, those hunters had weight, solidity, presence. They did not, however, leave tracks in the snow commensurate with the size of their party.

The cloaks and the boots were nothing short of miraculous. Ellerson, who had spent some time in Arrend, had expected the going to be rough. Walking through or across snow added a level of difficulty to any journey. But the boots seemed to skirt above the snow's surface, as if the snow itself were a cosmetic dusting over smooth, worked ice. It wasn't.

The cold could be felt, but at a distance—it was like pressing a hand against glass windows in the winter—from the inside. He knew it was cold; it was possibly as cold as the Rendish winter of his distant youth. The cloaks denied something as trivial as temperature.

Between these two things, Ellerson's estimation of their chances of survival rose. Food would be their worry.

But the rings concerned him as well. He understood that the Oracle was, in theory, the child of gods who had long since deserted the world. The mortal world. If he had considered the philosophical existence of other worlds—and he had been young once—he reevaluated now. A world in which the Winter Hunt—if that is what the passing hunt was—made itself at home was not a world in which mortals could, as anything but prey.

He could understand the cloaks. The boots. The blankets. He could understand the packs—packs which did not seem to increase in weight, no matter how they were laden. But the rings troubled him. What had the Oracle seen? How had she seen it? Had she somehow known that Carver would, or could, be found, carrying a leaf that did not look at home in this forest? Had she known that he would find the half-height door that to Ellerson's actual hands had felt like solid stone even as Carver passed through it?

He did not know much about the Oracle. Information about characters in children's stories—and at that, very old ones—was never going to be thick on the ground. The idea that she might know exactly where and when to meet him was not, at this point, cause for concern. The meeting had been a boon.

The fact that she was returning to the site of a previous visit in very different circumstances was also not alarming. The fact that the existence of the safe space beneath the hard, cold earth had come about because she had asked it, in awareness of that future meeting and future need was slightly more unsettling. Ellerson, however, did not question survival. If somehow these gifts led to death, they had been walking that road since the moment they had stepped into The Terafin's wardrobe. Anything that extended life extended the possibility that they could find a branching path off that road.

But the rings disturbed him.

He could not say, with any certainty, that they had been left for Carver. The impassibility of the thick, stone wall implied heavily that they had not. Only the metallic blue leaf allowed them to see and enter the small chamber in which the rings had been left.

If the rings had been made by the same makers who had crafted cloak, boots, and blankets, they had seen future need. It was a need that Ellerson could not see. The rings themselves were plain enough that he did not consider them decorative.

* * *

"You want to *wear* them?" Carver asked, lifting his head as if he thought he'd drifted off into an almost waking dream.

"Everything left in those rooms was meant to increase our chances of survival. Nothing, of course, is a guarantee—but the odds are so enormously improved I believe we will see home again before we perish."

"You don't sound happy about it."

"Almost nothing in life is free. There are costs to any interaction—some of which we are so happy to pay we do not count it costly. Any one of the three things—cloak, boots, blankets—would be a costly, costly commission were we to request such a crafting from the Guild of Makers. I do not believe any but the Artisans could craft them."

Carver whistled. "Not the mages?"

"We might have more luck there—but it would be the work of years, and even then, the magi are limited by the material they work. These cloaks have not stained or torn; they do not get caught on branches, no matter how tangled the branches are. I am not certain we could cut them or harm them without concentrated effort."

"And the rings?"

"Everything was left against possible need. I cannot see the need for them. I do not know what hold the Oracle had over the people who created a space for us. I do not know if they resented her or feared her; I do not know if she forced them to do what she demanded. I do not believe she did—but I do not know."

"If she did, perhaps the rings were a single act of defiance."

"And if not, they might be necessary."

"Yes. I mistrust necessity that I cannot identify or understand—but the whole of this place defies easy understanding." He paused. "Or rather, our part in it. The winter is winter, except for the passage of the Hunt. And at a far enough distance they, too, might seem a natural part of the winter order." His smile was slender as he straightened the fall of his cloak. "I am domicis, Carver. You are part of what I have chosen to serve. If you choose against the rings, I will, of course, accept it and continue."

Carver shook his head. "We'll wear them."

The rings were simple bands. Carver had assumed they were silver. Jay—or Finch or Jester—could have identified them by weight and color. Carver's ascension to the Terafin name had not, however, changed his essential nature.

What had Jay once said about gold? You couldn't eat it when you were starving; you couldn't wear it when you were freezing. You couldn't shelter beneath it.

He couldn't remember who pointed out that with gold you could buy the things that were lacking; he had a dim memory of Rath's voice, Rath's tone. And of course he'd been right. But the hang of ostentation had been slow to come to the den, and for some members, it had never arrived.

There were two things that became obvious immediately. The first, that the rings were sized for the two men who now wore them. Carver hadn't expected that. Ellerson, given his reaction, had. The second: they weren't cold. Carver hadn't expected them to be freezing—they were carried in a backpack beneath the voluminous folds of heavy cloak—but hadn't expected them to be warm. It was as if they'd just been pulled from someone else's fingers.

The second was more disturbing, at least to Carver. If Ellerson found it disquieting, he said nothing. But that was the domicis. He'd made his decision, weighing all known facts, and he'd live with it. The only time Carver had ever heard Ellerson come close to complaining was when the cats had first started destroying rugs and furniture in their boredom.

The thought made his lips twitch. Cats were predictable and annoying. Much like his den could be. But they were deadly and efficient when dealing with assassins, much like most of the den couldn't.

He looked at the ring. A band of writing had appeared on the rounded surface of the metal the minute Carver had pushed it home. "I don't suppose you can read this?" he asked.

Ellerson shook his head. "When we return, we might ask the House Mage if he is available. He was renowned for his study of things ancient and long-buried." He removed the ring to see if he could; the words didn't disappear. Both of them had chosen to put the rings on their left hands.

Thereafter, for the rest of the day's march, the wind did not howl, except at a distance. That night, when wrapped in the folds of cloak and sheltered against the roots of sleeping, ancient trees, Carver heard no distant horns. He couldn't say why, but sleep came easily, and when he woke in the long shadows of dawn, he felt refreshed.

The only evidence that this winter landscape had once been inhabited was the ruins from which they'd walked away. They found no other ruins, no hint that any other buildings might once have existed. Instead, there was snow. The only place the snow had been shallow was in the ruins themselves, as if even weather was afraid to overstep its bounds there.

By the end of this full second day of marching, Carver missed the wind and the horns. The only other noise in this world was theirs; everything else was silent. It was a silence that reminded Carver very much of held breath. He therefore filled it, talking first about the West Wing, and second, about the den. He asked Ellerson's opinion about the House Council's various members and listened—really listened—to the replies. There was nothing to distract him.

He talked about the cats.

And then toward nightfall, huddled against a tree trunk and gazing at a sky that held only one moon and no stars at all that he could see, he talked about the dead. About Lefty, Lander, Fisher. About Duster. But he didn't speak about their deaths; he spoke about their lives—or their lives as they had overlapped Carver's. He fell asleep smiling. He woke smiling. And hungry.

On the third full day, he asked Ellerson questions about his life; Ellerson was not a man to volunteer much, and generally when he did, it was worthwhile to listen. He began gingerly; he knew that there was a division between the serving class and the people they served—how could he not know that, by this time?—and he was aware that breaching that barrier was as much an act of condescension on the part of the servants as it was on the part of their masters.

But domicis were not servants, as Ellerson explained. He spoke of Arrend and his time there—the winter reminded him much of the Northern climate, which led naturally into the people who lived in it. "But there is spring and summer, no matter how brief, in Arrend. I do not think this landscape has seen either."

He spoke about his travels in the Dominion; about his travels on the merchant transports that had reached the fabled and distant Eastern Islands and even returned. And he spoke of his time in the guildhall.

He did not speak of family. He did not speak of kin. Carver didn't wonder at it, though. None of the den did—and Ellerson was clearly part of them. If Carver had never consciously said it or thought it, he accepted it as truth, as bedrock. The loss of this one old man would be as devastating to his den-kin as Carver's loss would be.

He lifted his hands and signed, experimenting with the movement of fingers.

Ellerson frowned.

"It was useful in the old days." He signed, *where*, followed by *where?* "You understand it, right?"

"Yes."

"But you've never used it."

"No."

"You could."

Ellerson shook his head.

"This one," Carver continued, as if the motion had never been made, "is yours. It's *Ellerson*."

Ellerson's silence lasted for another long beat. And then he lifted his own hands and signed, slowly and distinctly, *Carver*.

"You're not den," Carver said, smiling. "But you could have been, if your life had jogged a little to the right. Or the left."

"I am too old," the domicis replied. It was hard to tell whether or not he was offended, but experience gave Carver the necessary clues. Experience. Familiarity.

"You know we don't have any family but den, right?"

"I would quibble your use of the word family, but yes. You are *of* Terafin; in theory, Terafin is your family; it takes the place of blood ties and blood-kin. You are wed to it, responsible for it. It is why The Ten—and some of the other notable patrician families—adopt. Adoption allows them to choose those affiliated with the House Name, in a way birth does not. It fosters a sense that merit is the defining trait for which the House chooses."

Carver snorted. "Rymark. Haerrad."

"Ah, you equate competence with congeniality. They are not the same. Haerrad was—and is—a ferociously competent man. He is aggressive. He can be both vengeful and unkind. But, Carver, most men who are aggressive, vengeful, and unkind are very seldom *competent*. The force of their personality, if you will, their drive, is poured into the narrative of rage and resentment; they master nothing else."

"Rymark?"

Ellerson shook his head. "Rymark is not Haerrad."

"Not competent?"

"His competence requires control; it requires acknowledgment. Haerrad seeks respect, but he does not mistake obsequiousness for respect. He does not equate fear with respect. Rymark does. Do not tangle with him," he added.

"Tangle, no."

But Ellerson shook his head. "In the narrative of the den, it was you and Duster who were the heavy muscle. If death was necessary, Duster was your killer." He spoke without judgment.

"That wasn't muscle," Carver replied, after a significant pause. "And yes. I was the backup Duster."

"You knew you could kill?"

Carver's shrug was stiff. "I knew I had," he finally offered. "I knew I could. By the end, I would have done it without thinking if it saved any one of my den-kin. I was comfortable with that."

"And now?"

"I don't know. Back then, they were the only thing I had to lose. The only thing. I saw how each loss—of den-kin—scarred us, came close to breaking us. And you're changing the subject."

"Am I?"

"Yes. You can't, you've said, be den. I wouldn't have understood it, back in the holdings. I don't think I understood it until Merry. I can now, and I do." He turned to look at the domicis; it was dark beneath the branches, but the moon was always bright, the sky always clear. He could see Ellerson's face.

"So you're not den. But you're family, Ellerson. More than the rest of Terafin. You're the father we wish we'd had. Or the uncle. Or the older brother. You're not our life, but part of our lives." His smile was wan, but without edges. "Things have gotten strange since Jay came back from the South. Not the demons—they've been part of our past since we arrived at Terafin. But everything else. The forest. The cats. The change in The Terafin's personal rooms. Jay's afraid."

"She is not a fool, no," Ellerson replied.

"When she's afraid, we're tense. We can't help it. There's not much that scares her—and it usually involves death. I wasn't surprised when I walked into the wardrobe and found myself here. I didn't expect it, but it was in keeping with what our lives have become." He looked down at his hands; they were still. He began to sign. Speaking with his hands, however, he continued to speak out loud.

"The fear came when I saw the Hunt. The injuries came then, too. I thought I'd never make it back—I'd be dead and lost. Our dead? They're lost. We've never found their bodies. I was certain Jay would never find mine.

"And then I met her. I thought she was here. She was standing in the ruins." His toes began to dig at snow. He fell silent. His hands spoke. *She was scared.* "I told her to leave," Carver said. "And I meant it. I understood that she was somehow choosing between me and everyone else. But—it's cold, you know? It's cold, the den's not here. Duster died so that the rest of us could escape. I had her back, in every other fight. She had mine. It was the *only* time you'd ever want Duster at your back. It was the only time the two of us were a team. If I'd been with the rest of them, if I'd been with the den, I'd've died with her. I wasn't. I was with Jay.

"I'm not driven by guilt. Never have been. I know that if I'd been with

Duster, I'd've died too. That's it. We'd both be dead. But if I'd been with the rest of them, and not Jay, I *would* have died. Because it was a life-or-death fight, and I would have had her back.

"I think some of us just need something to protect. Duster didn't, until us, and even that took time."

"Sleep, Carver." Ellerson's voice was soft, a perfect whisper of sound. "The den is the master I have chosen to serve. It is a bit unusual—but not unheard of—for a domicis to serve a family rather than one of its individual members; for most, the burden of choice in difficult decisions makes the service too complicated, too difficult to untangle. The rest of the den is in Terafin."

"Not Jay."

"No, Carver. But if Jewel is part of the den, she is not part of my responsibility. I cannot and could not be domicis to her, and that pained me greatly at the time. But I have come to understand what my role is, what it must be, in this conflict. This is where I'm needed. If I have served the den in other ways, it is service that the Household Staff could provide.

"We will find our way home."

Carver said, so softly the words almost vanished into the winter hush, "I was so happy to see you. I thought I was delirious. I felt almost like I was home."

In the dark, when sleep had claimed the younger man, the older man kept watch for an hour longer. The moon silvered snow; ice caught its light and held it. There was a beauty in the silent hush; were it not for the cloaks, the boots, the food, it was the beauty of something so powerful and so distant it must lead inevitably to death.

The rings were glowing faintly in the darkness. The words were the color of sunlight.

"This is not a good time to be sleeping. I would wake up, if I were you."

Carver's eyes opened instantly. The voice was not familiar.

"That won't hurt me, you know." Carver's hand froze halfway to the knife he always carried. He flattened his palm. No horns, no hooves, no sound of armored men could be heard. It was night, and the moon was low and bright; the forest—and the snow that covered its roots—glowed gently with reflected light.

Ellerson was awake. Awake and utterly still. Nothing moved. For a moment, even the sound of breathing was absent.

But not the voice. "There's been noise, here, the past few days. Noise enough to wake me."

Carver's hands flew in den-sign. Ellerson did not respond in kind, but his stillness was enough. It said, *wait*.

"Why are you here? It is not safe, for you." As the voice approached, it was followed, at last, by a visible form. "And what do you have there?"

He looked up. He looked up and remembered that there were no walls. He met eyes that were round, gold, and lower to the ground than he had expected. It was an animal of some kind, the size of a large cat, the size of a small dog— the scrappy kind, not the hunters. Its fur was a silvered brown, and over the slight curve of its back, a very bushy tail rose.

Carver caught the direction of the talking animal's gaze. "A ring."

The creature blinked then. He nodded his head, which was at least a third of his size. "Well met."

Ellerson inclined his head. He shifted position, folding his legs in a very Southern obeisance. He did not rise fully, did not tender the small, furred creature a proper bow, or what would have been a proper bow in Averalaan. The creature tilted its head as he met Ellerson's steady gaze.

"I heard you," he said.

"If we have disturbed you or your slumber, it was entirely unintentional."

"It is certainly novel," the creature replied. "But it has been Winter for far too long. Tell me, what is that that you bear?"

"A gift of sorts," Ellerson replied. "And, as all gifts, it demands a measure of respect."

"Respect?"

"It cannot be discarded or traded as if it were simply an item for barter."

The creature laughed. It was a higher pitch of sound than Carver was accustomed to hearing from talking, furred creatures. "No, indeed. Even were you so foolish, it would not be possible."

"Oh?"

"The rings you bear were made for you. They cannot be so easily transferred. They cannot be so easily removed. Were I of a mind to claim them— and I am not, if that sets your mind at ease—I could devour you whole, except for the hand upon which that ring is situated."

"Ah."

"You do not understand what you bear?" Long whiskers twitched. "I see that you do not. Nor, I imagine, do you understand what I see in it, either."

"What do you see?" Carver asked, when the question failed to emerge from the domicis.

"Ah, no, no, no, that will not do. Are you a child?" The furry face was not a human face; it was not a grim, cold Arianni face, either. The lines and muscles around mouth and eyes did not move into expressions that were easily translated into ones Carver knew. But he had had experience with the great, winged cats—or great winged brats, as Angel often called them.

"I'm not certain. How do you define child?"

"Cozened. Protected. Ignorant." The creature tilted its head.

"But not young?"

"Youth is relative. Are the trees young? Are the distant mountains? Is the earth upon which you so carelessly rest?" The question was clearly rhetorical. "This is not the safest of places to rest," he continued, speaking to Ellerson.

"Perhaps not. But in the wilderness, there is very little safety."

"For such as you, yes. Tell me, is it Scarran? Lattan? It has been long and longer since I have seen your kind in these lands."

Ellerson, however, inclined his head. "As you must understand, time passes differently between our lands."

"Time passes, in yours." The creature's voice was lower, deeper, a hint of growl informing the words that now left him. His fur had risen, adding height and the illusion of size.

"My companion asked a question of you. You have asked a question of us. I propose an exchange of information."

The fur lowered slowly and not completely. "Only one of you is a child." Turning to glare at Carver, he added, "If you wish to claim otherwise, there is only one interpretation of your behavior."

"What behavior?"

"You asked a question of import."

"I asked a question, yes."

"Of import."

". . . Of import."

"You either expected an answer because you believed I was stupid—an insult, manchild, to my kind—or you expected an answer because you feel that I am insignificant, that your power is the greater power."

"I asked a question," Carver countered, "because I believed you were more knowledgeable."

"And indeed I am, but that would not be particularly difficult. Your companion is wiser. I would advise you to let him speak for both of you—where that is possible. There are passages through the high wilderness where it will not be, although that is largely irrelevant. You will not survive to reach it."

Carver said nothing then, but it was hard. He trusted Ellerson, but Ellerson's instincts weren't Jay's. No one's were. But as Jay had said, often, her voice broken with guilt and pain and loss, her instincts were only guaranteed to save *her*.

No, Jay, he thought. They had saved Finch. They had saved Teller. They had saved Arann. Yes, they had not saved the others, and death and time had taken them—but they had not been useless, not wasted. Haval had said, often, that Jay could not save everyone, that she had to accept that.

And how do I judge? she'd asked.

You don't. Accept that you will do more good than harm. Were it not for your gift, none of your den would have survived.

You can't know *that*.

No, Jewel. I can know it. You cannot.

He shook himself. Ellerson was speaking.

"If you are aware that time passes differently in our two worlds, you will know that I do not have an answer."

The creature was silent, waiting.

"But I will nonetheless hazard an educated guess in return for an explanation of what you see when you look at these rings."

"And if I lie?"

"I will have very little way of ascertaining that. But I might lie, as well. There is always a measure of good faith in an exchange of information."

The creature laughed. And it was a laugh, not the cat hiss of sound that passed for one. As he laughed, he changed.

Snow clung to his fur as his body grew larger, and larger again; his back retained its rounded curve, but where it had been close to the ground, it was now feet from it. The dusting of silvered fur gave way almost fully to a gold-tinted brown, and the shape of the face changed, the point of ears gentling their line to a roundness and a width that they had not possessed before. The small paws that had been almost buried in the snow now broke it with their size and the weight they supported.

"You are mortal indeed if you believe that. Or perhaps you have only bargained with mortals. They once hewed the forests, and burned them, and made homes of their corpses. Do they still?"

"Not forests such as these," Ellerson replied.

The creature laughed again. It was a warm sound, and had he not been so large, his fangs so prominent, it might have been a welcoming one. "You amuse me. It has been an age since I last laughed; laughter is a gift. We do not like to be indebted to anyone, and as you have given me a gift, I will return the favor." The creature's voice was lower now, a rumble of sound.

"You are being hunted here. This place is not what it once was; it is waking as we speak. Very few are those who could find their way here—and you bear the rings that mark you as the property of one of them. Should she find you, I believe you will be safe—but she is not here, and she is not hunting.

"There are others, however, who were guests here when the world was awake. And one at least has found a pathway into this place. I do not know how, and it is not my concern; he would not attempt to harm me." The bear—there was no other word for it—tilted his head. "Or he would not have before we met. I am not certain how much of your scent will cling to me, now that we have.

"But come. I would not lose my first source of amusement in eons to him. Not immediately." And speaking this, he turned on his haunches and ambled away, looking pointedly over his shoulder when Carver and Ellerson failed to immediately follow. The domicis, however, took the time necessary to pack what few essentials they had that were not already contained in their back-packs before he obeyed what was essentially a command.

Chapter Nine

IN THE ORACLE'S ABODE, darkness could be absolute; there were no windows through which light could shine.

"You need to *sleep*," Shadow said. He lay sprawled across the bed, ignoring the inconvenient placement of the person who was actually in it.

"I was asleep for almost three days, Shadow."

"That *wasn't* sleep, *stupid* girl."

Jewel was exhausted, and in the darkness, guilt was the whole of her world.

"You are *stupid*," the great cat replied. He lifted his head, which made it easier to breathe. Or move.

"Always," Jewel told him. "When I dream now, I can't see you."

"No."

"Why? Why could you walk into my dreams before?"

Shadow sniffed. Jewel thought his lack of answer meant he didn't know. "Your dreams are *different* now. Sometimes you go where I can't *follow*."

"Can you follow me at the beginning? When I fall asleep?"

Shadow hissed. It wasn't laughter, but it wasn't injured dignity. It was an entirely different sound. In the darkness, the cat seemed larger. But his fur was still soft, and he was warm. A little too warm. "You need to *sleep*."

"Did I kill those people?"

"Does it *matter*? There are *so many* people. If you *do not* sleep, you will become even *weaker*." He snorted. "And then they will *all* die."

"It matters," Jewel said. And then, voice softer, she added, "I don't know why you ask me questions when you already know the answer."

Shadow lowered his head again. He growled. "Because you *need* to *remember* the answer. You need to *think* it. You need to *say* it." His voice fell into a more familiar whine as he added, "It would be easier if your answers weren't *boring*. Now go to *sleep*. Or we will *die* of *boredom*."

There was, about the gray cat's expression—most of which was carried in his voice—something familiar. It was fractious, difficult, required patience and tolerance, but it was something she wanted. Needed. She reached up, placed her hand on his head, and began to scratch behind his ears. The motion was soothing; the cat's fur was soft. Like a small cat's fur, not like a predator's.

She slept.

She dreamed.

Her hand was still on Shadow's head when she opened her eyes. She knew she was not awake.

She stood in the streets of *Averalaan Aramarelas*. As a child, she had dreamed of crossing the bridge to the Isle, of being able to afford the toll to do so. She had assumed—what had she assumed? That the streets were paved with gold? That the god-born Twin Kings were actual deities? They might as well have been. If there were gods, they didn't hear the prayers of the poor and disenfranchised in the hundred holdings.

She would have said as much to Shadow, but the gray cat was fading.

She wanted to hold on to him and tried. In dreams, dignity wasn't a given; she didn't much care if people stared at her while she threw her arms around Shadow's neck.

She felt cold. Heat. Physical sensation at a remove, the way it sometimes was in dreams. She wanted the cat *here*. And here he remained, but it took effort. She knew the effort was successful when his voice became louder. And whinier.

"Better," the cat told her, when he had relieved himself of his opinions about her general intelligence. "This is *better*."

She was standing outside of the entrance to a building she recognized: the Guild of Makers. Some considered it the most powerful guild in the Empire; more powerful by far than the Merchants' Guild.

The maker-born, however, were not political. Gilafas ADelios was the nominal head of the guild and was rumored to be the guild's only living Artisan. Jewel had met him a handful of times, but only one was significant: he had come to her on the first day of The Terafin's funeral rites, drawn by sight of the dress she had worn that day. It was the dress Snow had made.

On that day, he had been at his most absent, his most socially irregular. She had seen him at a distance in the gatherings her position forced her to attend; there he looked like a slightly bored, slightly irritable, older patrician. On the first day of the funeral, he had seemed almost childlike in his fascination. That fascination had led him to examine the dress from all angles, without thought for distance or his own dignity.

She had never seen him so engaged.

Shadow said, "I'm *bored.*"

Jewel, accustomed to this, exhaled. The people in the streets were dream people. She knew, somehow. This *was* a dream. "Why," she asked the cat, as she squared her shoulders and headed toward the guild's gatehouse, "are you here?"

"You *made* me stay."

"No, why are you with me *at all?*"

The cat sniffed.

"We thought you would be *less* boring."

This, strangely, was true. She was in dream, but not in dream, and she remembered that this cat, of the three, had almost succeeded in killing her. She could not muster fear of him, in the face of all the facts.

"We are *yours,*" Shadow told her. The guards at the gatehouse looked down their noses at her; they were, however, accustomed to some eccentricities in the wealthy and powerful. Jewel was not wearing the Terafin seal, and she wasn't dressed as if she should be. She was dressed, she realized, as a traveler. She gave her name: Jewel Markess.

They sent her to the trade entrance.

The trade entrance was not unguarded. Thieves, or would-be thieves, had always been a problem for the guild and its rumored treasures.

The guards at the back gate demanded to know what her business was, just as the guards at the gatehouse had. The former, however, had asked very few questions before ascertaining that she was someone else's problem. That someone else was far more thorough.

It was the cat, she decided. Even in dream, the cat was not invisible. Or silent.

A word traveled between the guards. "Did they honestly send you to *us?*" the older of the two demanded. She was visibly annoyed, and muttered something about lazy young men, none of which was meant for Jewel. "Do you have a collar or a leash for that?"

Shadow swelled in outrage. He sputtered.

"Not exactly," Jewel said, placing her customary hand on the top of his head. "Shadow, please."

The best she could hope for was what she got: lowering of wings and a lot of muttering about how intelligent she wasn't.

The guard, however, shook her head; her eyes narrowed. "You said you were Jewel Markess?"

Jewel nodded.

"It's your business, ma'am," the guard continued, "but for our part, we're very, very sorry you were sent to the trade entrance. I'll have a word upstairs."

Jewel, however, smiled. "I'm not—"

"With that great cat by your side, there's only one person you could be. You're here for Master Gilafas."

She nodded because, in this dream, she understood that she was.

"You don't have an appointment."

"No, I'm sorry."

The guard looked at the gray cat again and then straightened up, making a decision. "Andrew, door's yours. I'm serving as armed page. Again."

The halls through which the armed page led Jewel and Shadow ended at a very finely appointed reception room. If the maker-born were not determined to wield their wealth for political power, they understood its trappings. The chairs were of a darkly stained, heavy wood, upholstered in fabric that would have beggared a normal family; the rugs were likewise delicately woven and knotted, their colors bright and vibrant. She could see the pale sheen of orange light that spoke of enchantments laid across them, no doubt to protect them from wear and sunlight.

And sunlight streamed in through the forbiddingly large windows. They were framed by colored, worked glass, a mosaic of sorts, but their centers were clear, as if to acknowledge the value of normal daylight.

She was not surprised to find that Master Gilafas was not resident in this office.

But a page was sent, and a page returned. The guild's version of Barston rose stiffly. "Master Gilafas will see you now."

Jewel wondered, as she followed the page up the stairs, how it was that the most prominent of the many guilds, comprised almost invariably of older men and women, had stairs so punitive in height, pitch, and length. By the time she was finished with them, she felt the climb in her legs; her breath was short.

The page who had been sent to guide her didn't seem to feel them the same way—but she was probably paid not to. She frowned apologetically when they finally reached flat floors again. "They're not always this bad."

"Do they change?"

"Oh, yes. Frequently. It's why the guards don't generally accompany guests to Fabril's reach."

"The stairs?"

"No—the fact that they change. If Master Gilafas is not expecting you, or if you have no legitimate business with him, you will fail to reach him. You might fail to reach anything that could be remotely considered an exit."

"But . . . you said he was expecting me? Or at least willing to see me?"

The girl nodded, eyes bright.

". . . And the stairs are worse than normal?"

"No, not worse—just different. But I know these ones," she added, smiling.

Jewel almost stopped walking; the cat hissed and butted her back with the top of his head. "Have you ever been lost here?"

"Yes. Twice. But the older pages found me; they recognized the stairs, so they knew what to expect."

"Have you ever lost pages here? I mean permanently?"

"Yes—but never while I've been here." She lowered her voice. "I've been told it was very different under the previous guildmaster."

"Oh?"

She nodded, and then, as if realizing that she had said far, far too much, flushed and lowered her head.

And Jewel remembered that she was The Terafin. But she was not dressed as The Terafin should be, and she wondered if the formal clothing and obvious wealth it implied was meant, in the end, as a kindness—an obvious wall that would inhibit all such slips of tongue, such casual conversation. She smiled at the girl and said, "My apologies. Curiosity is one of my besetting sins, and if I'm not thinking, I don't remember to keep the questions on the right side of my teeth." And she thought, as the tension across the girl's straight shoulders receded, that she had never been as young as this page. Not at the same age.

The page led her to Master Gilafas' room.

The door that led to the rooms of the most powerful man in the Empire was not what Jewel might otherwise have expected. It was narrow, short, and plain, and would have been at home protecting the contents of a closet. The surface of the wood had clearly been cared for, but it was deeply scratched in a familiar way. Jewel looked at her cat, lifting her brows in question.

Shadow hissed. "It wasn't *me*. It was *Night*." Since the cats generally blamed each other for crimes both real and imagined, Jewel thought there was only a small chance that this was the truth.

"I really like your cat," the girl whispered. "I'll wait outside."

But the cat, who preened slightly at attention from a young woman, flicked his wings. "We will leave a *different* way. If you wait *here*, you will starve." He glanced at Jewel and added, "which would be *better* than dying of *boredom*."

The room into which Jewel stepped was not empty; it was not, however, occupied by the guildmaster. It was a tidy room, lined with bookshelves; there was a writing table at its heart, with four worn and empty chairs around it. She hushed Shadow to listen for the sound of either movement or voice and was rewarded instantly by two things. The first: a small thread of sound, something musical that suggested a song. The second: a crash. It was the crash she responded to first. She ran.

She found the guildmaster standing in the midst of—of all things—a small mountain of paintbrushes and palettes which had clearly not seen use in a while. He did not appear to be aware of them, or perhaps that was wrong; they appeared to have been on a shelf or table that had been *in the way*. As she watched, he shoved two books off a table with an irritable sweep of his right arm; they joined the brushes and the palettes on the floor with an audible thud.

Teller would have shrieked in shocked outrage at the sight. Books were expensive and precious; to see them tossed off the table as if they were unwanted first drafts of complicated political letters would have been too much for him.

"Master ADelios," she said.

He continued to hum, but there was a frenzied pitch to the tune as she drew near. Shadow flexed his claws. "Don't even think it. I mean it."

"But *he's* doing it. He won't *notice*."

"They're his things. He's allowed to make a mess of his own things."

"Well, where are *my* things?" Shadow demanded.

It was the cat's angry demand that drew the guildmaster's attention. He frowned, blinked; his voice lost the subtle, rising hum that Jewel had first heard. "I don't know," he said—to the cat. "I do not believe I have anything of yours in my personal rooms."

"In the *other* rooms?" the cat asked, as if it were natural that Gilafas would indeed have something in his possession that belonged to a winged predator.

"Maybe. Some of the rooms are very old. And very strange."

Shadow hissed. "*You* call *me* strange?"

"He said the *rooms* were strange, Shadow." What she needed now was not a petulant, whiny cat, because that generally led to a petty, destructive cat.

"Ah, yes. I did. I was looking for something," he added, almost apologetically. He turned to Jewel. "Terafin."

He even started to bow.

But the bow froze before he could complete it; his eyes rounded, his mouth opened, and he stared. It was different from the very obvious stares she'd received—or rather, her dress had received—previously.

"What," he asked, half frozen, half bent, "have you made of *yourself?*"

This was a dream.

In dreams, you often knew things you knew nowhere else. You had parents who were not, in the waking world, your parents—but you didn't question them in the dream. You didn't deny them. You had den-kin you'd never seen, homes you'd never encountered. You had knowledge that was strictly of, and for, the dreaming.

And she *knew*, thinking this, that she might never truly dream again. She knew what she was here for. And it was knowledge she didn't have, or hadn't had, until the dream had enfolded her, but it was also real.

She straightened her shoulders, and for the first time in the presence of someone other than the Oracle, she reached into herself and withdrew her heart from the cavity of her chest.

Or she started to make that attempt. The guildmaster caught both of her hands in his. "No," he said. "Perhaps you know what you have made better than one who has not and could never make it. But it *is* a making, and I am a maker. Do not do this."

"This is the reason I left Averalaan. The reason I left home."

He glanced at the cat. "You could not find the materials you needed here? I have, once or twice, been forced to travel to do just that."

"No, Guildmaster. It was to make something of myself that I left. It is because I have succeeded that I am here."

He met and held her gaze. There was a weariness in his expression and an all-encompassing compassion that skirted dangerously close to the edge of pity. He did not, however, release her hands. "I believe," he told her, "I have something for you." He turned to one of the messy worktables and retrieved what looked, at this distance, like a key ring. He had released only one of her hands. "My apologies for any overfamiliarity. If we are not somehow attached, either you—or I—will become lost in these rooms. I cannot be guaranteed to find you again in time."

"I thought the pages—"

"No, Terafin. The pages are not permitted beyond my workrooms. They are allowed to wander the halls to find it; it is good exercise for them and keeps them out of trouble. But they do not enter the heart of Fabril's reach. Only the maker-born can."

"I'm not maker-born."

"I misspoke." He hesitated. "It is my belief that you could both enter and leave—but where you would emerge, I do not know. You might travel the whole of Fabril's creation and return. You might be lost to one dell, one landscape, and perish. Come. Before we leave, I wish you to see my butter-flies."

He led Jewel, hand warm in his, cat silent in their wake, to another room and, through it, to a small hall. The walls were stone, the ceilings short, almost squat. There were no windows; the whole of its short length was lit by mage-stones. Gilafas frowned. "You are not afraid of butterflies, are you?"

She wasn't, of course, but she no longer trusted butterflies to *be* butterflies—not in the dreaming. She did not explain this to Gilafas. She had explained it to almost no one. But Adam, were he here, might understand.

Before she could answer his question, he continued. "Do you know, I had a student once? I did not want her. When she came to me, I did not want her."

"She wanted to become a maker?"

"No, Terafin." The door opened. "Or, perhaps, yes. Tell me, have you ever desired to become human?"

The room was full of butterflies. Jewel must have breathed because eventually she had to exhale—but she did not recall anything about the first few minutes in that room except the butterflies. They were not, as they had been in prior dreams, glowing pale lights. They had the form, the shape, the implied deli-cacy of butterflies—but they were not, in the end, alive. As if each had been spun of blown glass, made whole, set down, these butterflies waited. Not all were translucent; some were green, some blue, some tinted gold; some were red, and some a delicate purple that was still too deep to be lilac.

"There are birds, as well, but they do not appear to be nesting here today."

She frowned, trying to pick up the shattered thread of the guildmaster's conversation. It was difficult. "You made these?" she whispered.

As if her voice was breeze—or wind—the butterflies *moved*. Some closed their wings, and some took to air, fluttering as if agitated or excited. She froze.

"If you don't *close your mouth*, they will *fly in*, stupid girl."

She snapped her jaw shut but inhaled sharply when she heard the cat flexing his claws against the stone floor. "Do not even *think* of harming a single one, Shadow. I mean it."

"They are not *real*."

"They are."

Shadow hissed. "They are not *alive*. I cannot *kill* them."

"Don't break them. Please."

Gilafas waited until this exchange reached its natural conclusion before he answered her question. "No, Terafin. These were made—at least I believe they were made—by my student."

"The one you didn't want."

"The only Artisan ever born who I believe might rival Fabril at the peak of his powers, yes."

The butterflies had an affinity for Master Gilafas which was immediately obvious. They surrendered their various perches, seeking instead like space across his arms, his shoulders, the top of his head. Some, like enterprising children, landed on the tops of shoes almost hidden by the drape of his working robes.

"Can you hear them?" he asked softly.

She listened. Whatever he could hear, she could not. But she did not doubt that he could, in this place. He was a portly, older man, but he looked like—not a god, not exactly, he was too solid for that, but perhaps like a fey sorcerer of stories of old. She was not afraid of him.

She was afraid for him. And that was unwelcome. She had not come here for that.

"Why *did* you come, stupid girl?" Shadow was staring at the butterflies, his claws twitching rhythmically.

Jewel was staring at the only other glass in the room. At first glance, it looked like the centerpiece for a large window; it was of colored glass, like the windows in the naves of the great cathedrals on the Isle. But it was small, she thought, as she approached it.

Small or no, it was so finely crafted she knew it for maker's work the moment she laid eyes on it. Years of merchanting supplied numbers, figures, some normal way of assigning a value, all irrelevant. The stained glass work depicted a young woman, eyes closed, head slightly bowed. She was golden in cast, in tone; her hair, her skin, her eyelashes. Her lips were the deep but pale pink of the young—those healthy and well fed.

She was the heart of this room. No, she was half of it.

The other half was watching her.

"Fabril made this place," she said because she could think of nothing else to say.

"So the guild has always believed."

Something about the phrasing gave her pause. "You don't believe it?"

"No. I have been told, however, that Fabril made it his own. Fabril was the greatest of the maker-born. He was without parallel."

A pause. Into it, Jewel said, "You don't believe that mortals made this tower."

His smile was youthful and wise at the same time. "Very good, Terafin. I do not know who made it. I, like many, assumed it was Fabril's reach for a reason. He was not guildmaster, in his time; I do not believe the guild as it is currently constituted existed. But the mortal maker-born were valued, even when the gods walked—or so I was once told."

"By who?" she asked; it was the only question she could think of asking.

"By the Winter Queen."

The temperature in the room plunged between one held breath and its escape.

"I have something I have created for you, I believe."

Her eyes widened as the merchant experience returned in a rush. It had been implied, heavily, that she might preside over the ruin of her House— that she might witness the fall of Kings and Empire—but she had never assumed that ruin to be financial folly. No, she told herself. This is a dream. It's a dream.

"*Stupid, stupid girl.*"

"Your companion is not terribly polite," Gilafas said. But he smiled. "Yet it is heartening to see that the heart of a cat, no matter its size or ferocity, remains the same."

Shadow could not decide if this was an insult or not; it was said as if it were praise. While he puzzled, his own insults diminished.

"I'm accustomed to it. It's when they're quiet that I'm really in trouble." She swallowed. "I don't believe I commissioned—"

He swatted the words away, and butterflies rose from his hands as he did. "That piece," he said, pointing to the stained-glass work, "was mine. It was a true making." There was, in his voice, no pride at all. Jewel wondered then if the maker-born were driven like the seer-born—if the gift mastered them, and not the other way around; if it drove them, hurt them, confused them.

It was the first time she had ever wondered.

As if he could hear the question she had not asked—and it was a dream, anything was possible—he said, "I was disappointed when I had finished. Sometimes we know what we will craft; sometimes we do not. But I recognized it for what it is: a true work. That figure," he added softly, "was the student of whom I spoke. Her name was Cessaly."

"Was?"

"I do not know what she is called now. She is in the Winter lands, ruled by the Wild Hunt and their cold, cold Queen." His smile was wan, and mostly sane. "Do you know, on the first day of The Terafin's funeral rites, when I saw you in that dress, I was reminded of Winter? I was reminded of snow, and cold, and also of blood and death.

"What I make, Terafin, is made; sometimes I do not understand its full purpose. But I understood the purpose of this window on the last night I saw Cessaly. Cessaly did not require a window such as this—and it is a window. She walked, one night, into the Winter—through one of Fabril's many halls. I am not certain. I tried to follow. I tried to find her—and she was almost impossible to find on some days.

"I would find her, hands almost bleeding, lips cracked; she had worked and worked and because we did not know where, there was no one to feed her, to make her drink, to stand guard at her back so reality itself did not destroy her.

"I have some of the things she made; she left them. But it is not for me to decide who they were made for."

"I don't understand."

"We make, Terafin. The creation is the drive. Only when we are finished—and some are never truly finished—do we understand who the creations are for. It is not irrelevant, not exactly, but it is not the reason we make when compelled."

"But the guild—"

"Yes. The makers make. They craft. They are in command of what they make when they undertake commissions. But these? This window? They are not commissions. Or perhaps they are commissions of the soul; things that drive us that we cannot name because we cannot see it, cannot hear it, except in rare, rare moments.

"This window was one. I came to understand what this window did. Or does. For the first time, I became profoundly grateful for my gift."

"What—what does it do?"

"It is connected, always, to Cessaly." His smile dimmed, but its ghost remained comfortably on his face; he was lost for a moment in memory, and some of that memory was good. But it was shadowed—as memories often are—by loss. She did not ask.

"These butterflies—"

"Cessaly made them. Cessaly *makes* them. They come through the window and into this room. The birds were later inventions, but they came through this window as well."

"Can they return?"

"I do not think they have ever tried. They are not, as you understand it, alive—but they are like little vessels. They are," he added, the smile deepening, "for me. While they come, I know she is well. She is making, and she is allowed to make what she is moved to make. She was always in search of materials here; she would wander dreadfully in her urgent need to find them, and she could not clearly tell us what she needed most of the time.

"I want to find her. I am sorry—I wander, it is my age. I have desired to find her since the night she—she left. I believe, with your help, I might do so, at last."

"The Winter is not a safe place for you," Jewel replied, before thought closed her mouth.

"I know. But the Winter Queen is said to value the maker-born, and it is clear Cessaly is alive, and in some fashion, she is content." He exhaled. "At least that is the story I tell myself, but I cannot completely believe it—it is too infused with my desire to be able to do so.

"When you return, you will agree to allow me to accompany you, or you will not leave through this door."

Jewel was confused. Shadow stepped—far more heavily than was warranted—on her foot. "Return?"

He turned to her, then, the smile sliding from his face. A man of power, an autocratic man who was accustomed to having his own way, remained. It was both frightening and comforting—because *this* man, she could fight.

"You will return to your home," he replied, voice soft. "You are searching, Terafin, perhaps as I have been searching. You have not yet finished; you require passage."

She stared at him, thinking *this is a dream*. And as the rest, it was both true and false. "It's not for my sake that I require it," she said at last, attempting to choose her words with care, as one did not, in a dream. "It is for the sake of this city, for the people who live within these walls."

"There has been enough sacrifice," was his angry reply. "There has been enough loss for the sake of this city, this Empire, these people. I had no choice but to pay the cost—no, even that is wrong. But I have sacrificed enough. I have searched, Terafin. Did you know? I have studied. I have besieged the Order of Knowledge with demands for information and lore.

"Only one of their members was even remotely useful, and he is no longer resident within his rooms there. He is now, if rumor is to be believed, resident within yours."

Meralonne.

She felt a breeze then; winter breeze. The butterflies seemed to shudder with it all at once, as if they were a single individual. They did not, however, freeze or shatter.

"I once opened this window." He turned, again, to the stained-glass image of a young woman, his face hardening. "I have never been able to open it again. The mage believed that I could not—but he counseled against its destruction, as if that were necessary.

"He said, Terafin, that he thought it would be open again—but once—and not by me. Do you understand?"

"When it does open, what will happen?"

"I will find her." He bowed his head. "You are not required to do anything else, anything other. I believe it is your hand that will open this window—if any now can; the mage could not. He said it was a making, and it was peculiar and specific in nature. Nothing immortal and nothing dead might pass through this portal.

"One cannot trust the magi, of course. I did try. The butterflies," he added, "come. But I believe you might open it. I do not know if the window itself will survive the opening." Even as he said it, she saw the way his pallor shifted, pink giving way to something far more ashen. "I do not know. It is my greatest work—but I will accept its loss if it serves this one purpose.

"Perhaps you will find another road. And perhaps, if you do, you will resent me. But if need drives you here, I will not allow you into these rooms again without your word."

Student, Jewel thought. She had been his student. And she understood that for Cessaly, Gilafas had been a different version of Rath: a man who had, against his own wishes, come to care. He was old. As old as Rath would have been. For the first time—perhaps for the only time—Jewel was grateful that Rath had predeceased her; he would never know the pain of her loss or death.

"Where is Cessaly?"

"She is with the Winter Queen."

*   *   *

"Yes, I will take you with me," she told the Artisan. "But, Gilafas, no threats are necessary. I would counsel against your company, given what I have seen and what I am becoming, but were I in your position, I would do what you desire to do. But I do not know if I will find my way back to Fabril's reach in time."

Gilafas closed his eyes. Opened them. "I have said I have something for you, have I not?"

"Yes."

"I did not intend to give it to you if you would not agree—and that would have pained me greatly. It is a work, Terafin." His voice held no pride at all. "It is a working. Had Cessaly made it, it would have been wondrous, powerful, a thing outside of time and place; it would have been *art*. That was what she was. I am not Cessaly. Nothing I craft will ever be as flawless, as perfect. But: it is a work.

"It is not here. You must follow." He held out a hand. She took it with vastly less discomfort than she had the first time; it was warm. It was callused.

The workrooms which contained the mirror and the butterflies—but not the birds, apparently—were warm and bright in comparison to the inner corridors of Fabril's reach. She thought it interesting that Cessaly, in stained glass, was the icon of Summer—golden, glowing, warm.

The rest of the halls were not. Where she had been gold and light, they were gray and dark. They were not lit by the magestones used as a matter of course by the wealthy; they were barely lit at all. Gilafas opened one door—one heavy, scored door that was wider than the door to his own rooms had been—and the temperature plunged.

It was not a short journey, and it made clear to Jewel that Fabril's reach was very like a dream itself. Its halls were dark and secret, the hush in them hovering over that moment when dream walks, suddenly, into nightmare.

No maps could be made of these halls. No maps would remain relevant; the halls were very like the halls in the Oracle's domain. They changed between one hour and the next.

Jewel watching the play of shadows cast by torchlight, flickering as if moving with independent life. She was not surprised when those shadows did, indeed, lift themselves from the walls, retaining only an echo of the shapes that had originally cast them. One of them was her own.

Gilafas was watching her. "I see I am meant to let you lead," he said. "But do not let go of my hand."

"Lead?" she repeated, as if she were once again the child that Rath had first found beneath the bridge of the river that cut through her city.

"Yes. You know where we must go. Or part of you does."

She followed her shadow. She lost it several times in the darkness ahead, and it did not return—but the torch was bright enough, once her eyes had acclimated to the darkness, that another shadow was cast, and another shadow came to an odd sort of life. In fits and starts, she followed where it led.

Master Gilafas had fallen almost as silent as her cat; gone was the oddity, the scattered attention, the flow of words that touched on personal history. He waited so patiently Jewel could imagine him as someone's keeper or caretaker. She could imagine that he could hunt through these halls—for these were the halls, she was certain of it—in which his apprentice had wandered to work.

She did not wander into the wrong room by mistake; there were doors, but the doors would not open for her. Shadow lifted his forepaw but did not speak; Jewel shook her head. She glanced at Gilafas, but he did not seem unduly perturbed, and she continued to walk.

The absence of snow did not distract her; she felt the winter in the air.

She had considered the transformation to The Terafin's personal rooms—rooms that she had never truly considered her own—to be unsettling, and even upsetting. But once they had undergone that transformation, they had become a place of light, of air, of breeze and the hush of distant forest. The skies were amethyst, clear, the trees grew bookshelves; the floors were pale wood and went on in any direction for as far as the eye could see.

This felt like a dungeon, a crypt; the open skies did not touch it, and the wind that did was not gentle. She could hear its howl, as if the stone of these walls was so thin it could keep nothing out.

"Are the halls always like this?"

"Like what?"

"Dark. Stone. Cold."

"Ah. No, Terafin."

"So . . . it's just for me."

He chuckled, which surprised her; his hand tightened briefly around hers. "The reach has a will of its own. It cannot communicate as we do. It is given no voice, no way of making its desire known. Confound that unknown desire, and you will never leave this place—even the maker-born have difficulty navigating its endless corridors."

"And you?"

"I have no desire to force structure or meaning on it. When I leave my own rooms, I do not know what to expect. I try to see it as it is; I accept that it will differ each time. There is no part of my will I attempt to force upon it. I choose to walk; it chooses where my walk will lead me."

"How did you search for Cessaly, then?"

"The same way—but with greater fear and desperation."

When she heard the horns, she froze. Gilafas' hand tightened, and he stopped as she came to a stop. Shadow was silent, but his wings, tense, had risen; his fur was like a second skin. She gave him no commands. Here, in the wilderness, he was wild, and she was content to allow him to be so.

She was content, she thought, to allow her forests to be so. To allow her personal rooms—and they were hers, even if they didn't inhabit her inner heart the way the rooms in the twenty-fifth holding, or even the West Wing, had—to be wild. She could at times find herself robbed of breath when she stopped to notice—but as with all things, familiarity often bred a comfortable disregard.

She could not see the halls as she saw any of the other things—but she knew, by Shadow's countenance, his fur, and his sharp silence, that he could and did. He expected trouble. He expected martial trouble. But he was still at home in this darkness, this place. And, she thought, she must learn to be at home in it as well.

Her legs ached. She had no idea how long they'd been walking and searching for the one room that would allow her entry, but her body told her it had been a while.

Throughout it all, the guildmaster held her hand. In the dim light, she was reminded of walking through the city streets, her hand in her father's or, more often, her Oma's. They wanted to protect her; to keep her safe. She'd felt, at the time, that they *could*.

But she was Terafin now. She was seer-born. She was on a path that would either elevate her or break her. She saw the whole of the city as one fragile being and knew that there was no safety. And yet that safety had not been a lie.

Or perhaps it had. But it felt like truth.

She stopped walking. Gilafas stopped as well.

"There is no door here," he pointed out, voice mild, the final word rising slightly, as if in question.

Jewel smiled up at him; he was taller than she by a good head, but she had not really noted the physical difference so distinctly before. "Not yet." She lifted their interlocked hands. "You don't want me to become as lost as some poor thief—and I am grateful for that, Master Gilafas. Of all the gifts offered me, it is the one I should value most."

It was his turn to look confused, and confusion suited the odd lines of his face. "But I have not yet given you what I made."

"No, you haven't. But you have given me your confidences. You have shared both joy and sorrow. You have tried—as you can—to protect me from the dangers you perceive."

He shook his head. "It is far too late for that."

"Yes. Yes, it is. But you have tried anyway. I will remember it."

"*Promise?*" Shadow asked, uttering the first word since the halls had enveloped them.

Jewel Markess ATerafin lifted her chin. "I promise it. I will remember."

And lightning struck the hall.

Chapter Ten

JEWEL HEARD IT THE way one heard thunder in the stormy port skies in the rainy season. She felt it; had her hair not been pulled back and bound against the vagaries of wind, it would have been standing on end. Shadow's certainly was. The great cat yowled in outrage.

Only Gilafas seemed unfazed by the lightning. But his eyes held it; they were pale, almost white as he turned to look at her—as if the lightning that had struck now resided within him. As if he had absorbed it before it damaged Fabril's reach.

Fabril's reach *was* his home. In that peculiar moment after the lightning, before the cat's screech, she understood that, *knew* it. He did not order his home; he did not restructure it; he did not demand that it be. But it was his place. He would leave it upon his death, or not at all, even if he traveled with her, as she knew, now, he must.

If the lightning had not killed her or harmed her, it had changed, in one swift stroke of light and wild grace, the halls in which she had wandered. Large cracks appeared in the stone, stretching from the floor where the great flash of moving light had landed and spreading in all directions, as if floor, wall, ceiling were made of thick glass, and the glass had been broken.

It was a swift process; the cracks expanded.

Gilafas was watching. He did not seem panicked by what he had seen, but perhaps he saw things she didn't or couldn't. That was the gift familiarity gave, when one had surrendered the ability to feel awe or surprise.

The walls fell away in chunks—but they did not fall inward. Jewel closed her eyes. She couldn't cover them while carrying the torch, and her other hand was still ensconced in the guildmaster's. The halls to either side were now short outcroppings of newly jagged stone.

Beyond them, as far as the eye could see, was snow.

"It is going to be a bit noisier," Gilafas told her, almost apologetically.

She nodded as the sound of horns drowned out thought. "This is where you left whatever it was you made?"

"It must be," he replied. "Lead, and I will follow."

"Will you be able to return?"

"Yes, Terafin."

"Call me Jewel," she said softly. "I did not come to you as Terafin."

"And I did not come to you or the young woman who tends your gardens as guildmaster. It is, however, what I am."

"It's not all you are."

"I cannot untangle it from every other thing. Can you?"

Could she? She considered the winter to either side of this broken hall. She had come to Terafin with her den—those who'd survived. She had been desperate for shelter, for safety, for someone powerful to hide her den behind. She had worked, at the command of The Terafin. She had traveled to the West and even the South. She had learned merchanting and better math.

None of those things were part of who she had been upon her arrival at the gatehouse half a lifetime ago. That had changed. Slowly—so slowly she could not pinpoint the moment—she had come to think of Terafin as home, as hers.

But she had taken the seat only because she had promised Amarais Handernesse ATerafin, the woman who had saved all their lives and preserved them in the face of demons, that she would. That she would take the seat, and that she would protect what Amarais had spent a lifetime building.

Mortals could not, she had been told, make binding oaths.

The only binding was, therefore, their conscience.

". . . No," she said.

He nodded, as if he had expected her to arrive at no other answer. "Terafin."

She did not ask him to use her given name again.

The hunting horns grew distant as she stood; the wind howled. She looked— was looking for Carver and caught herself. She knew, as she did, that he was not here. Everything she had said to him the last time they had spoken—in a dream, like this one—was true. He was *one life* against which the lives of every person in this city must be weighed and measured.

But truth was not a shield, not a comfort, because it was never singular. There were other lurking truths, each as strong, each as rooted. "Does it get any easier?" she asked, mostly of herself; her breath adorned the sound with thin clouds.

"No, Terafin. I have walked these halls in dream and nightmare, even if both were waking. I have searched, and the search has been fruitless, constant; the loss becomes so sharp, the pain so present, I might be living in the past. There are days when I hate the Kings. Days when I hate every other person who lives and breathes in the Empire.

"Hatred does not dim the pain. It does not lessen it."

"What does?"

"Nothing. I do not think it will truly end until I have found Cessaly again. But you are Terafin, not guildmaster. Where will you go?"

"What did you make, Gilafas?" She saw snow and cold and heard the Wild Hunt. Celleriant was not here. Avandar was not here. She had Shadow—and perhaps Night and Snow were hovering near him somehow. Neither the black nor the white cat had ever entered her dreams the way the gray one had. She did not like her chances for surviving a second encounter with the Wild Hunt.

But she would not have given much for her chances to survive it a first time, either.

"It is a crown," he told her. "It is delicate; perhaps tiara would be the better word."

Jewel froze for reasons other than the plunging temperature and turned to stare at him. "I am Terafin, *not* monarch."

"I did not say that it was you who were meant to wear it," was his mild reply. "But you are meant to *have* it. What you will do with it is no longer in my hands, if it ever was. It was made from the leaves of your many trees. I did not steal them," he added, as if that were necessary—and perhaps it was. "They were freely given to me by your gardener. I gathered what I needed and returned to Fabril's reach, and here, Terafin, I worked.

"Had I first made crowns when Cessaly came to me, I would have been pleased. I would have considered them significant in a way I did not consider a portrait of the most difficult student known to guildmaster in this or any other era to be significant. I was wrong. The only comfort, the only solace, I have been given *is* that portrait. It is the only hope.

"So perhaps the crown will have no value, or much less value, than I might have assigned it; crowns are pretentious things. I did not know who it was for until I heard that you had come to our doors. I knew then. You hesitate."

She shrugged, uneasy. "I wouldn't dare the Winter lands for something as simple as a crown. I won't—I will never—wear it, and I can't think of anyone who might who would require it. Had you said—"

"Had I made something useful, you mean?" There was an edge to the question that had not been there before.

She closed her eyes. Opened them. She handed Gilafas the torch, and after a moment, he lifted his free hand to take it; it was no longer necessary. Snow illuminated the darkness: snow reflecting the silver of moonlight and the hanging veil of stars.

"You're *certain* you can return?" she asked him.

"I am. I never leave the reach, no matter where I wander. Only others can."

She was dressed for cold; the older man was not. He did not, however, seem to feel it, and after fifteen minutes, Jewel asked.

"Ah. I am wearing robes that Cessaly made," he replied. "Because it was cold. She made two: one for me, one for her. She did that often, and without thought. She did not want me to be cold, and perhaps—just perhaps—I complained. Finding her in the warrens of the reach could be an endeavor of hours, or even days in the single worst case."

That, Jewel thought, would be useful. Practical. That, she would have dared the winter for. And had Gilafas not said the crown or tiara was made from the leaves of her living trees, she would have let the crown lie. She would not forget that she was Terafin, ruler of the most significant of The Ten. She could not. Nor would any of her traveling companions. Anyone she was likely to encounter would not be impressed—in any way—by a crown; it would be insignificant, as almost all things mortal were.

But she glanced at Gilafas; some of the butterflies still clung to his robe at the shoulders; one was perched in his receding hair. Two looked to be of spun glass, but one looked other. They had remained with him.

And if he had made butterflies, she thought. If he had made butterflies such as these, would she risk the howl of wind and the distant hooves that implied a host of riders?

She lifted her free hand, as if in question.

One butterfly—the one perched on the top of Gilafas' head, as if it were the only crown he was to be allowed—rose, its movement erratic as butterfly motions always were: fluttering and inexact. It flew lazily toward the hand she had lifted, landing in the cup of her palm.

Master Gilafas had been nearly casual about anything that had not involved his lost apprentice; he looked almost comically shocked now.

When the butterfly landed, however, she could hear what she had not heard before: its voice.

It was a soft voice—so soft it was a whisper in the wind's howl. Jewel shouldn't have been able to hear it at all; were it uttered by a person, she would have missed it entirely.

"Shadow can you hear—"

"Yesssssss." His eyes were focused on the butterfly, his tail twitching.

She listened. The voice did not have anything important to say, which was a terrible thing to think, but true. It was, on the other hand, light and joyful; it appeared to say, *look, look* as children do when they discover something for the first time. There was wonder, not in the butterfly's existence, but in the voice it now spoke with: wonder and awe.

Joy.

She was moved almost to tears, which surprised her. "These were made for you," she said softly to Gilafas, who had recovered some of his composure.

"Yes."

"She wanted you to know—she *wants* you to know—that she is alive, that she is happy."

"Yes. But, Terafin, I do not believe it. In public, I am successful, confident, powerful. That is one truth. I speak with the voice of a patrician. I interact with Kings when the mood strikes me. It is one part of my life—and I would not say it is the most significant although, to outsiders, it is. So, too, the butterflies. She is allowed *to make*. And she makes. This is the heart of it, her making: the wonder, the joy, the curiosity, the *drive*. This is what she tells me.

"But I do not know if she is allowed to make or she is forced to it. I do not know what she makes for the Winter Queen, if she makes for her at all; I do not know what the Winter Queen demands of her. I do not know if immortals understand that mortals must eat and sleep. I do not know if they understand that mortals seek—and require—understanding and affection."

Thinking of the Winter Queen, Jewel hesitated. "Affection? No," she finally said. "But she understands love. It is a Winter love; harsh and absolute. I think only the immortal could survive it." Thinking of Shianne, she added, voice softer, "and perhaps not even them. You've seen the Winter Queen."

Gilafas stiffened.

"I have," Jewel said, voice softer than even the butterfly's.

"And you survived."

"Yes. But . . . the memory of her, astride her mount, her gaze across the landscape as if it were an insignificant field of mortal battle—it's burned into my thoughts. I can see her, now, if I close my eyes. I can hear her voice. I think—" She hesitated. So much hesitation now. "I think it would be almost impossible not to love her. Not to want her. But . . ." she smiled down at the butterfly. "But I don't think Cessaly sees her the way I did."

"Is this relevant?"

"Yes. I think if we found Cessaly and persuaded the Winter Queen of the necessity, she *could* come home."

"You are not saying all of what you think or know."

"I ride a great stag," Jewel replied. "I call him the Winter King. Once, when the gods walked the world, he used to be human. Mortal. He can speak—but only to his rider, and at the moment, his rider is me. I have, in my service, a man who once rode with the Wild Hunt. He failed his Lady, and he was—was given to me. Both the stag and the warrior serve me. They serve me because that was her command.

"And they live, regardless, for the moment they might set eyes on her again. They serve willingly *because* it was the only thing that she demanded, in her anger.

"I don't know if Cessaly will want to leave the White Lady's side."

"They are—the stag, obviously, but the man—enchanted. Enspelled."

"Yes. But I do not think anyone—god or man—could now remove that enchantment. It is what they want. It is almost all they want. You could have dragged them away from the Winter Queen's side only by death—unless she ordered it. Nothing else would have moved them."

"You fear that Cessaly will be the same."

"I assumed she would," Jewel replied. She lifted her hand. "Now? I am uncertain. What she sees is what she makes, what she desires to make—and she could not ever create the Winter Queen."

"Who did?"

"Gods, probably. I don't know."

Gilafas inhaled sharply. Jewel looked up.

The maker was staring at the wrist she had exposed by lifting her hand to raise the butterfly. His eyes were wide, almost glassy; his mouth hung open, as if he had been in the process of speaking and had momentarily lost the ability or desire to form actual words.

He reached out almost involuntarily, and Jewel was once again reminded of children: he had that utter intensity of focus, as if nothing else existed or mattered.

She had never seen one of the maker-born at work before. The maker-born did not have public galleries in which the idle and the curious might watch them, as if watching an opera, a play. But she knew, she *knew*, that this was about to change, if she allowed it.

She did not withdraw her wrist, did not offer him warning.

He moved toward her, stood, his face inches from what was twined around her wrist in a near-invisible braiding: the three strands of the Winter Queen's hair. She had called them a gift and felt in truth that they must have been—but they had not been offered. She had, mouth dry, reached almost blindly for Ariane—as if she were a child—and her hand had brushed the Winter Queen's hair.

These three strands had remained in her otherwise empty palm.

He did not ask her where she had come by them. He did not ask her why she carried them. He did not ask anything at all for another long moment.

"Terafin. Give them to me." It was a demand. It was a plea.

"They are mine," she replied, with neither force nor heat.

"Yes, of course. But they are not what they must be. Can you not see it? Can you not understand?"

Jewel did not see what Gilafas saw. Would not see it, she thought, until he was finished. But she did not want to part from these strands. Had been told that she must never do so.

And yet, she thought, this was a dream, a half-dream.

"I cannot leave without them," she said. "I need them to find—"

"Cessaly, yes. You will need them. But they will not serve your purpose yet."

She hesitated, and the hesitation was bone-deep, visceral. These were the only things of Ariane, beyond memory, she had. The only proof.

No stunning insight returned to her. No certainty that this was what she must do. She was left adrift, her desire to keep these strands of hair at odds with every other thought that clamored for attention. She did not *know* that she must part with them.

She did not want to let them go.

"I can't untwine the braiding," she finally said, her voice thick.

Gilafas frowned. "What do you mean?"

"I mean what I said."

"With your permission, Terafin?"

It was like a question, but his hands—larger, callused, older—had already begun the work she had said she could not do. As if in speaking, in commenting at all, she had given him the answer he desired.

Shadow hissed but did not harm Gilafas—and Jewel wasn't certain at the moment that the guildmaster even noticed the presence of the great, gray cat.

"I could *make him* notice *me*."

"Please," she said, and her voice trembled, "don't."

"*Why* do you *care*? It is *only* hair, and it is *ugly* hair."

Jewel, accustomed to the cats, said, "Yes. That is true. I'm certain I would value your feathers far more highly."

Shadow hissed. Hissing, he raised his wings as if he intended to swat her— or worse, the guildmaster—with them. And from the shadows of those great wings, which seemed—for a moment—to be larger and more complete than even those of the Warden of Dreams in nightmare, she heard the rumbling roar of things so ancient and wild she was frozen in place.

And yet, even so, she heard Cessaly's tiny, soft voice of delight, and she held her ground. Gilafas had not heard the roaring, but he had seen the raised wings; he turned toward them, and toward Shadow, and Jewel realized that he was done. He had extracted his three strands, and they lay against his palm as they had once lain against her own.

His eyes were narrow now, as if he could almost see the shape of something in the shadows but could not quite make out what it was.

And then he bent knees and reached out; Jewel couldn't see what he was reaching for until he held it in his hands.

It was a feather.

It was a gray feather.

She was not surprised—and should have been—when the next feather he gathered was white, and the one after, black. She was slightly surprised when he bowed—to Shadow—and asked his permission to take what he had just picked up. And maybe it was required.

Shadow sniffed, however, as if listening to the guildmaster was tedious beyond endurance and shooed him away with his wing; the guildmaster bowed again and retreated, carrying all three feathers. He then turned and left Jewel; he had retrieved the hand he had offered her so that she might not be lost.

He was lost, she realized, in a fashion; she followed instantly, remembering what he had said of Cessaly and her making—her work—in this place. She did not want to lose Gilafas.

"You *can't*," Shadow said.

"I can," Jewel said grimly. "But I don't intend to."

He did not walk into the snow. For that, she was grateful. Although she appeared to carry her pack, she did not have the wide net for boots that made snow such as this passable—but neither did Gilafas. He seemed to forget that she was with him or had been with him; he moved—he strode—with purpose, his hands close to his chest, cupping the materials that he had gathered.

She reminded herself to breathe; she was uneasy, and not because the halls suddenly shifted, the prior architecture, which evoked crypts—and, at that, old, disused ones—vanishing almost between one step and the next. But unlike the snows of winter, into which the first halls had been nestled, this new stretch was almost like a public gallery, an open thoroughfare through which even the most monied or pompous might feel at home.

Light fell from high windows; the day could enter, but the eye—at Jewel's height, and even Gilafas'—could not gaze out.

Gilafas did not seem to notice.

Shadow, however, did.

"Do you recognize these halls?" she asked.

He sniffed, which probably meant no. "Fabril was *dangerous*," he said. "It is a *good* thing he is *dead*."

She stiffened, but the guildmaster did not appear to have heard the cat. It was a small mercy, but Jewel had learned to be grateful for them. "Was Fabril more dangerous than I am?" she asked. It took her mind off the constant itch in her hands; she wanted Ariane's gift back and had to fight the impulse to grab Gilafas and extract it. Since her return from the distant south, she had carried those three strands of hair with her everywhere.

She did not want them in Gilafas' hands.

But she also thought that this was where they must be. It was like, and unlike, crossing a very dark room in order to pick up a dagger and stab herself in, or around, the heart. Every instinct in her—all the instincts she had always obeyed without thought—had screamed against it, until she was all but paralyzed. She knew, at that time, that she had to force herself to walk, to work against those visceral instincts.

It was simpler here. She did not feel that those strands of hair, in Gilafas' hands, were an immediate threat to her life or her sanity. But their absence invoked the specter of both loss and its attendant grief.

Perhaps because she was seer-born, had always been seer-born, it had never been her own death that she'd feared. It had always been the deaths of others, the sense of abandonment that came in the wake of those deaths.

She almost walked into Gilafas' back; he had stopped moving abruptly. She stopped; Shadow collided with her—probably on purpose. When he did not feel endangered, he was sulky. No, that wasn't fair. When he did not feel that *she* was endangered, he was sulky.

"Why did you let him take the feathers?" she whispered. Gilafas appeared to be staring intently into the empty air directly in front of him. "This won't do," the older man finally said.

He turned. There were no other doors and no other halls that Jewel could see. She wondered if he meant to take them back to the crypts, as she now thought of the winter halls.

"They are not crypts," Gilafas said, as if Jewel had spoken the words out loud. She reddened; she probably had. "They are winter halls. But, Terafin, there is life that remains in the winter. There is life that the trees hold, the ground hides; it is merely waiting for summer. The winter is deep in this place; not for the promise of false summer will such life stir."

"But—where are we going? Why have you stopped?"

"It is never wise, in Fabril's reach, to step outside. I have seen the truth of that myself. It is why—it is how—Cessaly was lost. I am willing to be lost," he added softly, "but not yet. And I do not think I wish to lose you the same way."

She shook her head. "I'm already lost, Gilafas. To me, this is a dream."

He nodded absently.

"When I wake, I will be where I was when I went to sleep. Will you get lost?"

"No. It is not yet my time."

She frowned. "Your time?"

"Artisans—unlike the maker-born—do not die. They simply vanish one day. The pages cannot find them—no one can." He shook himself. "Come. This is not the place for us; I am not quite sure why we are here." This last was said apologetically.

Shadow hissed in annoyance; his body practically quivered in outrage. He stalked across the very fine floor, leaving marks in the stained wood and worse in the carpet runners that protected most of it.

"It is *here*," he said, adding a growl to the end of the sentence as he lifted a wing. "*Here.*"

Gilafas followed the direction of the cat's wing, and his expression lightened instantly. "My apologies," he told the cat. "I had all but forgotten. Yes. It is here."

Jewel was staring at a pedestal in a carefully placed alcove that had been built across from one of the high windows through which light streamed. That light now fell on something that had not, until Shadow's interruption, caught her attention, so intent had she been on what Gilafas was carrying in his hands.

Atop the pedestal, on a small ivory cushion, sat a gleaming piece of jewelry.

It was, or appeared to be, all of gold until Jewel approached more closely; there was gem-work here, but the gems were small and subtly placed; they were not meant to be the centerpiece of the work but, rather, simple adornment.

It wasn't a crown.

It was a tiara.

She wondered how different they were, to the wilderness and the ancient and wild creatures who occupied those hidden lands. She was silent, still, considering the crown, the guildmaster, the great gray cat, the nature of dreams. Anything but fear.

Fear was there. Fear had become a constant companion, although perhaps that wasn't true. Fear had always been a constant companion, but as a child, as a much younger woman, she had believed that with enough power, she could know a life free from that fear.

"Yes," Gilafas said. "It was made for you."

She did not move.

"Terafin, I cannot touch it now." Hearing her sudden intake of breath, he added, "My hands are occupied. I do not wish to drop anything."

"What—what does it do?"

He shook his head. "It is like—it is a little like—my stained glass. I do not fully know what it will do, what it might do. I do not know if you will wear it, or if you are intended to convey it to someone else who might. But it was made of the leaves of your forest. It is either yours or no one's."

Shadow growled. "*Take* it, or I will *eat* it. You are *wasting* time."

She took the tiara. To her surprise, the light that had illuminated it had also warmed it; it was not cool to the touch.

Gilafas nodded. He then began to walk forward again. She didn't understand why he no longer feared to reach an exit, for he approached the same door that had been the terminal point of the gallery. He nodded to Jewel, and she opened it with her free hand. It led into a room.

It led into a workroom, the interior of which reminded Jewel instantly of Haval's workroom. She could not tell, for a moment, what the floor was made of because she couldn't see it. There were, however, two long benches against the wall farthest from the door, and these at least were of wood and had space for one tired seer.

"I will ask you to wait," Gilafas said, without pausing for an acknowledgment.

And so, she waited. She sat on one bench, and Shadow sat on the floor beside her legs. The gray cat cleared space for himself with a petulant litany of complaints, tossing the bits and pieces of paper and wire and beads to the side. Gilafas was not Haval. He didn't appear to notice or care. He cleared space at his own workbench; he threw paper to the left of what was a large, flat table-top. Some of it fluttered to the ground, to be instantly forgotten.

He laid the feathers with care to the left, in the space he had just cleared. The strands of hair—which should have been invisible at this distance—he placed directly before him. He then reached beneath the table and opened a drawer Jewel hadn't been aware existed until that moment. Surprised, she did acknowledge that this was a maker's guild, and the things the maker-born made didn't have to conform to expectation, or even reality.

The butterfly was perched on her shoulder. It had not left her. Nor had it fallen silent—until now. The soft, attenuated whisper of its voice vanished so suddenly she could hear its absence as if silence were merely a different language.

There was excitement in the hush, anticipation, the held breath of unexpected hope. Silences were hard to read, but sometimes they said more than words could. Jewel thought she wanted to meet the girl—the woman—who had created this butterfly. She could understand, in the silence, that she was capable of a great joy; that creativity, that creation, *was* joy in some fashion to her, no matter the cost.

Shadow sniffed.

"Is he like Snow?" she asked the gray cat. "I watched Snow weave a dress from nothing." The dress Shianne still wore. It was impervious to cold, damp, or fire, at the very least. When Shadow failed to answer, she continued. "You said only mortals are maker-born."

Silence.

"But . . . Snow made that dress. I think he made the one he gave to me the same way. How is that not making?"

"It is different," the cat said. "What we make is *part* of us. It is not made as you make. The old man will give you what he makes. He will not lose himself or part of himself in it.

"You have children," he continued, without his usual whine.

"I don't."

"Your *kind* has children. But they do not have children the way *she* does. They *cannot*. They create, and what they create is *part of them*."

"But—"

"If, for every child a mortal had, he was forced to cut off a finger or a hand to bring it to life—his *own* finger, his *own* hand—it would be similar. But not the same."

Jewel stared, not at the maker, but at the cat. "Are you—are you telling me that Shianne is *wearing part of Snow?*"

Shadow hissed and muttered a very soft *stupid*. "What did you *think* the dress was? Mortals are *stupid*."

"Shianne had to have a child the mortal way so that the child would not be of her."

"Yes. But that is *not* our strength. She *could not* do it and remain as she was. You think we are strange? She has given up eternity—and the child will be weak and stupid, and it will die. She will leave *nothing* in the world."

Jewel laid a trembling palm on the top of Shadow's head. "Enough."

"It is *different* for *you*. You have no *choice*."

Watching Gilafas, Jewel said, "Does he? Did Cessaly?" And when Shadow failed to answer, she asked, "If I return the dress to Snow, can he unmake it? Can he take it back into himself?" She better understood Shianne's awe and wonder at the dress Snow had made. And she bitterly regretted asking it of him without understanding the cost. That was the difficulty with her strange company of mortals and the immortal, the wild, the ancient. Even if they shared a language, or could, the familiar words they used meant something entirely different. Other.

"He made *your* dress. He *wanted* to make it."

". . . And he made Shianne's dress."

Shadow was silent.

"And it was my fault."

"Yesssssss." Shadow's gaze was now upon Gilafas. "But the old man does not make as Snow makes; he makes as mortals do. As mortals would, were they gods. Watch him, Terafin."

The butterfly whispered, trembling with excitement, and Jewel rose from the bench. Snow's work was magic, magical; it was an act of concerted will, a demand that the very air surrender the materials he needed with which to work, to create. Gilafas could not, or did not, do that. Not precisely.

But the leaves—yes, there were more leaves, these of gold—that he took seemed too light, too fine, to be of substantial use. Only the feathers seemed large enough, strong enough, to survive craftsmanship.

A thought occurred to her. "Shadow—your feathers—"

"Yes?"

"Is it like—are they—"

He butted her, shaking his head. "You are *soooo stupid*."

"And her—her hair? Is it like that, too?"

Gilafas said, as if he had heard and been part of the entire conversation,

"No, Terafin. Can you not see it? It is both more and less intimate. They have surrendered a part of themselves to you, to do with as you see fit. It is not creation as they deem it. Creation is an act of deliberation, of choice. You lose your hair," he added mildly. "So do normal cats.

"But the Wild Hunt does not. Hunters shed blood," he continued. "And they, like mortals, will die from the loss of it—but perhaps not for the same reason. They are immortal; time cannot or will not touch them. But they are not invulnerable."

Something about his voice was strange; the cadence was different. He spoke without the weariness, the pain, that had shadowed all his words and expressions since she had arrived.

"Who are you?"

The butterfly stiffened and shut its wings.

He spoke as if he had not heard her question. "The three strands of hair are of Ariane. The three feathers are of the eldest. Mortals have possessed at least the latter before."

Shadow growled.

"But those feathers were seldom surrendered peacefully, and most did not survive the attempt to take them."

"Why would they even want—" She shut her mouth.

"The Winter King had feathers from the three. He had, of course, seen them before; they are not fond of the Wild Hunt, and the Winter Queen is not fond of them, not precisely. What he did with the feathers, I cannot fully say; I was not there.

"But what you have, you were given."

"Gilafas was given. What Gilafas has, Gilafas was given."

"Pedantry changes no facts. The cat would not have surrendered the feathers if he was not certain that what was to be made of them would become, in some fashion, yours."

"And the hair?" she asked softly.

"Had she not desired to leave you some token of her regard, they would not have remained in your hand. I expect she did not think you would understand the significance. She is beautiful, as a force of nature is beautiful—she understands that this has some effect on mortals. But she has not become beautiful in order to have this effect.

"The regard of mortals was never necessary to her survival. The enmity of mortals was insignificant, except in the great Cities of Man. She did not care how she was seen by you. And yet, in the palm of your hand, she left three strands of hair. You cannot be either Summer or Winter King. She had reasons of her own for leaving some small part of herself in your hands.

"But you have never parted from them."

Jewel lowered her head. "No."

"Until now."

". . . Yes."

Even speaking, Gilafas had not turned to face her; his gnarled and callused hands had never once ceased their almost rhythmic, deliberate movements.

As they caught her eye, she watched. He wasn't Snow. He physically melted the golden leaves; he did not touch—not yet—the leaves of diamond, although Jewel was certain that they would be of no use.

Slowly, slowly, the butterfly on her shoulder once again exposed the interior color of its wings.

This time, Jewel asked no questions, although she had many. She did not know what he would make but wondered if he had known before he stood in front of this worktable. It seemed to her, as he returned to the drawer that shouldn't have existed, that he wasn't trying to find the exact things he needed; he seemed to be staring at what he had, as if waiting for it to speak, to tell him what was lacking.

"This is *boring*," Shadow said.

She didn't agree.

But when he drew the vial from the drawer, the Artisan froze. Lifting it, he considered it, his expression shadowed by a memory of events to which she was not privy.

Shadow hissed. He wasn't angry, but he wasn't mocking, either.

"Eldest?" For the first time, he turned to face his witnesses.

"*You* make," Shadow countered. "You decide."

"You know what this is."

"Yesssssss."

He set the vial back in the drawer—or tried. Jewel saw his look of consternation, followed slowly by one of resignation. "You seem young, to me," Gilafas finally said. "You should not be here. You should be at home, among kin. But the longest shadows are falling, Terafin; you at least should be able to see them."

Jewel said nothing.

"Can you see what casts those shadows?" He set the vial beside the hair. "There is death here, war here. In all of these things. Do you understand it?"

"The war?"

"War itself."

"Yes."

"Good. Only in your leaves do I see something other than echoes of, eddies of, ancient wars—and even then, the wars define their shape. We must know how to fight," he added, so softly Jewel had to strain to catch the words. "And we must know when it is futile."

"Who are you?" Jewel asked again.

"Gilafas," he replied.

"You said—"

"And more. He will be aware of what has happened here, and he will accept it. But it is his power that makes; that power is no longer mine. It is said only Artisans inhabit Fabril's reach. Understand that the difference between Artisan and Sen is very, very small when the world's power is at its zenith. What I make, you could make, albeit in a very different fashion."

Jewel shook her head.

"Ah. Not yet? No, not yet." He fell silent; he did not speak again, not while he worked. Jewel found it difficult to watch him yet couldn't say why.

Shadow sauntered over to Gilafas' side. "*Why* are you making *that?*"

Gilafas did not answer. He wasn't ignoring the cat; he had not heard him.

"Shadow."

"It is *boring.*"

"Could Snow do this?"

Shadow hissed.

And Jewel thought of the necklace she wore. Had Snow been able to craft jewelry, he would not have had to steal it. She pulled the pendant from the folds of cloth that kept it hidden; light flooded the room, almost blinding her.

"Where did you get *that?*"

She had, once again, interrupted Gilafas at his work.

"From one of my cats," she replied, blinking, blinking again. "Do you recognize it?"

"You should not have it." Which was similar to "yes" but far more forbidding. "Where did your cat get it?"

She cringed. "He made me the dress you saw. You remember it?"

". . . Yes." There was more reverence in this word.

"He hated all my jewelry. He hated all of Finch's. He couldn't stand— I can't remember his exact words. But he insisted I wear something worthy of his dress, and then he went to find it."

The silence was shocked, choked. And yet, through it, the man who was guildmaster and Artisan and, also, other moved.

"I want to return it," she added. Theft had saved her young life, and the lives of her den but this theft had been unnecessary.

"You cannot, now. It is done, Terafin; if there is a price to pay, you will pay it. I am sorry."

He came to stand before her. Without permission, almost without aware- ness, he cupped the gem between his palms. His face was gray, grave. "I will take this," he told her. "Perhaps it will doom you; perhaps it will save you." Before she could reply, he had removed the necklace. "Stay, now, where you are. The eldest is free to go as he pleases; his nature is fixed. I will tell you when it is safe to move—if it becomes so."

"Gilafas, even the firstborn—the children of gods—would not willingly touch this necklace."

"No. They are wise. But they are not desperate—and we are. One does not take pointless risks, Terafin." Light seemed to wash the age from his face, his expression, it was so bright. But he did not squint, did not blink. He returned to his table and set the gem down, where it pulsed faintly, like a beating crys- tal heart.

He then ignored it while he made.

She saw the ring take form and shape; it was a simple band. Words appeared to be written on it; she could see them from where she sat, and it made her uneasy. She could not read them. But words, she thought, were written on the inner face as well.

He made only one ring, but he was not yet finished; he set the ring aside with care and began again. The second creation was a chain—a necklace, she thought, given its length. There was nothing delicate about it, nothing fragile; the links were oddly formed and locked together. The third was a bracelet; unlike the chain, it was solid, and hinged, the gold thick. It might have resem- bled a manacle, but the craftsmanship was too fine. Into this last, gems were set, all of one color: green.

And then, when the three were done, he returned to the necklace Snow had stolen. "Understand," he told her softly, "that even the ancient valued the Artisanal. Understand," he continued, "that groveling and abasement will avail *nothing*." And so saying, he gestured sharply and brought the flat of both palms down.

The gem shattered.

* * *

She could not say what he had done, not then, and not later. His hands had been—and remained—empty. She had handled the necklace, but seldom; she had taken it on the road with her only because she feared to leave it behind. She feared its unknown owner might descend upon her House in her absence, hunting the thief.

She did not scream; she did not speak. Words deserted her.

But as she watched, the light that had shone so brightly here and almost nowhere else did not disperse; it seemed to be a living thing, set free from a crystal cage. It moved, a miniature sun; it scorched the tabletop, without seeming intent.

She was rigid, frozen. Gilafas had ordered her to remain where she was; it was superfluous. She could not move now. Her body had locked itself in place, her seer's instincts screaming her into immobility.

Gilafas began to sing or to keen; as he did, the butterfly resting upon her shoulder pushed itself up and off. It fluttered its way to Gilafas, to his table, and when it reached that table, it landed.

"Not you," he whispered, looking down, his face hidden, his odd song paused. He did not pick his song up again, but the butterfly did—in its whisper-thin, childlike voice. "Not you," he said again. But he made no attempt to remove the butterfly, no attempt to preserve it as the white light moved inexorably over its folded wings.

Everything in Jewel Markess strained against the imperative to remain seated: everything. But the butterfly was *not* a child, and not hers, and it had—in some fashion—chosen. She understood that an Artisan had crafted it, had assumed that it had one purpose, and one alone. She understood that to save the butterfly was not to save an actual life—but that understanding was not visceral.

The butterfly, however, was not destroyed by the light; it seemed to absorb it, to drink it in. As if that light were jealous, possessive, it consumed the original color of the wings, and left white behind. But the butterfly did not melt or shatter, although it was made of glass.

It could not and did not absorb all the radiance of the light; much diminished, that light continued its passage across the table and across the three items so newly made. At each, it left some of its essential brilliance behind, none so dramatically as the butterfly. Only at the last—the ring itself—did it gutter.

The butterfly returned to Jewel, then.

"These, also, are yours, Terafin. You must take them."

"What do they do?"

"Lie," he replied. "Where you travel, it is the ring that will keep you safe from all but a handful of enemies."

"How?"

"It will tell them the cost of your death; they are ancient, and they will understand. Only those who feel they can escape the Winter's reach will act against you without provocation."

"And the other things?"

"I am maker, not seer. They have a role to play, but it is not clear—to me. Perhaps you will come to an understanding of it, perhaps not. You are not required to take what I have made; it is a gift."

She understood that there was a future in each of these things that touched hers. "And—and this?" she asked, indicating the butterfly that had returned to her shoulder.

"It will accompany you, I fear."

"But it's yours!"

"Yes. It was made for me, but all things made have an existence of their own. Perhaps, in time, it will return to me. Perhaps it will return, instead, to its maker, carrying within it a gift, a light she might craft into her next making."

Jewel looked at the items she had been given, at the gift of hair that had been returned to her, unrecognizable. She turned the ring over, examined the odd writing around both its inner and outer faces, and then slid it over a finger on her left hand. The ring fit perfectly; it was warm.

The chain, much thicker than the chain she had previously worn, she returned to its place around her neck; she was surprised at the weight of it, the thickness. It disappeared into the folds of her layered clothing. The bracelet she contemplated for a long moment. Of the three pieces, it was the most ornate; of the three it was the only one into which he had worked gems, glittering pieces of color and clarity that nonetheless suggested beauty was hard. She studied it carefully, saw that it was etched in some fashion with lines that implied leaves, possibly flowers; they were faint and dependent on the light.

This one, in the end, she slid into her pack, where it clinked against the tiara.

The purpose of the three items was not clear to her, but she understood that at the heart of the ring, a strand of perfect platinum was somehow encased. It was hers, and until and unless she set the ring aside, it was safe.

"You will return to me, Terafin, when next you return to Averalaan while you wake."

She nodded. "You have my word."

Jewel woke to the light of the butterfly, which rested on her chest, wings spread as if to alleviate the Oracle's darkness. She was not alone. Adam was sitting by her side, both of his hands cupped around her right hand. The left, which lay above the thick covers, bore a new ring.

The necklace was not around her waking neck; the bracelet, and the tiara were not in the pack into which she'd placed them in the dream that was not a dream. *Gilafas*, she thought. She knew that she must return to him—if she could return at all.

Chapter Eleven

"COUNCILLOR, WERE YOU AWARE that Jewel paid us a visit?"
Haval, standing beneath the benign flames of the tree of fire, glanced toward his feet. Of the elders—or eldest, as they were often called—that dwelled within Jewel's lands, this one concerned him most. He knelt. It was not a gesture of obeisance; Haval would not grovel before any of the wild powers that inhabited Jewel's lands. He did not serve them, and he did not wish to confuse the issue of position, if he could be said to have one.

The golden fox, however, disdained to shout, and if he was the wrong color for a fox, he was otherwise the right shape and size. He therefore preferred to be carried, as it brought his mouth closer to people's ears. Haval understood that preference was not necessity, and the fox did not demand it; he merely waited upon the expected courtesy as if he were a fussy, elderly aunt.

Haval considered the fact that cats were also accorded the title of Eldest. It was surprisingly difficult for Haval to remember that the cats were ancient, wild, powerful. But he did remember. He had watched the white cat, Snow, weave a dress out of literal air. The memory did not dim with time; instead, like legend, it grew brighter, larger.

"You really ought not to carry him like that," a familiar voice said.

Haval didn't bother to turn; he did, however, raise a brow at the golden fox who now curled in his arms. "I am expecting a guest," he said, the severity in tone aimed entirely at Jarven.

"And here I am."

"A guest, Jarven. I do not believe I included your name on the invitation, such as it was." He exhaled. To the fox, he said, "Has he shown promise as a student?"

"Remarkable promise," the fox said. "But I find him exhausting—the young often are."

"And I am not young, Eldest?"

"You wish me to say that, to me, you are all children, is that it?" The fox smiled, or at least exposed his small, perfect teeth. "And I would, Councillor, but some are born old."

Jarven laughed. His laughter was infused with the type of delight that generally meant a man's ruin—a man who was not Jarven, of course.

"Finch is expecting you at the Authority building today."

"Ah, yes. Did you know that I can walk there from here without ever touching the city streets?"

"I had heard, yes."

"You should try it. You never know when it might come in useful."

"I cannot travel as you do, as you are well aware."

"Am I?"

"If you are not, you are being deliberately obtuse—and I am an old, busy man with a very short supply of patience."

"When this guest arrives, he is not to be harmed," Haval told Jarven. There was no humor or inflection in the words. Some words spoke of hidden depths; Haval's now spoke of endless, impenetrable walls. He had not otherwise shifted position.

"Does she understand what he is?" the fox asked.

"I have not asked, Eldest."

"I was under the impression that you ask far too many questions, yet you answer far too few." The fox's reply set Jarven chuckling again.

"If you wish my opinion, I will give it; the opinion is not a promise and not a guarantee."

"Very well."

"Yes, I believe she understands what—or who—Andrei is. It is entirely irrelevant to her. She once offered home and shelter to the living daughter of the god we do not name. She is aware of danger; she believes, because she is seerborn, that she can circumvent most of it."

"That is not wise."

"No—but as you have pointed out, the young are exhausting." He turned, then, to face Jarven. To the eye, Jarven had not magically shed years; he was still an old man. But there was, about the whole of him, a restless, enterprising energy that he had lacked this past decade. Only his eyes seemed instantly different to Haval; they were lighter and warmer in color than they had once been. They were not Birgide Viranyi's eyes. They might be called hazel, a notoriously imprecise description.

Haval measured the man standing before him in a dispassionate fashion, as if he were a cut of cloth, a suit, a dress. "Your eyes."

"Yes. It is a bit of an issue, but you know as well as I that almost no one will mark the difference a sentence after I've opened my mouth."

It was true. "The Merchant Authority?"

"I will go. The travel is practice. I will not tell you where I arrived in the city the first time I tried it. Apparently, there was hilarity." He looked down his nose at the fox, who looked up to meet his gaze.

"You must admit, Jarven, it was amusing."

"Not for me, and not for the other people I so rudely interrupted. I am, however, glad to know that some joy was taken somewhere." He lifted his head at the same moment the fox did.

Haval noted both.

"Why did you not desire what he desires?" the fox asked, genuinely curious.

"I cannot be *of* the forest and of my own life; the two would not mix well." Haval smiled, and added, "I am what, and who, I am. I am old and set in my ways."

"You do not enjoy the game."

"I enjoy it some of the time; it is a test of wit, of observational skill, of knowledge. But I am not a casual gambler, Eldest. The stakes must be very, very high if you wish me to sit at the table."

"And these are suitably high," Jarven added, his voice softer.

"Have you found Rymark?" Haval asked. Jarven did not even blink.

"I do not believe he is currently resident in the city. The forest's boundaries define the reach of my newly acquired skills."

"You might leave," the fox told him. "There are some things you will no longer be able to see or feel—but that is the way of the land. There are roads like the Terafin roads; they are owned by others. If you wish to pass through those lands—"

"I must ask and receive permission."

"Was he always this prickly?" the fox asked Haval.

"He was not considered prickly at all," Haval replied. "Nor is he considered prickly now."

"How is he seen?"

"With the exception of a very few, most view him as an increasingly scattered old man, long past his prime."

The fox's brows rose and drew together; it made the creature look disconcertingly human. "And this does not anger him?"

"He has, and has always had, his pride. But to find it disturbing at all, he would have to care about the opinions of others."

"Ah."

"Haval exaggerates, of course," Jarven said. "I care very much about the opinions of others."

Haval raised a brow. "When your plans require a specific opinion, yes. The accuracy of either your presentation or that opinion is otherwise irrelevant."

"Haval, on the other hand," Jarven continued, "has always been this prickly."

"I like his cunning," the golden fox said, ignoring Jarven's interruption. "I like his intensity. He *eats* risk."

"Yes. And on occasion lives—not, of course, his own."

"Ah, Councillor. We understand that Jewel does not trust him. But we understand that Finch does. And we understand that Jewel trusts Finch enough that she is willing to accept him—and that is enough for me."

Haval said nothing for a long beat. "Understand that you will have some competition."

Jarven's frown was mercurial. "I am not you," he said, voice as sharp as it might have been in his distant youth. "If something is worth having, it is worth fighting for—and many will."

"Ah. I mean only that Haerrad is searching for Rymark. Unlike yourself, he is free to travel; he cannot walk these roads and must, therefore, make do with the ones he has traveled all his life. It is my belief that he will find Rymark first, if you wish to devote your ferocious energy into more useful activities."

The fox lifted its chin and then turned its face to better see Haval's expression.

"Have I misspoken?" the tailor asked the fox, with far more respect in his voice.

"I cannot decide," was the slow reply. "You are Councillor for a reason."

"Yes. The Terafin."

"Ah. No—if it were just The Terafin, many might fill your complicated position. We were undecided," he added.

"You wished for Jarven?"

Furry brows rose alarmingly quickly. "*I* wished for him, yes—but *not* as Councillor. I might as well bite off my own tail!"

Jarven laughed. Haval heard, in it, the youth that was absent in every other visible way.

"He is cunning. He is bright. He is fast. He is both fearless and cautious—and that is highly unusual in the wilderness. He lies as if lies were truth; he tells truths as if he were dissembling. Also: I liked his jacket."

Haval was patience itself with the creature he cradled in his arms.

"He sees what you see, Councillor—but his grasp and his reach are different. You know that he must find Rymark first."

"I did not," Haval demurred.

"I do not believe you," the fox replied, unoffended. "Jarven is less certain. I have set him a task that is close to The Terafin's heart. He must find Rymark, and he must finish him. He will return to me with proof that the deed is done."

"Jewel would not countenance this." Haval's voice was flat and quiet; it was very much like walls.

"Yes, Councillor, she would. Do you doubt us? Do you doubt what we perceive? Here, we feel her rage, her fury. We feel her fear. We feel her desire."

Haval seemed singularly unimpressed. In truth, he was, and did not scruple to hide it, although he considered it prudent to soften its edges. "Eldest, you are immortal and eternal. You do not understand the slow walk of man from birth to death—but every step we take is on that road.

"When we begin, we are infants—but helpless. We cannot speak. We cannot eat; we drink, or we starve. We cannot think. But we can feel. The feelings come first."

The fox glanced at Jarven. Jarven's expression was uncharacteristically sober—which meant nothing or should have meant nothing. He was the master of artifice. But so, too, was Haval Arwood.

"When we can walk, we are still too small and weak to even open doors on our own. We struggle to master language; to speak at all. We learn to think, but it is slow."

"Some do not bother," Jarven added, sounding a trifle bored.

"We feel, even then."

"And your point?"

"The march to adulthood, to power, to competence, is our ability to *master* those feelings, those emotions. They are part of us from birth—but if they master us, instead, we will hold power for a brief, brief time, if at all. Jewel has long loathed Rymark. She has long suspected his hand in the death of the woman who once ruled these lands. She has, as you rightly discern, been beyond simple anger.

"And yet she has not once had Rymark assassinated. She has the power and the tools at hand to do so, and she has had them for some time. Why do you think Rymark lives?"

"You do not think she would have him hunted down, then?" The fox sounded doubtful.

"I think she would surrender him to the Kings or the magi. She would withdraw his House Name. But even then, I am not certain she would send someone to kill him."

"But you are not certain she would not."

"Given the events at dinner, and the possession of Haerrad, no. I am less certain. But it is my belief she would surrender Rymark, and knowledge of him, to the Kings and Sigurne Mellifas first."

Jarven cleared his throat. "This is all very well, Haval—but as you have aged, you have become almost determined to waste my time. What The Terafin wants is the safety of her House and her den. I have a particular fondness for one or two of the den myself, which signifies little. The House Council will see Rymark stripped of his name before the week is out."

"If The Terafin is not present, the Council's vote must be unanimous."

"Indeed. But Haerrad is the driving force behind that vote. He is enraged, and the whole of his focus is turned toward this one thing: Rymark. The demons are almost a secondary concern. Rymark will no longer be ATerafin by the week's end. Do you doubt me? Who would you expect to vote against? Abstentions will, by Council rule, not affect the outcome of that vote—unless the abstentions outnumber the actual votes cast.

"Can the House afford to devote the financial resources to such a hunt in the current climate? The Merchants' Guild is sewn together by very fine, very delicate threads—it could disintegrate at a moment. There are shortages of everything—food being the primary concern—and scarcity has caused an unfortunate rise in prices. There is panic, Haval. There is fear. A man of Haerrad's temperament is accustomed to fear, and the fearful; his attention at this time could be more effectively—and more constructively—spent."

"You almost move me with your reasoning," Haval said.

"And instead I have made you unduly suspicious."

"Yes, actually."

"You did not know me in my distant youth."

"No, perhaps not; you did not know me in mine."

"And a good thing, I think, in both cases; I am not certain we would be standing here now if we had. I have been tasked with Rymark's death. It has been a long time since I have killed a man."

"Or had a man killed?"

"Ah, that is different. I see you are determined to be tiresome."

"It is a character failing. Very well." He exhaled, losing inches and stiffness. The fox regarded them both with bright, inquisitive eyes. "My approval is not required—nor has it ever been, in your case. But for what it's worth, I accede. Find Rymark. Test your wings. But, Jarven—you have work to do that is at least as valuable. If the merchants are hanging together in such a fragile condition, you have been the thread that binds them."

"Oh, indeed. But I am a frail, tired old man, and the continuous burden of making my way to the Order of Knowledge—where all the primary meetings are currently being held at the largesse of Sigurne Mellifas—is too much for me. I have, therefore, found a reasonable replacement. I will find Rymark."

"I ask only one small concession."

"Yes?"

"Kill him cleanly."

"Haval, that is dangerously sentimental, coming from you. Dead is, after all, dead."

"Were he not ATerafin, it would be. There are things Jewel will accept—she is pragmatic, after all—and things she will not, not easily. As the entirety of the Isle is currently subject to her state of mind, it is unwise in the extreme to needlessly upset her."

"And at need?"

Haval did not reply.

"I would like," Andrei said, his expression so pinched and sour Hectore actually laughed, "to strangle Jarven and have done." He had taken up his position by the table, and his expression was scaring away the rest of the inn's servants.

"You must admit that he looks somewhat wan and fragile these days." Hectore, his erstwhile master, was seated, of course. He had taken the opportunity to have a glass of wine; Andrei did not drink often, and almost never in Hectore's presence.

"He looks wan and fragile while he's cheating men out of their fortunes in the name of Terafin."

"True, true. Come. You disliked—intensely, that I recall—leaving the governance of the guild in Jarven's hands. The governance of the guild has now been placed in mine—I cannot see the cause for your concern."

"You might recall the fate of the previous guildmaster?"

"Indeed," Hectore replied, without blanching. "But I will not be guildmaster, any more than Jarven is. I will be a steadying hand."

Andrei grimaced. "What does he gain from this?"

"Andrei, please. Jarven has been bored for the past two decades; I have only recently come to realize how much. He is not bored, now—and he is not looking at us. We are not his targets."

"You know what he intends to do," Andrei said.

"I do not know for certain; we have not discussed it. I have suspicions, yes—but where Jarven is concerned anyone sane and experienced has almost nothing but suspicion. Which, I suppose, would explain your current attitude."

24th day of Morel, 428 A.A.
Order of Knowledge, Averalaan Aramarelas

Eva Juwal was a thundercloud.

Sigurne Mellifas was a delicate, tired old woman. A brief glance between them would not indicate any similarity of tone, of upbringing, of commonality.

"I would rather deal with that murderous, half-senile bastard—"

"Eva, please."

"You know how I feel about Hectore of Araven."

"I do now." Sigurne drew her robes more tightly across her shoulders, as if to imply chill. It was unseasonably cold, but winter was past. And even were it not, she no longer felt the cold's bite. "I would have this conversation, and at length, were the Merchants' Guild not expected within the hour."

"I know when they're expected," Eva snapped. "Merchant, remember?"

"Ah, yes."

Eva's eyes narrowed, shifting the shape of her facial scars. "Sigurne, what game?"

"No game," Sigurne replied. "Or rather, no game of mine. The Kings are concerned. The destruction of the guildhall—and, more relevant, the men and women who died there—has caused instability at a time when the city cannot afford it. Hectore is universally—almost universally—well-regarded. Given some of the company you keep—"

"I keep most of it at arm's length."

"—I cannot see what you find so objectionable in him. I consider Jarven ATerafin to be the greater danger, if peace and prosperity is your desire. I am not sure why he chose to relinquish his temporary control—but I do not believe the Araven patris desired the responsibility."

Eva frowned. "What are you not telling me?"

And that, as always, was the difficulty with the cunning and the observant. "I see Duvari has arrived."

Eva frowned, trying to place the name. She was not one of nature's politicians; she *was* one of nature's pure forces. *"Astari?"* she finally asked.

"Yes."

"The *Astari* are involved?"

"I told you, the Kings are concerned."

Eva bit back an intemperate reply. She did not harangue her friends—if that was not too much presumption on Sigurne's part—in front of powerful strangers.

"Guildmaster," Duvari said, as he approached. If Eva was capable of a certain consideration, the Lord of the Compact was not. The lack was not, as many assumed, due to the fact he was so certain of his power, so assured of his position. His focus was ferocious, his sense of duty so all-encompassing, he did not deign to bend to lesser considerations.

Sigurne Mellifas was seldom thought of as a lesser consideration. She had chosen to find it refreshing, but on some days, that equanimity did not come naturally.

"Lord of the Compact."

"I'll catch up with you later," Eva murmured, withdrawing.

"Eva."

"Guildmaster?"

"I have a task for you."

"Of course you do." Eva shook her head. "And I have to be patronized by a wealthy old man and his cronies. If we both survive the next few hours, I'll come up to the Tower."

Matteos Corvel, utterly silent until that moment, muttered something beneath his breath. Sigurne did not actually catch the words; she was certain that Eva, farther from him, had not.

"Guildmaster," Duvari said, drawing her attention away from Eva's retreating back.

"My apologies. I am currently host to the Merchants' Guild."

"And Eva Juwal is a merchant, yes. It is not of Eva that I wished to speak—although I would hear what task you intend for her to accomplish."

"I'm certain you would," was her benign reply. It was not followed by the requested information, however. Duvari could come and go as he pleased in any of the guildhalls of Averalaan—but he was not master. Not yet. "You have come, no doubt, with a matter of pressing concern."

"I wish to speak with Hectore of Araven."

"He will be present."

"And his servant?"

Ah. "You no doubt have information on and about Hectore; I will leave you to draw your own conclusions."

"Where is Jarven?"

She found the question almost astonishing, and allowed this to show. "Duvari, age has perhaps addled me."

He waited.

"I do not understand your question. No, let me amend that. I do not understand why you ask that question of me. I am not The Terafin; I am not ATerafin. I am not, and have never been, a merchant, of either greater or lesser repute. I do not deal with the Merchant Authority directly in any way. Jarven ATerafin's path does not cross mine often."

"No. It has, however, crossed yours recently."

"Jarven is not my servant; he is not my operative. If you refer to the daggers that he used to moderate effect on the night of the disaster, yes. As you suspect, they came from me. Jarven has the appropriate writs and permissions to carry them. He has also made the appropriate reports."

"I have read the reports he made of their use."

"And?"

"They are remarkably free of information."

"I have read them myself; your claim is a gross exaggeration. He can, and frequently does, ramble when the mood strikes him—but on the use of the dagger, and on the dagger's effect, he was clear, even concise."

"You have heard that he has handed interim governance of the guild to Hectore of Araven?"

"I have. Hectore thought to inform me, purely as a courtesy."

"Is there a reason that he no longer wishes to subject himself to the Order of Knowledge's oversight?"

Sigurne considered the question with growing unease. "He did not offer reasons for his withdrawal. If you have conversed at any length with Jarven, you cannot expect that he would."

"No. I wish to be informed when he next visits."

"Interesting," Jarven said to his golden-furred companion.

"The Terafin does not care for Duvari."

"No. She is breathing."

"But you do not dislike him."

"The Terafin does not like many people, in case this has escaped your notice. She has certainly never warmed to me."

"She likes the old woman."

"She has a particular weakness where strong old women are concerned, yes."

"Should we kill him?"

"The Terafin would be beyond angry if you did it and she became aware of it."

"Ah. He is powerful?"

"He is powerful. He is mortal." Jarven continued to listen to the conversation that Sigurne was attempting to end. He had been drawn from the forest byways by a soft, faint light, and had chosen to follow that glimpse to its terminal point.

Its terminal point appeared, at first glance, to be Sigurne Mellifas, the dour Matteos Corvel by her side. First glances were often superficial. If she was the source of that strange light, it was only because she was wearing it.

It was an odd illumination; it did not grow stronger or brighter as Jarven walked toward it, and he had at first assumed that he was in pursuit. He was not. The guildmaster was wearing a ring. It was a simple band, but Jarven could see that words, written across its slightly rounded surface, blazed. He could not read the words, not because he could not see them at this distance; he could and did. They were not written in a language that had any meaning to him. Yet.

The golden fox was staring at it, in a round-eyed silence that spoke of surprise. The forest denizens were frustratingly unlike the humans Jarven had made his life's study. They did not often lie, except by omission—but omission was critical.

Jarven could walk the forest. He had walked through miles of forested land in his ambitious youth; none of those experiences were relevant now. He could not understand how he could be this close to the guildmaster and Duvari without their awareness. It both pleased and discomfited him.

"Why?" the fox asked.

"Sigurne Mellifas is observant to a fault. She is also cautious—to a fault. If I am here, and neither she nor Duvari have any inkling of my presence, it puts the concept of security and its resultant safety to question."

"Do you wish to be seen?" the fox asked.

"Not at the moment, no."

"Then I fail to understand your concern."

Had he been a mortal mentor, that would have been a lie, edged as it was with condescension and the implication that Jarven's concerns were beneath regard. Jarven found this frustrating. He was old, and took advantage of that fact, much as Sigurne Mellifas did, and to much the same effect.

But with age and experience had come a kind of power. His physical age was no longer the limiting factor it had once been. The fox heavily implied that his appearance could be altered, with some effort on either Jarven's part or the eldest's; Jarven was not sure which.

He could not, however, allow this without losing what he had spent decades building. He had considered the loss with care, but in the end felt it would greatly inconvenience him if he intended to live largely as he had once lived.

He had not, however, realized how very little his former life and his personal consequence would mean to the forest. How very little they *all* meant. Only The Terafin was significant; every other mortal of import was important only if The Terafin valued them.

It was a humbling thought, and humility did not suit Jarven—not when it was genuine. "Why does the ring surprise you?" he asked the golden fox.

"Do you not recognize it?"

"No. I have never seen it before."

"Then pay attention now, little mortal. You are not what you were; you have the power, now, to give offense to the powerful if you move without caution. That old woman," the fox continued, gazing at her for the first time as if she was of interest, "has been claimed; she is under the protection of a powerful Lord."

"If she dies?"

"If she dies, Jarven ATerafin, it will not be by your hand. Or by ours. And The Terafin, as I have said, likes her."

"If The Terafin disliked her, if The Terafin did desire her death, would we be likewise moved to stay our hand?"

"Yes. If she commanded it, we would of course obey—but the Councillor she has chosen would argue against it in our stead, and we believe she would listen to him if our words failed." The fox was silent for a long, long beat. "You do not recognize what you see."

"It is in a language I have not studied."

"Then listen and listen well. The Terafin retains the services of a mage."

Jarven nodded.

"She could, because he is sleeping. He is not imprisoned, as his brothers are; he was not disobedient to his Lord's command, as his brothers were. He was left freedom of movement—but not the freedom of power, of self. He had failed her," the fox added softly. "He had failed us all."

"You were never his master."

"No, of course not. But in times of great need and great danger, the denizens of the high wilderness can come together for common cause, and thus it was. Even the gods played their part. But he and his brothers failed. They failed because they could not do what they had been commanded to do.

"What was done was enough. Meralonne APhaniel, as he is styled, has been sleeping for centuries. Longer, perhaps. He remembers the old days, the old ways; he remembers the beauty of old glories."

"By sleep, you mean he is without power?"

"Essentially, yes."

"He is not, by mortal measure, powerless."

"No. And by the measure of the wilderness, he is not powerless. But measured against what he once was? He is as a mortal infant to a powerful man in his prime." The fox was silent for a beat. "Humans get lost in nightmare because while they dream, they believe the world they are in is real. Do you understand? The nightmare has terror because they believe in it. But when they wake, the nightmare recedes; it is gone.

"Meralonne sleeps in that fashion. He lives in the mortal world. He has the power that cannot be riven from him, and shards of his true light shine when he is pushed to battle. He has chosen—without choice—to believe in the truth of his sleeping perceptions.

"But he is close to waking, Jarven. And he knows it. He understands that the waking might well destroy everything he has built while asleep—and because he is not yet awake, he does not desire this."

"You believe that will change."

"Yes. But I have seen him as he is; I have seen him awake. That ring is a symbol of his waking self. Perhaps he hopes that if he sees it, it will stay his hand, or perhaps he hopes that it will stay the hand of his brothers—for they are waking as well; we can feel it. And they have not had the paltry freedom that he has had; they have no experience of, and no regard for, the mortal, except as quarry or prey. You see the words; memorize their shape.

"It would give every ancient being pause if their intent was Sigurne's destruction. Only the powerful would ignore that pause—because if Sigurne is destroyed, Illaraphaniel will be honor bound to hunt down and kill the one who committed this crime against him."

Jarven frowned. Duvari was everything he had always assumed he would be. Duvari suspected—on no grounds and with no experience whatsoever—that

Jarven had done something to himself that he did not wish exposed to the guildmaster.

It was, in fact, one reason he had chosen to withdraw from the position of interim guildmaster—the other being tedium. Birgide Viranyi was *Astari*. It was possible that the information Duvari now possessed had come from her.

"She was concerned," the fox said.

Jarven said, "I will ask you not to respond to things I have not said or asked aloud, if it's all the same to you."

"Ah. Why?"

"Because mortals spend years or decades learning what to say out loud, and how—and I have been considered a past master of that art. All of my given talents will atrophy if they become essentially useless."

"As you wish. We are not as you are."

"Can all of the denizens of the wilderness hear my thoughts?"

The fox looked almost aghast at the ignorance of the question. It had been too many years since Jarven had been an apprentice of any kind. "Jarven," the fox's eyes narrowed, "you are ignorant, and we accept that—but there is a depth of ignorance that will be tantamount to suicide, and that, we will not. It has been many, many years—beyond your ken—since I have last chosen to impart some trace element of myself and my power to one who is merely mortal."

"I would counter that it would be safest to gift the merely mortal with power; they are unlikely to cause harm to you in its use."

"Were I to bestow the same largesse on the wild and the immortal, they, too, would be unlikely to cause harm to me." The fox's smile was edged, sharp; it was predatory. "But that is beside the point; you understood, from the start, that any gift granted is also obligation or burden; that nothing is truly given between people like us. I am not The Terafin."

"I am not comfortable with charity."

"No? You are not comfortable requiring it, it is true. I do not think it has troubled you one way or the other until now, and even now, you consider the cost acceptable. But you have interrupted me. Some element of you is of me, now. Were you to put your own mind to it—and some small effort—you would be aware of me and my intent in the way we are aware of The Terafin's. It is not because you are in or of the forest; it is because you are mine.

"In turn, you are my responsibility. Your misbehavior, such as it is, would be laid at my feet; restitution for it would be made—should it be required—by me. I assure you that this has happened in the past."

"And did your apprentices survive?"

The fox tsked. "Of course not. I do not know why you persist in asking questions to which you know the answer."

"Perhaps I like the sound of your voice."

"You are bold."

"Yes. But were I not bold, Eldest, I would not be here." He shook his head in admiration. "She is managing Duvari almost perfectly."

"Is she? He has not left, and she wishes him to be gone."

"That is entirely in Duvari's nature. She has given him nothing. She," he added, "does not particularly approve of me; she is quite fond of Hectore."

"As are you."

"As am I. I am always fond of men who have managed to surprise me—even at cost to myself. And it happened in the distant past."

"And his servant?" the fox asked, with studied care.

"I have been comforted to discover that the paragon of service is not, in fact, mortal."

The fox studied him. "You are not afraid of him?"

Jarven was honestly surprised by the question. "Are you?"

"He is dangerous," the fox replied, which was both an evasion and an answer.

"The Terafin does not believe he is."

"The Terafin does not understand what she sees. Or perhaps it is better to say, she does not see everything. She does not know his history; did she, she would not have given him free run of all her lands."

"You fail to understand the woman at the heart of this forest," Jarven said quietly. "You understand her imperfectly because you are not mortal. She is appallingly straightforward, and entirely predictable; were it not for her talent, she would be dead a hundred assassination attempts ago. She does not know his history. Even did she, she would do as she has done because the history that carries the most weight with her is the history she has personally observed.

"Andrei serves Hectore. The whole of his life in the time I have known him has been devoted to Araven, and to its master. Hectore, in turn, values Andrei more highly than he values anyone but his grandchildren. He considered—seriously—having Birgide Viranyi killed."

"He would have failed utterly."

"Perhaps, perhaps not. It is significant to me that Andrei has chosen to serve Hectore. And, Eldest, he *has* chosen; the service *is* his life. I have always envied Hectore his Andrei. If you harm Andrei—if anyone who in theory owes allegiance to The Terafin harms him without cause—she will be very, very angry."

"Yes, we understand that," the fox replied, as if Jarven was observing that water was a liquid. "We merely assume that her attachment is a form of mortal ignorance."

"It is not. Oh, she has a plethora of mortal ignorances and beliefs, but not this one."

"You like him."

"I do not particularly like anyone."

"Why do you say that? It is not true."

"It is, Eldest. I can, for instance, say I like Hectore, but it signifies little. If he stood between me and my goal, I would push him off a cliff without a third thought; I might be troubled by second thoughts, but they would not stay my hand. But you know this about me; it is true of you, as well."

"It is, yes. I believe your Duvari is leaving."

"He will return."

"Will you follow him?"

"No. I have seen enough for the moment. I wish to visit some of the rooms in the Order."

"Jarven." Finch's arms were folded, her eyes narrowed. Had she not been forced to utter syllables—in this case, his name—her lips would have been compressed as well. It was not, in Jarven's opinion, a particularly attractive look; it suited Lucille, but Finch was not Lucille.

"Apologies, Finch," he said.

"If you are going to enter the office, please use the doors."

"It is my office, and I do not recall—"

"We have contingencies in place for unexpected visitors."

"I am hardly a visitor."

"Given your involvement in the office at the moment? Lucille has had to be almost forcibly restrained from calling in the magi."

"Meaning I have set off the protections within the office proper by entering it."

"I will speak with her in a moment," Finch continued, folding her slender arms. "I am not certain what skills you have gained. At the moment, I am not concerned with them, except in this regard. When you enter the office, enter it through the front doors."

"I am attempting to discern the limits of my own abilities, as you call them."

"I am attempting to set limits for the use of those abilities in my office. Lucille is . . . not happy. I have convinced her that there are no demons in the office—just you."

"And she did not believe you?"

"We'll see. If the magi dissolve the door and fill the room with Summer light, then no. But," she added, her voice softening, although her expression did not, "she let me into the office."

"Tell me, which protections did I cross?"

Finch exhaled. "Why did you visit here?"

"Because most of the city is deplorably trusting. I could have attempted to enter the right-kin's office, but I judged that to be very unwise. This office, however, is my own. Our own," he added. "And I am cognizant of all of its protective functions. How did you know it was me?"

"I could see you," was her flat reply.

"You have been the first person today to do so."

"Maybe you wished to be seen. I have no explanation and offer none. But when you enter this office again—"

"Use the doors. Yes. Will that diminish your impressive ire?"

Finch exhaled. "Not entirely."

"I will now go out and grovel and apologize to Lucille. Will *that* be enough?"

"Yes."

"You drive a very hard bargain."

"I was taught by a master."

"I believe I bargain with a good deal more charm."

"Charm was not my first concern." She shooed him out of the office and then turned to look down at the golden fox.

"You are not happy," the fox said as she knelt.

"No." She had, of course, lied to Jarven; she suspected he knew it. She hadn't seen him at all. She had not lied about the protections; he had tripped several—but not all. She had, however, seen the golden fox—and she understood that either the fox had set off the protections, or Jarven had. Either was a possibility.

She was not at all comfortable with the idea that Jarven could, at will, enter rooms such as his own without being seen. She wondered if he could touch or take anything when he paid these visits. Jarven was, and had always been, dangerously perceptive. His instincts were sharp; age had honed them.

"Is it so unusual?" the fox asked, his head tilted.

"It is."

"It is not, to us. If we hunt, we must not be seen until it is far too late for our prey. We are not dragons; it is not through size and breath that we triumph. We are cunning, a cunning people; we make our home in the quiet spaces, and we swallow that quiet, where we must."

"Jarven has been cunning beyond belief in his life," Finch replied. "But, in general, he doesn't swallow quiet so much as shatter it." She opened her arms, and the fox agreed to grace them with his august presence. "He otherwise seems himself."

"It is not to change what he is that I have made him my own," the fox replied. "Truly."

"I could not be yours."

"No, Finch. But you could not belong to any of the ancients who grace the high wilderness; you are The Terafin's. You will be The Terafin's until either she dies, or you do. To even approach you requires some courage; the younger ones will not do it."

"Courage?"

"You are fragile. You are mortal. Our games might break or destroy you."

"You are not so afraid."

"No. I believe I can survive any harmful intent on your part, and I understand mortals well enough not to inadvertently harm you. Mortals," he added fondly, "were once my prey, when the world was young. And they were a glorious prey—agile, cunning, resourceful. They could, and did, surprise. Not all surprises were pleasant, of course, but that is the nature of the game: it is only real when there is risk. I am not a cat; there is no test, no joy, in playing with mice."

"I can understand what you saw in Jarven."

"That is unkind, Finch."

"Is it?" She turned, arms cradled protectively around a creature that had spoken of hunting men for game, to meet Jarven's steady gaze. "Well?"

"I am not yet in command of the few abilities I have been granted. I cannot see magic as Birgide Viranyi seems to; I cannot touch it or disrupt it. I can walk unseen into almost any room—but clearly, there are difficulties. I am concerned, myself, about the quality of these magical protections. They are not well written or well constructed if I can step through most of them."

She blinked. "You weren't certain?"

"I was relatively certain."

"Jarven, at least two of those will *burn half the office to ash*."

"Well, yes. That would be a bit inconvenient."

"I happened to be working in the office!"

"Hush," he said, wincing. "Lucille will hear you, and she is only barely willing to be mollified. You have been wearing the clothing that Haval made for you; the fire would not have killed you." He glanced at a ledger on Finch's desk and frowned. "Ruby?"

"Nothing I can't handle. Haerrad has pulled in his fangs for the moment; if the dinner accomplished nothing else, it accomplished that. There are fewer avenues of resistance." She exhaled and surrendered. "Your presence on the House Council has caused different fires, but those fires give me some leverage."

"Compared to me, you are considered malleable and acceptable?"

"Not malleable enough, but much more acceptable. It was not necessary to attack Iain's records the way you did."

"They were, in my opinion, appalling."

"Iain is relatively honest and relatively straightforward, and he has done the House a great service. Honestly, Jarven." She was cross and allowed herself to look it. Unlike Lucille, she had the choice.

"My dear," he said, in his most indulgent voice. "You could not expect that I would join the House Council to little or no effect? I dislike invisibility."

"You have a very odd way of demonstrating it."

He laughed out loud. "I dislike invisibility that does not serve my purpose." He then frowned at the fox. "She is not yours."

"No, of course not," the fox agreed. "But neither is she yours."

"Oh?"

"I will not play that particular game with you—not over this mortal. Perhaps another, but perhaps not. We will have time when things are less uncertain."

Unwilling to leave the conversation entirely to the fox or Jarven, Finch said, "I understand the game you believe you are playing there. If I am to be regent, I must be seen to exercise a control that other Councillors could not likewise exert. I am not, however, you. I am not—and generally you are in favor of this—Lucille or The Terafin. If I appear to be in control of you, everyone who witnesses the interaction will assume it is actually you who are the power."

He raised a brow.

"It is too obvious," Finch said.

"Is it?" His smile was gentle, which put Finch on her guard immediately. "You are naturally suspicious. It is a useful trait. Do you honestly think the House Council will see in me what you see?"

"Only the dangerous ones."

He inclined his head.

"And it's the dangerous ones I need to control." She hesitated. "Rymark is not in the city."

The whole of Jarven's posture changed. "You are certain."

"Haerrad is."

Jarven's gaze dropped to the fox. "I will need to leave the city for a brief period."

"You are not ready yet," the fox said.

Finch tightened her arms in subtle warning; she did not otherwise move.

"Ready," Jarven said, "is alway subjective. I was not ready to take this office; I was not ready to become part of the Merchant Authority governing council. I was not *allowed* to enter the Merchants' guildhall but did it frequently. There is no 'ready,' Eldest; there has never been 'ready' for me."

"I thought mortals were more careful with their lives as their time is so short."

"I am exceedingly careful with my life," Jarven replied with a suspicious amount of dignity. His eyes were bright.

"Did you not have duties here?"

Jarven was restless. Finch would not have kept him in the office in this mood unless Lucille's life depended on it; she would not do it to save her own. In this mood, Jarven became the greatest danger; if he did not find trouble, he became it.

Jarven deliberately softened his voice. "Eldest, I need to understand my limits. What you have given me is appreciated greatly—but before I had it, I traveled as I pleased and survived it. I am not afraid of doing things the old-fashioned way; it is, after all, what I am accustomed to."

"Very well. Find your limits. I will not be pleased if you perish; no one likes wasted effort, especially when it involves their own." He lofted his small, pointed nose in the air. Finch met, and held, his eyes. "Go, go."

Jarven did not need permission but did not say this; he left.

"You think Jewel will be angry," the fox said, when Finch had returned to her desk and her ledgers. She settled the fox in her lap since he seemed to have no intention of leaving.

"I don't think she'll be happy, no. And before you ask, no. I don't wish to see Jarven destroyed, and given the choice, neither would she. What's done is done. What are the restrictions you've placed on his power?"

"Restrictions?" the fox asked, blinking.

"You cannot think to keep Jarven leashed without some."

"What restrictions have you placed upon him?" the fox countered.

She blinked. "He is not mine; he does not serve me. I came to him as a junior apprentice, at best, and he has condescended to teach me—mostly by throwing me into the middle of his various meetings as a serving girl."

"And yet you will occupy the position of power in the house; he will not."

"He doesn't *want* the power. He's come to understand that there's far too much fussy, boring responsibility associated with it. Were he thirty years younger, he would take it anyway; he's not. He considers the regency to be babysitting without appropriate compensation."

"Do you believe that?" the fox asked with genuine curiosity.

The question made Finch pause. "He has never sought power of that nature in the House before."

The quality of the eldest's silence was almost bemusing. Finch found herself stroking golden fur, almost as if the small fox was one of Jay's giant cats. "In his youth—or perhaps when he was slightly older than I am now—he could not have become Terafin. He did not have the birth and the connections that arise from it. Amarais did."

"The current Terafin does not."

"No. And that, in the history of The Ten, is unusual—but it's not unique. That we know of, though, being seer-born is. The patrician birthright wasn't as important, in the end, as the talent."

"Meaning that she was born to power."

"Do yourself a favor," Finch told the golden fox. "Never say that in her hearing."

"I do not understand mortality," the fox replied.

"You don't have to understand all of it—no one could. Jay doesn't like to think of herself as a power, because power is duty and responsibility, and she has too much of that already. She feels, often, that she is skirting the edge of failure—but the greater the responsibility, the greater the cost of a misstep. I don't know if she was ever afraid to die," Finch mused. "But she was always afraid that everyone else would. Her own death, she was certain she could prevent—and she has. Every time. But the deaths of others?

"Not reliably." She looked at the fox and said, "You knew she was here."

The fox nodded. Paused. Frowned, which looked odd on an animal face; it was mostly a movement of brows and eyes. "You did not."

"Oh, we did—but not immediately."

"She was here this afternoon."

Finch closed her eyes. "Was she dreaming?"

"You are clever," the fox replied. "I think I understand why Jarven kept you."

"If you must know, he kept me because he wished to prove a point or two.

I was not the choice any of the House Council would have made for the position into which I was thrust at The Terafin's command. In truth, I wasn't Jarven's choice either—but it *was* his choice, in the end. His office was powerful enough to survive the addition of an orphan street urchin with poor numerical skills.

"He was bored. I was different. And I reminded him, in some ways, of himself—as I said, he was not born to the patriciate. He was not born to power. Where was she?"

"She went, I think, to a large building on the Isle. We think she entered Fabril's reach and walked upon his roads. They are not," the fox added, "our roads."

"But they're in the city."

"Yes. But they are not ours. They are claimed and guarded until the reckoning, and that reckoning has not yet arrived." The fox leaped off her lap and onto the desk. "Jarven can move without being seen. He can move quickly now. He can understand the language of the wilderness, and he can make himself heard by it.

"And he cannot be taken. He is claimed, and this will be known. What happened to Haerrad will never now happen to Jarven."

"Is he even alive?"

The fox chuckled. "You are astonishingly perceptive. Why would you ask that?"

Finch didn't answer the question. "The Terafin would not sacrifice even Jarven willingly."

"No, she would not; it is a pity. But she has need of dark things, dangerous things; she understands that the pure and the joyful do not always make good soldiers—and if they do, it is because they have changed. Or broken. Jarven is a dark thing, but he always was. He did not come to her because he does not want what she offers, so he cannot be *hers*."

"You did not do this as an act of servitude or charity."

"No, Finch, I did not. But consider: the Councillor, in the end, thought it necessary. We do what we do for our own reasons—you, me, Jarven—but that does not mean that we do not, in our own fashion, serve. If you must be troubled by her choices of companions—" But he stopped, then, and would say no more.

"Could Andrei face Jarven?"

"Yes. He could face Jarven and survive; he could face Jarven and triumph although it would no longer be a certain encounter. But you could not."

"I survived Jarven because he desired that I survive. For me, nothing you have done to or for him changes our essential relationship. What has changed it is time, familiarity, experience—but at any point during our long association, had he wanted me dead, I would have died. The fact that it is still true does not bother me."

"No, it doesn't," the fox agreed. "You are now concerned that the same is true for people other than yourself, who will not *know* the risk they take. It is a pity; you are concerned about things over which you have no control."

Finch nodded and returned to her books.

Chapter Twelve

THERE WAS NO MORNING in the darkness of the Oracle's many rooms; Jewel thought of the cave they had first seen and thought the illusion apt. She rose in a darkness alleviated by more than simple torchlight, dressed, and joined her companions. They watched her in silence, except for the cats, who had made boredom their personal cause.

The butterfly remained on her shoulder; it moved only to allow her to dress. It was as beautiful as it had been in dream, as solid, as delicate. She found it almost a comfort in the darkness of this place.

The ring, however, was not. It was odd; the wearing of the strands of hair had been marked and noted, but it did not invoke what the ring did.

Avandar noticed it instantly. "Where did you come by that ring?" His voice was soft, which was no comfort, because it was also winter cold.

"I didn't steal it," she replied, as defensive as if she'd been sixteen and newly arrived at the Terafin manse. She flushed as the words left her mouth.

He stared at her. "I did not—and would not—imply that. Your cats, however, are far less careful in their habits of acquisition."

Shadow hissed. Night swatted Snow. Snow, however, lowered his belly to the ground.

"In this case, you could not wear that ring if it were not intended for you. Do you understand what it is?"

"Jewel."

The Oracle had entered the room. She did not enter it the normal way—through the door—and made no noise until she wished to be heard. It was astonishingly easy to overlook her.

"Oracle." Jewel bowed.

"It is time. It is almost past time. You must leave—and soon. The window that is open will close, and you must be there before that happens."

And she thought the Oracle knew.

"I see you have chosen." The Oracle stared then at the butterfly on Jewel's shoulder. Her eyes, for a moment, were round with wonder, but beneath that wonder was dread. "What did you do, child?" The words were a whisper.

Defensive words came; this time, they were discarded before they left her mouth. "I didn't make the butterfly. A maker did."

"An Artisan."

"I think so. I wasn't there when it was made."

"Were you there, then, when it was remade?"

Jewel exhaled. "Yes. I gave the maker the necklace that I wore."

Snow shrieked—it was hard to tell whether the sound was one of outrage or horror.

"Did you not see this?" Adam asked the Oracle. It was a mild question that implied it could be ignored with ease.

The Oracle smiled. "Yes. Yes and no. I see many things. I see everything that might happen. But I do not experience my visions as Jewel experiences her own. If time is not a yoke I bear, it is nonetheless relevant.

"This? It was a glimmer of possibility. It was not something I could influence; it was not something I could bring, by planning and the careful deployment of those very few who serve my interests, into being." She lifted a hand. "And perhaps this will be enough."

The butterfly left Jewel's shoulder and fluttered in its winding, chaotic aerial dance toward that open palm. It rested there as the Oracle studied its closed wings.

"He will know," she told Jewel.

"Who?"

"The owner of the necklace. You have heard his sleeping voice if I am not mistaken. He will know." She closed her eyes, her mouth; the lines of her face grew heavy with gravity. "It is too late. You gifted what you could not gift to a man who could not, at the time, understand the consequence of accepting it. But it is you who will pay the price of it, if a price is demanded.

"Guard this butterfly."

"It's not just a butterfly."

"No. But done is done, Terafin. I cannot change it, nor can you. You are not Evayne; she is god-born. You are Sen. Do not seek to be what she is; do not seek to do what she does. I had hoped—" She shook her head. "But so many hopes are ash and bitter daydream. You have bought—although you cannot realize the cost of it—time for yourself. Now you must spend it wisely."

The butterfly left her hand. Jewel could hear the echoes of a wordless tune as it once again landed on her shoulder.

She turned to the gathered group, who had fallen silent—as they often did—in the Oracle's presence. The exception, as always, was the cats.

Kallandras was staring at the butterfly. Just . . . staring.

"You can hear it," Jewel said.

"Can you not?"

"Only if I listen very carefully—and the room isn't full of bored cats." She glared at the cats, which did nothing to decrease their volume.

"What do you hear?"

"Mostly? Singing. A young girl singing. Her voice isn't particularly strong—but it's happy. If that makes sense. I'm not even sure she's aware that she's humming."

Kallandras said nothing, and after another silent moment, Jewel lifted the butterfly very gingerly from her shoulder, carried it to the almost stricken bard, and set it on his.

"Terafin—"

"Jewel," she said firmly. "I'm Jewel."

"I cannot—"

"The butterfly doesn't belong to me. It's just another responsibility, another burden to shoulder." She grinned briefly. "And I am choosing to share. It is vitally important to us—to all of us—that no harm come to that butterfly until we reach . . ." She stopped; the words died. She was no longer aware of what she had intended to say.

"Can you protect it, Kallandras of Senniel?" the Oracle asked. "It is no small task she has set for you, and if you decline, she will accept it."

Kallandras nodded.

Celleriant had, from the moment he had seen the ring on Jewel's hand, been transfixed in his regard; the rest of the conversation had passed above or around him as if he were a standing rock at the center of a small, fast moving river. He blinked and glanced at the bard to whom he had always been unaccountably drawn.

"It is no small charge, brother," he said softly.

"No," Kallandras replied, "it is not. Can you hear it?"

"I cannot. It does not speak to me. But it speaks to you, and passion is oft that way. If you will accept, I will aid you as I can."

Kallandras bowed to the Arianni Lord; it was not a formal bow, nor a stiff one, but it was not perfunctory, either. It said and implied many things to Jewel as she watched, but she couldn't untangle them all, and after a moment, she gave up trying.

To Celleriant, she said, "The ring was made to protect the Winter Queen's gift." She could think of it as hair, as strands of hair, but found it difficult to say it out loud—as if somehow something of the Winter Queen's could never be so mundane, so simple. But Celleriant understood this far, far better than Jewel.

"The protection was not required," he replied. "And, Lord, that is not all that the ring does or will do."

"It is what I wanted," she said—and knew, instantly, that it was true.

"He has written her vow and her claim upon that band. He has written her declaration. Any who see it—any who can—will know that you belong to Ariane."

"The Winter King didn't wear this ring."

"No. I do not explain well what requires no explanation to most of the immortals." He turned to Shianne, who was staring at the ring, her mouth tight, her eyes narrowed. "Lady?"

"Had you no part of the White Lady, the ring could not exist," she said. Her voice was cold. It was ice. It had swallowed Winter and might never be free of it. "And the ring *should not* exist; it is a lie."

"It is a lie," the Oracle said, "with a thread—a strong thread—of truth in it. The Terafin is mortal, and she is Sen, but it is not upon her own lands that she encountered the Winter Queen, and not upon her own lands that she was gifted three strands of the White Lady's hair. You cannot know what the White Lady's intent was although you might guess and guess well. Do not take offense in her stead, Shandalliaran."

"I take offense," Shianne replied, "in my own."

"Jealousy and envy are not, in the end, offense."

Shianne swelled with rage.

Celleriant, however, bowed to the Oracle. "We will take our leave, with your blessing." He caught Jewel and Kallandras by the arm and almost marched them out of the room.

"Why can *she* have *fun* when *we* can't?" Night muttered. He stalked out of the room, followed by Snow, who bit his brother's tail.

"No one in that room is having fun," Jewel told the cat. "Adam!"

Adam had stepped between Shianne and the Oracle, his hands spread; Jewel could see his back, and some hint of his profile. Angel caught up with her before she could turn. *Trust him*, he signed.

"He's too young—"

"When you were in a mood, we let Teller deal with you. He always could. When Duster was bad, we let Lander intervene. Trust him." When she opened her mouth, he said, "He's the age we were back then. He's as much a child as we were. He's chosen. He's not a fool. And he's damn hard to kill."

"He's—"

"Not as hard to kill as you, but short of removing his head by main force, his own talent won't let him die."

Terrick's ax was strapped across his back. He did not look as worried as Jewel felt; he looked both tired and strangely excited. "Listen to him," he told Jewel almost impatiently. "The boy is her favorite. She will not harm him in her rage."

But Jewel had seen the Arianni in a rage. She tensed, briefly, and then nodded. She remembered being Adam's age; she did not remember being young the way he seemed young to her now.

She had dreamed of a world in which the young could *be* young, for just a little while longer. And why? What had youth ever gotten any of them?

"She will not harm him," Terrick repeated. "You shoulder burdens that would break the backs of many. Do not shoulder burdens which are not yours."

When Jewel emerged from the mouth of a cave, the landscape was no longer white; the snowshoes which she'd strapped to her feet with Terrick's help no longer served a purpose. It was spring here.

No, it was Summer.

She felt a moment of lurching panic at the thought of the passage of time, because she knew what the cost of *too late* would be. But Avandar did not seem unduly disturbed. Terrick was bewildered, but his innate stoicism made his state of mind far less obvious. Angel began to remove layers of clothing, looking at the packs with some disgust; the morning's work would have to be redone.

"You are not late," the Oracle told The Terafin. "You did not leave the way you entered. These lands are not the lands in which the ancient serpents live in their splendid, winter isolation."

"Whose lands are these?" Jewel asked.

The Oracle's smile was soft as she inclined her head. "You are learning, Terafin. Jewel. Can you not feel the answer? Can you not hear it?"

Jewel shook her head almost impatiently. "I don't ask questions if I already know the answer."

"There are some questions that cannot be answered by others," the Oracle countered, "even if those others do have the answers." She glanced at Adam, who stood to her left; he was between the Oracle and Shianne. Shianne was not happy—but the instant, almost boiling rage that had possessed her had subsided. Barely. "You could not walk this road if you had not walked your own." Significantly, she glanced at the butterfly.

"Who owned the necklace that was destroyed?"

"Owned?" The Oracle shook her head. "I will not answer that question. Should you desire it, you might search yourself—but as you have come to understand, that way is fraught. It was not, as you must know, a simple necklace; it was not a thing of craft and mortal metal. If you knew how to listen, it told a story—and the story is simple and as old as the wild gods.

"It fell into your hands. No one of my kin, ancient or young, would have dared to touch it or to wear it; you did. Do you believe in coincidence, Terafin?"

Jewel nodded.

"I am not certain I do. Be that as it may, the lands you walk now are claimed. There is some contest of that claim along its borders, where you now stand. For that reason, the lands are guarded. It would not surprise me if you meet some of those guardians as you travel."

Jewel wanted to ask her where they were meant to go, but she knew: to Averalaan. Home. They had done it once. She shoved hair out of her eyes and grimaced. *Adam* had done it once.

"Matriarch?" Adam asked.

She shook her head. To Shianne, she said, "Shall we call truce and have done? I did not know what the guildmaster would make of what I gave him, but I knew—as seer—that it was necessary, once he had finished. I make no claims, now or ever, upon the White Lady, and if it were not necessary, I would never have surrendered her gift to his keeping. We could not reach her any other way." She spoke the words as if they were truth, as if they were certain. No visceral sense of rightness followed them.

"Guildmaster?" The single word was cool, but the curiosity in it was real, felt.

"It's a mortal term," Jewel replied. "Come. If you can stand to do so, walk with me and I will explain what it means."

For three hours, Jewel did as she had offered to do. Side comments came from Terrick, who had dealt with the most fractious of merchants—and the most powerful, although they were not always the same—in his decades at the Port Authority wickets. Avandar added his own opinions as if the discussion bored him with its necessity.

The cats, not to be left out, let Shianne know how incredibly *stupid* mortal hierarchies were. And how *boring*. But Shianne dropped a hand to Night's head when he came into range and asked softly that she might be allowed to listen to the boring and the stupid; she had been asleep for so long the world had changed, and changed, and changed. It was, to her, a new world, a new age.

"*Ssssso whaaaat?*" Shadow said. "It is *boring*. It is *stupid*."

"Eldest," Shianne said, with mild reproof, "I do not know enough to judge it. Perhaps, if you will allow me that small amount of time, I will come to hold your opinion."

"Time? *Time?* You are *mortal*. You *have* no time. And you are *wasting* it."

"The Terafin is mortal."

"That is *different*. She is *Sen*."

Since Jewel had made clear that she did not understand the term, Shianne nodded. But the woman who had once been immortal Arianni clearly found Jewel's ignorance as frustrating—in her graceful, elegant way—as the cats did. It might have ended badly, as Shadow at least was spoiling for a fight, had a new and familiar voice not stemmed the tide of their growing spat simply by existing.

"Jewel."

Jewel smiled. She felt instantly wary, instantly on her guard—but the smile itself was both whole and genuine. "Calliastra."

She did not come to Jewel as Duster, not this time. Nor did she adopt any of the other guises available to her—and Jewel guessed that they were many, like the clothing in a rich woman's closets. She was pale, her skin a perfect color, her eyes an almost shocking cornflower blue. Her nails were long, and her dress, far too revealing—but they better suited the Summer skies than they had the Winter ones. She did not bow. She did not, as Jewel turned toward her, move at all.

Her eyes were wide with consternation, and then, as seconds ticked, narrow with fury. That fury was turned almost in its entirety on the cats. "What have you *done?*"

Shadow, who had been in the midst of his own private argument with Shianne, turned only his head to glare at the newcomer.

"What have *we* done?" His wings rose, stiffening. His fur fell until he looked so sleek and deadly he was almost breathtaking. "*We? Us?*"

Jewel placed a hand—quickly—on Shadow's head. "They didn't do anything."

"The consequences of the things they *have* done will be far larger than you can imagine."

"I'm seer-born," Jewel replied. "I don't need to rely on imagination for horror."

Silence. The comment was eventually rewarded with one of Calliastra's languid smiles. "You seem to be well. I had wondered how your time in my sister's domain would affect you."

"So had I. Still do."

"You will not find this road as contentious as the last you traveled—but it is not safe. The forests are waking to the sound of your . . . butterfly." She hesitated and then added, "The ring you wear will be cause for much conversation. Can you not feel the curiosity?"

"Curiosity is better than outrage."

"I am not so certain. Are there not mortals who satisfy their curiosity at dire expense to others?"

"Yes. Thanks for that." Jewel made space, and Calliastra slid into the position by her left; the right was occupied by bristling, gray cat. Angel drifted to the back of the group, where he walked beside Terrick in a companionable silence. This had been his way of dealing with Duster, in the long-ago past, as well.

Adam did not appear to find Calliastra terrifying, but he had not found Shianne terrifying either. Shianne kept herself between Calliastra and Adam at all times. Calliastra chose to find this amusing; Jewel thought that took effort. And she was grateful that the effort had been, and was being, made.

"He will be angry," Calliastra said conversationally.

"Who? Who exactly will be angry?"

One perfect black brow rose, aimed in its entirety at Snow. "Have you still not told her?"

It was Shadow who answered. "Why? She will just talk about it. And *talk*. And *talk*. And then he will *hear*."

"No one will tell me," Jewel said quickly. "The Oracle wouldn't. Shianne won't. I believe Celleriant has some suspicions, but he keeps them to himself."

"Perhaps that is wise," Calliastra replied. "Perhaps not. I considered it astonishing that your cats could be so bold as to steal from him—but if he slept so deeply that theft was possible, there was the chance—however slim—that the return of the item would allow its theft to go unremarked.

"Now, however, there is nothing to return. The ring, he would destroy before wearing; I do not think he would condescend to retain it."

It was not the only thing that Jewel had carried from Fabril's reach.

"The butterfly, he would keep—but I think it too delicate to survive him long. Still, he would see its beauty; I myself have never seen a work so striking."

"It almost looks alive, doesn't it?"

Calliastra looked at Jewel, both brows lifting.

Shadow hissed laughter.

Jewel didn't ask Calliastra why she was waiting for them. Possibly because of that, no one else asked either. Although the Winter King and Avandar were willing to share their unspoken views—often at length—they understood that Jewel had accepted Calliastra. The only voluble complaints came from the cats—but the daughter of darkness had chosen to find the cats—or their opinions—entirely irrelevant, and as they spent most of their whining, long complaint accusing Jewel of stupidity in a screeching kind of harmony, she merely felt included. At least that was Jewel's guess.

Calliastra's eye was drawn to two things when she was not moved to glare at the cats: Shianne and the butterfly. Since the butterfly sat on Kallandras' shoulder, her gaze would shift to linger on the harder lines of his face. Twice in the long day's march she drifted toward Kallandras.

Shianne was content to allow this; she would not let Calliastra stand anywhere near Adam without interposing herself between them. Jewel was grateful. She knew that Shianne was protecting what she saw as her own best interests, but it didn't matter. If Shianne kept watch, Adam was safe. He was one less thing to worry about—not that it stopped the worry.

"Where are we going?" Angel asked, and she blinked, shaking her head as if to clear it. They had shed winter clothing, adding bulk to packs that were not light to begin with; for obvious reasons, no one suggested abandoning that gear. Beneath the skies of this odd forest, it was summer, but summer in the wilderness could turn a corner into bitter cold without any of the usual warning signs.

She turned to look back at the group and realized Angel was beside her because she had been leading. Calliastra had taken the other side, and Night was stepping, or trying to step, on Angel's feet. In the cat hierarchy, the rest of the den was obviously of lesser import than the cats, although they did grudgingly protect them if anyone else tried to hurt them.

She signed, *I don't know.*

He shrugged. He had long since given up questioning her instincts; he asked for information so that the rest of the den could plan. Their fights were not always her fights, but her fights—when they knew about them—they adopted as their own. Always had.

"We have to keep going," she added softly.

"Terrick reminds us that we have to eat."

Jewel nodded. It was remarkably hard to stop her feet from moving forward; she had to concentrate. She didn't like it.

Kallandras surprised her. When they had finished eating, he sang. He had a lute, one she couldn't recall seeing on the journey so far. She didn't ask. Even had she wanted to, she found his voice so riveting it obliterated all other thought—and she sank into the sudden stillness on the inside of her head.

She was not surprised when Calliastra joined her; she was slightly surprised that the scion of darkness and love sat at a respectful distance. "Jewel."

"Call me Jay."

Calliastra frowned.

"It's what Angel calls me. It's what all my den call me."

"Den?"

"Family," Jewel replied, not wanting to explain what the word "den" meant otherwise. "We're not related by blood, but in every other way, we're kin."

"And they call you . . . Jay? Why?"

"When I was a child, I hated my name."

"But why?"

"Jewel?" She shook her head.

"You still hate your name."

"I've learned to live with it. At home, though, no one uses it."

Something about Calliastra's guarded expression brought elements of that home back to her, and not in a good way. But she said, "I'll consider it." She fell silent as if doing so, but then she lifted her head. "Have you ever been where we are now?"

"No."

"Tell the ax-man not to cut wood here."

"He wouldn't. It's not cold, and none of the food we currently have needs heat."

"Tell the Arianni not to hunt here, either."

"If you're about to tell me to tell my cats the same thing—"

"No. The Lord of this land has always had a fondness for those beasts; if the cats came with you, she will nonetheless hold you blameless for their mischief." Her hands were massaging the folds of her blood-red gown.

Shianne did not seem to be discomfited in the summer heat; the light of the sun was insistent and even, until the clouds rolled in. Where they had experienced snow and bitter, howling wind, they now had rain. Jewel thought she preferred the snow; in the cold, it didn't seep into clothing.

"All living things require water."

Jewel stopped in her tracks. Everyone did, with the exception of the cats, who appeared to perk up a bit—which was generally not a good sign. They didn't, on the other hand, shift into their predatory postures.

"Yes, even us," Jewel replied, although she could not see the speaker. "But we prefer for the most part to drink it rather than wear it."

The speaker chuckled. Jewel tried to track the direction of that voice, but it was impossible; it seemed to come from everywhere.

"It *does*," Shadow said, clearly annoyed. "These are *her* lands."

Snow said, "They are *mostly* boring."

"And may they remain that way," Jewel muttered.

"A sentiment I share." A woman stepped around the trunk of a tree of middling size. Jewel couldn't identify it and didn't try; the only trees she knew by name were where she'd left them. At home.

"Well met, Jewel."

Jewel bowed. "And you, Corallonne."

She did not look familiar to Jewel, but Jewel recognized her nonetheless.

"It has been but a short time since the Stone Deepings," Corallonne told her. She nodded to Avandar. "Viandaran. Ah, and I see young Celleriant is with you as well."

He offered her a perfect—but short—bow. "Firstborn."

"You have come to my lands on a path that is seldom traveled, and only at need."

"We visited the Oracle, yes."

"Then you must be weary. Come. Shelter here for the evening." She glanced at Shadow and added, "I would appreciate it greatly if you did not hunt here."

"We will only hunt *bad* things," Shadow replied.

"What if *we're* hungry?"

"You are not mortal, to perish from something as simple as starvation." She then turned to Calliastra. "Sister. You are welcome here."

"Oh? That's new." Calliastra had folded her arms; her lips were a compressed, pinched line in an otherwise astonishingly beautiful face.

Corallonne's face was neither pinched nor beautiful; she appeared to be Jewel's elder by perhaps two decades. There was silver in her hair, but it was a scattering of light across an otherwise perfect brown. Her skin was darker than Calliastra's, darker than Ariane's, but it seemed warmer to Jewel. It implied home.

And was she now a child again, to be so homesick while the world hung in the balance?

Before she could speak, Shianne stepped forward. She had never been awkward, but was stiff and hesitant now. It put Jewel on her guard. She found no suspicion in herself for or about Corallonne.

That is never wise, Avandar said. The Winter King was not far behind. But neither man appeared to be unduly worried; the eddies of their interior conversation were simple nagging. Jewel had grown up with that; it held no horror for her, although it was trying.

Corallonne seemed neither surprised nor displeased to see Shianne.

"Shandalliaran," she said. She held out both of her hands, palms up, and after a notable hesitation, Shianne placed her own in them.

"Firstborn."

"You are concerned."

"There is a debt of blood between us. We have never been friends."

"No. But we have been allies in larger causes; we have managed—with effort—to put enmity to one side."

"And it has ever returned."

Corallonne nodded again. "But you seldom visited my lands. Perhaps twice, in my recall."

Celleriant was staring at the two women with growing concern. He did not, however, draw sword or shield.

"I have come—"

"As a member of Jewel's delegation, yes. And I accept Jewel's stay here without reservation. She will be held responsible for any war you bring with you." There was warning, in that.

Shianne, however, nodded. "Understand that I do not serve her. I am not bound to her."

"No. But Jewel is an odd creature, as mortals oft are. The bindings she holds are her own; she does not command or control in the ways of our kind. But she is, if I am not mistaken, Sen.

"And she is, if I am not mistaken, attempting to find a path to my sister,

Ariane." She failed to notice the effect the name had on Shianne, probably deliberately. To Jewel, she added, "there are no paths, not now. We have been searching for a way to enter her lands, and we have failed, time and again. But I perceive that you carry hope with you, in all its complicated forms."

"Yes."

"Introduce me to your friends, then, and we will withdraw for the time to a safer, quieter place."

Angel offered a bow which was almost perfect in form if a little stiff. Terrick knelt, which surprised them all. "All-mother."

Coralonne's eyes widened, and her lips rose at the corners, her eyes narrowing in a genuine smile. "You are far from home," she told the Rendish warrior.

Terrick did not lift his head; he did not rise.

"Come." She offered him her hand, and he placed his—reluctantly—across hers; hers was dwarfed. Terrick was taller, wider, larger in all possible ways than the woman who stood before him—but seemed, at the same time, to be younger and awkward with that youth. It was a striking contrast. "Rise, Terrick."

He did, but again, absent his usual powerful grace.

"You are far from home," Corallonne said again, "but home is here, for the while. I bid you welcome, you and your kin."

He was silent, as he so often was. It was not a comfortable silence.

"Do not tell me that the boy is not your kin," was her gentle command. "I see you in him."

"He is not blood, All-mother."

"No? You made blood oaths to his father, and you remained true to those vows. Some of his father's blood runs in your veins, and it certainly runs in his. I hear no lie, Terrick, and offer none. You are welcome here."

She moved then; the cats seemed drawn to her, but they followed docilely—for cats. To Kallandras, she said, "If you are willing, I would hear you sing before you leave."

His bow was an Imperial bow in form and texture. The warmth that Jewel was drawn to did not likewise compel the bard; he was guarded and would remain so. But he was, as always, polite. He demanded none of her attention and certainly none of her respect.

"Kallandras," Jewel said, when it became clear that Corallonne was waiting on his reply.

"I would be honored to have such an audience," he replied. And he sounded as if he meant it—but he was a bard. If he couldn't do at least that, he would never have been given his rank: Master Bard of Senniel College.

Coralonne stopped last in front of Adam as if it were a deliberate decision.

Adam offered her a very Southern bow—it was brief, a bob of motion. "Why does he call you the all-mother?"

"I am not certain," she replied. "But it is what his people have always called me, since our first meeting, and I accept it—it is spoken with respect, and there is affection in it if one knows how to listen. To you, however, I am not that. You are far from the Sea of Sorrows; far indeed from the Voyanne. I do not think you will ever return to it."

"I will not," Adam said. He was young, yes. But he was firm with youth and certainty. "Arkosa has returned home, and when I return to my kin, it will be to that home. We wander no longer."

Her smile was soft, but it was sad, as if she remembered something ancient that still caused pain. "No. The Cities of Man are rising—and they must rise. I can feel the god's footsteps from here. You have accompanied Jewel, and you will travel with her some small while yet—but when it is time, you must leave her."

"And how will I know?"

"You will know. Ah, no, perhaps that is not correct. She will know."

To Jewel's great surprise, Adam shook his head, a brief *no* in the gesture. "She would send me from her side now if she had that choice. How will I know that she does not do it out of worry or fear for me? How will I know?"

Corallonne chuckled. "You will not know, Adam. But you are wrong. You could not be here at all had she not desired your presence, and I have been made aware of what you have done on the unclaimed road. You are necessary, or you would not be here. And when necessity dictates otherwise, she will send you away—and you must go."

"To where?"

"Arkosa," was the quiet reply. "They wait you, even now."

He frowned. "You are not the Oracle."

"No. You wish to know how I know?"

He nodded.

"We can feel the Cities of Man when they wake, when they rise." She looked, then, to Calliastra. The daughter of darkness averted her gaze, but she did nod. "To enter those cities—those ancient, lost cities—we require permission. I was welcome in all but one, and that welcome has not been revoked. They do not know *how* to revoke it. They do not know how to govern the city."

"The Matriarchs know how to lead. They know how to rule." He spoke with more heat, his brow furrowed.

"I did not say that they did not know how to lead their people, nor would

I. That four cities will rise is a miracle in and of itself—one that we might never have predicted. I spoke of the governance of the *city* itself."

Adam appeared confused; he wasn't the only one.

"The Cities of Man were built by the Sen. All of them. In no other way would such places have been able to withstand the power of, the war of, gods. They are not a simple collection of buildings as Celleriant says your cities have become. The Cities bear the marks of their creators. But understand, Adam, that the women called Sen within the Cities of Man were not Sen. They were seers, yes. But they governed their kind in seclusion; they protected their kind. Sen was both an ancient title, in mortal terms, and a state of being. Those who *built* the Cities of Man were Sen. And my sister believes—the Oracle believes," she added, as Calliastra bridled, "that your Jewel is *Sen.*"

"Are the Cities alive?"

"They are, in some fashion, alive," Corallonne said gently. "They will not bleed; you cannot knit them whole with the strength of your talent-born gift. But they are not simple hovels or shelters. You have touched the sleeping earth in one of the Winter lands."

"And the cities—Arkosa—will be like that?"

"Like and unlike, yes. The Cities had defenses. Some of those defenses are active now, because they are part of the fabric of the city's creation; only when the last stone is razed will those defenses falter. But some defenses could not be woven into the fabric of the city itself; they were added later. They are not unimportant.

"You are not Sen," she added softly. "That is not your power. But you *are* powerful. Jewel is, or will be, Sen. The girl who made that butterfly is not, but *she* is powerful. Do you understand?"

Adam didn't, but that was fair; Jewel didn't either.

Corallonne shook her head, a rueful smile altering the geography of her face. "And I will talk until you are weary with lack of food and sleep, both. Come." She gestured, and the forest stepped away, trees moving back, their roots the only thing that remained in their passage.

Above their heads, branches began to stretch and, eventually, to twine; they formed a canopy.

"Come," she said again.

Jewel was reminded instantly of what The Terafin's personal chambers had become. She felt, if not at home, then as if she were in a home, someone's personal dwelling. The air was warm, but the heat was lessened by the canopy.

She did not expect to see walls. Indeed, there were none—but ivy, or something similar, seemed to gird tree trunks as if those trees were, like the walls of the houses in the city, solid and unchanging. There were stumps for tables and a small brook around which large, rounded stones had been laid; across these stones was moss.

"You will forgive the lack of hearth or fire; we light no fires here."

Jewel nodded.

"The food that sustains us does not require your cooking; the water that passes by us is pure and clear. It is never cold here."

"Not never," Shianne said quietly.

"Where there is cold," Corallonne continued, as if she had not been interrupted, "it comes with the visitors—and leaves with them, as well. Only one of you was born, in the end, to Winter."

"I was born in the Summer," Celleriant said.

"Yes, Winter Prince, you were. But it was in the Winter that you blossomed, as intended. There is no war here."

"War will take everything," he replied.

"Yes. But the heralds have not yet sounded the final horns, and we remain. There is no war here," she said again, "and those who might bring it cannot yet find the heart of my domain. I am not your Lady—your former Lady—to be chained and trapped in the confines of my lands, with no passage out, and no path in, but these are my lands, and permission to traverse them is required."

"Is that not so with your Lord's lands?" It was a sharper question, a more pointed one, than she had yet asked.

He did not answer.

Corallonne then turned to Jewel. "I would have you answer my question."

"I believe permission is required."

"You believe?" She took no trouble to hide her surprise, which verged on a kind of stunned outrage.

Shadow hissed laughter. "She is *very stupid*," he told the firstborn. "Permission *is* required, but she doesn't *know* how to *withhold* it. She is *afraid* to *own* anything."

"My dear, that will not do. Do you not understand why the Cities of Man could withstand the assault of walking gods?" Her voice gentled. "I see that you do not. Well. I will not withdraw my welcome. Come. Rest. It is safe for you to sleep here."

Jewel ate in a silence that was as close to peace as she had felt since she left her home. The Oracle had not starved them, but the Oracular halls spoke of danger and the consequences of bad choices, all of which could easily be made at any moment. Corallonne's forest was nothing like those stone halls.

She slept.

She woke to the sound of voices, both familiar.

"She will not be strong enough to do what she must do," Corallonne said.

"She will, sister," the Oracle replied. "I have seen the full measure of her success, the full measure of her failure. The one shadows the other; they are intertwined. She cannot be all of one thing; she will not be all of the other."

"She will break. She cannot do what must be done."

"She is the only hope we have."

"Our sister will destroy her. She has brought with her the tools of that destruction. Why did you allow her to wear that ring? Why did you allow it to be made at all?"

The Oracle's chuckle was low, rich, compelling; there was affection in it, and warmth. It reminded Jewel of her Oma in an indulgent mood, when everything was safe and might be forgiven. She did not move; she listened, wondering if everyone alive sometimes yearned for the illusory safety of childhood.

"You fail to understand her nature if you believe that I could have forbidden it. She is *Sen*, Corallonne."

"She is *not*," Corallonne snapped. "She does not understand what it means."

"No more, in the end, do we," the Oracle replied. "We have the powers of our parents to some degree; we have the power of creation—or destruction. But we are not Sen and cannot be. She has begun; this is the path she must walk. There is no other.

"But you labor under a misapprehension, sister. You believe—you must, given your reaction now—that the Cities of Man were built with will, thought, intent; that they were planned by people who had all the knowledge of architects, magi, and seers. You think that there was deliberation, choice."

"You do not."

"No. I saw the Cities birthed, and if you desire it, I will show you their creation."

Silence. A beat. Two. "It would tax you greatly."

"Yes, it would. But your fear and your anger make your land too wild for mortals to cross; if it will calm them, I will pay that price."

Silence again. "You frustrate me," Corallonne finally said. "As you delight me, at times. No, sister, I will not ask that of you. Not yet, and perhaps not ever."

"Do you understand the price I must pay?" the Oracle asked softly.

Jewel rose to her elbows; both women were watching her without apparent surprise. She shook her head, felt sleep recede as she joined them.

"You can look into the past."

Jewel nodded, because she had done it, once, and understood only now the reason that Amarais had left her a ring, a sword. To show her that she could look back, look over her shoulder; to demonstrate that there was information in the past she could find, should she care enough to search.

Corallonne opened her mouth, but words did not leave it; Jewel had lifted a hand in quick den-sign. She was obviously still half-asleep, and flushed, but the women seemed to understand the gesture.

"Everything you see causes pain."

Corallonne's brows rose; she glanced, quickly, at her sister. The Oracle's face was smooth as weathered stone. "Yes, child."

"Everything."

"Yes. Even hope is a type of pain, and it cuts bitterly when it dies. Better to dream of a future where pain might, at last, be laid permanently to rest; better to believe that that world exists, or might exist, around each and every corner."

"You can't."

"No."

Jewel had had days—weeks—of believing in nothing but loss and pain. She'd had weeks and months of knowing, *knowing*, that she should have been able to do something, anything, to prevent that loss. That she'd failed, as she always, always failed. The weight of that was something she could not completely shed.

"Yes, child. It is thus with our kind. But you fight on."

Jewel nodded.

"So do I. Your greatest failure is part of your greatest success; it is continuous, this pattern."

And Jewel understood. "The failures are permanent."

The Oracle's smile was slender, but present, as she nodded.

"They're fixed, they're set in stone, they can't be changed. They're forever. But the successes aren't. Everything I've gained, I could lose tomorrow. Everything I've built could be destroyed. Everything I want, everything I'm willing to work and bleed for—everything."

"Hope is dangerous," the Oracle replied, "where vision is clouded. Yes, child. To look at the future, at the possibilities, is to have the hope that one can affect the outcomes; that one's choices make a difference. But the past is, as you have said, fixed. It is a single thing; it cannot be moved or changed by such as we."

And Jewel said, "Evayne."

"What of her?"

"She walks through time. She's never the same age when she appears."

"She walks through time but experiences life as you would. She ages; she is weathered and worn by experience. She cannot change the past. Do you understand that?"

Jewel shook her head.

"She cannot change the past; she is part of it, wed to it. She is encased in the things that cannot be changed. You think she has choice in what she does—but Jewel, there are things that she *must* do, because they *were* done. She has less freedom than you, and less hope than I—but she endures. Of all my descendants, she is the one I wish—" The Oracle stopped. "Will you see the Cities of Man?"

Jewel swallowed. "Will it tell me anything I need to know?"

"What do you think?"

"It won't."

"I believe you are correct. The Cities of Man are perhaps not aptly named, and no two were the same. There is a reason for that. My sister is also correct; you do not understand what ownership means in the wild. The land on which you walk now is hers; it is of her. But it is kin to your dreams: your dreams are of you, but you do not dictate their growth or the direction they turn, and you cannot—yet—command what shape they will take; you cannot demand that they never transform into nightmare. Could you, you would.

"This is the high wilderness, Jewel. And Terafin is part of the high wilderness, now. It cannot be tamed; it can be survived and in places conquered—but it cannot ever be fully controlled."

"But it can be owned?"

"Yes. In the same fashion that you own your nightmares—and your dreams."

"In time," Corallonne added, "you will know which parts of your own lands are dangerous, unsafe; you will be able to guide your guests so that they might avoid that danger. But the danger is part of you; it remains, always." She hesitated, as if afraid to offer advice although she clearly wanted to do so. "The wilderness is *not* you. It is not all that you are—and it cannot become so, or you will cease to be Lord. But it is *of* you, regardless."

"But there are people who live in my lands."

"Yes? There were people who found shelter in the ancient cities, as well. And there were men and women of power who could coax and coerce those cities into shapes that more easily accommodated life—but never trivially. Come, Jewel," she said, as if reaching a decision she had struggled to make. "I wish to show you my winter."

Shadow woke then—if he had ever been sleeping. He yawned, exposing both his many, many fangs and his inexplicable boredom. "I don't *like* winter," he told Corallonne. Beside him, Snow and Night stirred as well.

"Yes, Eldest, I know. I will be guide and guardian; you need not accompany us."

"But it is *boring* here."

"I believe your Jewel craves boredom."

"Because she is *stupid*."

"Boredom has its place. You really should not let the cats speak to you like that," Corallonne added.

"So I have told her, sister." Calliastra stepped from the shadows. She had avoided the Oracle and the Oracle's domain; Jewel had expected her to avoid Corallonne. "But she does not listen. And when the cats visited you, they were hardly better mannered."

"They are not mine," Corallonne pointed out.

"No. But I am not entirely certain they are hers, either."

Shadow hissed; it was not the laughter hiss. He neither confirmed nor denied; he did complain about stupidity—with care not to include Corallonne overtly in his criticism.

Corallonne, however, frowned.

"What? She *is* stupid."

"She is a guest, Eldest. She is a guest in my domain."

"*Soooooo?*"

"What happened the last time you mistreated my guests?"

Jewel dropped a hand onto Shadow's head; the gray cat's muttering grew far less distinct.

"What if *she* doesn't care?" Snow asked.

"Are these her lands, or mine?"

". . . Yours."

"And she is *my* guest. I am certain you would not wish to embarrass me in front of my guests—and treating my guests with so little respect would be an embarrassment."

"But we're *bored*."

"And that," Corallonne said firmly, "is neither her fault nor her problem while she is here." She sounded like a severe Oma—one not yet angry but threatening storm. "If you wish, you may play at the edges of the tangle—but only at its edges. It is not notably safe for visitors; your master will not see it while I am with her."

"The tangle?" Jewel asked.

"It is a snarl of wilderness and ancient rage," Corallonne replied, as if she were describing a variety of plant. "We work around it. But it is not safe, even for one such as I. My sister," she added, indicating Calliastra, "has traversed it and survived—but only once."

"There wasn't much to see," Calliastra said, in the offhand way that meant she felt challenged or judged. "I'm sure your cats will find it boring. And who knows? It just might be able to kill them."

Night yowled in outrage. "If it didn't kill *you*, it *can't* kill *us*!"

"You cannot possibly believe that your power is, in any way, equal to my own?"

Corallonne grimaced; she met Jewel's gaze, and Jewel saw both resignation and weariness in the older woman's expression.

Night opened his mouth on a literal growl. Jewel lifted her hand from Shadow's head and murmured, "Stop your brother."

"Why *me*?"

"Because you can."

The black cat launched himself at Calliastra, who stood, arms folded, face hard and bright as a cut gem. He didn't reach her; he was intercepted by a hurtling gray mass. Their combined weight and trajectory took down a young tree, and probably a lot of the foliage at its base.

"I'm really, really sorry," Jewel began.

Corallonne's smile was grim, resigned. "Were they any other creatures, I would hold you responsible for the damage they now do. But my sister is correct; they were welcome visitors, and they were not markedly better behaved, in the end. They were, however, far more careful with their words." She offered Calliastra an arm, and to Jewel's surprise, the prickly child of gods slid her own around it.

"Walk with me?"

"Who will watch your guests?"

Corallonne smiled. Jewel knew the answer: the forest would watch—and was watching; it reminded her of her own forests, although the trees were not so markedly magical and otherworldly. Thinking of them, she opened the satchel she had carried from Terafin; it clinked as the leaves of her unnatural trees rubbed against each other.

Corallonne turned almost instantly; her eyes were a peculiar shade of golden brown, because they were glowing. Jewel almost dropped her satchel, but instead drew it closer. She opened the flap to look at the contents, as if to assure herself that she had not left them behind in the Oracle's halls.

Celleriant stepped into the space Shadow had vacated as branches—or whole trees—cracked and fell in the background. *Cats.* But it was not the sound of the two brothers sparring that drew either Corallonne's attention or her ire; she was angry.

"What," Corallonne demanded, "have you brought into my forest?"

And Jewel thought: Here? Is it here? Is this where these leaves were meant to go? The doubt and uncertainty were paralyzing enough that she had no ready answer. As she so often did, she settled for the truth.

"They're leaves," she told Corallonne "from the trees in my forest."

Corallonne stepped forward, looking down at the contents of Jewel's hand without extending her own. To Snow she asked, "Is it true? Do these trees grow in her forest?" There was an urgency to the question.

"Yesssss." As Corallonne opened her mouth, no doubt to ask another question, Snow swatted air and added, "She *planted* them." He glanced once over his shoulder, his tail twitching, but the sounds of Night and Shadow brawling had already started to fade.

"How?"

Jewel cleared her throat, and the older woman turned; the cat appeared to be inspecting his claws for signs of the wrong kind of dirt.

"I had a dream of the Winter King. The cats were his, but they were made of stone. To reach him, I had to pass through a forest of silver, a forest of gold, a forest of diamond. And when I woke, I had taken a leaf from each. Or . . . a leaf from each was with me."

"Do not leave those leaves in my forest," the woman who owned these lands replied; her expression was as grim as Jewel had ever seen it.

Not here, then. She hesitated. She slipped the three leaves back into her satchel and drew from it one other leaf: the *Ellariannatte*.

Corallonne's expression changed instantly. "And that leaf?" she asked, her voice almost hushed.

"We call them the Kings' trees," Jewel replied, modulating her voice to match her host's. "They grew in the Common, and only there, when I was a child. I used to gather the leaves that fell as if they were flowers." They had been the only flowers she could gather in her childhood; any dirt given to growing things had been used to grow vegetables—and there was precious little of that.

"And that did not come to you from dreams of Winter and death."

"No."

"They grow in your lands, these trees?"

Jewel nodded. Her smile was layered, informed by memory and sentiment and something that could have been peace. She held out one leaf to her host, and Corallonne hesitated.

"I have no like gift to offer," she said. "And I am not at all certain that these trees will take root in my own lands. The soil here may not suit them."

"They will grow in your lands if you permit it," Jewel replied, and knew it for truth the moment the words left her mouth.

Nor did Corallonne question her certainty. "Why are they called the Kings' trees in mortal lands?" she asked; her hand shook as Jewel placed the leaf into her open palm.

"I really don't know. I think it's because they grow nowhere else in the Empire. Nowhere—until I became Terafin—but the Common, which is the capital of the Empire."

"And they grew even after the sundering."

"They grew like normal trees—they just couldn't be planted anywhere else. I have a gardener who would love to meet you—I'm sure she could tell you in great detail all the places the trees couldn't be planted." Jewel hesitated and then continued. "You recognize the leaf."

Corallonne nodded.

"Do you recognize the tree it comes from?"

"I did not realize they still grew at all. I will forgive you your trees of cold metal and cold stone if you also shelter these. Plant this one, Terafin, with my blessing and my gratitude."

Jewel almost asked her why she didn't care to plant it herself, but her mouth would not open to let the words out. And she felt comfort in that; the instinctive certainty that had guided the whole of her life until recently had all but vanished in the wake of the Oracle's caves.

She took the leaf back from the firstborn. It was so light it should have been weightless; the breeze should have carried it aloft, borne it away. It was to that breeze that she had surrendered the leaves of silver, of gold, of diamond; she did not consciously remember planting *Ellariannatte* at all. She was not Birgide, not a botanist; trees and their study had not informed any part of her life.

These had come with the forest. These had grown in all their majesty when she had become the ruler of the Terafin lands. Not The Terafin—that had come later, and by surprising, if reluctant, acclaim—but the ruler of the lands in which silver and gold grew.

She closed her eyes. She heard a breeze. She heard the heavy rumble of cat complaint. She heard the voice of the butterfly—soft, high, inquisitive, and joyful in turn. She could not hear Shadow or Night; she could not hear Calliastra. She thought she could hear the full measure of Angel's breath. Angel.

She let the leaf go.

Chapter Thirteen

E YES CLOSED, JEWEL COULD see the arc the leaf made in the wind. The white of its outer edges seemed to glow for a moment; eyelids did not diminish its lazy but deliberate arc. Its flight was not the delicate meandering of butterflies, but neither was it the deliberate plunge of birds of prey.

She could not see the rest of Corallonne's forest. She could not see her companions. She thought she caught a glimpse of Shadow—but only Shadow; Night and Snow were absent.

She could see Corallonne and almost stopped breathing for one long minute. The woman that she thought of as maternal was not, not here; she was gold and brown and green, and she radiated life, as if it were an elemental force. If nature had a face, if nature could be forced into an almost human form, it was her face, her form. She looked neither young nor old, and her body was all things at once: slender, youthful, thick, and strong; her hair was night and day as its strands interlocked and fell.

She was a god, a goddess, who did not live in the lands the gods now inhabited.

Her voice was thunder and velvet when she spoke. *Jewel.*

Jewel had no words to offer in reply; her mouth was dry. But she shook herself. If this wasn't the Between, it wasn't the first time Jewel had seen and heard gods. She turned away, but only to watch the leaf fall, to see it touch foreign soil, foreign earth.

It was part of the wilderness.

It had always been part of the wilderness. Even in the mundane Common, the roots of these trees touched other soil, drawing strength and sustenance from it.

She whispered.

Yes, Corallonne replied, her voice too strong to be gentle, although there was no anger in it. *The Sleepers.*

"My trees are no part of the Sleepers."

No, Jewel, they are not. But they exist in the fashion they do in your world because of the Sleepers. And, now, because of you. She fell silent, and her silence was a hush, the space between lightning and answering thunder.

And the thunder did come, but it was not carried by Corallonne's voice: it was carried by the swift breaking of earth as a single leaf melded with Corallonne's forest, Corallonne's home, Corallonne's self—the three were not separate. As they had in the Terafin forest, this single tree bypassed the sapling stage, the fragility of youth; it gained width and height as it stretched up, and up again, as if seeking the distant sky.

And she heard its voice. She heard the name it spoke.

Yes, Corallonne replied, although Jewel had not spoken of it aloud. "Yes. Come, Jewel."

"But it's—"

"Yours, yes."

She blinked; her companions and their natural setting were restored. The thunderous quality of Corallonne's multitude of voices was hushed, muted. "But why?"

Shadow and Night had returned from their violent outing. They were stepping on each other's feet. Snow whacked the side of Night's face with his tail. Shadow muttered *boring* under his breath. Or as much under his breath as he ever did.

Corallonne ignored them all. "Why do I allow something so foreign into the heart of my forest?"

Shianne was clearly wondering the same thing; she looked as if she were on the verge of speech but could not yet decide how costly words might be.

Jewel nodded. She could, if she strained, now hear the breeze of her own forest; she could hear the tinkling of decidedly metallic leaves.

"You do not understand the nature of gifts, of giving, if you can truly ask that question."

"I do not understand your decision either," Calliastra said.

Jewel tensed.

"No, sister," Corallonne replied, the words soft and heavy with despair. "But

I am not you; you are not me. What I require would not, and could not, sustain you." She turned once again to Jewel. "You have given me some small part of yourself. I have allowed it to grow here because I understand what it means, and what it has meant, to you. You will not remove it—you cannot, now—and you will not demand, of me, something similar in return."

"It would not be wise," Shianne said, voice neutral, eyes downcast.

"And you, child of my sister, are as confused as Calliastra. You feel that this will diminish me."

"She feels that it could," Jewel said, coming to the rescue of a woman who needed none, and aware of it. "That I might use it to find purchase in the wilderness that otherwise bears your name."

"Yes, Jewel. It is a possibility. It is a vulnerability, if you will. But you cannot know life without vulnerability, and you cannot know joy. It is a risk, always, to accept the things that are given; some things are not given freely. It is an act of hope, if you will, and I am ancient, you are young. I seldom make mistakes."

"Not never," Calliastra said.

"I do not hold you responsible for that," Corallonne replied, her voice softer, her eyes darker. "You are what you are; you are the child of your parents."

Jewel said, "Can't we be more or different? I'm the child of my parents, but I'm not—"

"You are mortal. Mortals have a freedom of choice, of hard choice, that the ancients do not have. We envy it," she continued, "but we do not envy or even understand its cost." And, so speaking, she glanced at Avandar, who said nothing.

The *Ellariannatte* was at the height of its majestic growth; its buds had opened, and its leaves were in full flower high above their gathered heads. One leaf, and only one, broke loose of the branch that held it aloft, and it fell.

Jewel reached for it without thought, catching it before it touched the earth.

"These are ancient trees, and they have voices, and their song is sweet. It reminds me of youth, and the hope and dreams of youth before we spent them so foolishly. It reminds me of home, Jewel."

But this was her home.

"Yes. It is my home now. It was not always so. You think the trees were called the Kings' trees because of your Kings. That is not, however, the whole of the truth, or even the majority of it—and the trees do not care, one way or the other."

But we do.

Shianne's eyes widened; Celleriant's did the same. Although one was pregnant and mortal, for a moment they looked almost like twins.

Corallonne's expression lost joy, gained gravity. She turned to the lone tree and held out her arms, as if to embrace it.

The tree did not change; its bark did not alter; it did not open in any obvious way. But a man stepped out of its shadows, its shade, and she recognized him. Jewel had seen him once before, in the dream in which she had found and woken those stricken by the sleeping sickness, a world, or many worlds, away.

His skin was brown, bark brown, where once it had been gold; his eyes were green. His hair was green as well, but it was not precisely hair; it was vines or new branches or some mix of those.

But his lips were turned in a ready smile; his expression was gentle. He looked down at Corallonne—he looked down at them all, he was that tall— and he offered her a bow. There was the hint of a creak in it, as if branches were moving, but it was a graceful and complete motion.

"Do you, then?" Corallonne asked, an answering smile in her eyes, supported by the warm, full curve of lips.

"We do, All-mother. It has been so long since we have woken, so long since we were asked to watch and guard in our slumber. It has been so long since we have heard all but the barest whisper of the wilderness, we feel young again." He then turned and offered a second bow—to Jewel. "Lord."

She was discomfited.

Corallonne was not. "Will you remain as guest in my domain?"

"It is not as guest that I was planted," the tree replied. "But I am content. You offered such joy and such hope before you allowed me to be planted, and that pleased me greatly." At Jewel's expression, he chuckled. "You did not ask my permission?"

She nodded, wordless at the thought of the other leaves she now carried.

"My permission, Terafin, is not required. Do you think I will resent you? Are you afraid to abandon me?"

She was afraid of all these things but she hadn't been until he had stepped through the trunk of the tree.

"I am not a slave," he told her. "I am a servant."

"But I didn't—"

"No. I am not mortal. While you live, I am yours. If you perish and no other is strong enough to hold the lands in which I am planted, I will be other. But being yours is not a burden to me, and it does not greatly change my nature. I am content to be here, far from the horns of war. I will carry word to you if word becomes necessary."

"You cannot expect that war will reach my own lands so soon?" Corallonne almost demanded.

"It is our belief—it is the belief of the oldest and most dangerous of my kind—that war will reach all lands in less than the span of a mortal lifetime—her life. I am hers, Corallonne—and I am yours while you allow it. What she cannot do, I will do."

Corallonne seemed greatly pleased, even joyful. She caught his hands in both of hers, and he allowed it.

"And now?" she asked.

"I ask a boon of you," the tree replied as if this were expected. "My Lord needs travel, and she is unfamiliar with the roads she must traverse." He glanced at Adam. "The boy is coming to know them."

"You do not wish to chance your Lord's safety on the knowledge of young Adam."

"No, I do not. But I trust Adam because she trusts Adam. It is not his intent that is in question; it is the destination to which he must, in the end, travel. They are not, I fear, the same, although the roads overlap for some while yet."

Corallonne stiffened, but did not release his hands, "You were young," she said softly, "when I was young. You and your kin. I marveled at what you built; I grieved for what you destroyed. But that was ever the nature of the ancient and the wild—as powerful, as beautiful, as the storms."

"But perhaps more enduring," he replied, smiling down at her. "Yes. I wish you to take my Lord home. The way is clear to you; it will never be so clear to her."

"If she is home, she will not fulfill the task she has set for herself. It is not from home that she will find the Winter Queen."

"No," he replied gravely, his voice smooth as new bark. "And yes. You will not reach your sister, and you," he added, turning to Calliastra, "will not, even if you condescend to try."

"I will not try. I am generous enough—but only barely—not to interfere with the attempts of the mortal. Ariane can rot in the netherworld, neither Winter nor Summer Queen—it is what she deserves for her pretension."

"Pretension?"

"She wished to *be* Winter. To *be* Summer. And because she was Ariane and firstborn, the whole of the world knit itself to her desires. And her desires? They were exalted, respected, valued." If words were containers in which bitterness could be held, these ones were too small for what Calliastra attempted to pour into them.

The ancient gazed down at her almost sadly; Corallonne stiffened. "She did not attain her role, or undertake the responsibilities of it, without permission; she traveled, she bartered, and she warred—but war was her last option. It was costly."

"Yes. And we see the costs now, and I see no reason that she should not pay them."

"But I do," Jewel said quietly. "Your world was vast and ancient. You've seen the rise and fall of empires. I know one Empire. It was there before I was born. I don't want to watch it fall—everything I love is in it."

"And your *love* is to be reason enough?" And oh, the scorn, the derision, in Calliastra's voice. Her hands were balled in fists, and those fists shook; Jewel understood instinctively that now was not the time to reach out to her in any way.

"It's reason enough for me," she said quietly. "I'll spend my life on it, one way or the other."

"And would they do likewise for you?" She meant to needle; it was petty.

Jewel said, voice much softer, "Yes. Some already have. They're probably waiting by the bridge for the rest of us to join them—and when we do, I want to be able to tell them that I fought, too. I did *everything* I could."

"Mortals." Calliastra's anger fled into the lines of her quieter petulance and resentment.

The newly planted *arborii* attempted to come to Jewel's aid. "The Oracle herself has seen no road that she can travel. If she had seen a road that Evayne a'Nolan could travel—"

"What road is forbidden *her*?" Calliastra demanded. There was so much resentment in her, so much anger.

So much pain.

"The road," he replied, "that might lead her to her half sister. It is she upon whom the Oracle pinned her hopes these ages past—but even she cannot find the way."

"And you expect *Jewel* to do what you believe—incorrectly—that none of *us* can?"

"No, Firstborn. We hope. There are things that even the Oracle cannot clearly see—you understand why. You intend to accompany my lord on her journey."

"I am *not*—" Calliastra pulled herself up short. She spoke her mind, much as Duster had, but could see when her own declarations might embarrass her. "I have nothing else to do. I am restless, and there is war where she walks. There is war almost anywhere she stands."

"Ah. Then your interests are kin to the interests of the eldest."

Cats yowled in outrage—but so did Calliastra. Jewel kept her expression stiff, but it was difficult—and Shianne chuckled, which made it worse.

Jewel muttered a brief Torran imprecation and stalked over to the nearest cat. She placed a hand firmly on Shadow's head. "It was not an insult," she told him firmly.

"It *wassssssss*."

"It was an *observation*, Shadow. If you don't want people to make observations like that, you'll need to change the behavior that allows it."

"And me?" Calliastra asked, voice of velvet death.

Jewel squared her shoulders. "And you as well, of course."

This put Shadow in a better mood and Calliastra in a worse one, which was not ideal. But Jewel understood that she could not back down when she was right, not in front of people like Calliastra. Not in front of people like Duster.

"I'll take you," Jewel continued, when Calliastra's speechlessness extended the brittle silence. "I'll take you with me if you want to come. But my home is my home; the people in it are not food. I'm sorry," she added, her voice softening in spite of her screaming instincts. "I may be leading them all to death, in the end—but not that death. Can you live in a city without feeding?" It was a flat question.

"As well as you can," Calliastra countered.

"I can't."

The firstborn did not reply, not directly. She glared at Shadow and said, "What do you eat in her pathetic, mortal city?"

"We don't *need* to eat. We're not *mortal*. Only mortals are *stupid* enough to *need* food."

"It's how we were made," Jewel told him, frowning.

"Yes, *and*? You *have* power. You. The healer boy." He sniffed. He was never going to like Adam. "Why don't *you* change?"

"You don't honestly think that we can physically alter ourselves enough that we don't need to eat?"

Shadow yowled. To Corallonne he said, "You *seeeeeee? Stupid.* Stupid."

Corallonne's lips twitched, which did nothing to discourage the gray cat. "You have patience, Terafin. I grant you that. Your race is often in such a rush to live to the fullest the small number of years granted them, they lack that patience, and the lack is costly." To the man whose hands she still retained, she said, "I will do as you ask, if it is at all safe for me to do so. I am not welcome in the high wilderness where it is not claimed."

"It is not unclaimed," the man replied, the bark of brows rising in near-outrage.

"But it is not claimed as I have claimed my own, or as my sisters have claimed theirs. You cherish her as Lord because you are awake—but you are not of her; she has not remade you."

"Ah, but she has, Corallonne. When we are with her, we dream of home, and some of us have begun to make it. It is not *her* home, not as she sees home—but we have taken what we can out of her desire. It is like fire's warmth, without fire's cost." And his eyes glimmered then, with a hint of red.

The red caught Calliastra's attention. Shadow, however, sniffed and turned his nose up.

"Then sleep, if you will, you and your companions. In my dawn, I will wake you and we will walk. There may be some small difficulty, and I believe at least one of your cats has managed to snarl himself in the tangle."

"Nothing can kill the cats," Jewel said, with utter conviction.

"The cats can be transformed; they are part of the ancient wilderness."

"Yes. Is the tangle sentient?"

Corallonne did not appear to understand the question.

"I've had the cats turned against me once, by the Warden of Dreams."

"You have seen our brothers?"

"More than once."

"They trespassed, then."

"More than once," Jewel repeated, with more emphasis on each word to give the sentence a kind of ugly color.

"They were never completely cognizant of the boundaries and borders that divided lands."

"Meaning they couldn't be bothered to respect them?"

"I think it likely that at times, when focused on their own pursuits, they did not perceive them. Are they well?"

"At the moment, yes." She turned to the tree.

"They are well. They are perhaps a trifle bored, but they have done no further damage."

Corallonne's eyes widened as the implication of the ancient's words sank roots. "You have imprisoned my brothers?"

"I have offered them hospitality," Jewel countered, "where they offered me death. And worse."

"Worse?"

"The death of my kin. But if you will travel to my lands, you will be able to speak with them."

"Then it is settled," Corallonne said. "Tomorrow I will do more than try, Terafin; I will succeed." To the tree, she said, "I will require your aid."

"Indeed."

The Hidden Wilds

Carver walked ahead of Ellerson, in the tunnel forged by the passage of the weighty, gold-tinged bear. He had no other word to describe the creature and, in truth, wasn't certain that *bear* was accurate; bears were not creatures that he had encountered in his life in the streets of the hundred holdings. He'd heard stories—everyone had—but had assumed that bears were almost mythical. More mundane than dragons, far less real than dogs.

No dogs would have broken decades—or more—worth of winter ice simply by standing or walking on it. And no dogs who somehow could would move so damn quickly. Were it not for the boots left them by ancient peoples who had deserted this place, the tunnel would have been a godsend.

It was Ellerson, not Carver, who called a halt to their rapid progression. "Eldest."

The bear paused and turned, its golden eyes baleful. "Yes?"

"If you cut this track through the snow for our use, it is not necessary." When the bear failed to acknowledge this—and Ellerson waited some seconds before he continued—he added, "We were gifted boots that make passage across the snow possible. It is how we traveled as far as we did. And if we are being hunted—if we *will* be hunted—we wish to disturb as little of the landscape as possible."

The bear cocked his head to the side, as if struggling to translate the words into something that made sense. His eyes narrowed, his brow furrowed; it was an oddly human expression. "I am not," he finally said, "certain what you fear.

"These tracks will be seen, yes—but you cannot make them as you are now; it is likely that anything that hunts you will assume these tracks were made by me."

Ellerson was silent. It wasn't a hesitation. Carver had seen this silence a few times before. He waited now, as he had every other time.

"We have no wish to seem ungrateful," the domicis began.

"Mortals often say this when they intend to seem exactly that. You are suspicious?"

"Say, rather, that we are cautious."

"How cautious could you be and end up here?" The bear snorted, his breath visible in the winter air. He also scratched his nose, a black, damp patch of skin. "How could you end up here at all? It is vexing, and it taxes my mind. I am famously lazy," he added.

Ellerson's response was a dubious glance at a trench that now seemed to stretch for a mile. Or more.

"That is not effort, on my part. In this place, it is what occurs naturally. Thought, however, requires me to be fully awake. I dislike the cold. I dislike the Winter. I have always thought it best to sleep through it." The bear yawned. "And I have been sleeping. I would remain asleep were it not for the damnable noise."

Carver could hear nothing.

"Sleep," the bear added, "can be boring." The creature's eyes narrowed as his massive head swiveled in Carver's direction.

Carver had the grace to flush. "Apologies," he said, tendering the bear a half bow.

"Did I say something that offends?"

"No."

"Did I say something that reminded you of something else?"

"Yes, I'm sorry."

"Ah." The bear sat on its haunches. "And that would be? It can't be sleep. Hmmm. Boring?"

"I've spent time with winged cats," Carver explained. "Their most common word is *boring*." He stretched the two syllables out in a passably catlike whine.

The bear's eyes rounded. "Are they here?"

"No. They followed their master."

"Master? *Master*? Mortal boy, you had best have a care when using that word around the creatures you do not name. They take very poorly to it, and there is nothing about you that implies you could survive their great petulance." He frowned again, his upper lip moving in such a way that it exposed fangs. "No," he said at last, "there *is* something. And you have made me think . . . and also wasted time."

He turned and once again began to tunnel through the ice and snow.

Ellerson cleared his throat. "Eldest," he said. He had not moved to follow.

"Ye-es?"

Carver wondered then why so many of the ancient creatures took the form and shape of animals.

"What do you seek to gain from us?"

This time, the bear smiled. "Very good." He turned to face them and once again sat. This time, however, the earth trembled at his weight.

"I heard three things," he said, and his voice, like his weight, assumed a rumble that implied thunder, storm. "Three things, I heard, while I slept. The first was the name of the Winter Queen. The second was the voice of the dead. And the third was the voices of those who are trapped. As I am trapped. I did not come to these lands when their Lords slumbered; I came at the height of their power. It was not Winter then, but Summer at its height, and you will not know beauty or power who cannot see these lands in Summer.

"And they will never be seen in Summer again, mark my words."

Ellerson waited. If the words of the bear—if the voice of the bear, which caused tremors in the snow—held any fear for him, he kept it from his face, from the line of his shoulders and neck. Carver wasn't certain he had done the same.

"Her name, you bear. It is an echo of what she once was, an echo of those who called her. I was not one of them," he added, in case that were necessary. "But it was her name that drew me to you, here, in a world that *cannot* speak it. It has been forbidden the Lord of these lands, even in dream. Do you understand?"

Ellerson nodded as if he did.

Carver signed *truly?* Ellerson did not reply.

"The puzzle, of course, is how you are here at all, but you have no answers. No," he said, before Ellerson could speak, "I have not finished yet. The second thing I heard, the earth will hear; it rumbles in its sleep, even now. These lands are waking, and that means their Lords are also waking. But it is early yet; the earth would not rise had it not been for the second thing: the voice of the dead.

"In truth, I am curious, and I would wait. I thought that the voices of the trapped accompanied the dead, as they often do, poor, lost souls—but that is not the case."

Ellerson waited.

"You drive a harsh bargain, mortal. For your scant years, you accrue wisdom at an astonishing rate. Very well. I seek to leave these lands."

"So do we."

"Yes, I imagine you do. The Lord will wake, and you will not survive the waking. There is some small chance that *I* will not survive the waking; one wakes from the deepest of slumbers in a state of confusion. But if you are here, there is, somewhere, a *there*, for these are not lands in which you belong. Not bearing those rings that speak the Winter's name for all who have ears to hear.

"They will not protect you from the dead who come seeking you."

"These dead of whom you speak were not called thus by mortals."

"Ah, no. I forget myself, I have had so little company for so long. No,

Mortals called them demons in their many tongues. When they made their long choice, when they chose to forsake all kin, all alliances, save one, they lost their names. I cannot tell you which of the demons have come unless I see his ghost. And I do not counsel that we wait; I am likely to survive, being somewhat good at that; you are not."

"You offer us aid in return for aid? We cannot guarantee that we will find what we seek."

"Wise, but tiresome. Yes. You will do me the favor of alleviating boredom, and if you are very lucky, more besides. And I will not allow the demon to harvest your souls—if I cannot somehow save your lives."

"Very well. That is the sum of our responsibilities to you?"

The bear nodded impatiently.

In the distance, Carver could hear the winding of horns.

"The land remembers the Hunt tonight," the bear said. "They will not harm you."

Carver said, "They already have."

The creature spoke a word that Carver didn't understand, but the tone made its meaning clear. "Did you wear that ring when you first encountered them?"

"No."

"They will not harm you now. They are memories, dreams, things of power only here. But to them, the ring you wear supersedes all hunts, all pleasure." He exhaled as the horns sounded again. "If we are lucky, they will stumble across your pursuer. He will note them, and perhaps he will be delayed. But come, come. We must leave the trapped behind, or we will not escape."

Corallonne's Land

Jewel did not dream in Corallonne's forest.

She woke three times: once to the ancient that was, in some fashion she didn't understand, the spirit of the *Ellariannatte* she had planted, once to the pale luminosity of Calliastra's eyes, and once to the furious howl of outraged cat.

The third waking was the final one; she was on her feet, blankets thrown haphazardly to one side, before she realized where she was. She had attempted to leap out of bed.

Shadow was staring intently into her sleep-blurred eyes. His mouth was closed.

"Where are your brothers?" she asked, shaking herself free of that dreamless, peaceful sleep.

"They are *not here*," he replied, his voice a low rumble.

Corallonne stepped out from behind a tree. "They woke in their usual state. They were bored. Shadow chose to remain while you slept, but his brothers did not; they went to find something to fight. They have not returned." Her face gave expression to the uneasiness that had driven Jewel from sleep.

Jewel turned to Shadow. "Where are they?"

"Not *here*." He failed to meet her eyes.

"Shadow."

"They *might* have chased something *into* the tangle."

". . . where they're not supposed to be." Of course.

Corallonne spoke, her voice the kind of soft that had steel underneath. "Understand, Jewel, that the tangle is not unlike your cats."

Shadow hissed in outrage but did not otherwise disagree.

"How? It moves, destroys things at random, and makes a lot of noise?"

Hiss.

"Yes." The older woman smiled. "And no. It is, in its entirety, what it is. It can be—carefully—confined; it cannot be remade or otherwise controlled. It resists all such interference. The greater the power one attempts to exert over its shape and its existence, the greater the danger of its response."

"Is it sentient?"

"Not in a fashion that you would recognize."

"In a fashion," Jewel demanded, dressing, "that you would?"

"Yes. It speaks with a voice that I can sometimes hear—but only with effort, and it is costly. Its voice is slow; slower than the voices of the ancient trees; slower than the voices of the stone or the mountains built of it. Mortals could not speak with it—but I have never had Sen as guests before; I do not know what it might make of you."

"I'd like it not to make anything of me, if it's all the same to you."

"Of course."

She hesitated. This wasn't the first time the cats had disappeared, and when they did, they could be gone for long stretches. Long, *peaceful* stretches.

"We don't have time to look for them," Jewel told Shadow, who watched her. He said nothing. The height of his fur didn't change; his posture remained stiff and feline. Even his whiskers, which twitched constantly, were still.

But she hadn't been thrown out of sleep without reason. This was not the first night that her talent-born gift had roused her. On those other nights, she woke from dreams that would not release her until she had spoken of them. On those nights, she had had her den.

Only one of the den was with her now, and she turned to him. He was packing.

What are you doing? she signed. Her hands were trembling.

"You need Shadow," he replied, an indication that the answer was too complicated to sign. "And Shadow needs them."

Shadow glanced at Angel, his wide, round eyes narrowing. To Jewel's surprise, he didn't contradict Angel.

"They can take care of themselves," she said. "They always have before. When they vanished into the darkness—"

"It's not the same."

"How do you know that?"

"Because you do, Jay."

She stiffened.

"There is a way to approach the tangle safely," Corallonne said. "You might be able to call the cats back to your side from its edge. There is no safe way to enter the tangle, but it might not be necessary for you."

Calliastra said, "No." The word was snapped out, harsh; she was pacing, her hands in fists.

"Did she not come from our sister's domain to learn what she must learn? Has she not succeeded at least well enough that she can continue her journey?"

This was not the first time Calliastra had had this argument. Jewel could feel the weight of history in her denial, see it in her posture.

"Our sister did not tell her everything she needs to know."

"She could not; Jewel is mortal, and time is pressing for her kind."

"What," Shianne said, her voice as hard as Calliastra's, her eyes colder, "do you feel she must know?" She spoke to the firstborn daughter of darkness, command in her voice, in her words.

It seemed to calm Calliastra, but it would; it was something to stand against. Corallonne provided no counterbalance to her growing anger. Her fear.

"You know nothing about the Sen. Nothing about mortality—which is ironic, considering your state. You'll learn. It will kill you, but you'll learn because you have no choice."

"And you know the Sen?"

"No. I know insanity. I know how to break a mind. I know how to break a man, a boy, a woman, a girl. I know when hope is a gift and when it is a curse.

The strongest of people can be broken by the smallest of things—if you understand them."

Jewel cleared her throat.

Both women turned toward her—as did Corallonne. Shadow came to sit by her side, his tail twitching.

"The reason I came to the Oracle was to learn the use of my gift. The full use. To be able to command it, rather than drifting in its currents to be tossed up on some random shore."

"Do you honestly feel that you will be in command should you choose to expose your heart *here*?" Calliastra's voice was almost the definition of scorn. Jewel took comfort from it, which she knew was perverse. Maybe scorn was one of the capstones of her early life; it reminded her so much of her Oma.

"The location won't make much difference," Jewel replied. Her voice had a bit more edge in it, but it had a bit more color as well. If she didn't know what to fight for, she knew what to fight against.

"I do not speak of *location*. Honestly," she added, speaking to Shadow, "I do not know how she has survived to reach her present age. It must be very difficult for you."

"It *is*," Shadow replied.

"The Oracle understands tragedy. She understands fear. She understands the weight of hope. But she does not understand people."

"And you do?"

"Of course I do," she snapped. "I had to snare them to hunt them. I had to learn everything about them in order to live." She glared at Jewel; Jewel's gaze didn't falter. "You cannot act in fear."

Jewel was silent.

"Do you understand? There are those who *can*. Their lives revolve around their fears; their dreams revolve around their fears. Their hopes, as well."

"I'd say that about covers me."

"Then your cats are right. You *are* stupid."

Corallonne's brows had risen, her lips had thinned. She said nothing, however. Jewel recognized the quality of that nothing—there were a lot of words jostling for position behind it. Some of them might even manage to break the wall that kept them hidden.

"You are right. It is why you came. But understand that *how* you approach the question will define what you see. You will look into your heart, but your heart is not a perfect, pristine place; it is not a place where fear or anger or hatred is absent. It is a place in which you have sheltered those things, hidden those things, imprisoned those things—do you understand? Your heart is not separate from you; it *is* you. But it is you without bounds.

"Did you honestly think that you could just rip out some essential part of yourself and suddenly have perfect clarity of vision?"

"I didn't rip it out," Jewel replied, but she flushed.

"I'd let you discover this on your own—you're not a complete fool, you'd learn—but you constantly whine about *time*. If you do this now, in this frame of mind, you will *lose* time. You may lose more than time. My sisters—the ones you've met—don't understand your kind. It's probably the *reason* the Sen who approached the Oracle went insane."

"You never spoke with them."

"Not directly, no. I was just one element of their personal nightmare. I was part of the reason they built their very specific walls." The words were both bitter and proud. "But I saw enough."

She was lying, Jewel realized. She was lying about something. But the quality of her voice, the rawness of it, made the lie seem almost like truth—and it probably felt like truth to Calliastra. Whatever that truth was, Jewel left it alone.

"How am I to make use of the gift?"

"Control it."

Jewel exhaled slowly. "That's the reason for the crystal: control."

"You misunderstand me. In theory, you have control over your powers; in theory, you have made the choice to take that control, to make it conscious."

Jewel thought she understood, suddenly, what the lie was.

"But in practice the control is required most when you choose to look into your own heart. A mortal heart is an incredibly ugly place. And at the same time, it is incredibly beautiful and illuminating. There is no heart anywhere that is not both of these things. Control, Terafin, is choosing *which* of these places you will dwell in. But you will see both, in yourself. You have no choice.

"And if you ask the questions in fear, or with fear, you change the nature of what you see. Is your fear real? Of course it is. It is real, and it is true because it exists, always, at the heart of you.

"But so, too, the strength, the purpose, the focus. The hardest thing you must learn is to see the truth past the veil of fear, because *some* of those fears *are* truth. But not all."

Calliastra had clearly spent some time in the company of the Sen—at least one. Jewel wanted to ask; didn't. The past was the past. That had always been her rule.

Corallonne, however, stared at the woman she had called sister.

"Mortals," Calliastra continued, knowing that she had her sister's full attention, "hide what they are. They call it adulthood. They call it self-control. They learn, in time, to present only what must be seen. Sometimes, that *is* anger. Sometimes it's fear. Sometimes it's kindness—less often, but not always. With time, the heart grows to encompass many things, it moves and changes, but the process is slow, and it is invisible. What they develop as they age is the ability to choose what others see—but they are always choosing among a pleth ora of emotions, of states of being."

This did not change Corallonne's expression.

"If a mortal woman asks, *what will become of my child*, and she is seer-born, she will receive not one answer, but many. If she asks in fear, all that she sees will be the culmination *of* that fear. She will think that his life, from infancy on, is lived only in that state of privation. She will search in desperation for an avenue that does not end in starvation and death."

"We *all* do that. We don't need to be seer-born," Jewel said, with more heat than she'd intended.

"No, little seer, you do not. You might fear it. Fear might shadow you and dog your steps. But you will *also* see your son walk, and speak his first word, and smile at the leaf of a tree. He will be himself, and he will grow. In your own heart, he will not—he will be the sum of your question, and in the example I have given, he will be the sum of his mother's fears. Not more than that. And those fears will define how she moves forward; it will guide all the choices she makes, for good or ill; she will not *see* her child; she will only see *her fear.*"

Jewel stared at the daughter of darkness, then, and understood.

"You are Sen. The tangle is far less dangerous to you personally than you yourself have become." Calliastra waited; Jewel did not reply, not in words. But something in her expression must have changed, for the daughter of darkness fell silent.

Jewel drew one long breath and said, "Take us to the edge of the tangle." Remembering belatedly that she did not speak to the Chosen or her household staff or her House Council, she flushed and added, "please."

Angel was silent; he often was.

Adam, however, lifted his hands, moving them in a particular way which immediately caught Angel's attention; it was den-sign. He frowned, glancing at Jay, at Calliastra, at Corallonne. Angel had told Jay—and he fervently believed it to be the truth—that Calliastra was not, and would never become, Duster. She was the child of gods—and at that, the one god mostly likely to end all known human civilization without careful opposition. Duster, like most of the den, had been uncertain about at least half of her parentage.

But it was Duster who most often took on the thankless job of arguing—pointedly, angrily—with Jay. And at least half the time, Duster had been right. The other half? Not so much.

He wasn't certain if Calliastra was right, but she didn't have to convince him. And Angel knew the moment when she'd done the job she'd set out to do. He could see it in the lines of Jay's face, the corners of her mouth, the slow unbunching of her shoulders.

Adam said, "Is the Matriarch not correct?" the question soft.

"I think they're both right. Jay knows why she came here. She knows what she thought she'd be doing. And she knows that you don't get something for nothing."

Adam coughed; it was a politic sound.

"If the Oracle had said, *I'll trade you: give me your right arm and I'll give you the ability to see the true future*, that would be more along the lines of what she expected. But she didn't. One night in a dark room—by Jay's account—"

"She cannot speak of everything."

"She's not one of your Matriarchs," Angel replied, voice even, irritation lurking at the core of the words. "She's one of ours. She speaks of everything she thinks might affect the rest of us. It wasn't a *good* night, but—it wasn't enough. Calliastra is reminding her of that."

"Of what?"

"That she didn't get something for nothing." He shouldered a pack. "Come on."

"Why are you taking those?"

"It's just a hunch."

"You think something bad will happen?"

"I think," he replied, as Terrick joined him, "something bad *has* happened. But it might affect where we end up, and we don't want to starve when we arrive there."

"Why do you believe that?"

"Because Jay does."

"You said she speaks of everything—"

"Aye, and she does—but not always in words. She thinks the cats are essential. And she thinks the cats are in trouble."

Adam looked dubious.

"She hasn't accepted it yet, but the cats *are* den-kin. They're hers, same as we are. She couldn't control Duster, not precisely. She couldn't demand Duster change who she was or what she could do. But she had rules we *all* had to follow—the weakest of us and the strongest of us. The cats? They're kin, to her. And unless the fate of the world hangs in the balance, she won't leave 'em."

"But . . ."

Angel glanced at the boy.

"The fate of the world does."

The spirit of the *Ellariannatte* accompanied their host. He was bright-eyed, his expression one of open wonder, even joy. He asked questions, and paused only once, losing the strands of his focused curiosity as the bright butterfly left the bard's shoulder and came to rest upon Jewel's.

Words fled his open mouth, and no schooling in manners caused that mouth to shut; he appeared to be gaping. After a long pause he spoke again, but this time he spoke in the language of, apparently, butterflies.

Jewel had come to understand that it had a voice, of a kind; Kallandras could hear it. It didn't so much converse as sing, as if it existed in its own little world—a world it carried with it. She couldn't hear its voice, most of the time.

She heard it now.

The *Ellariannatte* spoke again, shifting tone and texture of voice without adding recognizeable words; Corallonne and Calliastra seemed transfixed.

Shadow, however, growled.

Jewel's hand fell automatically to the top of his head at the sound.

"They are making *too much* noise," he told her.

She couldn't hear it. "They make less noise than you or your brothers."

"They *don't*. Not *here*."

Jewel looked down at the cat and froze.

Beneath his feet, beneath the tips of his claws, the forest floor was flickering.

Without thought, she said, "Stop. Stop walking now."

Celleriant, by Kallandras' side, drew his sword and his shield.

Shadow stepped into her side, narrowly missing her foot. "You *hear* it."

"What am I hearing?" she asked, eyes narrowed, as if sound could be seen.

"The tangle," Corallonne replied, but her voice was muted, hushed. The *Ellariannatte* had fallen silent as well, and he retreated.

"Adam. Angel." She signed *danger*. Words were visual, here. To the Senniel bard, she said, "Quiet your voice."

She didn't see his answering expression.

Corallonne said, into the ensuing silence, "The tangle is not yet here," as if the location could move.

And it could, Jewel thought. It could. It was not a place as she understood geography, not even a place like her forest, her private rooms. She felt it as a presence, or as a comingling of presences, as if she could see the hushed gossip of a large, gathered crowd. As if that gossip carried anger, rage, helplessness— all things that turned a crowd into a mob.

And she could see the butterfly's glow, could hear the sudden storm of its song. Where she had heard the voice of a young girl, raised in a fluting sort of wordless, joyful song, she now heard the rage and despair—utter despair— that underlay it, or perhaps existed by its side. It was an odd thought.

Kallandras was staring at the butterfly.

Other eyes turned to it as well, hearing now what Jewel heard. She lost the sound of its song for one moment when the dragon roared.

Shadow hissed. His fur was sleek and flat, his claws scratching stone, although the rest of the forest floor was of dirt.

"You are sensitive," their host said. "We are much closer to the heart of the tangle than I perceived. It is no longer safe here, Terafin. I bid you withdraw." She glanced once at Celleriant, her lips thinning, but held her peace; she did not do the same for Shianne. "Shandalliaran, it is no longer safe for you."

"Where they go, I must follow," the former Arianni said; she was white as bleached bone, pale with the absence of color.

"Will you not then warn them?"

"Of what? The White Lady is trapped; she is all but lost. To reach her, there are no safe paths. Even contested paths, where our peoples war, will no longer lead us to her." She had paled with each sentence; her hands were fists. From the corner of an eye, Jewel saw Adam move to stand beside her; saw Shianne drape an arm protectively—or possessively—across his shoulder.

"There might be no existing paths," Jewel said, her voice even but low. "But we don't walk across water, either."

Angel understood. Terrick lifted an iron brow.

"There are some places we can't go. We can't build what we need to build there, no matter how desperate we are. We can't walk across water. Even if the land is at war and the ground is treacherous, water can't be made into what we need."

"It might be touched by ice," Celleriant offered. He was waiting, measuring—both Jewel and the environment. His desire to reach the White Lady's side was no less visceral, no less desperate in the end, than Shianne's. But Celleriant, unlike Jewel or Shianne, had forever.

"Fine. Water was a bad example. Fire? Would fire be better?"

Angel lifted hands, signed; Adam signed back. She watched what they both said and did not say, then shook her head. Her own hands were bunched in fists; she couldn't join their conversation.

But she felt it, in the pit of her stomach, in the beat of her heart, the tightness of her hands: certainty. It was not safe to continue. And continue, regardless, she must.

"My companions," she began, turning to Corallonne.

Angel said, "I'm going with you."

"You're not Sen."

"So?"

Jewel glanced briefly at Adam, remembering the dream that had almost killed them both. Shadow growled, low and wordless. Adam was not Angel. He was pale—although that might have been because Shianne's grip was so tight her knuckles threatened to pop out of her skin.

It was Adam Jewel wanted to leave behind. Adam and Shianne. She opened her mouth to ask. The words would not leave her lips. She could not find breath to speak them. She tried twice; the third time she lifted her hands and signed.

Adam was not Angel. She considered him part of her den, her made family, but every member of that den was individual; they had their own thoughts, their own way of doing things. Adam's had been formed by his family, his blood-kin—Jewel was Matriarch. Whatever she told him to do, he would do. Angel? He'd never been that person. He never would be.

But it was Angel who was staring at her, eyes slightly narrowed; Angel whose hands lifted in reply. Adam was silent, pale, steady. He was the most truly gentle person Jewel thought she'd ever met. His sister and his cousin had been nothing like him, nor had most of his kin, male or female. But gentle was not stupid. Gentle was not, in the end, weak.

It was Angel's hands he watched, now; Angel's gaze he met. He turned his back to Jewel, and his elbows moved; he was still signing. In the end, he nodded.

"I will go with you," he said quietly.

"I don't want you to go with me."

"No. You don't. You are even less suitable to be Matriarch than Margret." As he said the words, he smiled; it was a rueful smile, a type of surrender. "You don't want me to go with you—but you need me to be there."

"I don't even know what we'll need—"

"Yes, Matriarch, you do."

"I'm *not* your matriarch. Margret is. And she's halfway across the world right now, waiting for you to come home." It was true. It was all true.

Adam lifted his chin. "I am Arkosan. I am of Arkosa. But you have been kin to me, and you *are* kin to me now. You are Terafin, not Arkosan, yes. But Yollana was Havallan, and when she gave commands, the Matriarchs listened, even Margret."

"Adam—"

"You are Matriarch," he repeated. "And you are afraid to be Matriarch." To the great, gray cat he said, "She needs me."

"She is *afraid* to *need* you because you *almost* died."

"Had I not been there, she would have died."

"Yesssssss."

"I do not always trust your fear," Adam said, speaking once again to Jewel. "But your intentions and your instincts? Those, I trust." He switched to Torran. "I will go where you go." Frowning, he knelt.

"That is not wise," Corallonne told him, her voice smooth as worked stone, and just as hard.

"No, Lady," Adam replied, without looking up. "But being healer-born isn't wise, either. My kin consider it almost a curse." His lips twisted in something that might have been a smile, if someone had broken it before it fully formed. He had become something strange, something other, in his absence from Arkosa, and he wasn't certain what he would be to the Arkosans when he returned.

Would he lie? Would he hide? Jewel's hands were shaking enough that she had to force them from fists. Would they reject him? She'd keep him. She'd keep him if they didn't want him.

But even thinking it, she *knew*. Adam was Arkosan. Adam was loved. If he had become something strange and other, he was still both of those things. The people who had known him, some since birth, would love him regardless. Her Oma had known that Jewel was seer-born; she had feared *for* Jewel, but she had never stopped loving her or watching over her. Not while she drew breath.

Adam placed both of his hands, palm down, against the forest floor.

The roar—of dragon, of monster, of angry demon—returned in force, in fury.

Jewel froze.

Corallonne and Shianne were white as alabaster. Celleriant moved instantly to stand before Jewel, his sword like lightning, but with a hilt attached.

It was Kallandras who spoke; Kallandras who gave voice to the thought that was forming above a sudden pit of terrified certainty.

"That," he said softly, "was Snow."

The Hidden Wilderness

The winding of horns grew louder and more insistent as the bear trundled— with astonishing speed—through the ancient snow. The shadowy fingers of branches through moonlight grew softer and more attenuated; the bear's gold-tinged fur became, as he worked, the only source of light. Ice glittered yellow as he labored, but the moonlight was gone.

Carver looked up to see clouds, or what he thought might be clouds, as the night sky lost the heart of silver light. He froze. What diminished the moon's light in this winter world was not cloud, but . . . wings. Long, fine wings that seemed to stretch almost across the horizon.

He had seen those wings before, although they had not been so large. He had seen this demon in the heart of Averalaan, on the day of the victory parade that marked the true end of the Southern War—or at least this iteration of it. A warning, then, that the war was not finished; the Southern part had been a skirmish; the real battle was to come.

"Ellerson."

The domicis turned in the direction Carver was now facing, the tunneling, talking bear almost forgotten.

"We've seen him before."

The bear shouldered them both out of the way, knocking them to the left and the right as he shoved himself between them. Walls of snow caught them before they could otherwise reach the ground.

"This," the bear said, "is bad." He swiveled a head that seemed larger and brighter in Carver's direction; his eyes were narrow, his fangs exposed. Carver thought he could see the echoes of a different shape, a different form, in the golden light that seemed to stream off his fur. His nose rose, and he seemed to exhale a golden mist as he gazed upon the creature that now graced the skies with his dark flight.

He was beautiful, Carver thought, even through the fear he caused.

The fear and the winding horns. Carver could hear metal against metal; the clink of chain, the subtle scrape of greaves against barding. He could see the Wild Hunt in its full majesty; they were the color of moonlight and Winter.

"They do not ride to hunt," the bear said softly. "They ride to war. Look, boy, and look well; this is what the Lord of these lands remembers best." His voice grew quiet. "This and the creature above them now." And as he spoke, tears nestled in the folds of fur beneath his eyes—eyes that seemed, suddenly, to be ancient.

"I had not seen him," the bear whispered. "I had heard, but I had not seen the truth of it for myself. Better that I had slept, then wakened now." He fell silent, and to Carver's surprise, lost substance, becoming again the much smaller animal he had been when he had first appeared.

Without thought, Carver bent and retrieved the beast as if he were a cat. A real cat, not the winged, fanged variety.

"You are warm, boy," the creature said. "And foolish beyond measure. It is never safe to invite the ancients into your bosom. Remember it. Remember this, too: no matter how quickly you flee, you cannot escape your memories or your fears; they are within you, part of the measure of who you are." Although he spoke to Carver, his eyes were upon the demon and the Wild Hunt as demonic wings slowly folded, and their bearer came down to the earth. The moon was once again visible, its light harsher and brighter, as if it, too, bore witness.

From a distance, storms could be beautiful. And this was a storm of rage and pain and fury. Carver had seen the demon once before, but not like this. His voice was raised in wordless pain, long before the Wild Hunt had closed with him. Their voices clashed with his, as potent a weapon as the swords—and spears—they bore. Their shields were raised, and Carver thought he could see the heraldry across the long, smooth surfaces that glinted in the silver light.

Silver became red; the color of blood and the color of fire. The demon had drawn sword, called shield. He flew above them but skirted the reach of their weapons because his chosen weapons did not give height the vantage if he wished to destroy.

And he did, Carver thought.

"Yes," the creature said. "And no. That is memory, for the ancients. It is ever new, and ever renewed. He was a fool to come here now. His presence will hasten the end of this dream."

Carver stilled. This was the dream of a Sleeper, if he had understood anything that had been said in the West Wing in the past month—and there was only one way this dream was going to end. "Can you stop him?"

The small creature hissed, very catlike, in outrage. "Stop him? *Stop him?* Perhaps if I attempt to throw you beneath his sword, it *might* catch his attention. But not yet. The ring you bear will not protect you from the Wild Hunt at the moment: this is elemental; they will not even see you. This is what happens when dreams turn to nightmare. You have not seen pain yet." He shook himself then. "And I am grieved to miss it. But it will buy time."

"Where do you lead us?" Ellerson asked; he had been silent, watching as Carver watched.

"To safety, of a kind. This is not the place to make a stand unless we have no choice. I will survive. Probably." He did not resume the bear's shape. "You said you can walk across the snow, and I would like to see it for myself." To Carver, he added, "I like your cloak. It smells of nostalgia."

Chapter Fourteen

Corallonne's Land

ADAM AND ANGEL LOOKED instantly to Jewel as Adam lifted his hands. He was trembling, almost shuddering.

Jewel's throat was dry. Her mouth was drier. She forced words to cohere from the chaos of thought, of fear. "It was Snow," she whispered. She looked at Shadow.

Corallonne looked ahead, straight ahead, as if she could now see what had roared in such pain and fury.

"We must leave," Shianne told Jewel. "We must leave immediately."

Celleriant frowned. His sword did not waver, but he turned to look back at the woman to whom he had sworn his life.

Jewel nodded. Terrick and Angel were geared, although the larger man had dropped his pack at the first roar; his ax was in his hands. "Adam?"

The boy was staring at his hands; turning them over, and over again, as if looking for an injury he was certain he'd sustained.

"What did you *do*, you stupid, *stupid* boy?" Shadow demanded.

Adam ignored him; it wasn't deliberate. He turned to Corallonne and said, voice shaky and slight, "What *is* the tangle?"

Corallonne did not reply for long enough that Jewel thought she wouldn't. But she exhaled. "Shianne is correct. It is time to retreat. I do not know what your cats have done, but they have destabilized this region, and it is on the move." She frowned at Adam. "Do you understand the endless?"

He blinked.

"No more do we, although we have more experience with it. The gods are not endless. The firstborn are not endless. We persist; if nothing kills us—and, Adam, even we can be killed—we endure. But we had a beginning. We are not endless; there was a start to us, a will to our creation."

Adam nodded.

"The tangle is endless, as we understand it. It is not like us or like our parents—but we believe that our parents were born of it, indirectly. Have you spoken with your gods?"

Adam was silent.

Jewel said, "I have."

"They are not the parents of my childhood, my youth. What knows life, knows change, even gods. Even firstborn. We do not change so readily, so easily, as mortals—and that, Terafin, is the gift of mortality. Some among your kin thought it a curse: the shortness of the span of years. But in that short span, you change, are changed, so easily. It has been conjectured that change *is* mortality.

"The gods changed slowly, as mountains change, or shorelines. They are their natures; to rise above them, to move the forces that they are in a different direction of their own choosing was never simple, and it is never complete. You speak of trust, you who are mortal, as if trust were simple.

"Our trust is different. We see what a thing is, and we understand how much its base nature controls it. We understand both the struggle and the intent; oftimes intent is not enough. The tangle is unlike the gods. It is unlike the wild gods. It exists and has existed since the time before the gods themselves saw this world and found it fair."

"Why did you choose these lands as your home?"

Corallonne's smile added years to her face. "Because the tangle is here, as you suspect. It is compelling to one of my kind; it exists as it exists, and it does not compromise. I have walked the tangle."

Calliastra's breath was sharp, singular; it was followed by no words.

"It is a force that exists without history; there are stories of the tangle that might be dream, and stories that might be nightmare. What it can, it devours."

"And what it can't?"

Her smile deepened. "It accepts. I have set rough boundaries around its edges—these are my lands, and I am capable of at least that. But, Jewel, it cannot be changed. It cannot be—as you must be considering—destroyed. It is, in its entirety, what it is. You might drain an ocean more readily than you can alter the tangle.

"But the tangle can alter you; the ocean can destroy you. A storm sings harmony to the ocean's waves. Perhaps that is what I seek to do. But it is not mine. It is not owned. It cannot be."

"You like it," Calliastra said softly, "because it lacks ambition."

"Say rather I like it because it is, in its entirety, what it is. What care does it have for respect? What care for rulership? What care for ownership? There is no contest, and no war to be fought that would change its essential nature—and it has been tried, many, many times." She hesitated.

Jewel marked it.

"No, Adam," Corallonne said, although the boy hadn't spoken. "You feel—you felt—what it is. If it cannot be changed, it changes what it touches, where it can; that is the nature of the tangle. But the change is not predictable; it is wild and unknowable. Except," she added softly, "perhaps by one such as you. Would you dare it?"

He was utterly silent. He glanced once at Jewel and then away, as if this was again wholly the business of Matriarchs.

"But if the tangle is unpredictable, there is a raw storm of power at its center. It was once called—and you will, I think, hear this again in time—the forge of the gods."

She froze.

"Yes, Jewel. Yes, Terafin. I will not speak of what was forged there; it is known, in some fashion, to you and your kind."

"A forge." It was Terrick who spoke.

Corallonne raised brows, inviting him to continue.

"And what was created in that forge?"

She shook her head. "The tangle could not, cannot, be controlled; its will is its own, if will is even the word to describe it; do mountains have wills? Do oceans? Arguments were made, for and against, but in the end they were discarded because no interests—no singular interests—would rise to elide all others. And I remember that day. It echoes, even here."

Adam said, "The sword. The sword of Moorel."

Her brows rose, then, her expression darkening. Her face was forest night—a night that contained predators, broken sleep, nightmares.

A roar broke the silence, broke all conversation. Jewel thought all her hair that wasn't pinned down would be standing on end if most of it weren't covered.

"Snow?" she asked Kallandras.

He shook his head. "Night."

Jewel met Adam's eyes. To her surprise, he nodded, his expression grave and pale.

"We will leave you," she said to Corallonne, "and approach the tangle."

"You see its heart?"

"No. I don't want to see any more of it. Nature, except where it would kill me, wasn't inherently interesting to me. I want my cats."

"Your cats?"

"My cats."

Shadow hissed. He did not, however, interrupt.

"Sister," Corallonne said to Calliastra, "come. Keep me company."

Calliastra was staring, almost openmouthed, at Jewel. "They are ancients, they are *eldest*. If *they* cannot survive, what hope do *you* have?"

And Jewel said, "If they do not survive, we will not survive." She hadn't meant to speak the words, had meant to offer something more bland, more impersonal. But she welcomed the words that did come because they were viscerally true. She *knew*. The words did not frighten her; they did not terrify her; the truth was simply what it was.

"They cannot be killed!" Calliastra shouted. Her hands were fists, her skin both pale and flushed. She turned on Shadow. "Tell her!"

Shadow hissed at the child of gods. "I will *bite* you."

Not here, Jewel thought, placing a very firm hand on the top of Shadow's head. He flicked his wing and almost knocked her off her feet. Angel stepped in to steady her if it became necessary; it wasn't. Barely.

"Do not go," Calliastra said. It wasn't a plea. It was, however, as close to a plea as Calliastra could ever come, and Jewel knew it was costly. "You do not need the stupid cats; they will never serve you."

Jewel shook her head, offering a pained smile. "That's not the way I work," she said, voice low. "Most of my friends don't serve me. You—you came to me as Duster, do you remember?"

Calliastra stiffened.

"Duster would have slit my throat if I'd ever implied that she *served* me. But she was my muscle. She was my heavy. She could only do one thing well—but she was willing to do it for me, and not to me. Not to any of mine." That was an exaggeration, but the heart of it was true. It had always been a struggle, for Duster. She had done the work. She'd done it imperfectly, but she'd done what she could. "The cats are like Duster."

Shadow hissed in outrage.

"They're what they are. I'm surprised the tangle has any effect on them at all." As the words left her lips, she froze, caught in the thought, in the oddness of it. She did not know the tangle, but she understood that this knowledge, like the certainty that had come in flashes that had guided her life, was the gift of talent, of birthright.

She turned, slowly, to Shadow, upon whose head her hand still rested.

"The Winter King said he made you, he created you."

Calliastra rolled her eyes in open contempt. "He was always a vain fool of a man."

"You knew him?"

"I had reason to interact with him when he was actually alive. And speaking of vain fools, where is your Winter King?"

Jewel turned to look. He had not entered the Oracle's domain. He had not, she realized, entered Corallonne's.

"Yes," Corallonne said quietly. "He will not go where the White Lady will not go, unless you command it. You have not done so."

"I'm not comfortable giving orders about trivial things."

"And it is trivial, to be without the Winter King on this road?" Corallonne shook her head. "Mortals have always been strange to me; they are slight and perish so easily; they are driven by preference at the oddest of times." Her expression shifted, her voice gained depth, edge, strength. "Call him, Terafin."

"He can't walk where the White Lady hasn't walked."

"Yes. I know. Call him."

The Winter King came.

He came at her command, and when he approached, he lowered himself to the ground to allow her to mount. She bid him rise unburdened, and he did, but his eyes were almost black. *You should not be here*, he said.

You know where we are?

You should not be here. It is not safe for you. It was not safe for the Winter Queen the one time she was forced to traverse these lands. Do not trust the firstborn.

Corallonne.

Yes. To her, all corpses are fertilizer for her gardens, and her gardens are in constant need. Do you understand? She is not your friend. Jewel, you must away. This is not the place for you.

I'll leave the minute I have my two wretched cats, and not before. Do you understand why the Winter King considered them his greatest creation?

He had been the Winter King, in his time; one in a long line to accept Ariane's challenge, to love her, to possess her, and to fall at her hand.

No. The Winter Queen did not love the cats; they were little better than vermin to her.

You can walk this road.

I do not know.

You can walk any road that she has once walked.

Yes, Terafin. But I do not know if even I can walk where you desire to go. The land remembers Ariane, do you understand? The wilderness still echoes with her footsteps, where she but rode. I am of her. If she dies, I will die. While she lives, I will not.

You can't be killed either?

No. I might lose this form. I might take a century to return to her. But in that century, no matter what I do, I will not escape her. There is no bridge to the beyond for one such as I. I do not know if I can carry you as I have carried you if you step on this road. I would not step on it, given any choice at all.

We have to.

Why? In all of history, there was only one who could walk into the tangle and emerge unchanged. Only one.

But you said Ariane did it.

I did not say she emerged unchanged.

What if your history is wrong?

Those who do not learn from the mistakes of others—

Are doomed to repeat them, yes. It had been one of her Oma's favorite phrases. *My cats are in there, and we need to find them.*

You will not find them unchanged. What they have become, what they are becoming—you cannot hope to control them.

I don't control them now, she snapped.

Corallonne watched, as if she could hear the unspoken conversation. And maybe she could. Or maybe the content was obvious enough that she could guess. It didn't matter. "I will not accompany you further," she said.

Jewel nodded.

"But know this: my lands know you. They know your companions. Should you traverse the tangle unchanged—should you survive—you will be welcome in them as honored guests." She turned away then, without preamble or further leave-taking. The trees parted to allow her unimpeded passage.

All but one: the tree that had come from Jewel's leaf—the leaf that had come from the *Ellariannatte.*

"Some of my distant kin once dipped roots into the tangle; the tangle was not confined, at that time, to one realm. It is the all-mother's burden now; she cannot change it—and will not try—but she hems it in, she restrains it."

"Could it be used?"

"No, Terafin. It is like, and unlike, the rest of the lands."

"What happened to the distant kin who had their roots in the tangle?"

His smile was strange, brilliant and yet reserved. "They woke, Terafin."

"Pardon?"

"They woke. They could see, they could feel, they could—with time and effort—communicate with the firstborn."

"But that's not bad—"

"No, perhaps not; it is not, we believe, what trees were meant to be when they were first created, first conceived." He bent at the waist, but it was a cumbersome movement, where all other movements were supple and graceful. "We do not fear the tangle, but we are not like you. What point fear of something we cannot contain, cannot control? What point fear if we cannot change what moves toward us?" He rose. "I will remain planted in the realm to which you have carried me. But I can hear my brethren across the wilderness."

"You're speaking to the trees in my lands."

"Yes."

"But you're here."

"Yes?" He looked vaguely confused.

Celleriant's lips were twitching although he retained his weapons. "She is mortal; she does not understand the nature of true forests, true wilderness."

"Ah."

"Never mind. Go, with my blessings. And know that if these lands prove inhospitable—"

"You will come for me?" He shook his head. "That is not the nature of gifts such as the one you have given. I am of your lands, but I am now Corallonne's. Do not," he added, his voice becoming lower but not in any way softer, "attempt to take from the firstborn that which you have surrendered. It will not end well."

Jewel hadn't intended that the *Ellariannatte* bloom; she hadn't expected that what did grow from her leaf would be a person. A thinking being, something that had will, and desire, and thoughts of its own. She was not comfortable with it, either. Giving a plant away was one thing, but one didn't give *people* as gifts. That was generally considered slavery, and it was illegal.

Even if it weren't, it was hugely, personally distasteful.

She wanted assurances now to assuage what she recognized as the seeds of guilt. She wanted to be told that he would be safe and happy. She wanted to believe it. And she didn't have time to be patted on the head by a child of the gods. Or anyone else, either.

What you meant to do doesn't matter, her Oma said. *What you did counts. What are you going to do about it now?* And the answer was: nothing. There was nothing she could do about it now.

"You are thinking you will be more cautious in the giving of gifts in future," Celleriant observed, which surprised her.

"Yes."

"That is wise. You may perhaps survive to accrue some wisdom."

"You're not afraid of the tangle."

"Fear is irrelevant, Lord. Where you go, I will go. What you consider necessary is therefore necessary."

"Angel—"

"Already had this conversation."

"Fine. We're moving out."

Out was, for another ten yards, forest. Trees. The same undergrowth, the same oddly colored insects, the same fluting bird cries. Even the sound of a passing brook or stream remained unperturbed by anything but the roars of rage that broke the deceptive, steady noise of forest life.

And they weren't cat roars. She'd heard the cats in all their various moods. She'd almost been killed by them—but that had happened in a dream, and the threat of it, the fear of it, remained in that dream. She both knew it had happened and could live as if it had not.

"Shadow, what are they saying?"

Shadow hissed.

Jewel exhaled. "What exactly did the Winter King do to you? Besides turn you into stone?"

"He *liked* cats," Shadow said, as if this were proof of superiority on the part of the fallen king.

"So does Teller."

The gray cat stepped on her foot. He seemed to be considering her question. "We are not stone now."

"No."

"Why?"

She blinked. He seemed to be asking that question as if it honestly puzzled him.

Have a care, Terafin, the Winter King said, just as Avandar said, *be cautious*.

Jewel stopped walking. Shadow *was* asking as if he didn't understand it. They were already in the tangle. The trees, birds, and brook notwithstanding, the journey into the unknown had started. It didn't affect Jewel in the way it seemed to be affecting Shadow; nor did Celleriant seem discomfited.

But Calliastra's eyes had darkened—literally. And above the line of her perfectly straight shoulders, the hint of midnight wings cast shadows.

Jewel's hand rested on Shadow's head. She remembered the cats of stone, but they were distant, a dream. She knew cats of flesh—one gray, one black, one white. She could hear the echoes of their childish, constant complaints; could almost see the sum of the damage they had done to furniture and flooring on the center of her desk.

She could see Shadow's eyes, in all their various states; she could see him as he walked by her side in dreams, usually calling her stupid, or some variant of that word.

"Shianne," she said, her hand fixed to Shadow's head, "when you first met Shadow, you were surprised at his size."

"Yes."

"But you recognized him."

"Of course. He is eldest."

"Is that what Snow and Night are becoming? What they were?"

Silence. Three beats of silence. "I do not know. They were old when I was young. They did not look as they look now, and their claws were never sheathed. In the court, we were told stories of the glory of their many hunts— and, Terafin, they claimed to have injured the dragon. I thought, at times, that they were his distant kin."

This caused Shadow to yowl in outrage, and that was a comfort to Jewel; it was his normal outrage, his normal voice, his normal hissing spit. He was insulted, of course.

"Did they have fur?"

Again, silence. Two beats. "They are not now what they were when I first caught sight of them, by the White Lady's side. She did not care for them then. I do not imagine she would care for them now."

"But did they have fur? Did they have scales? Was there a reason that you thought they might be related to a dragon?"

"Fur. Scales. I do not know. What I saw, in my infancy, was what lay beneath their outer appearance. It is what I see, now, when I look at them. It is what they are, not what they appear to be. But . . ."

"But?"

"They are not what they were. Oh, they are," she added quickly as Shadow began to sputter. "But they are . . . more. There is more to them than there was, then. The force of their ancient selves lies coiled within them, still, but it is buried."

"It is *hardly* an improvement," Calliastra said, with withering scorn, as if she, too, remembered.

Shadow's head, still beneath Jewel's hand, swiveled as he eyed Calliastra.

"Not *now*," Jewel told him. "We need to find your brothers."

"It won't be safe if they're making that much noise," Calliastra said.

"Safe for who?"

"Are they yours?" The darkness-born woman demanded. "You have always refused to answer that question. You prevaricate. You make excuses. Here, in the wilderness, and there, in the tangle, there is only *yes* or *no*. And, Terafin, if the answer is not yes, you will die. You will all die."

Shadow said nothing, but his side-eye was turned on Jewel, not the child of gods. He seemed to be waiting for her answer, and she had none she wanted to give. She understood loyalty. She understood kin. She understood the ways in which the ties of blood could supersede all else.

She understood—she thought she understood—love. She loved Finch. She loved Teller. She loved Angel and had grown to love Adam. But in none of those examples—and, of course, there were others—would she have said she *owned* them. Did she love them? Yes. Did they love her? Yes, although the reasons for that were far less clear to Jewel herself. But were they *hers*?

They followed her orders—when she gave them. But she'd certainly asked Jester and Carver to tone things down in the past, and their answer had not been compliance. Nor had she expected it. If asked if she owned her den-kin, she'd've answered swiftly, viscerally. *No.*

But if the answer was yes, did it even apply to the cats?

"What were they?" she asked Calliastra. "What were they before?"

"Can you not hear their voices?"

"We can all hear them, yes."

"Have you ever heard them speak like that before?"

She started to say no, paused, frowned. "Yes."

"Oh?"

"When angry. They roared thus at the Warden of Dreams."

Shadow nodded, as if satisfied.

"They are not angry now."

"Oh, they are," Jewel replied grimly. "It's just lasting longer. And at least this time, it's not my mansion that's going to take the brunt of it." She began to walk, and in her wake, her companions followed. Only Shadow walked by her side; he had to. She wasn't moving her hand.

*   *   *

Jewel couldn't mark the exact moment when the forest changed; she was aware that it had, but the change had not been instant; trees grew taller, thicker, and sparser. There was a footpath between them, and she followed that until Terrick pulled her up short. The older Rendish warrior had his ax in hand; he had shouldered his heavy pack in such a way that dropping it would be a matter of seconds, no more.

He spoke in his native tongue to Angel; Angel replied. They weren't arguing, not exactly, but they weren't agreeing, either.

"What's the problem?" she asked.

"If the tangle is not a fixed geographic location, Terrick considers the footpath suspect. It's clear that Corallonne considers the tangle all but impassable. If people do not walk here—"

"She did not say they do not walk here; she implied heavily that those that do do not return," Calliastra said. She was pale, her skin the white of death, her hair the black of darkness; the shadow of her wings was still a soft blur. "It is more than possible that the tangle itself carries the imprint of those who have traversed it. Little is known of the laws of its landscape. It has no Lord."

And Jewel said, reflexively and without thought, "Yes, it does." It was never wise to disagree with Calliastra; it required finesse, and a better choice of words. But this was visceral certainty, words born of gift, not observation or experience.

Calliastra's expression rippled with obvious displeasure. But there was, in the lines that finally settled, some hint of curiosity and even acceptance. "You are certain?"

Jewel nodded.

"And has your vision produced something as simple as the name of the Lord of these lands?"

"No. That's not the way it works."

"Can you look? Can you look for the answer?"

"Here? In the tangle? Is that what you would advise? You didn't seem all that keen on the idea before we entered it."

Calliastra stared at her for one long, silent beat, and then she threw back her head and laughed. Her laughter, like the raw, loud roar of the cats, was at home here. It was right. And it was every bit as dangerous. "No mortal of any sense has ever asked my advice, and when I have offered unasked, no mortal of any wisdom has followed it. I am death, Jewel. Love is death." She paused to look up the length of tree, her laughter folding, in an instant, into pain and fury and resentment.

*   *   *

An hour later, or perhaps less, the footpath remained. The forest remained. It was not Corallonne's forest, but there were marked similarities. No birds sang here, however. No insects buzzed. The only butterfly that flew was the one that Jewel had brought from Fabril's reach—but it did fly here, landing on tree and branch and bent stalk of wild plant that might have been grass were it not such a deep shade of blue.

It did not sing, in this place. Jewel asked Kallandras if he could still hear its voice—her voice—and he shook his head. The distant cats roared once, twice, and fell silent. The path led in the direction of those voices.

"What does the tangle do?" Jewel asked.

"Do? It exists."

"You implied that there was a use for it—at least to the living, walking gods."

"Did I?"

"Yes."

"It is irrelevant. You have no god's blood in your veins, and even those of us born to gods cannot safely touch the heart of the tangle."

"And the gods could."

"I did not say they did so in any safety. They did not. But it was their risk to take. Rulers sacrifice pawns," she continued. "And in order to rule efficiently, in order to rule without heartbreak, they keep the pawns at a distance; they appreciate them for what they are, but they move them to ruthless purpose.

"Even among the gods, there was hierarchy, an order of importance. Where beings of power gather, it is always thus, is it not, Lord Celleriant?"

He seemed suspicious of her question, which was fair; his suspicion stemmed from confusion, which was less so. To Celleriant there was clearly only one answer to the question, and it was so obvious he could not divine the game being played.

Jewel ground her teeth as Shadow hissed laughter.

"It was always so," he finally replied.

"And so, gods died. Did you know that they could die?"

Jewel nodded.

"Do you understand what happened to those that did die?"

"What do you mean, what happened?"

"When mortals die, do they not leave corpses?"

"Depends on how they died." It was Angel who answered. Calliastra accepted his answer as if Jewel had offered it herself.

"Do you believe that gods have bodies to desert, the way mortals do? Do you believe that their existence is somehow twin to yours, but larger and more powerful?"

"She does." This time, it was Shianne who answered. Calliastra found this interruption more annoying, if one judged by expression. "I believe they all do."

"Not all," Celleriant said.

Shadow hissed.

Avandar said nothing, but in the silence of thought, she felt his curiosity and his caution. He had seen gods die. He had never spoken of what he had seen. Nor did Jewel now ask, although she thought she would. Later.

"They believe that this," Shianne continued, raising hand to the height of rounded belly, "is how *all* offspring are born. They believe this is the only way. They believe that you were born in this fashion. They believe that I was."

Calliastra's eyes were round and obsidian.

"If birth, to them, is this, death must be the same: an echo of their lives, but larger, grander."

"That is not the way the gods died," Calliastra finally said.

Have a care, Terafin.

"What happened to them? What does death mean to the gods?"

"An ending, of sorts," Calliastra said. "As there was a beginning, of sorts." She hesitated, then. Glanced at Shianne, who seemed only confused, and Celleriant, who was more shuttered.

"They are not their bodies, although their bodies can be damaged. In some battles, their containments could be shattered, rendering them ineffective. Were they mortal—or immortal in the way of the firstborn—that would *be* death. They were not; they were gods. But in some cases, Terafin, more than those containers was shattered, disrupted. Then, gods fell to their enemies."

Jewel understood where Calliastra was leading this discussion; it required Jewel's participation. She accepted it. "What happened to the fallen gods?"

"Where they could be, they were consumed. Those elements of their being that were in harmony with the victor of their long war became part of the victor."

"And those that weren't?"

Calliastra shrugged. "There is no bridge, for gods. What do you think happened to them?"

"I honestly have no idea. We're not accustomed to thinking of gods dying."

"Oh?"

"To die, you have to live."

Silence, then, as the words sank roots.

Calliastra, however, smiled. "It is an odd wording, but it is apt. The gods do not live as you perceive life; they do not die as you perceive death." Her smile grew edges—but those edges had always been there, beneath the darker velvet. "Much has been said about gods, Terafin. About their wars, and their acts of creation and destruction. As you watch the firstborn in awe when they go to war, we watched the gods.

"And when the wars ended, when peace—of a kind—was brokered, we watched the world perish. Magic left it, seeping out of the earth and the skies and the waters, as blood seeps from mortal wounds. We, scions of the gods, were scions as well of the world itself; we were anchored in place, in time; we could not transcend them.

"We were deserted. But not all lands could be so easily divested of some part of their essential nature. The Stone Deepings. The Green Deepings. The hidden ways.

"The tangle, Terafin."

"What exactly is the tangle?"

"That has never been fully ascertained—but many believe that the tangle contains the deaths of ancient gods."

"It killed gods?"

"No. It is what their deaths left behind."

This was wrong in some fashion. Jewel could feel it yet could not articulate much beyond that; it was instinct. But the instincts of the seer-born were never simple. She turned to Shadow. "Call your brothers."

"Are you *stupid?*" he demanded, in obvious outrage.

"Demonstrably. Is it dangerous? Will they not recognize you?"

"It is dangerous," Shianne said softly, "because they will. If what I hear is correct, your cats are in the process of being reborn."

"As what?"

"As themselves, as they once were." She did not look intimidated by the prospect; there was a glimmer of something that might have been anticipation, had she been human and not merely mortal.

"Shadow."

"Yesssssss?"

"What did the Winter King do?"

He hissed.

"I mean it. I need to know. I need to know yesterday, but I'll settle for now. What did he *do?*" Her skin was tingling in a very peculiar way, as if she were lightning that clouds had not yet released.

"He *died*," Shadow growled.

"Terafin, there is a risk—"

Jewel did not remove her hand. Shadow's eyes had grown rounder; she thought at first it was his outraged expression taking root. It wasn't. His eyes were larger. His fangs had lengthened, and his claws—his claws were scraping the stone beneath his feet as if he could shatter it just by scratching.

The only feet that stood on stone were Shadow's. Not even Calliastra changed the ground on which she stood, and she was daughter to gods, one of whom Jewel did not have the courage to name—not here, not in the wilderness.

The stone beneath great cat paws was scored, scarred.

The cats had once been made of stone.

She knew—thought she knew—what must be done.

"Yesssss," Shadow said, although he had volunteered no information. "But you *cannot*, foolish girl. *These* lands are *not* your lands. *These* lands are not *anyone's* lands. But they could be *ours*." And he roared.

Snow replied.

Night replied.

There was an ebullience, a joy, in a sound that was otherwise death. Shadow struggled a long moment with silence, as if he meant to cling to it by main force.

What had the Winter King done? "He was in his own lands," she said, speaking to herself, but speaking out loud.

"Yessssss."

"And when I was in my own lands—"

"Yesssss."

"Are they yours, Terafin?" Calliastra demanded. Her voice was both distant and more urgent, as if she cared about the answer. No, as if she cared about the *right* answer. Jewel turned to her, and then away. These lands were not her lands. What she could do in her own with barely a thought—with less than a thought—she could not do here.

She suffered no delusions. She could not ask Corallone to cede some part of her lands. Even were the firstborn willing, it would make no difference; they walked the tangle, now—unclaimed wilderness in the heart of Corallonne's stronghold.

Could the tangle be claimed?

Yes. Yes and No. The No was relevant here because it was Jewel's answer. Jewel couldn't claim it. But she didn't think the cats could, either. Instead, it claimed them, was claiming them. No, that was wrong. It wasn't making them; it wasn't unmaking them. It was unmaking what had been made *of* them.

"Shadow," she whispered. "What do *you* want?"

"I want you to be *less stupid*."

"Want something attainable."

Shadow hissed laughter. The laughter ran through the whole of his body; his claws momentarily stilled. "You want *permission, stupid* girl."

"Yes."

"That is not the way the wilderness *works*. While you are *waiting*, it will *devour* you. And your *stupid* friends."

"How does the wilderness work, then?"

Shadow's eyes were luminescent; they implied darkness by being its opposite. "*Speak*," he hissed. "Be *heard*. If you are *loud enough*, it will hear you. If you are *strong enough*, it will listen. If you are determined enough, it will obey. It will be yours."

Calliastra said, again, "Are they yours, Terafin?"

And Jewel answered.

Yes.

The cats were not cats. They had never been cats, not even truly in form. They had been stone, when she had first seen them; flesh and fur—and noise—when she had encountered them again. She had wondered, often, why they had come to her; had wondered if they somehow existed as part of a forest of metallic trees.

They didn't.

They were very like the Stone Deepings and the road she had walked through them. The Stone Deepings, like the Green Deepings, were part of the wilderness, and in them, things grew that were not mortal, and not of the mortal world. There were wonders, and dangers, and death. But when stone spoke, it killed the unwary, that was its nature.

She had not consciously tried to take the Stone Deepings as her own.

It would not have worked, Avandar told her, some hint of ancient frustration coloring the words.

She knew. Maybe some part of her that was only seldom touched by words, and therefore thought, had always known. But it was on the roads in the Stone Deepings that she had faced the Winter Queen. It was on those roads that she had remembered who she was, where she was from, and what she was fighting *for*.

And the road had answered not the imperative of the Winter Queen and her Wild Hunt, but the imperative of an orphan who had built a home and family in the distant, distinctly mortal streets of the twenty-fifth holding. She had held the road, although she could not own it.

It had been hers for that moment in time because it was of her. Had she asked permission of it? No, of course not. It hadn't occurred to her that she needed permission. If the Stone Deepings spoke—and she was uneasily aware that they could—they didn't speak to her in that way.

They didn't speak the way the cats did—and could. They didn't squabble. They didn't destroy furniture—although she was uneasily aware that they could destroy so much more. What she wanted from the cats—what she wanted from Shadow—they didn't even understand.

And yet, the cats conformed in some fashion to what she wanted. They always had. She had been afraid to test that, to push it, to stretch those boundaries; had been aware of the ways in which they might break.

But she needed Shadow. She knew it. She needed him only a little less than she needed water. She couldn't say why; she didn't examine it. Examination didn't matter. It was rationalization after the fact, and at the moment, the fact was too large, too unstable, to sustain the words and their structure.

What the Winter King had done was more than simple containment—it was complicated containment. In the tangle, the stone that had once encompassed the cats remained wherever Shadow placed his feet—as if he were somehow shedding it. And when it was gone, he would be something other. He would be what he was meant to be.

Meant to be.

What did that even mean? Was Jewel Terafin because she was meant to be Terafin? Had she been orphaned because she was meant to be orphaned? Had her mother and father died such lonely, mundane deaths because that was their lot?

No.

No.

No.

Shadow was like the Stone Deepings. He was not, quite, like the forests behind the manse, like the wilderness that had become her permanent home. But he was wild in the same way. He could hear, had heard, her voice. He understood what she needed: what would make her, what would break her. He was not old and wise and avuncular in the way of Hectore, but it didn't matter.

What she needed of Shadow, he had given her.

He had always given her.

Shadow was *hers*. While she lived, he was hers.

It wasn't a complicated answer. It wasn't a difficult one. It was visceral, instinctive, possessive; there was anger in it. It was a familiar anger. She didn't need to tell Shadow what she meant. The word *mine* didn't have a lot of structural underpinnings. It wasn't a word that could be used in a cultured debate. It wasn't meant to convince anyone.

It was a fundament on which she could stand—as she'd stood on the roads in the Stone Deepings. She hadn't asked permission of the Deepings; it hadn't been required.

That is where you are wrong, Avandar said quietly. *But the Stone Deepings heard you, Jewel, just as your forest did.*

She nodded, brushing Avandar's words away.

Shadow was like the Stone Deepings. She didn't cajole. She didn't demand. She did not, in any way the House Council would understand, talk to him at all. She needed no answers from the great, gray cat; she asked him no questions. He was not her den, not mortal, not human. She did not ask permission. She made no plea.

She looked at him, his head beneath the open palm of her hand. She saw Shadow. Memories of her time in his company came and went, as if memory were a mortal river. No, she thought, not quite. The riverbed was memory. What flowed through it? Jewel.

The cats were like geography. They spoke, they interacted, they destroyed things; they squabbled like siblings. They suited her, suited her den—and Shadow had, for no reason she could understand, taken Ariel under his literal wing. Only in the presence of the gray cat had the child felt truly safe in the strange confinement of the Terafin manse.

She understood why. She couldn't put it into words. It didn't make rational or logical sense. But it was felt, and it was truth.

Shadow hissed. He was neither angry nor amused; it was a quiet sound, an exhalation of held breath. "Do you *know* what you are *doing*?"

Hush.

What had driven the Winter King? No, that was the wrong question. How had the Winter King found the cats? How had he met their ferocity and divined that it could somehow be contained? How had he understood that they were like the land itself—or the lands—in some essential way? Jewel had never, until this moment, seen that in them. Had she encountered them in their primal form—had she heard Night and Snow at a distance—she would never have seen it, either. She would have avoided them entirely, keeping as much distance between her party and their angry roars as she possibly could. Death was in their voices, not peace. Pain was implied.

The cats had gone absent before. She had been surprised at just how much she missed their squabbling and complaints; the world had gone quiet in their wake. Until they had arrived, she hadn't realized that it was the quiet that made the role of Terafin so difficult. She could not speak her mind. She could only say what she thought when she'd shifted through all possible variants of the words she could safely use. She was surrounded, except in the West Wing, by people who saw the House ring; she was *Terafin*, not Jewel.

Shadow—and Night, and Snow—could not care less about The Terafin. They didn't treat her with the respect the firstborn all but demanded; they didn't bow or scrape. There was nothing they wanted from The Terafin. On most days, there was nothing they wanted from Jewel.

No, she thought, and she smiled, that wasn't true. They wanted attention. They wanted flattery. They wanted to be told they were the *best cats ever*. They sulked when they didn't get what they wanted—but even that, at a remove, could be endearing.

She had grown up in the streets of the twenty-fifth holding. She had reached her majority there, but she had not yet developed the self-control, the self-denial, that was required of the woman who held and ruled the House. She had developed those things because they were practical, they were necessary.

But at heart, she was at home only with the den because with the den it *wasn't* necessary. She didn't bear the crushing weight of their disappointment every time she spoke her mind. She didn't fear their judgment if she picked up the wrong fork or knife, nor did she fear it if she was not dressed in the finery, the trappings demanded of The Terafin.

And she didn't fear it from the cats; never had. They were almost like earlier iterations of home, for Jewel. They spoke their minds instantly, unselfconsciously; they did what she could no longer do.

She couldn't imagine that the Winter King had needed from the cats what she needed. But perhaps what he did need, he saw in them. He was gone, now. Maybe he had become another stag, another mount in the eternity of the Winter Queen's host. She couldn't ask him and doubted that she would, if they ever crossed paths again.

He neither needed nor wanted her gratitude. Her gratitude, if it existed at all, was entirely her problem, not his. She looked at the cat, and saw him; around him, above him, beneath him, she saw and understood the shape of her own needs.

She accepted them in their entirety. Were they a weakness? Maybe. But she was human, she was mortal. She was born to weakness and the interdependence of tribe, of family, even if there was no shared blood to bind them. She was born to a small apartment, a cantankerous old woman, and the parents whose faces she could not recall, except in dream.

She had hated the silence of Rath's home before she had begun to gather her den. These cats were like Avandar. She felt the domicis bristle in annoyance at the comparison, and surprised her companions by laughing out loud, which didn't improve the bristling much.

They can't die, she told her domicis. *They're like you in that way.*

You don't fear to lose them.

Not to death, no. And that loss was always a fear. It would always be a fear. Death had shaped her early life, merciless and pitiless.

The stone beneath Shadow's feet began to melt, losing solidity, shape, texture. What remained in its passage was forest floor. He was not a creature of stone now. "Could you move before?"

He muttered *stupid* under his breath. Under his breath, however, was relative.

"Could I be *bigger*?" The gray cat asked.

"You're too big as it is."

"But we have to *carry* them," he countered, wheedling. His expression was guileless as he added, "Could I be bigger than Night or Snow?"

"Shadow."

"Yesssssssss?"

"Find your brothers."

Shadow leaped into the air, and it devoured him.

Chapter Fifteen

HECTORE WOKE WITH A start, as he so often did in these latter days. His wife stirred, lifting her head; her eyelids flickered. He smiled. "It was a dream, Nadianne. Nothing more. Go back to sleep."

"And you?"

"I cannot sleep at the moment, more's the pity. I am fine."

"If you go out, take Andrei with you."

"Of course, dear."

It was of Andrei that Hectore had been dreaming. He did not tell his wife this. She was not a politician; she did not terrify or terrorize the patriciate. In most cases, where his wife was absent, men generally ignored her existence. This was as Hectore desired it. Enemies of old—long dead, for the most part—had attempted to draw Hectore's first wife and child into their small wars.

But not the smarter enemies. Not, for instance, Jarven, now ATerafin. People saw only that Hectore was sentimental; that his great affection for his family could be used as a weapon against him. It had happened to other men in the long and checkered past of the merchants who governed commerce in the Empire, after all.

Hectore had asked Jarven, casually, years after their first few clashes, why he had not chosen that route. To Jarven, any tool could be, and often was, used.

Jarven's smile was steely, polite; he matched Hectore's tone, his mimicry of it so exact it was clear that he understood that the Araven merchant's casual non-chalance covered a trench so deep it could kill a man who fell into it unawares.

"We are both merchants, at heart," Jarven replied. "And older men. We have seen trade wars. We've counted the fallen."

Hectore nodded; this was general enough that it was true. It was in the details that Jarven became especially slippery.

"You and I have crossed each other before. You have been—you remain—a worthy opponent, a rival."

Hectore nodded again. He was pleased and let it show; Andrei was sour and likely to be worse before Jarven had finished speaking.

"You have never been an enemy. Many merchants make the mistake of assuming that *opponent* and *enemy* are one and the same; they allow the personal to dictate their interactions. I am perfectly happy to have you as an opponent, as you have not been obliging enough to lose. Not often.

"But targeting your wife or your children? That would make me an enemy."

"Surely that would be true of most men?"

"As I said: most men confuse the two. You do not and have not. And you treat your enemies with a dangerous respect and an utter thoroughness; I note that most of them are no longer with us."

Hectore did not demur; it was true. Once a man—or woman—had attempted to kidnap or kill his family, he felt no compunction in having their lives ended. The deaths themselves had not been entirely subtle or private affairs, but he wished those who considered the same hostilities, the same approaches, to understand their cost. And there was only one cost.

"I admit the challenge might have been bracing, but in the end, I did not consider it worth the effort."

"You speak as if you consider it impossible that you would have lost."

"No, not impossible at all. But not a certainty, either. I am willing to go to war."

Hectore nodded.

"But even I must have cause I consider worth the expense. I had no like vulnerabilities, no weaknesses. Some of your enemies did, that I recall." There was a question in the words.

"If I could not countenance the inclusion of innocents—my wife, my children—I would not then stoop to use them myself."

"No. You did not often consider assassination attempts against you personally outrageous."

"I was at war," Hectore replied, shrugging. "When at war, one expects that one will face weapons and possible death."

Andrei had, indeed, been sour and monosyllabic for the whole of that discussion, his dislike of Jarven so strong one could practically cut it with a knife. Jarven found it amusing—or chose to find it amusing.

Hectore had never quite understood Andrei's animosity toward Jarven. Many were the merchants who considered Hectore's position a personal prize to reach for, and Andrei might consider them foes, but he accepted them as part of the landscape, something to move around. Or level.

Now? Andrei did not stay long in a room that contained Jarven.

But Jarven had changed, as well.

Hectore did not yet play at age the way Jarven did; he suspected strongly that if he did he would be subject to the worst of Andrei's temper until he ceased. But he felt his age more keenly than he had even a decade past. Jarven had not been, and was not, young. But there was something in his eye, something in his carriage, that reminded Hectore strongly of the younger man. Not a man to cross, then, unless one had no choice.

He shook himself. Jarven had never been a man to cross, unless one had no choice. And when one had no choice, one stepped carefully. Cautiously. One thought, and planned, and only in the end let instinct have its way.

Hectore was in the middle of choosing clothing for a day with an abnormally early start when Andrei entered the room. His frown implied outrage, without transforming the rest of his face, and Hectore understood why: it had been a long time since Hectore had been responsible for dressing himself. On the merchant roads, one seldom took one's servants.

Andrei, of course, was the exception to that rule.

Hectore had been expecting him since he woke. He had drawn the curtains, to let in what light there was; it was meager and gray, although sunrise would change that.

"What has happened?" he asked his most trusted servant.

Andrei was silent. Andrei was often silent, although his silences had obvious texture and tone if one knew how to read them. This one, however, was new. It was measured, constrained, uncertain.

"I should have known," Andrei replied, after the silence had stretched between them.

"Where are we going?"

This startled Andrei, and Hectore was petty enough to enjoy that. But he had always been a man to take what amusement he could when it was offered in an otherwise grim situation, and he had no illusions. This was grim.

"We are going nowhere," Andrei replied.

Hectore raised a steel brow and continued to dress. The clothing he had chosen was a type of anonymity; he was dressed for the open road. He was dressed for the caravan.

"Where," Hectore asked again, as if Andrei had not spoken, "are we going?"

"You are going nowhere," Andrei told him. It was surrender . . . of a sort. He turned from Hectore, hands clasped behind his back, and began to pace. As he did, he spoke.

"You have given me everything that I asked for. You have given me everything that you promised."

This, however, was not a promising beginning. Andrei seldom referred to their past in this fashion, although Hectore's past provided ample opportunity for criticisms should the mood strike.

"No, you have given more. I have been happier in this life than I can remember being in any other."

"It is not the life that most men dream of, when they dream of happiness."

"No? But Hectore, I am not a man."

Very, very unpromising.

"What has happened, Andrei?" Hectore all but demanded.

Andrei said, "She has walked into the tangle."

Hectore knew that "she" was The Terafin. Andrei had become aware of Jewel Markess ATerafin in a way he was seldom aware of other people; she drew his attention. He did not consider her a threat, and as threats demanded the bulk of Andrei's attention, she stood out. Had she not been Terafin, this would still be true.

But she was.

"You allowed me to be what I wanted to be," Andrei continued, into Hectore's thoughtful silence. "You did not care what I was."

"That is not true."

"Had I chosen to walk by your side as a great, gray cat—an odious, disrespectful, destructive gray cat —you would have accepted it with as much ease."

"Not, I think, the destructive part. That would upset my wife."

Andrei smiled. The addition of a new wife, these many years ago, had been a study in territoriality—on both Nadianne's and Andrei's part. But Andrei had, inasmuch as he could, approved of Hectore's choice. And had he not?

Hectore would have married, anyway. If Hectore accepted Andrei—and he did—Andrei accepted Hectore. Andrei was, perhaps, louder in his complaints about Hectore's many decisions—but complaints were not unexpected.

"You did not desire to be a gray cat of any size or description."

"No, Hectore, I did not. What I desired, I have had."

"You make me uncomfortable. Where are we going?"

"I cannot take you where I am going. I do not think you would survive it."
Hectore opened his mouth and Andrei lifted a hand. "It has been many, many
years since I last traversed the tangle. I do not understand why she has entered
it now."

"She must have had her reasons."

"Yes. I will say that about your Terafin. She has her reasons, even if she
cannot clearly express them—or see them for herself."

"I am not of a mind to let you leave on your own, I'm afraid."

"Your wife would never, ever forgive me should I take you with me."

"Oh? She made it very clear that if I was leaving, I was to have you accompany me."

Andrei's smile was genuine, but brief. Yes, they had had their territorial is-
sues, but in time, they had come to see that they occupied space in Hectore's life
in entirely different ways—and they both wanted Hectore to survive. And thrive.

"The Terafin did not leave the city on her own," Hectore continued, when
Andrei did not immediately argue. "She took some members of her House with
her. I do not speak of the pale, cold man, and I do not speak of the mercurial
domicis—those, I think, she would have regardless. Nor," he added, as Andrei
opened his mouth, "do I speak of the cats. She took Adam."

"Adam might survive."

"And she took a member of her den. I believe Finch called him Angel. He
is not talent-born; he is as ordinary as I. She is ferociously protective—even you
must admit that."

"She is not worse than you are."

Hectore frowned. "Be that as it may, her retinue will travel with her, and if
she is entering this territory of which you speak, she will not do it alone. If she
is content to allow them to take that risk, I do not believe it will kill me."

"I would take Jarven in a second," Andrei countered.

That stung. "Only so you could lose him."

"Yes."

The sting vanished. "You will have to accustom yourself to Jarven at some
point. He is unlikely to go away."

"You speak truer than you know. Hectore—I must go. She has entered the
tangle, but her path has not yet been unmade, remade; it has not yet been
transformed. She is not lost to me—but she will be if I tarry."

"I do not advise you to tarry—but I am going where you go."

"You do not generally accompany me when I do my work at your behest."

"This work is not at my behest," Hectore replied. He did not speak of the nightmare which had dropped him unceremoniously out of sleep.

"Hectore—"

Hectore smiled. It was a very particular smile; it implied a wellspring of gentleness, of kindness, of humor. It was, of course, deceptive; Andrei recognized the expression immediately. So would his wife. His children were not always as perceptive, but that was fair; children did not see "person" half so much as "parent."

And it was not a smile he ever offered his grandchildren. Andrei deplored his indulgence and was probably correct to do so.

"I cannot concentrate as I must if you are with me."

"I have seen you at your worst," Hectore countered, his smile genial, agreeable.

Andrei said nothing for one long moment. "Why do you insist on accompanying me?" he finally asked.

Hectore considered the possible ramifications of answering the question. He considered, as well, the cost of remaining silent. Everything that existed between them existed in a space that words did not generally touch. Those words were not allowed entry, as if to speak was to break that fragile peace.

He chose not to speak. His smile spoke for him; it deflected all rejection, all denial. He did not say that he followed because he was concerned. No, he was afraid. He was not at all certain that Andrei would find his way back without Hectore as anchor.

Before he left—and he extracted Andrei's very, very sour promise to wait—he accoutred himself with a number of small stones, each purchased at great expense from the Order of Knowledge. On numerous occasions throughout his adulthood, stones such as these had saved his life. He wasn't certain what their function would be on the road he now traveled, but certainty was not required. They might be useful, and if they became so, it would be worth the cost and the inconvenience.

He retained his caravan clothing. Tangle, to Hectore, implied an unkempt, wild place, and he did not wish to wear ostentatious and impractical clothing there. Yes, he could replace anything that was destroyed, but it was the principle of the thing.

You sound like a doting mother.

He smiled, remembering.

* * *

Andrei was tense, which was not unusual. His eyes were all black, which was. Hectore cleared his throat, and Andrei shook himself.

"Your eyes," Hectore said.

"My—" Andrei glanced in one of the decorative mirrors placed in the hall to make it seem both larger and grander. He frowned, and his eyes cleared. They were, at the moment, a very passable, nondescript brown. "It will not matter, where we are going."

Hectore rolled his own eyes. "What have I said?"

"You have said so much in my life were I to recite it all, we would never leave. You will, no doubt, remind me by repeating it."

"I will, indeed. In the warm months, clothing is almost irrelevant for purposes of protection or shelter; the night, and the temperature, will not kill. How many people walk the streets of our fair city without clothing in such weather?"

"Ah, that. I am, as you see, clothed." He exhaled. "But there are no streets where we now walk, Hectore. There are no people of your particular variety. There are glimpses of the familiar, but they are fractured, fragmented. In nightmare, terrain shifts and changes beneath your feet, to your sides, in front of you—it is one of the features that marks it as nightmare. This might be very like that. There are oases within the shifting, changing space; places in which the current mode might remain stable for hours, perhaps days."

"You do not make this sound pleasant."

"No. It is not, or will not be, for you."

"Is there some intent in these changes?"

"There is war," Andrei replied. After a pause, he added, "there is the detritus of ancient war. It is an echo of things past, of ancient struggles. But there is no loss as we define loss, and no victory, as we define victory; it is the struggle itself that has primacy."

"And you can just walk there."

"There is no 'just' about it." Andrei began to tie rope around Hectore's waist; Hectore allowed it, noting that he tied the same rope around his own shortly after. "If I ask it—"

"No."

Hectore followed where Andrei led. This was almost novel. While it was true that in day-to-day life Hectore allowed Andrei to guide him to the various appointments that he might otherwise neglect, he was unaccustomed to giving Andrei free rein. While they were together, they served Araven's interests—or

Hectore's. Every decision made reflected that. Andrei did not merely help in the shaping of the merchant empire; he offered aid in the building of bridges between Hectore and his offspring.

Between Hectore and his godchildren.

He thought of Ararath, as he walked behind Andrei. "We are going?" he asked his servant.

"To the Terafin manse."

"Wearing rope around our waists."

"Yes. Apologies, Hectore—but without the rope I cannot guarantee that you will not be seen."

"People can't see me?"

"No. There will always be exceptions; it is a subtle, quiet magic, meant to deflect vision rather than defeat it."

"Why the Terafin manse?"

"It is there that we will find, or fail to find, a way to reach your godson's ward."

Hectore repented of his clothing choice. He almost ordered Andrei to remove the rope; he had no reason not to visit the manse in the open. But perhaps Andrei did. He was ill at ease, thus roped, and Terafin was not a minor patrician house, to forgive all oddity and all possible offense.

Andrei chose to avoid the manor itself. Hectore was grateful, but unsurprised. He was *very* surprised when he entered the forest, attached by rope like a child in thick, leading strings, to find himself instantly confronted by the Terafin gardener.

Her eyes were the color of bright blood, not dark; it made the rest of her skin seem unflatteringly pale. She glared openly at Andrei, who offered her a very formal, very correct bow. Or rather, it would have been correct had she been The Terafin. The grace of the gesture did nothing to mollify her, but Hectore thought nothing would, where Andrei was concerned.

He found it very difficult to like the woman, which was irrelevant in any practical sense.

"I have been granted permission to traverse these lands, while The Terafin lives."

She nodded, glancing at Hectore and frowning at the rope that joined him to his servant. She did not seem to note his clothing, but her own was no better. "What do you intend, Patris Araven?"

"My servant," he replied, "believes that your Terafin may be in trouble."

Birgide Viranyi stiffened. "On what grounds?"

"An interesting choice of words."

"Patris Araven. What a pleasant surprise!"

There was only one thing that could further blacken Andrei's mood. Hectore, however, felt his automatic grimace fade into a resigned smile. "Jarven."

"I see Andrei is in fine form this morning. It is, however, rather early for you."

"I could say the same thing but will refrain from doing so. We do not, sadly, have the time to spar; Andrei feels that The Terafin is in danger."

"And he feels he might come to her aid? Does he even know where she is?" Jarven's tone didn't change; it was jovial, friendly, even warm. His eyes, however, were sharp, and the glint in them was cold.

"She is," Andrei replied, "in the tangle."

The whole of the forest erupted in noise then.

Leaves rustled so loudly they sounded like ocean waves in a storm. Birgide, in spite of her eyes and her duty, didn't understand the significance of those words. Nor, it appeared, did Jarven. But the trees did. The earth beneath their feet did.

Hectore was not surprised to see Haval Arwood, accoutred in an apron and armed with sewing needles, appear from between the trunks of two trees. Haval bowed—to Hectore. He glanced at Jarven with about as much affection as Andrei had shown.

"Patris Araven."

"Hectore, please."

"Very well. Hectore. The elders seem alarmed at your servant's words."

"If, by elders, you mean trees, I noticed."

"They wish to me to ascertain that his words are materially true."

Hectore stiffened. "They do not mean to insult my servant or my House, surely."

"No. But The Terafin is seer-born. They have heard some whisper of rumor that she approaches the tangle, but opinions had only barely begun to be expressed. They are now worried."

Haval studied Andrei; Andrei returned the regard. The older man, Hectore thought, had the better of it, in the end. Haval Arwood did not often condescend to open conflict, but he was clearly well-practiced. Given his obvious knowledge of Jarven, that should not have come as a surprise.

"You did not, of course, lead her into the tangle." At those words, Hectore relaxed, inasmuch as one could in The Terafin's forest. This forest had will; he could feel it bearing down on them all, in anger or fear. Or both: fearful men were often prone to anger, which led in turn to acts of folly.

Andrei nodded, wary now.

"The elders, therefore, wish to know—"

"We wish to know," a voice from somewhere beneath Haval's knees said, "how *you* know and *why* she has entered the tangle."

Hectore looked down to see the fox. He offered the fox a respectful bow. The fox regarded him with lively eyes in a gold-furred face. "Tell me, Eldest," he said, mindful now of how the fox had been addressed by others. "Do you ask The Terafin how she knows what she knows?"

The fox regarded Hectore as if coming to a decision about his impertinence. He could find it either offensive, which would be difficult, or amusing. Amusing might cause other difficulties, but those would be in future. "As you must know, we do not. But the Councillor questions her often, and she feels compelled to answer his many, many questions, even when they are not respectful."

"Does she have an answer that is acceptable to you?" Hectore continued. He had injected a note of mild curiosity, and he kept his voice soft. He could not treat the fox as a child; he could not treat the fox as a peer. He had always been a man sensitive to the currents of power, and in this clearing, they swirled around the fox.

Jarven said nothing; he observed. This was not unusual.

"All of her answers are acceptable," the fox replied, as if the question made no sense. Given the forest, the wilderness, the great trees that had sprung full grown from the soil itself, perhaps it didn't.

"My servant," Hectore continued, with emphasis on the second word, "has my absolute trust. I do not ask him how he knows what he knows."

"You are not likely to understand most of the answers." The fox was definitely condescending now. And this, too, Hectore accepted, although in other circumstances he would have been offended.

"Ah. But, you see, The Terafin is like unto me. What I will not understand, I fear that she will not."

The fox turned his nose toward Haval and lifted it, in obvious question. Haval met Hectore's gaze for a brief second and then nodded. "Jewel is fond of Hectore," he added.

"Yes. We are aware of that. She wishes to preserve him. But she is fond of his servant, as well."

"Yes, she is. Hectore, like myself, is not a young man. And Andrei is unusual. But inasmuch as she trusts, she trusts them both. And, Eldest," he added, as the fox opened its mouth, "you cannot tell me that she does not see. You might accuse Hectore of that ignorance—but you would be wrong, in my opinion. I think Hectore sees more than any of us."

"He cannot," the fox said, clearly cross and irritable.

Haval did not disagree; it wasn't necessary. But he straightened shoulders, fussed a moment with his apron, and turned—to Andrei. "Can you reach The Terafin?"

"From here, yes, but I must move quickly."

"What do you intend?"

"I intend to lead her out of the tangle. It is not safe. It was not safe for gods, when gods walked, and she is no god."

"She is Sen," the fox said.

Andrei nodded. "She is Sen," he agreed. "And it is possible that she might claim some part of the tangle as her own and make it strong—but that will not help her in the end; it will not help you. It will not save this city, or this Empire, when the god walks."

"What is the tangle?" Haval asked.

"It is what remains in the wake of the death of gods. Death does not mean to the gods what it means to even the firstborn; the firstborn, when dead, are gone. But the gods cohered. They were not born as you understand birth; nor did they give birth as you understand it."

"You know where she is."

"I know where she has walked; it is not, in the tangle, the same thing."

"And you know the tangle."

"One cannot *know* the tangle," Andrei replied, with obvious frustration. He looked at the fox as if expecting aid.

To Hectore's surprise, the fox said, "Very well. Warden, if the Councillor accepts it, we will accept it. The Terafin does hold Araven in some esteem. He has not lied to you," he added, to Haval. "But understand: he is *namann*. He does not need to lie. All truths are his, and some of those truths will destroy you."

"He is Andrei," Hectore said, voice cold.

Andrei placed a hand on Hectore's shoulder; Hectore shrugged it off.

"It does not offend me, and it does not cause me pain," the servant said.

"Not anymore, no."

"And you will not hold the entirety of the ancient world responsible for my . . . childhood."

"As it happens," Hectore replied, "you are not the keeper of my opinions."

Haval pinched the bridge of his nose. "You will have to tell me how you first met your servant. Ah, no. I would dearly love to know, if you are willing to speak of it at all. I do not require the knowledge." To Jarven, who had not moved, he said, "It is highly inadvisable."

"But he will take Hectore into the tangle, and Hectore is one of the few—the very, very few—who have provided me with any challenge in decades. I would not lose him to that. It seems too impersonal."

"Have you tired of this man?" the fox asked Andrei, indicating Hectore. It was not asked in accusation, but curiosity.

"If you would refuse him passage," Andrei replied, "I would consider it a boon, and I would be indebted to you."

The fox considered this.

Haval, however, said, "No."

"But if he does not wish to lose the mortal, the mortal *cannot* follow."

"The mortal in question is Hectore of Araven, and he has chosen."

"And *namann* would be in our debt."

"He will be in our debt in the future, regardless, if I am any judge of The Terafin," Haval countered.

"She would not wish Hectore to be put at risk."

"And she would allow it, regardless." To Andrei, he added, "You will allow it, as well."

"You are not my master."

"No. But I believe I understand what is now at stake."

"And me?" Jarven said, his voice soft.

"That decision, I leave in the hands of the eldest. I am aware of some of your abilities, but they are not in the area of my expertise."

"And you don't particularly care if I'm lost?" Jarven smiled.

Haval did not. "I do not feel it would aid our cause—at all—to lose you. It might afford me some personal peace, but I am accustomed to long periods without peace. Eldest?"

"No."

"No?" Jarven asked.

"No."

"You do not think I will survive?"

"It is the tangle, Jarven. It is not mortal—or even immortal—politics, where you pit knowledge, will, and raw power against the same. It is no more an opponent than typhoons; you endure it—or you die. I see no reason at all to take that risk, given the usual outcome. Firstborn have been devoured by it. Foolish gods."

"Foolish gods?" Haval asked.

"Yes. Very, very foolish gods." He hesitated. "Oh, very well." And his tail flicked once, twice, and a third time, and the forest changed.

*   *   *

"Eldest," Andrei said, in a tone entirely unlike his usual servant's tone.

The fox ignored him.

They no longer stood beneath the bowers of towering trees; they stood by the side of what appeared to be a lake—and a lake whose opposite shore could only barely be seen.

"The gods were not born as you understand birth. Birth in your lives *is* a beginning. The gods do not remember their beginnings, although in some fashion they remember their youths."

"And you?" Haval asked, for Haval was with them. He did not seem startled or surprised by the sudden change in the landscape. Nor did Jarven. The woman with bloodred eyes was no longer present.

"I remember my youth," the fox replied, which was the only answer he tendered. "Imagine, then, what death meant, to those gods; an ending, to those who had no clear beginnings. And there was war, always, among the gods. It was war that divided them, war that informed them, war that hardened their shapes, defined their possibilities. Where there is war, there is a need for sides, after all."

"You did not war?"

The fox chuckled at Haval's question, although his eyes were not warm. "Of course. War defined us all—by either its presence or its absence. You interrupt too much," the fox added.

Haval bowed and fell silent once again.

"Where there is war, there is death: an ending. And it happened, long, long ago, when the gods still walked the world, that gods died. And so: there was grief. It was not instant, of course—the gods could not easily conceive of *absence*, of continual absence. But death was absence, and in time, when that absence was not alleviated, one god approached the tangle."

"The tangle existed?"

"The tangle existed. It has always existed. It will always exist. It was only in the presence of the tangle that the god could feel any hint at all of his lost companion. He attempted to speak with the tangle, and the tangle replied."

"It is sentient?"

The fox chuckled. It was not kind. "Are madmen sentient?"

"Yes."

"Very well. Perhaps one could say it was sentient. The god asked for the return of his companion; the tangle did not reply. And it did reply. And that is the nature of the tangle. The god walked into the tangle."

"And did he return?"

"We heard his cries of fear and pain and bewilderment; we heard his cries of delight and joy. We heard his voice for three days and three nights, and then we heard no more of him. Some said that he had found his companion. Some said that he could not hold onto his companion.

"And yes, Haval, he did return."

Andrei had grown stiff and cold as the fox related his story; Hectore had grown more and more irritable. His humor was not improved when the fox turned toward Andrei, his eyes narrowed. He cleared his throat, and to Hectore's lasting surprise, Jarven bent and picked him up.

Hectore would not have been that fox for all the money in the world. He saw, in Jarven, the beginnings of a web. Jarven was not, and had never been, content to serve. He was entirely unlike Andrei. When he served—and he did—it was never his intention to remain in the subservient position.

And that, Hectore reminded himself, was not his problem.

"Will you tell the rest of the story, or shall I?" the fox asked Andrei. There was no friendliness in the question; there was the undercurrent of threat.

Hectore said. "Neither. We are short on time, as I'm sure you are aware."

"Hectore," Jarven said.

"No. I do not understand what enmity exists between Andrei and the rest of the denizens of this forest; I know that *none* exists between Andrei and the forest's ruler. I will not have him judged or condescended to in my presence."

"Hectore," Andrei now said, forced to join his protest to Jarven's, for which Hectore was likely to pay later.

"You do not understand what he is," the fox said.

And Hectore of Araven had had enough. "I understand *who* he is far, far better than you, Eldest. The Terafin understands *who* he is far better than you. What she did not demand, you should not demand."

"It is not a demand," the fox replied, voice cooling.

"Hectore." This time Jarven and Andrei spoke in concert.

"He has come at risk to aid The Terafin, and if we whittle away the time, the aid might come too late."

There was a fixed, rigid stiffness in the silence that followed. The fox finally said, "Very well."

Jarven's expression over the head of the golden fox was halfway between glare and resignation. "Know your limits, Patris."

"Know your boundaries," Hectore replied.

Andrei pinched the bridge of his nose. "Hectore, if it does not offend me, I ask you not to take offense on my behalf. Come."

Jarven set the fox down on the forest floor at some unspoken command. "I will accompany you."

*   *   *

Andrei led in a tight-lipped silence; he did not approve of Jarven's company. The forest did not change, not immediately, but something did because Jarven began to speak.

"You are far too experienced not to understand the import of the fox in this forest." His tone was clipped; he was annoyed.

"Yes."

"He is not simply another cantankerous, powerful merchant."

"Yes."

"Some caution and, more to the point, some manners are called for when dealing with the ancient and the powerful. They have longer memories than Lucille."

"I did not find his manners up to scratch, and I am not Terafin. I am not of a mind to extend a courtesy that has not been extended in turn."

"Or first? Andrei is not a child to be coddled or protected."

"Nor is he an enemy or a nonperson."

Jarven chuckled. "He is *namann*, Hectore. He is the definition of—"

"Enough."

"I have always found your lack of humor bracing, when it does come to the fore." To Andrei, he said, "I have always admired the service you provide to House Araven. I have always been aware that you would never willingly provide such service to me. Whatever price Hectore pays, I cannot pay."

"No," Andrei replied. "To Hectore I am servant, not pawn or tool."

"Were you created to walk the tangle?" The question was casual.

Hectore struggled to contain his momentary rage, to isolate it. It would help neither Andrei nor House Araven. "Jarven."

"Yes?"

"He is family to me." It was, in its fashion, a threat.

But Jarven nodded slowly, remembering perhaps earlier conversations, earlier observations.

"I was not created to walk the tangle." Andrei surprised Hectore by replying. "I was created in part to end war."

Silence.

The forest was often seen at night; only in the presence of the ancient was the cast of the evening sky guaranteed to change. This night, glimpsed through branches, held the face of one bright moon. There was no other.

The tangle had implied to Hectore a mass of ever-changing surfaces. It had implied chaos, a lack of physical sense. But he knew, by Jarven's expression, by

Andrei's tension, that they had walked into the tangle. Were it not for the single moon and its almost harsh light, Hectore would have assumed that they were taking a leisurely—if inexplicable—stroll through the Terafin grounds.

"Remarkable," Jarven said, almost to himself.

Hectore grimaced. "If you would refrain from treating me as if I was less observant than the lowliest of your clerks, I would appreciate it."

Jarven laughed. Andrei, predictably, did not; amusement or mirth existed as constant between the two, and at the moment, Jarven had taken the lion's share. "It is not condescension. It is an invitation to conversation. You have, in the past, not been averse to conversation."

Hectore stopped, inhaled deeply, and exhaled as much of his irritation as he could. The fox's treatment of Andrei had annoyed him. And why? In most cases, the patriciate failed to even see Andrei, because Andrei was a servant. Invisibility was the natural order. He was not given respect because he was not considered—ever—an equal.

Jarven, however, had always granted Andrei the compliment of considering him an equal, as much as Jarven considered any man an equal.

"Apologies," Hectore said. "I am, perhaps, still fatigued by lack of sleep."

"Oh?"

"I woke poorly. I woke," he added, "dreaming of the tangle, although that was not the name it bore in nightmare."

"What name did it bear in nightmare?"

"Hell."

"And what, Hectore of Araven, is hell?" Jarven asked the question as if it were one of the anchor points of a contract negotiation, rather than one of the fiddly details that clerks went to war over.

"A strange question."

"Not at all. Hell is, in theory, the torture, the despair, of mankind. But what causes me to hate or despair would be, in the end, very different from what invokes the same response in you. Oh, there's physical pain," he added, almost dismissively. "And in that sense, we are all equal. But the architecture of hell—at least as artists render it or poets recite— is individual, in the end. It requires some knowledge."

"Why did you come?"

"I am bored."

Hectore's laughter was a bark of sound in a silent night. "You have been in the odd position you hold for perhaps a handful of days, and you are *bored*? Jarven, you will never fail to surprise me."

"One would hope not. You wish to know why I am bored?"

"Oddly enough, I do."

"The acuity of my normal senses is heightened. They are expanded. I can see things that occur within the bounds of the city in a way that I have never seen them. I can see, for instance, the paths that lead from Terafin to the Common or to *Avantari*. The latter, I take care in approaching.

"I can see traces of the demonic on some of those paths. I am faster than I was at my peak; I do not tire easily, if at all. But I am restless, Hectore. The elders do not feel that I have learned enough to be allowed free run of my own city."

"And you do not agree with this assessment."

"I consider the assessment irrelevant. I am meant to be the Terafin version of *Astari*."

"But without the element of absolute trust?" Andrei asked.

Jarven raised one brow, as was his wont. "I have been told that my abilities, such as they are, are tied in some fashion to the forest in which the ancients have their roots. I will retain some, but not all, of the advantages I currently enjoy when I step beyond the boundaries of the lands that enclose them."

"Perhaps you should consider their advice."

"Why? They have not considered mine. I consider most of their advice irrelevant. I am not a simple dagger or sword, to be lifted and wielded at their leisure or need, and if I am to be effective, I must know my own limitations. I must test them."

"Against what?"

"That would be the question. You will note that Haval did not demur when I professed some interest in joining you."

"And you now accept the opinion of a tailor?"

"I accept all opinions. I do not accept them as instructions or commands, however. And you will note that the tailor is called Councillor by the ancients. They are willing to accept his advice."

Ah. "But not yours?"

Jarven was silent.

"One day, you will have to tell me what your history with that tailor is. I can't imagine it's good; he seems to feel about you the same way Andrei does."

"Yes. Both men lack any sense of humor whatsoever." Jarven stopped walking.

So did Andrei.

Hectore looked ahead. He saw forest, much the same in composition as the forest through which they'd been walking. Turning, he looked back. The forest there had not changed, either.

"We have entered the tangle?" he asked, voice soft.

"Yes." Their voices overlapped.

"I am sorry to be so ignorant—or perhaps so blind—but how can you tell? With the exception of the single moon, there is no difference to my eye."

Andrei frowned, as did Jarven; the expressions were very different. "You see only one moon?" the latter asked.

"Yes."

"And you see no other changes? The forest floor? The nature of the trees?"

"None."

"Can you see the path?"

"There is no path," Hectore replied. "When the sun rises—as I assume it will—I might be able to discern footpaths, but at the moment, no. This is not what you see."

Jarven nodded. "Can you touch the trees?"

Andrei said, "No."

"It is a reasonable question," Hectore told his servant. "I have carried some protections with me, and we are joined at the waist." Andrei had refused to remove the rope. "It is clear to me that Jarven's vision has been altered in a way that mine has not. Jarven merely wishes to know if my vision is accurate."

"Jarven can touch the tree himself."

"I am not at all certain that Jarven sees the trees," Hectore replied, the frown shifting texture. "And it has become clear to me that you do not." He then reached out and placed his hand against the bark of the nearest tree.

The bark was solid, rough, and remarkably treelike. Hectore had once climbed trees like this in his distant youth—although the trees he had climbed were younger, their lower branches closer to ground, the girth of their trunks narrower.

"I can, as you perceive, touch the trees. You do not see them?"

Jarven was frowning. Hectore understood why. "No."

"Do you see anything?"

"I see that you are touching empty air in a fashion that implies solid object. You do not have the sense of mischief that would be required for this to be a joke. Andrei?"

Andrei said, "There is a tree. Hectore is touching it."

"You perceive the tree?"

"Yes. Yes, and no."

"Well, this is unfortunate," Jarven then said. "I will have to have a word with the elders upon my return."

"How so?"

"I wish to retain my actual vision; I do not mind if that vision is sharpened or refined—but if I cannot see as men see, if I cannot see as I once saw, it is far less advantageous. And I would like to know how you see the tree."

Hectore said, "Jarven, let it be."

But Andrei said, "Because it is there, ATerafin."

"And you do not see the boundary? You do not see the words pressed against the floor like a guiding path or a warning?"

"I see them, as well."

"And the skies?"

"They are amber. Amber and amethyst. The skies will not retain a single color; they will shift. Nor will it be night or day in any recognizable order. There are pockets within the tangle that are almost natural—to your kind—and they might last decades, centuries, or days."

"Is that the whole of the danger the tangle presents?"

"No. But if you are here, if Hectore is here, there are some geographies which are unsafe."

"And they are not unsafe for you."

"No. Some are infinitely more painful than others, but no. There is no place in the tangle that I cannot walk; there is no path that I cannot follow before it is consumed. And the paths are consumed, remade, consumed, remade."

"I would like to know the rest of the elder's story," Jarven said.

"Then, perhaps, when you return—if you return—you may ask him. Legends are not history, and history is not event."

"Did a god search for his lover in the tangle?"

"No doubt dozens of gods searched for their lovers in the tangle," Andrei replied, but distantly. "Come."

They walked for hours. Hectore's sense of the passage of time had always been sun-dependent, and there was, at the moment, no sun. But the trees, while they thinned here and there, did not magically fall away. By the end of the third hour, Hectore turned to his servant.

"You looked peaked," he said, as if examining a child. "And I assume that you are somehow choosing a path that is not entirely convenient for you."

"I am forced—by your presence—to choose a path that you can walk and survive, yes."

"And it is draining to do so." The moment the words left his mouth, he understood that he had made the wrong assumptions. It was draining for Andrei to be here, yes. But not because of the chosen path.

Because of the form and shape he now wore. "I remember what shape you were in when we first met." His smile was genuine, but it was three parts pain. "I accepted your service then. If you fear my reaction, do not fear it. If you fear Jarven's, again, do not. He understands that you are kin to me. What I accept, he will accept.

"It is not easy to retain that shape in this place."

Andrei, tight-lipped, nodded.

"And that is why you wished to leave me behind. Which is disappointing, and I am struggling not to take insult."

"I wished to leave you behind because you cannot traverse ocean. You cannot traverse desert for any length of time—not as you are, and not unprepared. You cannot fly above lava, cannot walk airless, lightless surfaces. It has nothing whatsoever to do with my appearance."

Hectore let it go, which was difficult. Had Jarven not been present, they would still be arguing.

"While you are present—and to a lesser extent, while Jarven is—there are only so many paths we can walk; the others are death. But The Terafin is mortal, and her companions are mostly mortal. The Terafin could, in theory, go where I can go; she has the Winter Queen's mount. But the others cannot. She does not know the tangle as I know it—because it cannot ever truly be known—but she will choose paths that can be walked by those who follow her.

"Understand that when I say I can follow her path, I do not speak of the actual steps she has taken or will take. I cannot. No two paths into the heart of the tangle are ever the same, even if they reach the same destination. There is no map of the tangle because such maps are meaningless. They are biography, not geography."

"But you said the path would be unmade. Surely that implies something solid."

Andrei grimaced. "I did say that. In some fashion, it is accurate. I am not following in her footsteps. I am following the echoes of her choice.

"I told you. The tangle changes. There are places and phases and shifts that will kill you. They will kill The Terafin. She does not, therefore, choose to walk them. Whether or not she makes conscious choices or instinctive ones is irrelevant. She is speaking to the tangle; were she not, I would not have known that she had entered it.

"The tangle is replying. . . as it can. I can hear her request. I can hear, far more clearly, the tangle's response. I am following its response," he added. "And, Hectore, I retain my shape and form because you are here. It is a reminder—a necessary reminder—that I cannot take shortcuts."

"Almost, I wish I had taken your advice and gone back to bed," Hectore replied. But he smiled.

* * *

He had not chosen to pack food—or rather, to have food packed—and he regretted it as the day wore on. Andrei, however, had not forgotten. When he found a rock, or a series of rocks, that both Hectore and Jarven could see, he called a halt and brought out the type of food one generally took for winter travel. By foot. In the wilderness.

Jarven did not complain. Hectore watched his old rival as he ate. "How long did you work the caravan routes?"

"Some number of years. I started when I was too young for the Kings' armies. I had managed to avoid being reluctant ship crew and did not consider my chances for continuing to do so high."

"And this reminds you of your youth?"

Jarven shook his head. "No. This reminds me of no part of my lived life. I do not see what you see," he added, voice softer than his wont. "I almost wish I could; I would like to be able to compare and contrast the two things." He glanced at Andrei, who was not eating. "You see both things."

Andrei said, "I see far more than two things, ATerafin, but I ask for silence. She is not close enough that we can bridge the distance—not safely."

"Ah. And had we not accompanied you?"

Silence for two beats. "I would be by her side now. But there are pathways which Hectore cannot walk."

"And me?"

"I am uncertain. I would not risk Hectore."

"No." He paused. "What do the demons see, when they walk here?"

"They do not walk here," Andrei replied. His voice was a wall—it often was when he chose to speak with Jarven.

"Because they are dead?"

Andrei stilled.

"He was always observant," Hectore said mildly. "As you continually pointed out."

"I believe I used slightly different phrasing."

"Well, yes."

Jarven was enjoying himself. Andrei was not. The two sentences, side by side, described most of the interactions between Jarven and the Araven servant. On very rare occasions, the sentences could be inverted—but that would not occur today.

"If you would occupy the Terafin Council member, I must listen. It is noisy here, and likely to grow more so, rather than less." He was frowning. "I do not understand the choices she is making—or has made. She is not walking the rim of the tangle; she seems to be walking toward its heart."

"That's bad."

"Yes, Hectore. At the heart of the tangle, there are no safe choices for The Terafin. At the heart of the tangle," he added, "there are almost no safe choices for me."

"Is she being pursued?"

"If she was, she has lost her pursuers. It is the *only* reason to enter the tangle at all. But if she retains Avandar and Lord Celleriant, such retreat should not be necessary. Retreat might be—but not into the tangle." He frowned. It was a familiar frown.

It was the frown he offered bad wine, poorly cooked food, or unacceptable hospitality; it was the frown reserved for things that failed to meet some basic standards. The frown gave way to almost open disgust.

"Excuse me."

Hectore laughed. The gravity of the situation did not warrant laughter, but he had seen a like expression on his servant's face only once in his life, and it had involved mice, food, and a restaurant kitchen. Hectore considered the war against mice to be a constant battle—but he was not the commander of the army that fought it.

Andrei had said, *there is a reason the word* vermin *was invented*. He had been disgusted to the point of near-fury.

His expression grew more pinched, not less, as Hectore's bark of involuntary laughter quieted.

"I resent having to do this," Andrei said.

"You resent coming to The Terafin's aid?"

"Please, Hectore; I believe I have given you enough amusement for the day. I am more than willing to come to The Terafin's aid. I know what you are like when your godchildren or grandchildren are having difficulties—in general, it is I who suffers. I will go and return. Do not move from this place."

"I don't think—"

But Jarven placed a hand on Hectore's shirt. He did not speak.

"Keep Jarven with you—if at all possible. I am not certain I would not feel a similar resentment should I be called upon to find him."

Chapter Sixteen

The Hidden Wilderness

CARVER'S ARMS WERE TIRED. If the gold-furred creature was the size of a housecat, it was heavier. He had had some experience running with full arms—but it had been decades since he'd been forced to practice. Nor did his passenger give them time to break—not until Carver's run had become a forward, gasping stumble. Ellerson was likewise winded, but he offered to carry the creature; Carver's *no* was visceral, more felt than stated.

"We have not run far enough," the creature said. "Nor fast enough. But you *can* skirt the snow with your weight."

The moon's light was silver and bright, although the moon itself seemed to be descending, just as the demon had done. Carver looked over his shoulder; he could not see the demon although he had no sense at all that they had evaded him. They were, for the moment, beneath his notice—and Carver desperately wanted to remain that way.

"Where," Ellerson asked, "do you take us?"

"We are *trying*," the creature replied, with obvious exasperation, "to evade the trapped. And they are *following* us. If they follow, he will find them, and when he does, he will find *you*. This was a terrible, terrible idea. One should never make important decisions when newly roused from slumber." He shook his head, rumbling. "Put me down, boy."

Carver was only too happy to oblige.

The creature once again became a bear. His weight, however, no longer sank beneath the snow's icy surface. "I dislike fighting," he said. "I am not one of the Winter people." He began to sniff the area, as if in search of food. Some of that area included the two men who occupied it.

His nose stopped at the center point of Carver's chest, and his words fell into a growl that contained no syllables.

"It is *you*," he said. "It is you. What *are you*?"

Carver met golden eyes. As his gaze lowered to black, snuffling nose, he understood. He reached, slowly, into the folds of his shirt. Hand trembling, he withdrew the blue leaf that Jay had given him in her dream. In the moonlight, it glowed, the light brighter in the veins of a leaf that could only grow in a forest like Jay's. Except this one hadn't.

The bear's jaw dropped open, as if unhinged. His eyes rounded. His brows—and he had brows of a paler gold than the rest of his fur, almost disappeared. His jaw worked, but he had, for a moment, forgotten the rudiments of speech. It returned in stumbling syllables, but it took a moment for an actual sentence to emerge from his attempts.

"Where did you get that?" he finally asked.

"It was given to me by—by my Lord."

"And what, exactly, is your Lord? Do you serve one of the dead?" The question was sharper, harsher.

"No!"

"Then get rid of it, boy—if you can. Is it bound to you? Are you trapped? Is it your life that gives it form?"

Carver shook his head in rapid succession. "It was a gift."

"It is *not* a gift that can be safely used or kept. I better understand why the dead seek you here, where their safety is not guaranteed. Do you even understand what it is?"

Carver shook his head again. "It's . . . it's a leaf."

The bear turned a baleful gaze on Ellerson. It needed no interpretation. "Do you understand?"

"No. He does not lie. We were sundered from our own lands, and our Lord sought him while she slept. She left this in his keeping, but retained something of his in return."

"Did *she* make this? It is a work, you understand? It is a terrible, terrible working. Put it away if you will not abandon it—but I suggest that you do."

"If it is so terrible," Ellerson replied, "it might be best not to leave it here. We do not wish the Sleeper to awaken."

"Aye, this might wake him. He hears it. I heard it. And the creature who follows you—Darranatos that was—hears it as well. He hears it, if I were to guess, far more clearly than either of you." The creature cocked his head to one side. "Do you hear it at all?"

"No. It makes as much noise as a single leaf does."

"Mortals are so limited," the bear said. "So limited."

"The Lord we serve is mortal."

The bear glared at him.

"Truly."

"Impossible. Unless she is a maker."

Carver shook his head. "She's not a maker. She's—" here, he hesitated. What was the word that Meralonne used? That Avandar used? Ah. "*Sen.*"

The bear stared at Carver. When Carver failed to add more, he swiveled his head to look at Ellerson. The domicis nodded.

"We cannot escape if you do not let go of that leaf."

"But if we drop it here—"

"What was it intended to do?"

"I don't know."

"Did your Lord not tell you when she gifted it to you?"

Carver shook his head. "I'm not certain she knows, either."

The creature shouldn't have been able to look more outraged—but discussion had calmed it somewhat. His expression once again adopted the shape of shock and disgust.

"We are mortal," Ellerson said, voice soft and respectful, as if the bear were one of The Ten. "We do not know. But perhaps you, who are infinitely wiser, might tell us."

The creature sniffed. It reminded Carver so much of Shadow. "If you find the right soil," he finally said, "you might be able to leave these lands. I can't guarantee where you'll come out, though."

Carver's breath quickened. Jay had left him this leaf. And maybe, just maybe, this was why. If so, she hadn't done it deliberately—but she was seerborn. His hand tightened around the stem of the leaf as hope descended.

"Where," he asked, voice dry, "is the right soil?"

"I will lead you," he said. "But there *is* a danger."

"You mean besides the demon and the Wild Hunt?"

The bear growled.

The Tangle

"You are not *always* stupid," Shadow told Jewel. He had decided, for no obvious reason, that he needed to walk on the other side of Jewel, and had shouldered Angel out of the way, had stepped on Adam's foot, and had taken his chosen position. Jewel had no doubt that he would immediately decide that he needed to change that position, and the process would repeat itself.

Calliastra was not amused.

In the minutes—or hour—that had passed since the forest floor beneath Shadow's feet had become earth, she had grown silent. The wings of midnight that had been a hint of shadow were now as solid as Shadow's wings. Her eyes were black, her lips bloodred. She was disturbing, compelling, and angry.

Angry Calliastra was not unlike angry Duster. In an emergency, anger could be held in abeyance.

"We should stop," Terrick said, "and eat while it is safe to do so."

Jewel shook her head. "It's not safe. Not yet."

The roars of the missing cats—Snow and Night—continued to break the silence. They did not grow any louder, but they didn't grow distant, either. It was only when they ceased that Jewel's fear sharpened. She had been following their voices.

"You've been following *me*," Shadow said, his voice threatening growl the way heavy clouds threatened storms. Regardless, they'd not been gaining ground. Following them through this odd forest had taken a type of concentration she seldom used.

Every step she took—every step—had to be measured. She might take three steps, or four, but her foot would freeze before it came down on the fifth, and she would withdraw that foot, would test a step to the right or the left.

No one else seemed to be forced to be as careful—only Jewel. But this, at least, she understood. She was leading. If she didn't take a wrong step, those who followed couldn't, either.

Shadow purred.

She could, and did, lift her hand from his head; she no longer felt it was unwise to do so. Shadow was not materially different; he was a very large hunting cat. His wings were larger but not markedly so; his eyes were gold.

"Why do you *need* them?" he asked, as she was forced to take three steps to the right, as if circumventing a barrier.

She had no immediate answer; she wasn't really concentrating on the question. She was concentrating on the placement of her feet, on the forward movement that was, for the moment, denied her.

"Jay."

She looked up. At the edge of this forest was a clearing, seen between trees that were almost mundane. She could see white between the trunks of two of them; it wasn't the white of snow.

"Stone?"

"Ruins, I think." Angel didn't offer to scout ahead. Nor did Terrick.

"Avandar?" She squinted. She wasn't certain Angel was right.

Her domicis was so silent Jewel wondered—with a start—if she had some-how lost him.

You will lose everyone but Celleriant and the Winter King first, he replied. He was mildly annoyed, which was comforting.

"Can you see what Angel sees?"

Silence again.

Jewel, feet planted, turned to look at Calliastra and froze.

The darkness-born child of gods was no longer there. In her place stood a young woman Jewel did not recognize. Gone were the great, shadowed wings, gone were the eyes so black they had no whites, gone were the snow-white pallor and bloodred lips.

"Calliastra?"

The young woman blinked. She looked around in confusion.

Avandar cursed, but silently; he was stiff now.

Shadow cursed loudly, which drew the young woman's attention. Her eyes were brown, looked brown, and her skin was freckled; her hair, while long, was also a shade of dark that didn't immediately evoke the Lord of the Hells. And her nails appeared to be bitten. "Eldest."

"Yes, *yesssssssss*," he said, with weary resignation. He pivoted, leaped, and pounced.

She laughed—laughed—and leaped up so quickly she wasn't standing where the great gray cat had landed.

"Shadow."

He glanced back over his winged shoulder and then forward again to the girl. "She won't let us have *any* fun." He folded his wings and sighed. Loudly.

And the girl who was—who must be—Calliastra then clambered up onto his back.

What do you see? she asked her domicis.

I see what you see. She is . . . not what she was when we entered the tangle.

Jewel turned to Shianne then; Shianne was watching the two: girl and cat. But her lips bore the full shape of suppressed pain or sorrow. "Yes, Terafin. She is Calliastra. I did not know her in her youth, but the White Lady did, and I share some of her memories."

"But—but what's happened to her?"

Shianne shook her head. "We are in the tangle, and she is of the gods. I might now be grateful that I am mortal. The tangle can kill me, but it will not alter me as it might alter . . . others. No, before you ask. Only if you are killed or altered will Celleriant fall prey to that particular fate. He is yours."

"I don't even understand what that means," Jewel said quietly. "He's immortal. He's ancient. I'm neither. How can someone like Celleriant be mine?"

"It is the nature of the vow," Shianne replied, her voice soft. "You are mortal. You change, and are changed, simply by existing. It does not require effort on your part; it is natural for you. It is what you are.

"But his birth—like mine—was not yours. His nature is fixed, and to change requires effort, will, or external interference. He has said that he is, until your death, *yours*. And the tangle understands that. To alter Celleriant, it would have to alter you—and I think, in the end, that it is not possible to alter you without destroying you. If you die, it will be different."

Jewel was watching Calliastra. "If immortals are unchanging, why is she . . ."

"I did not say we did not change. We are living beings."

Calliastra was speaking to Shadow, who looked entirely too long-suffering. He treated her almost as he treated Ariel, and it was clear that she responded in kind. Jewel knew that Calliastra was the daughter of darkness and love. She understood the tragedy of that life, or thought she had.

But she had not seen Calliastra as this girl. This girl was . . . young. This girl could be joyful. This girl had yet to be broken by the knowledge of what love *meant*. What she loved, she killed. What she loved died. Always.

Jewel knew that fear. It had shadowed her adult life. "Will it change her again?" she asked softly.

"Will it? I do not know. Can it? Yes. It is the tangle, Terafin. If we could predict it, we could control it."

"You've walked the tangle before."

"Yes. Once."

"Why?"

"Because it is only in the tangle that what I desired could be achieved. You have not moved."

Jewel nodded. There was no place to put either of her feet; she had lifted both, and instinct gave her no clear path forward. Nor did it now allow her to take a step back.

Shadow hissed.

"What?"

"I'm *bored*. You're *boring*."

Calliastra *giggled*.

"Lord," Celleriant said quietly.

She looked up at him.

"She cannot remain as she is. Even if you do not move, the tangle will."

"That's not why I'm standing still." But she heard the low murmur of the godchild's voice, and it broke her heart. And she realized, then, that Celleriant wasn't wrong. It worried her. She had fallen back into her patterned reaction to visceral instinct, but if visceral desire had the same strength, she would lose that compass, lose that certainty.

You don't always get what you want, her Oma's voice said. She grimaced, shook herself. Her Oma's voice, her Oma's lectures, her Oma's criticisms, would never leave her. And they were, in some fashion, as much of a compass as her talent.

Nor did she argue with it now, although she sometimes did. She wanted this child to be happy. She wanted this daughter of darkness to have a few moments of a life in which love was not death. In which love was not an issue. And these were the only moments she could offer.

She lifted her foot and moved forward.

It would have helped her progress if the world changed on a footstep. It would have helped her to understand the tangle as a danger. But the landscape changed slowly when it changed at all. The rest of the mortals, as Jewel, saw what Jewel saw, even Avandar, who had been mortal at birth, before hubris and a desire for eternity had changed everything.

But the Winter King had been mortal at birth as well, and that mortality had been burned from him, along with his human form. He did not see what Jewel saw. Celleriant did not, without effort. Shianne, however, didn't speak of what she saw. She watched Jewel and Adam as if they were toddlers, her shoulders stiff with unexpressed anxiety. She did not want to lose either of them here and clearly thought that was the most probable outcome.

It wasn't affection, of course. Jewel knew that. Shianne owed loyalty—and love—to one person only. But to *reach* that person, she needed Jewel. And to deliver her unborn child, she needed Adam. They were necessary to her goals.

But even knowing it, Jewel felt a flush of warmth at the obvious worry.

The trees thinned, and thinned again, as if they were making themselves smaller and less significant. Celleriant had slowed to a very graceful, very stately walk. Terrick was fidgeting; he was clearly accustomed to scouting an area before it was fully entered, and that duty had been forbidden him.

Avandar, however, felt no qualms.

That is untrue. I am willing to trust your talent, but I cannot conceive of any way in which those cats are worth this risk.

Shadow was with Calliastra, who was no longer young. Her expression denied joy; a smile would have withered before it started. Her eyes were dark, her skin too pale, but she did not have the shadow wings that spoke of her father's power. Nor did she speak. She walked beside Shadow in silence, looking at her feet.

Is she yours?

Jewel frowned. It wasn't Avandar who had asked the question, nor was it the Winter King. She glanced at Shianne, but no, and Kallandras appeared to be listening to the butterfly that now sat on his shoulder.

Calliastra was the child of gods. She was the daughter of the Lord of the Hells. She was death—how could she not be, and sustain her own life?

But she was more Jewel's than Shadow, Night, and Snow.

She's mine. Just as Duster had been. Duster had been free to walk; she wasn't caged or confined. No one could confine someone like Duster. But she could be worked with, valued for what she did, and nudged in the right direction— that direction being the one that Jewel needed her to walk.

Calliastra would never be Duster. But she was Jewel's in the same way that Duster had once been. And the frown growing on her face was very like Duster's frown, couched in different features. The godchild looked at Jewel, the frown deepening.

"I'm not worried about you," Jewel said, before Calliastra could speak.

"Do not lie to me."

"I'm not. I know what I see. It's more than that, though. You could kill us all—"

"Not *me*," Shadow said.

"I could," Calliastra told him, looking down her very perfect nose at the gray cat.

"Could *not*."

Very clever, Avandar said.

She hadn't done it deliberately, and what her domicis thought clever, Jewel thought the edge of total disaster. She turned but did not take a step toward them; she couldn't. "Fine. She could kill all of us easily except you. She'd probably have to work for that."

Shadow hissed.

"You've been changing as you walk here. None of the rest of us have. I don't know what it costs you. I don't know how you experience it. But Shadow hasn't changed."

Calliastra's smile was bitter, turned inward. "Is that how you perceive it?"

Jewel nodded.

"I have not changed, Terafin. I have simply been. We are not yet overcome by the tangle. But it seeks truth, and our truths are not yours." She glanced at Celleriant, who had not changed in the way she had. "So, it was true. You are sworn to her service."

"While she lives."

A roar interrupted the conversation that had been punctuated by Jewel's slow footsteps.

She looked to Kallandras.

"Night," he said, frowning. "He is not happy."

"He's *never* happy," Shadow said, sniffing. The gray cat did not look concerned.

"He doesn't sound afraid."

"No. I believe he is angry."

She listened for a second roar as Night's died into silence. "I can't hear Snow."

"No. I do not believe Night is angry at his brother." The bard's frown was slight.

It was enough. He didn't tell her to hurry. He didn't tell her that she was running out of time. But he didn't need to. She felt it in the pit of her stomach. Taking a deep breath, she closed her eyes and bent into her knees.

"We're going to pick up the pace," she said. "If I understand anything I've been told, don't run ahead of me."

She could not run in the tangle. That was the first thing she discovered. She couldn't safely *stumble* here, so she had to open her eyes.

She closed them instantly.

The trees had given way utterly. There was no longer any forest. The ground beneath Jewel's feet was rocky. The sky was clear. The air was very dry.

Adam whispered something, and Jewel nodded. She had seen landscape like this once before—as the Arkosan caravans had approached the Sea of Sorrows. There, rock gave way to sand in places; Jewel had expected the desert to be nothing but sand. As always, experience changed expectation. It wasn't true that nothing grew in the desert—but nothing broke the line of distant horizon except the haze of heat.

Jewel turned. In the distance, to her right, she could see what looked like a cloud of moving dust.

"Windstorm," Adam said.

But Jewel, lips compressed, shook her head. "Cat."

The first thing she discovered was that she could move more freely in this space than she had when attempting to lead the way out of the forest. Or into the forest. She had never been particularly good at navigation; she had relied on familiarity, and she had been familiar with the holdings. She was familiar with the manse. She was not familiar with her own forest, but familiarity in the forest of the *Ellariannatte* had never been required.

She glanced at Terrick. "You've seen desert before?"

"That is our word for the snow plains," the Northern giant replied. "But yes, I have seen the deserts in the Dominion. I have never seen a leader of The Ten in the desert."

"I wasn't The Terafin then."

"Do not waste water," Adam told them all. He looked to Shianne.

"I have seen the vast, empty plains," she replied. "I understand their stark beauty and their danger."

"You were not with child then." Adam said. Gone was the stammering, blushing youth.

"No. I was not mortal then. It is difficult to accustom oneself to the idea that simply standing outside can kill. And before you speak, Terrick, I have seen the snow as well, unadorned by tree or shrub." To Adam, she said, "What would you advise? I cannot lose your Matriarch, and she has chosen desert."

"It wasn't a deliberate choice," Jewel said. She reddened—but a walk in this sun would have that effect in the end anyway.

"It was deliberate," Shianne replied, frowning slightly. "You did not know that it would lead you here. Had you, would you have walked away?"

The wind howled.

Kallandras was right. The storm was Night.

"Shadow."

"Why do *I* have to *go*?"

"It's you or me." Celleriant started to speak; Jewel lifted a hand to cut him off.

"Then *you* get him. He is not right. He is *dangerous*."

Before Jewel could answer, Celleriant did. "Ah. My apologies, Eldest. I did not realize he could be a threat to you. I will go."

Shadow, however, sputtered in wide-eyed outrage. "He can't hurt *me*!"

"But you said—"

He spit to the side. His wings rose.

"Terafin," Calliastra said, her voice somber, quiet, "this is not wise. Not here."

"No. But it's not wise to be here at all. If I relied on wisdom to govern my life and my decisions, I would never have left home."

"Not true, as you well know. If you are killed here, none of your companions will escape the tangle."

"Will you?"

"In time, yes. But I am not what you are. I am not what any of your companions are. I believe your cats—in some form—would also escape."

Shadow's outrage continued. "*Escape? We don't need to escape!*"

Jewel nodded.

Shadow did not pad forward, as he might have if they had been at home. Instead, his haunches bunched. He didn't coil silently, and his language was foul, even given his mood, but as it was all aimed at Jewel and she had heard worse in her time, she shrugged it off.

He leaped.

"Terafin—"

She shook her head. He leaped into the windstorm, and as he did, she shouted a single word.

"*Night!*"

The storm, a thing of sand and wind, moved as Shadow approached it; it halted the moment Jewel shouted its name.

Jewel stood her ground as the storm's trajectory changed. "What are the cats?" she asked Calliastra.

"I have often believed," the god-born woman replied, "that you fail to pay attention to the construction of words. But think: Catastrophe. Cataclysm. It is how I saw them, in my youth."

"You played with—"

"Yes, of course. There is an odd, ruined beauty in destruction. They did not build. But their intent was not destruction. At heart, they are playful, proud, vain—but they are restless. They have learned with time—as all ancients have learned—to make . . . room in themselves for more.

"But no force on earth in their youth—or mine—could own them." There was an implied criticism in this, and a question.

"They're not young now," Jewel replied. "What did the Winter King do?"

"I believe you have your suspicions."

*   *   *

The storm enveloped Shadow. Jewel lost all ability to breathe as the great, gray cat disappeared in winds that carried abrasive sand. It howled with Night's voice, a hint of Night's triumph.

She had sent him there.

The Hidden Wilderness

Carver froze when a howl rent the air at their backs. Unlike the roar of a demon or the angry cries of the Wild Hunt, this was a familiar sound. Not entirely a safe one—but familiar. He froze in place. So, too, Ellerson, although the domicis' expression was neutral. Carver thought his exhaustion had given way to hallucination; he shook his head to clear it.

The yowling, however, repeated itself. As it did, it drew closer. Carver could feel a shift in the breeze. So did the snow on the branches of the trees overhead; it fell. The bear wasn't pleased with this. Or perhaps he wasn't pleased with the sound of a whiny, angry cat. A winged cat.

"This is just what we need," the bear snarled. Carver and Ellerson dodged to the side to avoid being bowled over as the bear turned in the direction of that familiar voice. "Take advice from me," he continued, as he shifted his stance. "When you have the opportunity to sleep, take it."

"No, wait," Carver shouted. "Wait!"

"This had better be good," the bear replied.

"Shadow?"

The gray cat emerged from the shadows for which he was named.

"Why are *you* here?" the cat demanded, glaring at Carver, his wings high, his ears almost perpendicular to his head. His claws created instant runnels in the icy snow, although he hadn't moved them.

"Shadow? *Shadow?*" The bear demanded, in turn. His defensive posture stiffened, but he did not attack. He seemed almost dumbfounded. "Why is he calling you *that*?"

"Is he speaking to *me*?" Shadow asked Carver, a sniff at the end of the final syllable.

The bear growled.

Carver stared at Shadow. "Why are you here?" he asked, mirroring the cat's question without the annoyance. "Did Jay send you?"

Shadow sat, folding his wings. He examined his left paw for dirt. "She sent me to get Night because Night is *stupid*. He is *almost* as stupid as *she* is." His eyes, all of gold, narrowed. "Why do you have *him* with you?"

"Shadow—do you know where you are?"

The cat shrugged. "I am *here*."

"Why?"

"We were in the tangle," Shadow said. He offered no other explanation.

"Tangle?"

"Yes. The *tangle*, stupid boy."

Ellerson now cleared his throat, but before he could speak, the bear did.

"He isn't as stupid as you are, if you were in the tangle. What were you thinking?" The bear, like the cat, sat.

"The tangle is better than *here*," the cat replied. "Here is *boring*."

Not boring enough, Carver thought.

"Is *too*."

Ellerson, however, turned to Carver. He lifted his hands in den-sign, and Carver felt a pang, but answered his question. *Yes.*

Certain?

Yes. Den-sign didn't have much room for subtlety.

"Shadow," the domicis said, in a far less outraged voice than the bear, "why are you here? Have you come to take us home?"

The cat hissed. "Can't. You shouldn't *be* here. *I* shouldn't be *here*. Night is *stupid*. It is *his* fault."

Ellerson bore with this as if patience was the very air he breathed. To be fair, he'd had practice. They all had.

The cat frowned then, and, once again, the whole of his attention returned to Carver. No, not to Carver, but to the leaf he held in a shaking hand. The cat's eyes transformed; they were, in the Winter landscape, all blue. The blue of leaf. Of this leaf.

When he spoke next, his voice was free of the whine that characterized most of the cats' speech. "Why do you have that?"

"Jay gave it to me."

"She gave it . . . to you? Now?"

"She came to me when she said she was dreaming in the Oracle's abode. She left it with me." He added, before Shadow could speak, "I think she wanted to leave me something."

The cat continued to stare, but his wings had once again unfolded, and they were rising into the night sky as if there was no end to their length, just as the wings of the demon had done. Shadow growled. It was an animal sound; speech had deserted him, or he had deserted speech.

Carver remembered, then, the night Jay had lain abed in the dreaming. He remembered the wounds that had appeared across the whole of her body. She had said the cats had done it. No.

She had said Shadow had. She had no fear of the great, gray cat in the wake of that nightmare, but Carver remembered: these were lands created and held by someone who slept. And dreamed.

The cat's tail swished back and forth as he regarded Carver. The bear, however, had had enough. He pushed himself up off the snow and leaped. Shadow, still growling, turned instantly to face him, and the two collided in a moving, roiling mass of gray and gold.

Ellerson exhaled.

"You don't think they're going to kill each other."

"No more than I think Shadow will kill Night," Ellerson replied. "But if we are attempting to survive in this place, now is not the time for this; it will almost certainly draw far more attention than we have managed to draw so far."

"It *won't*," Shadow hissed, in his normal voice, a snarl breaking the syllables. "*Nothing* will draw *more* attention than what the *stupid, stupid boy* carries! Why? Why is it *here*?"

"I told you—"

"She is *stuuuuuupid*!"

Jay was, apparently, the most stupid creature to ever draw breath in the history of the universe. Ellerson, however, was right. The bear picked himself up as Shadow continued his tirade. He batted Shadow's shoulder with his left paw, and the cat staggered, breaking his stream of invective and disgust to return the favor.

"Do *not* ignore me!" the bear roared.

"Why *not*? You are *boring*. All you do *is sleep*!" He turned back to Carver to continue his dissection of Jay's stupidity. After what felt like hours of this, though it couldn't have been more than five minutes, Carver dropped his head into his hands.

The bear's roar, coupled with Shadow's whine, joined in a disharmonious mess of sound; he could feel their words resonate in his jaw, which was clenched too tightly. Which made this day almost normal, if one didn't count the Winter, the demon, the ghosts of the Wild Hunt, and the utter absence of anyone that he counted as kin, except Ellerson.

That would have been bad enough—relief giving way to the actual, less pleasant details of daily reality—had it not been for the other voices.

He could hear them, almost as a chorus, but they didn't speak the way Shadow did; their voices were felt as a thrum that paced his breath, his heartbeat. They were a tidal wave, moving inexorably to where he stood rooted in this Winter world, this half-dream, this place of death. He could not understand a word they spoke, but he knew that he would. Let the tide reach him and sweep him away, and he would hear it *all* clearly.

This was what the bear was trying to escape.

This was the voice—the many voices—of the single leaf that Jay had left him.

"Don't *do that*," Shadow growled. He leaped above the bear and headed directly to Carver, bowling him off his feet, where his back cracked the sheen of ice over snow as he fell. The cloak protected him from the cold; it did not manage to protect itself from the cat's claws.

Carver rose, cursing the cat in two different languages. He retained his grip on the leaf; the leaf, which seemed so delicate, had not been damaged by Shadow's fall. "What are you doing?" he demanded. He put the leaf back between chest and shirt, glaring at the cat, who immediately launched into another furious tirade about Night and Jay and stupid that was endless.

"She *gave* it to *you*. To *you*."

"That's what I said."

"You *don't understand*, you *stupid, stupid* boy! She gave it *to you*."

Carver did understand this.

"Why? *Why? Why* are you *so important?*"

Carver had heard a variant of this ever since the cats had first joined the den—but something was different. He approached Shadow and knelt across the broken ice, sliding in place while the cat snorted.

"Why is this important? Where does this leaf come from? It's not the same as the leaves in the rest of the forest."

"Of *course* not."

"Why is this leaf special?"

"Why did she leave *this* one with you?" the cat countered.

"The bear—the bear says that we—we can use this to get home. She couldn't take me with her when we met the first time."

Shadow stared at him, unblinking.

"This is what she left me. Maybe she knew—"

Shadow snorted. "She is too *stupid* to know."

"She is," Ellerson said, clearing his throat, "seer-born. Perhaps she understood on some level—"

"She understands *nothing*. If she understood what it was, she would *never* have made this leaf. *Never*. She is Sen. She *knows* what she needs even if she refuses to accept it. Or to *think* at *all*. But she left it with *you*."

"Perhaps," Ellerson said, because Carver suddenly couldn't, "she made this leaf for Master Carver."

Shadow's growl was lower, longer. He turned to the domicis. "She did not. If it were not what it is, *he* couldn't even *plant* it. But he *can*. Maybe Night is *less* stupid than I *thought*. A little less."

"Night sent you here somehow."

"*She* sent me here," Shadow said. He stared at Carver. "She told *me* to search."

"She didn't tell you to search for me."

Shadow said nothing.

"How can you be here?"

"The *tangle*."

"Can you get back to Jay?"

"*Yesssss*." Shadow glanced over his shoulder, shifting a wing out of the way. "But maybe not *yet*."

"Shadow?"

The bear said, "The demon has finished injuring himself against the Wild Hunt. He'll be coming this way."

"You are *stupid*," Shadow said to Carver as his wings unfolded. "You cannot *lose* what she has given you. Do you understand? And *he* is stupid, if he thinks you can."

"Which he?"

"*That* one," Shadow replied, as the moon went out.

The wind began to howl. Branches lost snow, trees lost branches; Carver and Ellerson scrabbled for footing and found it because they wore boots that had been crafted by people long dead. Only the bear seemed untouched; his fur didn't ruffle at all. He growled.

"Not *yet*!" Shadow yowled. He pushed himself into the air, where he hovered a moment in front of the bear. "You are not *completely* useless when you are awake. Take them and *go*."

"Go?"

"This is not safe for you—for any of you. But *you*," he said, to Carver, "do not plant that leaf. She will survive—but none of the rest of you will. *None*." He pushed himself off the ground, becoming a darkness of wings against the night sky.

"We can't leave," Carver told the bear, as the bear turned and began to move. "He wouldn't even close with that demon when we were at home! He can't fight him alone!"

"And what will *you* do? Die? Clearly, he doesn't want that, I don't know why.

You will have to tell me about your Lord when we have time. He must be unusual."

"She is."

The Tangle

Jewel understood family. She understood kin.

To her Oma, both required blood. It was blood that defined family, defined kinship. It was blood and responsibility. You owed your mother, your father, and your Oma your obedience and your love. They owed you. It was a chain—a happy chain—that bound people together. If it weren't for blood ties, her Oma implied, the world would be ugly, selfish chaos.

Jewel had—only once—pointed out that her mother and father didn't share blood. They'd come together, from two entirely different families. If they could do it, if they could become family, why couldn't anyone?

Her Oma had not been happy. Jewel was the bond that cemented two strangers. In her, the blood of both ran. It was how family was created and continued.

Jewel had no children of her own. The family into which she'd been born was gone. But she *had* family. She had kin. Did they fight? Yes. But her mother and father had argued. Her Oma had shouted at everyone. Everyone.

Would it be quieter without the cats? Yes.

Would it be quieter without the den? Yes.

But she could have quiet in the grave.

Family, for Jewel, was something that both gave strength and demanded it. It was like an unspoken vow. It could hurt—how it could hurt—but it could soothe. It was the soil in which she was planted. It was how she knew she could stand.

And Night was, like her den, kin. Family.

"*Night!*"

The Hidden Wilderness

Carver didn't see the moment two shadows became one. The bear did, with the back of his head.

"He's gone."

Carver knew. He knew—he had heard, contained in Shadow's terrifying, guttural roar, a familiar refrain: *Stupid Night!*

"Did he take the demon with him?"

"What do you think?"

"Thinking's not my strong suit."

The bear didn't stop, didn't pause; he seemed to be able to run forever. Ellerson surprised Carver; he kept pace with the bear. Carver, however, struggled, which would have been humiliating if he'd had the energy for it. He didn't.

"Master Carver."

"I'm fine—I'm fine."

"Let me take your pack."

Carver shook his head. "Pack weighs nothing," he said. It was true.

He knew what the weight was.

Jay had left the leaf for him. It was a deliberate choice on her part. But it was a deliberation born of pain, of guilt, of desperation. The den didn't question Jay. Not often. She was home, she was whatever rough safety life could offer. She could *see*. They'd trusted her sight for so long, it took effort to doubt it. It took no effort to examine it—they'd all done that, gathered around the kitchen table, first too small and then too large. But to doubt it?

Shadow did.

Shadow had.

The Tangle

The storm stilled. Sand fell away from air, pooling as if it were liquid in the bright, harsh clarity of sun.

In the heart of what had been storm was a great black cat—wings high, of course. He leaped as Shadow almost landed on him, and the two passed each other in the air, claws—and fangs—extended.

"That is *not* what I meant, Shadow!" Jewel shouted.

Shadow—like his brothers—had perfected the art of selective deafness.

"I *mean* it! Night, cut that out. We have to find your brother!"

Night roared. His voice was deeper, louder, fuller, than Jewel had ever heard it. She should have found it disturbing. Maybe later, she would. But the cat was appreciably cat now; the storm had passed.

"He *started* it!"

"She *told me* to!"

"You are certain you want to keep them?" Calliastra asked, but she was staring at Night, her eyes rounder, her mouth half-open in what, on a less jaded face, might be wonder.

"I was," Jewel replied.

"Then you must hurry, Terafin. I admit that I did not think you could call him back. Do you know where Snow is?"

Jewel turned to Kallandras.

The bard shook his head. "I have not heard his voice for some time."

And that silence was far worse than the roaring of a desert storm.

Hectore sat on the rock; Jarven stood on it.

"What do you see?" the Terafin merchant asked.

"Rock. Trees. The passage of a trickle of water too meager to be called a river. You?"

"I see the rock."

"And the rest?"

"I see only rock. It extends in all directions for as far as the eye—my eye—can see. I wish to explore it."

"I will not stop you," Hectore replied. "But I do not think it wise. Given Andrei's reaction to the tangle—as he has called it—I think you might well be lost."

"He believes it," Jarven replied.

"And you?"

"I believe that he believes it." His smile was sharp, slender, but it lit his face like sunlight. Or flame. "Where did you find him?"

"Jarven."

"I do not seek to poach. I am curious."

"I found him when I was a much younger man. I was working the caravan route to the south. He was injured."

"Was he as you see him now?"

"As I see him? Yes."

"Ah. And as I see him?"

"I will not play these games with you," Hectore replied. "I do not wish to answer these questions."

Jarven's shrug was entirely his own: fluid, dismissive. "Do you fear to lose him, now?"

"Of course I do. I would appreciate if you also declined to play games."

"Is this his home?"

"You must ask him yourself if you wish an answer."

"He will not answer me."

"Then that is answer enough. He is kin, Jarven. He is family to me. I will not surrender him to anything without a fight."

The rock upon which Hectore was sitting began to tremble.

"Interesting," Jarven said.

That was not the word that came to Hectore. He rose.

Jarven's hand fell to his shoulder. "I am willing to explore," he said. "But I understand the possible consequences, and they do not trouble me. You, however, are not in the same situation."

The rumbling grew stronger.

"How so?"

"You have something to lose."

This distracted Hectore from his growing concern. "And you don't?"

Jarven smiled. "I have always considered sentiment to be something of a weakness. I have seen young men—and young women—betrayed by their desire for love and family. That desire is a tool in the hands of men like me. It could have been a tool in your hands—but you were too enmeshed in the same game to see it."

"I have never considered myself foolish enough to desire what you desire. I have taken some pride in my own impregnability."

"If you have not built family, you have built position and power. You are an authority, Jarven."

"A faded authority whose glory days are behind him." This amused Jarven. "There will be rejoicing when I retire. That is what I will leave behind."

"Lucille would not agree."

Jarven shrugged.

"And I think young Finch would be saddened."

"She is not a fool. But yes, Hectore. Had I never met you, I would have considered it my duty to beat the sentiment out of that girl. You, however, have proven, in some fashion, that not all sentiment must become weakness. So has your Terafin. That life, however, is not for me. I am not capable of it. You are. And I consider it unsporting of you."

"Unsporting? I am beginning to understand why Andrei finds you so frustrating."

"Unsporting, old friend. If I am not you, if I am to leave no tears in my wake, I nonetheless understand why there will be tears in yours. I believe if you walk from this place, you will never find your way back to it. And I am not certain that Andrei will be able to find you."

"He can find The Terafin."

"Yes, but she is Sen. You are not; you are mortal. You will be lost here—and if you are lost, he, too, will be lost."

"And you would care?"

"Only inasmuch as I am willing to remain here—to see that you do—until he returns. And I resent it."

Chapter Seventeen

"HOW LONG HAVE YOU been glaring?" Hectore asked Jarven. Jarven was silent. He was not, to be fair, glaring at Hectore. He was glaring at the endless sea of stone with obvious displeasure. Hectore considered—as was his habit—what Jarven might gain from a display of annoyance; he considered, as well, what Jarven might gain from a smile, a laugh, a display of fear or fragility.

"Have you spent much time with The Terafin's winged companions?"

"Very little," Hectore replied. "I consider the gray to be dangerous."

Jarven's laugh was brief, harsh. "Only the gray? You are not that dim, Hectore."

"I consider the gray to be tactically dangerous," Hectore conceded. "The white and the black seem overly focused on the moment. Any of the three could kill me with ease."

Jarven's left brow rose.

"Any of the three could, absent tertiary precautions, kill me with ease."

"That is better. One of those precautions, I assume, is Andrei."

"But not the only one, as you are well aware. And you have not answered my question."

"I have no idea how long we've been waiting, and I resent the implication that I have wasted it glaring at you."

Hectore's smile was genuine. "What do you see, ATerafin?"

"Sand," Jarven replied. "To the horizon, there is nothing but sand."

"You do not see Andrei."

"No. Of the two of us where Andrei is concerned, your vision will undoubtedly be clearer. Why, exactly, did Andrei wish to meet The Terafin in this place?"

"I believe he hoped that she would not be lost in it if he could find her first."

"Hubris," Jarven said.

"Andrei has never notably been a humble, modest man, no. For my part, that hubris has saved my life many times; I am inclined to trust it. I am uncertain, however, why you are."

"Do I?"

"You are here, Jarven. You are here, and you believe that here is as dangerous as Andrei believes it to be. Your own hubris is considerable, yet you have chosen to obey what was almost a command."

"I am comfortable obeying commands," Jarven countered. "I have taken orders from The Terafin since I joined the House."

"I am grateful Andrei is absent," Hectore replied.

"Oh?"

"You have subverted orders when bored or ill-tempered; your idea of obedience is entirely idiosyncratic, and I believe it would annoy my servant."

"Almost everything annoys your servant."

"True."

"There is a storm on the horizon," Jarven said.

Hectore found the silence of this place grating. His legs were stiff; he felt as if he had been sitting, inactive, for hours. Were it not for the presence of the Terafin merchant, he might have disobeyed Andrei's request. He was concerned.

Andrei often left Hectore's side; he was not chained to it. He disappeared and reappeared, taking care to be present for any significant meetings or appointments. It was Andrei who had gone to the aid of Hectore's more difficult grandchildren; it was Andrei who had interacted with Ararath when that godson had chosen to forsake Handernesse.

It was Andrei who could stand between Hectore and the magi; it was Andrei who could face—and survive—the demon-kin. Hectore had the tricks the rich might avail themselves of, but they were entirely defensive. He did not have the ability to fight as Andrei fought. Nor would he.

Thinking this, he turned to study the Terafin merchant. Jarven was—had been—in Hectore's shoes. He could see the coming war as clearly as Hectore could, but where Hectore accepted his limitations, Jarven chaffed at them. It was not in Jarven to sit on the sidelines, a mere observer to events that would affect his life in multiple ways. If Jarven was to be affected, he would have a say. If he had a stake, he would find ways to play the game.

No, it wasn't just that. He would find ways to win it.

Hectore, as Jarven pointed out, had much to lose. But even knowing it, his desire to do what Jarven had done was vanishingly small. It was not that he distrusted The Terafin; she made suspicion nearly impossible to sustain. But she was not her forest, and she was not her forest's inhabitants.

And, also, her forest did not trust his servant. No, worse, they appeared to hold him in some contempt. Hectore could not bind himself to anyone who held that opinion. Only long years as a merchant made it possible to appear pleased to have their company in any fashion.

"Do you think," Jarven said, his voice suspiciously conversational, "you will retain his services?"

"While I live, yes."

"Ah. Why?"

"Because that was his wish. I do not pretend to understand it myself. I have not been particularly solicitous or careful with his time. I have treated him as a servant because that is what he is. He has almost no sense of humor, but he has a particularly pinched expression I have come to enjoy. He is vastly more suspicious than I can bother to be; nothing is too small to escape his notice, and he can hold on to offenses, real or imagined, for far, far longer than I."

"This also amuses you."

"It does. My wife considers it unkind, but she has—with time and effort—developed a fondness for Andrei."

"It was not there at the beginning."

Hectore chuckled. "You remember that?"

"There were bets placed at the time."

Hectore shrugged. "She was younger then. We both were. And she felt uncertain. She knew me well enough to know that Andrei was important and would remain so; she was less certain that she would. But that is water under the bridge. Once she understood that Andrei was as consumed with my success—and survival—as she herself was, she also accepted him. At first, he was a necessary evil. But a handful of years later, he was simply necessary. She did not treat him poorly in the interim; she did not abuse her position—or his."

"And had she, would you have kept the servant or the wife?"

Hectore shook his head, clearly amused. "You do not understand, ATerafin. My first wife was chosen for me, it is true. But my second wife? I chose. And

I would not have chosen a woman who could abuse a servant behind his master's back. Not then and not now. She certainly let *me* know that she was unhappy, and in private, she could be quite harsh when unhappy. But she divined correctly that the problem was with me. And that, I could accept."

"And now?"

"Now? She will barely let me leave the house if Andrei does not accompany me." Hectore's frown was brief. "They discuss my clothing. They discuss decor. They discuss my menu—although I have had to be somewhat more firm about their choices. She would be as bereft as I were Andrei to vanish."

"I doubt that."

"Yes, old friend, you do. What you do not understand is that I am Andrei's master. I consider him kin, but that is my choice. My wife, however, considers him a friend. Friends have a different interaction than master and servant. She does not treat him as a servant; she has her own maids to tend her. She values his opinions—of me, of the merchants—and she discusses them with him as if they are equals. He did attempt to discourage this, but she pointed out quite forcefully that she did not have these discussions when they were not both at home. In public, of course, he is a servant."

"And so you have forced ties on him that he did not seek for himself."

"I have given him the opportunity, rather, to sink roots. The choice was always his."

"What is he, Hectore?"

"Andrei."

"Yes, you've said that. But that is a name, not a state. You know more."

"In the old world," Andrei said, stepping seamlessly into existence across the bed of stones, "they were not so separate." His frown was pure Andrei. "I wish you would speak less with Jarven. I have never understood your affection for him."

"Affection," Hectore replied, "is a strong term. Might we say appreciation, instead?"

"I would not understand that, either," was the rather prim reply.

Jarven stared at Andrei. Until the moment Hectore's servant had reappeared, the Terafin merchant had had no sense, no awareness, of his presence. This was annoying. Jarven had some experience with annoyances. On occasion, everything in the Merchant Authority was annoying.

Hectore said he saw stone, stretching as far as the eye could see.

Jarven could see stone with great effort, great difficulty—and it did not seem profitable to expend that effort. He did not see stone. Nor did he see forest, tree, anything that spoke of natural life. He could, and did, see Hectore—but Hectore had been, until the return of Andrei, the only solidly visible object in view.

Andrei, however, was arresting. If Hectore was solid, Andrei was not. He was present, yes—but the whole of his form seemed to shift in place, colors rising and falling across his body. With those colors came shadows, hints of shape, things that had the solidity and texture of mist. This sounded peaceful in description; it was not.

The whole of Andrei's form seemed to be at war with itself.

And yet, it was part of this place. Hectore was not. Nor, Jarven thought, was he.

"I see a storm on the horizon," Hectore said to his servant.

The servant's face drew together, the colors once again returning to something that normal flesh might take, and cohering into a very familiar expression. "That," Andrei said, "is not a storm. It is a disaster." He spoke, as he often did, judgmentally. He did not, however, speak with any great fear.

"Ah." Hectore was silent for some moments. "It's not, by any chance, The Terafin?"

"No, of course not."

Of course, Jarven thought. He was irritated, but also intrigued. Either of the two were preferable to boredom and the ennui that arose from it. "Is it," he said, "one of The Terafin's cats?"

"They are not cats," Andrei replied.

"Andrei likes cats," Hectore added. "You have not, however, answered Jarven's unfortunately worded question. Is it one of The Terafin's winged companions?"

"I very much fear the answer to that question is now no. I do not know what she was thinking to bring them into the tangle. It is clear she is almost entirely ignorant."

Jarven coughed politely. He had the choice between that and laughter. And that, too, was odd, not right; Jarven had perfect control of any outward expression of his internal state of mind.

"If rumors are to be granted any credence," Hectore said, "she tends to let the cats run wild."

"And where have you heard those rumors?"

"You are ATerafin, Jarven. You cannot honestly expect me to answer that question."

Jarven's smile was, once again, a simple tool.

"She has not allowed them to injure or kill anyone in her House. She has been unable to prevent them from destroying assassins, on the other hand."

"So I had heard. I had not heard that they were otherwise particularly destructive."

"If you are not in the habit of attending to the physical maintenance of your manse, there would be no reason you would do so; they are, however, responsible for a fair amount of incidental property damage. Tables. Chairs. Carpets and runners. One section of wall in the public galleries—although that, at least, they have not repeated. And that is neither here nor there," he added, looking almost embarrassed to be mired in such trivial details.

One look at Andrei, and Jarven realized that the servant did not consider these details trivial.

"Do you think," Hectore continued, "that she entered the tangle to find her cats?"

If possible, Andrei's expression became even more sour, and Jarven found himself laughing again, which did nothing to alleviate the grimace that seemed to have taken up permanent residence in the lines of Andrei's face.

"Those creatures were not meant to be companions to mortals."

"That was not no," Hectore pointed out.

Andrei sighed; it was almost theatrical. To Jarven, he said, "Many assume that Hectore's success in the past is due, in large measure, to my interventions."

"I have never made that assumption."

"No. It is why you are dangerous." To Hectore he said, "I believe you are correct."

"It is not making your day any happier."

"No."

"You do not think she can control her cats—"

"They are not cats, Hectore."

"—If she is not present."

"Given the obvious disrespect they show her when she is? No. They were not known for their kindness or their consideration, and they were feared. By mortals," he added, "they were feared. It is best that we find The Terafin before that storm finds us."

"Can you control it?"

"I? No. They are like very powerful demons. When you bend your will to any other task, they slip free of their constraints in subtle ways."

Jarven said, "The cats are not known for their subtlety." He paused and added, "Some caution however, Andrei."

"You are not notable for your caution."

Jarven was almost offended. "I am well noted for it. I am not noted for timidity—but when I choose to approach danger, there are none as cautious as I. Be that as it may, you are speaking of demons and their control, and that topic is severely frowned upon by the august Sigurne Mellifas and her Order of Knowledge. I am curious, of course, but assume that the knowledge is second-hand."

"It is. But, Jarven: I know what demons once were. I would not summon them."

"And The Terafin's cats?"

"I would not keep them. I would not make the attempt."

"By all accounts," Hectore said mildly, "she did not choose to keep them; they chose to stay." He rose at Andrei's slight gesture, but did not otherwise move his feet. Not until the Araven servant gestured.

"We will not have long," he said to his master. Hectore nodded, as if this type of direction were an everyday occurrence. When Andrei nodded again, Hectore took a step forward. He was instantly lost to sight.

"I will not leave you here," Andrei said, gazing at the spot that Hectore had occupied. He spoke to Jarven. "But now you must be cautious. I consider you as dangerous as the creatures you call cats—and as tractable." He paused and then added, "In some ways, you are more dangerous. The eldest—for reasons I cannot fathom—have attached themselves to The Terafin; they are willing, inasmuch as they can be, to serve her. You, however, do not understand service in even that most basic of fashions."

"Do I not?"

"No. Nor have you ever. You search, always, for advantages gained. You make alliances where they will be of benefit—but they are unwise allies who turn their backs on you, because allegiances are guaranteed to ebb and flow, and you are easily carried away with the tide."

"And you?"

"What do you think?" Andrei looked at the shifting ground beneath their feet. "Follow if you can." He took a step forward.

Night was not appreciably different when he and Shadow had finally condescended to stop their midair brawl. His roar had implied many things, but those things had receded. He was sulking, of course, because Jewel was more critical of his behavior than his brother's—and Shadow was appreciably more smug.

"Do not step on his tail again," she told the gray cat.

Night's tail, however, was low to the ground and twitching, and when it smacked Shadow's nose, she sighed. "I mean it, Shadow."

"But he *started* it!"

"We can't afford another big fight right now. I have no idea where you'll end up."

"No," Shadow said, with infinitely more weight in the syllable, "you *don't.*" He turned and batted Night's wings, his paws almost whistling with speed through the air he disturbed. "And *you* are *stupid. Why* did you send me?"

Night growled, his voice an echo of the storm in this place. "You *needed* to go. *You* are *stupid.* You could have *told her.*" He returned Shadow's blow.

Jewel exhaled. In less than ten seconds they would resume their brawl, but this time they were close enough to the rest of her companions that someone else was likely to be collateral damage. She walked between them, which caused Angel to sign frantically, and put a hand on each of their heads. "Cut it out *right now.* We don't have time for this.

"Snow is still lost, and we need to find him."

Night snickered. "*We* won't get lost," he told her. "We never get lost."

"Fine. He'll lose the rest of us, and we can't afford that."

"Why not?"

Shadow snickered.

"I ask that question myself although, perhaps, not in the same fashion," Calliastra added. Night gave her the side-eye.

"You *have* to come here," Night said, ignoring the godchild and instead focusing his gaze on Jewel.

"Why?"

Night glanced at Shadow, who shrugged, still sullen. "She is *stupid.*"

"She is *very stupid.*"

Calliastra glanced at Celleriant; Celleriant was annoyed, but he frequently found the cats annoying, and he hadn't drawn his sword. "You tolerate this?"

"I tolerate," Celleriant replied, "what my Lord tolerates."

"She will have to fight her way across the unknown."

"She will not," he countered. "But I may well. Lord, where is Snow?"

Jewel glanced at Kallandras, who shook his head. She then turned to Night. "What? *What?*"

"Where is your brother?"

"Why do you need *him?*"

"Does it matter? We need him. Do you know where he is?"

"You know."

"If I knew, I wouldn't be asking."

"You *could* know."

Jewel's feet stopped moving.

Hectore found himself in a forest. The plain of rocks and pebbles had vanished between one step and the next. Andrei had strongly implied that geography in the tangle was highly subjective, and he was not known for his sense of either mischief or humor. Even so, Hectore found the sudden change of landscape disturbing.

He turned to say as much, but Andrei was not behind him.

He did not take another step. Hectore—like all men—was a creature of habit. He was not accustomed to landscape reasserting its existence in inexplicable ways, and he felt the lack of solidity strongly. It was, therefore, not a surprise to him when a path opened up beneath his feet—and beneath the heavier shade of the trees above.

It was not a footpath, such as might be seen in more heavily traveled wilderness; it was a road of stone. Wagons could make their way through this terrain at speed, even in inclement weather—but roads such as these were costly endeavors, and merchants were not inclined to part with their own money to create them.

Its existence implied power, ownership—and neither of that was Hectore's. "Andrei."

"I am almost there," his servant replied. Hectore glanced back, saw trees, and shrugged; he twined hands behind his own back, his left foot tapping almost impatiently.

"Some caution is required," Andrei said, although in theory he could see neither of these gestures. "And, in future, I advise you to leave Jarven behind. He sees too much, too clearly, and it makes it far easier to lose him. While that is my inclination, it has never been yours."

"True. Is he causing you trouble?"

"Deliberately? No. It is his essential nature."

"Oh?"

"He wishes to see all and know all, and he is—as I have no doubt made clear—enormously greedy."

Hectore chuckled, but the brief amusement left him. "I think you had better hurry."

Silence.

"Hectore, where are you?" This was not the question the Araven merchant wanted to hear.

"I am in a forest. It looks remarkably like the forested lands of the Western Kingdoms, except for one detail: the road."

"Road?"

"Road. And a well-built, well-maintained road, at that. It is beneath my feet and continues forward and behind where I am now standing. It was not, however, here when the forest itself coalesced."

"Do not take a step."

Hectore nodded. "It is not my steps you need fear," he told his invisible servant. "Can you hear them?"

The reply: a very heartfelt curse. And a very dry chuckle, the latter from Jarven.

The sound of hooves on stone was distinctive, even at a distance. Only in cities and keeps was this at all common, and in Averalaan, other sounds cushioned the aural impact. Here, nothing did. There was a curious lack of birdsong and insect drone, and even the wind that caused leaves to rustle against one another was absent; it was as if the world was holding its breath.

Hectore was not the world; his breaths were slow and measured. He slid a hand into his pockets; his hands were dry but steady. He had seen and survived demons, but the survival was not due to any particular skill on his part; he had planned for the unforeseen. He was aware that his survival had been entirely dependent on his wealth and the desire for the mage-born to accrue some part of it.

He was not Jarven. He had the instinctive and visceral desire to avoid the dangerously strange. Danger, no: he had been the target of assassins in his younger years, and he could not turn a blind eye to possible enemies. But they had the tools that he had at his disposal. Not one of them could create a home in which every step changed the environment. Not one of them could create roads such as these without notice.

He knelt, placed the flat of his left palm against that stone, being right-handed. It trembled beneath the weight of approaching hooves. He was under no illusion; in this place, on this road, the last thing he wanted was to meet the riders that accompanied that sound.

Andrei, however, had told him not to move—or rather, not to take a step. Standing as he was, there was every chance Andrei would reach him before the riders did. He was not certain that would be the case if he left the road. But every merchant's instinct he had honed through the decades told him to leap to the side—right or left, it didn't matter. Every instinct but one.

He straightened his shoulders, his back, slid his hands to his sides; he watched the road.

*   *   *

Jewel met the eyes of the gray cat. Of the three, it was Shadow to whom she felt closest. She had never said this out loud; the chance that Snow or Night would hear it and descend into the loud caterwauling destruction that passed for cat sulking was too great.

The gray cat muttered imprecations; some of the words were very familiar. He finished with his favorite. *Stupid. Stupid, stupid, stupid.* He then turned and headbutted his brother.

Night's fur rose, his eyes widened, and his claws extended.

"This is not the time," Shianne told them both. Her voice was not a human voice; it was laced with thunder, the syllables crackling with the type of sound that followed the lightning strikes in the bay.

And both cats froze on hearing it. Night's belly almost struck ground. Shadow's, however, did not. He glanced at Shianne as if she were just another sand dune.

"She *could* find him," the gray cat said. "If she looked. But she is not *ready* to look."

"And you do not know where he is, Eldest?"

Shadow examined his paws, lifting the right one to flex claws. "Maybe he doesn't *want* to be found."

"He probably doesn't," Jewel told Shianne, trying to sound natural. Her voice was too thin, too reedy, in comparison; everything about the syllables except their content felt superficial. "Night was making enough noise to wake the dead. Snow . . . isn't."

"And it is unlike your cats to be silent."

Jewel nodded.

"Do you fear for his safety?"

"No." Jewel paused for one long breath. "Not until you asked."

The men came into view, shimmering in the distance as if the road was hot as desert sands. Hectore could not count them; they rode two abreast, but their ranks seemed to extend into that shimmering. They did not gallop or trot; they moved as if they were escorts—carriage or caravan. But they carried spears, and those spears reflected light beneath a forest that had, in an instant, become canopy.

Hectore had seen gods before, in the Between.

These men were not gods, but they were so perfectly rigid, so seamless in uniformity—of height, of armor, of weapons and even of mounts—that they did not seem real. He had, however, become familiar with things that did not seem real. They did not seem to be aware of him as they approached. He chose to stand with his hands by his sides; he drew no weapon, well aware that he had none of any use against this number of men and the arms they bore. He felt a twinge of fear, . . . and a twinge of curiosity. Both grew.

"Hectore."

"I have not moved," Hectore replied. "But I am going to be asked to move soon."

"What do you see?"

He described it.

Andrei cursed. It had been decades since Hectore had heard such liberal cursing from his servant, a man many suspected was entirely composed of starch.

"Banners, Hectore?"

"Yes, now that you ask. But I cannot easily see the standard. It is held high," he added, "but it seems composed of silver."

"You are certain?"

Hectore did not deign to reply. "You are having difficulty reaching my side?"

"Yes. There are no paths here; there are rivers, brooks. There are oceans. But those moving streams are the only way to progress through the tangle. And this is a poor analogy; I will think of better, in future. But if you stand as you are standing for a day, for two, for three, the tangle will change around you constantly.

"There are some who can follow the ebb and flow of a particular stream, seeking its estuary—but there is a risk in that, for once you reach ocean, you cannot easily return. In this place it is better to keep moving—and it is deadly to keep moving, both."

"I do not believe," Hectore replied, voice mild, "that it was my idea to come here."

"It was entirely your idea."

"It was my idea to follow; had you decided against it, I would now be attending to a meal or less pleasant negotiations. I do not understand why you fear for The Terafin here; the girl is seer-born. She will not take a wrong step unless there are no correct ones."

"There are frequently no correct ones; there are less disastrous choices. There are some streams—to continue my analogy—into which no mortal should step, and all streams flow through all points eventually."

"And the ocean? No, never mind. I believe our riders have noticed my presence."

They had. They did not lower their spears, but one man raised a hand, and the entire procession came to a slow stop. Hectore was surprised; he would not have considered it strange had they simply chosen to ride him down.

The banner stopped; the riders—two—came forward.

They did not ride horses, although Hectore might have been forgiven for assuming it. They did not—as The Terafin sometimes did—ride great, ant-lered beasts, either; Hectore could not name the beast they rode. It was, in general shape, an animal; it was hooved, like a deer or a horse, and it had a long tail, which could be glimpsed clearly by its motion. But the head was too narrow for a horse, too thick for a stag.

And Hectore could understand why. The creatures' riders were not mortal, not human. They reminded Hectore of the cold armsman who occasionally attended The Terafin herself. They had the long white hair, plaited in warriors' braids; they had the same perfect skin, the same silver eyes. They wore gaunt-lets, helms, their visors open to air and sky.

And they looked at him with faces that might have been carved of ice or blown in perfect glass.

"Greetings, stranger," the man on the right said. "We have need of the road today and ask that you move to allow our Lord passage." The words were mu-sical, beautiful; they implied song, or wind chimes, caught in syllables for a moment before being released.

Hectore's throat was dry. He felt oddly self-conscious, standing here, his clothing meant for merchant caravans, his skin aged and weathered by sun and wind and time. These men had never known age—and would never know it—if they were men at all. But he thought, watching them, they had not known youth, either. He framed a reply with care; he chose the same tonal formality that they had chosen. His knees did not bend, for he understood that to show weakness here was death.

"I regret that I cannot accommodate your reasonable request. This road is not the road I must walk, but I dare not lose it."

The man stiffened, his eyes narrowed.

"It was not a request," his companion said.

"Ah. Might I know in whose name you command me?"

"The Winter Queen."

"The Winter Queen?" Andrei asked, as he stepped—at last—onto the road itself.

Hectore noted that his servant's hair was both unbound and long; that his face had lengthened, that he had gained three quarters of a foot in height. His clothing at first appeared to be ragged—but no. It was indeterminate now; it flirted with shape, with texture, with color, but did not seem to settle on any of them, as if they were all too fleeting to catch and hold.

The two riders had shown no alarm at all at Hectore's presence; they had been about to descend into contempt or even annoyance.

But Andrei? Andrei was not Hectore.

"The Winter Queen is not Lord of these lands, and even were she—and it is, as you well know, impossible—she is not with you."

Hectore allowed Andrei to take the reins of the conversation. He glanced to the side and saw that Jarven had joined him. To his mild consternation, Jarven's feet did not seem to touch the road—or the earth to either side of it; he appeared to be floating slightly above it, his lips compressed in obvious concentration.

It was the concentration that Hectore found most disquieting. Jarven had taken injuries without blinking or altering his expression; he might have been pleased and pleasantly surprised by the pain. He was an accomplished liar; he understood men—and women—well. His words could not be trusted, but they could be sifted. What he wanted you to know or to believe was information; what he thought you might believe was also information. What he did not say was information. He had always been master of every stage on which he chose to stand, and he was not particularly protective of his dignity. If a man could be said not to care about the opinions of others, it was Jarven.

"Do not think so loudly," the Terafin merchant said.

"I was not aware that my thoughts could be heard."

"Your expression is remarkably unguarded, and it is giving me a headache."

"I am afraid I cannot indulge your headache at the moment."

Jarven fell silent as the two men dismounted.

"We carry her banner."

"And it is a lovely piece of cloth; I see her hand in its weaving, and it is seldom that she chooses to weave. But the cloth is not the man; she is not present."

"Her will is."

"Her lieges are." Andrei's hair rose as if at a gust of wind; that wind touched nothing else. No, Hectore thought; it touched the air, chilling it instantly. They had called their Lord the Winter Queen, and Winter, he thought, must descend.

Andrei did not move. "The road you follow will continue here; the road we follow will not."

"What," a new voice said, "seeks to hinder us?" And this voice? This voice was almost human. Jarven's gaze narrowed, mirror to Hectore's. The voice was male, masculine—but it was chill.

"What, indeed?" Andrei replied. His voice shook the road beneath Hectore's feet. Without thought, Hectore reached out to place a hand on his servant's shoulder. He intended, now, to take back the conversation he had surrendered.

A man appeared, walking between the unnamed mounts and their riders, his feet heavy on the stone road. He did not wear armor, gauntlets, helm, and his face was neither perfect nor inhuman. His hair was black, his brows black, his eyes brown; he bore two scars as a bracket to his face across his lower jaws. He was not a young man, not a youth; he was a man in his prime, at the peak of his power and the certainty that came with it.

His brows rose as he saw Hectore. "This is not your forest," he said.

"No," Hectore agreed. "But neither is it yours. I have been told mortals do not enter the tangle." He did not bow, but said, "I am Hectore of House Araven."

"And I am the Winter King."

Andrei stiffened beneath Hectore's palm as the man—the mortal man—reached the last rank of his guards. The two immortals parted, the motion subtle and far too silent for the amount of metal they were wearing.

If the stranger was a man in his prime, it was Jarven's prime; his eyes were narrowed, but there was a focus, an intensity, to their flickering gaze that implied that he missed nothing. Where the guards were white and silver, he was obsidian and copper. He was, however, Lord here. No one could question that.

His gaze traveled between Hectore and Andrei, narrowing on the latter, before it moved to Jarven ATerafin. It remained there the longest, and Hectore glanced at Jarven, his lips turned in the slightest of frowns. Jarven's were not; he was smiling broadly. On occasion, Hectore's wife was uncomplimentary about men and their various rivalries; she opined that civilization occurred because of the women. He was grateful that she was safe at home because she would certainly have been moved to comment about this.

Or perhaps not; she understood that there was a time and place for frustration and condescension, and being in the presence of the Winter King was neither. She would not, however, have been impressed.

Hectore, not notably his wife, was. Jarven could—and frequently did—play the aged, fragile fool with little care for his reputation or the reputation of the men or women around whom he chose to do so. But Hectore understood, watching the two, that the Winter King would never be among their number.

As if Andrei could hear the thoughts Hectore did not put into words, his hair stilled; after a moment, it braided itself neatly into a thick plait that fell down his back. His back was no longer a moving patchwork of fabric—or worse—beneath Hectore's hand; it became a very, very fine wool, a somber gray that suited the Araven servant's regular duties. He did not shed the inches of height he had gained, and his face remained longer and somewhat more angular, but it was recognizably Andrei's face.

Whatever staring contest the Winter King had begun to engage in was forgotten as Andrei once again established himself. Jarven would be annoyed, but his annoyance at the moment was not Hectore's problem. He willed the Terafin merchant to speak, to intervene, because Andrei was servant here, not master, and must remain so.

Ah, Hectore thought, shaking his head slightly. Andrei was servant, yes—but Jarven was not his master. Hectore was.

"And what is this House Araven?"

"It is a mortal family," Hectore replied. "Perhaps your sojourn with the immortal has been long enough that you have forgotten." He used the last word deliberately and was rewarded—if reward was the correct word—with the edge of very narrowed eyes.

"I am aware of the significant clans in every one of the cities." The tone of his voice made his title appropriate; it was ice. "Araven is not among them."

"I am unaware of your cities," Hectore replied. He smiled. There was no warmth in it.

"This . . . man . . . serves you?"

"He is my servant, yes."

A whisper started in the distance. It broke against the Winter King's back; Hectore could catch syllables, but they did not or would not cohere.

"I would accuse you of lying if I had not seen the truth of it myself. I would have the whole of the truth."

"Perhaps. But you would have it at another time. There is a task we must accomplish here."

"Oh?" The Winter King's hand fell to his sword, which had been hidden by the fall of his cape, the shadows of which did not follow any light Hectore could see in the clearing.

Andrei stiffened; Hectore lowered his hand.

"The road is not ours," Hectore continued. "Nor is it yours. We must stand here a moment longer, and then we will be on our way."

To his surprise, the Winter King's brows rose, as if in astonishment. His attention fell, once again, to Andrei, and it was anchored there. "The road is mine." Before Andrei could speak, he continued. "Only the road. The lands, as you surmise, are not; they belong to no one. They are not solid enough to be bound, not sentient enough to remember something as complex as a name— even a mortal one."

"The road is yours?" Andrei asked. His voice was polite, neutral, and none-theless full of doubt.

Hectore wished to move his feet. He wished to take a step, to bend knees; he felt as if he had been standing in place for a very long time. And perhaps he had.

"The road is mine. You will allow a mortal his vanity; I am proud of it. But I am not as you are. The tangle is not my home."

"Yet you are here, where mortals do not walk."

"I am."

"If you can force a road upon the tangle, might you be persuaded to alter it slightly? I do not have the same ability, and the road we must walk is not this one."

"Is it not? As you must guess, the making of such a road is not a trivial endeavor. The road will carry me between two points, and only when I walk it am I safe from the primordial. It is . . . odd that it crosses a path you feel you must take." He gestured then.

The two immortals withdrew, mounted, and returned to the distant carriage.

"Does the tangle have will?" he asked Andrei.

"Yes. But it is not a single will; it is a plurality, and there is no majority. It is not a place of consensus, but a place of power. Where will is strongest, it will override all others—but even that cannot hold at the edges; strength is tested, battle commenced, victory achieved—but it is the victory of the wounded and the dying, only. Will is broken, subsumed, devoured, but there is never co-hesion."

"Would that I had had you when I began this endeavor."

"You wish to conquer the tangle?" He lifted a hand as the Winter King unsheathed his blade. "He is my lord. Attempt to destroy him, and I will de-stroy you before returning, in full, to the tangle. You will not find me, Winter King. No road you build, no matter how strong, how solid, how bloody, will reach me.

"But no wall you build will keep you safe, if Hectore of Araven is dead."

To Hectore, the Winter King said, "I would know how you did this."

"Did what, exactly?"

"How did you bind *namann*? How did you bind the godspawn?"

"You would never understand it," Andrei replied, before Hectore could. "No more would you," he added to Jarven, although the Terafin merchant had not spoken a word.

"You claim to love him, then? This is the sentimental drivel that has long plagued the foolish of our own kind."

Andrei said nothing.

Hectore said, "He has made no such claim."

"He has heavily implied it. I am the *Winter* King. I am, of course, heartless. I exist in isolation when the last hunt is called."

Silence. A beat. Two. It was Hectore who broke it. Of course it was.

"And before that last hunt?"

"As you see: the Winter Queen's servants serve me—at her command. I am their Lord; my word is considered her word. There is nothing I cannot command of these men saving only that they raise sword against her. I live in her Winter Court when I choose to be confined."

Something in his voice caught at Hectore, and the Araven patris could not look away. "Does she confine herself to her Winter Court often?"

"She is the Wild Hunt, the heart of it," the Winter King replied. "I have hunted at her side these many months."

That was a no.

"Do you understand what she desires of a Winter King?" the Winter King continued. "Do you understand how she chooses?"

"No."

"Have you not explained it?" he asked Andrei, incredulity in the question, as if the Winter Queen was the whole of the world, as if her desire, her choice, was the center of it, the heart of all life. It was the first time that he had seemed genuinely human.

"It is irrelevant to his life," Andrei replied. "Hectore is not, could not, and will never be Winter King. It would be neither his desire nor hers."

"And yet you serve him."

"Power to you, to Winter, is measured in the simple act of survival. But survival among your kind—among your former kind—is not a simple thing."

"It is."

"No, Winter King, it is not. It is complex. You think of survival as war. That is one aspect. But among mortals it is not the only one. A man with an army behind him can destroy villages. It has happened. It will happen. That is your definition of strength. If you have an army with which to greet him, you cannot be so easily destroyed."

The Winter King frowned but nodded.

"There are other ways to survive. An army is not the only gathering of men; it is not even the most common. An army is not the only threat man faces. There are others. Hunger. Disease. Isolation."

"Isolation? *Namann*, I was never alone."

"No. You were never alone." Andrei's quiet statement did not sound like agreement. "Did you have children?"

A pause, brief and cold. "Yes."

"How many of them did you kill?"

Hectore said, and did, nothing because he could not lift a foot.

The man that Andrei called the Winter King did not answer the question, but his silence had texture, weight. It was answer enough. Winter, when seen through a window, could be—was—beautiful. But it could kill, and only the drunk or the foolish forgot that.

"How many of his own," Andrei continued, when no answer was forthcoming, "has Patris Araven killed?"

"Andrei, I feel that this line of questioning is far too personal. I cannot see its relevance."

It was Jarven, therefore, who answered—and he looked at the Winter King. "He has, of course, killed none. Nor has he been forced to end the lives of his grandchildren or great-grandchildren. He has killed no wives, no mistresses, and perhaps a handful of servants."

"He has killed no servants," Andrei said, attempting to retrieve the reins of the odd conversation.

"Oh?"

"They were assassins, and I dispatched them."

"I consider that killing," Hectore said. "If you are my servant, you do not kill on your own recognizance, but on mine. The sword is not responsible for the deaths it causes; the man who wields it is."

"And you claim to wield *namann*?"

"He is my servant," Hectore replied.

"You believe this." There was a faint—and almost insulting—condescension in the statement. Hectore, however, was a merchant. He had heard far worse.

"And you?" the Winter King said to Jarven ATerafin.

"I am Jarven ATerafin. I am not of Araven, and I am not his servant."

"His liege, then?"

"No. Hectore will accept alliances of convenience when circumstances require it, but he would not accept a pledge of allegiance that was, at base, without merit. I will not, and do not, serve."

"Yet you travel by his side."

Jarven shrugged and, to Hectore's surprise, said, "Yes. I was bored."

The Winter King laughed.

Hectore swore later that his laughter shook branches; he could feel it rise up from the road beneath his feet.

"How much longer?" Hectore's question was a whisper, meant for Andrei's ears.

Andrei lifted a hand, gestured. *Soon.*

"You do not bear the scars of a warrior," the Winter King said, mirth still evident in the corners of his eyes, his lips. He spoke to Jarven.

"No. When pressed, I can wield a weapon, but any fool can. I am unwilling to entrust any single weapon with my safety or success. But I understand that any choice is a gamble; Patris Araven has chosen different risks. If Andrei had offered me his service, I would have accepted in a heartbeat. But what Hectore offers, I cannot. It is not a matter of wealth or freedom; it is not a matter of stature—clearly.

"I have no wife and no children. I saw them as inevitable weaknesses. Anchors. But power in the Empire does not depend on children. Bloodline is of little consequence to me. I have no dynastic ambitions. You must have, once— but dynasty is irrelevant to the Winter Queen."

The Winter King nodded.

"Tell me. Tell me what the Winter Queen wants from her King."

"In the end? To kill him."

"And before that?"

The Winter King's smile was difficult to describe. "Companionship, of a kind. While I live, she is mine; she is Winter. I am not subordinate. The men who form my small company obey my commands as if they were hers. I hunt," he added softly.

"To what end?"

"It alleviates boredom."

Jarven's smile was almost a reflection of the Winter King's. "You do not walk as a lamb to slaughter."

"No. That is not what Winter requires. She will hunt me when the seasons turn, and if she is capable of it, she will kill me."

"And if she is not?"

"Who knows?"

"It has never been done?"

"In the history of this world? No. There is Winter. There is Summer. Each has a king. At the end of the season, the king is sacrificed; the seasons turn."

"And no Winter King goes peacefully to his death."

"Would you?"

Jarven chuckled. "No. What sport would that be?"

The Winter King nodded. "Winter draws to a close soon. They know it. I know it. We have hunted across the many, many planes. But she yearns, now, for Summer, an end to the bitter cold. She will not have it, while I live. I am last in a long line of powerful men. I surrendered all hope of dynasty to accept her offer. But legacy?" He shook his head. "What man surrenders that? She will remember me. I will be *the* Winter King."

"And that is why you have come to the tangle?"

"No." Winter smile. "Something crossed my domain and, in passing, destroyed things I valued."

"You are not here for revenge."

"Odd. That is not what most would assume."

"You do not have a concept of justice, and revenge, at base, requires it. Something has piqued your interest."

"Just as something has piqued yours, yes. I have been told by those who dare to advise me that those responsible for the destruction are like snowstorms or avalanche; they are forces of nature in the wild world."

Andrei stiffened beneath Hectore's hand.

"I seek to capture nature for my own amusement."

"And you have entered the tangle to do so."

"It is to the tangle that they fled," the Winter King replied. "But if I could not traverse something as insignificant as the tangle, what hope would I have of capturing them?"

"She does not understand how dangerous you are," Andrei said.

"You are wrong, *namann*. She understands exactly how dangerous I am. I am Winter King. For no other reason was I chosen." He turned, and then turned back.

"Patris Araven. You have killed none of your own offspring?"

"None."

"And none of your wives."

"No."

He was silent, as if searching for words. In the end, he did not find them. To Andrei he said, "Our roads have almost parted."

Andrei nodded.

"Were we in any other lands, I would have swept you from them."

"As you say," Andrei replied.

Jarven shook his head in pinched disapproval. "That is not the appropriate leave-taking."

"No? Perhaps you wished me to say he would have tried?"

"What I prefer is irrelevant to what is proper. Manners have their place in any situation. Do you believe that the Winter King could move you should you choose to stand your ground?"

"It is irrelevant. We want different things of the tangle, and the tangle is not easily traversed. Not for the sake of his own pride would he commit himself to a battle of that nature here. I have given him reasons to avoid that battle, and he has accepted them; he has chosen to grace us with his company while the tangle churns beneath our feet.

"He could attempt to kill Hectore because it is Hectore that forms the anchor here. It might amuse him. It might not. But even you would think twice about such a decision when there is no obvious gain."

Hectore lost the flow of their bickering words, as if they were the rustle of overhead leaves, the babble of passing brook. He watched the back of the man who called himself the Winter King and understood, watching, what that King had not—could not bring himself—to ask.

As that back grew more remote, as the hunters once again closed ranks behind it, Hectore raised his voice, "I loved them both. I love my children."

"And were you foolish enough to believe that you loved them from the beginning?" the Winter King asked. He did not turn back, did not glance over his shoulder; he continued to walk, as if to put distance between himself and the words that had left him.

"Yes."

"Did the first wife die in childbed, then?"

Hectore was silent, remembering. But at length he said, voice thicker, "No."

"And not, as you've said, by your hand?"

"No."

The Winter King said, "There will be no second wife, no second Queen, no second Lord for me. There will be no other desire, no other Winter, no other kingdom. In my life, while I draw breath, there is the Winter Queen, only the Winter Queen—and she is *mine* while Winter reigns."

Hectore said nothing. The forest remained above his head, but the road inexplicably faded. His legs were stiff. "Andrei?"

"Yes. It is safe to move. Mark my footsteps and follow them as you can."

"And if I cannot?"

"This small stretch of forest will hold."

Hectore's voice was soft when he spoke again. "He longs for Summer."

"That is the failing of mortals," Andrei replied. "But he understands that he will never see that Summer. He was not, and could not be, Summer King; he did not have that death in him."

"Or that life?"

"Or that," Andrei said. "But mortals often feel that if they give everything they have to give, it is—or should be—enough."

"And it is not?"

"Hectore, please."

"It is a serious question."

"You have some familiarity with Jarven ATerafin. Could he give your family what you have given them over the decades?"

"Of course not."

"Even if he desired to do so?"

"Might I remind you that I am present?" Jarven said.

"You disagree?"

"Pragmatically, no. I have no desire to descend into sentimental drivel for the whole of my life; it has its uses, but so does poison."

"You have never been in love," Hectore said. Jarven did not trouble to hide his disdain. "No, I will take that one step further. You do not, and have not, loved. You allow yourself affection; you have affection for Lucille. You annoy her when you are bored, but you have never set yourself against her. You would, however, if you felt it necessary.

"Lucille would not turn against you."

"Ah, Hectore. You are so perceptive, and yet so wrong. If Lucille felt that I was a danger to the House itself, if she felt that I was a danger to the Empire— if, perhaps, she thought I was demonic—she would. You have always liked her; she has always regarded you with suspicion. But she is not like me; she is like you, with far less tact."

"I will take that as a compliment."

"Lucille loves, as you define love. I will not disagree. Could I give what you give? Yes. But not, I fear, for long. It is not what I want. It is small, quotidian, uninteresting."

"I argue that this means you cannot give it."

"How so? I assure you, no one would know the difference."

Hectore stepped over a tree root, which required more concentration because the root stretched to mid-thigh. "You would know," he said, when he had managed to find level ground again.

"Love requires self-deception, then?"

"Do not test my patience; I find it is in short supply. You would take no joy in it. You would take no delight in it. You would find no measure of self-respect in shouldering the responsibilities on days when joy or delight are markedly absent."

"Let us assume this is true. Surely, if the wife—or children or Lucille—can discern no difference, it is not different."

"It is different," Hectore replied, grimacing briefly as he approached the next root. "The joy is not in the possession, it is in being. Husband. Father. Brother. Godfather. It is in the connection."

"I have seen how inconvenient even your godchildren are."

"Yes. But that is family, Jarven."

"I wouldn't know. Yet you, a family man, are here in the most wild of the wilderness, with your foremost servant, who is not, and will never be, mortal. I sense fraud."

"Fraud? Why?"

"You want what I want."

"I want some of what you want, yes. I fail to see fraud in this. We have different desires, of course. Boredom would not be enough of an excuse to bring me to this place. I am here for reasons you consider, at base, contemptible. Your contempt is irrelevant, of course."

"Of course."

"I am willing to learn. I am willing to attempt to understand this landscape and the reason for it; it has a practical, obvious effect on my life. In that, we are not dissimilar. But I do not relish it."

"Liar."

"I do not *often* relish it. Andrei, will the roots continue in this fashion?"

"No."

Jarven did not seem to have the navigational difficulty that plagued Hectore. "You believe that the Winter King wants . . . what you want?"

Hectore was silent while pulling himself up to the roots' height. "Relationships are best begun as you mean to continue."

"And that is relevant?"

"He longs for Summer," Hectore said again.

"He is Winter King," Andrei added. "Summer cannot exist while he lives."

"Were I he," Jarven said, after a pause, "I would ensure that the world remain in Winter."

"If you can't have it, no one can?"

"Or something similar, yes." Jarven's smile was dry as kindling.

Andrei glanced at the Terafin merchant once, but he said nothing.

Chapter Eighteen

ANGEL TOUCHED JEWEL'S SHOULDER; she looked back as he signed. She then looked at Kallandras; the bard shook his head. He couldn't hear Snow. Neither could she. Shadow implied heavily that it was obvious where Snow was, but cats never owned ignorance—at least not their own. Night, however, was subdued. The only thing that held his attention for long was Shadow, and Jewel hesitated to let them brawl. She was certain that they would survive it—they always did—but not certain that she wouldn't lose them here.

Shianne walked in Jewel's footsteps. Kallandras did the same. Adam, however, walked by her side or sometimes stepped ahead. He did not disappear, nor did he appear to be altered. Jewel did not understand the tangle.

"His path," Shianne said, "is your path, for a little while yet. Here, he is yours, and he knows it. The cats are yours in similar fashion—but no one has ever truly owned them."

"*We* are not *really* hers," Shadow hissed.

"Oh?"

"*She* is *ours*."

"She is not yours." Shianne's expression was grave, magisterial, but Jewel could sense her uneasiness.

"Shadow."

"*Yesssssss?*" His eyes were silver, ringed by an aurora of gold, centered around pupils that defined the color black. His shadow was long; it flickered around the edges, reflecting no obvious change of shape while implying many. Night's shape, however, seemed blurred.

"Stop bothering Shianne."

"Me? *Me?* I am not bothering *her*—she is being *stupid*." He was spitting around the sibilants, his claws gouging earth in a dance of frustration. He seldom called Shianne stupid; that was a word reserved for his brothers, Jewel, and her den.

Night, however, hissed laughter, and Jewel watched the lines of his fur shift, hardening. "What did you *expect?* They are *all* stupid."

Shianne was not Jewel, of course; Shadow's frustration was met with a wall of ice. There was nothing about her expression that implied resignation and much that implied death. Not her own, of course.

It didn't help much that Calliastra's lips twitched at the corners.

Angel, however, was sane. He grimaced over the head of at least one cat, but he said nothing.

"Leave Shianne alone," Jewel told the gray cat, "and find your missing brother. We need to leave the tangle."

Long-suffering cat was only slightly less difficult than bored cat. It certainly wasn't any less loud.

The tangle was difficult in ways that Jewel had not expected. Had she entered a nightmare landscape in which the world shifted from one step to the next, she might have found it more comfortable because the weight of each step would be concrete, visible, immediate.

And the world did change, but the changes were slow, subtle; the path beneath her feet remained anchored in a forest version of earth. At times it was wide enough that her entire company might walk without restriction, and at times so narrow it was difficult to find a foot-width's space in which to take that step.

And the step was permanent, irretrievable. She had looked back once, over her shoulder. The path that she instinctively followed could no longer be seen—or perhaps felt. There was only one way out, and it was in.

Hope, when it came, was a mixed blessing.

A roar of rage, more felt than seen, punctuated the silence in which the company now walked. The earth beneath Jewel's feet shuddered for long enough that she was afraid of earthquake. If she lost her way here, while the ground broke beneath her, she would never find her way home.

But the roar subsided.

Twice more, the roar shook the earth itself. There were syllables buried in that roar, which made it somehow worse. Kallandras, when asked, simply nodded: it was Snow. But the reverberations of misplaced cat faded into unnatural silence quickly, as if all noise was being hungrily devoured.

There were no birds, no forest rodents, no droning buzz of the insects that should have otherwise been present; the hush itself was oppressive. But there was something about it that made the silence very hard to break. She lifted her hands in den-sign, her fingers moving slowly, deliberately.

Can you hear it? she asked.

Angel shook his head.

Silence returned, laden with the weight of worry. It had been chief among the crimes one could commit against Jewel's Oma, when that old woman had been alive, her pipe her scepter, her regalia. One did not make her grandmother worry and escape unscathed.

Avandar was not entirely pleased at the comparison.

The path is so narrow here, she finally said. *It's hard to find a place to step, let alone stand.*

Wait, then.

We don't have time, *Avandar.* His name, as all names were when used, was a type of punctuation, of emphasis. She had never been one of nature's liars. Lies required subtlety, or a peculiar form of belief in the moment, that Jewel had only rarely achieved. That or desperation. Even as a merchant, she had not quibbled to lie. She had been told, time and time and time again, that she would fail the House if she did not learn.

And perhaps there was truth in that, for a different person. Jewel, however, had decided early that having the House on her side meant that *she* was not the person who had to learn. If people wanted to trade with Terafin, they accepted the odd, flat bluntness of the particular merchant to whom they spoke.

She did not lie to Avandar. They didn't have time.

No, he said. *That is not, however, what you fear.*

It was the only thing she truly feared. She didn't bother to tell him as much; she expected him to know it. Uneasiness was not fear. It was caution, and Jewel had always had need of it.

"Terafin," Kallandras said.

She turned only her head to look at him.

"The forest is speaking."

Her shoulders sagged. "Yes."

Shianne said, "I do not hear the voice of trees."

"Nor I," Celleriant added. His sword came to hand then. Jewel could have told him to put it away. What she feared could not be faced by weapon, no matter how ancient or powerful.

"What do you hear?" the Senniel bard asked.

"Echoes," she whispered.

"Echoes? Ah. That is not what I hear."

"What do you hear?" She asked the question in the flattest of her many tones, as she looked at ground inches ahead of her immobile feet.

Shadow growled at the bard before he could answer. Jewel's hand rested on the top of the gray's head, but the cat ignored it. "It is not for *you*," he told Kallandras.

"No," the bard agreed, unruffled. "But neither it is for The Terafin."

The growl intensified, and pale, long fangs seemed to sprout from the cat's upper lip. Night, sleek and black, turned to the bard as well; he made certain to remain outside of Jewel's reach.

They must never be outside of your reach, a new voice said: the Winter King. *They must be yours, Jewel, and they have not been. It is why we traverse this cursed place at all. You do not understand the danger.*

No more do you, Jewel snapped.

Silence. No, not silence; the Winter King ceased to speak, but in the background, words more felt than heard caused tremors in the forest floor. Without thought, she reached for the trunk of a tree to steady herself, standing in place, moving neither forward nor back, balancing between hope and fear, twin sides of a flipped coin.

Her hand shook. She was, she admitted in the interior of her thoughts, tired. It wasn't the walking; it wasn't even the journey or the things she had faced thus far. It was the certainty that her ignorance would—without intent— doom her people. She had never believed she was perfect; she had made far too many mistakes in the past. But those mistakes, she had paid for, had more-or-less survived. It was not Jewel—not Jewel alone—who would pay the cost for mistakes made here.

She took a breath; it barely seemed to fill her lungs. *I'm sorry*, she told the Winter King.

Do not be. She heard his amusement; it was dangerously like affection. *No, Jewel, it is not. You desire affection; you therefore see it when you look. I am not yours. I will never be yours. There is no room in the life I have chosen for something as paltry, as slight, as affection. You are weak, but you have turned that weakness into a strength—and in the world you have inhabited, it did not destroy you. This world is not that world. What do you hear, Jewel?*

I hear . . . the cats.

Your cats?

Not—not mine. Not my cats. But . . . the cats.

What do they say?

"We *say*," Shadow replied, "that she is *ours*."

Snow roared. Jewel heard words in it, and she recognized them, although she could not repeat the syllables.

She is ours.

"She cannot be *yours*," Calliastra snarled. Her eyes were almost literally red, a color they did not often take—if ever.

"*We* found her," Shadow snarled right back. "*Us*."

"I was dreaming," Jewel told the gray cat, in a much milder voice, "the first time I met you."

"You are *Sen*."

She thought of the three leaves: silver, gold, diamond. She could not, even now, remember picking them, but they had been with her when she woke. And from those leaves, she had built a forest, and in that forest, ancient voices rose from their long, long winter slumber.

"You were his. You were the Winter King's."

Night hissed.

Shadow, however, stared at her. "Is that what you thought?"

"Yes."

"Stupid, *stupid*." Night's voice was far more his own, as was his shape, the sleek solidity of his fur. His wings settled lower upon his back as he stared at his brother's moving tail. She wanted to weep in relief.

"He came for us," Shadow said. "And we were *bored*."

"Bored," Night agreed. He sat, heavily, on his haunches and examined the underside of his paws. "We had never seen a human enter the tangle before." His eyes were golden. "I thought it would *eat* him."

Snow roared again.

She is ours.

Jewel did not disagree. She felt, in this story of the Winter King, there was the thread of an answer—and at that to a question she did not know how to ask.

"It didn't."

"Nooooo. And *we* didn't either." Night glared at Shadow, who shrugged.

"He was not *boring*," he offered.

"Why were you stone?"

"Were we?"

"Yes. When we met, you were stone. You were all stone."

Night hissed laughter.

Shadow, however, looked thoughtful. "You are *very* stupid," he said at last. "Almost as stupid as Snow."

The entire forest shook with Snow's answer, although the white cat himself was nowhere in sight.

"Shadow, this is important. Did the Winter King make you his own?"

Night was instantly outraged. Shadow however, was not. Insulted, yes, but his long-suffering glare made it clear he expected no better. "We were never *his*. But we left the forest with him because we were bored."

"Shadow, important, remember? *Why* were you stone?"

"I might be able to answer some part of that question," a very familiar voice said. Jewel did not take a step because visceral instinct prevented that motion, but she spun in place to meet the gaze of Andrei, servant of House Araven.

He bowed.

He bowed to her as if she were in the Terafin manse.

"Where is Hectore?" she asked. It was, suddenly, the only important question.

"I am here," Hectore replied. She heard only his voice; she could not see him at all. For a moment, the entire world seemed to center on Andrei; even her own companions were lost to the sight of him.

"What," Andrei asked, voice soft, "do you see?" He might have been asking about the cut of a dress, or the length of its hem.

"I don't see Hectore."

He lifted a brow in a very characteristic way, although the expression was most often turned on the master she had just named. And that was more of a comfort to Jewel than she could have expected. She drew a breath, tightening her hold on Shadow, who—unlike Jewel's companions—had freedom of movement, and had started to use it.

"Why are you here?" the gray demanded, his voice entirely free of the whine that Jewel hated on most days.

"To find your Lord," Andrei replied, "before she is lost in the tangle. She should not be here—as you should well know."

"She is *safe* here," Shadow replied, his fur rising.

Andrei stared at the gray cat for one long beat. "Do you feel safe, Terafin?"

"No."

"Andrei," Hectore's voice said, "has come to lead you out of the tangle."

"I can't leave without my cats."

The air grew chillier as Andrei regarded the cat; to Jewel's surprise, it was Shadow who looked away. "You led her into the tangle."

"Not *me*," Shadow said. He glared at Night. "*They* did it." But his voice had once again fallen into his characteristic wheedle.

"You let them."

Shadow hissed.

"What are you planning here, Eldest?"

Night growled; Andrei ignored him.

"*We* are not planning *anything*." Shadow sniffed. "But *she* is *stupid*. She must be *less* stupid, or she will not *survive*."

"She is lacking in wisdom to follow you here." His tone implied *anywhere*, but he failed to use that word. "She is not yours."

And Snow, at a great remove, said, *She is ours*, and the ground beneath their feet shook—and shattered.

When earth broke, it could kill. This was not, therefore, earth. The cracking that preceded the sudden breakage sounded far more like fallen glass—or pottery—than the movement of trees and roots, the fall of branches, the upheaval of buried stones, which would have been an earthquake in any other forest.

Andrei cursed; Jewel couldn't catch all the words and didn't try. She was shocked to hear them because they came from Andrei, and if they survived all of this, it would be some cause for humiliation on the part of the Araven servant. Survival, however, was not guaranteed.

The shards of what had once been forest floor—and trees—did not cut or tear as they traveled past Jewel. They seemed, instead, to fly—and they flew, all of them, toward Andrei.

No, she thought, as he lifted one slender arm. They flew into his shadow, and his shadow was vast and almost endless. In their absence, no other reality rushed in to assert itself. Jewel stood moored in fog; she lifted a foot but could find no place to put it.

"The path," she said to Andrei, a question in the words.

"It is still here."

She turned to her kin, her companions; she could see them clearly. She could also now see Hectore. Had he not been standing beside Jarven ATerafin, she might have wept with relief, but Jarven put her instantly on her guard; he always had. She froze when their eyes met. Not even the roaring of a distant, almost unrecognizable cat had chilled her so instantly.

His smile was familiar, his expression bright; of all the people here, he seemed the most solid, the most present. She had never trusted Jarven. Finch, within limits, had and did. But she wondered if Finch would trust *this* Jarven, because he was not the same. In looks, if one glanced past him, one wouldn't notice the difference—but Jewel did not look away. The whole of his face, his form, seemed like a mask of flesh, something into which something different, something other, had been poured.

And yet he was Jarven ATerafin; he was just the essence of Jarven, laid bare.

He knew that she knew it. His smile sharpened, his posture shifting only slightly as he offered her the polite nod that passed between members of the House Council and their theoretical ruler.

"It was not," Andrei said, "my choice to bring him."

No, it wouldn't be. Jewel's smile was slight; it acknowledged the suspicion and hostility with which Andrei had famously viewed the Terafin merchant.

From out of the vast shadow of which Andrei seemed to be the point or pinnacle, Hectore of Araven stepped.

"Hectore."

"It is, I think, safe to stand here."

"It is not safe to stand anywhere in the tangle for long, as I believe I have made clear."

Hectore rolled his eyes. "What," he asked Jewel, "do you see here?"

"Fog," she replied, understanding why he asked. "You?"

"Beach. It is a sandy beach; there is a distinct absence of rock or anything but a very unusual ocean."

"Unusual?"

"The color. Can you hear the ocean?"

Jewel shook her head.

Kallandras, however, said, "I hear what you hear, Patris Araven. It is not the ocean." He lifted a hand, and the butterfly that had taken up residence on his shoulder shifted position onto his finger, without once flapping its wings. Hectore blinked, twice, and stared hard at the bard's lifted hand, and Jewel realized that he couldn't see the butterfly, or at least not as she saw it.

She wondered, then, if this was how people were lost in the tangle; no two of them seeing the same thing, no two stepping into the same reality.

"They are *all* real," Shadow said, in his grumbling voice. The presence of Andrei had dampened something about him. Or perhaps simply focusing on Andrei had; Shadow had never liked the Araven servant. And that, Jewel thought, was not her problem.

"It *could* be."

"It had better *not* be. I mean it."

"Yes, yesssssss." Shadow glared at Andrei. "She doesn't *need* you. She has *us*."

"Eldest, she is mortal."

"She is *Sen*."

"She is mortal. Why did you enter the tangle?"

"The tangle," Shadow replied, after a lengthy pause, "is *moving*. She *wants* to leave. She *wants* to go home."

"You cannot expect that she could walk from the tangle to her own lands?" Andrei's astonishment overrode the respect with which he generally treated the great, winged cats.

"Why *not*? *You* did."

Andrei's mouth was half open as he stared at the two cats. His expression rippled—literally rippled. Jewel had seldom watched the Araven servant with as much care as she did now, but she knew that she did not see what the ancient saw when they looked at him. He made even Calliastra uncomfortable, uneasy.

She had claimed, boldly and definitively, that she knew who he was, and she'd meant it. But who, and what, were not the same. He was not, as the demons were, dead; he was not a mockery of life, not proof of the end of it—the eternal emptiness that followed when death took the living.

She had known on some level that he was not mortal, not human. She had not seen it so clearly at any other time.

"Terafin."

She swallowed.

"What," he asked, as he had asked at the beginning, "do you see?"

Her throat was dry, her mouth dry; for a long moment she couldn't force words out. "I'm—I'm not sure," she finally managed.

He had stiffened, but the shadows that were now everywhere behind him undulated, moved, lengthened, rising in place as they did, as if they were a tidal wave in the making.

"You are not going about this the right way," Hectore said, his voice mild with the type of disapproval he offered only to Andrei. "If it is your intent to frighten the wits out of The Terafin, you have severely misjudged her mettle."

"Or her wisdom," another voice muttered. Jewel thought it was Calliastra's.

Jewel closed her eyes. It was easier to speak. "I don't know what I see, I'm sorry."

"Does it change anything?" Hectore asked, his tone casual.

Jewel had no illusions. That type of casual had death standing to one side. But she understood it viscerally, because it was the same reaction she would have had had someone threatened any of her den. She exhaled. "I sheltered the daughter of the god no one is stupid enough to name in the wilderness." She increased the pressure on Shadow's head as she spoke. "I knew who she was. I knew what she was. But I offered her a home and as much family as she could stand. What she was wasn't who she was. And that matters, to me.

"People assume that because I'm seer-born, I see what Andrei is. But to me you've always been Andrei, the man who came to rescue Rath on the same night I did, so many years ago. You serve Hectore the way my den serves me—you're not shy with criticism, and you have your own mind. You make your own decisions. But I trust your decisions. I trust your intent."

"Even now?" Andrei asked, and she heard layers in the syllables; he spoke almost with the voice of a god in the Between.

"Especially now," she replied. She opened her eyes. She looked at a man who was not, in any way, a man. She saw that the shadows he cast were all his shadows; they were representations of the layers of physicality that Andrei of Araven possessed. She saw feathers, she saw scales, she saw eyes and an absence of eyes; she saw limbs, legs that ended in the shape of paws and in the shape of feet and in the shape of claws. "You came to find me."

All of Andrei nodded. She heard whispers, as if the varying parts of the whole were arguing among themselves. But there was a strange familiarity in this, because she did it to herself all the time. No decision that was not visceral, instinctive, immediate, didn't cause second thoughts, third thoughts, fourth thoughts. She could act as if free of those doubts, but it was an act, an illusion she wanted to sell to observers.

"You came to find me," she continued more deliberately, "because of Hectore."

Hectore coughed politely.

Jewel ignored him. So did his servant.

"If you are lost, I believe we will lose the Empire," Andrei replied. "And the Empire is Hectore's home."

"And yours?"

"Home is where Hectore is. I will not lie; he can be difficult."

Hectore coughed less politely.

"But he is utterly himself."

Jewel nodded, understanding intuitively why Andrei needed that. "Can you lead us out of the tangle?"

"I can."

"Can you help me find my missing cat first?"

"He is not missing," Andrei replied. "Hectore."

Hectore, not apparently bothered by his servant's shadows—or perhaps not aware of them at all—had taken a step toward Jewel, frowning. "Terafin, what do you see when you look at something other than my servant?"

"Fog," she said. "Fog with Andrei in it." Almost as afterthought, she added, "You shouldn't move around here. It's not safe."

"Thank you for your opinion. You can see me?"

"I can see you with difficulty; you're standing in Andrei's shadow."

"And Jarven?"

Jewel grimaced. "Jarven, I can see."

Jarven chuckled. It was a dry sound; it was also a sharp one. "You need me, Terafin." Jarven's voice was so clear, it might have been the only voice in the fog.

"Terafin has always needed you."

He waved the words away as irrelevant, and Jewel accepted this; they were. What The Terafin—what Amarais—had required of Jarven ATerafin she might have had from a handful of her best merchants. What he could offer now had changed, and Jewel was not at all happy to see it, because there was, about the merchant she had never trusted, something that spoke of, spoke to, *her* forest.

He knew. Of course he knew. He was very like Haval in his ability to observe. Haval didn't trust him, but Haval didn't trust anyone.

Nor should you, the Winter King said, echoing every argument about power and rulership they had ever had.

"What Terafin needs, Terafin, is defined by two things. The first: the House ruler. In this case, that would be you. But the second? Its enemies. You do not wish to make an enemy of me."

Shadow stiffened, turning; he slid out from under Jewel's hand before she could stop him. She had not been offended by Jarven's words; she considered them as a merchant might. They were the opening steps of a negotiation, and at that, a negotiation that was purely business as usual.

"Shadow!"

The gray cat stalked across the foggy, shadowed terrain as if he owned it. But his steps did not turn whatever it was beneath his feet to stone—she knew the distinctive sound of cat claws against stone flooring.

Jarven glanced once at the cat, his eyes narrowing. "I would not suggest," he began.

Shadow leaped. Night, growling, began to pace toward Jarven, but Jarven was no longer where the great gray cat landed.

"*Shadow! Night!*" She almost leaped forward, then stumbled because her feet did not move. Cursing—loudly—she repeated the names she had given the cats in such an offhand way. "Jarven is *not* an enemy, and I will be very, very angry if you hurt him!"

"Hurt him?" Shadow growled. "We will *kill* him."

"We will *eat* him," Night agreed.

Calliastra laughed.

Adam's voice, thin and whispery, reached her—as did his hand. The hand steadied her completely. Adam was not a child, but he was not the age of the rest of her den. Maybe, she thought, as she reached for the hand that now rested on her arm, she needed his presence, not because he was healer-born—and powerful—but because he reminded her, by youth, by optimism, by his ready acceptance of life, of all the things she wanted to protect.

All the things that would perish if she made a wrong move here.

"I see," he whispered, "what Hectore sees."

"Do you see—"

"I think Hectore has always seen his servant as you see him now. But I see ocean, Matriarch. I see sand. I see distant spires on the horizon."

"In the water?"

"No." Silence. A beat, two, while Adam struggled with Weston. Weston was his language of respect, because it forced him to think about his choice of words. "The sand is in the Sea of Sorrows. The spires are there." He hesitated. "I see trees, Terafin, such as we have never seen in the desert."

Jewel did not think of any of this terrain as real. But Andrei was here, with Hectore. "When you say the sand is in the Sea of Sorrows—"

"Some part of these lands overlaps the desert."

"You're certain?"

"Yes. I'm sorry."

She frowned. "Why are you apologizing?"

"Because I do not think this path will lead to where you must go. I do not think it will return us to the city at the heart of your Empire."

"*Averalaan*," she said automatically. "*Averalaan Aramarelas.*"

"Yes." She marked his hesitation as the fog around his face cleared enough that she could see his expression. "I think you are bringing me home."

Home was hundreds of miles away from where she needed to be. Home was nowhere near the Winter Queen. She swallowed.

Shadow's roar swamped anything she might have said. She meant to tell Adam that it wasn't possible, but knew, of a sudden, that he was right. She was, somehow, taking him home. Or rather, Adam's home was now their only escape.

But she saw the great movement of cloud and fog as the gray cat leaped, once again, for Jarven—and this time, she saw blood. It hung in the air like a fine, beaded necklace, absent the flesh that had shed it.

"You are *stupid*," Shadow roared—at Jewel, of course. But his attacks on the Terafin merchant ceased the minute he drew blood. The blood remained. Jarven, who had clearly shed it, did not; he was nowhere near the cats. He looked mildly surprised; given the cut of his clothing—and the rents in it, which were not part of the initial design—Jewel would not have been surprised at outrage.

Night hissed at Jarven. It was the laughter hiss.

Shadow came back to Jewel's side, impervious to her very real glare. And her fear, which was never far behind.

"Terafin," Andrei said, "I believe you must gather your cats now. We will not have long." He glanced at the blood that remained in the air, and added, "Have a care what you weave, maker. His blood is not kin to your blood, and his existence is thin and slender compared to your own."

And the air said, "Of *course* it is not like ours—he is *mortal*."

"He is mostly mortal," Andrei replied, with gravity. "But so, too, is your master."

"She is *not* our master."

"You are not her master," Andrei told the cat. He was talking, Jewel realized, to Snow—and Snow was answering. She felt relief in the midst of confusion.

As if he could hear her, Andrei said, "The fog that you see, Terafin, is not fog. What Hectore sees is what I—or some part of me—can see. What you see . . . is Snow."

"Snow?"

"Yes."

"The fog is . . . Snow?"

"Yes."

"Do you see him as fog?"

"I? No, Terafin."

"What do you see?"

"I see the tangle," he replied. "I hear its many, many voices. They speak to me—or parts of me. You asked what the Winter King did to the cats. You asked why he turned them into stone, moving statues."

"That's not exactly what I asked."

"Ah. Perhaps I am too aware of the answer to remember the question's exact wording clearly."

Hectore cleared his throat; as this was the third time he had done so, Andrei ceded the figurative floor to him. "I believe I met your Winter King." He spoke with certainty.

Impossible, Jewel's Winter King said.

"He was clearly a man, but his attendants were not. They were Lord Celleriant's people—but far more fell in mood. He had built a road into the tangle, as Andrei calls it, to find the cats." Hectore hesitated, eyeing the two that were visible to Jewel. "I do not see your white cat," he finally said. "Andrei does. I . . . do not believe that the Winter King saw your cats as you now see them."

"Your cats," Shianne said quietly, "entered the tangle some long, long while ago. Before they did, they were not as you see them now."

"How did you recognize them?" Jewel asked.

The question seemed to surprise Shianne, judging by her silence. As Jewel waited for her answer, she, too, grew in solidity, in clarity—as if the fog were reluctantly moving to cede some space to her. "I do not understand the question," she finally admitted. And it seemed an admission, and even a costly one.

"You knew the cats when you saw them. You offered advice on how they should be handled. Andrei seems to recognize—to see—Snow, when I can't. If the mist, the fog, is Snow—and it must be, I'd know his voice anywhere—I can't recognize it *as* Snow." She could, however, recognize the hissing sound of the white cat's laughter.

"You are *too loud*," Snow then said. "And I am *working*."

This caused Shianne to fall instantly silent. It didn't have the same effect on Jewel. "What are you working on?"

The hissing reply was not laughter, this time. But the roar, the wild sound that reminded Jewel of breaking earth and fire, was gone. If she could not see her cat, he was present. Shadow came to sit by her; he was inspecting his paws—or perhaps claws—as if they displeased him.

"You were *here*," Shadow told her. "You were *stupid*."

"I am here," she replied.

"Yes. You are here. And he is here. He is here. He will not recognize you."

"Who?" But even as she said it, she knew. Without thought, without anything but instinct, she reached for the air—because the air was fog, and the fog was the third of her triumvirate of loud, whiny, obnoxious, and destructive cats. And the air coalesced—not smoothly, and not all at once, but in discrete chunks of white fur and the flesh that underlay it: a leg, an ear, a whisker, a feather. They hovered, bloodless and almost distinct as their own separate entities.

Snow hissed. "I am *busy*," he snapped, and feathers smacked her wrist; her hand tingled. "I am *too busy* for *you*."

Shadow snarled, and Night hissed laughter, and a white tail joined the other disparate parts, at a remove from the two solid cats, black and gray. At the center of these pieces, obviously alive, obviously part of a greater whole, while entirely separate from it, were beads of crimson and scarlet. Jarven's blood.

"I don't think this is a good idea," she said to the white cat.

"Because you are *stupid*. She says you don't tell *us* how to *behave*, but she ignores *him*." The she was not immediately identifiable, the *him* was. Jarven. "You are *stuuuuuuupid*. He is *dangerous*."

"He can't kill me while I have you."

This seemed to offend Shadow. "Of *course* not!"

"He is *too mortal* to serve. You should have demanded his oath before you allowed this."

"Snow—I didn't allow anything."

Snow's shriek was comforting. The assertion that she was stupid, which came again, was also strangely comforting. Jewel had never, in her life, felt smart.

Calliastra chuckled as she, too, became completely visible, completely present. Beneath her feet—which were curiously bare—Jewel could now see sand. "You should feel honored," she told Jewel, as she watched the beads that had once been blood—and might still be—come together in a short strand. "The eldest does not make, often, and if I understand what I have seen, he endeavors to create for you."

"I don't want it."

Three shrieks, then.

"May I ask what it is?" Jarven said; it was the first time he had spoken since Shadow had launched himself so murderously.

"I have no idea," Jewel replied. She was uneasy. People did not try to kill Jarven, not more than once.

"No, of course not. I did not mean the question for you." In shredded clothing, he had a stillness, a straightness, that implied none of his dignity relied on the merely external.

Snow did not dignify the question with a response, and Jewel, in Snow's position, would have. A very carefully worded, very carefully offered response, with as little actual information as she could manage.

"They serve *her*," Shadow said—to Jarven. "You serve *them*. You *should* serve her."

"She is Terafin. I am ATerafin. Of course I serve her."

"You don't understand *service*."

"Because I am mortal?"

"Because you are Jarven," Jewel said, before Shadow could. "You only barely understand alliance." This, on the other hand, was not carefully worded. Her legs hurt. She was tired, even exhausted. She had become amazed at just how much pain standing in one place could cause. She wanted to walk, to move, to find a place where she could sit and massage stiff legs, stiff feet.

Jarven's smile was sharp, but fluid. "I understand alliance as men of power understand it. I understand alliance as Finch ATerafin understands it."

"And as I don't?"

"As you choose not to, yes. You are, I believe, an orphan. You chose to build family—a choice I did not myself make, when I found myself in your circumstance. And, perhaps, had I met you at the age I found myself alone in the world, I might have become like your Finch. Ah, no, like your Jester. I did not. I chose to see—clearly—what was set before me. I chose to see danger when it was present. I chose to be dangerous myself.

"I did not choose responsibility for others; I expect no one to take responsibility for me."

"Lucille," Jewel said, flat-voiced; she folded her arms.

"I do not expect that; I attempt, where possible, to avoid it. As you suspect, I value her. I do not value her enough to guarantee her life or safety were she to work against my interests. There is no one in my life, Terafin, who is of more value to me than I am. There are many in yours, and it makes rulership very complicated.

"A ruler has no friends."

"And Hectore is not your friend?"

"Hectore is an old, worthy, adversary. He is comfortable to me because we both understand the rules of the game by which I play. But he is kin to you in some fashion; he is canny enough—powerful enough—that he can survive it. I was not." Jarven's smile deepened. "I see that I have surprised you."

He had. He had not, judging by Hectore's expression, surprised the Araven patris. And he had, judging from Andrei's, annoyed the Araven servant.

"I am capable of a great deal of charm. I am honest when honesty will best serve my interests; I am dishonest, otherwise. Honesty bores me; it is singular."

"It is not," Jewel told him, her voice softer. "It is singular only when there's one truth, but there are many." She thought of Carver then.

"Perhaps. I see your cat has almost coalesced."

She glanced at Snow; Jarven was right. His face, his jaws, his ears, and of course his fur, seemed to have knit themselves into mostly contiguous pieces, and in the right positions for them. But his jaws were open, and in his mouth was a string of red beads that ended in a pale, ivory clasp. It was ivory the way bones were, when bleached by sun and sand and wind.

And she remembered Gilafas' words—the words he spoke that were not his own while he endeavored to create—and felt a pang. Snow trotted to her, as if he were carrying a dead—and old—fish. She held out her hands and he spat the bracelet—it was too short to be a necklace, at least for anyone over the age of four—into them.

"Could you—could you unmake this and—and take back . . ."

Shadow and Night hissed laughter—uproarious laughter, apparently. Snow simply looked disgusted, especially when Calliastra's low, deep voice joined the black and the gray. "You will never understand how fortunate you are that the eldest have chosen to find your ignorance amusing."

"If it's all the same to you, I'd rather be less ignorant."

"That," Andrei said quietly, "is almost inevitable. I am sorry." He glanced, once, at Jarven, and then his gaze moved to encompass the three cats. His expression, never friendly, soured as he considered them. "You should not have brought her here."

"We *found* her here," Shadow countered. He sniffed the air, his expression shifting into weary disgust. To his brothers he said, "He is almost *here*."

"We should kill him," Night said.

"We should *eat* him," Snow agreed.

"I should very much like to see you try," a new voice replied.

And Jewel, Terafin, seer, turned instantly toward a voice she recognized, and a man she did not. And she took a step. Finally.

He was not a young man, in either appearance or bearing; there was none of the slenderness of youth, none of the softness or the uncertainty. Jewel herself was not a child, but she was not, and would never become, this man. He had none of Jarven's ready charm, none of his apparent flexibility—but it was of Jarven she thought first.

Thinking it, she slid the bracelet around her bare wrist. The clasp, like the bracelet, was magical; it shut itself with an authoritative click that ivory shouldn't have been able to make. She glanced once at Snow, who was staring—with some fascination—at the man Jewel had met, briefly, as the Winter King. The last Winter King. The final one.

The thought discomfited the stag who resided at the back of her mind, but he did not argue; he, too, recognized the man. *This is what he was*, Jewel's Winter King said. *This is what he was in the beginning.*

You recognize him.

As do you, but not in the same way. He is *Winter King. Can you not feel the season?*

In the chill of his expression? Perhaps. But in her dreaming—and she thought of it, still, as a dream—he had been skeletal, all but dead, the armor that encased him holding his bones in place.

Yes, the former Tor Amanion said. *He was strong, in the end, in a way none of his forebears were. He wished to win, and the desire for victory was absolute; he cut himself off from the Winter Queen, and no yearning, no desire, could force him to return.*

But Jewel said, *No, I don't think that's it.*

Oh? Chilly word.

He trusted that she would be strong enough, in the end, to reach him.

The Winter King that she rode did not, ever, criticize the master who had, in a moment of pique, ordered him to serve Jewel. He was therefore silent.

In the end, she did reach him. But not, Jewel added, *on her own.* She spoke without spite, and without satisfaction. Even the scions of gods were not islands. They were not absolute. And how could they be? What defined a ruler was subjects. In isolation, there were none. What defined a victory was defeat, and again, without the defeated, what point victory?

She looked up from her wrist, letting her hand fall to the side as she did.

The Winter King's narrowed gaze moved from that same wrist more slowly, traveling up her arm and to her gaze.

She offered him the stiff nod she might have offered any of The Ten; it was a gesture of wary respect among equals. This man thought he had none—and that was his problem, not hers.

Be wary, her own Winter King said.

This is *wary,* she replied.

As if he agreed with the stag, the Winter King's gaze traveled past her own without acknowledging it; it came to rest upon the cats—and froze there.

Shadow hissed, the sound partway between laughter and disgust—but he meant both for this august stranger and his men.

And the men were, as Hectore had said, Arianni, all.

"Lord," Celleriant said, the syllable tailing up in question.

She nodded, and he moved to stand in front of her, as he had not done for the entire trek through the tangle.

"It is seldom I encounter your kind outside of the Cities," the stranger said, speaking to Jewel, failing to acknowledge the man who had drawn sword to protect her. But if he did not acknowledge Celleriant, he understood—who better?—that Celleriant served Jewel. This made Jewel the ruler, here.

Beyond her back, however, Shianne moved, her steps soft, light, and taken without permission—as if she knew the ground in this space made of Winter and mortal was, for the moment, solid.

And she spoke. She was mortal, she was pregnant, but her voice was the voice she'd been born with. Or created with. Jewel accepted that she did not now, and would probably never, understand the Arianni concept of birth. Shianne did not speak Weston, which only meant that her words were not for Jewel or her kin.

Celleriant, however, understood them. He did not lower his sword, but his wariness made clear his respect for the men gathered behind the Winter King. No, Jewel thought, for the Winter King himself.

The Winter King is the only *mortal that the White Lady's people willingly serve. Until you,* the white stag added, almost as afterthought. *But you are barely mortal.*

She frowned; the frown remained in place. She wanted to ask this man if he remembered her, but already knew the answer. Time, it seemed, was of no more relevance to the tangle than geography, or anything else Jewel considered reality. The tangle had something to do with the gods, but the gods viewed time in as linear a fashion as their many followers.

Shadow turned his glare on her and let it sit there; he did not, however, call her stupid while the Winter King and the Arianni were present, and this, more than anything else, told her that they were a very real danger in the eyes of the cats.

Not that the cats were particularly respectful at the moment.

"It is seldom," Jewel began, "that I venture—"

"She is *Sen*," Shadow informed the Winter King, before she could finish.

The Winter King, however, nodded, his expression momentarily enlivened by what might have been surprise on the face of a lesser man. "That explains much." When he turned to Jewel again, he offered her a bow. "You are far from your city."

"Am I? The tangle is so unpredictable I might leave it and find myself in the streets of my own home at any time." She knew that he thought of her city as one of the ancient Cities of Man and had no desire to disabuse him of the notion. But it made her uneasy, and that uneasiness had been growing with the passage of time—if that had any meaning now.

"Your companions," the Winter King then said, indicating the cats, "are unusual."

A hundred sarcastic comments attempted to escape Jewel's mouth all at once; she managed to contain them. ". . . Yes."

"Are they yours? They must be if you can keep them in the graveyard."

"Graveyard?"

"It is oft called the tangle, for obvious reasons; it defies logic, it defies reality. But the reality of our lives—and our deaths—are not the realities of the lives of gods past. It is here, wherever here is, that the dead who cannot die dwell; their echoes alter landscapes. What remains in the wake of passing gods is very like their lives: ancient and wild. The mortal dead have no desire to destroy, no intent; if they can be found at all, it is not here."

"No," she said. "They can be found—" and then she stopped.

He watched her.

He watched her, and then turned to the Arianni who accompanied him. For the first time—for perhaps the only time since the immortal aide had appeared—he seemed unaware of his Lord's presence. Unaware of anything but Shianne.

They did not speak.

Nor, after the first foreign syllables, did she.

They would not survive the tangle, Jewel thought. They could not; had they, Shianne's state, her existence, would be known—and it would be known by the Arianni, known by Meralonne, known by Celleriant. Yet the Winter King would survive, must survive, for Jewel had seen what would become of him—a man who could not die, save at the hands of the Winter Queen; who ruled, deathless but unliving, in a castle of ice and glass.

"Do you dream, Sen?"

She had not given him her name; nor had he asked.

"Yes, as you must guess."

"Did you dream of this?" His smile was wintry, but it added warmth to his face.

"I am dreaming of it now."

"And these?" He indicated the cats.

"I first met them in a dream," she told him. "A dream of the Winter King."

"I had cats when I ruled mortals." He glanced at her. "I had sons and daughters, as well. I did not have to kill my cats, except as an act of mercy. I lost a handful to poison." He was silent for a long moment. "I dreamed," he finally said. Before she could ask, he added, "Not of you, Sen. But of them." She thought his smile both predatory and genuine.

Shadow hissed.

"They are yours."

Night and Snow joined Shadow.

"I want them."

This decreased the volume of hissing. Had Jewel been the cats, it would have had the opposite effect—but clearly, they were flattered, and that had always been their weakness.

"I have seen nothing like them. In my time, I have seen the whole of the ancient world by my Lady's side—and apart from it. I have seen the firstborn. I have seen the gods. But I have not seen your companions' like in my many travels, and I finally understood that it was here that I must come."

"Only fools travel into the tangle of their own volition," Calliastra now said.

His expression chilled. The silent Winter guard became far less still as Calliastra stepped into the space between the two: Sen and Winter King. She was no longer a bruised urchin; she was no longer the Avatar of the god they did not name. She existed in the wide range of space that separated them—but her eyes were lidded, almost lazy; her hair was a spill of perfect, lush night.

"And yet you are here, Firstborn."

The Arianni shifted formation; they might have formed up in front of the Winter King had he not lifted a hand. He spoke no word, uttered no command, but the gesture was enough.

"You are aware of the danger with which you travel?" he asked Jewel.

"Of several, yes."

"She is not in the danger you are," Calliastra added, her voice sharper. It would never be shrill; it would never be less than compelling. Not as she was now. And the now, Jewel thought, felt eternal, as if it were Calliastra's only truth. It wasn't. But she was the scion of gods, and the moment, the present, almost overwhelmed the memory of other aspects, other faces. What she was now was complete.

"I am not in any danger," the Winter King replied. "I am Ariane's King, as you well know." He had subtly shifted his stance; his hand had fallen to the hilt of a weapon, invisible until that moment beneath the careful drape of cloak.

"Do you think that means you are free of danger?" Calliastra's eyes were black. She raised her arms, and her wings—which had been no more than looming shadow since they had entered the tangle, when they were visible at all—rose with them, polished obsidian.

The Winter King remained unruffled; his men, Arianni all, did not. Swords were drawn in the stillness of a sandy clearing. The Wild Hunt should have looked ridiculous on what was, essentially, a beach or a sandbar. They didn't.

"I cannot kill you," Calliastra said. "But there are many fates which might cause a man to long for, to beg for, death. Ask Viandaran."

And the Winter King turned, Calliastra and her threat momentarily forgotten, he was so certain of himself. His eyes did widen. "Warlord."

Avandar offered a very grim nod to the Winter King. "Did we not desire," he asked, voice soft, "eternity?"

"You achieved it."

He nodded again. "You understand the bitter disappointment children can be—especially when they must be put down, as any threat must eventually be. I am not seer-born; that was not my particular burden to bear. But you will understand the burden of eternity, near the end, old friend. You will understand why mortals were never meant to achieve it."

"Will I?"

"You will."

"Why are you here? Why are you dressed like that?"

"The City, which was my home, fell."

Jewel turned then, remembering. She did not say why it fell although she knew. She could not even feel that it deserved better, given the rulers and their abuse of the power they wielded. But the fall of the city had not killed only the rulers. Everyone in it had perished. People who had as much say as Jewel had had at ten years of age. People who had less.

"And you come to the tangle seeking power for vengeance?"

"No. I am servant to the Sen."

A pin dropping into soft sand might still have been perfectly audible in the silence that followed. "I would laugh," the Winter King finally said, "but you are serious."

"I am."

"And are you then oathbound?"

"I am bound by my own oath, yes. But I have long valued my own desires and choices more highly than a god's."

"And you did not demand that he swear a binding oath?" the Winter King asked Jewel, Calliastra ignored or forgotten.

"No. I am mortal. I grew up in the lowest of city streets. I made mistakes. I survived them. If I understand the oathbond, it has no room for mistakes and allows none. Failure is absolute, and failure is death."

"It is not death," Avandar said. "Not always."

Jewel didn't ask. She wondered—had often wondered—how many different ways Avandar had attempted to end his own life, but that was neither her business nor her immediate problem.

"I would never swear a binding oath," she continued. "I could not therefore demand that anyone who follows me do what I am unwilling to do."

The Winter King looked confused for the first time.

He is, the great stag said, sounding far more amused than he had in a while. *What you say makes no sense at all to him. And no, Jewel—were I in his position, it would make no sense to me either. I have served you at* her *command, and I have come to understand your life and the way it defines the choices you make. He has not, and will not, have that experience.*

They will die here, Jewel replied, indicating the Arianni.

Yes. They will die, or they will be lost. They entered the tangle at the behest of the King, but they did not leave it. Only he did. And they are not your problem; do not seek to make them so. They are not your Lord Celleriant. They are not, in my estimation, Illaraphaniel. Do not attempt to warn them, he added. *They will not serve you. They will give you nothing of themselves, and you require that gift to function as ruler. I did not.*

The warning she considered had nothing to do with their survival. Shianne, who had stepped between the Winter King and Jewel, now approached them. The Winter King's gaze grazed her face, her obviously pregnant belly, and moved away as if she were of no consequence and very little interest.

She spoke a name. Jewel recognized it only because one of the Arianni, so grim-faced, so perfect, turned at the series of cascading syllables she spoke. The Wild Hunt was silver and white, but it seemed to Jewel that there was a shift of pallor across his features. What he saw in Shianne the Winter King did not see. Perhaps could not see.

The Arianni spoke. He spoke her name. And at the sound of her name, fully half of the gathered Hunt turned. If cacophony could be utterly silent, this was cacophony.

The Winter King noticed. Everyone did. His gaze moved back to Shianne, but, even so, he did not see what the Arianni did. He didn't see what Jewel herself saw, having met the Winter Queen only a handful of times.

You are Sen, the white stag said. Of all her company, he alone failed to appear.

But—but he's the Winter King. *He serves—*

He does not serve.

He's the Winter King.

You have never *understood the heart of Winter.*

Fine. He loves the Winter Queen.

His silence made clear that he was annoyed. *You of all people should understand,* he finally said. *There is no artifice in her—for us. There is danger, there is the promise of death; it is inherent in her affection. She is bitter, cold, harsh; she is as grand and glorious as the ancient vistas the gods so casually destroyed.*

And, Jewel? She cannot be killed. I lost wives, in my youth. I was not foolish enough to believe they loved me—that word is not for men like us. But they were fond of me, and in reward for that folly, they died. Not all of the deaths were quick. The children that I was not forced to put down died. Those who were powerful enough to survive my enemies were powerful enough to become them.

But she is all things: enemy, lover, rival. And no hand, save perhaps our own, will end her. You do not worry about Viandaran because he wants death. You do not worry about Celleriant because you believe, viscerally, that he cannot be taken from you by anything trivial. You do not profess to love them, even in the privacy of your thoughts— but you trust them in a way that you do not trust the people you do love. You are afraid, always, of loss. You are afraid of death. You are afraid to leave them because you believe that your presence preserves their lives.

Silence. A beat. Two.

I was never weak in the fashion you are weak. I would not have survived it. I learned, early, not to love as you love; to love is to despair. You will not learn that lesson. Perhaps in some fashion you are strong; I cannot see it. You are a power, even if you do not choose to acknowledge it. For one such as we, she is safe to revere.

And she would kill.

If she can, yes. But we are worthy, all, to stand and face her; she would not choose a Winter King who was not. That is the nature of Winter.

And Summer?

I was not Summer King. But she gives willingly to the Summer King what she cannot give in Winter. And the Summer King can give what we cannot. But there is a reason that Winter reigned so long in the Hidden Court, the hidden world. No Summer has lasted so long, no matter that she desires it.

And Jewel? I do not believe that it is wise to let Shianne continue to speak.

Jewel turned. Shianne had fallen silent after speaking a name, or names. Or so she'd believed; she had heard nothing further.

She speaks, the Winter King said softly. *Perhaps only those who belong to the White Lady can hear her voice. Ah, no. The bard can hear her, too.*

What is she saying?

She is telling her former brethren about the Winter Queen's fate.

Gods.

Chapter Nineteen

I F SHIANNE'S VOICE WAS inaudible, the response of the Arianni was not. Swords struck shields. They ringed the Winter King, but—and this was strange—the Winter King did not seem to hear Shianne's words; he was as much of an outsider in this regard as Jewel herself.

"What," he said to Jewel, the texture of his voice the season of his title, "have you done?" It was a reminder that threat could be expressed in the softest of voices.

Jewel had long learned that I *don't know* was not an acceptable response from a leader, even if it was the truth. Only with her den did she say it, and this man would never, ever be among their number. But there were other gambles she might take; other avenues she might pursue.

Winter King.

Into the clearing, the great white stag came. He walked slowly, head high, tines casting odd shadows against the sun-drenched beach; his hooves did not touch the ground. He did not acknowledge the reigning Winter King, and the look he gave the woman who was theoretically his master was almost the definition of simmering resentment.

"I have done nothing," Jewel then told the reigning Winter King. "You have seen my companions. Did nothing strike you as unusual?"

He said, "Your winged cats, of course."

"And beyond that?" She pressed, aware that at least one of the three was purring loudly. Probably Night.

"That you are foolish enough to travel with Calliastra. That you are accompanied by one of the White Lady's people." He did not mention Avandar.

"Nothing else?"

Men of power did not, as Jewel had not done, acknowledge ignorance.

"You cannot hear her," Jewel continued, as if she herself could.

One of the Winter King's men turned to Jewel then. His eyes were silver light, his weapon a brilliant blue that almost hurt to gaze upon. "What," he demanded, "have you *done?*" Although there was Winter in his voice, there was also rage and the heat of it; the combination was striking. It was not comforting.

No impulse moved her to speech. No certainty gave her confidence. She exhaled, but tension kept her spine rigid. She turned to meet the hostile gaze of her own Winter King, and told him, *I think we need them.*

His anger at her stupidity was instant, searing, silent.

He doesn't recognize you.

No. He is Winter King. We, none of us, accepted our fate. We accepted the Winter Queen's offer because we felt we could best her. Those in the long line who had failed before us were irrelevant; we believed ourselves to be stronger.

He was stronger, Jewel said quietly, *than any that preceded him.*

How odd.

Odd?

Your definition of strength does not usually agree with mine.

Do you know what happened here?

No. But I understand that, in the tangle, this is *what happened. His history—his long history—of defiance began here. What I see in him now—what you force me to see—he cannot see in me. Nor should he.*

"I am seer-born," Jewel said quietly.

This did not seem to impress the Arianni Lord. He lifted his sword, and Shianne stepped between them; Celleriant had not moved. Not once. He held his sword, his shield; that much, she could see. That and the chain that adorned the back he had turned toward her, as part of his duty.

Shianne turned to Celleriant, and then away.

"Lord," Celleriant said, his voice so soft she was surprised she could hear the word at all.

A cry broke from the rest of the Arianni, and Jewel understood. Celleriant was young, in the terms of the ancient world. But these men? They were not. And some of them had been alive when Shianne had walked the ancient world as a child of, sister to, the White Lady.

They spoke and spoke again; their words traveled, igniting a depth of feeling that must remain otherwise hidden in their service to the Winter King.

And Jewel understood then. They served the Winter King; they loved the

White Lady. They could not forsake this man—and his commands—at their own whim, no matter how dire, how necessary, the act now seemed. Three of the ancient Princes of that vanished court lay in unending slumber, cast aside for that very crime.

She wondered, then, if they knew. She wondered at the chronology of the last Winter King. He was of the Cities of Man, and the Cities had existed in tandem with gods and ancient elemental wilderness. But he had resided in the heart of the hidden pathways.

"How long do you wish to rule?" she asked the Winter King.

"Eternally."

"The world will exist in Winter."

"Better Winter than death." And she heard, as he spoke, other words. She understood that he longed for Summer, and that it would not come again while he lived, and this seemed strange to her, given the life he had led, the life he *would* lead.

"I have seen you," Jewel finally said, "in vision. I did not come to seek you, but I do not believe in coincidence." This was a lie. Coincidence had troubled her life, much of it bad. She closed her eyes. Opened them again. At the edge of her vision in all directions, she saw glittering, icy blue. "I have need of your men."

Whispers rose in the stillness and died just as quickly.

"They will not serve you."

"Not without your direct command, no."

"Not without *hers*."

"I am willing to take that risk. They obey you. They must obey you." This was a gamble, but she dredged out all of her merchanting experience to make it. "You desire my . . . cats."

He hesitated, the first real hesitation. "I do not desire them more than I desire my life."

"No. And perhaps you will not have the strength required to keep them."

His eyes narrowed. He was not, more's the pity, a fool; he understood that she had begun negotiations. She had, however, something he lacked, and moreover, something he wanted. It was a luxury, yes—but men had beggared themselves for luxuries before. And would continue to do so in future, if the future arrived for any of them. "The cats serve you, yes?"

"They serve me in a fashion. They are not, as you perceive, caged; they are not—"

"They are disrespectful, quareling, arrogant creatures," Calliastra interjected. Attention had moved from her, shattered by conversations Jewel couldn't even hear; the firstborn didn't like it. "You would be well quit of them if you were to leave them here."

Night hissed. Snow hissed. Shadow's tail lashed out at the firstborn. He remained more-or-less silent.

Jewel automatically dropped a hand to the gray cat's head and pressed down. He hissed. "They will not remain with you," Jewel continued, as if there had been no interruption, "if you do not have the strength to bind them, the will to keep them."

Shadow angled his head awkwardly, attempting to meet Jewel's gaze. Or to catch it. "You are not *stupid* all of the *time*," he said, as if this came as a great surprise.

Jewel grimaced. The Winter King, however, frowned.

"If this is your idea of strength, Sen, it is . . . lacking. No man or woman in my service would dare to speak with such obvious disrespect."

"I am not Winter King," Jewel replied. "But the cats exist, now, in the tangle."

"And you found them here?"

"I? No. They found me. They found me the moment I claimed some small part of the high wilderness as my own." She closed her eyes again. "I grew trees, there, of a moment. Trees of silver, of gold, of diamond. A tree of fire burns at the heart of my lands, and the trees, *Ellariannatte*, have begun to wake."

"They cannot—it is Winter."

"It is Winter in lands that are not mine," she replied. She chose, as merchants do, to speak the truth, but to speak it at a slant.

"If you did not seek your companions, why are you in the tangle? You are Sen, if the gray cat did not lie; you have no need of them."

She gazed long at the Arianni, who were now listening to every word she and the Winter King exchanged. "I had some need of them. I do not know what you know of the Sen; I do not know if the Sen are all of one thing, or all of another. Until I met you, I did not know what I sought." And this was true, although it was also a lie. She had come—as he had come—seeking the cats. No, she thought, she had come seeking *her* cats. The cats of the Winter King were stone and silent unless he desired sound.

Shadow hissed, as if he could hear her.

"The Wild Hunt will serve me," she continued, "if you command it. And that command will last until your death. Until the coming of Summer."

"Summer will never come." He spoke with a strange intensity; it was not arrogance, not confidence, and not—quite—desire.

"Then they will serve me."

"And in return?"

"I will release the cats. If you can find them—if you are strong enough, clever enough—they will serve you. They will serve you in a fashion they have never, and will likely never, serve me. I cannot build cages."

"You undervalue the Wild Hunt."

"You undervalue the cats," she countered. She drew breath, but before she could speak, she heard a familiar—and unwelcome—voice. Jarven ATerafin stepped onto the beach. He had always been there, but Jewel realized, from the reaction of both the Winter King and the Arianni, that he had remained unseen, undetected. He offered Jewel a deep, almost reverent bow, and when he rose from it, no hint of anything but respect touched his expression.

"Lord," he said quietly, "if you will allow me to handle these negotiations? They have never been your interest, and they have never been your strength; your abilities and your power have always been necessary for far greater things." He glanced at the cats as if they were a simple housekeeping chore, and Shadow—of course—bristled. He even waited for her nod before he turned from her to face the Winter King.

To Jewel's surprise—and there had been far too many surprises in the recent past—the Winter King *relaxed* as he faced Jarven.

"You serve the Sen?"

"I bear her name," Jarven replied. He had not said yes, which did not escape Jewel. It did not escape the Winter King.

"And that name?"

"ATerafin," Jarven replied. "It is the only name of relevance."

Jewel did not, instinctively, trust Jarven to negotiate anything of personal importance to her. But she felt a hand on her shoulder before she could speak, and although she did not look to see who the hand belonged to, knew anyway. Andrei.

"And you, *namann*? You also serve the Sen?"

"No. But we are allies, and we are friends."

"The Sen are clearly workers of wonders and miracles beyond even the ken of legend." This was said almost sardonically. The Winter King did not seem to harbor the same almost-hatred of Andrei that every other immortal did. Or perhaps he felt there was some profit in hiding it.

"Let Jarven do his work," Andrei said softly. "You do not trust him, and that is both fair and wise. But he is the blade you must wield at negotiations such as these. I wish I had seen that more clearly sooner. There is a reason you brought him here."

She had not brought him here, and Andrei knew it; nothing in his voice, which was pinched and slightly disapproving, as if this were merely a matter of conflicts among the Household Staff, gave this knowledge away.

The Winter King smiled. "If it is acceptable," he said, to Jewel, "I will deal with your agent."

Jewel nodded.

Jarven was a merchant at heart. Whatever else he had been, he was good at his job. The changes made in him—and they were neither insignificant nor irrelevant—had not robbed him of acumen. The skills that he had honed, sharpened, and used to disastrous effect for his opponents in his early years shone here. She could believe that he had faced death so often it was a matter of course; she could almost believe that he treated with immortals and ancient, wild beings on a daily basis.

He had never had Haerrad's ego; he had always had ambition.

She was very surprised when he opened with praise of the cats and their abilities as guards. She had never discussed them with Jarven, and while she had not forbidden Finch from doing so, was almost appalled at the depth of his knowledge. He extolled their many, many virtues, but did so almost casually, which was, of course, a merchant's trick.

And when the Winter King frowned, calling into question the value of simple guards—given that he was served by the Wild Hunt itself—Jarven nodded. "They are the equal of the Hunt here." This predictably riled the Arianni, as it was no doubt intended to do.

"But they are problematic in other ways."

"Ah, yes. The Sen has always liked cats; it is the reason for their appearance. They are not, otherwise, as they now appear. It takes power to hold them in this shape, at this size; it takes power to confine them at all. But no power, I have been told, can confine a cat unless one does not care about the cat's survival. I myself have never understood the appeal." He waited a beat.

The Winter King's gaze remained narrowed.

"They are wild," Jarven continued. "They will always be wild."

"They would not be so with a true Lord."

Ah.

"No? But they are hers, regardless. If she desired what you desire, perhaps they would be different—but they would not be as compelling to you." Jarven stopped speaking for long enough that Jewel thought he had finished; she opened her mouth and shut it as his words once again resumed. "But they serve a different function. You will have noted, no doubt, that the Sen is not like the Sen of the City you once ruled."

"I have. But it was never wise to disturb the Sen; the Sen seldom disturbed the rule of my City, and never deliberately. For obvious reasons, the only Sen I have addressed has been the Sen of my City; I had assumed that all Sen were similar. You imply the cats are somehow responsible for this difference?"

"Yes. The gray cat walks in dream."

Silence. "He walks in the dreams of the Sen?"

"Yes. He walks where the Wild Hunt cannot walk. And he guards what the Wild Hunt cannot guard."

Jewel's jaw would have fallen had her mouth been open.

You are surprised. Did you think your mistrust of Jarven was baseless?

Does the Winter King dream the way the Sen did?

I did not. But we were not all of one thing, just as the Sen were not and clearly are not. In broad strokes, yes—but not in specificities. This Winter King spoke of a dream that led him here. And you spoke of a dream in which you met him. Tell me, Jewel, did you not bring leaves from that dream?

He knew the answer.

"Yes," the Winter King said. "I will take them."

"I cannot simply hand them over," Jewel said, before Jarven could speak. This time, Andrei's hand did not tighten.

"Loose them, then; I see them, and I know them. Only loose them, and I will find them, no matter where in the tangle they choose to hide. The Hunt that serves me, I will command to your service, and they will serve you while *my* Winter reigns." He spoke without doubt.

"That would leave you without your guard."

His eyes were flashing, almost literally; there was a hunger in his face that she saw seldom, a desire that was so focused it seemed all-encompassing. She thought, again, of Jarven—a man who affected boredom and the infirmities of age entirely for his own amusement—and shook her head. Would she trust this Winter King? No. She might mimic trust if her life depended on it.

But she would never trust her own Winter King were it not for the geas Ariane had laid upon him, either. She felt his vague, unvoiced approval at the thought, and shook her head.

Shadow hissed. He was unpleased to have lost even a fraction of her attention, which was normal.

Snow said, "I'm *bored*. Even *here* she is *boring*."

Night added, "*Booooooooored*."

The Winter King watched them with an expression that was sharpening, hardening; his grin was almost feral. She felt a visceral desire to call it off, to tell him *no*. Half of her time with the cats involved fantasies of somehow strangling them. But they were den. She did not want to hand them over to this man.

Shadow hissed. In a low, low voice the word *stupid* repeated itself often enough it seemed a continuous echo. This, too, the Winter King heard.

"You must care a great deal for cats," the monarch observed, as if from a lofty height.

"Only the ones that can't be poisoned or easily killed," she replied. Her hand was warm with the softness and heat of living fur. "It is true. The gray cat guards my dreams. When the dreams are a threat to me, when they present a danger that I cannot clearly see while dreaming, he reminds me of what I am." She inhaled, exhaled, lifting her chin, letting her shoulders slide fully down her back. "I have need of the Hunt, now."

"Do you?" He turned to one of the Arianni then and spoke. Jewel did not understand a word he said. Celleriant, clearly, did. So, too, Shianne. They were white, almost breathless; they might have been clothed alabaster.

The Arianni thus addressed was silent a beat. Two. He then turned to his compatriots. He did not speak. Nor did they. But in their stretched, tense silence she felt the heat of urgency, of panic. Although no words were interchanged among the Arianni, some agreement was reached, some consensus developed. Or perhaps not.

Jewel wondered, not for the first time, how the Arianni had become *Allasiani*, and knew better than to ever ask.

Celleriant put up his sword. Or, rather, sheathed it. Jewel had never quite understood where the former phrase had come from, but she was not a swordsman, not trained in the weapon. He then turned to her. The tension that gilded the faces of the Winter King's men was in him, bone-deep. "Lord," he said, offering an exaggerated sweep of bow which he knew—had to know, by now—was both unnecessary and unwanted.

It is now neither, Avandar said sharply. The Winter King had words to add, but he allowed the domicis to speak them over the undercurrent of his frustration. *Celleriant came to you at her command. These men will come to you at the command of the Winter King—and, Jewel, he is dead.*

Not here. Not now.

There is no now *in the tangle, as even you must understand. What he commands of them—and he has the right to command—they will offer. But what he said is true: they are his while he lives. And he is dead.*

The Winter King had fallen silent, and Jewel turned to him. It was, how-ever, to Avandar that she spoke. *Is he?* He understood the force of her argu-ment; she didn't even have to make it.

He is dead, the domicis repeated.

The Tor Amanion—

Mortals were not born of the wilderness except in a small, insignificant way. The Tor Amanion, as he styled himself in life, is dead. He cannot pass beyond. He cannot cross the bridge. He belongs to Ariane for as long as she desires to hold him here, but he is dead. The Winter King who cedes the Hunt to you is likewise dead. Unless you wish to spend the rest of your years in the tangle, when you return to the lands you have tamed, the Arianni will no longer be yours to command—if they ever were.

Ah. She said again, "We *need* them." She turned to Shianne.

"They will not be yours," the former Arianni said quietly, divining the only relevant question Jewel might ask. "They *cannot* be yours." But she glanced, briefly, at Celleriant. So, too, did Jewel.

"He is young," Shianne continued, when Celleriant did not speak. "The youngest of our kin, I think. The last of her fair Princes. What he offered you has not, in my experience, ever been offered. It was not, to his elder brothers, even conceivable."

Silence. A beat. But silence would not serve here. "The *Allasiani.*"

Shianne's expression did not cool but grew somber instead, and Jewel regret-ted the words.

"We are not—they are not—what you are. And what you are, little mortal, is chaos and change. You are not all of one thing, nor all of another; mortals are not predictable en masse, and only barely individually. Ariane was all of Ariane. She was—she is—the White Lady. Perhaps her descent into seasons changed her. Perhaps the losses she took in her war with the god we do not name changed her. I cannot say.

"But these are my kin, and I tell you again, they will never be yours. Not as Lord Celleriant is."

"Will they serve until we reach the Hidden Court?"

"They will give up their lives and everything they might ever dream of becoming in a bid to reach it now. And if you are the only method, the only possibility, they will serve that cause with a devotion that eludes mortality. You can trust them to do that. But you cannot command them as the Winter King does."

"Do you counsel against it, then?" Jewel asked, which was unkind; she knew the answer. But she was moved to see Shianne struggle to give it, and she lifted a hand, forestalling words. "They will live in my forest. There are powers in it that not even the Princes at their peak would dare to offend. The forest *is* mine."

"While you live."

"Will they kill me, then?"

". . . No."

A different thought struck Jewel. "Will they kill you?"

"I do not know," Shianne replied. "I am mortal, but I am not without power. Do you understand why you need them? I did not speak to sway them; I spoke to convince them to allow you free passage, where it did not conflict with the White Lady's command."

"I'm sorry, but I don't believe you."

A slender smile graced Shianne's lips, illuminating her face. "You are growing in wisdom." She turned to Celleriant. "Brother," she said. "I leave it in your hands. Your experience with mortals is far greater than mine—and I suspect far greater than those who now serve one." She indicated the Winter King.

The Winter King had not once removed eyes from the cats—Shadow in particular.

"In my hands?" Celleriant asked.

"It is you who will suffer. Tell her."

But Jewel understood. If the men who served the Winter King came to Jewel, it was not by their will, but his; they served him—as Celleriant had first done—at the command of their White Lady, their Winter Queen. Celleriant, however, had offered Jewel his oath, and his service, while she lived.

And after? Jewel had assumed that he would return to Ariane. She saw, now, that was in question. The *Allasiani* could no more return to their Queen than they could return to life; they were demons now, and their home—when they weren't summoned to wreak havoc—was the Hells. What would become of Celleriant?

He shook his head, his perfect features twisting in a brief, brief grimace, an echo of the familiar expression on mortal faces. "Do not offer me either your worry or your pity. I am the White Lady's. I am as I was made to be. Shianne's," he continued, his voice breaking oddly on the syllables of her shortened name, "story of birth and creation has confused you. We are *of* her, we are of her in a way that no mortal may be of his or her parents. But we are *not* her. We have freedom of choice, of will. Had we not, there would be no war between my Lady and the Lord of the Hells; there would be no sleeping, sundered Princes. Do you understand?"

"As much as I understand anything immortal."

"I made my choice, when I chose to enter a binding oath with you."

"You are not oathbound," Shianne said.

He did not correct her. Jewel felt the brief sting of cut across her palm, the shock of warmth and blood and determination returning as if she were wrapped physically in memory. What Celleriant did not do, she did not choose to do, but she knew Shianne was wrong. Instead, he smiled—at Jewel. "I will see the End of Days by your side and no other. I will see gods again. I have seen the tangle, where no one of my kin except the four walked willingly or openly. Things ancient and wild bow before you, and in their lee, I am a sapling. I am *of* her. She will be angry, perhaps—and cold—but she will not be surprised."

"She isn't here. They are."

"By serving you, we find her," he replied. "They will understand."

"They had better."

Shianne laughed. The sound was arresting, compelling; it drew all eyes, even those of the Winter King. He blinked, and blinked again, as if the laughter, and no part of her appearance, had awakened recognition at last. And why wouldn't it? It was ice, it was perfect, brilliant, and shining, as if it had captured all the sun's attention on the whole of a winter day.

His eyes swept down her face as if dragged toward her protuberant belly before he shook his head. But some hint of his obsession with the Winter Queen did not allow him to look away.

"There is a tale here," she said, voice soft, but hard at the same time; it implied that it was not a tale of which he could partake.

"Who," the Winter King asked of the Wild Hunt, "is she?"

Silence.

"You have not yet left my service. The bargain has not yet been struck. I will keep you in stone and darkness for eternity if you fail to answer me now." He did not even look at the Arianni; he spoke without doubt. Even so, they did not choose to answer until Shianne briefly lowered her chin.

One man said, "She is Shandalliaran." Which is what Jewel heard. But she heard, as well, other syllables, other songs; there was a depth to his voice that implied a chorus. Or a distant god.

It was the first and only time the Arianni would remind Jewel of her cats. The Winter King was not amused, but amusement had always seemed beyond him.

"It *is*," Shadow sniffed. "But he is a *king*. He doesn't *need* joy."

"Kings don't need joy?"

"What do *you* think?"

The Winter King ignored them both. He swept Shianne an impressive, supple bow. Jewel's jaw would have hit sand had it not been attached to her face.

Careful, her own Winter King and domicis said in unison.

Why? He can't see me. He sees nothing but her.

He is a power, Jewel. If you believe anything that transpires in his presence escapes his attention, you are a fool. The Winter King.

He has not lived as long as he has by being unaware.

They were wrong. And it was irrelevant.

His bow seemed to mollify Shianne, which was an odd thought. Or perhaps it wasn't his bow; perhaps it was his command of the Wild Hunt—Shianne's one-time kin.

"Will you tell me, Lady, why you have entered the tangle? For I perceive that you are at the center of the Sen's journey."

"I am woefully unfamiliar with both your Cities of Man and their Sen," Shianne replied, "And I am not . . . what I once was. The tangle is not safe for such as I have become."

"And was it ever?"

Her smile was almost warm. "You are bold, Winter King. Bold and yet graceful. I can see why she chose you."

Please tell me he's not blushing, Jewel said, to her internal council. Neither, however, dignified the comment with a response. He turned at once to the Arianni; whatever he said to them was inaudible, but it was clear that he had chosen to speak; their formation changed. He then offered Shianne his arm.

"Is that wise?" she asked, the smile still at play on her lips.

"Were I *wise*, Lady, I would not be here. Traversing the tangle is not trivial. It is not, however, impossible, as you have surely seen."

Jewel felt Andrei's hand grip her collarbone as if the Araven servant intended to break it. She understood that he desired silence, immediate silence, and although she was not Hectore, she obeyed. She trusted Andrei. She had trusted him from the first moment she had laid eyes on him, as a twelve-year-old orphan.

Rath had trusted him.

The thought of Rath in this place robbed her of breath. She struggled with the sudden, immediate sense of abandonment, of loss, as if the intervening years had never happened, as if she were not The Terafin, and not of that House; as if she had just been turned out of the last home she had shared with her blood-kin, when any of them had been alive.

Shadow *growled*. His voice shook the sand; Jewel had raised her hands above her waist, and stopped before she clapped them, instinctively, over her ears.

"Not *here*, you *stupid, stuuuuupid* girl. Never *here*."

This a familiar voice added, *is what you get when you let things run wild. Don't you forget it, girl.* It was her Oma's voice. Disembodied but never fully dislodged from memory. And it steadied Jewel in a way that Andrei and Shadow could not. Her Oma was dead, long dead, but the words she had offered, the advice she had thrown like darts—or daggers—remained buried forever in Jewel's thoughts.

Yes, Oma, she said, squaring her shoulders. *Yes.*

"Terafin," Andrei said, mouth almost pressed to her ear, "we cannot remain here for much longer. What the Winter King has done is solid—more solid than almost any other incursion I have witnessed—but it is beginning to fray. If you will negotiate, you must do so *quickly.*" When she hesitated, he added, "You are likely to survive it. I most assuredly will. Nothing can kill Jarven," his tone implied this was regrettable, "but Hectore will perish and so, too, your mortal kin. Decide."

"I've already decided," she whispered back. "But I'm not the only person here, and not the only person who has decisions to make."

"You fail to understand. The Winter King is here *because* his is the only decision or desire he values; he can see *no other.*"

"And how are you here, then?"

Silence. Silence and one sharp, drawn breath that cut.

It was Hectore who answered. Hectore who had moved—against all wisdom and all orders—to stand by her side. No, not by hers, but by Andrei's. "Andrei can see all others. The tangle doesn't confuse him; in some fashion, he reflects it. It was once thought that this was his home, and his only home. He is not the Winter King; to leave, he had to focus on one desire, and one alone. But he hears and wants all things, Terafin. When he speaks of danger, you assume there is no danger to Andrei. So does he. His arrogance, I excuse; it is one of his sterling features. Yours, however, I cannot.

"It is Andrei who will be lost here."

She started to argue. Stopped. Raised her voice. "Winter King."

The silence that fell at her tone was instant. It was not a tone that could be ignored; it demanded attention. It spoke to power of power. She wondered how surprised those subject to it would be if they knew that at base, it was her Oma's voice that guided her, not her experience in Terafin. She lifted a hand in densign; didn't even watch for an answer. Angel came, as did Adam; they clustered in a small space that would grow more crowded with the passage of minutes.

Nor did the Winter King now ignore her voice. It did not surprise him as Shianne's laughter had; he had presumed that Jewel was, as he, a power. In his eyes, she had merely removed the silk velvet gloves to reveal what he was certain lay behind them.

"You will either grant me what I have asked or continue your search on your own terms."

"And if I choose to set my Hunt against you?"

"You will die."

He raised a brow before his eyes narrowed.

"You lay down your life for the things that you value. I will lay down your life for the things *I* value. Your Hunt would serve my ends well, but with or without them, I will do what I must do."

"They have hunted gods and godlings, little Sen."

"They have been felled by cats," she countered. "They have been felled by gods."

"You think I am averse to risk?"

"No. You think I am. I'm not, but I won't risk everything for a moment's amusement; I find it self-indulgent."

Jarven coughed.

"Power," the Winter King said, "covers a multitude of indulgences. Is that not why you chose to become a power?"

"I was born Sen," was her curt reply. "Power came to me; I did not seek it. But where we are given power, we are given responsibility."

"I will know more of Shianne's story."

"No, you will not."

Silence again. She could feel the uneasiness of her two internal advisers; it was too late for remonstration. She could almost see the magic that Avandar now invoked. It was the domicis who said, "You will be lost here. You do not serve the White Lady, Lachlaren; I *do* serve the Sen.

"She will not take what she cannot hold. The Hunt—some small part of it—is yours while you live. Decide."

"Very well." This time, when he spoke, Jewel could feel and hear the words. *Kill them.*

She saw Shadow's fur rise; she heard Night growl somewhere to the side. She saw Snow bunch on his haunches as if to leap, and she commanded, demanded, that he stop. Blue sword came, and blue shield—and only one of each was raised in her defense. Adam stumbled into her, as if accidentally; he placed a hand on her hand, his healer skin touching hers. He said nothing, signed nothing, did nothing else.

Behind her, she felt the earth begin to rumble. She heard Hectore's swift, almost inaudible curse. And she saw, as well, the wings of shadowed darkness that were at the heart of Calliastra.

Terafin, be ready, the bard said. He was so diffident and so quiet she had all but forgotten him. She did not forget Terrick, who wielded his ax. Angel, however, had not drawn sword.

Shianne spoke and spoke loudly; none of her words were meant for the mortals present because none of them could understand her. Not even Jewel.

But the swords of the Wild Hunt did not waver.

Jewel held out the hand that Adam did not touch. It was not a command; she offered it palm up. Shianne's eyes were the silver of polished steel. She glanced, once, at the Wild Hunt and then turned away, turned her back. Only then did the swords list slightly, but no words accompanied that minute motion. She walked away from the Winter King; he raised an arm to impede her progress, and she wheeled on him.

What she said to him, however, did not travel. After a brief moment, she did; she was glowing faintly, glowing gold, her white hair almost blonde in the magical light. Jewel was not surprised when she drew sword.

The Arianni were; the sword was golden.

Jewel was upset for an entirely different reason, but pent it decently behind closed lips. Shianne had joined the aerial combat against the storm serpent. She was pregnant, yes, but she was not helpless. Not human.

Mortal, Jewel thought, but never simply human.

"Terafin," Avandar said.

"No." Before he could speak again, she added, *not that sword. Not here.* To Hectore she said, "Do what you can to contain your servant."

Hectore's brows rose, as did the corners of his lips; it was a gallows smile, but there was humor in it.

The butterfly began to sing.

As if the song were spell, it killed all motion on the beach; only the sound of water could be heard at all; even breath was dimmed. Jewel glanced immediately to Kallandras, but the bard's eyes were wide as he looked at the creature of spun glass and Artisan magic. It rose from his shoulder, shedding light that was both golden and white, and as it did, its wings spread. They were not wings such as Calliastra possessed; they did not widen until they implied something draconic in size.

But they widened enough that they might have been bird wings were the shape not so specific. All eyes fell upon the butterfly, even the Winter King's.

Swords fell as the song continued, disappearing into thin air as all the Arianni weapons did when they were not required. Axes did not. Shianne turned toward the butterfly, her own sword fading; she lifted one white hand to the base of her throat, and her mouth opened—but it did not move.

What is it saying? Jewel demanded of her own Winter King. She had no doubt that he could hear what most of her party could not.

I pity you, was his strange reply. *I am not man anymore; I have not been man for centuries except in the realm of dream. But you cannot hear, Jewel. You will never hear what we now hear.*

I don't care if I can hear it. Can the Winter King? The other one?

Of course. I will not tell you what I hear; I doubt I could, even had I the words to fully encompass it. Perhaps Shianne might—but later, if at all.

Jewel looked at Shianne and knew she could never ask. Instead, she turned to the Winter King.

"An interesting first attempt at negotiation," she said, her voice as dry as Jarven's might have been, had he chosen to speak. He did not. He did not appear to be aware that she'd spoken, either. As the Arianni and the Winter King were, he was transfixed by the butterfly. His eyes were wide, bright, his mouth slightly open. She had no doubt that this expression mirrored what he felt: shock, awe, astonishment.

As if aware of her—as if struggling to become so again—he closed his mouth, narrowed his eyes. But she had seen it: the slippage of a mask that was so perfectly controlled it was easy to wonder if anything else lay beneath it.

The Winter King was the first to reply, the only one to make the attempt. He bowed—to Jewel, in full sight of those who bore his standard and willingly died in his service. "It might have been a glorious battle, Terafin. We will now never know. I grant you the command of the forces that have come into the tangle by my side. In return, I will seek the cats."

"You will, eventually, find them," she replied.

"Will I?"

"Yes. They will serve you until your death."

Shadow yawned and flicked the underside of Jewel's chin with the tip of a feathered wing.

"You cannot enforce that servitude as I can."

"No, Winter King, I cannot. But I am Sen."

The butterfly came, at last, to rest upon Jewel's shoulder. It shed its light, its size, the power of voice, closing its wings as if exhausted.

"You are bolder than even I could imagine," he told Jewel. "To have that upon your shoulder. But it is . . . fitting. When I return to my Lady, I will tell her the tale of our encounter. Perhaps she will make sense of it."

"Or perhaps she will think it a consequence of your sojourn in the tangle." She turned to the Arianni, who blinked. They did not need to steady themselves. "Come," she told them.

"Where?" one asked. He was not armed or armored in a way that distinguished him, and his flawless, unlined features did not immediately suggest the seniority of age or command. But she recognized him: he was the man who had answered the Winter King's question. He knew Shianne.

"My lands," she said. She spoke with certainty although she felt none.

"Which City?" he asked.

"Averalaan," she replied.

His frown made it clear that the name meant nothing to him. She was content with this ignorance. She would have been content were it to remain that way, but knew, *knew*, it would not.

Her biggest fear at the moment was the leash that remained in the hands of the Winter King. He had died, was dead, in her own time. The Arianni might cross the paths out of the tangle and arrive in the heart of her forest, her home. But they would arrive without the compulsion of the dead king's command as their binding.

And it didn't matter. On a visceral level, she was committed.

Shadow began to growl. It was a low-throated sound, lost to the gentle lap of ocean waves, more felt than heard. Her hand, where it rested again on his head, tingled. She frowned.

Night sighed—theatrically—and joined his brother's low thrum of a growl, and after a second, Snow did the same.

"What are their names?" the Winter King asked softly.

"I don't know," she replied, as Shadow stepped on her foot.

"You don't know?"

"They aren't demons. They're giant, winged cats. Most cats I know ignore their names unless it's convenient not to."

The growling intensified, deepening. She felt a hand on her shoulder; it was Andrei's hand. She glanced at him, and forced herself not to glance away, because the two hands he normally possessed were by his side.

She was surprised when the whisper of butterfly joined the growl of cats; surprised when the wings of the butterfly opened. She could, if she twisted her head toward her own shoulder, see the echo of silver *feathers* in the small, contained wings of blown glass.

She shook her head to clear it. "Andrei, you will break my collarbone." The grip eased but did not vanish. She had the strange sense that he was holding her here, on this beach; that he intended to protect her in any fashion she allowed. She swallowed, nodded, and looked at the cats.

Their fur had risen. Their wings had risen. Their lips were pulled back over long, long teeth. All of these, she had seen before. Even their eyes —golden, all— seemed familiar. But there was an intensity of light to those eyes that did not belong in a living face, and as it brightened, that light became harsh: a warning.

She might have panicked—was, in fact, starting to feel the tight clench of fear in every muscle of her body—when one of the cats said *ssstuuuuupid*; his voice was an earthquake.

They shook, she shook; she saw the spread of wings that might have been blades, they seemed to reflect light so harshly. *Sooooo stupid*. That might have been Snow. Their voices were unfamiliar, acts of nature; were it not for the familiar words, she might not have recognized them at all.

The ground shook, the wind roared; sand flew up, and Jewel lifted a forearm to protect her eyes. The sand, however, was damp; it was beach sand. When she lowered her arm again, her hand was not empty. She carried three long feathers. Or what might have been feathers; their shape shifted even as she tried to categorize them.

She blinked, shut her eyes, and felt Andrei's grip tighten once again. She forced her eyes open. Felt a wave of nausea, of disorientation; she could no longer see Andrei. She could no longer see Hectore. Adam remained by her side, his hand wed to hers and tightening. But Angel and Terrick, like Hectore, were no longer visible.

Calliastra was; her wings were high and wide—wider, of course, than the wings of the cats. Her hands had elongated, although they still looked like hands; her lips were bloodred, implying a hint of fangs. Neither could equal the cats. But her eyes were black; they appeared to be all pupil now, and those pupils threatened to change the width and length of her natural eyes.

Or perhaps these were her natural eyes. She looked like death—or rather, like artistic renditions of death; there was a poetry to her appearance, and it was a poetry of absolutes.

"Terafin," a familiar voice said. She could not see Jarven. She could, however, hear him. "It is time, I think, to leave."

Chapter Twenty

SHE COULD NOT DESCRIBE what the cats became in the moment Jarven's last syllable dropped. The light that spilled from their eyes seemed to consume their forms—but it seemed to consume everything. Vision blurred as her eyes watered.

"We can't leave—"

"Remain, then. I, however, have seen enough. Hectore, stop fussing. Andrei can take care of himself here." Before she could ask, he added, "You have lost no one. We are all present. The cats, however, are not safe at this time."

"Shianne—"

"She is with the Wild Hunt. They *are* the Wild Hunt, yes?"

"Yes. I'm not certain it's safe for her."

He laughed. He laughed, and his laughter made him sound decades younger. There was a warmth to it that she could swear she had never heard in his voice before.

The water that had lapped the beach moments before began to rise; she couldn't see the ocean, but she knew water when it hit her.

She could hear the voice of the storm in the concerted harmony of howling cats. Icy water hit the back of her legs, trickling into her boots; she felt the familiar spray of active sea across her hair, her cheeks. She lifted her hand from Shadow's head, and the storm stilled instantly.

Yes, her Winter King said. There was no surprise in his voice, only a studied, deliberate neutrality. He had never liked the cats.

The cats spoke in concert. She heard the words, although she could never repeat them, no matter how hard she tried. *Come, mortal King. It has been long and long since we have been truly uncaged. You wish to own us? Try. Try.*

And she understood. To the Winter King, the living one, she lifted a hand. Opened her palm. Wind took the feathers that graced it, and they passed from her to him. What he grasped, however, bore no resemblance to flight feathers.

"Yes," he said softly. "Even so." He was not speaking to Jewel.

She blinked; the light was gone. The butterfly remained, but it was nascent, sleeping, its light spent. Angel was once again beside her; Terrick, the only armed man in the clearing. And it was a clearing now; there was no sand. There were no cats.

No cats.

She glanced at Adam. "I'm sorry."

He understood why and smiled. "I would go home," he told her gently, as if he were the elder of the two. "But I think . . . I think if we cannot win your battle, there will be no home to return to, except the Voyanne, and even that will not be safe for my kin. Where are we?"

She looked around. "Forest," she finally replied. She turned suddenly, breathed again when she caught sight of Shianne. Stopped breathing when she saw the Arianni that stood behind her. True to the Winter King's word—his ancient word—they had accompanied Jewel.

She remembered, vaguely, Evayne a'Nolan asking what the date was. She now understood why.

"You are both right and wrong," a familiar voice said. Coralonne.

They were standing in Coralonne's forest, their feet planted in a brook that had nonetheless crested the height of their boots. "The tangle has moved, for the nonce." Her voice was soft. It was not, however, gentle or welcoming. "What have you brought with you?"

The Arianni seemed to take no offense at the question. They drew neither sword nor shield and indeed seemed to be preoccupied with their surroundings.

It took Jewel a minute to realize that her ire was not meant for them. Gently shaking her hand free of Adam's, she moved and caught Andrei's before he could step away from her. And he had already begun to make that attempt.

"Not here, Hectore," Jarven said quietly.

"You are not responsible for me," Hectore replied, less quietly. "I recall that I had a mother. And a grandmother who would make me weep with guilt at my inadequacy. You are neither, and it is unlike you to attempt something when you are doomed to remain out of competition."

This caused Coralanne's expression to ripple briefly. Hectore had made a very handsome fortune by his ability to read the reactions of strangers. He now tendered Coralonne a very deep bow.

"You are mortal," she said. "At your age, such obeisance would be unnecessary."

"You are immortal," he countered, rising, "and what you are due does not trifle with the infirmities of age." His smile was warm.

Hers was almost reluctant, but it did come. It died when she returned her attention to Jewel. "These are my lands, Sen, not yours. What crosses my borders must receive my permission."

"You have given permission to me and my chosen companions," Jewel countered.

"Have I?"

"Yes. He is one of my chosen companions. I trust him. My life has been in his hands before, and he has saved it, or I would not be here at all."

"Truly?"

"Truly."

"And have you changed him, then? Or is it merely mortal arrogance and lack of vision speaking?"

"Firstborn," Andrei said, speaking for the first time.

Both Jewel and Hectore lifted a hand in his direction, as if his words were houseflies. Neither looked away from Corallonne.

"It is experience speaking," Jewel said. Hectore was willing to cede the floor to her for the moment; she didn't suffer under the illusion that he would continue to do so if she did not handle the discussion well. But she didn't require Hectore's approval.

Coralonne's gaze didn't waver, either. "He is not one thing, or the other. In the long history of gods, he has betrayed many. My parents. Her parents," she added, although she did not mention Calliastra by name. "It is in the very fabric of his being. He was created—"

"I don't care how he was created," Jewel said, aware that cutting off the woman who ruled these lands was unwise but unable to summon the will to play at politics. "He has saved my life. He came into the tangle to come to my aid. I trust him enough that he has been given free passage throughout the lands I claim; there are no conditions laid against him. He is as much my compatriot as the mortals you see gathered here; he is certainly more helpful than my cats." She spoke with a pang.

Corallonne's silence stretched. "Do you take responsibility for your cats?" she asked, as if Andrei had never been mentioned.

Jewel blinked. Hectore, older and wiser, did not. "Do you take responsibility for the creatures that dwell within your lands?"

"Of course," Corallonne replied.

Jewel was silent for another beat. Responsibility had been her Oma's marching drum, while she lived. But she was not her Oma. She had come, with time and Haval's nefarious questions, to understand that responsibility had layers. "I am responsible for my decisions and my actions. I am responsible for the damage done by those under my command. I am responsible for and to the power I've been granted through no work or choice of my own.

"But I do not own those I command. And those I've no hope of commanding? No. I would not claim responsibility for the ancients whose roots are sunk in the earth I've claimed. I don't *own* them. If, however, mine come in conflict with you or yours, I will consider reparations as part of my responsibilities as ruler.

"I am in no wise responsible for actions taken before I was accepted as ruler."

"And what guarantee will you give me? What will you stake against his behavior?"

Jewel folded her arms. She caught den-sign to her left and ignored it. She was wet, she was exhausted, she was hungry. In theory, she shared enemies with the woman who had not, until this moment, seemed grim or forbidding. Arguing about Andrei was not what she wanted to be doing right now. Or ever.

But she thought of Duster then. Of all the harm Duster could do, had done. Andrei was not, and would never be, Duster—but she'd had to negotiate over Duster, and she'd kept her.

"If you will not have him in your lands, we will leave. He will do no harm while he is with me. I will vouch for every aspect of his behavior until it is irrelevant to you and your concerns."

Corallonne's brows rose, her expression just shy of active condescension. She had, however, nothing on Haval when he was in a mood.

"You do not know what he is."

"I don't know what he *was*, no. And, frankly, it's none of my business."

"Terafin," Andrei said again. He fell silent when Hectore cleared his throat. It wasn't even loud.

"I don't know," Jewel continued, "what you were, either. I have some inkling of what Calliastra was because she's not exactly private about it. It is far, far safer to have Andrei at the very heart of my home than it would be any other immortal whose path I've crossed."

"You are Sen," Corallonne said, after a long pause. "What do you see when you look at him?"

"I see Andrei," was Jewel's firm reply.

"He cannot look mortal to you. He cannot appear as my sister and I do."

"No. I don't see how this is relevant."

Jewel.

"You are in the heart of my lands. It is relevant for that reason, and that alone."

"Terafin," Andrei said, a third time. She saw Hectore lift a hand in his servant's direction, but this time she didn't choose to ignore him.

What was a Sen? What did it mean? She was seer-born. She'd come to terms with that, over the years. She'd come to understand that the power offered was not a curse. As a child, with a child's responsibility, it had been. She had been able to see the future, but she had not had the power to change it. She couldn't make people listen—not even the people she loved and depended on.

But what did the seer-born *see*? She could see demons. She could see them even if they resided at the heart of mortal bodies. She could see shadow; she could see magic. Magic had color and texture. She hadn't chosen those colors; hadn't considered whether or not the vision was voluntary.

But she had looked at Andrei before, and she had seen . . . Andrei. Perhaps she'd seen what she wanted to see. Or perhaps she'd seen what was necessary to see.

"Terafin." This time it was Hectore, and she heard the warning in his voice. She lifted her chin in acknowledgment; there was no obedience in the gesture. Nor had Hectore the right to demand it. No one did now. The Kings, in theory the rulers to whom she had pledged allegiance, were in *Averalaan Aramarelas*.

She turned to face Andrei. She was not Haval, not Jarven, not even Hectore; she had not learned to school her expression as carefully as they had. But the woman who had had power in her early life was her Oma, and her Oma had hidden nothing. She had not been kind, had not been gentle, had not, perhaps, been nurturing; her power had never risen above street level.

But she had been the bedrock beneath their family's feet. She could be angry, yes. She could be more than angry. But life did not break her. Shock did not break her. Pain did not break her. Jewel was her granddaughter.

She looked.

What she saw now was some hint of what she'd seen in the statuary beneath the Kings' Palace: something that was not bird, not beast, not reptile; something that cohered as parts of all these things, as if limbs, torso, even face, had been composed of the bits and pieces of random corpses. She felt no shock; it was almost as if she expected what she now observed.

And if that had been the whole of it, she would have been fine.

But what she saw was not visual. It wasn't as simple as form. She saw shadows in him; she saw death in him—demons, at base, were dead; she saw an almost sickening blend of the colors that magic shed when cast, but they pulsed and moved and shifted in a way that made her dizzy, almost nauseous. And even this, she could have accepted. She *knew* Andrei.

And she did not know him.

He spoke her name. She heard him clearly. But she heard, as well, the multitude of voices that underlay the familiar one, the known one. She heard her name spoken with disdain, with disgust, with—uncomfortably—desire, obsession. She heard her name spoken through tears, through something strangled that sounded like a scream. She heard all this and more, and she understood that it was *all* Andrei. All of it.

She stood, frozen for one long minute, the seed of doubt planted by Corallonne attempting to take root. And it did. It took root. It sank those roots into her viscera. She was, for one long, silent moment, afraid.

This was worse than Kiriel had ever been. Kiriel, upon whom she could turn her back only by ignoring every screaming instinct that had kept her alive through demons, assassins, and gods. Even Calliastra's danger paled entirely into insignificance. Was this what the immortals saw, when they looked at him at all? Was this what they felt?

"Terafin," Hectore said. Once again, there was command in his voice.

"Hectore." Andrei's voice. And this time—for this single word—she could barely hear the rest of the cacophony that gilded it. She blinked, looked; it was an act of endurance. But she needed to see him, if only once. She needed to understand what other immortals saw.

And she realized that there was a thread of ugly, colored light that reached for, that bound itself, around Hectore of Araven. It was knotted there, in the center of his chest; indeed, it seemed to pierce cloth and even flesh, as if it had bored its way past anything so insignificant.

Yet it had not devoured Hectore.

Would not, she thought, devour him. He stood encircled by its possessive, devouring weight, and as the Araven merchant studied Jewel's face, she realized that he both knew what she now looked at and accepted it. As if to underline this, he lifted a hand to his chest.

"We all make choices," he said softly. Almost too softly. Andrei's internal voice was loud, broken into so many syllables she wanted to cover her ears with her hands to make the sound *stop*.

Jewel did not reply—not with words. But Hectore's voice was blessedly simple. Was there anger in it? Yes. And fear—not of her, but for Andrei. Or perhaps both. She lifted a hand, as she had done several times in the past hour. But this time she did not speak with it. Instead, as Hectore had done, she reached for his chest, his heart, and the ugly, ugly threads that bound him to Andrei—or that bound Andrei to him.

She had not expected that her hand would touch something physical but did not startle when it did; she had regained enough control that she could manage this. She kept her expression as neutral as she could, fighting the lines of her face, the pace of her breath, as she touched . . . something. It was both cold and warm, hard and soft, painfully spiky and yet slimy; it was fur and yet coarse and stiff as feather; it was hard as teeth and sharp as knives. It was all these things.

It cut her hand. She bled.

But she'd bled before, and for lesser cause. Or maybe for the same cause. She glanced at Celleriant who was utterly still, utterly silent. Surrounded by his kin—his estranged kin—he said and did nothing that would harm the dignity of his master. No, she was perfectly capable of doing that on her own.

But the pain was bracing. The fall of blood seemed natural. As natural as it had when she had accepted Celleriant's oath.

It was Shianne who spoke or started to speak; it was Celleriant who cut her off as if he, too, understood what Jewel intended—even if she had not, until that moment, intended anything.

Andrei could not pull away from Hectore. And if he could not, he could no longer pull away from Jewel. He wanted to. She saw that. And she saw the desire in multiple forms, because she could hear them all. But the one she clung to, in the end, was his concern. He was *worried* for her.

People, she thought, were like this in much smaller and much less visible ways. Had she loved Duster? Yes. Had she despised her? Yes. Had she been afraid of her? Yes. But, also, afraid *for* her. Had she wanted to strangle her? Yes, especially when she had gone after Lefty, the most vulnerable member of their den. Had she trusted Duster?

Yes.

Yes.

All of these things were true. Many of them were contradictory; she had always contained those contradictions, brokering a peace between them because they were all inside her, all part of her. They could change from moment to moment. They did.

Andrei's contradictions were stronger; they were not contained within him. But . . . the metaphorical struggle was one she could, with effort, understand.

Just as she could understand the choice he had made, somehow, with every internal voice so visceral, so real.

Corallonne spoke. Jewel recognized the voice of the firstborn because it contained the multitudinous plethora of voices; it was like— –and entirely unlike—Andrei's voice because Corallonne's words were a concert of sound, each part a spoken harmony. Andrei's were not. Could not be.

And yet he had struggled, she thought. He had struggled, he had chosen; he had fought the impulses that pulled him in different directions to remain by Hectore's side. And she intended to help him remain there. She intended to honor that choice. All revulsion aside—and she felt it as sharply, she thought, as Calliastra, as Corallonne—she accepted that it was the struggle itself that defined Andrei. That possibly ennobled him.

"Terafin," Andrei said, sounding strangled.

She shook her head. "I'm sorry. You are Andrei to me."

"You have seen—"

"And heard, and—" she glanced at her palm, blood deepening the lifelines it contained, "and touched. You are Andrei. I have granted you free and unconditional passage through my lands. I cannot grant the same through the lands of any other."

"I am not—"

"All one thing? No. But neither am I." And as she said the words, the vision faded, taking sound and noise and ugly, continuous struggle just to exist with it. "I know what I *want* to be. And I know that I'll never be it—not completely, not entirely. I struggle all the time. To do the right thing. Hells, to even *know* what the right thing *is*. And I don't always get it right. Sometimes my anger gets the better of me. Sometimes my sorrow does. Sometimes it's all I can do to put a foot forward, in *any* direction. I'm not—I know I'm not—facing what you face. But . . . I think I understand some small part of it.

"Hectore was Rath's godfather. I would have him as kin and be proud to own him. I cannot take you from him—I would never try—but while you are with me, you will be like kin to me. Blood of my blood. And, Andrei? When Hectore passes, when he dies, I will *still* claim you as kin to me. As den, if that is your desire. If it is, come to me then."

Andrei was silent. Utterly silent. All voices dimmed. Those that returned were a cacophony of sound; some derisive, some disgusted, and some desirous. And he fought. She saw that. He fought. He did not reply.

"Give me your word," she said. "Give me your word that you will at least seek me before you make any other decisions."

"I will not speak of Hectore's death—"

"You will," Hectore said quietly. "You will speak of it here, to this woman, at this time."

"Hectore—" But Andrei fell silent. "I cannot swear a binding oath," he said to Jewel.

"I don't need it. Give me your word as Andrei."

Andrei nodded. Hectore cleared his throat. Again. ". . . I give you my word. As Andrei."

Jewel then looked across the forested clearing to Corallonne. "Yes," she said. "I know what he is. Is this acceptable?"

Corallonne watched Jewel bleed; her face was waxen, pale. It was no longer, however, disapproving or judgmental. Jewel had always hated pity, but in this one instance, pity was a useful emotion for her cause, and she could live with it.

"You are unlike any Sen I have ever encountered," the firstborn said quietly. "And perhaps, had they all been like you, the Cities of Man would never have fallen."

"They couldn't," Jewel replied. "They couldn't be like me. They lived in—in isolation. They lived inside their own fantasies, but those fantasies became reality, over and over again."

"And you don't?"

"I don't want to," she countered, thinking of The Terafin's personal chambers, remade into a patch of wilderness that housed a growing library, replete with trees that sprouted shelves for branches and had roots that extended beyond sight. "I have help." Saying this, she slowly lifted her hand; her palm was throbbing.

Corallonne then turned to Andrei, stiffening as she did. "Understand that any harm you do in my domain will be laid at the Sen's feet. Any responsibility, any debt, will be hers to pay."

Andrei nodded, but did not speak. Instead, he looked to Hectore. Hectore shrugged dismissively. His servant frowned. "There is blood on your shirt." As if this was the most unacceptable thing that had happened today. Or possibly ever.

Hectore chuckled. "Yes, but this time it's not mine."

This soured the servant's expression. Jewel laughed. She curled the cut hand into a loose fist.

Angel signed; she signed back. He couldn't see what she had seen, and Jewel was profoundly grateful for it. "Do you have objections to any of my other companions?"

"Yes, as it happens." Corallonne turned now to the lesser threat: the Wild Hunt.

To a man, they remained unarmed.

"Are you hers?" the firstborn demanded.

Silence. Jewel was profoundly sick of the question of ownership. And yet she considered Angel hers, Adam hers. The den. Terafin. But the Wild Hunt? No. She didn't answer for them; she waited.

It was Shianne who said, in a voice barely louder than a whisper, "No." It carried in the silence left by Corallonne's question.

"Why are you here?"

"We have been commanded to the Sen's service by our Lord."

"Your Lord?"

"The Winter King, firstborn."

"And you have not accepted their service?" she asked Jewel.

"I have," Jewel said, picking up the reins she had dropped.

"Then, for the nonce, they are yours."

Jewel did not say that the Winter King who had given the command was dead; there was no profit in it. But she knew that it was folly to lie to the firstborn in the lands that they had claimed; she didn't know what the cost would be.

Jewel, Avandar and her own Winter King said in unison.

She squared her shoulders, lifting her chin while her hand continued to bleed. "They are mine," Jewel said evenly, "for as long as the Winter King lives, and no longer."

At that, Corallonne smiled for the first time, and the smile was a reminder of everything Jewel had lost: family, kin, home. And that, in turn, was a reminder of everything that she, almost empty-handed, had built after that loss. While Avandar and the Winter King spoke in her ear, she felt herself relax.

"If I could," Corallonne said gently, "I would open my lands to you and offer you a home."

"I have a home."

"I know, child. I know. I am sorry." She turned again to the Wild Hunt. "You are my sister's," she said quietly. "No service into which you are pressed by my sister changes that fact. You will make no oaths of allegiance to any but the Winter Queen—but she is now trapped in the wilds of her Hidden Court. She might never emerge, and the night is falling; the only god she truly called enemy while he lived once again shadows the living world. Can you not feel his presence? Even here, in lands he has *never* walked, I feel it.

"I will not hold the Sen responsible for your actions or your decisions while you are here. You are not hers and cannot be hers. But these are my lands, and there is a cost to walking them, as there has always been. It is not to the Sen I will look should you cause damage here. It is to the White Lady, my sister. Your behavior here—all of it—reflects on your Lord."

And that, Jewel thought with reluctant admiration, was how you threatened the Arianni. It was not a tactic she herself would have tried, although it had faint echoes of one of her Oma's favorite phrases: *Your mother would be* ashamed *of you if she could see you now.*

The man who had spoken Shianne's name bowed to Corallonne. "We understand."

"I am not a mortal, to be content with the mere surface of words, the shape of obedience.

"The Sen is your hope," Corallonne continued. "She is the only possible key to the White Lady's freedom." She turned, then, to Jewel. "The White Lady has taken the field against the Lord of the Hells before. She has held it. She is one of the few to do so and survive." Jewel opened her mouth, and Corallonne smiled. "Yes, Terafin. The Cites of Man held fast against the god who approached their walls. But those cities fell, regardless, for mortality is not of one mind, one heart."

"The *Allasianni* also exist," Jewel said. She felt Avandar and the Winter King's disapproval. And she saw, in the rigid stiffness of every single Arianni present, even Celleriant, anger, outrage.

Corallonne, however, nodded. "Things living know change, little Sen. Even the gods. But you are mortal, and your changes are greater, wilder, than ours. A word of advice, however. Should you succeed—and I have doubts, but no vision to ennoble them—do not ask my sister about the Lord of the Hells. Discuss strategies, discuss war, discuss pragmatic enmity. Ask about nothing else, or you will not survive.

"If you do not survive, I think very, very few of your kin will. Will you take one last meal with me?"

Jewel glanced at the Arianni and saw the No that was forming collectively behind closed lips. She then turned, not to Corallonne but to Andrei. "You came here to find me," she said quietly.

He nodded.

"How do you intend to get back?"

"You are so certain that that is his intent?" Corallonne asked.

Jewel nodded. "For himself, these lands might hold bad memories, but they hold no threat. It is not the same for the man he has chosen to serve. To strand himself here, in our company, he would likewise need to strand Patris Araven."

Andrei did not smile. He had slid, once again, into impenetrable servitude, and clearly intended to remain there. But he served Hectore, and Hectore frowned. "Andrei. She is The Terafin. Please."

"I intended to leave the tangle," he replied, "after we had made contact. I did not realize that one of the firstborn would be waiting for you."

"The tangle she entered was in my lands," Corallonne said, her voice noticeably chillier.

"We did not have time to have a strategic discussion," Andrei replied, his tone neutral. "Had I known, I would not have dared the tangle at all."

"Dared? It is your home."

Jewel saw Hectore's eyes narrow, and she stepped between Corallonne and Andrei. "His home," she said quietly, "is my city."

"That is unwise, but I will not belabor the obvious. You will vouchsafe his presence here, and I accept it—but understand that he alone can do more damage, cause more harm, than the Wild Hunt itself, of which you have only a handful."

Hectore did not say a word.

Jarven, however, chuckled. He swept Corallonne a magnificent bow, and in that motion Jewel could see proof of all the changes wrought in him; it was the bow of a man in his absolute prime. No age marred it, no infirmity, no hesitation. Her brows rose, and she smiled, a hint of surprise in her expression.

"I see that you have met the eldest," Corallonne said. "I believe I know which one. You are a bold man, and a fearless one, to accept what he has so clearly offered. The Terafin has claimed the lands in which he slept?"

"Indeed."

She looked at Jewel once again. "Have a care, Jewel," she said, voice softer and warmer. "Does this man claim to serve you?" The question was so carefully worded, Jewel offered the firstborn a rueful smile. Jarven did not serve anyone, not truly, and clearly Corallonne could discern this.

"I am of her house," Jarven replied. "But as you must guess, I do not serve her the way the Wild Hunt serves their Lord. I am not, frankly, capable of it."

"No. No more is the eldest."

"We make alliances of necessity."

"Even so," the firstborn conceded, glancing at Andrei. "But you are far from his forest, and far from your Lord's. Why did you come?"

He smiled; the smile was slight. "I was curious. I have heard very little about the tangle—but I have heard of it. And I wished to see if it could be traversed in an advantageous fashion."

"How so?"

"I require entrance into a specific area in the Northern Wastes that has otherwise proven impenetrable."

Jewel stiffened. So, too, did Corallonne.

"Having considered the experience, I do not believe such travel will suit my purpose."

"And that purpose?"

"Ah. The eldest has set me a task. To graduate from his infernal lessons, I must pass it. Passing it, however, has proven a challenge."

"And how do you intend to return?"

"Walk," Jarven replied pleasantly. "The wilderness is not geography as mortals understand it, but it has laws and rules."

"None of which you generally respect," Jewel said before she could stop herself.

Jarven chuckled again. "I respect the power behind those laws. I respect the possible consequences. You are gathering forces for your own war, Terafin. I am gathering forces for mine. For the nonce it is one and the same; the Lord of the Hells is large enough that he can be enemy to all with no diminishment on the part of those who claim it.

"I will return to your forest. I will not, however, travel the paths you will now travel." His eyes were bright, his smile unfettered. Jewel was suddenly certain it was genuine.

"He won't be happy."

"At a remove, that is not my concern. But he will accept it. I am beholden to him for the moment, but it is not—precisely—my obedience that he desires, and, frankly, obedience is not my besetting sin. I need knowledge, Jewel. I will not be able to stand against the servitors of the god we do not name without it. You've heard the old, trite phrase? Knowledge is power."

She nodded, uneasy.

"It is true. For me, knowledge is power. And I have never been a man content to wield the lesser power." She opened her mouth and he waved her to silence. "You are going to ask me why I am not Terafin. Or why I am not a hundred other things. The answer: it would bore me. You are a glorified babysitter, if history is to remember you with any kindness. So, too, the Kings. You are not free to do as you like. You are not free to choose your battles on a whim. You are not free to give in to your anger—and your anger, Terafin, is insignificant; it is a shallow puddle in comparison to my own.

"Not for me those things. Could I take power? Yes. I could have taken Terafin in the last House War had that been my desire. But then I would have had to *hold* it, and it is not such a prize that I would willingly dedicate my life to it."

Andrei now looked disgusted, which was comforting; it was his common expression where Jarven was concerned. Hectore, however, looked resigned. Jewel had never understood the relationship between these two men and thought at heart she was much more like Andrei than his master.

"Does any such prize exist?"

"I do not know. I have not found it yet. I have come by hard-won knowledge of myself, and I accept it: it is the hunt that motivates me. Not the kill, not the possession, but the hunt itself. It is illuminating, it demands all of my attention, all of my skill; it is intricate, like the steps of a very complicated dance. When that dance is performed to perfection—" He exhaled. "I am being extraordinarily sentimental at the moment. I will seek knowledge. I will seek power.

"And I will seek you, when I have achieved them. You are The Terafin, and I am ATerafin. I will make my report when I return."

And just like that, he was gone.

Corallonne nodded, as if she—and she alone—had seen him leave. And she probably had. To Jewel, she now said, "You have not answered my question. You cannot return to the tangle that you left; it is not where or when it was. How, then, will you proceed?"

Adam touched her elbow. She glanced down at his hands, and he signed.

This was not what she wanted of Adam. This was not what she wanted for him. And it didn't matter. What Adam could do, she could not. And what Adam could do was necessary.

How much would she sacrifice, in the end? How much would she demand of those who had chosen to serve her, to follow her?

Angel signed as well, but she ignored it. She could take no comfort from his unspoken words, because to her, Adam *was* a child. An Arkosan son, born of the open road and the desert skies. Loved, because it was safe to love him: he would never be Matriarch. He would never be the person who made the cold, hard decisions on who to sacrifice, and when. He would never become Yollana of the Havalla Voyani.

Yollana terrified her. She terrified the Matriarchs of the other Voyani clans. She was ruthless, unwavering, unflinching.

And she had, no doubt, been Jewel at one point in her life. She was seer-born, as Jewel was. And what she had seen had whittled away compassion or love or comfort until only the desert remained. It was merciless.

"Adam," Jewel said, pronouncing his name with a Torran inflection.

"Matriarch."

She flinched but did not correct him.

"Can you take us home?"

He nodded, a hint of doubt in his expression. "If we do not need to return the way we came." The hesitation grew pronounced; she saw him struggle with it. But he was the scion of Matriarchs and knew better than to ask for explanations. It was death to know the Matriarch's business—even if the Matriarch was mother or sister.

Shianne stepped between Jewel and Adam in that instant, the round fullness of protuberant belly pointed in The Terafin's direction. "You have not completed your quest." Her voice was full and warm; the words were cold and judgmental.

"I have completed what I can of it," Jewel replied. There was no doubt in her voice, although no seer-born certainty drove the words themselves. "I came to walk the Oracle's path. And I came, in the end, to find you, although I did not know it when I started.

"There is nothing I can do in the lands of Corallonne. Even could I, I would never be so foolish. No, it is in my lands, my wilderness, that we will find a path—or forge one." She had folded her arms without thinking, and attempted to correct this oversight to posture, but it was an old, old habit.

Shianne tilted her chin, but she did not speak. After one long, almost breathless moment, she turned her attention to the woman who did claim rule of these lands. And rulership in the wilderness was not the rulership that Jewel had been aware of at the periphery of her entire life. In some fashion, the wilderness *was* Corallonne. It reflected her. It obeyed her. It took shape and form in a fashion that pleased her.

Only the tangle did not.

"I have an interest in the White Lady," Corallonne said to Shianne, the White Lady's daughter. Or sister. Or echo. Jewel was no longer certain. "I have an interest in her freedom. We are kindred spirits, she and I; we came of age in the same fires, the same wars. We survived, where so many of our kind did not.

"But my interest will not open the ways. I am not certain that the Sen's will. But I am all but certain that the Sen is the only hope, the only window."

And Jewel knew, suddenly, that she was wrong. And right. She bowed her head and allowed the conversation to pass above or around her. She needed to go back to Averalaan. She needed to be at home.

And she needed to visit Master Gilafas as soon as humanly possible.

Exhaling, almost unmindful of the conversation that continued with its complex cadences, its stilted give-and-take, she said, "Adam."

Adam bowed to her, Southern style, as if she were in truth his Matriarch, and she remembered that the former Matriarch had been his mother, the current one, his sister. He then knelt, his hand hovering inches above the forest floor.

Corallonne said abruptly, "What are you doing?"

"With your permission," he said, not lifting his head, not meeting her eyes, "I wish to create a path to the Sen's home." He spoke Torra.

"Oh? And how do you intend to do so?"

Adam placed his left palm flat against the ground. When nothing appeared to happen—when Corallonne herself did not speak to deny him, his left hand joined his right. His eyes became a sweep of dark lashes as they closed.

But Corallonne's eyes widened. She lifted a hand, and silence fell instantly in the clearing. No birdsong, no cricket, no sound of distant, burbling brook or river, touched them at all. She stared at Adam's bent head.

"What is he doing?" she asked softly, so softly.

Jewel drew breath, held it briefly. Shianne remained by Adam's side; he was crouching in the lee of her skirts as if those skirts were a natural outcropping of rock, of cliff. Shianne did not speak, but rather, let a hand fall to Adam's head. It was an odd echo of the way Jewel handled her cats when she was afraid they might become dangerously fractious, but it did not have the same meaning.

Corallonne noted Shianne's position, and understood what the gesture meant: it was possessive. Declarative.

"He is healer-born," Jewel replied, wishing she had not called him by name.

"A healer? Truly?"

"Yes."

"The mortals do not have healers."

"We've always had—"

"No, little Sen, you have not."

And Jewel remembered Levec then. Alowan. She remembered Shadow. She remembered Isladar. And her gazed turned to Adam again, grief and surprise and love and fear crowding into it. "We have had healers," she said, when she could force herself to speak. "Just as we have had Sen."

"Can you feel what he is attempting?" Corallonne asked as if Jewel had not spoken.

Jewel shook her head. "He is mine. If what he does displeases you or causes you harm, I will pay. It is on my command that he acts—and has acted."

Corallonne did laugh then. But it was a warm sound, a rich one. "You understand so little of the wilderness and the firstborn, Sen. I would suggest that you avoid them were it possible; I know it will not be. He does not harm me. He does not make that attempt. This close to me—and he is touching me now in a way that none of you ever have or ever will—I can almost hear him.

"I would keep him," she added softly. "I would keep him here and keep him safe. There will be no safety where he travels, no safety where he rests—your shadow is too long, and other, longer shadows are even now being spread across the lands." Before Jewel could answer—or perhaps before Shianne could—she lifted a hand. "He would not stay. Even were he to desire it, he would not stay. Can you not hear him? He yearns for home. It is in his breath, in his hands, in his thoughts. He has remained by your side, but it is not by your side that he will stay."

"No," Jewel agreed, relaxing. "I thought—"

"You thought to take him home."

"I thought it was the reason the tangle became desert, yes."

"Desert? Interesting. But no. He will remain by your side because you walk toward the only home in which he belongs. A pity, really." She watched Adam, a maternal smile at play around her lips and eyes. Jewel understood it. Jewel had no children, had no desire to have them—she could not imagine bringing a child into a world the Lord of the Hells also walked—but thought she felt the same.

"Has he attempted this in your own lands?" Corallonne asked. The question sounded casual.

"No. We've had no need."

"I almost suggest you let him try." In the distance, Jewel heard birdsong and insect buzz and something that sounded like howling. Corallonne had let sound return to the clearing. "They will know, of course. Your ancients, your elders, your trees; they will become aware of Adam. Do you understand what he is even attempting?"

"To get us back home."

"Ah. No. That is the effect it will have. It is not what he attempts. And perhaps," she added, worry marring affection briefly, "the effect is what he feels he is attempting. You said he was healer-born. I can feel the truth of it as he works. But Jewel, we have had no healers for a very, very long time. It was always thus; we attempted to either keep them or, if they were not in our hands, destroy them. They were ever a danger in the long wars that divided our kind." She closed her eyes, tilting her chin up, as if, behind her lids, she was looking at something so vast and so awe-inspiring it was only safe to see it thus.

"You have not finished your journey. I will not ask how you will attempt to do so. But . . . I see the light you bear. I will not ask how it came to be in that shape; I will not ask how you returned voice to it—but what I see, I hear. Have a care, little Sen. The world is waking, and I fear your Adam will be the force that finally opens its eyes."

It didn't look like fear, to Jewel.

"It is natural to fear what we desire," Corallonne said, as if she could hear what Jewel was too wise to say. "Only when desire is the medium through which we live at all do we welcome it with open arms." Speaking thus, she opened her eyes to look at Calliastra.

"I do not need your pity," Calliastra snapped.

"It is not pity, sister. We are, all of us, trapped in the moment of our birth— and struggle as we might, we cannot overcome our essential nature. But it is always easy to envy those who do not live within the confines of our own personal cages."

Calliastra's laugh was sharp, harsh, discordant. "Envy? You envy me?"

"No. I do not envy the consequences of your existence; I envy the purity of it. And yes, sister, it is a whimsical thought, a whimsical desire. What will you do?"

"I do not require your permission—or your knowledge—to do as I will."

"You are in my lands. With my permission."

Jewel saw Calliastra's eyes shift, saw them lengthen, darken; saw the hint of shadow wings begin to take concrete form as they gained substance. Without thought, she lifted a hand in den-sign, her fingers dancing as she faced the daughter of darkness and desire. She realized her mistake before she'd even finished.

Calliastra frowned as Jewel's hands stilled. The anger had literally hardened the lines of the firstborn face, but Calliastra was all about anger. Anger, pain, loss, and a hope that could not be eradicated, determination notwithstanding. This could go either way—but reaching out to someone who was nothing but pain always could. Jewel had learned that years ago and could not forget it; it was part of who she was.

Angel did not come to stand at Jewel's side; Shianne did. But Angel understood, as instinctively as Jewel herself did. Jewel had made the decision, and the consequences that arose from it were now hers to bear. It had never been wise to get between Duster and Jewel, and no one tried.

Jewel exhaled, lifted her hands, signed again.

Calliastra stared at her hands before lifting her gaze, aiming the obsidian glare more deliberately.

"Adam?" Jewel said aloud because Adam couldn't see the motion of her hands.

He didn't appear to hear her.

Or perhaps he had. She heard the distinctive rustle of leaves—metallic leaves. She heard the shift of birdsong, and in it, heard other songs, some wrapped in words that she couldn't understand. Or that she shouldn't have been able to understand.

"Yes," one of those voices said, and she glanced then at the tree that she had planted—had been allowed to plant—in Corallonne's forest. "They are aware of you, Terafin. Jewel. With Corallonne's permission, you might return to her lands once your Adam has built a path between them."

"Is that what he's doing?"

"That, and more. He will not be safe, soon, if he was ever safe."

"He'll be at home. He'll be in *my* lands."

"And he is yours?"

"Yes."

But the tree's lithe spirit shook his head, and Jewel was inexplicably reminded of the shaking of boughs. "And no, Terafin. The time is coming. He will not be safe. The ancient world will feel this."

"It's not the first time he's done it."

"No. But the Oracle's lands are not these lands. She is a power that none of the kindred understand; what occurred there might have been her bidding, her will. She can make paths between any world, at any time of her choosing, and has oft done so on what appears whim.

"This, however, is different. We did not see this in the boy, and we should have. But we know, now. Even at a distance, I can feel it. He is waking the world by slow degree, and first among those wakened will be yours."

Corallonne took a step back, and the tree spirit joined her, head bowed. His lips moved, and his hands, but Jewel heard wind, breeze, leaves upon leaves like a whisper.

The ground beneath her feet changed; the change was slow and gradual, but it was also unmistakable. The Wild Hunt—all but forgotten—gathered now around Shianne, although she had given no obvious commands. Jewel did not spare them more thought, although she knew she should; they would not be leashed by the commands of a dead king the moment they appeared in her lands.

Or perhaps, she thought, they were unleashed now. She didn't understand the tangle, didn't understand the how of it. She did not want to walk there again; she had had nightmares that were more easily navigated. She had released the cats to the tangle.

But no, she thought, and *knew* it for truth. The cats could traverse the tangle because they didn't care about the solidity of anything but their personal now.

She heard water, looked; in the distance she could see a brook with a very ornate bridge built to cross it. She had not seen it in her wilderness before but did not feel surprised to see it now. The wilderness that she had claimed had never been fully explored—not by the person who styled herself its Lord.

And that would have to change. Was perhaps changing even now.

"Matriarch," Shianne said, using the term she had learned from Adam.

Jewel, however, shook her head and once again turned her attention to Calliastra. Her hands had stilled, but remained half-lifted, as if ready to continue a conversation that was meant, at base, to be private. But she had, of course, never taught Calliastra what those movements meant. They might seem childish; all hidden language implied at base a reason to hide, and that implied a lack of power.

But it implied other things, as well. Duster had never been good with words; words had been a deflection, a way of creating space for herself, of driving people away. Of keeping them at a distance because if they ever got too close, they would be just one more thing to lose. Jewel didn't offer Calliastra words.

She's not Duster.

No. Jewel held out a hand—her left hand—and waited. Although the godchild's eyes did not change shape, her wings folded. She reached out with hands that were almost skeletal in shape, and cold—so cold. Her nails were long, sharp, reminiscent of claws or talons. Where they grazed Jewel's wrist, they cut cloth and broke skin. She felt it; it stung. It stung, she thought, the same way touching Andrei's invisible tendril had.

She wondered if everything in the old world revolved around blood. But she did not withdraw her hand. She wasn't certain if Calliastra meant to cut her; wasn't certain—and didn't care. Adam was here. If the darknessborn godchild cut through her wrist and severed her hand, he could fix it.

It had never been smart to show Duster fear.

It had never been smart to keep her, either.

And yet, stupid or no, Duster had saved what remained of the den. Were it not for Duster, none of them would have survived the demons that had come for their lives in the twenty-fifth holding.

To Corallonne, without looking at her, Jewel said, "We're taking your sister with us."

"So I see. Sister?"

Calliastra didn't spare her sister either glance or word. She stood, hand in Jewel's, blood on her nails. But even as she did, those nails receded; her eyes lost the almost crystalline darkness that characterized her rage. Her wings folded, and folded again, until they had vanished. What was left?

A very beautiful, very sensual young woman. Hair of ebony, eyes a strange color that Jewel couldn't quite describe, their undersides bruised. Her lips were red, her skin the color of death.

"Adam," Jewel said again, although she did not take her eyes off Calliastra. She understood—as she had understood with Duster—that inasmuch as Calliastra could willingly show vulnerability, this was it. And Duster had been at her most volatile, her most dangerous, when she had taken that risk.

"Matriarch," Adam said, in response.

"Take us home."

"Do we have to come back?"

"No."

"But the cats—"

"No, Adam. They found us the first time. They'll find us again."

Chapter Twenty-One

THERE WAS A MOMENT of dislocation, a moment in which Jewel was no longer certain where she was. She could see the Wild Hunt; she could see the silvered leaves of ancient trees; she could hear the gentle voice of breeze, could feel the deep slumber of earth beneath her feet. To her side, she could see darkness, desire, the commingling of impulses that lead to death; she could feel them touch her face, feathered, cold wings. For one long moment, everything about the world was winter, the ice invisible, the cold inevitable.

She turned toward Angel; he was frozen, fixed in time, his hands half-lifted, as if he meant to sign. She reached out to touch him, lowered her hand, examined his slender face. The peak of Rendish hair would never, she thought, return, and she missed it. She was surprised at how much it had visually defined him.

And even thinking it, she could see the ghost of its presence hovering in place above his familiar face, could almost see his hair rise of its own accord. He had not shifted position, not even in the subtle movement of chest that spoke of breathing. She wanted to take a step, either toward or away, but Adam was in front of her, head bent, eyes closed, hands pressed into the earth. Corallonne had said that the wilderness would hear him, would know him, by what he was now doing.

And she had let him. More: she had commanded.

She wanted to bend, to wrench his hands up, to break whatever he was building. She wanted to do it herself, instead. And she knew, she *knew,* she could not. But the wind's voice was growing, and she recognized, in its cadence, the harbinger of storm. She had brought it. She had brought it *here.*

As she watched Adam, she realized that he, unlike Angel—or Terrick, or even Avandar—was breathing. He did not move his hands, but she could see when they trembled, could see when they stilled. She turned, then, although she did not leave his side, to see that the Wild Hunt, all, were as motionless as Angel. To a man they looked like Celleriant to her eye: cold, judgmental, deadly; there was no joy in them.

Shianne, too, was caught in the momentum of spell—Jewel had no other word to describe it—as still, as frozen, as Angel.

She turned, last, to Calliastra, and froze again. But she was more prepared this time.

Calliastra was not a single woman. She was like—very like—the gods in the Between, but more limited in scope. In the face of a god, if one chose to look for long, expressions were carried by a limitless, unending shift of faces, some old, some young, some male, some female; nothing remained unchanging for long. When gods spoke, or rather, when mortals could hear them, they spoke in a chorus of all possible faces, all possible voices.

Calliastra, as still as Angel, could not speak. But silent, those multiple presences still overlapped, shifting and changing as Jewel watched. Shifting, changing, and yet, somehow each static as it came to the surface and retreated, like a tide.

Daughter of darkness, Jewel thought, as the god-born child's eyes narrowed, enlarged, became, for a moment, all of night and shadow, with none of its peace or tranquility.

What would it be like, to love and know for certain that love—any love given, any love accepted—was a death sentence? What did that leave? Hatred?

Yes, Jewel thought. Hatred—but mostly, and always, of oneself. If Jewel were Calliastra, she would eschew company, friends, family. Any family but the Lord of the Hells, the only being she would be certain she could not destroy. And there was no love to be found there.

But no, she thought. Calliastra needed to feed. The hunger that drove her was nothing like the hunger that had driven Jewel or her den-kin in the leanest of years, but the inability to eat would have the same results: she would starve. She would die.

Caught between these imperatives, where could she go? What could she do? What were the limits of sustenance for a child of gods?

If Jewel were Calliastra, the isolation alone would have driven her, broken her. The long, empty afternoons of a childhood in Rath's apartment had been so difficult. She had wanted, needed, family. She had built that. It meant as much to her as family had meant to her Oma.

She's not you.

No. But some part of Calliastra was that bruised, terrified, self-loathing child Jewel had glimpsed briefly in the tangle. And had *that* child been able to love, to be loved, in any safety, this godchild would not exist. What she needed was a different form of sustenance. What she needed was the ability to interact with the living, the mortal, without destroying them.

I'll accept what you are, Jewel thought. *But I'll judge what you do. And what you do in* this *house has to be different.*

And she thought—of course she thought—of Duster. Duster, who had been broken and had survived, as so many of the broken do. Duster, who wanted what Calliastra wanted, and who was also certain she deserved none of it.

Sometimes, her Oma said, *we get what we don't deserve.*

And that cut both ways. Always had.

She reached out for Calliastra. She touched her cheek with the dry palm of her hand. She said, "Your father is not welcome here. He will *never* be welcome here. But you are *not* your father. You are not your mother. The forces that drive you are stronger than the forces that drive me because they are so absolute, and so eternal—but you are not simply the one or the other."

Calliastra did not, could not, respond.

"What you've done in the past doesn't matter to me. What you do in the future will. You don't have to stay. I'm not building a prison. I'm building a home." She exhaled; her breath, as it left her lips, felt warm. "No one in my home is perfect because no one is capable of perfection. Not me, not any of my den. Will it be harder for you? Yes. Yes, absolutely. But they'll accept you. They'll trust you."

She brought her other hand to the still, cold cheek. "Will you stay?"

Calliastra blinked. Shifting faces stilled, hardened, forming a single image—a single, familiar image. Her eyes were obsidian, and the shadow of great wings rose. Jewel was certain that she meant to pull away, but she did not tighten her grip; she was aware that she should never have touched her at all.

The shadows pooling in those eyes grew; the wings developed color, texture. Calliastra was angry.

But even thinking it, Jewel knew this was not precisely right. It wasn't Calliastra.

She said, voice soft and far, far colder than she intended, "You are *not welcome here.*" And even as she spoke, the darkness receded, as if suddenly confronted with harsh light.

Calliastra's face did not change; this appearance was the one she had chosen, the one with which Jewel was most familiar. It wasn't Duster's face. It wasn't the face of a young woman, broken on the shoals of her coming of age. It was the face of someone who had seen life and understood how very bitter life could be.

And it was that woman who said, "I will stay." She met and held Jewel's gaze as if waiting.

Jewel didn't know for what. But no, even as she thought that, she knew she was wrong. Calliastra was waiting for oaths, for oathbinding. For an act of blood or an act of divinity that would take all choice except this one out of her hands. It was not something that Jewel could do. Or, perhaps, in this strange half-world created by the dint of Adam's power and Adam's will, it was something she simply didn't want to do.

"I don't understand you," Calliastra said, when Jewel failed to offer—or demand—what she expected.

Jewel said, "We all build home in our own way. Even were I a god, I could not demand what gods demand. It would change the nature of home; it would break everything I've tried to build." And that, too, was true. "But here," she continued, words falling out of her mouth before she could choose them carefully, "you will not feed. You won't go hungry. You might hate it here—gods know Celleriant does."

"My hunger—"

"Not here," Jewel said again. "It is not welcome here. You are. Do you understand? The hunger is not *all* of you. When you are in my home, it will not destroy you."

"You do not understand. My father once again walks the world. He is not distant. I feel his power. I *am* some part of it. What he was, he gave to me."

Jewel nodded.

"Mortals are not so bound. You cannot understand—"

"I understand," Jewel said, cutting her off because she was heading down a path that was much, much harder to follow, "that the Arianni were created as echoes of, shadows of, Ariane. And I also understand that there are three sleeping Princes beneath my home. They didn't do what they knew she wanted. They didn't do what she herself would have done.

"Is it harder for you? Yes. Yes, it bloody well is. I can't offhand think of a harder life, a more terrifying existence. But it's all you've got. When you're with me, when you're in my lands, the hunger will not destroy you."

"Am I to starve, then?"

It was a good question. A fair question.

Jewel felt the edge of an answer take shape; it was visceral. It cut. "No." And she offered Calliastra her hand, red with drying blood, and sticky with it. "But if it is my decision to shelter you, the consequences are likewise mine. I will feed you. I will sustain you."

Jewel. Avandar's voice. And cutting into the two syllables, the voice of the Winter King. They had returned.

And Jewel said, *We need her.*

The Winter King understood the value of, the power of, the firstborn. It was Avandar who said, *We, Jewel? She is* not *what you once lost. She is, inevitably, death. Understand what she is. See her clearly, if you hope to survive her.*

He understood that no argument would sway her. And he understood, as the Winter King did not, that it was not simply about power.

The difference, Jewel, is that I have observed you for most of your adult life. And I have observed the Sen. I believe that you can, now, survive the decision you have made because the wilderness is—finally—waking. It shakes itself free of the shackles imposed by the gods in concert, the gods who abandoned the world.

I'm not a god.

No? Tell me where you are.

She looked down at Adam's bent and slightly trembling back. She frowned. In the palms of her hands she could feel the cool skin of the godchild. But Calliastra stood, some distance away, surrounded by the Arianni who considered her the greatest threat to their well-being.

She lifted her head to meet her domicis' eyes. "Home," she whispered.

Almost, yes. There is no other place you could do what you have just done. Can you not see her, Jewel? Can you not see your hand in her features?

But Jewel looked at Calliastra and saw many things. Too many. She had created none of them, had saved none of them, had killed none of them.

"Home."

4th day of Lattan, 428 A.A.
Merchant Authority

Finch was at her desk in the Merchant Authority when the ledger to her left flew open on its own. There were windows, of course, but they did not open to the streets—or the sky. There were only two ways this book could open. She glanced at it, frowning, and set aside the draft of a contract on which she'd been working.

Tea was cooling in the cup to her right, and food sat untouched. She glanced at it with some guilt; if she didn't eat, Lucille worried. Lucille, at the moment, did nothing *but* worry. As she could not rationally argue against worry or fear, Finch did what she could to soothe the worries within her grasp—but Lucille was not truly worried for Finch.

No, she was worried for Jarven. And worried about him. Both existed in balance, and always had. It was, to some, odd that a person could both love and fear the same man, but it felt almost natural to Finch; she'd lived with Duster, after all. Duster would stop any other gang from murdering members of her den, but she was always a hair's breadth away from stabbing them herself in her frequent bouts of rage.

Jarven did not rage.

He did not seem to give in to anger; she had seen him angry only a handful of times and was never completely certain that the anger was genuine. Emotions and states were just one part of his perpetual disguise; he adopted them where it suited his purpose and shed them where it did not.

She reached for the ledger, drew it closer, and after pursing her lips, set it atop the contracts she had been reading. Jarven would have chuckled; if there was an actual threat, she instinctively attempted to protect hours and weeks of work.

Lucille would have shouted at her. The thought drew a smile from some hidden well—and it had to be so well hidden it was not immediately obvious even to its owner; very little made Finch smile these days.

She lifted her cup, as if drinking, focused her gaze on the page—the two pages—that had been revealed, and set the cup down.

Jarven had acquired these books. He had claimed they had come with the office, but Finch did not believe him. Could not, in fact, imagine that someone could be as bloody-mindedly thorough as Jarven when it came to matters of security. Some of his odd protections would never have occurred to Finch—and Finch had seen ancient, wild magics. She had seen a living god.

She had not seen Jarven for almost a week.

She knew—through Terafin channels—that Hectore of Araven had also been "convalescing" within his impressive estate; Birgide had made clear that convalescing was a euphemism. The Kings were concerned by the absence of both men. Lucille was not yet frantic; apparently, in a distant youth, Jarven had frequently disappeared for weeks at a time—and always, in the end, to the detriment of his enemies.

Finch believed it, but she did not believe it of Hectore.

There was a knock at the door. Finch said carefully, "I am occupied, Lucille. A matter of pressing importance has come to my attention." Her words were taken by the weft of the room's magic; Lucille would hear them. No one else, in theory, would. She had tested some of the magics laid across the whole of this room, but not all of them.

The door did not open. Lucille did not reply. Finch wondered absently if she were even now walking past her desk to the doors the Chosen guarded. She would not have been completely surprised had Jarven materialized in the room, to one side of his desk. He did not.

A familiar figure did. A small, golden fox. He glanced around the room as Finch rose instantly from her chair and made her way to him. Sunlight gleamed off his fur and silvered his whiskers. She knelt immediately although she did not attempt to touch him or to offer him any aid that he did not demand.

He nodded with august approval. "Finch."

She made no mention of the book, no mention of defense. She wasn't entirely certain that the spell was a defense. Clearly, it was meant to indicate the appearance of something unnatural, but she highly doubted it was meant to reveal demons. Or perhaps it was, but in that case there was more involved.

"If you are looking for Jarven," she began.

His whiskers twitched. He looked pointedly at her lap, and she immediately held her arms out. He was an almost negligible weight as he leaped into them; she had held small cats that were heavier. And she knew this could change on a whim. "I am not looking for Jarven."

"Apologies, Eldest. My service to The Terafin does not include the wilderness or your forest; I do not completely understand what you seek."

He snorted, and warm breath touched her cheek as she rose, still holding the gold-furred creature in her arms. "Even were your service to include that wilderness, you would not. You are mortal. To turn the whole of your life to such an understanding would avail you little, in the end. You simply do not have long enough. I have come," he added, "for you."

"I have duties here—"

"Yes, yes," he replied, with some irritation. He grew heavier, as if weight were punctuation. "But you are wanted now."

"Now?"

"Now."

"And have you orders?"

"Orders? No." Again, whiskers twitched. "Can you not hear the forest, Finch? Can you not sense it?"

She looked around the walls—four walls —of her shared office. "No, Eldest. I am not of the forest. I cannot sense it at all. Perhaps you want the Warden?"

"If I wanted the Warden, I would be with the Warden. Tell me, are all mortals so stupid?"

Finch had been called worse in her life, with the same degree of accuracy. "Almost all of us, yes."

At this, the fox chuckled. "I can see his hand in your responses, you know. Jewel wouldn't like that."

"She doesn't like it much, no. But she doesn't trust Jarven."

"Because she is not, at base, stupid. But oddly, Finch, I don't think you trust him, either."

"I trust him to be Jarven," she replied.

"Yes, yes. You are wanted. You must come."

"What has happened?" She shifted the fox's weight carefully enough that she could touch the door. Lucille was there before the door was fully opened, and yes: so were the Chosen. Torvan and Marave. They all blinked as they saw Finch, unharmed. Their eyes fell in unison to the fox in her arms.

They could see him now. They could see the fox clearly.

"I'm sorry," she said to Lucille. "I did have a very important visitor."

"Is that a fox?"

"It is *the* fox," Finch replied, just a touch of warning in her voice. "And he has come with word. I am, apparently, wanted at the Terafin manse."

Torvan stiffened. Marave said nothing. Lucille turned toward the outer office as if they were no longer present. Finch was safe, and her visitor was a small golden animal. The former was of great concern to Lucille, and the latter was none of her business, in her own determined estimation. "We have received no word from the right-kin," Torvan said.

"No. I imagine that someone has carried word to Teller, though."

"The Warden," the fox agreed.

Lucille stiffened and paused, but Torvan and Marave might have spent their casual, waking hours in the company of talking animals for all the reaction they offered. Torvan, however, had seen this fox before. Neither demanded an explanation from either Finch or the fox.

Lucille, however, folded her arms, all but planting herself in the doorway through which Finch would have to walk. Finch's arms formed a cradle for the fox, or they would have tightened—but she would have let them do so at her sides, where the tension would not be immediately obvious to observers.

As if he could understand the vein of her worry, the fox said, "I will not harm her. Jewel likes her and considers her necessary. And Jarven is fond of her."

This did nothing to still Finch's worry, and the fox knew it. The corners of his wide, round eyes shifted. "Yes," he said, to the unspoken fear. "Everything that can be used should be preserved against possible future need." To Lucille, however, he said, "The Terafin has returned."

*   *   *

Nothing would have been guaranteed to get Finch out of the Merchant Authority office as quickly, but she remained silent until they were in the crowded city streets. Since she was not leaving at the arranged time, there was no carriage, and while a message could be sent—quickly—to the manse to arrange one, Finch was not of a mind to do so.

"If you will leave your guards behind," the fox said, "we can travel by foot much more quickly."

"No, thank you. The Terafin will know where I am; she will know how much time it will take to disentangle myself and arrive." The fox nodded, as if he had expected no better. Finch, who learned early to appreciate the condescension that made her invisible to Jarven's many rivals, was not upset. "Do you know where Jarven is?"

"Yes." He lifted his head.

"Is he with The Terafin?"

"Not quite yet, no. He is a reckless young man."

Jarven was not young by any stretch of the imagination, but reckless was, if harsh, accurate.

"Do you understand why I wished to own him?"

"No. The immortals I've met—and I have not had The Terafin's experience—don't think like the rest of us do. If you were mortal, the word would not be 'own.' It might be 'employ' or 'hire.' Ownership implies a distinct lack of choice; among mortals it would be called slavery."

"Ah. Tell me, little mortal, does The Terafin not own you?"

"No."

"Yet all around you, invisible to eyes as weak as yours, is a wall that all but screams *mine* to the wilderness. Do you not just argue semantics?"

"No. Ah, yes, sometimes I do—but that is often a matter of entertainment or education. I am hers because I am family to her. She is mine because she is family to me. The use of the word *mine* doesn't mean ownership. It doesn't really mean control."

"Yet you obey her."

"She is seer-born," Finch countered. "When you say you want to own Jarven, what you want is not what The Terafin wants from us."

"You are not Jarven's equal."

"No. But I have never attempted to be that. He is Jarven. I am Finch. I can do things he can't do." Not that she felt that confidence on most days. But she felt it now, debating words with a talking fox. "No, that's unfair. What I do, he *could* do. He is unwilling to do it; there is no reward in it for him. No challenge. He is aware that the things that need doing are necessary even if he is unwilling to see to them. It's one of the reasons he's fond of Lucille."

"And yourself?"

"I couldn't be Lucille. In a different life, The Terafin could. When it comes to the Authority offices, Lucille is fearless. She defends them from all attacks, subtle or otherwise; she doesn't care whether the attacks are from internal sources or external. If you're not part of her office, you are an outsider." She smiled. "And yes, I'm fond of Lucille. But The Terafin could have been Lucille. She has the temper and the rest of the instincts. Instead, she's . . ."

"Finch, it is seldom I offer mortals advice; they are not of a mind to take it when it is good because they find it unpalatable."

"I wouldn't offer Jarven advice if I were you."

"Oh? Even if he requests it?"

She smiled. "Even then. But I suppose you could offer the advice that best aligned with your future interests."

"Yes. However, although I seldom offer advice, I am inclined just this once to do so."

"And that?"

"Your Sen will not be your Terafin for much longer, in anything but name."

Torvan stiffened. He didn't stop, didn't turn back, didn't break stride. But he was listening.

"She will be Terafin—"

"I express myself badly. And no, not deliberately at this time. We did not oft keep mortals; your kind was far too delicate to survive even a passing ill temper. We have, therefore, never learned to communicate well with you. Yes, she will be The Terafin. She will be Sen. She will reside in the dwelling she has claimed. All of this will be true—if she survives.

"She hopes, even now, to avoid the fate we all see. Do not," he said quietly, "entertain the same hope. You are pragmatic, but quietly so. What she must be if you are to survive is not what she is. Accept it."

"Do you only give advice you know can't be followed?" The question was casual; she was genuinely curious.

"No. You do not understand the wilderness. You do not understand the Sen. I am ancient. I could have chosen, upon waking, to relocate; my roots are deep, Finch. Very deep. But there was, about the voice, something very like the first spring; I found it compelling. And I realized that the person who had taken these wild lands, who had claimed them, was mortal.

"I was curious. And mortals do not last. If the choice was unfortunate, well. It would correct itself in short order."

"There's something I don't understand."

"There are many, many things beyond your comprehension." Her smile deepened; the fox's ears twitched. "You are not like Jarven."

"No, although more like him than like you."

"You are content not to understand, then. Ask your question."

"Why could you not claim these lands, this wilderness?" Feeling the way his entire body tensed, growing heavier in an instant, she added, "If the question offends, accept my apologies. I *am* ignorant."

"I am of the land," the fox eventually said. "I am of it in a way you and your kind will never be."

"But the White Lady—"

"Yes. She is not. Nor are her sleeping, disobedient Princes."

"Could they do what The Terafin has done?"

"No, Finch. Nor could Viandaran, no matter how he gained in power or wisdom. You do not understand what the Sen are . . . or were. But that is perhaps to be expected; they did not understand it themselves." He fell silent for some time, and then said, "The gods created the world—all worlds. They were not, however, rooted. They were not their own creations. The firstborn were like unto gods. They were a thing in and of themselves. But many, many of us were not. We woke in the wake of creation, but *our* creation was not their intent.

"And that is neither here nor there. You are not rooted in the same fashion we are, but you are hers. We take shape, form, wakefulness hearing the echo of her desires. She does not give commands to us as your kings would give them to you, but what she does give is absolute. Not from within will these lands fall, except by the treachery of the rootless.

"You will understand, in time."

It was obvious to Finch that Jay had returned when she entered the Terafin manse. There was an excitement, an eagerness, a stiff formality that suggested something like joy poured into rigid lines, and it permeated the Household Staff. She did not immediately set the fox down and enter the forest; she went, instead, to find Teller.

He was waiting for her in the great room.

She lifted her hand to sign, but stopped, as she had an armful of fox. He smiled and signed in reply. *Yes. Home.* Hesitating, he added, *cats.*

Finch grimaced. She was intimately aware of how much damage the cats caused when they were sulking, having seen the financial cost of replacing what had been destroyed. Before she could ask, the door to the room was flung open, where it slammed into the nearest wall.

Shadow, bristling, wings high, stood across the threshold, glaring at everything with so much malice, Finch was surprised that anything in the wing was still standing. She did not have Teller's affection for cats, and even had she, one as obviously maddened and dangerous as this required caution. Or flight.

The fox said, as Finch stiffened, "Do not put me down."

Finch said, "I'm not sure I could, even if I wanted to. I'd have to be able to move."

The soft sound of a surprised chuckle could be heard over the rumble of Shadow's anger. "You will have to move."

Protestations aside, she did. She moved toward Teller, who had abandoned his chair when Shadow slammed the door open.

"That is far enough," the fox said. "I apologize in advance."

"For what?"

The small fox opened its delicate mouth and roared. Had Finch not already been half frozen, her arms clenched too tightly in the position in which she carried him, she might have dropped him. Teller was not in the right-kin's office; his hands came at once to his ears and remained there while the fox spoke.

And he did speak; she had no doubt of that; Shadow's attention swiveled immediately, and he roared in reply. The hair on the back of Finch's neck was, she was certain, standing on end; the rest of her hair was so firmly fixed in place a gale wouldn't have moved it.

But when Shadow's voice ascended into words, she knelt.

"I told you not to put me down," the fox told her, without apparently looking in her direction.

"Yes, I know," Finch replied. "But you didn't say that for our safety. If Shadow is speaking—and he is—he won't harm us. He might destroy the great room, yes." Which would be enormously politically costly, but would not, in theory, kill them.

"I begin to understand why Jarven chose to teach you," the fox said. He did not sound at all pleased.

"No, you don't. But if you want the truth, he did not choose to teach me. He was ordered to provide employ and place for me."

"He has disobeyed the orders of the powerful before."

"Well, yes, of course he has. But he would have had to have reason, pragmatic reason, for doing so. And it pleased him greatly to annoy Lucille, through me."

Shadow said, "I'm *sssssspeaking.*"

Finch placed the fox on the carpet. To her surprise, he immediately became almost transparent. This was probably for the best; Shadow leaped instantly, landing—heavily—on the spot the fox was no longer completely occupying. And then, as Finch rose and took a step back, he snarled in rage and ran claws through the rug. Teller winced.

"You will *never* bring *him* here *again. Never.*"

"He came to the Merchant Authority and summoned me home. He said Jay's here." It was odd. When speaking to outsiders, she used the title Jay had chosen to carry; she used Jewel when speaking to Haval. Only among the den did she use the name Jay—the name she'd chosen for herself so many years ago.

"Birgide stopped by the office," Teller said.

"But you didn't go to Jay's rooms?"

"She isn't in her rooms. And . . ."

"What?"

"Haval told me to wait for you."

Shadow was still hissing and spitting. Finch would have attempted to stop him, but the rug could not be saved. "Haval?"

"I'm not sure I understand what's happened, but . . ."

She lifted her hands.

Yes, he signed back. *Bad.* Shadow, however, held most of his attention. "The fox is one of the forest elders."

"*Yessssss?*"

"He serves The Terafin."

The great gray cat's eyes widened so completely he seemed to be trying to eject them from the rest of his face. Finch wasn't surprised when he expressed his outrage at Teller's stupidity, but it was impossible to take personally since he used the words so often.

Night peered around the doorframe. "Did you *find* it?"

"Of *course.*"

"Snow says—" The rest of the sentence was lost to the enraged roaring that was only barely identifiable as the aforementioned cat.

Shadow screeched in frustration.

Finch's fingers were flying. So were Teller's. Clearly, Haval understood something neither the right-kin nor the regent did.

"Wait, Shadow—where is Jay?"

"She is by her *tree.* Go to her while *we* do *all* the work."

They did not comply immediately. Teller went to speak with the Master of the Household Staff. Given the noise the cats were making, it would be necessary. The older woman was terrifying enough that fear of disobeying her would be greater—barely—than fear of enraged cats.

She was not surprised when the Chosen changed shifts. Nor was she surprised when they accompanied the regent and the right-kin into the forest. She *was* surprised at how they were armed; the swords with which the household guard were armed had, in some hands, been replaced by different weapons. They were not here as a dress guard. Torvan, in fact, insisted on preceding them on the path that led from the manicured grounds to the forest.

Shadow joined them.

To Finch's alarm, he had a passenger. Ariel, the girl who had lost fingers in the Dominion of Annagar, before she had been rescued—if that was the word for it—by Jay. Both of her hands clutched gray fur; her arms were trembling.

"Shadow, what are you doing?"

The gray cat gave her the side-eye, which was, in some ways, an answer. "It is *your* fault," he sniffed.

She understood then and accepted it as truth. She had done as the fox demanded, and she had done so without consideration of the cost. But the fox was not Shadow, or rather, not wild in the way Shadow was. He was Jarven. He was as much Jarven as the wilderness, ancient, unknown, could be. She bowed her head.

"Why do you *think* he looks like *that*?"

"For the same reason Jarven looks frail and helpless."

Shadow snorted. "He *is*." He muttered imprecations against stupidity. He growled as Ariel lowered herself across his back and hid her face. She had never been comfortable around the Chosen; had never learned to accept their presence. Finch was surprised that she had come with Shadow at all. His wings rose to either side of the child, and this seemed to calm her.

"Do you trust him?"

Finch startled at the new voice, turning in its direction and stumbling slightly as she did. The stranger caught her before she could fall. "The roots here are exposed," he said gently, his lips turned in smile. "And we should know." The smile deepened in the gold-and-brown face. He was a tree.

"Yes, Finch. We are not eldest, but we are not saplings. We slept in the long, cold winter, and Jewel has called us to spring. She has returned. Can you not feel it?"

Finch shook her head. "We're mortal. There are things we can't hear, things we can't feel, things we don't know."

"We do not pity you," he replied. "For there are also things you can see, and things you can hear; you are free to move and move again; you look up to different skies, and you do not sleep when the winter comes. Not permanently. But more than that: you have Sen."

"Why is everyone gathering?"

"She has not returned alone, and there may be . . . difficulty."

Shadow snorted. "There is *already* difficulty. Because she is *stupid*." He wasn't specific about which "she." Then again, it wasn't necessary.

Teller signed, and Finch nodded. She didn't apologize to the gray cat; there was no point. Other trees joined the Chosen, and she saw that they walked in step, although they had the longer limbs, the greater height.

She saw, in fact, that the few who joined the front ranks were *armed*. She stumbled, and the tree that deliberately served as an escort—how had she missed that?—caught her again. His hands were smooth, but not soft; it was like being escorted by a tabletop.

Haval, she thought.

"The elders are canny," the tree said. "They are of the land. There are stories—many stories—about the mortals who attempted, against their very nature, to transcend their limitations. They desired eternity, endless life."

Finch nodded, thinking of Avandar. She did not say his name.

"It is folly, always, to reject what you are."

She nodded again.

"But it is not folly to test the boundaries that define you. And yet, one can lead to the other and often inevitably does. One reaches boundaries by pushing. How, then, is one to accept that a boundary is a boundary? How is one to accept the limitations when it is entirely by struggling against them that one gains power? There are rocks that I can break," he continued. "And rocks that I cannot, alone. But older, wiser trees can do what I cannot."

"He's not a tree."

"No." The man laughed. "He is not a tree. And there is no friendship lost between the great ancients who once woke to the sound of the White Lady's voice and the elder you think of as fox. We are not enemies, while Jewel rules us. It is novel." His smile did not fade, but his eyes changed shape as he added, "and it cannot last.

"Understand, Finch, that you are Jewel's, here. You were hers before she found us, before she woke us, before she claimed us. The ancients, the eldest, have no call upon you; they can kill you, but they cannot compel."

"Most mortals find threats of death very compelling."

"Ah. Yes. But that is simple fear. It is very, very unwise to give in to fear in the wilderness; fear has its own scent, and it is powerful. Fear, and you *will* be hunted." He glanced down at her and smiled. Although his hands, his arms, appeared to be hard, polished wood, there was a warmth and animation in his expression that implied youth, delight, joy.

"Eldest, why did you bring the mortal child?"

Shadow hissed, tearing up ground as he all but stomped down a path Finch couldn't discern, an opening through the trees. Mindful of the tree's comment about fear, Finch gazed with worry at Ariel's bent back.

But the child didn't seem to be frightened or, rather, not more frightened than she usually was. Shadow—winged, fanged, and deadly—did not frighten Ariel as much as people did. She had become accustomed to servants, but even then, did not leave her room if they were working in the wing.

Only around Adam did Ariel seem to be a normal child. And, perhaps, that was fair. In the end, people had caused Finch as much damage as the wild and the ancient. Certainly more damage than Shadow or the rest of the cats.

Shadow was not inclined to answer, and the tree accepted this. Teller signed to Finch; she signed back. Arann was with the Chosen. Jester was not immediately visible. Nor was Birgide; she had requested Teller's presence—respectfully, politely—and returned to the gardens that were, in theory, the reason for her employ.

Finch was not, however, surprised to see Haval when he appeared in the center of the path—a path that naturally widened to accommodate the growing number. He did not wear the apron that was his uniform while he worked within the West Wing, which was warning enough. He did not look martial. Nor did he look mythical, magical. Compared to the supple height and flexibility of the tree spirits, he looked decidedly mundane, an older man with a prominent nose, and slightly tired eyes.

The tired eyes, however, were enough of a warning. Finch adored Haval's wife; she respected Haval. She had never truly feared him, but she felt a small spark of unease settle somewhere within her. Jarven liked Haval. Approved of him. Considered him almost an equal—or perhaps an equal; with Jarven. it was hard to tell.

All these facts coalesced. Haval was a danger. Had always been a danger.

As if he could hear her thoughts, as if the realization were a physical bloom, a visible sign, he tendered her a very proper, very correct bow. "Regent," he said. He did not rise. Would not, until she had given him either permission or command.

"Haval. Rise." She didn't add *please*, but it was close. The trees were watching Haval. They were, therefore, now watching her. Her own escort's attention she had found strangely comforting. This was nothing like that.

Teller signed. Finch did not respond. She knew—had always known—that their secret language was not secret, that it was not private. Haval could read it all. He could use it. That had never seemed like a weakness before this moment.

"He is Councillor, Finch," the tree by her side said softly, as if only just aware that Finch might not know this.

"He is not part of the House Council."

The tree laughed; the sound carried, as if it were the rustle of leaves in strong breeze. "No."

"He is mortal."

"Ah. I understand your confusion. Yes, he is mortal. But so, too, the Sen. He is canny, as mortals oft could be. You live short, short lives—but in them, your minds move so quickly, absorb so much. He is considered wise."

"By the forest?"

"Yes."

But Haval said, "By The Terafin. It was to advise her—advise only—that I joined her staff. She is Terafin, yes. But she has never given in to her fear where I am concerned. Or even where Jarven is concerned, although in that case, she has taken few pains to hide her mistrust." He came to stand by Finch's side, subtly displacing Teller, who stepped back without demur. "It is not yet done," he continued, glancing at the trees who bore actual weapons. His gaze moved to the Chosen. "Every man and woman in this small cadre serves The Terafin.

"Some are bound by oath, simple mortal oath. It confounds the eldest, and even the older trees; they wish an oathbinding. Do you understand what that is?"

Finch did not reply.

Haval nodded, acknowledging the silence for what it was. "It is not—quite—enough."

"Where is Meralonne?" she asked.

He smiled, as if in approval, and she curled her hands into fists by her sides. She knew this trick, had seen it used by Jarven so often. She had learned not to trust that smile. And yet, in some way, she still craved it.

"He will come," Haval said.

"And that's the reason you've armed the forest?"

"Ah, no. You mistake me. It is not Meralonne that we need fear—not yet, although I am told that the time is coming when we will bitterly regret the choices the Sen has made in this regard."

"Haval, what are you doing?"

"I am building," he replied. "It has been many, many years since I have done so. I do not know if I have the tools I require; however, I have always adapted the needs to the implements at hand. I have spent some time in conference with the elders who are rooted here." He frowned. "Your hand is bleeding."

"Yes."

"You are not Jewel. You see more pragmatically than she does. You are, however, like her. Your loyalty cannot be bought, cannot be sold. Every creature in this forest is, at heart, like Duvari."

She blinked.

"And every creature is likewise similar to Jarven."

"Even you?"

He smiled. "Even me, Finch. Duvari will not, I think, be allowed entry into this forest without escort, but he is not necessary; Birgide is Warden. She is The Terafin's law here, in the absence of The Terafin."

"And Councillor?"

It was his turn not to answer. "Come. They will be here soon."

Armed tree spirits—and unarmed—joined them. They looked to Haval, and although he did not speak, they acted on the slightest tilt of his chin. His gaze was alert; she was certain that he, like Jarven, missed nothing. And she wondered, again, where Jarven was.

Jay trusted Haval. Finch trusted him because Jay did. But Jay had always had a rule for den: the past didn't matter. Only the present and what you intended to build going forward.

And that was folly of a different kind, she thought. It was a luxury that they had had because the den itself was composed of the poor, the under-aged, the under-educated: people who *had no power.*

Now? Jay was Terafin. If there was a more powerful House in the whole of the Empire, Finch didn't know about it—and it was her business to know these things. Decisions made by The Terafin could move armies. People would live or die by her mistakes.

Haval, she thought. Haval Arwood. She needed to know who he had once been, and what he had once done. She might never share it with Jay, but the information was necessary.

He glanced at her, and she lifted a hand before he could speak in his mild, neutral voice. "Do not tell me that I am wasted where I am."

"Ah. No, Finch, I do not believe you are, although perhaps I have said as much in the past. Where you were? Yes. Where you were was not a match for what you are. But where you *are?* You are not, and will not be, wasted. Jarven will miss you," he added.

She frowned. "I have no intention of leaving the Merchant Authority."

"No, you do not. And I pray—inasmuch as a man of my temperament does—that you have the option of remaining there. But you are now regent, and it is not only the Terafin merchants that are your concern. This forest— those trees—are wed to and rooted in Terafin itself. While you are regent, they are also your concern, your domain.

"She will confirm you in your position."

"The House Council has, at Haerrad's insistence, already done so."

"Do not imagine, in the end, that it is the House Council whose decision now matters."

"The House Council *does* matter."

His smile was benign . . . and surprisingly annoying.

"What The Terafin has built, what The Terafin before her built, she values. The wilderness has not stained or lessened that value. It is of import *to her*. If what you say or imply is true, it will remain so. And I can oversee it. I intend to preserve it."

He inclined his head. "You are Jarven's student. I speak perhaps too freely. You will see, in the end, what is in front of you."

She exhaled sharply. "Where is Jarven?"

"In the wilderness," Haval replied. She realized that she had not expected an answer only when she was surprised at receiving one. "I believe he will return soon."

She bowed her head for several beats. "Haval."

"Regent."

"What will Jarven be, to you? What will he be to Terafin?"

"Jarven."

"You don't like him."

"No, if we're being honest—and if you are Jarven's, you will understand that no man of power is ever completely honest—I do not. He has always been frivolous, egotistical, competitive. What has saved him, time and again, is ferocious competence. Nothing he does can whittle away that particular truth." The frown deepened. "I will not say he has not tried."

"Then *why* Jarven?"

"Ah. I did not choose him, Finch. He was chosen—and possibly chosen for the selfsame reasons he held the position he did when we first met. But there is a use to restless, caged energy when it is coupled with the aforementioned competence." He nodded, once again, at trees. Trees who bore spears that seemed to catch sunlight and contain it. They swept him magnificent bows—bows such as bark and trunk would never have allowed had they still been sleeping within them.

"You do not serve me," he continued. "Nor should you, ever. The trees do not serve me."

"They follow your orders."

"No, Finch. They follow my advice. They understand that The Terafin values it highly, even when it causes her pain. In all ways, their view of me is informed by Jewel." He gestured once, watching now. "The elders have explained, inasmuch as they can, what we will face in the very near future.

"There is some hope that we might save a large portion of the city—but without Jewel, the hope is scant in my opinion."

"And Jarven?"

"He is the wild card. Ah." He lifted his head. "She has returned."

Shadow, silent until that point, hissed. Finch glanced at him; to her surprise, Ariel had caught one of his ears in her hand—the hand that had lost fingers on the night she had lost her family. She did not speak of it, ever, but Jay had.

Without thought, she said, in Torra, "It hurts his ears when you do that." Her voice was mild.

Ariel's forehead creased at this obviously new to her information. She bent forward and whispered something into the ear that she still grasped.

Shadow said, "Yesssssssss."

The girl let go. Still frowning, she looked at Finch, and then away. It was the most rebellion Finch had ever seen Ariel show.

The sound of rustling leaves stilled suddenly, as if the entirety of the forest were holding its collective breath.

The stillness was broken by the sound of a very familiar voice, speaking very familiar Torra. Jay was swearing.

Finch forgot herself. Teller, beside her, did the same. The strangeness of pastoral tree spirits bearing weapons of war fell away. The moment Jay's voice could be heard, the forest was home. As much home as the manse. As much home as the dingy apartment in the twenty-fifth holding, or the shared space in the thirty-fifth had been. Finch lifted skirts to run in the direction of that voice, and Teller joined her.

She wasn't surprised to see that Jester was already ahead of them; nor was she surprised to note that Haval remained where he was. The Chosen surged forward, but they had an excuse. They were there as escort to the right-kin and the regent, after all.

But they were there because they were Jay's.

The trees understood this urgency, this inexplicable relief, this strangely sharp joy; they parted.

Adam knelt, his hands pressed flat into the ground; Jay stood over him, inches from his bent back, her expression forbidding. Adam was hers. Angel stood to one side of Jay, and the grim Northerner to the other. There were others, but that didn't matter.

Jarven would be angry, she knew. There was no excuse—there was *never* an excuse—to be anything less than precisely, instantly observant. But here, for just this moment, nothing would—or could—harm them.

Jay looked up, eyes widening, lips turning up at the corners; the first thing she saw, or seemed to see, were her den-kin, rushing toward her, arms out. They met in a tangle that almost knocked her over and did unbalance poor Adam, who ended up at the bottom of the sprawl. Finch was in full Merchant Authority clothing, Teller dressed to entertain dignitaries of note—and it didn't matter.

The captains of the Chosen kept the distance they had always kept; they saw nothing out of the ordinary. Even Jester chose to join them, at a remove. He had never been one for displays of obvious affection and probably never would be. But he joined Angel and lifted his hands in sign.

Angel signed back. Finch caught the dance of fingers forming a single word, a single name.

Carver.

She might have said more—would have said more—but the clearing had not yet finished filling. If Jay and Adam were back, if Terrick and Angel stood to either side of Jay, if Kallandras and Celleriant and Avandar, grim and unusually distant, stood a half circle back, they were not the only ones.

The pregnant woman who had stood only briefly in the forest during the night of the assassination attempt—on Finch, this time—was with them, which did not surprise Finch.

But the small army that materialized slowly at Jay's back did. She thought, at first glance, that they were somehow echoes of Celleriant—but their style of armor was different, and something about them spoke of the very heart of Winter. She felt her arms go slack as she recovered the composure she never lost in the office.

Teller, less reserved, was slower to disengage, and even when he did, his hands were dancing.

Shadow *roared*, and Jay's eyes widened. The great, gray cat padded toward her, foundling on his back, and then took a swipe at Jay's thigh. He was irritated. She laughed, mostly because he hadn't actually hit her hard enough to knock her over and reached out to catch his face in both of her hands.

He told her she was stupid, repeatedly. But even that was a comfort because it was so normal.

The men, however, were not.

And the woman who seemed to stand at their heart wasn't either. Finch met her gaze and froze, her lips half open. There was a story here, and she was suddenly afraid to hear it, to be part of it. But fear was not her master, not her lord. If she had one, it was Jay.

Jay noted the direction of her gaze and nodded. "We're back."

"Have you . . ."

"Finished what I left to do?"

Finch nodded.

Jay's chuckle was brief, brittle. "No. Not yet. But it appears I'm to be allowed to do some of it from home. I'm starving," she added. "Can we talk about this over dinner?" She bent and offered Adam a hand, helping him to his feet. He brushed dried leaves and dirt from his pants, stood, and then smiled—at Ariel and Shadow. Jay gave him a tiny, almost invisible shove, and he joined the two: the gray cat who didn't like him, and the child who only felt at home when he was present.

Ariel lifted her face and chattered in quiet, half audible Torra. He asked her if she had been eating. Finch let the rest fade as she turned once again to The Terafin.

Jewel felt home in the arms of her den-kin.

She felt home in the soles of her feet although her feet, booted, were not in contact with the actual soil of her forest. She felt warm, not hot; breeze moved the wretched tangle of her hair. Dressed as she had once dressed for caravan roads, she did not look, did not feel, Terafin.

She glanced, involuntarily, at her hands. She wore the ring Gilafas had made in a dream that was not a dream. She did not wear the Terafin signet. "I left it with the Oracle," she said before Finch could ask. Finch, as regent, had the right.

She didn't seem to care.

Jewel turned; Terrick was waiting for her command. So, too, Avandar. The den existed as part of her, but Calliastra was waiting as well.

"You look exhausted," Finch said, the concern in her voice muted but clear.

Jewel nodded.

"Food?"

"We'll eat here, for tonight." Calliastra was here. And Jewel could not leave her in the West Wing now because she was not there. Not yet, and maybe not ever. "I'm too tired to change and look respectable for the rest of the House."

Finch hesitated and then nodded.

"Tell me everything else that's happened in the morning."

Chapter Twenty-Two

5th day of Lattan, 428 A.A.
Terafin Manse, Averalaan Aramarelas

T HEY ATE BREAKFAST IN the West Wing.

Jay, dressed and bound in the fetters of clothing she almost detested, was nonetheless in better humor. She did not look markedly better rested. While the whole of the manse knew she had returned, she had made no official announcement; she did not wish to speak with the House Council or its many Councillors, with one exception. That exception, however, did not appear to be in the manse.

She was happy to see the Chosen; she was happy to see Haval. Haval was relaxed enough that he agreed to join the den for breakfast, which, if not a first, was rare. He seemed genuinely pleased to see her.

Finch wondered if he was. She was very surprised when Jay demanded, point-blank, "Has Jarven returned?"

Haval, however, might have been expecting the question. He said, "I expect him shortly. But Jarven—"

"Yes, I know. He does what he damn well pleases."

"That's not entirely fair," Finch began. Jewel's den-sign was abrupt to the point of rudeness, and one didn't need to know den-sign to understand it. In spite of herself, Finch smiled. Jester, however, laughed out loud.

He had been the last to join them, hanging back on the inside edge of their circle—just enough that he was definitely part of them but not so close that he could be surrounded or overwhelmed. He had dark circles under both eyes which implied a serious lack of sleep or a serious abundance of alcohol. Knowing Jester, it might be both, but might just as easily be neither.

She signed only one word to him: *wait.*

He nodded.

It had taken them some time to clear the forest, to find the manse proper; by the time they had, they had lost most of their gathering to the subtle barrier of the *Ellariannatte.* The men who looked like Celleriant chose to remain in that forest. The woman who looked like Celleriant—but obviously pregnant—chose to do the same. Adam didn't approve, but he was clearly intimidated enough that he voiced only a minor protest.

Kallandras bowed to Jay. He spoke, but Finch couldn't quite catch the words; Jay nodded. She then turned to Celleriant, a question in her eyes. Celleriant looked at his kinsmen, and Finch thought she would remember the momentarily desolate expression that crossed his perfect features for the rest of her life—no matter how long that life might be. But he did not speak—not to them, not to Jay.

It was Kallandras who drew him aside, Kallandras who led him away. It surprised her, but why should it? Kallandras was a Master Bard, and he was rumored to be indestructible. No mission upon which he was sent, no battlefield upon which he related perfect orders at the distant command of Kings, no political situation which might end with small armies and butchery, had ever managed to kill him.

And Celleriant prized power, prized the powerful.

She shook herself, waiting, as they were all waiting: Jay's mortal kin.

Jay listened with ferocious interest when Teller brought up the question of the regency. Her hands were dancing, her expression alive, when he said that Haerrad had, as agreed, supported Finch as regent in Jay's absence. She asked, pointedly, if there had been further assassination attempts.

Finch replied, as mildly as possible, that if there had been, they had been both unsuccessful and so subtle they had entirely escaped her notice. She added, before Jay could speak—and her mouth was open—that in Jarven's considered opinion, there had been none.

Huval backed her up.

Gossip, such as it was, was exchanged, but no one asked her where her journey had taken her or what she had discovered.

Calliastra was introduced to the den. Calliastra reminded Finch of Kiriel, for no reason that she could put her finger on. But she knew, having known Jay for over half her life, who Calliastra reminded Jay of.

She seemed almost hesitant to sit, but room was made; Adam chose the chair closest to her. Her brief glance at his exhausted but open expression was filled with suspicion: did Adam pity her? Did he *dare* to pity her? And that, Finch thought, was an echo of older, sparer meals. But Adam was practically falling into his soup in exhaustion. Jay demanded that he eat, and he obeyed, but even eating, he seemed to be going through motions that only barely made sense.

Finch was happy when Snow and Night joined Shadow in the dining room. She was less happy when she realized they were very angry—at each other—because the dining set had only just recently been replaced, and the entire West Wing would be in considerable disgrace should a new replacement be immediately necessary.

But she was flat out surprised—and not inclined to hide it—when Jewel told Shadow to go with Adam. "Make sure he gets safely to his room," she said. "I think Ariel is already there. With his permission," she added.

Jay looked refreshed and well rested in comparison to Adam, which said more about Adam than Jay. He had slept, but the sleep had clearly not been enough.

Shadow hissed. "Why *me*?"

"You know why. But if your brothers can stop hissing and spitting at each other, and you can talk them into doing *at least* as good a job as you could do—"

"They could *never* do that!"

Finch winced. Teller winced. Jester rolled his eyes.

Calliastra shook her head, her own eyes wide with wonder—and disgust. "You *do* let them run wild. Even in the heart of your own manse."

All three cats gave her the side-eye.

Finch had to admire her courage. It did, however, resolve the argument between the white and black cats. Calliastra did not seem concerned with the cats at all.

Jay, however, said, "Shadow."

"But I don't *like* him."

"Yes, but he seems to like you, regardless. I want him *safe*. If you can't do it, I'll have to ask Meralonne."

This caused an entirely different ruckus, but in the end, when Adam had stopped his forehead from hitting the table for the third time, Shadow knocked him off his chair and headbutted him toward the door nearest his room.

"Do bruises count?" the cat demanded.

Jay didn't answer, but it was pretty clear Shadow didn't expect one.

"I do not understand what you see in those creatures. You *have* the eldest who are rooted in the lands you have claimed, and I assure you they would be vastly more respectful, vastly less fractious, vastly more obedient."

Finch glanced at her hand; the cut had closed. "I'm not so certain about that," she said softly.

The West Wing was not small; a room was made ready for Calliastra's use. To Finch's surprise, Jay shook her head. "I want her with me," she said. There was no suspicion, no implication of distrust, in the words—and had there been, Calliastra would have ferreted them out.

"Jay—"

"I need Shadow with Adam. And I need—"

When Avandar cleared his throat everyone turned toward him. Everyone but Jay.

Finch signed; Jay caught the motion of hands and looked up. She lifted her hands, but lowered them again, as if their weight was too much for her. "I don't know."

Watching her, Finch knew she was afraid. It wasn't an immediate, visceral fear; it wasn't the sight, with its attendant certainty. The shadows beneath her eyes seemed longer, darker; it took them time to bleed into the rest of her pallor.

"I have the House," Finch said. "I promise. I have it, I'll hold it against all comers until—until you're home again." As she said it, she knew that Jay wasn't truly home. Jay's smile was wan, wrong, but there was gratitude in it. She pushed herself up from her chair. Avandar stayed where he was. So did Haval.

It was Teller who rose, Teller who came to her side; not even Angel moved.

"I did something," Jay said, voice so soft it was almost inaudible. "I did something I think I shouldn't have done."

No one asked.

"Carver's alive."

"Jay," Teller said. "Stay here. Stay with us."

Haval cleared his throat, and Jay met his hooded gaze. "I do not believe that is wise."

"None of this is wise," Jay said. "*None* of it."

His expression softened. His eyes, however, did not.

Frowning, Finch turned toward the far doors; they had not opened. But she recognized the voice that seemed to come from them. "Wisdom, in my opinion, is often too highly prized." And Jarven ATerafin materialized, his back to those closed doors.

Finch rose at once, as if she were Lucille, and walked briskly across both carpet and hardwood to reach the Terafin merchant's side. He was bleeding; his jacket and shirt were rent, the wounds beneath them running in three parallel lines that implied claws.

He looked down his nose at her, eyes as cold, as hard, as Haval Arwood's. As she had done with Haval, she ignored them.

"Finch, please."

She ignored that as well.

The temperature in the room seemed to plummet as if warmth had been dropped off a very high cliff. Without meeting his eyes, she examined the jacket, the blood, the edge of wounds that were only slightly sticky.

"Come, Jarven," Haval said. "If you claim that wisdom is too highly prized, you cannot then demand that your apprentice show any."

"You will forgive me if I fail to play your games of consistency. Wisdom is necessary when power is uneven; it is power that rules."

"And it is not," Finch said quietly, "your power that rules here." She frowned. "You should visit the healerie."

"I will not. Have you clothing here?"

Haval said, "Given what you have done with the clothing you are wearing, I am uncertain that I should answer that question. This is unlike you," he added.

"It has been many years since I have been forced to test myself in a simple physical contest—but it has been many years since I have lacked the information to take the measure of my foes. Finch."

She heard the edge in the word, the command. Lifting her face, she met his grim, cold expression and offered him the sweetest, meekest of smiles.

His anger broke against it, although the roots of it remained. "I will replace Lucille if this is what she has taught you."

"You know full well that it is not from Lucille that I learned this."

"Then I will replace the fool who encouraged such inappropriate boldness."

"Surely," Jay said, speaking for the first time, "such replacement would be my decision."

His lips folded in a smile; the rest of him folded in a perfect bow. "Indeed, Terafin. I have come to make my report. If it is not convenient—"

"Convenience is irrelevant at this point." Jay sat, graceless and heavy. To Haval she said, "The wilderness is too strong here."

"Yes, Terafin. But the changes wrought in your personal chambers might be as easily wrought in the West Wing should you choose to remain here."

*   *   *

He is correct, Avandar said. *And you are aware of this. It is, in the end, your risk to take. No one of your den will gainsay your decision. Were demons to pour in from the Hells in number, they would prefer to have you here, even if the influx were entirely due to your presence.*

I want Calliastra with us.

Avandar said nothing.

Jewel turned to Jarven, assessing his injuries. She considered commanding him to the healerie and decided against it. The trick to ruling someone like Jarven was to studiously avoid giving him commands he was not inclined to follow. One could—Amarais had, on occasion—but it had to be done judiciously, because one couldn't afford to have Jarven publicly disobey those commands. It was always a risk.

"The wounds look more severe than they are." He smiled. "I am not one of your den, Terafin." A warning. "Haval will—at a later time, when it will not bore me to insensibility—explain the weaknesses in your protective impulses. I am an operative. I am a weapon. I am a tool." He lifted a hand before she could speak. "If you mean to point out that tools are neither sentient nor fractious, I will respectfully disagree. The best tools are often both. Leadership is not merely the giving of orders; it is the giving of the correct orders to the correct recipients."

She exhaled. "Was it a demon?"

"I cannot be definitive at this time, and I would stake very little on the accuracy of my answer, but no. I do not believe my assailant was demonic in nature."

"It wasn't the fox."

"No, Terafin. The eldest serves you. You understand territoriality. Given your origins, you could hardly do otherwise. That understanding is the root of your ability to handle the occasionally ugly competition between The Ten. The wilderness is different only in degree, not substance. You have claimed these lands, and the wilderness has, for reasons of its own, accepted your claim. Your rule is absolute here, in a way it cannot be—"

"Over you."

His smile was slender, sharp, his nod slight.

"You think, however, like a mortal. It is not a criticism," he added, in the mildest of voices. "I think as one as well. It is an advantage."

Calliastra made a noise that was categorically rude.

Jarven glanced at her, his brows changing shape, his eyes narrowing. "You fail to see advantage in it?"

"I do. But I have spent much of my existence among mortals; I feel I understand your kind too well."

"You understand desire, certainly. You understand impulse. But impulse, I would argue, is the province of the immortal. You live forever if you are cautious—although caution is not, in the end, a signal strength of the immortals I have met. The choices you make have consequences, but with the long passage of time, the consequences become contextually irrelevant. Unless, of course, they destroy you."

"Would you not then acknowledge that we have more to lose? If you are foolish, you lose a handful of years. If we are disastrously foolish, we lose eternity."

"My dear," he said, in a tone that was dangerously close to patronizing, "In The Terafin's service is a man who has spent centuries, perhaps millennia, attempting to lose that eternity without success. The only people who appear to value eternity are those who are guaranteed not to witness it."

Jewel's face was a mask as she studied Jarven. She glanced once at Haval, who did not appear to notice. She had never discussed Avandar's past with Jarven. She had discussed it with very few, Haval being one.

"Meaning yourself?"

Jarven's smile was sharp, his nod precise. "Those who live often desire things they do not possess. It is, in the end, the heart of what I have spent much of my life doing."

"And now?"

"I spend some of my life in other endeavors." He turned, once again, to the woman who was his theoretical lord. "There are roads," he told her softly, "that lead to the boundaries of your lands. They are not subtle. I am uncertain that mortals could find them with any ease; I am completely certain that the predators who lurk in the wilderness could.

"I am not cognizant of how those predators mark territory; I suspect that land, such as it is, is owned as you yourself now own the forests which house your trees of silver, gold, and diamond."

Before Jewel could speak, Haval said, "Your injuries were not caused by the ruler of those lands."

"I am not entirely certain those lands have a ruler. There is some element in them that seems nascent, inactive."

"And you would know this how?" It was Jester who asked.

Haval lifted a hand, the movement of his fingers succinct, brief, and unmistakable. It shouldn't have surprised Jewel, but it did.

Jester, however, was in his fashion the fiercest guardian of the boundaries of *den*. He did not appear to notice.

Jarven was amused by her den-kin's question. Jester's dislike had always amused him. "When I walk these lands—when I stand in this manse or in my own rooms within it—I hear an echo of The Terafin's voice." He frowned as he turned to Jay again. "Voice is not exact. It is the closest approximation, however. The echo contains no actual words, no command, and had I no acquaintance with you, I would not recognize it. But I do. These lands are yours while you can hold them.

"In a like fashion, other lands are held. Were I to walk within Corallonne's domain again, I would know. Her presence marks the boundaries. But in lands adjacent to your own—if that is a word that has any geographical meaning in the wilderness—I hear similar echoes. Or their utter absence." His gaze drifted to the wounds he had taken. "The creature that attempted to end my existence did not dwell in lands that were claimed or owned."

Haval cleared his throat, and Jarven lifted a brow. After a pause, Jarven said, "No, I do not believe I was attacked because I was considered a territorial threat. At this point, I could not claim—or hold—the lands in which the creature dwells."

"At this point . . . or ever?"

"My inclination is to say ever, but I dislike the finality of that restriction. I will therefore say that I do not understand the paradigm fully enough to exploit it."

That drew a smile from Haval. It was not a pleasant expression. These two men stood, facing each other, youth cut away from them by the simple passage of time and—with it—softness, even warmth. Like blades honed and sharpened, they had waited for the moment in which they might at last be wielded, as if they existed for no other purpose.

Jarven had always been that man.

Haval had not.

Or perhaps he had, and the slow shift of the hidden world's many seasons had finally shed light on him in a way that could not be avoided.

Avandar exhaled, shedding his own particular brand of invisibility, the armor of servants. "Never. You will never be able to hold the wilderness. You might trap it, cage it, bind it; you might block all possible paths that lead to it, and claim ownership in that fashion; it has been done. But to be what the Sen is, what the firstborn were? No. No more could the Arianni, save only a handful, and they are immortal.

"Calliastra could, should she so choose."

Calliastra had paled, except for her eyes, where darkness absorbed all other color. The hands that had looked slender became something other; the wings that had been shadow absorbed light and air for sustenance. Jewel understood. Calliastra had, once, claimed some part of the wilderness as her own. She had, once, attempted to make a home for herself. She did not live there now.

Without thought, Jewel lifted her hand; her fingers rose in a weave, a dance, den-sign and visceral instinct twined. In an instant, the shadows fled Calliastra's eyes, the wings fading from view.

"Sometimes," Jewel said softly, "we can't build what we want. I built a home for my den. And when that didn't work, I built a better home. And when we all almost died, I came here. And here? Demons, gods, firstborn. Greater threats, all."

"I have never been as you are." Condescension and something much rawer fought for dominance in her voice. Calliastra was struggling to hold on to the former, but no surprise there.

Jewel accepted it. Hesitated. Held out a hand. Calliastra stared at it as if it were one of the half-eaten mice Teller's cat had graciously decided to share. Were that expression on any other face, Jewel would have laughed out loud. But laughter, to Calliastra, was poison; she had not learned how to feel the warmth or the affection inherent in familial mockery. If she were truly like Duster, she never would. Her laughter would draw figurative blood. Given that she was the daughter of gods, it might draw literal blood as well.

Finch said, "I'll stay in The Terafin's chambers as well."

Teller signed. Finch's hands remained still.

All advice, all caution, all the warring certainties pulled at Jewel. The wilderness was not the home she wanted. It had never been the home she wanted. But . . . she *had* a home. Had almost always had one—she could see that now, Calliastra's tentative hand in her own. Only after her father had failed—permanently—to come home from the docks, when she had faced eviction, and had lived beneath the bridge in the poorest of the holdings, had she been homeless. Rath had found her.

Rath had found her, had held her at a distance, and yet had opened his home to her, had allowed her to be part of it. He had never been father, or father figure. He had been *den*. He had been hers in the way the den was, but she had been too timid, too frightened, to see that clearly.

She saw it now. He had found her, had taken her home.

And she *knew* that Calliastra had likewise been found, but not by Rath.

Rath was dead. Jewel had not killed him. She was almost certain that whoever had attempted to offer Calliastra a home was likewise dead—but Calliastra was not equally blameless. No, that was wrong. There must have been a time when her intent had been almost the same as Jewel's. And that hadn't helped her at all.

"Yes," she told Finch, surrendering. She wanted Calliastra with her den. But Calliastra could not stay with her den if Jewel wasn't with them. Avandar was right.

"And that," Jarven said, with both warmth and a flash of irritation, "is our Finch; ever willing to broker compromise even if the only—"

"Enough," Jewel said, and meant it. "How close were you to my own lands when you were attacked?"

"At the boundary," he replied.

"Which boundary?"

His eyes widened slightly, his lips curving. Everything about him reminded her of blades, of blood, of conflict. He did not answer.

"Interior or exterior?"

He stared at her as if he had never seen her before. No, Jewel thought, recognizing some of that expression. He stared at her as if he had always discounted her knowledge, her experience, even her competence, and was now being forced to revise his opinion. Jarven's chief strength—she saw this now—was that he could. He had always been vain, arrogant, decisive in a fashion. But he was flexible enough to review and alter both plans and opinions when necessary.

One gray brow rose. "I am not concerned with appearances, except as they suit me. *Appearing* to be the best is not enough. I will *be* the best."

As if she had spoken out loud. She would speak with the fox. She would ask him what he had done to Jarven, or for him; she felt she needed to have a clearer understanding. Her instinctive reaction provided confirmation, but not information she could use moving forward. Shadow, however, had made clear that the fox was not allowed in the manse. Jewel blinked, shaking her head as if to clear it. She was certain Shadow had made this clear, yet she could not precisely remember when or how. The fox did not treat the cats with the contempt Calliastra did.

"Shadow."

"I'm *busy*." He was. She had sent him with Adam. But his voice was a rumble beneath her feet. She felt the ground list, saw Jarven's expression shift, and saw Haval's remain flat, neutral, and entirely unsurprised.

It was Angel who caught her, Jester who helped; it was Finch's arm around her back and beneath an armpit; there was sound and noise, light and shadow, familiar scents of both kitchen and forest, the taste of blood in her mouth.

"Shadow!" Finch's voice.

"Why can't someone *else* do it?"

Calliastra's hand was cold in hers, and it tightened. But as Jewel's free hand found the center of her own chest, the firstborn said, "Do not. Do not do that here. If you can, do not do it *ever*."

Do what?

"It does not show you what is. It shows you what will be, what might be, what has been. It does not give you clarity, only a different way of slicing through chaos. And no," she continued, her voice shifting, walls of distance snapping into place around the words, "do not send for the healer, if that was your intent. He cannot help her, but he will be close enough that he might, if not very, very careful, be lost as well."

She had no intention of sending for the healer. The thought had not occurred to her.

Jewel whispered something but could not then or later say what.

Calliastra said, "I told you, I have some experience with the Sen. You are not yet what they were." The hand that Jewel had offered had been taken, and that hand was solid, real, singular. It was here and in this moment. Even thinking it, she rebelled; Finch was here. Angel. Jester. Her den, her Chosen.

But their voices blurred and even their touch came at a remove. Calliastra's did not.

"I think I understand," the godchild said, "why you need me."

"I need—"

"You don't need death," she replied. She pulled Jewel by the hand. "Or rather, you don't need me to cause it."

"She has *ussssss*."

"Oh, please. You can't even guard one exhausted man-child without practically abandoning your master."

"She is *not* our *master*!"

Shadow's voice, like Calliastra's hand, was solid, real; it had no fuzziness around the edges. It was, however, loud, and the odd, growly humor that often informed it was bleeding into nothing. She did not want the cat and the first-born to clash in *this* room. Or this hall. Or this manor.

"Clearly, she is not a competent master if you can behave as disgracefully as you normally do. However. You are perfectly capable of stealth and silence should you so choose, and you are easily capable of disposing of her enemies.

She has Lord Celleriant. She has Viandaran. While none of her servitors are my equal individually, in aggregate they are impressive.

"I have little to add to that mass. I did not understand," she added, her tone shifting, her voice developing something that sounded like cracks, small fissures across the surface. "But I—I do, now." Her voice wasn't gentle. Jewel didn't think that Calliastra had that in her. But it was—in its own way—as astonishing. It was clear, and it was whole, while implying all the broken things that lay beneath it.

"If you step on my foot again, I will cut off your wings."

"*Try*."

Jewel's hand tightened on Calliastra's almost involuntarily; there was no command in it.

"I will. Later."

Angel signed. Jester signed. They watched Jewel. She was exhausted enough that they didn't bother to hide their concern. Why would they? Angel was home. He was finally home. His intimidating Northern friend—who seemed to have stepped out of childhood stories of barbarian invasions—spoke to him, but in Rendish. Finch understood a smattering of that language, but not enough to catch the gist of what was said; it was too quiet, and too quick.

She turned to Angel, signed *sleep*.

He signed *Jay*.

She shook her head. *Me. I'll watch.*

And he was willing—they were all willing—to have Finch as regent. As if relieved to be momentarily quit of his duty, he turned toward his own room, his own door.

Jester waited until Angel was gone and lifted his hands again.

They had no den-sign for outsiders; Finch did not therefore sign. "Find Birgide."

"I don't understand why she wasn't there."

"I don't think she needs to be," Finch replied softly. "And she's very reserved. She perhaps wanted to give us . . ." She shrugged. "But find her."

"And you?"

"We'll take Jay to her room. I think—I think she needs more sleep."

Haval's face was blank, neutral. Jarven's was not. His eyes were like lightning: bright, flashing, and so alive. Age—his own—seemed almost a lie, he wore it so poorly. "And what would you have of us, Regent?"

"You are not under my oversight," Finch replied.

"You are regent."

"Yes. When The Terafin is absent, I am regent. But she's here now."

Haval nodded as if he agreed with her spoken statement, and simply waited. Finch shifted Jay's weight; Jay was too hot to the touch. Where Jarven's eyes were bright with excitement, Jay's were bright with something else. Finch liked neither.

But she had grown to accept necessity when it fell on her, figuratively or literally. "I would have you both speak with Birgide. Find out where the attack took place, if it is possible. I highly doubt it was a lone, wild beast—but I admit I am out of my depth when it comes to the forests and the wilderness. I will see The Terafin to her room and her much deserved rest.

"Birgide will also have to see to the needs of the guests who remain in the forest itself. They are very like Lord Celleriant, if I am not mistaken—but they are mercenaries to his soldier. The Terafin would not have allowed them entry if she thought they could not be contained or controlled. But she is exhausted. It is in Birgide's hands at the moment. They are *not* to leave the forest until The Terafin wakes."

No one spoke for one long beat, not even the Chosen. Finch then turned the whole of her attention to the only thing that now mattered.

"Teller, help me."

Finch wanted to cling to Jay, to hold her in a grip so tight she wouldn't be able to leave. The visceral urge surprised and even dismayed her because it was so familiar. She had clung just so to her mother the last time she had seen her.

She had never gone back. She had never done the groundwork that would allow her to find the parents who had abandoned her. No, worse, who had sold her. She understood, in an intellectual way, why they had done it. She could even, when feeling charitable, believe that they believed it was necessary; could see how threats and cajoling could be combined when the burden of debt might lead to injury, death. But she did not forgive.

And on that day, she had been afraid. Too afraid to acknowledge the truth that was, even then, unfolding and undeniable.

She bit her lip and then, falling back onto years of studied practice, smoothed the worry and fear from her expression. Jay had nothing in common with Finch's parents except Finch's own fear—and she would not let that be a binding. Jay had no intention of selling them out, no intention of abandoning them.

Without thought, as instinctive in the motion as she had been in her desire to cling, she glanced at Teller, at Teller's color, sallow, strained. He had looked into the Oracle's crystal ball, the thing Jay called her heart. The Oracle had allowed it. He had spoken very little about what he'd seen, and although they'd all wanted to know—and still wanted to know—they had shied away from asking more than a handful of times. Each time he had offered small glimpses, contained and shaped only by words. The words were chilling enough.

"It's not the future," he'd said, expression fierce and defiant. But it was a ferocity born of fear, not certainty; fear and hope. "It's *one* future. We've faced dark futures before."

But she remembered: Angel's hair. And that, at least, had come to pass. He wore it in Northern braids. The complicated spire that had been the one identifying trait easily seen at a distance was gone. The heart of his attachment to Jay remained; it had grown stronger, if Finch was any judge. He had finally taken the Terafin name as his own.

But Teller had seen his hair in the Oracle's crystal.

Teller had seen more.

Teller, she thought, had seen this, or something that led to this.

She was very surprised when Snow stepped on her foot. Not because he had never done it, although feet tended to be Shadow's specialty, but rather, because until she felt the weight of his paw, she had not seen him at all. Just as she had not always seen the fox.

His eyes were gold. Sometimes they were brown, and sometimes that brown was so dark it was a warm, solid black. Her worry deepened the moment he lifted his foot, when he realized he had her attention. Somehow, squalling, whining cats meant the world was normal. Expensive, but normal. Consideration? That was for funerals, for the dying, for those moments in which the world was so grim, so dire, the loss so imminent, that respect was the only thing that could be offered.

Her hand drifted to the top of his head, in unconscious mimicry of Jay.

The great cat purred. His voice so soft it sounded like an entirely different voice, he said, "Cling, Finch. She does not *want* to leave you. She will *need* you here when it happens."

"When what happens?"

But Snow had said enough, or more than enough, in his own opinion. "You have eyes," he sniffed. "What do you use them *for*? She is mortal. She is *weak*. She made family, and she *needs* it. If you are afraid to need her, if you are afraid to ask, how will she *know*?"

"We're not children anymore, Snow."

Snow hissed brief laughter. "You are *always* children."

"She doesn't just have us—she has all of Terafin."

Snow spit, and stepped on her foot again, but harder this time. She stumbled, and Jay, leading Calliastra, pulled away.

And she thought of them at twelve, at thirteen, at fourteen. They had not felt young then. But desperation had given way, in the company of the den, to a strange kind of hope. Not for this, not for Terafin—they hadn't had shared dreams that big. But for each other. For the people who would have your back when things got tough; for the people who would share their food when food was scarce; for the warmth, at night, when there was no fire, and the only heat came from thin walls, thinner blankets, and adjacent bodies.

They did not feel young now. The power that had been so far beyond them it wasn't even a dream was in their hands—but the power came with a responsibility that had also been impossible to understand without actually beginning to carry its weight. The powerful didn't have to answer to anyone, in that distant, small apartment. The powerful had money. They wouldn't starve. They wouldn't freeze. They had *no worries*.

"We were children," she said again, but in a softer voice. "Even you must have been young once."

"We were never young as you are young," Snow replied. "Except Shadow. He was *stupid*."

The roar of the great, gray cat was unmistakable although they had put half the manse between them. Snow hissed laughter. Jay, however, turned back to glare at the white cat. "Now is not the time to fight with your brother," she said, and she headed down the hall to where Snow stood, at Finch's side. She released Calliastra's hand and dropped her palm to the top of the white cat's head.

"What are you doing to Finch?" she demanded.

And her voice *was* her voice, her expression familiar, contained. Annoyed, yes, but where the cats were concerned, that was normal. She lifted her eyes, met Finch's. "Don't let them walk all over you."

"How will *she* stop *us*?" Snow asked.

Jay glared at him until he looked away. Given he was a cat, it took a while. He sniffed, turned, and stalked off, clipping Finch with a wing on exit.

"It was a good question," Finch said, shrugging.

"It was a bad question," Jay answered, lips compressed, arms momentarily folded.

"If you were willing to exert power or authority over them, it would never have been asked," Calliastra said. She glanced at—and through—Finch, as if Finch were inconsequential. As Finch was accustomed to this, and often found it pragmatically useful if not pleasant, she accepted it without comment.

Duster had never quite done that to Finch. She'd done it to almost everyone else. Duster had died to buy enough time for everyone else to escape. Even so, she would have bitten off her own right hand before admitting that she loved them. She flinched, even thinking of the word "love" and "Duster" in such close proximity, knowing—half a lifetime later—how furious Duster would have been.

How furious, she thought, Calliastra would be in the same circumstance.

"They're cats," Jay replied, shrugging. The shrug seemed to adjust her clothing, even her skin; it seemed to shake them into place, to fix them in the here-and-now. "I'm sorry if my rooms are a mess," she added.

"You have servants, surely?" Calliastra said.

"I don't want them to wander around in my personal chambers too much."

"Oh?"

"You'll see." She started forward and then turned back, this time to face Teller. She signed; Finch saw her arms move although she didn't see what she'd said. "I want an appointment to visit Gilafas ADelios tomorrow."

He winced. "The guild of the maker-born doesn't generally consider any emergency its problem. I believe they've been known to keep the Kings themselves waiting."

"He'll see me."

"If he hears about it." Teller didn't ask her why she was so certain; it was Jay. "But the guildmaster doesn't set his schedule. He has his own small army of Barstons, each more intimidating than the last."

"Sic our Barston on them, then."

He nodded. Hesitated. She reached out and hugged him. "I'm home," she said, voice soft.

For how long? But he didn't ask and, in the end, neither did Finch, although they were the two people who probably needed, for pragmatic reasons, to know. It wasn't the pragmatic that drove them.

"Who is Gilafas ADelios?" Calliastra asked.

"The Artisan currently known as the guildmaster."

Calliastra's expression changed. "You have an Artisan?"

"The guild does. He's not mine."

"And you wish him to make for you?"

"No. He's done that already. He asked me—" She shook her head, lifted a hand, shoved stray, curled strands out of her eyes, and started again. "I told him that I would take him with me if I ever went to find the Winter Queen."

"You did not." Jay might have said she'd tried to stab him in the left eye to less effect, less shock.

"Probably not in those exact words, no. But it was what he wanted, and—in the end—no one says no to the maker-born without a seriously good reason."

"He will die. You yourself have only survived your sojourn into uncharted wilderness because of the firstborn." She seemed unwilling to disentangle herself from her growing outrage.

The outrage made as little sense to Jay as it did to anyone else in the hall who wasn't Calliastra. "He's not a child. He's the head of the most powerful guild in the Empire. I am not responsible for his decisions."

"He's an *Artisan*. You can't seriously expect that he would make cogent, rational decisions!"

"He's an *adult*, and he is not ATerafin. I have no responsibility for him, but more important, I have no power over him. And he seems, for the most part, a cogent man." She winced and added, "Most of the time."

"You cannot take an Artisan into the wilderness." Her voice was flat with certainty.

"Why not?"

Calliastra's eyes widened with surprise and, yes, disgust. "Do you not understand the value of an Artisan? Do you not understand the rarity? Only the seer-born were as rare."

"And never as valued?"

Calliastra ignored the mild barb in the question; it was clearly irrelevant. Her hands were fists, her eyes all black. Her wings, however, did not return, even as shadows of their former selves. "They are the *only* way in which the wilderness has ever manifested itself fully in entirely mortal form."

"And the Sen?" Finch asked.

"That is different."

"How?"

It was Jay who said, "The Sen were actually dangerous; they couldn't be owned."

Calliastra nodded. "The Sen were not considered mortal."

Jay froze. It was a brief lack of motion, a visceral reaction, but she suppressed it quickly. She didn't speak. Finch, however, did. Her tone was neutral, her words far more formal, and far more respectful, than Jay's.

"Why were they not considered mortal?"

Jay lifted a hand in den-sign. *Don't.* But oddly, so did Teller.

Calliastra frowned at their identical motions, but she said nothing. She was accustomed to being an outsider, Finch thought. An outsider whose presence would always be a threat, a risk. If she could not have anything else, she would have the respect of fear.

It was familiar. Finch attempted to set it aside as unprofitable. Calliastra was not Duster, not even an echo of Duster. She was the child of gods.

It had never occurred to her to wonder what that meant. The poorest of the citizens of Averalaan had seen the god-born all of their lives. But the god-born children of the Mother were mortal, and the uneasy alliance of mortality with the powers of the gods, however dilute, burned mortality away more quickly, not less. Calliastra had no mortal parents.

Jay said, "The Artisan is like the cats."

"Meaning you will not exercise control or authority over him."

"Meaning that I can't without somehow demanding that they alter their base nature."

"The Artisans are of incalculable value. The cats—"

Snow growled.

"Don't think that has any effect on *me*," Calliastra snapped. "She might tolerate your disrespect. I won't."

Jay's expression pinched further, and the pinching seemed to squeeze out the remnants of the frightening dislocation, the otherness that separated her from the rest of the den. She was smart enough not to add to her problems by remonstrating with either the cat or Calliastra, but Finch could see the difficulty of that balancing act, and it would likely increase in the future.

Avandar, who had disappeared with Jay and had reappeared by her side, remained by it. But he was silent, unobtrusive. He disappeared for perhaps five minutes, reappearing in clothing more suited to his station within the manse. Jay, however, hadn't ditched her traveling clothing, and they made a very odd pair. Then again, they always had. Avandar, unlike Ellerson, rarely faded into invisibility.

Ellerson. Finch exhaled.

The captains of the Chosen, after a short, almost inaudible discussion, had reached some command decision, and Torvan accompanied The Terafin. Arrendas disappeared, but Marave stepped into the place he should have occupied.

The Chosen were not invisible; if they did not speak, the sound of their armor spoke for them. But they were so much a part of daily life in the Terafin manse Finch only registered their presence when they spoke. They spoke when something was wrong. When they were silent, it was easy to forget they were there. It was easy to forget that Avandar was present. They were like shadows; their presence depended on Jay's.

The Chosen at the door saluted smartly as Jay approached. They stood straighter, taller, and Finch understood why. They were *her* Chosen. She had returned. In her absence, they had had to shepherd and guard Teller and Finch, but that was neither their calling nor the reason for their choice.

They did not welcome her home; they did not ask if she would be staying. They asked nothing at all, but did not impede her progress to the doors, did not demand to know her business. She was the only person who could expect that.

The doors rolled open.

They followed Jay into the wilderness of amethyst sky and trees that grew shelves. Or they should have.

The first thing Finch heard was the drawing of swords.

The second was the roaring of water. It was not the wave of ocean, not the steady lap that became so much a part of the background noise of the city it was almost inaudible. This roar was the sound made by falling water.

Jay's back was stiff, still, and at her side, no longer clasping her hand, Calliastra lifted her head, as if in surprise or wonder. Avandar had raised a hand, and it had fallen to Jay's shoulder; he released her when it became clear that she would not move without word from the Chosen. That word did not come immediately.

Mist and water rose, and if Jay did not move, they would soon be drenched. It was not the water of rainfall. Someplace ahead and beneath their feet was a waterfall.

Finch had read of these, but she had not pursued life in a merchant caravan the way Jay had. She, like Teller, had been tied to the office to which she had been sent as an apprentice half a lifetime ago. She had seen paintings, often as Jarven's escort to various functions of import to the House, or of interest to the wily, bored merchant.

Torvan's *all clear* drifted back, and they began to move.

There was a path beneath their feet; it was made, not worn there by the passage of many people. The stone itself was not all of a piece; it was like patterned tile work, in unpolished pale marble. Cracks existed, but those cracks were also part of the art of the creation; they glittered gold, or blue, or black, not a sign of age or wear, but rather the deliberate presentation of color, of highlight.

"Have you noticed a change in my chambers recently?" Jay asked, her voice drifting back, her hands stiff by her sides. She hadn't curled them into fists, as she often did when surprised—as if surprise by its very nature was conflict.

"No, I'm sorry," Finch replied. "We are not often here. We would have warned you, otherwise."

"Can you see the river?"

"The branches where I'm standing are too thick; I can see white between them."

Jay began to walk again. The branches did not immediately thin out, but as Finch approached the spot at which Jay had first stopped, she could see a river. It was not calm, not still. On the far banks, she could see people, or what she assumed, at first glance, were people. They did not wear livery, of course, and the river was wide enough that they were not instantly familiar.

Neither, however, was the sky. The deep and constant clarity of amethyst had given way to a blue that occasionally graced the skies of Averalaan. That blue, unlike this, was tempered by scudding cloud, by different saturation of color, by position of sun. This was like the ideal of a clear perfect day—or might have been without the water.

"It is an interesting choice," Calliastra said to Jay. "But a little pastoral, I think."

Jay said nothing.

"Is that your residence ahead?"

Since it was the only building immediately visible, Finch assumed that it was. But in the past incarnation of the personal chambers, there had been both library and private dining room, the latter in a tiny building with a very crude, but somehow charming, fence.

There was no library here. She could practically hear Teller's wail of shock and distress. The lack of a small room meant for more intimate dinners had probably failed to register in the wake of the greater disaster.

"The books!" he said, his whisper almost a shout, it was so textured with pain.

"They're here," Jay replied. "Somewhere less damp."

He didn't ask if she were certain. Calliastra, however, said, "Books?"

"When the former Terafin ruled, this room was her library. Her personal collection rivaled the Kings, or so I've been told."

"Ah. And you?"

"The last time I visited, it was still a library, but with unusual shelves and no ceiling."

Calliastra's expression changed, then. "You did not choose this vista."

"Not consciously, no."

Not consciously, no.

The words echoed in the silence that followed Calliastra's question. Teller was watching Jay; Finch was not.

There were fields between the river and the building which Finch called a castle. She had seen paintings of those as well but disliked them. Jarven had taken some pains to expose her to those he admired—and they were all plain stone edifices meant in some fashion for war. Or to withstand it. He did not consider the Terafin manse to be defensible but accepted that—if an army somehow marched its way to the manse—it was unlikely that something as simple as an admirable architectural plan would save its people.

Finch, however, had been born to, had grown up in, the city. The artistic rendering of a castle had seemed, in the vast green fields and rocks that surrounded it, to be a statement of isolation. It stood alone. If one wished to stand alone, this is where one could safely do it.

There had been no safety in isolation. No safety in being alone. Not in Finch's childhood. Not in her adulthood—which often felt fraudulent when claimed—either. And yet, Jay had brought them to her home-within-a-home, and it was a castle.

There was a path that led away from the river that ended in a cascading fall of water. How far below, Finch couldn't tell and didn't want to know. She had found a strange beauty in the amethyst skies of the previous iteration of these rooms, and danger—which Meralonne insisted was present—existed at a remove. It could; it was not her problem, and even if it were, she was not its solution.

This sky, its mimicry of the familiar and the expected, made danger inexplicably real. And yet there was nothing that crossed this sky: not even birds. She wondered where the House Mage was.

Calliastra, disgusted by cats and by Jewel's attitude toward one of the most powerful men in the Empire, was warier now than she had been. On some level, she trusted Jay. If pressed, she would probably say—as Duster would—that it wasn't a matter of trust: Jay was harmless. Caution wasn't necessary.

And it would, Finch thought, mean exactly what Duster's words would have meant. She didn't need to hear them. Calliastra was not Duster.

Finch understood why Jay had brought Duster home. She was afraid she understood why Jay had brought Calliastra, just as she had once brought Kiriel. Kiriel shared one parent with Calliastra, and yet . . . it had been very, very difficult to even turn one's back on Kiriel. It had taken will, intent, deliberation. Finch did not have that reaction to this daughter of darkness, and she wondered why.

Wondered because it was a safer question, a more comfortable what if than any other question she might have asked herself.

Snow accompanied her, walking to her left. To her right was Teller, and to his, Jay. Calliastra was on Jay's other side, as far from Snow as she could be. This didn't stop her from sending murderous glares the cat's way. Snow clearly—and loudly—didn't care.

"Where did you go?" Finch asked the white cat, in an attempt to distract him. It was a mile, perhaps two, to the castle's gates.

Snow shrugged. "Somewhere *boring*."

"Are you bored now?"

"Yesssssss. It is boring here. It is *always* boring."

"Will it always be boring?"

Snow sniffed. Glancing at Finch out of the corner of his eyes, he said, "Why do you asssssk? You *know*."

Finch smiled. "Because I have hope that you'll give me a different answer."

"You *want* me to lie?"

Her smile deepened. "No," she said, placing a hand on his head—not because he was misbehaving and the gesture would somehow keep him in check, but because his fur was like small cat fur: soft. Warm.

Snow sighed dramatically. "Why," he said, although his ears twitched in time with his whiskers, "are you *all* so *stupid*?"

"We were born that way," Teller told the white cat. Teller was seldom called stupid, but to be fair, neither was Finch. Carver—until his disappearance—and Angel had generally been the targets of their petulance. "We didn't get a choice. No one asked if we wanted to be cats instead. Why are The Terafin's rooms a castle? What happened to the books?"

"Oh, *books*," Snow said, with mild disgust. He paused, and then added, "*Is* it?"

"Is it what?"

"A castle?"

Teller regrouped. "It's not what it was."

"It is."

"It's not to us. To us—"

"It *is*. You aren't looking *properly*." He flicked wings to either side, clipping them both.

They exchanged a glance over his head, and Finch faced forward again, willing herself to see as Snow did. She failed. It was a castle, and they would be at its gates soon.

"The Master of the Household Staff will have my head," Teller said. "Or Barston will have hers."

Finch cringed on his behalf. The first . . . shift . . . in the state of The Terafin's personal chambers had been a point of extreme contention between the Master of the Household Staff and anyone who had no choice but to stand in the line of her ire. Carver had explained why, which didn't really help.

Carver.

She missed a step. Snow hissed. "So *stupid*," he said softly. "What is *he* worth? What will *you* pay for him? What will you ask *her* to pay?"

Finch didn't answer.

"This is *war*," the cat continued. "Do you not *understand*? You cannot fight a battle and lose nothing, except in your dreams."

Her dreams had never been that kind.

"If she *cannot* forget him, she will be *lost*." He shook his head again.

And Shadow said, "Too late."

Finch had not expected to see the gray cat, and in fact, still couldn't. Jay didn't react to the sound of his voice at all. Snow did; he hissed in displeasure and flexed his claws. She wondered if Shadow had stepped on his tail. Was he, she thought, like the fox? But no.

"You're supposed to be with Adam," she told the invisible gray cat.

Shadow hissed. "I *am*. Ariel is with him. He sleeps the sleep of the mortal. He has fed her, he has bathed her, he has eaten. He is not Sen. She has accepted him. He will be safe."

"Then why aren't you here?"

He hissed. It was a sulky hiss.

"I can hear you," Jay said.

"He doesn't *need* me." And Shadow appeared, first as a gray, vaguely animal-shaped fog, which hardened into more familiar solidity.

"And I do." It wasn't actually a question.

Calliastra turned her nose down as she glared at the gray cat. "You cannot even follow a simple command. You are a disgrace to your Lord."

"We are not hers," Shadow replied, stepping on Snow's foot. "She is *ours*. And you are *stupid*. We *told* you this. We *told you the truth*."

"You told it in the tangle, where all truth is slanted because all truth is possible."

"Because you are *stupid*, I am telling you *now* when we are *not* in the tangle. I will say it again, and again, and again. She is *ours*."

Calliastra turned to Jay, the movement an outraged, but wordless, demand.

But Jay said, "Ownership never goes only one way. Not when the living are involved."

"It is not *just* the living," Snow observed. If Calliastra's obvious outrage displeased him, it didn't show; his wings remained sleek and unruffled. He did give Shadow the side-eye that indicated possible future trouble, but had decided—today, for this moment—that he was above all that.

"What's going to happen?" Finch asked Snow.

"If you are *very* good, I will make you a dress."

This caused Calliastra's eyes—and mouth, momentarily and wordlessly—to open.

"I think that's an excellent idea," Jay told him.

"I have a lot of dresses," Finch began.

"I don't *like* them. And you will be Lord, here."

"No, I'll be regent."

"It is the same."

"It's not the same. Jay will be Terafin, while she lives. But . . . this war that you spoke of requires her time, her attention, her absence. When she is not here, I will make decisions in her stead. But I will make the decisions I think she would have made, had she been present. She is The Terafin. I am Finch."

As they spoke, they had been closing the distance between the river and the castle. They were damp, but no longer almost drenched. Dry probably wouldn't occur until a change of clothing.

There were gates. Gates were constructed of wood and metal, walls of metal and stone. But as Finch approached, she revised that. She could not—quite—feel terrified when she was with Jay and Teller. But she could worry—she could always worry, having spent half her life in Lucille's company.

Calliastra said, "Where did you see this building?" Her voice was soft, almost hushed. Were she any other person, there might have been a hint of reverence in it. But no, Calliastra treated nothing with reverence. Respect, yes, if it was necessary. Buildings did not demand respect.

The gate's bars were dark. They seemed all of a piece, and they did open—but not on hinges. Instead, as if they were a hard, ebon cloth, they pulled back to either side, their poles silent as they gathered to the left and right. On the other side, an interlocking stone path extended ahead until it reached peaked, stone arches. The central arch was recessed, and its shape seemed to cascade down in a type of stone echo, each iteration less concrete than the last.

"I've never seen this building," Jewel replied. "Have you?"

"I have seen one very like it."

"Where?"

Calliastra did not answer.

                            *   *   *

On the other side of the recessed arch, beneath the shadows it cast in the too blue sky, the path opened into a wide circle, circumscribed by shrubbery that had been pruned into odd shapes. It was not silent, however. In the center of the circle was a fountain.

Finch said, "This is the library."

Teller did not; he was staring at the fountain, recognizing, a beat after Finch had, where he had seen it before. She recalled that they did not see precisely the same thing when they looked at it and wondered if that had changed; what she saw, now, was not what she had seen then. It was an impressive piece of carved stone that would be considered a work of art had there been no fall of water, nothing to imply that it was not the only element of the work itself which should draw the eye.

She lifted her hands in den-sign, but they were slow to form the familiar words.

Is that Jay?

As she asked, she glanced at Teller; he had not seen her hands move; hadn't seen the way they shook, the way they formed Jay's name as if it was new to them, to her, as if it was not a common word. Had this statue been in one of the courtyards of *Avantari*, the palace of the Twin Kings, she would never have asked the question.

No, the question she would have asked, had she cared to reveal her ignorance in an overtly political environment, would have been: *which god does this represent?*

Teller's hands were shaking as he lifted them, fumbling over his gestures enough that she couldn't actually read them. He lowered them, pressing the palms of each flat against his thighs.

Calliastra became bone white, silent. What she saw was not what Finch and Teller saw—if they even saw the same thing. Finch knew this not because Calliastra spoke, but because her head tilted back, and back again, until the line of her jaw was flush with her throat. Her eyes were wide.

Avandar was likewise still, likewise pale, and if his gaze did not drift up, and up again, until the whole of his throat was exposed, it rose far higher than either Teller's or Finch's had.

"Jay?" Finch had found her own voice. Jay wasn't looking at the fountain, if that's what it even was.

The woman who was Terafin shook her head. "Fabril made this," she said softly, so softly.

This did draw Calliastra's attention. "How did you transport it?"

"I didn't. When the change happened, it was here. Or rather, it revealed itself. It did not exist as part of The Terafin's personal chambers—"

"Until you became The Terafin."

Gaze averted, she said, "Come on, let's go look for my books."

But even books were not, for a moment, a strong enough incentive for Teller, whose eyes, wide and unblinking, were attached to the fountain as if it were becoming a physical part of him.

Chapter Twenty-Three

The Hidden Wilderness

THE BEAR CONTINUED TO run until the moment Carver stumbled. He fell, arms forward as if to stop himself from hitting ice, but came to rest against the gray of night snow.

Ellerson dragged him to his feet, which was necessary. Carver was only barely conscious. The domicis looked at the bear's golden back, and then turned toward the moonlight again; the moon had lowered itself toward the horizon, paling as it did. Framed by the moon, Ellerson could see their pursuer; it was a wonder that the advantage of flight had not yet allowed him to catch them.

Or perhaps catching them immediately was not his intent.

Through wings, glints of moonlight could be seen; Ellerson thought the demon's wings were torn. Perhaps they had been damaged in the confrontation with the Wild Hunt. In theory, the Wild Hunt in this place was memory, no more—but that memory had injured Carver, drawing blood. Here, if one consented, if one *believed*, the damage memory could do was not merely figurative.

The bear growled, the growl forming words that were more felt than heard. Ellerson looped an arm around Carver, taking on most of his weight. He did not glance back again. While the bear ran, he followed, but the bear gained distance; Ellerson could not run for two, and his attempts to rouse Carver failed.

"We must stop," the domicis finally said, putting action to words.

"You will die if we stop."

"We will die if we don't."

The bear looked over his shoulder and growled; the growl shook the earth. Ice broke beneath enchanted boots, cracks stretching out in all directions, as if something slumbering beneath the ancient snow was finally waking.

"That wasn't me!" the bear shouted.

Ellerson grimaced as ice continued to crack, the sound of its breaking growing fainter as the distance grew larger. "Is it relevant?"

"It is *very* relevant!"

"Tell me how, then. It is clearly occurring, regardless."

"It is relevant because *I* will not kill you. I will not bury you."

"Ah." Ellerson exhaled. "Has the demon's presence awakened the earth?"

"Not *just* the presence of the forsworn, no." The bear glared at Carver. "If you and I were to flee this place and leave him here, the earth would wake regardless. The creature you call a demon might not be enough to wake the earth on its own—ah, no." He shook his head; beads of water flew. "It is what remains of Darranatos. The earth would for him."

"But you think Master Carver is responsible for this."

The bear snorted. "And you don't?"

Ellerson did not reply. The leaf concerned him now. Shadow's words concerned him. Master Carver could lie; he was not particularly scrupulous about honesty. But he chose to lie when the lies themselves were trivial.

The leaf had come to him from Jewel's hands. Ellerson was certain of it. Jewel had walked these lands; she had walked them in her sleep, in her dreams. Her dreams were not—had never been—the dreams or nightmares that plagued the rest of the den. Not until now.

But the control she had over her dreaming self was not the control she had developed, through trial and error, during her tenure as ATerafin, and Terafin. It was not the control she expected to exert over her waking self. Had she given this leaf to Carver while awake—while they were both awake—it would not have troubled Ellerson at all.

Had Shadow not appeared so briefly, he would still remain untroubled. He would be certain that the leaf itself was meant for Carver, had been meant for Carver. But this leaf had been, if he understood all that had happened, created *in* dream.

And Shadow had strongly implied that were Jewel not dreaming, she would never have created the leaf; she would never have allowed it to be created. It was of, and not of, her forest in some fashion. What she understood while dreaming was not real, in some fashion, to Jewel.

The leaf, however, was real.

Three things, I heard, while I slept. The first was the name of the Winter Queen. The second was the voice of the dead. And the third was the voices of those who are trapped. The first two, Ellerson knew; ring and demon. But the third?

Jewel was afraid. She had been afraid for some time. Ellerson had seen the shadows of that fear when they had first met, half her life ago. But he had seen, as well, the shadows cast by the talent to which she'd been born. He'd understood, on that long-ago day, that he could not serve her as domicis. It was not lack of desire on his part, and no lack of commitment, either; she was raw and rough, but she was worthy, in her entirety, of the service he could provide. Had it been only her worthiness that was in question, he might have signed a contract that demanded the rest of his life and considered himself blessed.

But he had not been a young man, at the time; he'd had far too much experience with men—and women—of power. He had understood that what Jewel needed, what she *would* need, he could not provide. He knew that she would face assassins as knowledge of her power grew, and knew, as well, that that knowledge would inevitably grow. Jewel Markess had one outstanding, undeniable advantage to offer the House. Any House. But she had come to Terafin.

And in Terafin, she had remained.

He had watched her from afar. He had listened to reports offered—stiffly and resentfully—by the domicis who had replaced him. He had, twice, almost broken guild laws, in the first year, to attempt to explain why he had made the choice that was not, in any real sense, a choice.

As her power grew, as her position within Terafin solidified, he had seen proof of that. It had vindicated what, to the young ATerafin, had seemed callous desertion on Ellerson's part. And when the den had come to Ellerson with an unusual proposal for the guildhall, Ellerson had accepted.

It was to the den that he now owed his service, but the den served The Terafin. They served Jewel. First as kin, and second as ATerafin. The bonds between these erstwhile orphans and urchins had clearly solidified over the years, their boundaries almost unchanged, their duties codified by the former Terafin's authority and desire.

Jewel had come into contact with men and women of influence and power, but she had not deserted the family she had built. She would not. Was that, then, why she had given the leaf to Carver?

He could not ask; Carver was in no condition to answer, if he could hear the question at all. But he could infer. Jewel had somehow met Carver; she had come to him here. And here Carver remained. Could she, she would have taken Carver with her. Ellerson knew what the loss of Carver would do to the den and to their leader.

But she had come to Carver, and Carver had given her the only item of value he possessed. He no longer wore the locket around his neck; it was in Jewel's hands now.

Which meant, to Ellerson—and probably to Carver as well—that Jewel had had no intention of taking Carver home. If it were possible, she would have done it. If it were possible but costly, she would have done it, unless the cost itself was too high. She was no longer an urchin in the poor holdings; her responsibilities were larger, their weight heavier.

And yet, he thought, even so, she would not let go of Carver unless the cost could be measured in the lives of the rest of her den.

She had left Carver the leaf, the carrying of which appeared—to Ellerson's eyes—to be consuming him. Carver was hers, but he was not her; what she might carry without awareness, he could not. And if he were not meant to carry such a weight, what was its purpose? Why had Shadow appeared?

"We must stop," Ellerson said again. He dragged Carver toward the trunk of the nearest large tree, and positioned the younger man's back against it. He then dropped his pack, opened it, and withdrew one of the two blankets that had been crafted for their use.

He set that blanket upon the snowy ground, and then moved Carver so that Carver lay across its length, the colors of the fabric muted by the evening sky.

The bear turned then. "It is—what do they call it? Ah, I remember—your funeral." But he cocked his head to the side. "What do you have there? Why are you carrying that?"

Ellerson did not reply. The cloak Carver wore protected him from cold; the blanket might seem superfluous. But Carver needed rest. He needed —if it were possible—some respite from the burden he had unknowingly accepted.

It was not his, the domicis thought. It was not his burden to bear. Jewel had left it, regardless. The older man straightened his shoulder as a stray breeze touched his face, touched more than his face; the tree almost directly at his back seemed to creak and strain toward that breeze, which touched little else.

Ellerson then removed food from the pack, noting what remained as he did. "Master Carver."

Carver stirred.

"It is time for breakfast."

Carver turned his back to Ellerson and reached for illusory covers. The domicis smiled as his hands closed on air.

"We do not have time for theatrics, I'm afraid."

Carver's eyes opened a crack. They opened to sunlight.

Sunlight.

The bear trundled over to the blanket; he growled. Ellerson realized belatedly that the wordless growl was actually a request. "There is room," the domicis said, "but the blanket was not meant for a creature of your size."

The bear then shrank. "It's not convenient," he told Ellerson, "to continue to switch like this. It takes energy." He eyed the food.

"The food was meant for—"

"You, yes, yes. Clearly. I cannot imagine what favors you did the Lords of these lands, that they would gift you in such a fashion. It is not a terrible idea," he added. "If you must rest." He stepped onto the blanket, once again the slightly round, bushy-tailed creature he had first been when he had interrupted them. His eyes narrowed. "Sunlight!"

"I . . . had not expected that," Ellerson confessed. "But the area the blanket covers seems to create its own season."

"It does. Or rather, it is its own season. It has been cut and parceled from another time and woven into these threads. Here, were the denizens of these lands truly awake, it would be of great interest, great value, should you desire to trade it."

"Or should they desire to steal it?"

"Such gifts are not easily stolen, and the attempt to do so may be *quite* costly. You should have told me you possessed this. It would have made some decisions a bit simpler."

Carver sat slowly, staring at the creature. ". . . I guess it wasn't a dream."

"It is all a dream, of a kind," the creature replied. "This will not protect you from the dead," he added. ". . . not entirely."

Above their heads, the branches of the great tree drooped toward them. Ellerson looked up to see buds struggle to become leaves.

"It was a good choice," the creature continued.

Carver shook his head. "Look, we can't just call you 'bear' or 'it' or whatever. What are you called?"

The furry creature nodded, a vague air of approval in his gaze. "I am called Anakton by those permitted to call me at all."

Carver shook his head, stretched his arms, and yawned. "I feel like I've been sleeping for less than an hour."

"Much less," Anakton then said. "You look better. But you would. It is not Winter, here, not truly." He seemed to relax. "He will come, regardless. But we may have some help here." He waddled up to the trunk of the tree, lifted a much smaller paw, and batted the tree's dark bark.

It had no obvious effect. "If these lands are dream lands," Ellerson began.

"They are," Anakton said, without turning.

"How come you to be here?"

"I was here before."

"Before?"

"Before they became subject to dream and the dreaming," Anakton replied. "The Lord of these lands was not always asleep—and it seems he will not remain so. But he has slept the long, long Winter, and we have slumbered with him, who were trapped here when the gods decreed punishment.

"Of far more interest is why *you* are here. You are not creatures of the dreaming, and those mortals who did exist in these lands—and they were few, if favored—perished here when sleep descended. It is not safe for mortals."

No, Ellerson thought, it was not.

"Was it safe for mortals when the Lord was awake?"

Anakton chuckled. "If you were one of the favored few, yes. But you are not. And the rings you wear are not his rings; they are *hers*. They will not save you here."

"No." Ellerson turned his gaze toward the winter forest, the winter moon. To his surprise, he could now see neither.

"This selfish tree," Anakton said, as if divining the problem, "is not like many of the others; it is older, and its roots are more deeply planted. You have brought some hint of Summer with you, and it desires to keep the entirety of that Summer to itself. Were it awake—fully awake—this would be less of an issue. You are lucky."

Carver snorted.

"The dead would be upon you now were you not, boy."

"If I were lucky, I wouldn't be here at all."

"Ah, perhaps not. But if you were very unlucky, you wouldn't be here, either." He glanced once over his small golden shoulder. "And that luck will run out, one way or the other. You carry your death with you here."

Ellerson signed. Carver saw the gesture and nodded, but did not sign in return.

"We cannot fight both tree and demon at the same time," Ellerson began.

"You cannot fight either," Anakton snapped. "And in truth I am surprised that the dead have come here at all. What you carry must be of significance, boy, even to the dead. Or, perhaps, especially to the dead. Tell me, what has happened in the worlds beyond since I went to sleep?"

"I only know of ours," Carver replied. "And not all of that, either."

"I see. Ah. There. You hear that?"

They did—or Ellerson did.

Clever. Very clever.

"We will have some small time, and we must use it. Or rather, *I* must use it. But I am restless here, and the tree is being stubborn. Tell me what has happened in the outer world. Or in yours, since it appears you believe there is only one."

4th day of Lattan, 428 A.A.
Terafin Manse

Adam woke to the sound of knocking on his door in the West Wing. Shadow's eyes were a golden glow in the darkness; Ariel was asleep, as Adam had been. He rose slowly under the cat's watchful eyes and startled when the cat hissed. That hiss shifted into what passed for laughter from the cats.

"Do not wake her," Shadow said.

Adam glanced at Ariel and nodded. In this, at least, the gray cat and he agreed. He dressed in the dark, which caused more hissing; the sound was muted. Ariel slept.

Adam wondered, as he sometimes did, if she had a home to return to; he knew why Jewel had accepted her but knew as well that this was not home to her. It had become home to Adam, a second home; he yearned for the first, but he understood why he could not yet return.

The Matriarch waited.

Only when he stepped into the hall did he list, allowing the wall to take some of his weight. He was exhausted, and his arms trembled if he did not put effort into keeping them still. Above his head, the magelights used so freely in the West Wing glowed, but the glow was dim.

He turned to the Terafin Matriarch and froze. It was not she who had knocked on his door. Standing less than a yard away was Evayne, her robes curling in a motion that was almost a tremor around her feet.

He bowed to her, Southern style; she returned a nod of respect. He could not invite her into his room; Shadow disliked her, and even had that not been an issue under normal circumstances, Ariel was asleep. He glanced toward the end of the hall. The great room in the West Wing was often used by the den for conversations of import.

She did not speak; nor did Adam. But he turned and headed toward the great room, and she followed.

Adam started a fire. It was not strictly necessary, but the fire in this room meant it was in use; it was, like food or water in the South, an emblem of hospitality. Nor did Evayne tell him that it wasn't required; she watched while he worked. He watched in return, although his gaze was more frequently broken.

This Evayne was not the Evayne he had first met; nor was she the Evayne he had spoken with at much greater length during his stay in the Oracle's domain. But the robes were the robes he had carried to her, and he thought it likely that she still wore the birthday gift that had been given to her in such dire circumstances. Her eyes were the same violet, but her expression was older; her eyes were lined in the corners, her lips thinner.

There was no hint of tears. This woman, the one who stood before him now, waiting as fire's light began to illuminate the room, was harder, colder, stronger. But she would be: she was older. Youth and its fear had been burned away by the fires of experience.

He knew that the Evayne he had met a handful of subjective days ago must become the Evayne who had come for him in the Sea of Sorrows—but that Evayne had given way, again, to this one. And this one, he thought, might one day be a match for Yollana of the Havallan Voyani. It was not a comforting thought.

He rose, the fire at his back. "Why have you come?"

"I hardly know," Evayne replied. "But I can guess. Tell me, what is the date?"

"I think it is either the fourth or fifth of Lattan, in Weston reckoning. The year," he added, before she could ask, "is 428."

"So soon," Evayne whispered. "You have not yet found what she seeks."

Adam shook his head. This was the business of Matriarchs, yes—but he felt no hesitation; he answered.

"Why are you here?"

"This is where my path leads," Evayne replied. "I must go deeper into the Terafin manse."

Adam waited. Evayne, however, fell silent. "Do you require a guide?" he finally asked.

"Yes, perhaps. Will you guide me, then?"

Adam nodded.

They traversed the halls that led to the stairs, but the guards did not stop them; they did not appear to see them at all.

"It was more difficult when I was younger," Evayne said, although Adam had not asked. "But I find it expedient to avoid unwanted questions. I have been given permission to traverse these lands; not even the Warden will stop me, although she will, no doubt, be aware of my presence. Shadow is watching," she added.

"He does not trust you?"

"No, nor should he. I am not his enemy, but our goals are not the same, and he knows it. No, he watches me tonight because I am with you. Adam, what have you done?"

The question made no sense to Adam, although he considered it from many angles before he finally replied. "I brought the Matriarch home."

Evayne smiled. "Yes. Yes, you did." She looked over the top of his head. "I never thanked you, did I?"

"Thank me?"

"For the time you spent with me in the Oracle's land. I was . . . not at my best that day."

"No one would be!" Adam replied, with genuine indignation.

"No, I don't imagine they would." Her smile was slight, but rueful. Adam did not understand why she felt regret over what was completely understandable. But he did not see that young girl and this older woman as the same person, and perhaps, in some fashion, she did. The one had come from the other, planted and rooted there.

"You were there," Evayne continued, surprising Adam, "with Jewel, the Terafin Matriarch."

Adam nodded.

"And you have only just returned."

He nodded again, with more hesitance.

"Do you know I resented her? I met her once when I was younger, some handful of years away from Callenton and my birthday. I resented her," she repeated. "I saw her with her den. They were young—maybe your age, maybe a few years older—and the Terafin manse was under attack. I was to lose someone I valued there. He was very like you. I could see the loss—the inevitable, constant loss—much more clearly than I could see anything else that night.

"But I saw Jewel. And I understood who she was. Who she must be. Do you know that there were two seers born to the Empire in this time? I was one. She was the other."

Adam simply nodded.

"She had her den, her kin, surrounding her. Yes, she had lost her first family, and yes, the life that led her to Terafin was shadowed and darkened by demons and death. But . . . her fate was not my fate. She *had* kin. She had a life that was in some ways like the life I had been forced to abandon."

He did not tell her that she had made that choice because he didn't believe it was a true choice. The Oracle probably would, but Adam was not the scion of Northern gods.

"You think she is too weak to be Matriarch."

There was a question in the statement. Adam winced but nodded, thinking of his sister.

"Do you think that I was stronger?"

"I . . . can't tell. You are much stronger now than she is."

"Diplomatic. I was angry."

She had the right to be angry.

"It took me many years to let go of that anger. And perhaps it is not truly dead. Jewel was allowed the kin, the friends, that I was denied. The closest to friend I have is Kallandras, and for a decade, perhaps more, he hated me. And he had that right; I had destroyed the only life he wanted—just as my life had been destroyed. I gave him the same choice I was given. Of course he resented me.

"But Jewel was never given that choice. Not truly. She was free to make her attachments, to make her commitments, to *love*. The love I have? It is theory, now, it is so many years in the past. The reason I made my choice?" she shook her head. "Those people—even my own mother—won't recognize me when, and if, that final promise is kept.

"All of the love I was allowed, I was allowed at a distance: it is a story that I have told myself so often it has the strength of myth. But . . . it is not *real*. Jewel's family is real. You've been part of it. You understand that."

Adam nodded.

"Do you know what she did? No, perhaps you don't. And perhaps it is not in your nature to question. But you were there on the day she woke the dreamers. She did, permanently, what you could only do in passing. Do you remember?"

He did.

"She is not what you are. You've been told she is *Sen.* You've been told you are healer-born."

This caused a flinch, but it was mild.

"You understand neither of those words. But, on that day, she created something that she must have. Where is it now?"

Adam found the question confusing.

"Never mind, then. My anger tonight is an ember; it is not a flame. I know the answer to that question, and I do not understand how it was even *allowed.* And yet I *do* understand. Jewel could not stop herself. She made a choice—the barest echo of choices I have been forced to make, time and again—and it almost broke her. She understood the choice itself but did not understand the consequence of what she did next. In order to assuage guilt, she—" Evayne stopped.

"Do you understand, Adam? Everything that she has, I was denied. And in order that she continue to have it, I find myself in this manse, on this road. Whatever she left behind in hope or despair, I must take back. Were it not for me, she would have doomed you all without a second thought. Without a first thought."

"That's not true." Adam's voice was low.

"Is it not?"

"Evayne, you—" he shook his head. "On the day you left Callenton, you left because if you did, you could save the people you loved, yes?"

She nodded.

"When the Matriarch of Terafin came to this place, she was the age you were then. And she had already lost her kin. She came because she hoped to save the rest and she had nowhere else to go. She had lost her mother, her father, her Oma; she had lost her brothers and one sister. You had not—not yet."

"I lost them in every way but death."

"I know. But what if you had had to make that choice then? To abandon them to certain death and *tell them* that? What would you have done?"

"I was sixteen. She is twice that, and *Terafin.*"

"Pain is pain," Adam said quietly. "Loss is loss. When we get older, we get better at hiding it. We learn to protect the children from our pain. It's what we do as—as adults. But pain is pain. And no one surrenders family without pain. I know I have not had your life. I haven't had to make your choices. I haven't had to accept that the pain is something I have no choice but to bear. I'm not Matriarch. I will never be Matriarch. I can't.

"But I know that my mother suffered. I know that my sister suffered. I know that she's too weak to become my mother—but if she were strong, the way my mother was, I couldn't love her the way I love her. I could support her, but I couldn't love her. I understand that I will never know your pain. And that Jewel might never know it.

"But—I don't understand why you want others to feel what you feel when it has been so hard for you?"

Silence. A beat in which Adam wondered if he had pushed this too far. This Evayne and the one to whom he had talked for hours were not the same woman; he knew this. And yet. The silence extended until Evayne came to a stop before a closed door. She looked at him then. And smiled.

It was an odd smile, something that implied tears, not amusement. "No," she said softly, "You don't understand it, do you? I am grateful that I met you. I am grateful that the Oracle sent you to me. You are part of Jewel's den, no? I brought you here to be part of that den."

Adam nodded. "Jewel wasn't here." He seldom used the Matriarch's name, but he used it now. "Finch came. Finch brought me here. She was like a sister, not an Ona. But all of them—all of them, even Ellerson—made me feel welcome here. They tried to teach me how to live in the manse. I understood who they were to her by the time the Matriarch came home. I understood what the former Terafin's loss would mean to her. I understood that she was like— very like—Margret, my sister. She's not strong enough to be Matriarch. She hasn't been forced to make a Matriarch's choices. Until now.

"She's learned to hide pain, mostly. But . . . not among kin. Here, she's where she wants to be. This *is* what she wants. I think this is what we all want, at least to start.

"And in the end, she can't have it, either. She's *Matriarch*. She's more. I want—" he shook his head. "I want someone to be beside Margret as Margret learns what she must do and be if Arkosa is to be safe. And I can't be there, not yet. But I can be here. So . . . I am here."

"I can't save him," Evayne said.

Adam lifted his hands in den-sign. *Carver.*

"It's almost never to save someone that I'm sent. A path opens, and I walk it. I've done things that would horrify you. I imagine I will do things in future that will horrify you as well." She inhaled. Exhaled. "I wish I could take you with me. I think you might be able to walk as I walk, with the right permission. You are what you are. No," she added, seeing the shift in his expression, "I would not ask it. It's funny. I resent—have resented—many people in my life, but you were never one of them.

"But . . . it's often of you that I think, and here you are, Adam, looking not a day older than the Adam of my memories. Not a day older, not a day wiser, not a day harsher. I will see you again," she added softly. "And perhaps on that day, I can return to you some of the peace you left, and leave, with me. It's people like you that I think of when it is absolutely the hardest to make the choices I *must* make if we are to have any hope at all."

"But I have not suffered—"

"No. And maybe you are what you are because you haven't suffered what I—what we—must suffer. But I don't think that's it. I don't think that's all of the truth. I want you to survive. I want the world to somehow survive, even broken—but that's theoretical. You are not." She reached then, for the door, and it opened.

It did not open into the room that Adam knew should have been on the other side. "Go, now. The House Mage will come, or Jewel will. They will know that this way exists, and they must close it, or others will suffer the fate of your Carver and Ellerson."

The Hidden Wilderness

Carver had always associated buildings—with intact roofs and walls—with, if not warmth, then shelter. The blankets with which he had been gifted—by ancient craftsmen who had either abandoned their homes or perished in them—were not buildings. But they were warmer, by far, than the buildings which he had called home in his youth. He remembered the bitter, bitter winter, and the lack of heat. The wind had howled on the other side of slightly warped shutters, and he had huddled into the nearest warm bodies to take the edge off the cold.

Here, without roof or wall, the wind did howl. It howled as if it had a voice that was demonic. Ah, he was tired. He was tired now. The demon was somewhere in the forest beyond this warmth, this tree.

Demonic magic was simple: you paid for it with your soul. Since Carver could not see souls—in any way—and could not eat them, could not stave off hunger or starvation, it had seemed a reasonable deal. But the eternity-of-hell part, less so. If he was to be given useful magic for only a handful of years, being in agony forever seemed unfair.

How had he ended up in this place?

Ah.

Memory. There had been a reason he had followed Jay home on the first night he met her; a reason he had gone into Taverson's with her: she could not hurt him.

*   *   *

That's how it had started. He had looked at her in the alley, her eyes narrowed, her breath shallow. He had approached her because she could not hurt him. Had he loved her then? No, of course not. Had he admired her? No. Had he wanted anything from her? No. What had she to offer him, when she herself seemed so helpless?

He could see her now, in his mind's eye: twelve, straggly hair in her eyes— clean hair; clothing in decent shape, threadbare, but only a little, no torn seams. Shoes that fit. That wouldn't fit him. Brown eyes, even in the darkness of alley. He had nowhere to go.

It's not that he thought she'd keep him safe; it was that she couldn't hurt him. He'd had nothing else to do, and she couldn't hurt him.

She was stupid, really. She was alone. She could hold a knife, but he didn't think she could use it. Duster? He'd known. They'd all known. But Jay? She was barely armed, but she'd come to save a friend. That's what she'd said.

A friend she'd never seen. A friend who wouldn't know her.

It was crazy, it was stupid. She was afraid. He remembered that. But it was the wrong fear. She was afraid of failing. As if someone her age, her build, could do anything else. So: she couldn't hurt him.

He wasn't certain she could hurt anyone.

He didn't know about her gift, her curse, that night, that first night. He knew that she was willing to risk what little she had for a stranger. He believed her when she said it. And he followed her. He followed her into Taverson's. He burned his mouth on the first solid meal he'd seen in days.

And he'd helped.

He'd helped save Finch. Finch, who couldn't hurt him, either.

He'd seen magic for most of his life: streetlights, even in the poorest of holdings. He knew that magic existed on the Isle, where he couldn't even afford to walk, given the tolls required to cross the bridge that separated the Kings and their small part of the city from the rest of the hundred holdings. He had dreamed that magic existed like gold did, there; that no one was hungry or afraid.

He laughed at his own naïveté.

Magic existed, yes. Gods existed. Demons existed. And there was no one, anywhere, who lived without fear. Not in the highest position in the Empire, and not in the lowest. The fear in the lowest was worse, to Carver, but that's where he'd lived at his most helpless. Where they'd all been at their most helpless. Starvation had been a real concern. Cold. Dens.

But in the poorer holdings, he'd had no responsibilities to anyone, nothing to struggle for except his own survival.

That changed, permanently, the night he'd met Jay. She wasn't the first den leader he'd met. She wasn't the first person with whom he'd formed an alliance of convenience, and he had more to offer her because she was so physically weak.

Had he known?

Had he known, then, that by following her on that one night he would never be free again? Had he known that responsibility would weigh down that child, the gravity of its burden shaping the whole of who she would become? No. Of course not. They were urchins in the hundred holdings. They would amount to nothing, be swept away by adulthood in a realm without power. They would join the Kings' army, if there was need for soldiers. They might drift, as many did, to the churches, where shelter and knowledge were exchanged for service.

But on that night, exhilarated by their success and terrified by their enemies, Carver had returned with Jay and Finch to their first home. She had welcomed him in, and he'd decided to stay, just to see if she was real.

She was real. She had a temper. She had decent aim when angry. But she asked no questions about the past, and she accepted people as they were. No other den he could think of would have taken Teller or Finch. Or Lefty.

Lefty, the first to die.

He shook his head.

Jay was kin. Finch. Teller. Jester. Arann. He had—mostly—let go of the others; they were not the first deaths he'd experienced. Not the last. But they haunted Jay. And he thought she welcomed the haunting. Her memories made them real. Her memories made them important. Gods knew they would never be important to anyone else.

She'd guided them. Guarded them. Provided for them, as she could. She hit it big with the Terafin manse. Her visions were enough to guarantee that the House Name would be offered to *anyone* she wanted in the house. And . . . she'd wanted them. She'd wanted Carver.

By that point? He'd've died for her.

What he'd been drawn to, all those years ago, was the fire of Jewel, the need for family, the ability to build it, without the constraints of blood. What he'd wanted for himself, even if he hadn't the words for it, was someone who was loyal not because it was expedient, but because he was kin. No, it was more than that. Jay took commitment, and the responsibility that came with it, seriously. She always had. He had been one of those responsibilities, and he accepted that now.

He had seen her; she had come to this place while he was being hunted by the memory of the Wild Hunt. In this winter place that spoke of the ancient and the lost, a younger Carver would have assumed that hunger and cold and fever had created delusions; that his own desire for *safety* had produced the worst kind of torment: a glimpse of what was lost, would forever be lost.

But she had given him something, and he held it against his skin, beneath his shirt. When he doubted, he could touch it, could take it out furtively, examine it. A leaf. A blue leaf, in kind similar to the leaves that fell from the trees of silver and gold. In her forest—and he wandered there seldom because it was somehow oppressive—he had never seen a tree of blue metal; he wouldn't even know what to call it.

This was what he had of her. This was all he had of home.

What he'd been drawn to, what he'd loved—and he used that word only here, because it still felt cloying and naive at his age—was what, in turn, had made her make the only decision she could.

Had she not been Terafin, she would not have made that choice.

But no, he thought. Had she not been *Jewel*, she would not be Terafin. But Jay, with no money, no machinery of a powerful House behind her, had come to rescue Finch. He smiled, thinking of magic, and talent, of gods and demons.

He thought about bargains, about costs, about prices paid. He still thought that selling his soul was a bad deal. But maybe he had more of Duster in him than he thought.

She had gone to face demons expecting to die. Knowing that death was the best she could hope for. She had never used the word "love," and when the word "den" had become inextricably entwined with it for everyone else, had shied away from that as well.

He could imagine making the same decision she had made. He could imagine that it might be worth an eternity of pain. Not that he'd probably be aware of it, given the nature of agony—it didn't leave room for a lot of thought. He wouldn't have an eternity of knowing he made the right choice because, in the end, he'd probably regret it.

But that end didn't matter so much on this side of life. What did was what made life worth living. He could have been Duster, his rage and pain turned inward, and shoved back out in a survival reflex as old as man, all of them.

And the leaf that Jay had given him, on impulse, in pain? It could do what she herself had said she could not do.

He knew, now, that she shouldn't have left it with him. She was kin. He was hers. But this gift was not a gift left him because she was seer-born, or because she had thought it through and made a rational decision. It wasn't the decision of a leader, a ruler.

He did not want to let it go.

Fair enough, he thought, as he levered himself out of memory and into this shimmering, false summer. At the moment, there was no one to give it to. If the demon wanted it, he could pick it up from Carver's corpse.

Which, from the shift in the earth beneath the blanket, which was otherwise unmoved, he thought would be soon.

"What are you doing?" Anakton demanded.

"I'm arming myself."

"With that? You'd do better to pick up a stray branch!"

"This is what I've got."

"It won't be useful. It might hurt your companion, but it wouldn't leave a scratch on me."

"I do not think it wise," Ellerson interjected, "to pick up, as you say, a stray branch. Not from these trees."

Anakton gave Ellerson the side-eye and then snickered. "You are not as careless as he is."

"He is younger."

"I don't suggest you leave this blanket. We have a bit of help at the moment, but it's not likely to last if the blanket is destroyed."

"This help of which you speak—does it have something to do with the tree's roots? I cannot help but notice that they are being unearthed."

"With the tree, yes, since they're attached. Watch: the tree wants to keep this patch of Summer where it is. You really should have mentioned that you had this earlier. But even if you pick up a stray branch, it won't help. I might help," he added, crawling into Carver's lap.

"Out of the goodness of your heart?"

Anakton tilted his head. "What does that mean?"

"It means," Ellerson said, "without cost. To us."

"How does that even make sense? Things of value are not merely thrown away; they are traded for things of similar value."

Ellerson lifted a brow, and Anakton chuckled. ". . . when both sides understand the value of the thing given. Survival generally makes all things that might be of use far more valuable in the short term than they might otherwise be."

"And you do not believe your survival is in question."

"No. It is not."

The earth moved—and moved again. The blanket rippled as roots rose to the left and right, forming brackets. "Does the tree understand that we're here?"

"It understands that *I'm* here. I am less certain of how it views you. Do you have any way of quieting that leaf you carry? It's making my teeth ache."

Carver shook his head.

"Can you plant it?"

He shook his head again. "The blanket," he explained. "I think the blanket would be destroyed."

"Because it is a Winter spell?"

"When Jay plants her trees, they grow to full height in an eye blink, a heartbeat. If this is meant to be one of her trees, that will happen here as well."

"It might be interesting—"

Something roared.

"—or maybe not. I should probably go."

"You want to face a demon on your own?" In spite of himself, Carver's arms tightened.

"You really are remarkably foolish. It is almost enough to make me feel guilty." He sat more squarely in Carver's lap. "I may have misstated the reasons for my tenure here.

"Although it pains me greatly to see the fallen, he cannot destroy me. He cannot even hunt me. Were it not for my presence here, he could hunt *you*, but sadly, I am awake now."

Carver waited.

"And because I am awake, the earth is waking far sooner than it might have otherwise woken." When Carver failed to reply, the creature continued, misunderstanding the silence. "Yes, I know. The earth *does* dislike the fallen; they betrayed the earth, they forsook it. But, for the most part, the fallen and dead do not have voices with which to bespeak the earth. Some remember the skills and the powers they had in life—and attempting to use them again is almost certain to destroy them, for the earth hears their call and responds in rage.

"Darranatos could bespeak the earth. And his voice was a thing of glory; it held the earth rapt, while he but spoke. There was almost nothing he could not ask of the earth; the earth desired greatly to please and succor him. And now? It will desire greatly to destroy him. I do not understand why he came, but it must have something to do with you. Not Ellerson, but you.

"Do you know, boy, that it is not safe to bleed here? To offer even the sleeping earth your blood? It is like the beginning of an oath, and the earth is

ancient and its bindings subtle and broader than the bindings of the Oathbinders in ages past.

"The earth is tired of its long isolation, its long sleep. It wakes me from time
to time, simply to hear my voice. It woke me this time for a different reason:
it hears yours. Yours and the chorus of the trapped that you carry with you.
Their voices are a crowd; they are stronger and louder than even my own.

"If you offer the earth what you carry, the earth will protect you from everything except the Lord of these lands—and perhaps, for a small time, even
that Lord."

"And if I don't?"

"You will perish here, and the earth will take what you carry anyway."

Carver stared at the creature he now thought of as an oversize rodent. He
then lifted a hand in den-sign. *Lying?*

Yes.

"You'll have to do better than that," he told Anakton.

"Oh?"

"If I die here, the leaf will never be planted."

A chorus of voices said: *Yes.*

Anakton frowned.

"You are eldest, but you are not of the wilderness that owes *my* Lord fealty.
If you could have taken the leaf, you would have taken it one way or the other.
There would be no need to bargain, no need to trade. Am I wrong?"

Anakton was silent.

"What I don't understand is why Darranatos is here. Or how. But why
seems more important. I can't imagine he knows about the leaf."

"And I can't imagine he doesn't. This is not a safe place for one such as he
has become. Even absent the Lord, it causes him no end of pain, for he has lost
much, and the loss is fresh, it is new each time he remembers what he once
was. There *is no reason* for him to come here now, unless it is what you carry."

Carver shook his head.

Anakton shook his tail in a way that implied the gesture was somehow
equivalent.

"Mortal child, you think that the leaf *is* a leaf, for that is what you perceive
of it. And were the Lord of these lands awake, perhaps that is what we would
perceive, as well. But he is not, and here, the dreams are loud. Do you understand? It is only here that Darranatos has some hope of finding that leaf and
its bearer. Do you ask how he knows?"

"I do."

"That leaf was created by a mortal upon the mortal plane, the overworld. A

implied power—but a power that had will and sentience and the ability to create and destroy in equal measure.

He could hear the trees wake to her voice; he could feel the warmth of her Summer and the bitter, bitter cold of her Winter. There was no Summer.

And the Sleeper would not see Summer, even were Summer to finally arrive.

Woe unto those, and all but death, who disobeyed the White Lady, if she but made a command. Here he lay, and the displeasure of the White Lady was met—was matched—by the displeasure of the gods, all save one. His failure was her failure, and her rage was great.

And yet, and yet, and yet: who could obey the commands given to the fallen? Who, of her kin, of her kind, of *herself* could do what she had demanded? Not he, on the bier; not his kindred. None cold enough, none strong enough, none certain enough in their shock and grief save one.

Illaraphaniel.

The Sleeper stirred. Carver held breath, crushing Stacy's hand. To flee one death to meet this one? No. That could not be why Evayne had come.

To the earth, whose voice he heard at a remove and yet at the same time within him, he said, Why? Why is there no freedom for this child?

She is bound, bound, bound, the earth replied. Bound to the sleeping, as the Prince is bound whose name was taken from us, riven from us, by the children. Bound to the Sleepers as the earth is bound.

Carver wanted to wake the earth. To wake the earth, and not the Sleeper. He thought that the rhythm of the earth, its cadence, was not complete yet.

She cannot stay here, he told the earth. But she was trapped, trapped and bound—and to the earth, the binding that could not be broken did not silence her; she could speak with and to the earth. She and her kind. And she might ask what Carver could not ask—although he did and was: For the freedom of those who were not bound as she was. Her voice was light and airy; it was a thing of spring and sunlight. Although she did not speak *to* the earth, the earth drank her voice in as if it were liquid.

As if it were blood.

Was Anakton awake?

Yes. Yes, because the earth had desired it; that Anakton enter the dreaming of this place as it was and find the voices that had entered the dreams of the earth. But other things had entered this dream that should not; had turned it from a whisper of youth and spring, to a far darker winter; the shadows of death and death and death, roaring in a pain and rage that would never end, unless the worlds—all worlds—should end first.

How? How? How?

Carver heard the answer that lay beneath the earth's lament. Darranatos that was, Darranatos, lost for eternity, his name forbidden, lay at the heart of the Sleeper in some fashion that the earth could not and did not perceive. Darranatos had once been of these lands and even the earth remembered the height of his glory, the radiance of his brow, the brilliance of his eyes, his smile, his laugh—and his voice, raised now in song and in praise of the White Lady.

The earth's pain was the White Lady's pain, almost beat for beat: the earth had been loved and the earth had been betrayed, forsaken. There was no forgiveness in the earth, for even in death, the fallen would never return to it; Darranatos' body, as the body of those demons who walked the mortal lands, left nothing in its wake: nothing to hold and keep and protect. Nothing to nourish.

Pain became hatred in time, and time had passed. But for the Sleeper, with perfect memory, history unfolded like a weed in a tended, perfect garden; time and again, it was destroyed; time and again, it grew. The Sleeper turned, his brow rippling.

Carver attempted to disentangle himself from the question he had asked, because it had led to the question the earth had asked—and he had not asked it of Carver.

We do not name the Lord of the Hells when we speak of him at all, he began, and that was enough; enough to pull the earth away from the question. But Carver then stepped into a different storm; this shook the earth, a movement that all but broke the sound of drums, the sound of the earth's heart.

Ellerson caught him before he was driven to the stone of the grand floor. Ellerson, who was steady, whose feet did not tremble with the movement of the earth.

"He can't hear it," Stacy said, her voice very quiet. "He can only hear you. And only when you open your mouth and use words."

"A pity. He looks smart enough to talk sense into the boy."

Carver was not a boy. He proved it in two ways; he did not correct the old man, and he endured. He stopped asking questions and waited. He had no sense of time passing, and simultaneously, of centuries passing.

"I can try," Stacy offered.

Carver shook his head. "Not you."

"It doesn't matter which of us, boy. We're bound together. You can't just pick one of us out."

Anakton bit Carver's ankle, although Carver thought it unintentional; he was, like Ellerson, attempting to hold Carver to his feet. "It is not safe to *lie down* here."

"And you care?"

"I did not intend to harm you. If I had, you would be dead."

"And dead, I'd be no use to you?"

"Dead, you'd be little use to anyone; nothing can even eat you as you are. I certainly wouldn't. But the leaf—the trapped—does it matter *where* they're trapped?"

Yes, Carver thought, as he gained footing and held it without relying on Ellerson. Yes, it mattered. If Jay had done this—and he could not doubt that she had—he could not, in the end, believe that she had done it *for* him. He had come to her by accident; she had not found him because her vision compelled her to do so. He wasn't Finch or Teller; wasn't Arann. And given the earth's response to the prelude to the question he had not finished asking, he thought there was a chance, no matter how small. "The earth might be unhappy again."

He waited until the tremors had died; waited until he was once again enwrapped in the sound of steady, beating heart. *Could I do what Stacy could do, if she were here? Could I ask and open the way?*

And the earth said: you are not bound here. You are not, yet, *of* me.

Carver could see the truth in that; could feel it; he was outside of the earth; he could hear its voice because the memories of this sleeping almost-god were deadly. He glanced, once, at Stacy, and once at the old man; what he saw in both steadied him.

To defeat him, we cannot leave the trapped here.

The earth stilled then.

At his heels, Anakton started to snuffle. And then to wail. Carver grimaced as Stacy's dislike began to wilt.

"He's crying, you know," she said.

"They're probably fake tears," the old man told her, voice grim, words clipped.

"They're not fake tears—he's really crying." Her hands fell to her hips, the gesture so familiar, it tugged at parts of Carver he didn't want to express. If she pushed her hair out of her eyes—but no. She looked at Anakton, and then she crouched. "You have to let go of my hand," she told Carver.

Carver shook his head. "You can't pick him up."

"I can."

Carver grimaced and bent at both knees; he scooped the silver furred ball into one arm but kept a firm grip on Stacy with the other.

"You can't hug him like that."

"I don't think he wants me to hug him," Carver replied, as Anakton attempted to burrow into his chest.

Ah, he wanted to go home. He wanted to see Merry. He wanted to see his den-kin.

"You *could*," Anakton said, half whine, half growl, his body vibrating in the crook of Carver's arm. "Don't you understand? There's nothing you can do for her—she is never going to be free. But you could! *We* could!" Carver had no doubt which of the two was more important. Nor did he believe that Anakton was lying; he couldn't. Anakton said what the earth, wordless, also said.

He believed that Jay had left the leaf here for a reason. But he believed, now, that it was the wrong reason. He could see the detritus of love—of the fear of loss—in this glorious room, and in the man that lay upon an altar as if it were a bier. He had heard it in the rage of Darranatos.

And even had he not, he could not buy his own freedom with Stacy's.

Anakton shrieked in agitation at Carver's stupidity; it almost made Carver feel that he was home. "She is *not* free!"

"And she will never be free if she remains here."

Carver was not surprised to see Evayne emerge from the light; she had not come through the tunnel. The shadows her robes cast were long and dark, but they did not fall on Carver. Not physically.

"She will never be free at all!" Anakton snarled. He glared at Evayne.

"You are bold," Evayne said, voice cool. "Far bolder here than you have been."

Carver understood. Until—and unless—the earth granted him his freedom, the earth would protect him.

Evayne looked above Anakton's head to Carver; she met his eyes, her violet gaze unblinking and steady. She was scratched and pale, and one eye was blackened, but she did not bleed. He wondered, briefly, what her blood would mean to the ancient earth, but did not ask.

"This is not why Stacy made her choice."

"Jewel will be sad," Stacy said, her voice soft.

"Yes."

"And my mother will be sad anyway."

Evayne did not close her eyes, but Carver closed his.

"Yes. Would you rather your mother be sad some of the time, or dead?"

Both Carver and the old man stiffened, Carver's eyes opened, his expression shifting as he glared at Evayne. Evayne, who could face demons, had faced far worse than the fear of one child, and certainly worse than the icy disapproval of an old man.

"Stop it," Carver said.

"It is not for her sake that I ask," Evayne replied.

"If you're implying that you're doing it for mine, don't. It doesn't help me."

"It is not for your sake, either; not directly." Evayne glanced, once, at the Sleeper.

"Why are you here?"

She was silent for a long, long beat, during which Carver could feel the thrum of the earth.

"I am here," she said softly, "to bespeak the earth once you have made your decision."

"You can speak to the earth."

She nodded. "It will not readily do what I ask, if I do not ask in a fashion acceptable to it, but it hears my voice when I choose to bespeak it. I am not Jewel, to make an offhand command it both feels as imperative and obeys—she is not what I am, nor am I what she is.

"But here, in this place, it will hear me." Evayne waited.

Carver looked away from her, to Stacy.

Clutching Anakton, he knelt, to bring his eyes closer to the level of hers. "Go and save your mother," he told her. He rose. To the old man, he said, "Take care of her."

The old man nodded. "For as long as I can."

He then turned to Ellerson. He could feel the earth tremble beneath his feet, the rhythm of the beat shifting, less a rumble, more a tremor. "Here," he said, and detached Anakton from the front of his shirt.

"The earth will not release him," Evayne said softly.

Anakton was crying, but softly now; he was a wet, furry bundle.

"Yes," Carver said quietly. "With your help, he will."

Ellerson helped Carver detach Anakton; he did not set him down, and Anakton's almost instinctive grip became snarled in the domicis' clothing, not Carver's. "Master Carver."

Carver shook his head.

"I am domicis here, and far older than you; I have more experience, and what I might offer the earth—"

Carver shook his head again. "You're domicis. I've never completely understood what that means—but I understand one thing. Your duty is to help me carry out my decisions; to support me, in both the making and the execution. This is my decision, not yours. It isn't yours to make."

Ellerson said nothing.

"Even if it were, they need you."

"They need you, Master Carver. Jewel needs you."

He shook his head, hair briefly flying in both of his eyes, not the usual one. "She doesn't. She's already said her good-byes. Whatever's coming to Averalaan doesn't require me to stop it. But it does require you."

Ellerson shook his head.

Carver said, "I went into the closet after you. Jay's a seer. She could have stopped me."

"It has long been a source of pain to The Terafin that her vision, when it came, was not reliable for any save herself." It was a counter.

Carver nodded, but said, "I came after you. I think we needed to be in the same place." He glanced at Evayne; she did not speak.

"Only one of us can leave. Stacy, you have to let go of my hand."

Ellerson said nothing, but bowed his head briefly, an acknowledgment of all that Carver had said—and much that he hadn't.

"I don't want to."

"I know. But you have to because Ellerson is going to take you home. You've been sleeping too long, and you'll wake if you're home."

"But I don't want to leave you here!"

"Stacy," the old man said, and this was a sergeant's bark of sound. Stacy let go reflexively; Carver retrieved his hand before she could grab it again. He then slid his hand into his shirt and withdrew the leaf.

Where the leaf cut the fall of light, light broke, but not into simple shadow; as he glanced at the floor just below his outstretched arm, he saw both himself, made short and squat and almost unrecognizeable by the light's angle, and what he had called leaf.

He froze.

The leaf's shadow was not small, and it wasn't singular; if it resembled the leaves of the *Ellariannatte* in shape and size while it rested by its stem between his fingers, its shadow told a different story. His shadow was squat, short, and human. But the shadows cast by the leaf—the multiple shadows—were not. As if even the light here were strange, as if it fell from all angles, and the shadows themselves could choose which angle they bisected, he saw people, or the outlines of people, against the cold stone.

Some were taller than he, some wider, some more bent; some, quivering as if standing still took effort and concentration, were children.

He could not count them all. He didn't try. He could still see Stacy clearly, and she was enough. No, that wasn't true. He could see Ellerson. Ellerson's hands remained by his sides. Carver still carried the leaf.

With one hand, Carver began to sign.

Finch. Teller. Arann. Jester. Adam. Jay.
Jay.

And then, because he might never sign these names again where others would read the gestures and understand their meaning, he added, *Lefty. Lander. Fisher. Duster.*

Ellerson.

Ellerson, Anakton in one arm, crossed the distance that separated him and took the leaf.

Stacy disappeared, as Carver had known she would; she was, for the moment, Ellerson's burden to bear. She would return to Jay; he was certain of that. Only when Ellerson tucked the leaf inside his shirt, did Carver wonder why he had not thought to give the leaf to Evayne.

But no. Even thinking it, his eyes were caught by Ellerson's hands, Ellerson's gestures: *Carver.*

Carver.

Ellerson could not see Stacy. Nor did he feel the weight of the blue leaf as Carver had felt it; he was burdened now only by the duties he had willingly accepted.

He glanced at Evayne; her lips were trembling, but he heard no words. Thrice, her eyes widened, twice they narrowed. The third time they closed. She raised hands; the folds of midnight fabric fell back from her arms exposing them; they were pale, the color of the Winter people.

Carver nodded, as if she had spoken. He signed, *go,* and then turned toward the tunnel they had followed to arrive in this place. Ellerson followed.

The moment he crossed the threshold between tunnel and what was, for all intents and purposes, a crypt, no matter how brilliantly lit, how carefully detailed, he could once again hear the demon. Pain, however, had given way to rage, and rage to threats that he could understand. The ground beneath his boots shook with them, as did the walls of this tunnel.

"You do not have much time," Evayne said, following in their wake.

Ellerson did not look back in the direction of her voice.

Anakton was now cradled in both arms; he had, thankfully, ceased to weep, although his sniffling suggested that laundering would be necessary in the near future. It was a future that did not include Carver.

"You're not afraid," Anakton observed. "But you are older than he is. Not wiser, then?"

"Wisdom is accrued by experience." Ellerson exhaled. The only thing he feared when he had first arrived in this strange, Winter world would come to pass. He could not prevent it, nor would he try. Carver had decided.

And he would stand by Carver to witness the outcome of that decision. He did not tell Anakton that his lack of fear—for himself—was entirely intellectual. He carried the leaf. Evayne was present. It was not for Carver's sake, nor Ellerson's; the scope of her goals was broader by far, and it did not stop long to rest upon the shoulders of a single individual.

She meant for that leaf to return to Jewel, and there was now only one way it would: through Ellerson. Until he carried the leaf to its maker, he would be safe. It was not his safety that had been his chief concern.

He understood that the den had lost kin in their earlier years. He recognized the names of the lost, although they were seldom spoken. Only in the teaching of the names were they added; Adam knew them.

This would be the first of the den to be lost during Ellerson's tenure. Carver's name would be added, by slow degree and the passage of time, to the rolls of the dead. His hands full of Anakton, he could not make the gesture—but he would have, otherwise. He had come to understand the comfort of a language that was, at its heart, the tongue of orphaned children.

"He will not die," Anakton said quietly. "Dead, he is of no use to the earth; the earth cannot bind without consent or the aid of the gods. I am sorry. I did not mean to injure you. Either of you."

Ellerson said, "No." It was why, in the end, he had taken Anakton from Carver, and why he would carry him until he could be safely set down.

They walked the tunnel in silence, Carver in the lead, Evayne at the rear. In the lesser light of the tunnel, it was dark; shadows were thicker than light as they lay across floor and curved wall.

The demon's voice could be heard; it was louder, a rumble of thunder; it felt like a natural disaster in the making. The earth shook, continued to shake, as they walked, but the dislodged dirt did not land on the tunnel's occupants. The tunnel held.

Carver walked to the altar that had been at the height of the dais, and there he stopped, lifting his head as if he could see the demon kept at bay by the earth itself. The altar was far deeper beneath that earth than a grave would have been.

Hands shaking, Carver removed the cloak that had protected him from the cold. He removed, as well, the boots that had allowed them to pass above the crust of ice that had settled, over the years, across snow. Both of these, he set into the almost weightless pack across his shoulders.

"Take these as well," he told Ellerson, holding the pack.

Anakton allowed himself to be shuffled, like dead weight, to the crook of one arm.

To Angel, he said.

Ellerson nodded.

Carver glanced at the ring on his hand, and up again. But the ring, he kept. "The earth likes it. He likes the sound of it."

Evayne said nothing. Ellerson moved to stand beside Carver; beside and behind. Evayne remained where she stood—facing him, the surface of the altar between them. Carver took the dagger he carried; it was a small, clean knife. He grimaced as he drew it across his left palm. Blood welled slowly; it had been a shaky, shallow cut.

"I won't die," he told Ellerson, his gaze flicking briefly to Anakton. "The earth says I won't die."

"What does the blood signify?"

"It's living blood," Anakton said, as if this explained everything. Or anything.

"Blood of my blood," Carver said, his words following Anakton's. "I . . . don't understand it. But blood offered to the earth on death isn't the same as the blood of the living. In the South, in the Dominion—I think—there's power, some obligation of earth to the people who can't hear it or speak to it." He blinked. "I think—I think it wants you to know that."

"Why?"

"Because you'll go to a place where the earth isn't awake."

"The earth," Evayne said quietly, "does not wake often, even in the wilderness. Were it not for the leaf, it would not be awake now—but the Sleeper's dreams are light and fractured, this close to his waking. They are one."

"The earth doesn't wake when she carries the leaf."

Evayne's frown was a network of etched lines around the corners of her lips, her eyes. "No. I do not entirely understand the why."

But Ellerson said, "Perhaps it was Shadow."

She turned her gaze to Ellerson then, her eyes narrowing. "Shadow? The gray cat?"

"He was here," Carver said. "Not for long, but he was here."

"When this is over," the seer replied, "I will singe the fur off those cats. It should not have been possible for him to be here at all."

It was Anakton who said, "No one tells the eldest where they can—or cannot—go. But he did not expect to be here, and he was not pleased. He could not stay."

She looked at them all, exhaling slowly. As if counting. "What is done is done. And perhaps the oldest understand what we cannot immediately understand. There would be no way out of these lands—for you, for what you carry—if the earth could not be roused."

"And there is now?" Carver asked.

"For your companions—yes, even Anakton—if you desire it." She looked up again. "But this space will not hold for long, and you will not survive if you do not do what you intend."

Carver nodded, then. He placed the palm he had cut upon the altar.

At once, the earth stilled. The roars of the demon quieted, although they did not—as they had done in the room which housed the sleeper—vanish utterly.

Carver lifted a hand—the uncut hand—and signed, although he did not turn to Ellerson. He was watching Evayne. She was watching him. When he finished, he lowered his hand. And when his hands stilled, she raised hers. She signed—it seemed to Ellerson that she signed—a word he did not recognize. Carver did.

He closed his eyes.

"Yes," she said, abandoning den-sign. "You will buy their freedom with yours. It is why I am here." She then placed her bloodless hand upon the altar, across from Carver's; she lifted her head, closing her eyes. She began to sing.

Her voice was not practiced, not strong—and yet it carried. Ellerson did not move; the earth did. The room, if it could be called a room, around the altar began to shift, to change; dirt became stone as stone emerged from its deep, deep brown; roots seemed to withdraw, to give stone the burden that they had undertaken.

The altar began to glow. Carver winced, shutting his own eyes, the fall of his lashes a fan of color that the light appeared to leech from everything else. He levered himself up, onto the altar's flat surface; he then lay across it, although the cut hand remained palm down on the surface of stone.

"Living blood," Anakton said. "It is a promise and a binding. Blood of my blood. Flesh of my flesh."

Carver's skin became the color of stone, as if color were blood, and he grievously wounded. His clothing likewise changed color, but instead of gray, it was brown—brown, green, gold. His hair remained a shade of brown that was almost black; Ellerson could not see the color of his eyes beneath his lids.

Evayne continued her rough song, and her robes swirled around her, as if they sought to accompany that song in a writhing, sinuous dance of their own. He could hear their movement.

The ground shook beneath his feet. The ceiling shook above him.

Evayne lifted her free hand and signed. Den-sign. *Go. Now.* She could not speak and sing simultaneously and did not try.

Ellerson, shouldering two packs, cradling a talking beast, stepped back from the altar. But he could not leave, not yet. Anakton bit his hand. He did not draw blood, but that was a deliberate choice on his part; he did catch Ellerson's attention.

"We must *leave*," he said, a hiss of sound. "Did you not hear her?"

"I heard her." He did not understand the words of the song.

"We must leave, or we will not leave. Come, come, we must away."

They were underground, and there did not appear to be an exit. Ellerson considered this obvious and did not say it. "Where?" he asked, instead.

"That way, *that way.*" Anakton's head swiveled in the direction of the tunnel they had taken; it still remained. "She cannot keep singing. She should not be able to sing here at all—but she does it for *your* sake."

Ellerson did not argue. He glanced once at Carver, but Carver's eyes did not open; he was becoming part of the stone upon which he had lain.

"We will not be able to leave if she does not sing. And she sings, where she should not. It is dark—can you not see it? We must be away before the darkness eclipses us."

Ellerson nodded, a brief, curt gesture. He turned toward the tunnel.

If Evayne's song was darkness, the tunnel's response was light: it was as bright, now, as the great hall in which the effigy of the Sleeper lay. Ah, no. He could see, as the light expanded, that it enveloped them all—all except for Evayne. The tunnel shifted, changing as the floor and the walls of this room changed; with the expanse of walls came color, a mosaic of a pattern, and between those flashes of color, pillars. They were not the pillars that girded the Sleeper's hall; they were not so tall, not so fine.

But they were better, in every way; they were statues, forms of people, the likeness perfect: the den. Carver's den. Ellerson could see their past being built as color continued to spread. Only Evayne remained, untouched, untouchable.

"Mortals," Anakton said, "are fast. Always fast. Everything moves so quickly. Everything changes in a rush. Perhaps that is why the earth is willing to keep him. It makes me dizzy."

There, Finch, Teller, Jester, Arann—pillars all, but perfect in their likeness. Angel. Jewel. Ah, he thought. Merry. The cats. He was surprised to see the cats, but they weren't pillars; they were mosaics, one on each of three walls. This was Carver's room, Carver's hall. This was the amalgam of the earth and the man.

The altar was not the center of this evolving, emerging hall. Perhaps, when the transformation was complete, it would be. At the moment, however, Ellerson was surprised to see a trapdoor in the center of the floor, hinged to lift, its surface a simple, plain wood.

He approached the door, lifting it one-handed with effort until it lay flat against the stone. There were stairs leading down, adding distance between them and the demon above. But distance from Carver as well. He straightened his shoulders as he rose, and then turning once for a final glimpse of Carver, began his descent.

5th day of Lattan, 428 A.A.
Terafin Manse, Averalaan Aramarelas

Jewel had, as a child, daydreamed of living in a palace. Palaces were, after all, for the rich and the powerful. They had more room than she could conceive of, and in the early years, more rooms than she could count. Wealth and power had been, to her much younger mind, guarantees of safety. Her family could live without struggle and fear—because the fear of both cold and starvation had always been a looming shadow that threatened to become a shroud.

In that distant youth, surrounded by her family, the words *palace* and *castle* had been interchangeable. They were large places in which powerful people lived.

As she stood before the closed doors of this castle, she did not feel powerful. She felt apprehensive. The castle itself had come into existence in her absence. Or perhaps it had come into existence upon her return and she had failed to notice.

Teller and Finch remained at the foot of the stairs that led to this grand door. The Chosen—Torvan and Marave—stood to either side. Torvan had attempted to open the door; he'd failed. He did not try again. The castle was new to him as well, and he understood that it was not, in any fashion anyone understood, a building that could exist within Averalaan. It was, as was the previous iteration of personal chambers, part of the wilderness. Part of Jewel.

He did not expect that opening these doors would harm her, and he did not expect that anyone except Jewel herself could open them. But expectations aside, he was Chosen; it was his duty to protect her if his expectations were confounded.

Snow returned, shouldering Torvan to the side—as if Torvan were one of the den. Torvan failed to notice the white cat, which took effort, as he had to regain his footing.

She had come home, she thought, but home had, once again, inexplicably changed. Were it not for the West Wing and its occupants, she would not recognize it. She shook her head.

Home had always been people. Place had never been guaranteed. It was not the loss of the apartment that had almost destroyed her, but the loss of her father. Her mother. Her Oma. The silence they left behind persisted, even during the stretch of days she had spent beneath the bridge across the river, when the noise of the city had failed to drown out the constant echoes of loss.

Rath had found her.

Rath had offered her a home. He was not familial, not family—but there *was no family*. Her Oma's words about strangers, while persistent, had become irrelevant. She would starve—or die—when winter came, unless she wished to dedicate herself to the Mother's church and pray to gods that demonstrably hadn't listened at any time before.

She touched the doors with the flat of her left palm. They did not open, but she hadn't expected them to. Hadn't *asked* them to.

Rath's home had been utterly silent in his absence, and he was absent a lot, just as her father had been before him. Eventually she had filled that home—and he had allowed it—with people. Not blood-kin but chosen kin. Lefty. Arann. Carver. Finch. Jester. Duster. Fisher. Lander. Teller. Angel had come later.

The apartment had become a house full of noise, the lack of space obvious because of the constant press of bodies. It was the noise that she associated with family. Sometimes, she wanted to escape it—but only, in the end, so she could return to it.

Home was the people that occupied it.

Here, home was den. If her quarters changed, if her forest changed, if the politics of Terafin threatened to overwhelm and exhaust, her den was here. Her den was safe.

Carver.

Her den had been safe.

She bowed her head; touched wood with her forehead.

Home was where her people were. The roof might change. The walls. The shape and size of the room. The clothing might change. The food. But if they were here, this was home. And home was a thing she could not give up. To lose it—to lose it again—was more than she could bear. The first time, as a child, she hadn't understood what the loss meant; the lack of warmth, the lack of noise, the lack of comfort, of *love*.

But the time that passed without family had enfolded her in a world that was full of people, none of whom even knew who she was. They did not care for her, or about her—and why should they? They had worries and fears of their own. Families to feed. Children who might starve or sicken. They did not need, could not bear, another burden.

She could see that now, could forgive that now. But not then. She had been a *child*. Then, she had understood that she had no value, no worth. She couldn't work. She could not do what her father had done, until that work had killed him in the Port accident. She could not do what her mother had done. And her Oma? Her Oma had no longer worked, but people obeyed her Oma when she opened her mouth, her words staccato, intense, a rumble of sound, presaging a natural disaster.

Jewel had had none of that. She had had certainty, yes—but no way of conveying it. And her Oma had made clear that the one gift she had was *not* a gift; it was a curse. It was a curse and a stain that must be hidden.

As an adult, Jewel understood why. But she had not seen it clearly then. She had heard her Oma's worry, her Oma's fear—but her Oma funneled all emotions through an electric anger. She had heard that there was *something wrong with her*. She heard it now, at a great remove. And she still believed it.

She had turned her rooms—The Terafin's rooms, meant, in the end, as a legacy for the women or men who would occupy the seat—into an open space of amethyst skies, a forest of library trees. Even the collection had been somehow altered, and without intent; books were not, to Jewel, what they had always been to Teller.

And now: a castle.

A castle that not even the Chosen could enter, if she did not first open the doors.

This isn't what I wanted.

But, hand on the door, feet on the flat, wide steps that led to it, she could no longer be certain. Because this was what she had—without intent, without will, without *knowledge*—made. Yet even her yearning for the past, before death and demons and gods, her yearning for a life that had not, objectively, been easy—ah.

Who had lived in that apartment? Who had occupied it after demons had forced the den to flee, and had, in the end, killed Duster? It couldn't have been empty. Where were the occupants that her dreams had driven out? Where were they now?

Shadow stepped on her foot.

"Find them," Jewel whispered, her forehead pressing into the door, her hand becoming a fist. "Find them, Shadow."

Shadow did not respond. She lifted her head, looked down; he was seated on the flat of the step; he had pushed Marave out of the way. His wings were high and dark; shadows seemed to trail, like smoke, from his flight feathers. He did not move. His eyes were gold and shining; his irises were black, large.

He might have been a statue, Artisan crafted, caught in a perfect moment. A mirror that she could not see herself in. And that she could.

She turned then, to the door. Inhaled. Exhaled. This castle was now. It was what she had made of the rooms that had a history of occupation by those who ruled, those who bore the weight of the fate of House Terafin on their shoulders, on their brows.

"I can't," the gray cat said, when she turned away, no longer caught by the gravity of his gaze, his posture. "You must find them."

"I don't even know who they were!" Louder words. Tremble in throat, in shoulders, the gravity of Terafin dragging them down.

"You *must* learn. You must *remember.*"

"I can't remember—I never met them. I have no idea who they were!" Her voice broke. She gathered it, pieced it together. "Do you?"

Shadow, however, examined his left paw. "You must remember," he said. "In the end—and the end is coming—you must learn how to remember them *all.* You hurt yourself," he growled. "You hurt *yourself.*

"You do not understand because you are *stupid.*"

She felt the frame of her shoulders relax at the sound of his familiar disgust.

"There are only *two* ways. Only *two.*"

She nodded. "What ways, Shadow?"

"Stop *caring.* Those people? They were *nothing* to you, and *that* is why they are *gone.* People who did not *know* you did not *care* about *you.* But you? You are *stupid.* You think you *can* care. You think you *should.*"

If Rath had not cared, she would likely be dead.

"You are not a *god.* You do not *create* your people. They are *not* yours."

Arann. Carver. Finch. Teller. Jester. Angel. She hadn't created them, either. "What's the second way?"

He lowered his paw; she could feel it hit stone, and for just a moment, thought the weight of it would produce cracks and fissures.

"*Become.*"

She started to argue. Words would not leave her mouth, although they backed up there. *I'm not a god. I can't become a god. Give me something I can work with, work for.*

And she looked up, to the peak of this doorframe, to the height of it, and beyond, to as much of the height of the building as could be seen, when one was standing this close to its wall. It was so cold here, she thought winter had arrived, in an instant, just as the castle itself had cohered.

Standing, frozen, she could only watch as the doors opened inward, although she hadn't pushed them. To her left and right she could hear the sounds of metal against metal, swords leaving scabbards. She herself felt no visceral fear.

No fear at all, although that would come later. She did not throw herself left or right, did not turn to leap back, out of the way. But she did throw herself forward.

Standing in the frame, standing there in the clothing he had worn for all of his time in the West Wing, stood Ellerson.

She could hear Teller, hear Finch; could easily separate which steps belonged to each as they raced up stairs, shouting a name.

Shadow sneezed.

Epilogue

ELATION AT ELLERSON'S RETURN diminished greatly upon the realization that he had returned alone. Castle and its implications all but forgotten, Jewel lifted a hand, and the rush of slowing questions stopped immediately.

"Kitchen," she said. Calliastra had no interest in a kitchen; she did not understand the significance of the command.

Every other person present marked it instantly, a fact not lost on Calliastra, who could not bring herself to ask. If the castle was now open, she would remain within; it was small and quite probably insignificant, but it was more suitable for a person of her stature than a mere kitchen. Even so, she made no derogatory comments about Ellerson, either his appearance or his import. She understood—and probably resented—what the rush up the stairs meant.

With the exception of Calliastra, they turned, Jewel in the lead, and headed back down the path that had dampened their clothing, seeking the comfort of familiarity: the kitchen in the West Wing, where all councils of war had been held among the den since they had first arrived at the Terafin manse.

For the first time that any of the den could remember, Ellerson chose to take a seat at the table itself.

Jewel had summoned Jester, Arann, Daine, and Adam. Adam walked slowly, as if his feet were heavy; the circles beneath his eyes were dark. He was exhausted; an evening of sleep had not done nearly enough good. Jewel almost sent him back to bed, but she couldn't. While he lived in

Averalaan—while he traveled at her behest by her side—he was den. But no, it was not just that.

He was the age the den had been when it had been whole, and the shadow of death had been starvation—and there was, about his presence, the suggestion of youth, of renewal; the certainty that, somehow, the den would survive, and its legacy, the heart of what it had been, continue to spread, to extend. And she needed that today.

Jewel spoke first, but quickly, quietly, as if her own excursion into the Oracle's domain was insignificant, unimportant. Angel occasionally added details that he considered consequential. The events they had witnessed and survived were not unimportant to the den, but Jewel, Angel, and Adam had returned. They were alive, here, unharmed, the kitchen walls enclosing them.

They listened, but half their attention was upon Ellerson. Ellerson, who had not brought Carver with him from wherever the interior of a closet had taken them. Jewel herself was barely interested in her own tale in comparison.

To this council of war, to this kitchen, Haval had come, although he did not sit; the Chosen had come as well, but they were omnipresent if Jewel, Finch, or Teller were anywhere in the manse. They would never have fit in the old kitchen in the poorer of the hundred holdings; they wouldn't have fit in the old apartment if anyone had wanted to be able to move.

Ellerson began; his voice was the only sound in the room. Even breathing was quiet enough that it could barely be heard.

Shadow, Snow, and Night—like Avandar—remained as far from the table as walls allowed. When Ellerson's tale touched upon a creature he called Anakton, Shadow was not pleased, but his offer to hunt and kill said creature was an indication of either disgust or annoyance; Shadow did not fear him the way he feared the golden fox. He did, however, shriek in outrage when Jewel thought it: he was not *afraid* of the fox. He was worried that the *stupidity* of the den would allow the fox to use them.

Around the table, while Shadow ranted and his two brothers hissed laughter, she could see her den-kin relax. Were it not for Shadow's outburst, the table would be shrouded in silence. No words broke it, or could, for this silence was the silence Carver had left in his wake.

Jester, often the first to break such a silence, lifted his hands. *Carver. Carver. Carver.*

Ellerson nodded.

Not dead.

The domicis nodded again.

Arann's hands did not move; Adam's did. *Not dead.*

But Finch and Teller eventually joined those silent movements, as if only den-sign, the language of their youth, was strong enough to form.

Only then did they turn to look at Jewel. Jewel, whose hands, trembling, were still, silent. She was thinking of Merry. Merry, not den, but as much a part of Carver's life as the den had been. It was odd, to think of her that way, and Jewel had not fully done so until now—because the loss itself would mean as much to Merry as it did to the den.

But Merry could not—could never—sit at this table. Merry ATerafin was not den, and could not be den without giving up the life she had built for herself.

It was a better life than Jewel had built with her den in the early years, and Jewel understood the value of that life. Yes, she was now The Terafin and Merry was simply part of the Household Staff—but without that Household Staff, there would be no manse, not as it existed now. Everything Jewel did, and everything the den did, was built on that quiet, unassuming work.

Her hands trembled. She had taken something from Carver that he had asked her to return to Merry. She would. She would, but not yet, not now.

No, she thought, that was wrong. It was the only thing Carver had asked of her. It was the last thing he had asked.

She rose. "I have to speak to Merry."

Finch rose. "I'll come with you."

Jewel shook her head. "I am The Terafin. I can speak to any member of my Household Staff and the Master of the Household Staff must accept the intrusion. She might question me. She will not question Merry."

Jester snorted, the first normal sound he had made since they had come to this table, this kitchen.

"Merry will not bear the brunt of the Master of the Household Staff's displeasure. I will."

Teller winced because it was true.

"But if it's my choice, Merry can't disobey me. It's my name she bears."

The den was slow to disperse. Ellerson did not leave the table until the last of their number had drifted away, leaving silence in their wake. Haval, however, did not leave the room. He waited.

Only when the door closed on Arann's back, the last of the den to go, did he speak. "You did not tell all of the tale."

"It is not for the telling," Ellerson replied. He understood that Haval was Councillor and understood what that meant.

Haval did not appear to take offense, and Ellerson considered the lack of offense genuine. "Will you tell her?"

Ellerson nodded.

"Then I will send her to the great room before she speaks with the Master of the Household Staff."

Ellerson raised a brow.

"The Master of the Household Staff could, in a different world, command the *Astari*. She understands the hierarchical rules that govern the house, but she does not allow them to be used against her. Jewel will speak with Merry as she intends. The process would not be as cumbersome if she approached Merry directly. She will not, however. She will speak with you before she speaks with the Master of the Household Staff."

As Haval approached the door, Ellerson said, "How much do you know? How much do you understand?"

"I understand very little, but much can be gleaned from the whining complaints of her three cats. And much from the whispers of the *arborii*. I will not tell you that she is not your concern; you are domicis and you understand where your duty lies. Comfort her if you can.

"Were we, in aggregate, facing any other danger, any other enemy, I would tell you that she will break unless she learns to develop the emotional calluses that many of the powerful are taught, from birth, to develop. But for better or ill, it is not what I would advise here."

"Even were you to advise it," Ellerson said, voice low, "she could not accommodate. She is what, and who, she is."

"I agree," Havel replied. "Jarven would not. The forest elders would not. But she will not be Lord of a simple forest, if we survive; she will be Lord of lands in which mortals can—and must—be safe." He met Ellerson's eyes in the dimmer kitchen light and held them. "My wife is one of those mortals. There is very, very little in the end that I would not do to preserve her.

"But conversely there is very little, in the end, that she would allow. Were I to devote the whole of my intent and my general lack of compunction toward her safety, I would lose her. I would, in the quaint, angry words of Hannerle, break her heart. I would destroy, in that instant, what love she might have nursed—with however much difficulty over the decades—for me. And so, my hands are tied by the very thing I value beyond measure.

"But, in like fashion, so are Jewel's." Haval bowed to him. "I will send her to you."

*   *   *

Ellerson was waiting in the great room when Jewel arrived. She crossed the room and sat, heavily, in one of the chairs, but did not motion Ellerson to do the same; he had forced himself to accommodate the den's emotional needs by joining them at the kitchen table, but he was never going to be comfortable doing so.

He withdrew the blue leaf from its resting place.

She stared at it, her shoulders folding. "I left it with him."

"Yes."

"I shouldn't have."

Ellerson did not reply.

"Do you know that I effectively killed people without even being aware they were there?"

It was not the question he expected to hear. He shook his head, waiting. She was staring at her hands, at the single ring that adorned them. Nor did she lift her head when she began to speak again.

She told him. Of her dream. Of the fact that it was a *good* dream. It was the best parts of the past, before the worst parts had started. She was in the apartment she had found for them. She was, once again, at home.

But, as her meeting with Carver had been, it was more than a dream. Real and not real. And her den—her *living* den—had walked into that dream as well. And when she woke, the apartment was empty. Whoever had lived in it before she had started to dream, before her subconscious had taken her to a place for which she yearned, had vanished. They were gone.

She'd done this.

As she'd left the leaf in Ellerson's hands with Carver.

"I shouldn't have left it," she whispered. "I *know* I shouldn't have left it."

"Did you know then?"

She shook her head.

He approached her, as he seldom approached her these days. "Do not regret love. Do not think that it brings only pain. Your den is here. Carver is not dead."

"I told him to use it."

"Yes. But, Jewel, Carver understands that you are The Terafin. You are more than The Terafin. And he understands that you are kin. No decision such as the decision you reached in that dreaming could be made without pain."

"What *good is pain?*" she said, lifting her head in a snap of motion. "What good is pain if it *doesn't change anything?*" She rose then and began to pace. Or she would have had Shadow not materialized. He stepped on her foot. She looked down at the cat.

The cat looked at Ellerson, studiously ignoring the woman on whose feet he was standing.

"Do you think that Amarais did not know pain?" Ellerson asked.

She was silent, breathing, struggling with rage and, yes, pain. She shook her head mutely. No.

"Were she to be Haerrad, would that be better?"

"No!"

"No, indeed. It is always a difficult balance. It will never be easy. But, Jewel, I think, were it easy or simple to sacrifice others, you would not be what you now are."

"And what is that?" was the bitter, quiet question. "I brought them here because I thought they'd be safe. And they were. They were. Until—until *me*."

"You are not responsible for the Sleepers. Not even the gods could destroy them."

"If I hadn't planted those trees, that door would have never opened. You would never have been lost in a closet. Carver wouldn't have been lost there, either."

"Jewel—what you are becoming, I do not know. But I trust the *heart* of it. You will make mistakes. Mistakes are unavoidable. Learn from the ones you survive. It is all you can do. It is all anyone can do.

"But if you lose heart, if you inure yourself to guilt, you inure yourself also to responsibility. It is the flip side of the same coin. And I believe you are *Sen*, as the ancients call you, for a reason. Is it safe? No. It is not safe for you; it is not safe for us." He exhaled. "But a god walks the world, and that is far, far less safe. Can you face that god as you are now?"

She shook her head.

Shadow nodded. He then shouldered her, and she stumbled back into the chair she had vacated in her agitation. Before she could rise again, the great gray cat dropped his head in her lap. He said nothing.

"What you become, what you are afraid to become, will in the end be better than that god. It will be better than the wilderness and the denizens of the forest that you now claim. It will not be free. It will not be without pain—because no life is lived without pain."

"It's not my pain that I'm worried about. Those people are gone. And Carver—" She stopped. She could not speak.

Ellerson handed the leaf to her and, hand trembling, she took it.

"Carver entrusts you with the people he cares most about in the world," the domicis said. "And one of those people is you, yourself. He is not in pain, I promise you that. I would have stayed—"

Her head snapped up again.

"—but he reminded me: I am domicis, and the decision is and was his to make. And, Jewel, he has also entrusted me with the people he cares most about in the world. You are not yet finished what you must do."

"Nooooooo," Shadow said, "she is not. And what she must do *right now* is scratch behind my ears. They are *itchy*."

She did.

Ellerson did not tell her about Stacy. He could not bring himself to do it. It was a weakness, but he was not *Sen*, not The Terafin, and he allowed himself this because the cost of it was not so high. The pain she felt now was human, and as long as she picked herself up and continued to move forward, it must be allowed; he did not wish to add to it. Not now. Not ever.

Shadow growled. "Sleep," he said.

It took Ellerson a moment to understand that it was not to Jewel he spoke. But Jewel was now looking at the leaf and the great gray cat, as if they were all the world she could, at this very moment, contemplate.

And, in truth, Ellerson was weary. He, too, would retreat, with his pain, his sense of failure, his sense of loss. He was older and better by far at dividing it from the actions to which he must wake in the morning.

Ellerson did not go to his room immediately. He went, instead, to Angel's room. He knocked on the door. Angel's indistinct voice could be heard in reply. He entered.

The room was spare, clean and perfectly tidy, an indication that it had not been lived in recently. There were weapons on the floor, half under the bed, and a pack in the corner. Angel did not intend to stay long. His face was drawn; he was silent.

Ellerson cleared his throat. "Master Carver asked me to bring you this." He held out the pack that contained the cloak, the blanket, the boots—salvation in the bitter winter of the dreaming wilderness. He held it out, and after a long silence, Angel rose from his position on the bed's edge, and took the pack. He did not open it.

"What happened?"

"As I told you, Carver chose to remain. He opened a way for us to return to you, but he could only do that if he was in communication with the earth."

"Why did he send this, then?"

"The contents are proof against winter, in some fashion, and he thought you—of all the den—might require them in future."

"Why did he think that?"

"I do not know. We did not have time to converse; the demon was almost upon us. The earth will protect Carver—the demon cannot destroy the wild earth, and Carver will be part of it, inseparable from it—but it could not likewise protect us." Ellerson cleared his throat. "Nevertheless, his meaning seems clear to me: he is leaving Jewel in your care. Of all the den, it is only you she will allow to accompany her."

Angel closed his eyes. He said almost inaudible words and gave up halfway through. Instead, he signed *thanks*.

Ellerson did not sign in reply. Instead, he asked Angel one boon, should it ever be required. Angel nodded, and he bowed to Angel, and left the room.

The Master of the Household Staff was not happy. Jewel did not have Carver's familiarity with the back halls—no one in the den did, with the possible exception of Jester. In order to speak with Merry, she must first petition the Master of the Household Staff, in the small, enclosed space that served as her office, her war room, and her interrogation chamber, all at once.

The Master of the Household Staff had long disapproved of the den's inability to observe the starched lines that separated those that served from those that ruled. She did not seem to care for patricians at all, which was ironic, given that it was patricians who received the benefit of the staff's labor.

Her opening salvo was a query about The Terafin's personal chambers.

Jewel's flinch was entirely internal; she met the autocratic stare of her chief servant with a neutrality that would have made Haval proud, if Haval could be moved to feel pride at all. She also answered the question, her voice almost uninflected. Castles that were a mile or two from the doors that led to what had once been library might have been an everyday occurrence, a change of sheets or curtains.

It was clear from the Master of the Household Staff's expression that she already knew of the changes. On any other day, Jewel might have let Barston inform her; Barston was fully capable of meeting disdain with disdain and displeasure with displeasure. Today, however, she did not wish to involve anyone else.

"The change in quarters is not, however, why I've come. I wish to speak to a member of the Household Staff in person."

"Which member?"

"Merry ATerafin."

The Master of the Household Staff's expression, grim and forbidding, rippled ever so slightly.

The Master of the Household Staff was first to rise, her lips pinched, her eyes narrowed. "Will you meet her in my office," she asked, "or do you insist on being led to her rooms as if you are part of my staff?"

Those rooms were shared. "I wish to speak to her alone."

"Very well." She did not ask Jewel why although she could have. Her job was to supervise the men and women under her command. And her job was, as well, to protect them. Jewel had no answer she wanted to give, but want, in this case, was almost irrelevant.

The Master of the Household Staff left Jewel alone in her office, departing by a smaller door.

When she returned, Merry ATerafin came with her. She led her into the office, to a chair next to The Terafin's, and then retreated once again.

Merry was silent as she bowed; it was a perfect obeisance from a servant, and Jewel allowed it because she was The Terafin. She had always hated the formalities the servants were expected to observe; she had always hated the distance it implied.

But there had been no servants in her childhood home. The cooking, the cleaning, had been done for the family by the family. In places where cooking was done, there were no hierarchies that didn't involve her Oma. Merry was a servant on the Isle. She was so far above the den in birth and training that it seemed ridiculous that she should now have to bow or scrape.

Yet here, there was a safety to be found in distance. Merry worked in the West Wing, but she was not of it. She was not mother, not Ona, not Oma. She was not kin, because being kin changed the nature of her duties, of her responsibilities.

Jewel bid Merry rise, and further, bid her be seated. Merry obeyed, her face pale, her hands, which rested in plain sight in her lap, twined together. Shaking. As if she already knew.

No, Jewel thought; as if she understood that this was the moment that the shape of all her fears, growing darker and heavier with the passage of time and the absence of Carver, finally had a name, cohering at once into what it must become. Grief. Loss.

Watching her, Jewel understood. It was the same for her.

Seeing Ellerson had lifted that shadow, that fear; seeing Ellerson alone had solidified it. Carver was not coming home. Carver's voice would no longer be heard in the West Wing. Or in the back halls.

But he had given her the locket he wore. He had asked her to bring it to Merry.

In silence, she bowed her head and attempted to remove the locket she kept around her neck. It caught in her hair. Merry rose instantly to come to her aid, although Merry was not a servant trained to dress, to clothe, to tend to hair and powders and nails. Nor did Jewel forbid it; her hands were shaking.

Merry's hands were shaking.

How much of a coward was she, Jewel wondered; it was far easier to speak— and it was not easy—when she could not see Merry's face, was not required to meet her gaze.

"I met Carver in a dream."

Merry said nothing; her hands had not yet managed to open the clasp of the necklace.

"I met him in a dream. It was a dream like the castle is a dream. He gave me this locket. He asked me to return it to you, and to tell you—"

"Don't say it," Merry whispered.

But Jewel shook her head. "He has us. We have him. But you're the only person he thought of, when we met."

"That's not—"

"No." Jewel inhaled. "No, it's not true; he did think of all of us. He couldn't help but think of me—I was standing in front of him. But the only thing he asked of me was that I return this to you. He loves you," she said, before Merry could stop her.

Merry said nothing.

"He wanted you to have this," Jewel said, after an awkward silence. Too much to say. Too little to offer. She lifted her hands and lowered them again.

The clasp finally came undone. The locket listed to the side, but one end of the clasp prevented it from falling off as the chain was pulled—gently—away from Jewel's neck. She felt the absence of the locket, the absence of its warmth, and the absence of its weight; it had come home, as Carver had intended.

But Carver had not.

Hope was a knife. A simple knife, not a sword, not an ax. But its edges could cut and its point, kill. They were caught by that knife; the point was embedded in both of them, working its way with the passage of time toward the heart, toward the end. When did hope become a burden? When was its weight too costly to bear? When was a bad answer—the feared answer, the worst answer—less painful when it finally arrived, inevitable as nightfall, than the weight of the fear itself?

And when could she decide that for someone else?

She didn't know Merry well. Carver spoke of her, but seldom, as if protecting either her privacy or the familial nature of the den itself, the lines of insider and outside so clearly drawn.

Merry made no sound. No movement. Jewel understood. The Terafin did not cry, but long before Jewel had become The Terafin, she had refused to cry in public—and public meant anywhere anyone could see. Even family. Perhaps, given the nature of her Oma's anger at the sight of tears, especially family.

Jewel rose stiffly. She could not reach the door without turning; could not leave Merry without seeing her face, her expression. Could not, she found, leave without words.

Yes, hope was harsh. Where hope lay, pain was waiting; where hope died, there might be some chance of healing. But without hope, what did they have?

She drew breath, turned.

Merry had opened the locket. She was crying, yes, but the tears were not the tears of loss and pain—or not only those tears. Her face was lit by a gentle glow that seemed to soften its lines, to soften the signs of exhaustion and apprehension; she was, for a moment, radiance and warmth—approachable warmth. Comfort. Jewel understood in that moment why Carver had loved her.

Did love her.

The locket's open face glowed. Jewel could not see what either side of the locket held. She'd assumed that it was meant to house a picture of each of them, but if this was a simple picture, its nature was not flat, not static; she could see the colors of the magic that radiated from it. She could hear nothing, could see nothing more than the trace of magic that her talent had always shown her.

Carver did not create this.

Nor did Carver pay for its creation. Had he, Jewel would have known. She would have seen the bill—and the resultant outrage from the collective House Council, foremost among them Iain.

"He's not dead," Merry whispered. "He's not dead."

Jewel swallowed. "No." He couldn't come home. But she could not bring herself to say this. Could not bring herself to tell Merry the rest of Ellerson's story. Nor did she ask what Merry saw; it was an unbearably private moment, and she felt out of place, intrusive. Not unwelcome, but there was no place for her here.

Merry looked up as she moved. Yes, there were tears as reality reasserted itself. But Merry's hands were shaking as she gently closed the locket. Greatly daring for a servant, she asked, "Can you help me put this on?"

Jewel did, her hands far less unsteady than they had been. She wanted to apologize. Carver had asked her to apologize—she remembered that now. But the gift that she had given was a different kind of hope; it was a place of retreat, a place of comfort—the comfort she could no longer find in his presence.

"Thank you. Thank you for bringing me this. Thank you for letting me have it."